THE

BOYS OF BIRCHAM SCHOOL;

AND

OUT ON THE WORLD,

Young Englishman's Journal Edition.

1869.
LONDON: 145, FLEET STREET, E.C.

THE BOYS OF BIRCHAM SCHOOL.

CHAPTER I.

THE DOCTOR—THE USHER—AND A STRANGE BOY.

THE minute hand of the large sepulchral-looking schoolroom clock told that it wanted but three minutes to the hour for the day's lessons to begin.

The boys, in groups of threes and fours, came trooping through the folding doors at the end of the dingy hall—they came ruddy cheeked and full of mischief, fresh from the play-ground; and finding that neither the tall melancholy usher nor the doctor had yet arrived, caused the old place to ring with their joyous laughter.

It would require a score of pens to note down the impish tricks which took place while the long hand of the clock was slowly travelling to the hour.

They had not much time for their gambols, and, to do them justice, they made the most of the few moments at their disposal.

Some were finishing a disputed game of marbles under the very shadow of the doctor's high and awe-inspiring desk—others, who loved a practical joke better than their schoolfellows' limbs, were prowling about watching for an opportunity to upset any studious youngster who had taken his place on a form.

The biggest among them were standing in a group round a youth who was Captain of the School Eleven.

This young gentleman was wisely discussing how was the best mode of baffling a famous left-handed bowler of the Wiggleton club, said Wiggletonians having offered to play the School Eleven, and it was reported their captain had said they would "beat 'em, too!"

Near the door was another group, and by the swaying to and fro it was evident that some weighty matter was going forward.

There was. One of the young gentlemen having called another a sneak, the latter replied with a vigorous blow on the villifier's nose, which nose looked most awfully red after the receipt of the unexpected favour.

"All right," said the recipient; "wait till after school."

"Bravo, Podge!" cried the challenger's admirers. "We'll see fair play."

"What's the matter?" asked a youth who had cleverly upset a form and its cargo of six small boys, and sought by mingling in the crowd to escape observation.

"A fight!" exclaimed a rosy cheeked little fellow, rubbing his hands with delight. "Sidney Allen has hit Podge Kelly on the nose."

"Fancy! when does it come off?"

"After school."

The half-dozen capsized youngsters having by this time picked themselves up, the youth who had overset them walked quietly past, and at every group he passed he called out,—

"Fight between Podge Kelly and Sidney Allen after school."

Talk about the electric telegraph, it would have been nowhere against the speed with which this news travelled; not more than two seconds had elapsed since the blow was given, and every boy in the school knew of the coming encounter!

With these and a dozen other causes for much talking and noise, it was not possible to hear oneself speak.

The minute hand at last set the striking power of the clock in motion, and as the first chime rang out it acted like magic.

The groups broke up and scurried to their seats; and even one of the biggest boys, who was kindly showing Podge Kelly how to raise his muscle, and otherwise prepare for the combat, stopped abruptly in the midst of his explanation of the last new way to stop a blow and return a facer, and made a very undignified retreat to his seat.

What was this that had such wondrous power over these reckless, fun-loving youngsters? Not the great old clock, with his solemn bell and big spider-like hands; not this quaint piece of horology—for upon more than one occasion his venerable face had been spotted with pellets of masticated blotting-paper until it looked, to use the boys' simile, "Like a large slice of plum duff."

Neither was it the presence of Mr. Randall, the usher, who entered the school-room a second or two before the hour struck.

Poor harmless fellow! There was not a boy in the school but liked him, and would have left the most interesting game to have served the sad-looking, quiet usher: yet, with all this affection for him, they seldom obeyed his commands. Perhaps the primary cause of this may be traced to the fact that he never punished a boy, nor had he been known to report any misconduct to the doctor.

Had he been more severe there is no doubt but the youngsters would have feared as well as loved him, but under the circumstances they were wont to continue their pranks in his presence, and whisper,—

"Go on, it's only old melancholy."

As the last chime of the bell vibrated through the hall, the doctor entered, and every boy became intent upon his book or slate.

It was Doctor Bircham that held these young reckless spirits in check; yet he rarely spoke or looked towards the closely packed forms; but they knew from long experience that his dark piercing eyes and wonderfully acute hearing could at all times detect the perpetrator of any breach of school decorum.

By some mysterious (to them) process, he would quietly send for the offender and chastise him for his misdeeds; yet the culprit would have sworn that the master was either engaged examining a class, or intent upon a book or paper before him. It was this strange power that cowed and subdued them; yet, with all this fear, they loved and reverenced the doctor, and just cause had they for doing so.

He was alike their judge, their mentor, and their friend; he detested tale-bearing, bullying, and cowardice, and in sickness many a little fellow's pale face had worn a happier expression for the few gentle hopeful words he was wont to use. When he visited their bedside many an aching head had rested easier through the quiet arrangement of their pillows by the doctor's hands.

He had never been known to punish unjustly; but woe to the offender who wilfully overstepped the rules—woe to the big lad who used his strength to cowe and browbeat the weak!

Upon occasions when either of the above class of offenders were brought before him the doctor's usually quiet musical voice could be heard like a trumpet as he spoke to the culprits.

"You came here," he would say, "to become worthy of your parents, worthy of yourselves, worthy of your name as YOUNG ENGLISHMEN. I ask you is this the way to become so? What, think you, will become of a boy who cannot for a few hours keep within the simple rules set forth upon that board? Do you think, when you grow to a man, an Englishman, that you can fight the hard battle of life without using a little self-denial. If such is your idea you will find your mistake when it is too late, when the habit has become too strong upon you to be shaken off; it is then you will think of your school days, think of me, and wish I had checked the growth of so vile and prolific a vice. Let him be flogged, Mr. Randall."

The punishment would be carried into effect, and the boy would become both better and wiser for that day's lesson.

The flogging would soon be forgotten, for the doctor was a humane man, and depended more upon the influence of his words than the rod.

A wise proceeding, which, thank Heaven, the masters of the present day follow, and shame the brutal reign of terror to which the boys of forty years ago were subject.

When a bully was brought before Doctor Bircham, he would raise his tall form erect, and, his eyes kindling with anger and disgust, thus address him,—

"I had hoped that all within these walls were proud of the land of their birth, proud of the name which our glorious flag has gained for bravery under every clime—you, sir"—looking sternly at the culprit, and raising his voice until the vaulted roof rang with the trumpet-like sound—"have dispelled the hope. I find there's one bully here, and I am grieved at the discovery, grieved for you—how could it be otherwise? I received you from your parents, and promised to make you, with God's help, a good and brave member of society—good, because you obeyed your parents by assisting me and your tutors in the work of forming your mind; brave, because you would use the strength which God has given you to help and protect the weak and oppressed. Have you done so? Can you look round at your schoolfellows and hold your head erect with the knowledge that your brutal hand has been raised with violence against a poor child who was but a few days since beneath a fond mother's care. Go, sir, pass down the centre of the school-room, and look your companions in the face, and behold what they think of a bully and a coward."

The flogging in store for a gentleman of this description was child's play compared to that fearful ordeal; and none, to their credit be it told, were ever able to raise their heads as they were compelled to take that humiliating walk from the doctor's desk to the school-room door.

Under such a man, can it be wondered that many of the boys who left Bircham filled an honourable nook in England's historic page for gallant deeds by land and sea?

When school hours were over the doctor would lose his identity as the dreaded yet loved schoolmaster. He would at times mingle with the boys, and by a few judicious words as he passed through the play-ground, incite the weak and timid to emulate the strong, and join in the various rough but healthful games.

There was a certain corner of the large play-ground hidden by a shed; this corner had from time immemorial been the spot where all pugilistic encounters had taken place; beyond this shed the doctor never passed, although at times he must have known that something extraordinary was taking place.

Whether he guessed the cause of the shouts and various cries that came from the battle-field was a matter which the oldest boy at Bircham could never determine.

Perhaps he did, and thought that a fair stand-up fight was a quicker and surer mode of making enemies friends than putting a stop to the encounter.

Such was Doctor Bircham; and we may safely assert that he is a type of the schoolmaster of the present day. Remember, this is no ideal picture; Doctor Bircham did, and we hope still exists. Remember, also, you that are learning, that whatever tricks you may play each other, your master should be served both in word and deed.

You are too young to fully understand the difficult and responsible position the head of your school has taken upon himself in forming your minds; think also of the vexations and disappointments he must undergo, when after years of toil many of his pupils have not gone beyond the first rudiments of their education.

Stay: I have said sufficient at present. These pages are written with the hope of amusing you when relieved from the day's severe but profitable studies—so bidding you honour and obey your masters, I will introduce poor Philip Randall.

That a great and unfathomable mystery surrounded the usher every boy in the school was at all times ready to affirm; his pale anxious face showed lines that care, not years, had wrought thereon.

What the mystery was that caused a stalwart young man (for he was not thirty years old) to be in such a continual state of depression, caused the boys of Bircham much speculation, and various reasons were assigned—all of them, as after events proved, very far from the truth.

Some said he had been crossed in love; others—and these were by far the greater portion—averred that Philip had been very rich, and lost his money by gambling.

There was one thing that could not escape the boys' penetration; that was, the devotion the melancholy usher showed towards the doctor.

They also noted that the usher's secret, whatever it was, was known by the master; for often when Philip had been sitting sadly by the doctor's desk, his head bowed, and the tears trickling down his wasted cheeks, the master's venerable head would be bowed: and

Tom Stanton, one of the biggest boys, and consequently an oracle with the lower forms, was standing near, and heard the doctor whisper,—

"Be of good heart, Philip; your repentance will yet be received by Him who died to save us."

These words were transmitted from one to the other until every boy knew them by heart, and that evening little groups could be seen in the play-ground. They spoke with hushed tones as they commented upon them.

Being crossed in love and gambling went to the wall after this; and one idea took possession of the boys—that was, the tall melancholy usher must have committed a very dreadful crime, and the good kind doctor, though he knew all about it, was too noble to give him over to the police.

The football being thrown out drove the usher and his sorrowful face from their minds, and they were soon shouting and as happy as though sin, suffering, and sorrow were unknown in the world.

There was another object of interest to the boys of Bircham—this was a fair handsome boy, who had come to the school some two years before the opening of this story. He was unlike his companions in many things—seldom speaking unless first spoken to, and never by any chance mixing in any of their boisterous amusements.

During the first six months of his career he was called "Milksop," "Mammychick," "Lollypop," and other characteristic schoolboy names; but at the end of this time, when the school broke up and the lads went joyfully home for the holidays, the poor sensitive boy remained at the school with the melancholy tutor; and when the vacation terminated, and merry groups were recounting the jolly time they had spent at home, poor Godfrey Bransome sat in the farthest corner of the great hall, listening to their merry prattle, and looking so hopelessly wretched that one of the happy boys—thrice happy, for he had returned rich in the possession of a new fishing-rod, a whalebone-handled cricket-bat, and two live rabbits—went to Godfrey's side and asked,—

"What is the matter, young 'un? Didn't you bring anything back with you?"

The boy looked up, and, in a tone that went straight to his companion's heart, answered,—

"I have not been away."

"Not been away! Gammon, young 'un!"

"I have not, indeed," said Godfrey, his blue eyes filling with tears; "I wish I had."

"Why didn't you go?"

"Because—because," the poor little fellow said, bursting into tears, "I have nowhere to go—I have no friends—not one in the world."

The possessor of the live rabbits, the fishing-rod, &c., was a noble-hearted fellow, and in the fulness of his joy the fair-faced boy's desolate condition seemed almost too dreadful to realize

He felt his heart become heavy, and his eyes dim, and, afraid to trust himself to speak, he rushed frantically towards a group of laughing boys, and blustered out,—

"Look here, you fellows; here's poor Godfrey hasn't been away since we broke up, and he hasn't got a friend in the world, he says. Now, look here, what do you say; suppose we all give him something—you know it's awful to be like that."

"Why don't you set the example, Glyn," said one.

"So I will. Here, Godfrey, cheer up, I'll give you my rabbits."

The subscription list once opened, presents of all kinds flowed in, and Godfrey that night found himself the master of a miscellaneous collection, among which were three fishing-rods, the pair of live rabbits, six tops, a brass cannon, three books, and two white mice.

The poor little fellow, who had mildly and uncomplainingly endured the scoffs of his thoughtless companions for upwards of six months, suddenly found himself championed by nearly two-thirds of his schoolfellows.

He had no friends—that was sufficient in itself to arouse the latent chivalry in their nature; and those who annoyed him had to answer for it to a set of brave lads who had begun to carry out the doctor's doctrine that the strong should screen and defend the weak.

Thus in one short hour the strange boy found himself in possession of unlimited wealth and a host of friends.

Poor little fellow! he needed them, for his was a rough journey so far through life.

Now we will draw up the curtain, and participate in the joys, the sorrows, the scrapes, and the adventures of the BOYS OF BIRCHAM SCHOOL.

CHAPTER II.

THE FRENCH MASTER.

PODGE KELLY AND SIDNEY ALLEN SETTLE THEIR DIFFERENCE IN AN UNEXPECTED MANNER.

THE coming fight between Podge Kelly—so called on account of his stumpy figure—and Sidney Allen was the cause of many youngsters getting into dire scrapes that morning.

Lessons were but partly learnt, and the workings of sums were neglected to give place to fancy portraits on the slates of Podge and Sidney as they would appear after school.

Various small pieces of paper were handed from boy to boy, having reference to the coming event; and by an unlucky mischance one of these papers was hurriedly placed between the leaves of a book by a boy as he was called upon to be examined by the doctor.

According to custom the book was placed on the desk during the time the youngster repeated his lesson. The fight had been of more importance than his book, and as a natural consequence he stumbled at the third line.

"Yes, my lad," said the doctor kindly, his voice as low and musical as a woman's; "do not hurry. Words ending with a 'y,' preceded by a consonant, form the plural of nouns, the persons of verbs, verbal nouns, past participles—go on my lad."

But "my lad" could not. He stammered, shuffled his feet, and wished himself anywhere but before that kind face and dark searching eye.

The doctor never bullied; he knew from experience that system did more harm than good; so with a shrug of his shoulders—for he was surprised at the boy's forgetfulness—he handed the book back, saying—

"I shall expect you to finish your lesson before twelve; if not, you will have to stay until it is done."

The boy took the book, glad to escape so easily; and while he assiduously conned the lesson, the doctor was reading a slip of paper which had fallen from between the leaves of the book to the desk.

"I'll bet you"—so it ran—"my three birds' nests which I found yesterday against two fishing-hooks that Podge wins."

Under this, and in a different handwriting, was the acceptance of the wager; thus—

"Done. I bet you two hooks to three birds' nests that Sidney knocks Podge into nothing."

"So," muttered the doctor, "this is the cause of so many boys being sent back this morning. Sidney—let me see—that must be Allen. Podge——"

He paused—this aristocratic name was unknown to him.

"Podge"—he repeated—"Podge is a nickname, I presume. Mr. Randall."

The melancholy usher came to the desk.

"Do you," the doctor asked, "know the young gentleman nicknamed Podge?"

"I do, sir; William Kelly."

"Thank you; that is all."

The usher turned and went quickly to the lower end of the room to capture a huge marble —usually called a bouncer—which at this moment rolled from one of the desks to the floor.

The contraband article found its way to the usher's pocket, and the owner whispered ruefully to the next boy,—

"He's got it, and it was my last bouncer!"

"Serve you right," his unsympathising friend said; "what did you want to roll it about the desk for? He collared my biggest top last week, and I was only looking at it!"

"French class this way!" the usher called out; and the boys rose from their seats and went towards a dark-featured, thin, short-haired gentleman, who filled the post of French master in Bircham School.

If ever there was a man that was thoroughly hated in this world, it was "Frenchy," as the boys termed Monsieur Jean Gailland—a feeling that was reciprocated by Monsieur Jean; and he never allowed an opportunity to pass without bringing several of the class before the doctor, and while they were being punished he would show his white teeth and softly rub his hands.

Though the boys dared not show their aversion to him during school hours, they amply made up for it afterwards.

Prodigious were the plots that were hatched for the annoyance of Frenchy, not only by the boys in the French class, but by the entire school.

There was not a movement of Frenchy's but was reported by the scouts to the chief plotter; and when he left his room—no matter how short the time was before his return—his eyes would be greeted by seeing the words, "Waterloo," "Froggy," "Bony Sneak" chalked all over the door.

Monsieur Gailland only smiled at this; but his smile was not unlike the expression upon a tiger's face when slinking through the forest in search of prey.

"Very good," he would mutter, as rubbed the obnoxious words from the door. "To-morrow some of you will have the cane, and very much of it, too. Eh, young pigs; I would like to put you all in one room and bake you up till you died."

He would have much liked to have done this, for Monsieur Jean would have thought but little more of killing one of his tormentors than of poisoning a rabid dog.

More of the boys' tricks with Frenchy arose. There was one youth in the French class, a noble-looking lad, named Stanton Gleddell; against him the French master's heart was filled with the most deadly hatred, and, as may be expected, Stanton suffered in consequence.

The repeated complaints made against him by Monsieur Jean, and the boy's silence when asked the cause of the ill-feeling between them, had more than once angered the good doctor; and at length he was compelled to think that Stanton's stubborn rebellious conduct was the cause of the French master's reports.

How much he was mistaken will be seen hereafter.

The class had not long been formed when the high falsetto of Monsieur Jean was heard crying out, sufficiently loud for the doctor to overhear,—

"Stop—stop; 'tis impossible thing for me to teach if Master Gleddell will not pay a little attention."

The boy looked up, and a red spot came to his cheeks as he answered,—

"I was paying every attention to you monsieur."

The Frenchman shrieked and clasped his hands together, then, rushing to the doctor's desk, said,—

"I am sorry—very sorry; but you must send that boy from me. He will not behave, and when I speak he answers back and puts bad examples to the other boys. It is impossible to teach the belle language when this does go on."

Frenchy played his part well. The doctor had heard Stanton's voice, and thought the boy was answering impertinently.

Gleddell was too big to flog, so for the present offence he was bound to keep within the school gates for a week—a far harder punishment, as every boy knows, than the severest castigation.

Stanton heard his doom with compressed lips and kindling eyes, and his chest rose and fell with the violence of his hidden feelings.

Monsieur Jean returned to the class with a smile of triumphant malice upon his sallow face.

"That was done very well," he thought— "very well, and he will not get out for a week. Ah, poor mademoiselle; she will believe perhaps what I shall tell her."

There was treachery in the expression of his face as he held this self-communion.

Next to Stanton Gleddell, Jean Gailland's hate descended upon Philip Randall, the quiet inoffensive tutor; and the malicious Frenchman had silently vowed to ruin the poor fellow, either by discovering the secret that weighed so heavily upon his mind, or by treachery.

Jean Gailland hated the usher for

reasons: one, because he was his rival with a beautiful girl who dwelt near the school; secondly, because he was Stanton Gleddell's friend.

Weighty reasons these, my lads; and the French master was just the man to keep his silent vow. He was as remorseless as a tiger with its prey, and as cunning as a serpent.

Philip had not yet felt the Frenchman's black treachery, but the time was slowly and surely coming when both he and young Gleddell would rue the hour that brought them in contact with Jean Gailland.

Monsieur Jean had given out, when he first became an inmate of Bircham Academy, that he belonged to one of the noblest families in France. The Revolution, he said, had ruined them as it had ruined many thousands besides the noble race from which he sprang.

As none of the boys believed him, he had gained but little prestige from this statement.

Why they discredited it none could answer, unless it was as Stanton said—

"He looks more like a ragpicker than a count."

And as Stanton was an authority upon most matters, the prevailing opinion was that Monsieur Jean was a ragpicker, and the nobility he professed existed but in his own imagination.

I am afraid, my dear boys, that you will by this time have come to the conclusion that I am a prosy old man, and have taken you in by promising to tell you the fun, scrapes, and sorrows of the boys at Bircham. If you have formed this opinion, dismiss it at once, for much of the interest of this story will be found in the doings of the *dramatis personæ* I have brought upon the scene. There is no joy unless we know what sorrow means. In Monsieur Jean Gailland you will find the dark cloud which at times came across the sunny lives of the good old doctor's madcap pupils.

Anxious eyes watched the spider-like hands of the big clock, and, to the joy of those who were not doomed to stay in school to finish their lessons, the hour came; but ere the first stroke rang out, the quiet usher came behind Sidney Allen, and whispered, "You are to stay after school is over."

Sidney was so taken aback by this that he could not help kicking the next boy's shins, thereby adding another combat to the one on hand.

Philip went in the same manner to Podge Kelly, and that young gentleman immediately asked,—

"What for?"

"That," said Philip, "the doctor will answer."

"Well, I'm blessed!" said Podge mentally, "I wonder if he has scented the mill that's coming off."

The school was emptied in a very few seconds, and when the playground was reached a rush was made to the corner behind the shed, to await the coming of the young pugilists.

Much speculation was the result of their non-appearance, and there were such expressions as, "They've funked it," "I knew Podge would not fight," "Sidney ain't got the pluck to come out and take his punishment?" &c. &c.

The shouts and laughter were heard by those whom a cruel fate had kept after school hours, and though they tried hard to learn the unlearnt lessons, their eyes were more often turned in the direction of the playground than upon the hateful page.

Kelly and Allen sat the very picture of astonishment, for both had by some means got through their tasks, and for the very life of them they could not imagine the reason they were kept behind.

About ten minutes after the usual hour for ringing the bell, the doctor looked up from his desk and called,—

"William Kelly,—Sidney Allen!"

"Here, sir," they answered, dimly conscious that they were found out.

"Come here, my lads."

Both rose at once. The doctor's tone was quiet, and both came to the conclusion that as far as the fight was concerned they were all right.

A host of undiscovered sins came to their minds, during that short walk from the lower form to the high desk.

"Ah," thought Podge, "Ned Thompson upset some ink over my copy-book yesterday, and he's only just found it out."

"All right so far"—ran Sidney's thoughts, "he has found the portrait I drew on the fly-leaf of my grammar-book, and I'm going to be flogged for it—don't care—shall put it in all the heavier on Podge's nose."

With these thoughts in their minds they were considerably taken aback by the doctor asking in a quiet manner,—

"What have you boys to fight about?"

Sidney looked at Podge—Podge looked at Sidney—but neither spoke; the news came like a thunder-clap upon them, and they verily believed the doctor dealt in witchcraft.

Several seconds passed—still no answer. The doctor began to tap the desk with his ruler, and said, as quietly as before,—

"I am awaiting a reply. Kelly, you are the eldest—answer me."

Though the voice and manner were so gentle, the boys knew that, like the lull which precedes a storm, both could in a moment change, and when that change took place, it would be much the worse for them—Kelly especially, as he had been appealed to.

"I called him a sneak, sir," Podge answered, "and he hit me on the nose."

"Why," the doctor asked, "did you use that word?"

Podge stammered — blushed — shuffled about—and at last blurted out,—

"Because he is, sir."

"That is not an answer to my question." The ruler began to move quicker. "What excuse was there for the use of that vulgar term?"

Podge saw that nothing but the truth would answer; so, much against his will, he said—

"Because he split on me to the man at the tuck-shop."

The tuck-shop, for the uninitiated, was a small pastrycook's near the school gates.

"What had you done that he should inform against you?"

Podge became scarlet to the roots of his hair, and could not answer for some time.

"Come," said the doctor, quietly, "what was it?"

"I don't like to say, sir—you will have me flogged."

The doctor elevated his eyebrows.

"No," he said; "speak the truth and I will let you off, no matter what you may have done."

The doctor never broke his word, and Podge, thus absolved, grew bolder.

"We went there last night," he said, "after school, and because the man would not trust me I gave him a shower of peas from my shooter right in the face, and while he was rubbing his eyes I—I—I—"

"Yes, you—well, what did you do?"

Podge felt the tears coming to his eyes, and, driven to desperation, he blurted out,—

"I took some tarts, sir; but I would have paid for them, that I would, if Allen had not told him of it."

The doctor looked grave as he said,—

"So, for this you were about to deface God's image. Because Allen told the shopkeeper who had robbed him, you would have tried your utmost to have marred the beauty of his face. Listen, William Kelly; although the theft was but trifling, and in keeping with your years, what will it be when you become a man, if you cannot better control yourself? Reflect upon my words—think of your parents, and picture them, when age comes upon them, and their son—their only hope—stands before a stern judge charged with theft—for," he added solemnly, "it must come to this unless you restrain the evil which is inherent in us all."

Podge's head was drooped upon his breast, and the tears coursed down his cheeks. The picture the doctor had brought before him touched his heart to its very core.

"You, Sidney Allen," continued the doctor, "did right in reporting the theft, but wrong in raising your hands so hastily. Remember, 'a soft answer turneth away wrath,' and had you spoken to your schoolfellow kindly—told him the dreadful habit would grow upon him, and that you had acted for his welfare in years to come—he would have listened, and upon reflection would have found that you were right, and, shaking your hand, become your friend as long as you both remain under this roof. It is not too late," added the good old master; "come, Kelly, take your companion's hand and tell him how much you have to thank him for."

The boy extended his hand but could not speak—his heart was too full.

The doctor rose from his seat, and much to the joy of the laggards, who had been quiet but not uninterested observers of the previous scene, he told them to join their companion in the playground.

It was as much as they could do to restrain a gleeful shout until they were clear of the schoolroom-door.

Once outside they gave vent to their feelings, and the fleetest one among them rushed to the corner behind the shed, and, bounding in the midst of the admirers of the noble art of self-defence, he shouted,—

"We've got let out, and there won't be any fight between Podge and Sidney."

He was overwhelmed with questions by the disappointed party, the general chorus being, "how did the doctor find it out?" The boy was unable to answer: he only knew that the master had got the "tuck-shop" affair out of Podge, and wound up by saying, "I'm blest if I know how it is, but everything he gets hold of somehow."

"Some fellow splits," suggested a youth who had taken off his jacket preparatory to acting as one of the seconds in the fight. "That's what it is—I should like to know who it was."

"That couldn't be," said the bearer of the news. "The fight wasn't arranged till he got to the hall, and the doctor hadn't left his study."

This was upon deliberation found to be true; so they dispersed, fully impressed with the idea that Dr. Bircham was possessed of a wondrous power in finding out their plans.

CHAPTER III.

MONSIEUR JEAN GAILLAND'S PEACE PLOTTED AGAINST, AND THE RESULT THEREOF.

STANDING apart from the noisy crowd was Stanton Gleddell. He had no heart to join his schoolfellows. The French master's maliciousness, and the general coldness he met with from the doctor (through his foe's machinations) crushed the lad's spirit and made him moody and thoughtful.

The morning's occurrence, still fresh in his mind, and the punishment he had received without giving the slightest cause, filled his heart with bitterness; and the shouts of happy laughter from the crowd seemed to mock his sorrow.

"I can't bear this much longer," he had thought; and his handsome lips trembled with suppressed anger—"yet what am I to do? Poor mother, I know, has deprived herself of many comforts to give me this extra half's schooling, and if I were to leave the money would be wasted."

"Hi! Stanton!" shouted a merry fellow as he ran past Gleddell—"come and join us; we are going to have a game at hare-and-hounds—come on."

He shook his head sadly, and the boy who had called upon him to join in the game, said, loud enough for Gleddell to overhear,—"Well, you are a muff not to come. Frank Moorhouse is going to be hare, and we shall have such a jolly chase to catch him."

The youngster passed on, and a dozen or more soon followed him to the starting point.

"I have no heart for it," Stanton muttered, "though I dare say I should be better for a good run; but the thought of being gated for a week is enough to take the pluck out of any fellow. Poor little Minnie, too—what will she do, not seeing me for so long? And that rascal Jean Gailland—he will tell her the most abominable untruths."

Stanton clenched his hands, and his eyes kindled as he added,—"I hope I shall have sufficient control over myself to keep from striking that Frenchman, but I'm afraid not, and the consequence will be my expulsion. That must be avoided for my mother's sake, so I will try and bear with it a little longer."

"Halloa, Gled! Why, you look as though you were chief mourner at your own funeral!"

Gleddell looked up and beheld his chum, Tom Dickson, or, as he was better known, "Happy-go-lucky."

"I have cause to look so," said Stanton. "When a fellow gets gated for a week for nothing it's time to look glum!"

"Gated for a week!" repeated Happy-go-lucky; "how did you manage that?"

Gleddell told him.

"Well," said Tom, "I'll be hanged if I wouldn't make it hot for the ragpicker during the week!"

"The ragpicker" was the sobriquet for M. Jean Gailland.

"Yes," Stanton said, "and share the fate of several good fellows who have tried to be revenged upon the lying Frenchman."

"Stuff! They were muffs to get found out and expelled. Look here, Gled: leave me and two or three more to manage, and we'll give Frenchy enough to last more than a week."

"I don't want you to get into trouble on my account," Gleddell said, "so let matters take their course. I dare say I shall get over the week's confinement."

"But Minnie, Gled; what about her?"

"You can do me a favour in that quarter, if you'll take a note."

"Twenty, if you like, old chum; but as I'm going that way this evening, have it ready early."

"You're going that way?"

"Are you surprised?"

"Well, yes,—I am."

"Why, is there anything extraordinary in a fellow going past Woodbine cottage?"

"No, certainly not; but as the house is close to the town I should have thought you would have gone in quite another direction."

Happy-go-lucky laughed.

"You're thinking of old farmer Smith's niece," he said gaily. "It's all U P in that quarter."

"Indeed, how is that?"

"The old fellow showed me the way out last night, and as he followed me pretty close with a sharp-pronged stable-fork, I found the way much quicker than I should otherwise have done."

"No doubt," said Gleddell, laughing in spite of his misery. "So you're going to the town to see if you can't find a nice little girl who is not troubled with a stern uncle and a long-pronged fork?"

"No," Tom said, "you are wrong. As I shall soon be leaving school, I don't want to break any young girl's heart, so shall cut that sort of thing until I go home."

"A laudable intention. Now, you have not told me the purpose of your visit to town."

"It has some reference to you. I'm going to buy some pitch."

"Pitch! pitch! what have I to do with that filthy stuff?"

"Frenchy has, so it's all the same."

"Now, Tom, don't do anything to him. I shall be sure to be blamed for it, and——"

"Don't be a muff; we'll manage it all right, and if I can get Jack Williams and two or three more like him to join me, I will give Frenchy something when he goes love-making to-night."

Gleddell's eyes brightened, and his better sense vanished before the prospect of annoying Monsieur Jean when he went upon his visit to the eldest of the two ladies at Woodbine Cottage.

Happy-go-lucky's plot was soon told. In conjunction with Jack Williams, and several of the biggest and eldest boys in the school, he would lay in wait for the Frenchman as he walked daintily through the thick wood which he was obliged to cross before reaching the residence of the two sisters.

"It will be dark, you know," Tom said, "by the time he leaves here, and as he passes among the trees we will pepper him with small bags of flour; and if we are careful we can do it without his being any the wiser."

"Bravo!" said Gleddell, his recent sadness changing to joy at this prospect. "Even if he does find it out, it will be too dark for him to see your faces."

"Exactly—that's my idea."

"Well, we'll suppose he has gone upon his visit. After we've pelted him we can run back and get into his room——"

"You forget he always locks the door and takes the key with him."

"No I don't: old Clark the locksmith has made Jack Williams a key that will open any lock. With this he will get inside, and spread a good thick coat of pitch well over his sheets—then dip the candle-wick in water so that he can't get a light—and if he don't howl when he finds the sheets sticking to him it's ——There's the dinner bell, so come along, and I'll tell you more at dinner."

They made a rush towards the large hall—its significance every schoolboy will at once understand. The remainder of the plot was talked over during the dinner, and Jack Williams and the others referred to by Happy-go-lucky were won over to the enemy's side.

Monsieur Jean—Monsieur Jean! you had better have put your naked hand into a nest of hornets than have offended the boys of Bircham!

The evening came, and the lights began one by one to appear at the many windows of the school. Standing in the centre of the playground, thus secure from the observation of any lurking telltale, the conspirators were watching the gleam upon Monsieur Jean's blind.

They saw his shadow as he stooped over the looking-glass, scenting and brushing his short black hair; and with gleeful feelings they noted his movements as he put on his coat, and finally adjusted his glossy *chapeau*.

"Off with you," said Happy-go-lucky, "he's put on his tile!"

The six conspirators darted out of the gate and made tracks for the wood, and Stanton Gleddell, acting upon an idea of his friends went to Mr. Randall's room. They knew the usher's word would absolve him from having any share in the flour business, and knowing so much of Monsieur Jean's nature, they were sure he would assert that Stanton was the leader of the assault.

They had ample time to conceal themselves among the trees which stood upon each side of the foot-path; and with the mouths of the flour-bags open and ready for action, they waited the coming of the foe.

Monsieur Jean carefully placed a box of matches beside the candle-stick before extinguishing the light; then, double locking the door, and putting the key in his pocket, he sallied forth—a very Beau Brummel in appearance.

The gloss upon his hat and patent leather boots was sufficient to cause several small

THE BOYS OF BIRCHAM SCHOOL.

THE SCHOOL.

boys he passed in the great passage to pause and regard him with awe. His waistcoat was resplendent with a massive chain, which twinkled and gleamed in the half light. (The boys said the chain was brass, because Monsieur Jean never wore it during the daytime.) His gloves fitted without a wrinkle; and to add a splendour to his brilliant appearance, he wore a light-blue silk scarf, in which glittered a (Paris) diamond pin. A light Malacca cane, silver mounted, and ornamented with a silken tassel, completed the external get up of Monsieur Jean's thin person.

Ah! Monsieur Gailland! while you are conning over the sweet speeches you intend to make when you reach Woodbine Cottage, the lurking foe is waiting and watching, and is ready to destroy your resplendent toilet.

But he thinks not of this; so daintily picking his way among the small stones, fearful that a speck of dust should soil the purity of his highly polished boots, he comes nearer and nearer to the fearful ambuscade—— But stay—how I am running on, and quite forgetting that my friend the reader has not the most remote idea of the object which causes Monsieur Jean to thus "get himself up," and, during the time the omission is being rectified, M. Jean Gailland will be near the trees where lurketh the avenger.

Woodbine Cottage stood on the verge of the thick wood which separated the school from the town.

It was a sweet sequestered spot, and well fitted for the home of its present occupier, a bluff old lieutenant, late R.N.

He dwelt here in peace and happiness with his daughters; the eldest, Eleanor, just entering her twenty-first year, the youngest, Minnie, a charming brunette, not yet seventeen.

Lieutenant, or, as he liked to be called, Captain, Oakplank had, after being blown about from every point of the compass for nearly twenty years, received a lieutenant's commission, but, unfortunately for him, the golden epaulet attracted the attention of one of the enemy's marksmen, and poor Oakplank received a bullet in his right arm.

Being in the tropics at the time, amputation had been necessary to save his life; so with a false limb—armed at the wrist with a formidable steel hook—and a pension from his grateful country, he retired from the service.

George Oakplank soon after this took unto himself a wife, and all went well until two years before the opening of this story. Fate then decreed that he should become a widower, so, removing from the scene of his bereavement, he rented Woodbine Cottage, with the hope of passing the remainder of his days in quietude.

The young ladies were wont to walk in the wood adjacent to this dwelling, and one morning, as they strolled among the trees, plucking the modest violets, they were startled by a bull suddenly lowering his head and making a charge at them.

They would have been gored to a certainty had not young Gleddell come upon the scene.

He had been climbing the trees in search of birds' eggs when the girls' screams caused him, as he afterwards said, to come down with a run.

A close application of a stout bough upon the bull's flanks soon caused the animal to turn upon his antagonist, and gave Captain Oakplank's daughters an opportunity to reach the cottage.

Stanton was soon relieved of his pursuer by the old sailor coming to the rescue with a double-barrelled gun, and the bull limped off on three legs, the fourth being broken by a bullet.

By this means Stanton became a welcome visitor to Woodbine Cottage, and, as a matter of course, he was soon head over ears in love with Minnie.

Time wore on, and Stanton introduced his friend Philip Randall to the inmates of the cottage, and, much to the boy's satisfaction, he beheld Eleanor's eyes glisten when the pale usher had been upon visiting terms for a few weeks.

He beheld more than poor Philip, whose quiet retiring manners and disposition would have received a shock had he known that the fair girl regarded him with more than friendly feelings.

True, he had been her companion in many a stroll through the wood. For her he had culled the tiniest flowers, and in his heart he felt that these rambles did him much good, although his fair and lively companion was in the habit of bantering him severely upon his habitual moody mien.

So matters went on, Stanton and Minnie revelling in the depthless bliss of a first love, and Philip, with his grave earnest face turned towards Eleanor as he explained the meaning and purpose for which every shrub and flower they passed was sent upon earth.

She would listen with a mischievous twinkle in her laughing eyes to his long speeches, and at their conclusion the old trees would re-echo with her happy laughter, and, like a child, she would question and perplex the grave usher until he was fairly beaten.

The footing between them seemed such as would exist between a laughing girl of sixteen and a grave old gentleman of fifty; yet there was but a few years' difference in their ages.

Neither had the least conception of the true state of their hearts until M. Jean Gailland came like an evil shadow upon their dawning happiness.

The Frenchman had met them by chance, and having occasion to speak with Philip upon some matters relating to the school, the usher introduced him to the Oakplank family.

Jean Gailland was struck by the eldest girl's beauty, and fully believing that Philip was her accepted lover, he resolved to follow up the introduction, and if possible supplant the usher either by the charm of his conversation or the irresistible beauty of his lath-like form.

Parting from Philip, M. Jean went slowly homeward, soliloquizing—

"That is one of the prettiest of the English girls I have beheld since I became a resident in this land of fogs. Yes, she is very beautiful, and much too good for that usher; he is like a monk, and not possesses the lively manners and superior dress which should belong to a partner for such a very nice miss. Ma'lle. Oakeyplank, I think Jean Gailland would be much the better man for you—his grace, his figure, his dress, just the thing; and she thought so; did I not see her look at me when I stood in such a graceful *pose?* She did—oh, you pigs!"

He entered the playground as he brought this soliloquy to a close, and an unseen hand hurled a stone which knocked M. Jean's glossy *chapeau* from its pinnacle, and caused the exclamation which concluded his speech.

By assiduously watching Woodbine Cottage when Philip and Stanton were away, he succeeded in getting asked inside. Once established therein he began his siege, but up to the time of his introduction to the reader he had made but little progress with carrying the fortification.

Twirling his cane, and repeating a set speech in his very best English, he reached the trees; and the ringleader of the concealed band gave the word for the firing to commence.

First came a small bag of flour, which fell so softly upon M. Jean's shoulder, that he remained in perfect ignorance of the favour.

This success was followed by several shots of

a similar nature, and M. Jean's back view was a truly edifying spectacle.

From the collar to the skirts of his coat all that was black soon disappeared, and he looked as though he had stood beneath a gigantic flour-dredger.

Whistling softly the refrain of a Parisian love song, he continued his way until the end of the trees was gained. Here he came opposite the right flank of his foes, and this flank being armed with stale eggs, he received a volley that caused him to yell with pain and rage.

One of the missiles struck him a little above the right eye, and the fragrant contents trickling down his face gave him an idea of perfumes that were not among those of Araby the blest.

"Diable!" roared M. Jean, "pigs, English, I will kill you!"

He made a wild rush towards the trees, and striking out madly with his cane, uttered a succession of oaths which were none the less wicked because they were uttered in French.

Like a maniac he continued flying from tree to tree, but without coming in contact with one of his tormentors. So when tired out with his efforts to obtain revenge, he sat down upon a fallen tree, and cleansed his face with his perfumed pocket necessary, then began to reflect upon a sure method of punishing the ringleaders of this attack.

"Very well, very well," he muttered—and his white teeth gleamed savagely—"this is the work of my brave young Monsieur Gleddell. Ah! the morning will come, when I will tell all—say I saw him here—and the doctor, when he hears it, will send him away for breaking through the rules. Ah! *mon ami*, you have for yourself done this time."

In blissful ignorance of the sight his hat and coat presented, M. Jean arose from the fallen trunk, and carefully placing the soiled handkerchief in his pocket, he resumed his way to Woodbine Cottage.

Happy-go-lucky had shown great generalship in the disposition of his forces; so when the ammunition was expended he was able to withdraw without feeling the effects of the enemy's charge.

"Look here," Happy-go-lucky had said, when concluding his harangue to the troops, "after you have all fired, make a run for that large tree, then slip off your shoes, and cut back as quickly as you can for the school."

They obeyed him, and the result proved his forethought, for although M. Jean Gailland was close upon them, yet, thanks to their shoeless feet, they were able to escape without capture or recognition.

They were careful in the manner of their return through the gates. A general dispersion took place, and they entered one at a time, and at sufficient intervals to disarm suspicion.

In the centre of the playground the chief conspirators reassembled, and after placing sentinels to warn them should the foe unexpectedly return, they crept softly to the Frenchman's little chamber.

CHAPTER IV.

THE SENSATION M. JEAN CREATED UPON HIS ARRIVAL AT WOODBINE COTTAGE.

CAPTAIN GEORGE OAKPLANK had a sturdy British dislike to all things foreign, and M. Jean in particular; he resisted the French importation to the cottage with more warmth than elegance when M. Gailland took his departure after the first visit.

But when the French master continued the invasion of the captain's territory, the old sailor's wrath became higher each time, and the girls had to promise that "the confounded foreign jackanapes" should not cross the threshold again; but to his dismay, no sooner had his daughters most dutifully mixed the customary evening glass of grog and filled a long churchwarden pipe, than M. Jean's rat-tat-tat could be heard, and the captain, vowing mighty things, would seize his grog and rush to the little summer-house at the end of the garden.

About the time that M. Jean was preparing for the visit, the old seaman's daughters were manœuvring to get papa out of the way, in case M. Jean should arrive.

This was more than possible, for he had placed his hand upon his heart, and, with a low bow, had assured Eleanor that he should "do myself the great honour of calling to see if the ladies' health is in good keeping when I pass on my way to the town."

Fearful every moment that he would make his appearance, the sisters plotted to prevent an explosion of rage and many strong seafearing terms from papa. Thus they began.

The captain was seated by the open window, leisurely puffing huge clouds of smoke from between his lips, and with the formidable steel hook which served him for a hand he from time to time drew the branches of a climbing rose towards him, and instituted a strict search for any lurking caterpillar, worm, or other destructive enemy to his favourite flowers.

He had just concluded the investigation, and, with much gratification, he complacently growled,—

"I think I've hunted the foe this time girls."

"I am glad to hear it, papa," said the elder, dutifully; "and I am sure Minnie is pleased, for she is so fond of roses."

"That's right—good girl. I say, 'Lenor?'"

"Yes, papa."

"Why don't you try a pipe now and then? I think we could smoke them out if we were both to keep at it."

"I tried one, pa; but it was so nasty I was obliged to leave off. Then Minnie put a pocket-handkerchief over the bowl, and began to blow the smoke out from the other end—"

"Yes, I did, papa," said the youngest; "and, before I knew anything about it, the tobacco burnt a large hole in the cambric, and my lips were quite scorched for a long time after."

The captain gave vent to a hearty guffaw at their troubles, and Eleanor, exchanging a look of deep meaning with her sister, said,—

"Speaking of smoking, pa, have you noticed the white climbing rose outside the summerhouse?"

Captain Oakplank's lips parted, and turning suddenly towards the fair speaker, he growled,—

"No. What, are they——?"

"Yes, pa. Underneath the leaves I saw a great number of small green insects."

The captain was on his feet in an instant, and in a quarter-deck voice roared out,—

"Bring the ammunition, girls, and let us bear down upon the foe!"

The ammunition was a large jar of strong tobacco, which Minnie brought from the sideboard.

"You go with papa," said Eleanor to her sister; "I will soon join you with the grog."

Minnie made a grimace as she followed the captain from the room, and Eleanor whispered,—

"Don't leave until I come down the garden."

"But," suggested the youngest plotter, "suppose he comes?"

"It wants some time yet. Go on—there's pa calling. I'll bring the grog, and when we once get him searching for the foe, as he terms them, we shall be safe."

Minnie skipped down the steps, and her sister proceeded to concoct a glass of the favourite mixture.

The captain soon began his crusade, and Minnie had to follow him with a second "churchwarden," well charged—a duty, to judge from the many anxious glances she cast towards the long windows that led to the garden, which her mind was far from being interested in.

To her relief, Eleanor made her appearance with the tumbler, and the captain, pausing to taste the grog, growled out,—

"Another day, girls, and these beggars wouldn't have left me a flower."

He returned to the charge much refreshed, and, while closely occupied routing the enemy, the girls took an opportunity to slip away.

The old sailor missed them when the evening began to close in, and calling them individually and collectively a pair of petticoated swabs, betook himself to one of the seats to rest after the exertions he had undergone.

The combined effects of the fumes of the strong tobacco and the stiff glass of the favourite mixture caused the old fellow to fall asleep and dream of bygone events.

From his slumber he was rudely awakened by a scream of rage—then peal after peal of laughter coming from his daughters' lips caused him to spring to his feet, and, flourishing the steel hook high above his head, he stumped towards the house, and entered the front room just in time to behold M. Jean dash through the open window and retire, howling with passion, from the house.

Captain Oakplank looked in vain for an explanation from his daughters; both were upon the sofa, convulsed with laughter.

"What the —— are you grinning at, eh?" exclaimed the old fellow, as he strode angrily to and fro the room. "That French pirate here again! have I not told you that he shall not come to this house? Quite bad enough to have that boy, with his tricks, without having such a jackanapes, lanthorn-jawed effigy as that here! Why don't you answer me? What is the matter with you both—are you mad?"

Eleanor was the first to recover her speech, and she told her angry sire the cause of M. Jean's sudden exit, and their merriment.

The unfortunate French master had made his entry bowing, and giving utterance to the speech he had been rehearsing when the enemy's file-firing awoke him from his blissful reverie.

"Just called, young ladies," he said; "I could not pass your charming residence without paying my duty and ——"

He stopped abruptly, as the sisters, in spite of every effort, burst into a fit of laughter.

M. Gailland was horrified at this breach of good manners, and he looked from one to the other, as though seeking an explanation of so strange a greeting.

M. Jean felt convinced that his get up was perfect; therefore this merriment could have no reference to himself. So he thought, until by chance he raised his eyes and beheld his own reflection in the glass which faced the door.

Horror unspeakable! Could that grotesque being be the reflection of the incomparable Jean Gailland? He could not believe it, and to make sure he advanced a few steps closer to the glass.

There could be no mistake, and M. Jean, in the agony of the moment, gave vent to that scream of rage which awoke the old sailor.

An Egyptian family, or an Ethiopian serenader, with the burnt cork half washed from their faces, are sights calculated to excite the risible muscles; but M. Jean's appearance was tenfold more grotesque than these.

One side of his face was smeared with the yolk of the broken egg, and, like the hideous war paint, there were sundry streaks of soot, mingled with an equal portion of flour, crossed and re-crossed from his left eye down to the point of his chin.

To heighten the ludicrous appearance, the tip of his nose stood out in bold relief, untouched by either soot or flour.

The resplendent shirt front and white vest were dotted with black marks, and his coat, from collar to skirt, was covered with white dusty marks.

No wonder that M. Jean should have yelled when he beheld this strange apparition; no wonder, when he fully realized the ridiculous figure he presented before the fair girl whom he had come to captivate, that he dashed through the open window and beat a hasty but most undignified retreat.

The bluff old seaman laughed heartily when he heard these details from Eleanor.

"Serve him right, the ape," he said; "I'll warrant he has been doing something to the boys, or he would not have been served out like this."

"We shall hear all about it when Stanton comes," exclaimed Minnie.

"H'm," muttered the old fellow; "Stanton, eh! I hope that young chap does not think of cutting out my little girl; if he does I'll put a stopper upon him."

He made a significant gesture with the steel hook that did not promise well for Minnie's suitor.

Crushed, humiliated, his vanity and self-conceit terribly wounded, the ill-starred M. Jean rushed like a maniac from the scene of his discomfiture. In his frenzy he took no heed of the road he was pursuing, and not until he found himself in the midst of a newly ploughed field did his reason return.

A plough left by the labourers stood near him, and Monsieur Jean—a very different man to the scented and elaborately dressed dandy who started so daintily from the school—sank upon one of the handles, and, covering his face with his hands, wept tears of passion.

The tables were turned upon him, indeed. He had gone to the cottage, his heart filled with evil thoughts against young Gleddell, and his smooth tongue ready to traduce the poor boy.

How different had been the result! and as he alternately cried with rage and vowed the deepest revenge against (as he believed) the author of his misfortunes, the bell from the distant town clock chimed the hour.

Then M. Jean sprang to his feet.

He knew the school gates would be closed, and to pass the porter and, in all probability, a number of the boys, who, like so many cats, delighted to creep about the passages after hours, paying forbidden visits to their friends —how could he pass them in the condition he was in?

The thought was maddening, and M. Jean looked wildly around him, as though seeking relief from the sombre-looking hedge-rows.

Joy!—a pool of water gleamed beneath the pale moon's rays, and thither the Frenchman repaired to cleanse his face.

But misfortunes never happen singly—so M. Gailland discovered, for as he stooped over the cattle pond, his foot slipped, and the next moment he was scrambling in the thick mud.

Regaining the bank, a most deplorable looking object, he walked sadly towards the school —a fierce dangerous glitter in his dark eyes as he thought of Stanton Gleddell.

When the old porter admitted him, M. Jean, in reply to the man's exclamation of astonishment, muttered something about having fallen into the mud, and, brushing past, ran to his own room.

Here he struck several matches, in the attempt to light his candle, but failing in the accomplishment of his purpose, he undressed and plunged into bed.

Here again he was followed by the Nemesis, and, with a yell that awoke all within hearing, he sprang to the floor, bringing the sheets with him.

He repeated his cry as he found the bed-clothes clung to his lank body, and, in the attempt to remove them, his hands became covered with a coating of pitch.

Like a baited bull he danced about the room, the sheets adhering to his body, and the long ends, like a train, sweeping the floor as he moved.

In the midst of his agony, the door opened, and Dr. Bircham, in dressing gown and slippers, entered the room.

CHAPTER V.

FRANK SUMMERS RECEIVES COBBLER'S ALLOWANCE.

THE crowd of youngsters who were in the long passage, listening with gleeful feelings to the French master's terrified cries, took to their heels when the doctor made his appearance, and when safely covered with their bed clothes they gave vent to their laughter.

One or two of the boldest crept towards M. Jean's door, in the vain hope of hearing the result of the doctor's visit.

They retired when the one who was peeping through the keyhole gave the signal that the head was moving towards the door.

Dr. Bircham looked very grave when he left the French master's chamber—graver still when the flickering light revealed several white clad forms scampering towards the sleeping rooms.

He passed slowly towards his chamber, his brows contracted as though in deep thought; and when the last gleam of the candle disappeared, doors were noiselessly opened and the boys with cautious tread came forth and went to where Happy-go-lucky and the conspirators were assembled.

They had not thought that the kind old master would have come upon the scene, and there the little group were busy cudgelling their brains with conjectures of what the morrow would bring forth.

Happy-go-lucky was sitting up in bed, his knees drawn up to his chin, and listening sagely to the doubts and fears of his fellow-conspirators.

"We shall be expelled," said one. "If we are, it will be your fault, Happy; you set us on."

"Listen to the sneak," said another, more courageous than the first speaker. "I'll bet anything he splits."

"If he does"—and Happy-go-lucky clenched his hand as he spoke—"I'll give him something before I get expelled."

"I won't split, Happy," Frank Summers said, "but you'll see we shall be bowled out somehow."

"No fear," said the leader, "I don't see any chance of our being found out, unless some one splits; and the fellow that does that will have his head punched."

They knew Happy-go-lucky would keep his word, for he never bullied a small boy, or avoided a fight with a big one—he in matters of this kind always carried out his intentions to the letter.

Frank Summers, a fair-haired, pale-faced youth, was not over-burdened with pluck: though he had joined the conspirators, it was more from the fear of being called a sneak than any wish to distinguish himself in the crusade against M. Jean.

The appearance of the doctor coming from the French master's room had slightly affected his nervous system, and he debated mentally whether it would not be better to go to the Frenchman's room when his companions were asleep, and denounce the ringleaders of the plot.

By this means he thought he should escape any punishment when the discovery took place.

There is no doubt but he would have acted upon this feeling had not Happy's threat brought a reaction.

"I say, Mallet," said Happy-go-lucky, suddenly, "suppose you go and see what Frenchy is about?"

The youth, so named on account of his large head and long thin legs, expressed no willingness to execute the task.

"How can I see?" he said. "Isn't the door locked?"

"Suppose it is, there's a keyhole."

Mallet looked uncomfortable.

"I don't like the job, Happy," he said.

"He might pop out and collar me."

"Now, look here, young un'—if you don't go, we'll toss you in a blanket; so make up your mind."

The Mallet debated.

The ceiling of the room was very low, and he knew by experience that being tossed in a blanket was not the pleasantest means of passing through the air, especially when the ceiling was not much more than six feet from the floor.

"I'll go," he said, at last; "but I shan't be able to see much."

"You'd better," said Happy, "or it will be worse for you when you come back."

The Mallet departed, muttering something about people being too fast.

"I'll tell you what it is," Happy said, when the scout had gone upon his errand, "there'll be a jolly row to-morrow morning; so the only thing we can do is to stick together if anything turns up."

A proceeding they all promised to follow out, no matter what occurred.

The Mallet returned in a few minutes, and, carefully closing the door, came to the expectant group, his face expressive of the intelligence he had gleaned.

"I can't make it out,' he said. "When I went to Frenchy's door, and peeped through the keyhole, he was sitting in a chair and sharpening a knife."

"Sharpening a knife!" they repeated,

"Yes; a big-bladed one, too. I did not stop long when I saw this, for I wasn't going to let Frenchy catch me, and him with a knife n his hand.'

The knife question was discussed with a proper amount of deliberation before Happy gave his opinion upon the matter.

"It looks queer," he said, sagely; "and these foreigners are always ready to stick a fellow."

"Ugh!" gasped Frank Summers, sidling from the group, and precipitately retreating to his bed, where he lay shivering with fear.

"Perhaps," continued Happy, "he means to come here after we are asleep, and——; but no, that can't be it."

"Why, Happy?"

"Because he does not know who did it. So there's only one thing he sharpened the knife for."

The listeners drew closer.

"That," Happy said, "is to be revenged on Gleddell; for he hates him, and will be sure to think poor Gled was at the bottom of the affair."

Not a doubt remained upon their minds of the truth, and with bated breath they began to form divers plans for the prevention of the deed.

"Stop here," Happy said, "all of you. I'll go and see myself what he's up to. Give me the bottom joint of my fishing-rod, and if I catch him creeping about I'll break his long back."

In his trousers and shirt, and with bare feet, Happy sallied forth to intercept the French master should he go upon his dark mission.

"I say," remarked the Mallet, "ain't Happy a plucky one?"

"He is," assented one. "Fancy if he meets Froggy, and they have a fight—would you go and help?"

"Wouldn't I!" said the Mallet, bravely; "should think I would, too!"

"I say," came, in a faint voice, from Frank Summers, "shut the door, some of you."

"What for?" the Mallet asked.

"Because he might come in here with the knife. Do shut the door."

The Mallet, after the important service he had rendered the cause, at once assumed a higher position among his schoolfellows.

He felt a proper amount of contempt for the shivering coward, and to make an example of him, the Mallet turned to his companions.

"All of us," he said, "know that the English are the bravest people in the world."

"Of course we do"—chorus.

"Well," the Mallet continued, elevating his voice to give force to his words, "if the English boys were not brave the men could not be."

"Of course not, Mallet."

"Well, do you think Frank Summers will ever be brave enough to be an Englishman?"

"No, he won't"—from a small boy—"he's the awfullest sneak in school."

"Very well," and the Mallet groped under his bed for his slipper. "What say you, lads, if we give him some cobbler's allowance, for being a sneak and a coward?"

The proposal was received with a yell, and a rush was made for leather straps, shoes, &c.

Frank Summers discreetly rolled out of bed, and crawled away.

"Lug him out," roared the Mallet, as he aimed at a naked foot which gleamed for a moment under a bed some distance from the culprit's.

The Mallet's zeal and the dim light caused him to clutch too hastily at the offender's foot.

He missed his grasp, overbalanced himself, and fell upon his nose.

Before he had regained his feet Frank was pulled out from his hiding place, and despite his struggles, thrown face downwards upon a bed.

In this position he was held, and received a bountiful application of cobbler's allowance, the Mallet holding his red nose with one hand, while he belaboured the cause of his misfortune with the other.

Young Summers yelled lustily for mercy, but finding this did him no service, he changed his tune.

"Let me get up," he roared, and, making a sudden plunge, kicked Charley Adlane in the mouth, and sent him flying into the middle of the room. "Let me get up, you cowards; twenty to one! Oh, oh; all right, young Stikkers; you hit me with the buckle end of your——oh, oh; murder! I'll split on you to-morrow; see if I don't! I'll tell who put the pitch in Frenchy's bed. I——oh, oh, my back; murder!"

The Mallet, having to beat a hasty retreat to the washstand to stop the effusion from his nose, gave the signal for the punishment to end.

Frank Summers, vowing revenge, crept into bed again, as the door opened, and Happy-go-lucky entered the room.

There was a rush towards the knight-errant, and a dozen inquiries were poured forth at once.

"Hold on a moment," said Happy, handing his weapon to Alf; "steady now; it's all right."

"All right? But about the knife, Happy?"

"That's all right too; he was cutting his corns when I went to the door."

"What a sell!" remarked a youth of a sensitive turn. "I already began to fancy myself recording the recent attempted murder at Bircham Academy, the gallant behaviour of——"

"Hallo," said a voice, and a face was visible at the door; "all right, young gentlemen, I'll take down your names; out of bed after hours."

It was the porter, who had been attracted to the room by the row when the "cobbler's allowance" was going forward.

Old Bill—he never had any name but this from generation to generation of the Birchamites—placed his candle upon a chair, then stood before the door to prevent the escape of those who were absent from their rooms.

Pencil and slate in hand, he began to take down names.

"Let's see," he said, as he wrote; "C. Adlane—third time this week I've caught him. Well, he'll be gated when the doctor knows it."

"I say, Bill," Charley began; "don't put me down this time, old fellow."

"Let you off last time," growled old Bill; "shan't this time. It's the likes of you that keeps me awake every night. Now, go back, you, Stikkers, till I puts your name down.'

Young Stikkers had made a bold but unsuccessful attempt to creep past the Cerberus.

"Stikkers," grumbled the old man, as he finished the name; "I'm glad I don't often have that name to write. I hates making k's."

"Don't make 'em, Bill," said Stikkers, pleadingly; "you'll get the cramp in our fingers."

"Shall I?" the old man chuckled; "perhaps your back won't be cramped after the caning you'll have to-morrow."

"Be a good sort, Bill," said Charley, shall have some pocket money next week Let us off and you shall have the lot."

Cerberus peeped over the top of the slate, and counted the number of those who were absent from their rooms.

"Six," he said; "that's not sixpence apiece."

They began to hope that he would relent, and let them off without a report to doctor.

"Not sixpence apiece," he resumed. "Can't be done. Besides, I let four of you off last half, and never got the money."

"You shall have it this time," said Stikkers. "Look here, Bill, we'll give you our fishing-rods to hold till we pay."

"No," growled old Bill; "I know you. When I get the rods I'd be served as I was served once afore."

"How was that?" Charley Adlane asked, with an assumption of innocence that was quite refreshing.

"How was it, you young beggar. Why you was one of 'em."

"I wasn't, Bill—no, not me. I don't know anything about it."

"Well——"

He could get no further than this. The cool assurance the boy exhibited was too much for the old fellow, and he could only elevate his eyes in silent horror.

The matter referred to by the porter occurred a few days before the school broke up for the Midsummer holidays.

Charley Adlane and a few choice spirits had been detected in a room far from their own by the old man—I blush to transcribe the truth—detected sitting around Happy-go-lucky's bed, a can of small beer in their midst.

The beer came from the cellar. How obtained was a mystery.

Old Bill pounced upon the carousal, confiscated the beer, and began to put down the offenders' names upon the small slate he carried for the purpose.

It was a case of flagrantly breaking the rules, and the offenders offered old Bill a tremendous bribe to let them off.

Human nature is human nature; so Cerberus relaxed under the brilliant promises held out, and to secure the payment of the various sums he was to retain all the available property possessed by the offenders.

Mark the result.

Fishing-rods, cricket-bats, canes, tops, and other articles—quite a goodly heap—were deposited in the porter's room, redeemable upon the production of the stipulated coin.

Before twenty hours were gone by the owners of the property came in a body to Old Bill's room, and one (Charley Adlane), making as though to pay the money, knocked the candle under the fire-grate, then blinded Old Bill with a shower of peas from a shooter, and before he could recover from his fright they had carried off the whole of the effects held until the money was handed over.

After this, no wonder Old Bill could only exclaim "Well!" when Charley looked so innocent.

"No more gammon for me," chuckled the old fellow. "I've got six of you down here."

Charley and Happy-go-lucky exchanged a significant glance as the former said,—

"Well, I don't care; but you ought to hunt all of 'em down; there's more than us out of their rooms."

"Eh! where are they?"

Charley jerked his thumb towards the beds, thereby implying that more of the defaulters were hidden beneath the chintz hangings.

Old Bill gave an inward chuckle at this, and made a rush towards the first bed.

"Come out," he said, lifting the hangings, "or I'll pull you out. Oh—o-o-oh—murder!"

The moment his back was turned towards the door, Happy-go-lucky flattened the candle-wick and called out,—

"Burke him!"

A dozen of the youngsters pounced upon the old fellow before he could rise, and prevented him from making the least outcry by winding a sheet round his head.

Thus rendered helpless, he was rolled about the floor and pummelled until he cried out for mercy.

"Let us off, then," said Happy, "or we'll pour the contents of all the water jugs down your back."

"Yes—yes; I'll let—you—off!"

He was liberated from his bonds: the candle

put in his hand; then, as a shower of boots and shoes whizzed round his head, the old fellow precipitately retired from the room.

"Shocking!" the reader exclaims, forgetting that he has "made one" in many similar boyish pranks.

In high glee the youngsters soon after separated and went to bed.

CHAPTER VI.

MONSIEUR JEAN SIGNALLY DEFEATED.

THE morning came, and the sun, glistening through the quaint old school-house windows, awoke the sleepers to that dreamy blissful state which one feels after a long and refreshing night's rest.

Eyes were rubbed, and one by one the boys sat up in bed, wondering whether the school bell had rung.

The thorough awaking of those who had on the previous evening waged war against M. Jean did not bring a pleasant train of thought to their minds.

Little by little came the knowledge that something unpleasant would happen before the day was over.

The boys sought, by lying perfectly still and closing their eyes to forget the deeds of yesterday; and many felt sorry that they had been so far carried away by their feelings as to join the cause.

Others boldly sat up in bed, and calmly meditated over the best course to pursue should matters come to the worst.

The deep clang of the school bell came fresh and clear upon the morning air; the hurry of dressing, and the noise and laughter occasioned by those who had risen with the first sound pulling sundry sluggards out of bed by the heels, for the time drove all unpleasant thoughts from the culprits' minds.

It must be confessed that the breakfast did not suffer the less upon account of those compunctious feelings; quite the reverse—the most guilty possessed the largest appetites—a circumstance which caused much grief among certain smaller boys, who lost the greater portion of their "Tommy and scrape" in consequence.

The time between breakfast and school was passed as usual in the playground.

Happy-go-lucky stood in the centre of the conspirators, his hands deep in his trousers pockets, his cap pulled over his eyes, and altogether wearing a desperate devil-may-care appearance befitting the leader of the gallant band.

His example inspired certain small boys of the party, and they, too, thrust their hands into their pockets (as far as certain contraband articles would admit—tops, marbles, &c.), pulled their caps over their eyes, looked heroic, and ready to be led to the stake.

They felt bound to stand by their leader, and the most romantic had a vague idea that if they were expelled from the school they could become smugglers or brigands, and with Happy for a leader become a terror to the world.

"The time approaches, my brave companions," said Happy, "and we shall soon stand before those who have made themselves our masters."

Happy had been reading the Book of Patriots, and had become eloquent in consequence.

"If we have to suffer," he said in continuation, "we will suffer together, and the knowledge that we have struck a death blow to tyranny and oppression—and—and—"

Happy paused—lost for words sufficiently grand to express his feelings.

The admiring circle were awe struck by their leader's eloquence, and those of the smuggler and brigand persuasion felt ready to rush forth and proclaim themselves outlaws, and hurl defiance at the world at large.

"And we have," Happy resumed, "struck —struck the foreign invader with—with——"

"Stale eggs," suggested one.

"With awe," continued the leader, "with awe, I repeat, and reverence for—for defenders of—of our country—yes, our country—I have done, my brave companions; let our fate be what it may, you will always find your captain ready to share your suffering as he has your perils."

A faint cheer greeted this burst of eloquence, and the band, much invigorated, but scarcely understanding Happy's meaning, turned towards the school as the bell rang.

With the last chime of the clock echoing along the quaintly-corniced roof, the doctor entered the school-room.

His face was eagerly scanned by the evildoers, but without the least benefit to themselves.

The kindly doctor appeared much as usual, his pale calm features placidly expressive of the undisturbed mind.

Once he looked towards Stanton Gleddell, but there was more of pity than anger in the searching grey eyes.

The usual routine of the morning went on as it had been wont to do, from the time the old-fashioned gabled house had been devoted to the training of youthful minds.

What could be the meaning of this strange silence on the doctor's part?

The culprits looked into each other's faces as this thought crossed their minds, and meeting only blank, hopeless looks in return, felt less comfortable than before.

Their discomfort was increased when M. Jean entered the schoolroom, his face sallower than usual, and his dark eyes glittering snake-like as he passed the form upon which Stanton Gleddell was seated.

The French class was summoned—the lessons learnt—and as the boys retired to their seats, the great clock chimed the quarter to twelve.

The doctor looked up from the book that he was examining—glanced round the forms, then, rising from his seat, ordered the lessons to be discontinued.

The hearts of those who had listened with such favour to Happy-go-lucky's fiery words gave a thump when the deep voice issued this command, and many of those who were inclined for a lawless life began to debate whether it would not be for the best to escape at once through the window, and seek a lonely cave by the sea.

The crisis was at hand. The doctor's hitherto placid face became as dark as a thundercloud, as he ordered the boys to assemble round the high desk.

THE BOYS OF BIRCHAM SCHOOL.

THE FRENCH MASTER CATCHES "VON LEETLE CRAB" AND GETS UPSET IN CONSEQUENCE.

Fixing his gaze upon Stanton Gleddell, he said, in a voice that electrified the culprits,—

"There has been a gross outrage perpetrated within these walls—an outrage so cowardly in its details, that I blush when I think it could have been perpetrated by young Englishmen."

He paused, and his gaze wandered from young Gleddell's face to those who were grouped before the desk.

"The ringleader," he said, "of this dastardly outrage fortunately can be identified—he will be expelled."

Happy-go-lucky began to feel as though cold water was trickling down his back.

"To those who were misled by their elder companions I shall speak hereafter, and punish according to the share they have had in this grave offence."

The small boys of the party began to feel a tingling sensation creep over their backs, and the heroic smuggler gentlemen made up their minds to go in for knee-boots, pistols, cutlasses, and waist-belts with large brass buckles without delay.

Happy-go-lucky set his teeth hard, and thought,—

"Now for it—now for the sacrifice."

During the few moments of doubt and suspense that passed before the doctor again spoke, M. Jean sidled to the doctor's side, and, as his small, bead-like eyes glistened with exultant malice, he whispered,—

"I do not wish that the small boys should have to be punished; it is but the large one, whose example made them so very bad."

The doctor inclined his head; then, to the astonishment of all present, he called out,—

"STANTON GLEDDELL."

A slight flush was visible upon the boy's handsome face as he stepped out from the group, and stood before the doctor and the malignant M. Jean.

"Stanton Gleddell," repeated the doctor, raising his voice until the echoes reverberated with startling effect among the oaken supports of the vaulted roof, "can you stand with head erect and with unblushing face, when you feel, or ought to feel, the humiliation this dastardly, un-English outrage must bring to your mind?"

The doctor paused, evidently struck by the fearless look of innocence perceptible upon Stanton's face.

"What, sir," he resumed, "have you to urge against being ignominiously expelled from the school?"

"Everything," was the quiet answer; "everything that a guiltless mind can prompt."

The doctor's eye kindled with a fierce light, and his hand mechanically closed upon the heavy cane that lay upon the desk.

"A guiltless mind!" Dr. Bircham repeated; "dare you tell me that you are innocent?"

"I dare do so, sir, and challenge any person to repudiate my words."

"Monsieur Gailland," said the angry master, "repeat before the school the statement you made to me last night."

Without a muscle of his face moving, the Frenchman glibly told his cunning story.

With matchless effrontery he averred that Stanton had passed him in the long passage when he returned from his evening walk. There could be no doubt, he said, respecting the boy's identity with the perpetrator of the outrage, for Stanton carried "one little red pot in his hand, and I did strongly inhale the smell of tars."

There was a suppressed giggle from two or three at M. Jean's pronunciation of the word "tar"—a giggle which a look of the doctor's at once suppressed, and caused the gigglers to sneak out of sight.

Gleddell's lips twitched nervously as he listened to M. Jean's lying statement; then at its conclusion he looked the doctor fearlessly in the face and answered,—

"Monsieur Gailland's statement is false from beginning to end. I was not near his room last night."

The truthful manner in which he spoke somewhat staggered the doctor.

He was a great disciple of Lavater, and the boy's face bore the impress of honest indignation as he boldly answered the base statement.

Dr. Bircham turned towards M. Jean as he said,—

"You hear this, Monsieur Gailland?"

The Frenchman shrugged his shoulders and turned the palms of his hands outwards as he answered,—

"It is not more than I expected. I did not think he would say that it was him that I met coming from my room."

The doctor was puzzled.

He, with characteristic clearness, felt that the opposing statements were equally to be believed.

He saw but one course open, so turning to M. Jean he said,—

"I cannot help feeling that a mistake has been made by you, M. Gailland, respecting the identity of the boy you met carrying the tar."

He was on the point of saying "tars."

"There has not been a little mistake," said M. Jean, his sallow cheeks reddening with rage at the prospect of Stanton escaping his revenge, "I saw him—him, and no other boy."

"It's a base lie!" said Gleddell, his temper getting the better of his discretion, "and you know it, Monsieur Gailland."

"Hush! Gleddell," said the doctor, with more kindness in his tone than he had hitherto used; "remember that is not the way to answer."

"I beg your pardon, sir, but I could not control myself."

"I'll tell you what, Alf," whispered Happy to a companion; "if old Frenchy does make the master believe his lies, I'll go and surrender myself to the e."

"Do," whispered Alf, who was one of those romantic gentlemen with a proclivity for cutlasses and high boots; "do, Happy, then we'll go for smugglers, and take Frenchy prisoner —then hang him at the yard-arm of our ship."

"Ship!" repeated Happy, "smugglers don't have ships, do they?"

"Of course."

"Hush! the master is going to settle it."

"There is but one mode of clearing yourself from this charge," said the doctor. "Can you bring a witness whose word can be relied upon, to prove that you were not near the French master's room at the time he declares he saw you?"

Stanton's face brightened.

"Hang it!" he thought, "why didn't I think of this before?" then said, "I can, sir. Mr. Randall can prove that I sat with him from six o'clock yesterday evening until a quarter to twelve."

"Is this true?" the doctor asked, turning to the melancholy usher.

"Quite true," was the reply. "I wonder I did not think of telling you so before."

It was not a matter of wonder to the doctor; he knew the dark cloud that pressed so heavily upon the usher's mind and made him so gloomy and abstracted.

The boys would have greeted Philip's account with a cheer, had not the doctor at once put an end to the scene.

"Sufficient!" he said sternly; "you can go, Mr. Gleddell."

Then, with a wave of his hand, he dispersed the school.

Looking through the window that opened upon the playground, he saw Stanton carried shoulder-high by four of the biggest boys, and the remainder trooped by the side, shouting as only schoolboys can shout.

Leaving M. Jean to follow him to the library, the doctor left the school-room; his face wearing an anxious troubled look.

M. Jean followed; his white teeth and parted lips giving him much the expression of a wolf suddenly deprived of its prey.

Philip Randall started when he saw M. Jean's distorted face; then, turning sadly from the school-room door, he wandered listlessly towards the outer gates.

CHAPTER VII.

M. JEAN'S AQUATIC PERFORMANCE.

WHAT passed between the doctor and M. Jean never transpired; but every boy who saw him leave the library declared that he looked "awfully sheepish"—also that he slunk out of sight as soon as possible—also that he was not visible for many hours afterwards.

The substance of the French master's interview with the head of Bircham School may be told in a few words.

The good doctor was much annoyed at the termination of the charge against young Gleddell, and, giving M. Jean a caution respecting his future conduct, added that he should endeavour to make friends, not enemies, of his pupils.

M. Jean promised to do so; but the malignant expression upon his sallow face totally belied his words.

Within sight of the school a glassy sheet of water was visible.

Upon its smooth surface the boys were wont to amuse themselves by boating, either in frail outriggers or the more substantial four-oared boat which was placed at their disposal by the doctor.

Upon the evening of the day which had witnessed M. Jean's discomfiture and young Gleddell's triumph, the greater portion of the boats were skimming through the tranquil lake.

M. Jean's unlucky star caused him to wander among the trees which skirted the water.

He had not gone far when he came across Tom Dickson, sitting on the bank, fishing.

The boy looked up as the master approached, and, mischief twinkling in his merry eyes, he politely wished M. Jean good evening.

The master returned the compliment, and the young traitor soon engaged him in conversation.

"I hope, Monsieur," Happy-go-lucky said, his face expressive of perfect innocence in last night's transaction, "that you have felt no effect from the disgraceful conduct of boys whom I am ashamed to call my schoolfellows?"

This was not bad from the ringleader; and M. Jean, fancying he had at last met a friend, seated himself by Happy's side.

"Not at all, thank you, Master Dickson," he said; "the trick did not have the effect the least me upon."

"That's a lie," mentally observed Happy; and then aloud—"I am glad to hear it, M. Jean—very glad."

The Frenchman looked at the candid face suspiciously.

"You are glad?" he said. "I did not think that one of the boys did care for the poor Frenchman, who by the great Revolution has lost his title and fortune, and obliged been to teach the belle language."

"Given up his rag-bag and stick!" Tom Dickson thought, before he answered—"I have no cause to dislike you, sir; neither do I think any of the boys have."

"Oh, but they tricks do play upon me!"

"There are sure to be badly inclined boys among so many, sir; but the majority, I think, would scorn to commit such a mean act as that of last night."

M. Jean's doubts respecting Happy's sincerity were rapidly leaving him, and he began to entertain a vision of learning from his new friend the names of those who had made his bed so uncomfortable on the previous night.

"You speak well, very," said M. Jean, "and I think you would not do such a thing."

"I would not, sir!"

"Nor yet"—M. Jean was beginning to test his companion's sincerity—"see it done?"

"No, sir!"

"That is very good; and would you, if you did know of anyone that put horrible stuff in my sheets, tell me the names of them?"

"If I knew them," Happy said, "I would tell you; but the boys that do those things keep quiet over it."

M. Jean was slightly disappointed; but the case was not quite hopeless.

"Ah, yes!" he said; "they would not let boys like yourself know anything; but you—you could, if you like, find them out for me?"

Happy-go-lucky's face was a study when M. Jean thus spoke. The proposal completely took his breath away, and he could only look blankly at the Frenchman's face.

"I have a beautiful—very beautiful—fishing-rod," the tempter continued, "that comes all the way from France, and I would give it to you if you did find out what I want."

The bait was tempting—Happy had but a hazel rod, and he knew by repute the merits of M. Jean's proffered gift.

"What's a fellow to do?" he thought; "of course he can't split, especially upon himself; but the rod—I must have that if I can; but how?"

"What you think about it?" asked M. Jean in a soft persuasive voice; "you know you can listen to what they talks about, and soon find out."

"So I can," Happy said, as though yielding; "so I can, sir; and I will try—you will give me the rod directly I tell you?"

"The very minute!" said the delighted Frenchman. "I will give it to you, and the line, and the hooks, and the little—what you call them?"

"Flies, sir!"

"Yes, yes; you shall have them all!"

Happy felt delighted with the prospect, although he had not the least idea how he should become the possessor of such an elaborate fishing-rod.

He would not split on his fellow-conspirators; but have the fishing-tackle he felt he must.

"Look here, sir," he said, "I dare say I shall soon find something out. Would you mind lending me the rod to-morrow?"

Happy's coolness somewhat astonished M. Jean.

"Lend you the rod," he repeated, "what, before you tell me?"

"Yes, sir—you see it's this way. If I split on the fellow, and directly after they see me with the rod, it won't do."

"Why it won't do?"

"Because, sir, they'll know directly that I have told you, and then there will be a row. You know, sir, I can't stand up against the whole school."

Monsieur Jean reflected—viewed the case in all its bearings, and finally decided upon granting the boy's request.

"I will let you have it," he said, "but you know, if you nothing find out about the affair, I must have the rod, and the line, and the—the flies again back."

"Yes, sir," Happy answered, his eyes sparkling with delight; "but, you know, sir, it will take me a long time, perhaps, to find it all out."

"A long time! what you mean?—several days?"

"Yes, sir, perhaps; I don't know, but it may be more than that."

Monsieur Gailland had his share of cunning, and a certain amount of perceptive power, which enabled him to see pretty well beneath the surface, by, Lavater like, reading the faces of those with whom he came in contact.

In this instance his judgment was much at fault; though he keenly watched every transient expression upon the boy's face, he failed to divine Tom Dickson's thoughts.

They parted apparently with mutual satisfaction.

Happy was to receive the rod and lines after morning lessons, and if successful in his mission, to become the happy possessor.

"Well," soliloquized Tom Dickson, "I'm in for a pretty go—after tarring old Frenchy's sheets, I am to tell him who did it! I will—over here!"

He jerked his left thumb over his shoulder, and in so doing nearly put out Jack Stanfield's eye.

Jack was of a facetious turn, and seeing Happy's head adorned with a new hat, crept softly behind the unsuspecting youth, with the intention of bonneting him.

As Jack raised his hand, Happy jerked his thumb back, and to his surprise this act was followed by a yell.

Turning quickly, he beheld Jack Stanfield doing a war-dance and howling with pain.

"What's the matter, Jack?"

"Matter!" was the reply; "you've nearly put my eye out!"

"Well I'm blowed!"—Happy, like most of us, used this expression without having the least idea of its meaning—"knocked your eye out?"

"Yes, stuck your thumb in it."

"Well, that beats everything! You can tell 'em, Jack!"

"Can I? And do you think I should put my finger in my own eye?"

"'Tain't likely, but I don't see how I could have done it."

Jack wiped his eyes with the cuff of his jacket.

"You did," he said; "I was just coming behind to bonnet you, and before I knew where I was I saw about a million of stars."

Happy laughed.

"Served you right, Jack," he said, "you're always after a fellow if he has a new tile."

"You ain't!"

"Well, I sometimes do a little in that way. Never mind, Jack, don't blink so. Come and sit down; I've a stunning thing to tell you—a regular wunner."

Jack left off blinking, and sat down by his friend to hear the "wunner."

Tom Dickson related the whole of the fishing-rod transaction, and the doubts he felt about being able to keep it.

"I can't, you know, Jack," he said, "keep him long by saying I haven't found out anything—if I do, he'll want the rod back—and it's such a stunner—all brass ferrules and a wheel."

Jack Stanfield was one of the conspirators, and M. Jean's most inveterate foe; and he expressed his joy at the prospect of doing Frenchy in a very forcible manner.

Throwing himself upon his back, he kicked up both feet, and sent Happy's fishing can spinning into the water.

Relieved and refreshed by this action, he drew his knees up to his chin and gave due deliberation to the mighty matter.

"You must have the rod, Happy," he said, "but how you are to keep it I don't know yet—I think the best way will be for you to ask Jack Williams—he's up to everything."

Tom Dickson took a rueful farewell glance at his can as it slowly went to the bottom of the lake, then answered,—

"I don't say but Williams is up to a trick or two, but, between us, Jack, he is not the sort of fellow to go shares in the matter."

Jack nodded approvingly.

Williams, although a favourite with them, was always afflicted with impecuniosity to the highest degree.

He had, as a rule, as much money as most boys; but after the second day of the allowance being paid he was as poor as ever, and continually borrowing.

Happy and his friend upon mature deliberation, came to the conclusion that Jack would either require a share in the spoil, or take it away—he being the biggest of the three.

"No," Jack said, "it won't do for us to set up a joint-stock fishing-rod company, although Williams is just the fellow for a director——"

"I shouldn't wonder," said Happy, interrupting his friend, "if Jack Williams does not become director of a joint-stock company when he gets to be a man."

"Nor I either, Tom," assented Stanfield. "I pity the poor shareholders if Jack gets hold of the coin!"

"So do I——halloa, what's up?"

"Frenchy's in—Frenchy's in!" came from twenty boys, as they rushed past the two friends.

Happy and his companion jumped to their feet, the former exclaiming,—

"So he is—run, Jack, or I shan't get the rod after all."

Poor M. Jean! he had been tempted to trust his precious person in a small outrigger, and in trying to overtake one of the boys who shot past him, caught a "crab."

There was a moment's struggle between

M. Jean and the oar, but the latter gained the victory, the outrigger capsized, and the last that was seen of the Frenchman was his heels; and the boys, forgetful that the accident might end fatally, set up a shout of laughter that was heard by those in the school playground.

The fear of losing the fishing-rod, and, let us hope, that desire to save life so inherent in the youth of our sea-girt island, caused Tom Dickson, who was a capital swimmer, to plunge into the water, and rescue M. Jean from his perilous position.

The boy had a hard struggle to prevent the Frenchman from clutching his hands—a mistake which most persons make when being rescued from drowning; but by threatening to leave Mr. Jean if he did not remain quiet, the gallant boy held him until young Stanfield came to his assistance.

Between them Frenchy was brought to land, and the youngsters who witnessed the scene saluted Happy and his friend with a round of cheers—such cheers as were, years afterwards, when their lungs became stronger and their faces bearded and bronzed, repeated amid the grey smoke of battle, and told the foe that the sturdy Briton was gathering for a final and overpowering charge.

Sounds which have upon more than one red field foretold the overthrow of England's foe—sounds which have heralded the sudden rush of British seamen when boarding an enemy's ship!

A cry that but one nation uses; and those who cause it by a brave action may well feel proud of receiving for a reward the hearty English "Hurrah!"

CHAPTER VIII.

MONSIEUR GAILLAND PLAYS AT "CRICKETS."

The crowd of youngsters forgot their enmity towards M. Jean when he stood, "a woeful spectacle," upon the grassy bank.

Fear had changed his complexion to a hue as livid as though the cold fingers of death were closing around his heart; his eyes became hollow, and though the day was warm and bright, he shivered like one stricken with the ague.

The boys pressed close to the hapless Frenchman, and many suggestions were thrown out to bring him round, among which were,—

"Roll him on the grass!"
"Slap his back!"
"Make him run about!"
"Give him some brandy!"

Poor Jean looked from one to another of his medical advisers in blank despair.

Some of their suggestions he vaguely understood; others were Greek to him.

Happy-go-lucky and his friend Jack Stanfield took upon themselves the whole management of the case, and, despatching one of the lower form boys for the brandy, strove to keep back the crowd and keep up M. Jean's spirits at the same time.

"Now, then, keep back, you young un's," said Happy, forgetful of his wet condition; "we don't want you all crowding round."

"Ain't we proud because we've been in the water!" was the remark of one of the young un's. "I say, Happy, you'll get a tin medal from the Society for the Confusion of Useless Knowledge for it."

"All right, Stikkers; I'll put my fist on your nose."

Stikkers replied by making a Chinese face at Happy—stay, do you know how to make a Chinese face, courteous reader?

No? Well, it is very easy. Place your right thumb to your nose, the end of the former touching the tip of the latter; then work your fingers about as though you were playing a clarionet. It does not want much practice—in fact, any street boy will teach you, and make you quite proficient at the first lesson.

When Stikkers had elaborated his face by using both hands, he retreated, or, to use an Americanism, made a retrograde movement for a strategic purpose.

In plain English, Happy made a sudden rush at the impudent young rascal, but, owing to his wet clothes, failed to capture him.

By the time the brandy arrived M. Jean, escorted by his rescuers, was on the way to the school-house.

They stopped to divide the brandy among them, then resumed their march, M. Jean getting a little better after partaking of the stimulant. They saw him to the door of his little room, then, promising to be back directly, rushed away to change their clothes.

When they returned they found M. Jean much better; he had donned an old but comfortable dressing-gown, and was sitting by the window, evidently much pleased at the gallant manner in which he had been rescued from death.

He smiled when the boys entered the room, and said,—

"I am obliged much for this—I must learn to do as the leetle fishes do."

"Can't you swim, sir?" Happy asked, opening his eyes very wide; "why I thought everybody could do that!"

"In England," said M. Jean, "you all do learn to swim very young, but in my country it is very few can do this."

"Fancy that, Jack!" said Happy, astounded at the ignorance of the French nation.

"I know," Jack said; "the French ain't English, are they?"

Stanfield was a thorough young Englishman —he believed that no land except his own was worthy of a place on the great map which hung over the fire-place in the school-room.

A prejudice which I hope the reader does not feel, for it is not only antediluvian and ridiculous, but unworthy of any who have even an ordinary intellectual mind.

"Some of the English," said M. Jean, "are very good and brave—you are both so; but the young pigs who came to my room last night were the bad and not the brave English boys."

Happy and his friend exchanged glances— perhaps they felt a little shame for their share in the previous night's lark, for they were silent.

"I do not know," said M. Gailland, "what I can give to you both for this, unless I give you, Mr. Dickson, the rod."

Happy's eyes sparkled with joy as the French master took the rod from among a pile of sticks, foils, &c., which were in one corner of the room.

"You can have it," he said; "but you won't forget what I did ask you, and I will buy one exactly like it for Mr. Stanfield."

"Look, here sir!" said Happy, "I don't like to deceive you; and much as I should like the fishing-rod, I must speak the truth."

"That is right, very right! What is the things you have to tell me?"

"Just this, sir: I would not betray my companions for all the money you could give me."

"Not tell me of the bad boys who did so wickedly tar my bed!"

"No!" Happy said; "it would not be right; and another thing, I was one who helped to do it!"

"You!" almost screamed M. Jean; "you—and you look in my face and tell me that if I did give you this it was for to tell me all about it? Oh, diable! get out; you shall not have one little piece now of my rod!"

He jumped from his seat as he spoke, and flourished the rod high above the boy's head.

Jack Stanfield expected to see the bamboo joints descend upon his companion's cranium, so going up to M. Jean, he said,—

"Yes; I was another who helped to do it. As for your presents, keep them; we can, I dare say, get some quite as good. And look here Frenchy——if you don't drop flourishing about with that rod we shall slip into you!"

The sturdy youngster had assumed a position which poor Tom Sayers might have been proud of, and Happy, running to his side, placed himself ready to aid his friend should hostilities commence.

The lads' attitudes took all the pluck away from M. Jean, and, depositing the rod in the corner again, he said,—

"It is sufficient—I will not tell the doctor of that—you have pulled me out from the water, so I will not speak. But you go from this room—it is the false way that you spoke to me on the side of the water that makes me feel——"

"Come on, Jack," said Happy; "leave him to jaw away; we'll take good care we don't ever help you out again—and you might want us some day!"

They left the room in a state of indignation at the unexpected turn affairs had taken.

When they reached the class-room, Happy turned suddenly upon his companion, and said,—

"Well, what do you think of the beggar?"

"Think!" Jack Stanfield said; "I don't think at all, but I know he is a most ungrateful skunk; if I saw him in the water again he might drown before I would go after him."

"The ugly ungrateful beggar!" growled Happy, "after getting wet all through him, to turn upon us like that!"

"I wonder," Jack Stanfield said, "whether he will tell the doctor about us."

"He may if he likes; I know what the doctor would say."

"Do you—what?"

"He would tell Frenchy that he ought to be ashamed of himself, and—halloa, Gled! what's up?"

"I heard that the French master was drowned," Gleddell said, as he ran towards his school fellows; "I hope it's not true."

"No fear of that," answered Happy. "We pulled the beggar out, and he nearly thrashed us with a bamboo rod for our pains."

Stanton Gleddell looked interrogatively from one to the other.

"It's true," Stanfield said, "so you needn't look so surprised."

"Enough to make a fellow look surprised," Gleddell said, "to hear you say that a man whose life you have saved turns round upon you in that manner!"

Happy and his friend enlightened Gleddell upon the matter; Happy telling him of the compact he had entered into by the water's side.

"You did right," Stanton said, "to refuse his gift, if he still wished you to play the spy upon your companions: it also showed good taste on your part to tell him so—much better, Tom, than if you had accepted his present, and been compelled to keep up a system of lies to retain possession of the rod."

"I'm glad, anyhow," Happy said in his old careless manner, "to hear you say I was right, because you always give us fellows good advice."

"I try to do so, Tom."

The trio passed out, arm-in-arm, to the play-ground, and in less than five minutes the whole of the lads were in possession of M. Jean's perfidy.

The compassion which had been excited by his immersion died away, and twenty fresh plots were begun against Frenchy's repose.

Bircham School Eleven were happy in the possession of a famous left-handed bowler.

This lad, though small for his age, had great strength of build, and in handling the cricket ball he was unrivalled.

A staunch friend of Happy-go-lucky's was this famous left-handed bowler; so when he heard Tom Dickson's story he at once proposed a novel revenge.

"I'm pretty friendly," he said, "with Frenchy, in consequence of having given him an insight into the mode of playing cricket."

"What's that," Jack Stanfield asked, "to do with serving him out?"

"Everything," was the reply. "I'll ask him to-morrow afternoon to take a bat; if he does, you shall see some sport."

Beyond this "left-hand" would not explain, so his impatient friends had to wait until the next day for a solution of his words.

The day came, as all days will come, whether for good or evil; and to the surprise of the youngsters who were playing, they beheld M. Jean, bat in hand, waiting to begin the game of cricket.

Left-hand was bowling to him, and to lure M. Jean on, he gave him several very easy balls to hit.

M. Jean struck the ball—though not far enough away to get any runs. He was much delighted at his wonderful success, and began to feel more at home with the bat.

Left-hand allowed M. Jean to have his own way for some time, and Frenchy, elated at the superb manner in which he played at "crickets," planted himself firmly, and, covering the wicket with his bat, prepared for a stroke that would at least score a dozen runs.

Left-hand winked at Happy and Jack Stanfield as he bowled a twister.

M. Jean drew himself up as the ball came whizzing through the air, but before he could raise his bat the ball came into violent collision with his nose!

There was a crash as M. Gailland's bat struck the wicket, and Phil Matthews, although the field rang with laughter at the mishap, walked quietly up and remarked,—

"Out, sir!"

M. Jean by this time had both hands pressed to his nose, and turning savagely to the wicket-keeper, said,—

"Outs, eh! my nose broke by your —— crickets! I have no more of them!"

He gave a howl expressive of the pleasant feelings which filled his breast, and a second howl when he beheld the bluff old Captain George Oakplank and his fair and lovely daughters.

The old sailor had strolled to the cricket field, "just to see how the young swabs now-a-days played at cricket. Not as it used to be in my time, 'Lenor. Ah! it was a game then!"

You will all say the same, my young friends, when Old Time mixes streaks of silvery white among your clustering curls.

The captain and his daughters were laughing at M. Jean's mishap—the former indulging in loud guffaws, the latter behind their pocket handkerchiefs.

M. Jean was not aware of their presence until he had dropped the bat and applied his fingers to the swollen and bleeding organ of smell.

It wanted but this to complete the agony. To be laughed at by the boys was bad enough, but this was worse!

In the privacy of his little room, and while applying a deluge of cold water to his nose, which by this time had swollen and looked not unlike a small beetroot, M. Jean fairly howled with pain and mortification of spirit.

"The pretty English miss," he thought, "is always to see me and laugh! This is the second times—*quelle horreur!*—and I that feel the great love for the pretty miss burning like one large fire here!"

He struck his breast, but, owing to the copious flow of the crimson stream, he was compelled to raise his hand again much quicker than he lowered it.

Happy-go-lucky and his lieutenant, the Mallet, saw M. Jean rush away when he beheld the captain and his daughters.

"I say, Happy," said the Mallet, "isn't the tallest of those girls the one that Frenchy is spooney about?"

"It is."

"Do you think she is spooney over him?"

"No, fear. Gled told me who she likes, but I ain't to tell any one."

"I don't want to know," said Mallet, "as long as it ain't Frenchy."

"Well, I've told you."

The Mallet suddenly commenced a dance expressive of intense delight, much to the surprise of Happy, who asked,—

"What's the matter, daddy long-legs?"

The Mallet made a clutch at his companion's sleeve, and, dragging him away from the cricket field, said, "Let's turn this up and find Charley Adlane."

"What for?"

"I'll tell you bye and bye. Won't it be fine?"

"I'll tell you what, young un'"—Happy caught the Mallet by the ear as he spoke,— "if you don't tell me now I'll make you cry out pen and ink."

"Leave go, Happy, and I'll tell you."

Happy left go.

"Look here," the Mallet said, "let's get all the fellows together, and see if we can't get up a good spree with Frenchy and the tallest of these gals."

"What!" Happy exclaimed; "what! one of the Captain's daughters? I'll tell you what, my cheerful Mallet, it's a good job for you that Gled is not here."

"Why?"

"He'd double you up, that's all."

"No, he wouldn't."

"He would, and you——"

"Don't be so fast. The game won't have anything to do with Miss Oakplank; only we must make Frenchy believe she is spoons on him, and we'll get him to go to all sorts of places to meet her, and——"

Happy gave a yell of delight. "Mallet," he said, admiringly, "you are a stunner!"

"I thought you'd say so. Now, then, let's get the fellows together and talk it over."

They went to concoct a fresh scheme against poor Mossoo, and Happy, the Frenchman's ingratitude still rankling in his mind, soon devised a plan that would amply compensate for the loss of the fishing-rod.

MISS OAKPLANK little thought the mischievous part she was unconsciously about to play in the forthcoming plot.

The pale handsome usher, with his young friend Stanton Gleddell, was with the Captain and his daughters, Stanton delighting the old gentleman with the recital of M. Jean's mishap after he returned home.

The old sailor was very wrath when he heard how basely M. Jean had endeavoured to throw the whole of the blame upon his young favourite.

"The monkey-faced, frog-eating swab!" said the Captain; "if ever I catch him in sight of my caboose again, I'll fall foul of him with this."

He flourished the steel hook in a manner both suggestive and unpleasant for the party threatened.

The stumps being drawn, the old fellow left the ground, Philip and Gled politely escorting them to the gate.

"I say," the old sailor said at parting, "you two can come down and have a hand of cards and a drop of grog with me, can't you?"

"Not to-night, sir," said Gled; "I must stay within the school borders until the week expires."

"Ah—liberty stopped—I'd forgot; never mind—you come when you can—the old man will be glad to see you. Hallao, Minnie, what the sulphur are you signalling for?"

Minnie blushingly answered—and I am afraid it was not a truthful reply,—

"I dropped my handkerchief, pa—and Mr. Gleddell picked it up."

"Eh well, you need not grapple each other's flappers like that. Come on, make sail, you jades—good-bye, Philip—don't forget, youngsters, come as soon as you can—ah! at it again!"

Stanton laughed at the old fellow's mode of hustling his daughters before him, then, linking his arm with Philip's, they went towards the school.

Passing a group among which were to be found Happy, Jack Stanfield, the Mallet, Charley Adlane, and young Stikkers, the

Mallet rushed to Gleddell's side, and whispered,—

"I say, Gled, old son, isn't the tallest of the captain's daughters named Eleanor?"

"Why do you wish to know?"

"Well, I'll tell you, Gled. Tom Dickson says it's Jane, and I've bet him fourpence it's Eleanor."

"You've won the bet," Gleddell said, as he passed on.

Back ran the Mallet to the conspirators and exclaimed,—

"Yes, it's Eleanor!"

"That's settled, then," Happy said; "now we'll get some one to write a letter to Frenchy. Which of you fellows can imitate a lady's writing?"

"I can," said Charley Adlane, "and I know Miss Oakplank's writing; so, as Happy says, that's settled."

"Yes," Tom Dickson said, "settled so far as the letter goes; but you must mind, Charley, to impress upon Frenchy that he is not to speak or take any notice of the supposed author of the letter.'

"I understand all that, Happy."

"That's all right, then. Now, about the clothes?"

"I can manage that," said the Mallet.

"How?" asked Happy.

"Easy enough. I'm on pretty good terms with the old tuck-shopman's daughter, and she'll lend me a suit."

"I'll tell you fellows how to improve the game," said Jack Stanfield. "I don't think it will be punishment enough for Frenchy to get off without having a little hard work."

"What's the idea, Jack?"

"This is it, Happy. Suppose we make up a good-sized heavy bundle, and have a lot of boxes. Frenchy, you see, will be sure to grab them; and when he is loaded like a donkey, Mallet can bring him across the fields right under the playground wall. Then we can collect on the other side, and give him a salute when Mallet makes himself known."

There was a yell of spontaneous delight at this addition. Then the conspirators dispersed, to meet in young Adlane's room, there to concoct the love-letter for M. Jean Gailland.

CHAPTER IX.

A LOVE SCENE.

NOTWITHSTANDING the sorry appearance he had upon the last two occasions made before Miss Eleanor Oakplank, M. Jean had sufficient vanity to dress himself within an inch of his life, and with a large white rose in his coat, presented himself at Woodbine Cottage.

M. Gailland argued with himself before taking this important step, and the result of this mental debate somewhat reassured his mind respecting the young lady's attachment for his splendid person.

"She is always very glad to see me," he thought, "and she smiles so pretty, and shows her teeth like little pieces of ivory when I go. Oh, it will not do to stop away. My figure, my dress, and the irresistible manner I have will soon make her forgets the last two times she saw me."

So he went, and fortunately the Captain was from home, or M. Jean would have been grappled with the steel hook; for, thanks to Stanton Gleddell, the old sailor had been informed of the purpose for which M. Jean visited Woodbine Cottage.

Captain Oakplank's face became blue with rage when he heard this, and shaking his maimed limb above his head, he blustered out,—

"What, the confounded jackanapes! the pirate! Come after my daughters, will he? By George, sir, if I catch him I'll stick this in his hull!"

He flourished the steel hook, and not until he had smoked several pipes, and drank a corresponding number of soothing mixtures, did he recover his usual equanimity of temper.

He gave the girls strict orders to give the pirate a broadside from all the water jugs, should he make his appearance; and fully believing these directions would be carried out, he went to pay a visit to a brother officer who had lately retired from the service.

He had not long left the cottage when M. Jean arrived, and the girls, instead of giving him a broadside, politely asked him to walk in.

Minnie stationed herself at the window to watch for papa's return, and M. Jean was left to do the agreeable with the object of his heart's idolatry.

M. Jean did not lose any time in the endeavour to gloss over the undignified retreat he had made from the cottage; and Eleanor, her eyes twinkling with mischief, apologized for her seeming rudeness.

M. Jean placed his hand upon his heart, and, bowing very low, accepted the apology, and remarked,—

"It was very droll my appearance; very much so, that I do not wonder you did laugh."

"I hope," Eleanor said, exchanging a glance with her sister, "you were not hurt with the cricket ball, Monsieur Gailland?"

M. Jean shook his head.

"I was not hurt, mademoiselle," he said; "oh no; but the appearance—it made me look so bad before all the scholars—that was the worst!"

"Cricket," said Miss Oakplank, "seems a very dangerous game, M. Gailland; for my part I wonder gentlemen like to expose themselves to a chance blow from the ball when in the hands of unskilful players."

"Mademoiselle speaks true. It is the players that are unskilled in the mode of throwing the ball that makes it so very awkward. If it were not for that, 'crickets' would be a good game."

"You were playing very well until that accident; in fact, papa said he had never seen a French gentleman play so well."

M. Jean felt delighted.

"What," he asked, "did mademoiselle think of my plays?"

"I thought it was very good," she said; "but I am but a poor judge—papa is the best, though"—she added—"he does not like foreigners as a rule, he could not help admiring the graceful manner in which you stood before the wicket."

Shame, Miss Oakplank!

"I think," said M. Jean, smiling pleasantly, "that the English do not care for the grace

THE BOYS OF BIRCHAM SCHOOL.

THE FRENCH MASTER PLAYS A GAME AT "CRICKETS."

which the sons of La Belle France are so noted for. You see, Mademoiselle, if crickets were a national game in my country, we should study graceful positions when standing before the wickets."

"And get the ball on your nose!" thought Minnie.

"No doubt," assented Eleanor; "but the English, as a rule, are so very boisterous with their games. Now, football, for instance: it would be impossible to study any graceful attitudes during a game like that. Did you ever play at football, Monsieur?"

M. Jean glanced ruefully at his shins, as he answered,—

"Once, mademoiselle; and I did get so many kicks, that I gave it up."

Eleanor smiled; she had been told of the tribulation which had befallen M. Gailland when he played at football.

Minnie suddenly turned towards her sister, and said, much to their visitor's astonish-

No. 4

ment,—

"Eleanor, there is some one coming across the field—I think it is papa."

Eleanor blushed, and opening the long windows which led to the garden, said,—

"You will excuse me asking you to step this way, for—papa—that is—I—he does not approve——"

"It's not papa," said Minnie, coming to her sister's relief. "I think it is one of the boys from the school."

It was Thomas Dickson, *alias* Happy-go-lucky, who (of course by chance) was strolling past the cottage.

He gave a sharp glance at the open windows, and seeing M. Jean's gorgeous form, a peculiar smile flitted across his face.

There must have been something more than the picturesque beauty of the quiet old country lane to have caused the Mallet, Joe Stikkers, Charley Adlane, and a small band of heroes of lesser note to saunter down the dirty lane at the back of Woodbine Cottage, at the same time as Happy-go-lucky passed the front.

By chance, the latter met his schoolfellows at the cross-roads, and the Mallet asked,—

"Seen him, Happy?"

"Yes, he's spooneying inside."

"Bravo!" said Charley; "everything goes well."

"Yes," said young Stickkers, "except finding a messenger."

"You are a lot," Happy said, "not to have captured a lout to carry the letter."

"It's all very fine talking," said the Mallet; "we've sighted three young chawbacons, and no sooner did they see us than off they ran as though the old gentleman was at their heels."

"Well," Happy said, "one will have to be captured before we go back to the school, because we must have him the first thing tomorrow morning."

The young lads in the vicinity of the school had good cause to run at the sight of the Birchamites, for the latter were in their glory when pummelling the agricultural generation.

"What's to be done?" Charley asked; "it will soon be dark, and our chance of making a prisoner will be very small then."

"The best plan I can suggest," said Happy, "will be for you fellows to disperse and hide behind the hedges, and as the louts come home from work make a charge and capture one."

"But how about keeping him until the morning?" said the Mallet; "you know the young beggars would sooner run a mile than come near the school."

"That will be all right," said Happy; "give the prisoner sixpence and promise him another if he will come to the playground at eight o'clock to-morrow morning."

"All very well," suggested the careful Stickkers; "but suppose he closes on the tanner and does not come."

"Should he do so," said Happy, "we will make him remember it; there, it's no use talking about what might happen; we must chance these things or give up."

"Look, look, Happy," said the Mallet, suddenly; "twig Frenchy coming down the garden with the young lady."

All eyes were turned towards the Captain's garden, as M. Jean, with the politeness of his nation, handed Miss Eleanor down the steps which led from the sitting-room to the garden.

"Stikkers," said Happy, struck with a sudden thought, "go and scout—look sharp; and bring us round the subject of Frenchy's conversation."

Stikkers ran like a young deer towards the rear of the garden, and as luck would have it, the young lady and her companion came and seated themselves in the summer-house.

Stikkers chuckled with glee, and placing his ear close to the back of the arbour, he listened with much inward satisfaction to M. Jean's words.

The alarm felt by Eleanor when Minnie gave notice of the Captain's supposed approach had caused her to give utterance to words which she would have given much to have unsaid.

M. Jean saw by her excited manner that old George Oakplank was not a consenting party to his visits.

Standing in bodily fear of the bluff old sailor, M. Jean thought the best plan would be to make an arrangement with Eleanor for the courtship to take place away from the paternal roof.

The steel hook and the Captain's heavy boots were subjects of more than ordinary dread to the sensitive M. Jean.

When they were seated in the little arbour, the young lady began to feel very sorry that she had yielded to her sister's advice, and encouraged the Frenchman's visits for the sake of giving his vanity and assurance a check.

But as matters had gone so far, there was no help for it but to continue the deceit until the moment came to astound the too susceptible Frenchman by ridiculing his pretensions, and giving him an abrupt dismissal.

It would have sadly marred the conspirators' scheme had she done so during that interview, and I much fear that young Stikkers would have been punished by each member of the party had he brought such an unwelcome piece of news.

Happily for the listener, this state of affairs did not come to pass.

After pulling up his shirt collar, and running his fingers through his short hair, M. Jean began to open the subject by saying,—

"When mademoiselle's sister did say that the Captain was coming, mademoiselle became much confused, and did say that the Captain did not approve of something. Was that something mademoiselle's most humble servant?"

Eleanor cast her eyes downward, as she replied,—

"To be frank, Monsieur Gailland, my papa has a great antipathy towards foreigners, and would not be at all pleased were he to know that we admitted you during his absence."

M. Jean's eyes glistened at this confession. He laid the flattering unction thickly to his soul that the young lady must be very favourably disposed towards him to thus risk her father's displeasure.

"Ah, mademoiselle," he said, "am I wrong when I say that you do not share the dislike to our great nation which your father does?"

"I must not," she said, "do anything against my father's wish; but I thought when you came this evening it would be better to tell you papa's objections to your visiting us."

"Ah!"—M. Jean's face became red with suppressed passion—"I know it is to that boy —one of the scholars—that I owe this. I saw him speak to your good papa when I left the field of crickets."

"And when," thought Stikkers, "you stopped the ball with your nose!"

"You wrong Mr. Gleddell," said Eleanor. "I can assure you he did not mention your name."

"Then," said M. Jean, "it must have been the usher—the melancholy man, Mr. Randall —that said bad things of me."

"No," answered the young lady, a rosy blush stealing over her face. "Mr. Randall has not uttered one word against you. I can assure you it is a deeply rooted antipathy which seems inherent in papa—and, in fact, with all old officers."

M. Jean did not credit the young lady's words. Stanton Gleddell he believed was his foe, and this item was added to the deep hate he cherished against the boy.

After fidgeting for a few seconds with the rim of his glossy chapeau, he asked,—

"Can mademoiselle be of so cruel heart to banish me from the light of her eyes, and make me one of the most miserable of all the men that lives."

"M. Gailland," she exclaimed, drawing her hand abruptly away from his sudden grasp, "I cannot listen to these words."

M. Jean was down upon his knees in a second, and before she could rise and leave the summer-house, he made a firm clutch at her hand, then poured forth his declaration of love.

"I cannot help it," he said, "if you do kill me—for if you say no to my love, it will be my death. Oh, mademoiselle, how much I love you is impossible for my tongue to speak."

Half frightened, half inclined to laugh at his words and gestures, Miss Oakplank drew her hand away and said,—

"Monsieur, this is not——"

"Oh, lovely Eleanor," he went on, beating his breast with one hand, and pointing upward with the forefinger of the other, "I have looked at the stars up there at night, and I have looked at the moon, and they have been very lovely; but I have thought of you, and——"

"Papa's coming," cried Minnie, suddenly running down the steps, "Monsieur Gailland had better climb over the fence."

The interesting Stikkers, when M. Jean was abruptly stopped in his wild declaration, had reached the pinnacle of glee.

He found it a severe task to keep from laughing outright; so to prevent this catastrophe he refreshed himself by standing on his head.

In this position he heard Minnie's cry of warning, and throwing a summersault, he scurried off, keeping well behind the hedge, to escape M. Jean's observation, should that gentleman follow the young lady's advice and scale the fence.

The possibility of the fiery Captain catching him there brought the impassioned lover to his feet, and Eleanor, handing him his hat, added to his fear by saying,—

"Pray make haste—papa's sure to come down the garden, and if he sees you there will be something dreadful happen."

"Adieu, lovely Eleanor, I go—but were it not your father who comes I would stay and fight ten——"

"Pray make haste—here, this way—climb up the vine, and mind the spikes."

M. Jean scrambled up the fence with wondrous agility, and with the exception of leaving about two inches of his coat tail upon one of the tenter hooks which the Captain had fringed the fence with, he reached the other side in safety.

Pausing for a moment, he called out,—

"Again I say adieu, and I pray, if you love me, we will meet at the old tree in the wood to-morrow."

There was no response, so M. Jean scrambled up the fence and peeped over.

Miss Oakplank was busy with a flower bed, and fearing the Captain would see the saturnine face peeping among the lilac leaves, she said hurriedly,—

"Pray go, Monsieur Gailland; I will write to you."

He kissed the tips of his fingers, then suddenly vanished.

Eleanor heard a dull thud as his body came in collision with the ground; then a deep groan as he lay gasping for breath.

CHAPTER X.

A BILLET DOUX AND A PROJECTED ELOPEMENT.

THE last act of gallantry had cost M. Jean a severe fall. When kissing the tips of his fingers the branch of the lilac tree gave way beneath his weight, and he fell backwards upon the hard road.

It was some minutes before he could realize what had befallen him. By the shock he felt, it seemed as though he had been broken into several pieces, and each particular piece had flown some distance from his body.

First raising one arm, then a leg, and finally his head, he found that he was still in possession of the requisite quantity of limbs, and being much satisfied at the discovery, he scrambled to his feet and crept away.

The effulgent Stikkers had been a concealed witness of the catastrophe, and the joy his youthful bosom felt at the sight was exemplified by the manner in which he rolled upon the ground.

The careful youth had paused in his onward course, hoping that the Captain would discover M. Jean climbing the fence. This hope not being fulfilled, he was about to depart when the lilac branch gave way.

When Stikkers had sufficiently revived to resume the perpendicular position allotted to the superior order of animals, and at times that interesting section of Zoology known as Quadrumana, he observed M. Jean limping away from the scene of his misfortune.

Stikkers was quite close enough to the French master to observe the accident that had befallen the skirt of his little green coat.

Stikkers was a sharp youth for his age, so when he beheld the tell-tale rent, he at once came to the conclusion that the missing piece of cloth must be somewhere within reach.

In satisfying himself upon the subject he scanned the spot where M. Jean's full length portrait was traceable, but not finding it there Miss Oakplank's caution respecting the spikes came to his intelligent mind.

Yes, there it was, firmly fixed upon the rusty hook, and Stikkers was soon in possession of the prize; but not unobserved, for the Captain was slowly stepping down the garden, and seeing a small hand over the fence, he yelled out—

"Ahoy, you young thief; after my apples!"

The Captain's fiery face was soon visible on the top of the wooden boundary, but Stikkers had vanished.

The place re-echoed with loud shouts of laughter when the scout recounted the love scene, but the mirth reached its height when Stikkers graphically illustrated M. Jean's sudden fall.

"I thought," the narrator said in conclusion, "that Frenchy had tumbled to bits, and we should have had to have taken him to the sick-ward in a basket!"

The piece of cloth was seized by Happy, who, in the fulness of his heart, slapped Stikkers on the back so energetically that the slapped one lost all power of speech for some time.

"This," Happy said, referring to the piece of M. Jean's coat, "will do more for the success of our scheme than you fellows think."

"What will it do?" asked the Mallet. "I can't see that it will be any use."

"That, my Mallet," said Happy, "is in consequence of that portion of your anatomy being of the thickness of the article after which you are named."

"You'd better get a plaster for your jaw," rejoined the Mallet savagely; "I'm sure it will require one after that speech."

"No chaffing," said Charley Adlane, "let's get back to school and concoct the letter."

"We haven't got a messenger yet," said Happy.

"Here comes a lout," said a small boy of the party, "now's your time."

"Scatter," said Happy, "and pounce on him when I whistle; three of us will be enough; all except Mallet, Stikkers, and myself keep in cover."

They scattered, and, hiding behind the hedge, awaited the coming of a ploughboy who was blithely trudging homewards.

Sounds of the unsuspecting youth's power of song came down upon the breeze as he approached the ambush, and the broad countryfied manner in which he pronounced his words caused much quiet laughter among the listeners.

> Giles Scroggins courted Molly Brown,
> Ri fol di rol de rol de rey,
>   (This he sang)
> The finest wench in the country round,
> Ri fol lid al de ray.
> If you loves me as I loves you,
> No knife shall cut our love in two,
> Ri fol di,—oh———"

He was grasped by the Mallet and Stikkers, and Happy stood before him with a great piece of wood, which he presented as though it was a pistol.

"Surrender," Happy said, "or die."

Giles dropped upon his knees, and began to blubber out, "I haven't done nothing; don't hurt me."

"Get up."

Giles did so, and Happy continued—

"Would you like to earn a shilling?"

"Eh?"

"Would you like to earn a shilling?"

"Should zay so; goin' to gi'e us one?"

"That depends," Happy said; "we want you to take a letter for us to-morrow morning; will you do it?"

"Ee's, but give shilling fust."

"You shall have the shilling and the letter at the same time."

"When will that be?"

"At eight to-morrow morning."

"Where be I to get it?"

"At the school house."

Giles had recovered from his fear, but the mention of this dreaded place brought it back with redoubled force.

"At school house?" he said, "no—not if I kflow it, measter; last chap as went there got tossed up in a blanket; that won't do for I."

"Look here, Chawbacon," said Happy, "no one shall touch you—I'll see to that—so come and you shall not only have a shilling, but I have a necktie all blue, with red and yellow spots, you shall have as well."

"What be going to give us the shilling and neck hankerchief for?"

"To take a letter, that's all."

"Ah!"—Giles's hand disappeared beneath a matted heap of straw-coloured hair. "Be the letter for a girl? 'cos you chaps can send letters to 'em."

"You'll find that out to-morrow morning—now what say, will you come?"

Giles pondered—the inducement was very great, especially the blue tie with the red and yellow spots.

"Ees," he said, at length, "I'll come; but if 'ee touch I, thee had better look out, for I'll tell Farmer Dingle o' thee."

"Do you," Happy said, "live with Farmer Dingle?"

"Noa; but I works for un'."

"All right. Now, if you don't come and take the letter, we'll wait upon you when you leave work—so don't forget."

Giles promised not to forget, and when his captors had gone out of earshot, he recommenced his lament respecting G. Scroggins and Miss Brown, and at the conclusion of the pathetic ballad, thus held communion with himself:—

"They be rum chaps, to be sure, up at t' skule—they be; but I doan't care what they do to I, as long as they gie the hankerchic' and the shilling. If they doan't, I'll tell farmer, and he'll stir 'em up wi' long-pronged fork—darn 'em!"

The breakfast-bell had just rung, and Monsieur Jean Gailland was sitting at the open window, savagely watching the boys as they scampered towards the great hall to fare upon the matutinal meal with an appetite that proved how effective the hour's exercise was for the destruction of the small crisp loaves and their partners, the unctuous pats of fresh butter.

M. Jean saw his supposed foe, Stanton Gleddell, pass beneath the window, and, grinding his teeth savagely, he looked after the boy, and muttered,—

"Ah! to you I owe one great revenge. It will be paid—yes, paid with much interest, if

I have to leave the school for it."

There came a tap at the door and interrupted M. Jean's silent thoughts, and, imagining it was the boy ("Frenchy's moke" he was called in the school) who brought his breakfast, M. Jean growled,—

"Come in."

The door opened, and a red mass of unkempt hair delighted the French master's eyes. Following a downward line from this unexpected sight, he saw a dirty canvas cowgown, a pair of fustian trousers, much turned up at the bottoms, and filling up the intervening space; between the rolls of fustian were a pair of lace-up, hob-nailed, thick-soled, hard leather boots, which gave the beholder an uncomfortable idea that the wearer must certainly sleep in them.

Raising his eyes from the base to the apex of this apparition, M. Jean asked,—

"Well, what you want?"

"Be you," said the hob-nailed Mercury, "Monseer Jean Gay—Gay—Ger—dang the outlandish name—be you the French master?"

Wondering what on earth could be the meaning of this strange visitation, M. Jean said,—

"I am the French master, Monsieur Jean Gailland."

"You be?—that's roight. Then here."

He extended a very red—very fat—very dirty hand towards M. Jean, and, crushed out of all shape, lay a letter in the dirty palm.

This was part of Giles's instructions. The conspirators thought it would be a safeguard against M. Jean suspecting the handwriting were the letter considerably mangled.

At arm's length, M. Jean took the billet-doux, and, opening it, beheld a small piece of cloth.

"Diable!" he muttered, picking up the mutilated tail of his bottle-green coat. "I did not know I lose this. Ah! pig, some one has taken this from the pretty—the belle Eleanor."

The damage sustained by the bottle-green was instantly forgotten, as the delighted lover spread out the crumpled paper, and read these joyful words:—

"Monsieur,—

"Maidenly modesty prevented my earlier declaring the passion which I have long felt for you; but after the declaration you made last night, I should have told you the sentiments of my heart, had not our blissful interview been interrupted by the return of my cruel parent. Monsieur—or shall I call you dear Jean—I am now about to propose a means by which we can be happy. I know that my father will never consent to our union, therefore there is but one course to pursue—I must elope with you; therefore, dear Jean, be at the old oak in the wood at nine this night, and you will find me waiting your arrival, with all my clothes and jewellery packed up. Until then, loved of my heart, adieu.

"ELEANOR."

Forgetful of the interesting Giles, M. Jean capered about like a maniac, and enlivened the performance by giving vent to spasms of idiotic laughter.

When he became calm, he read the postscripts, which ran thus—

"P.S. 1. I send you the piece of cloth you left on the spikes, as I wish you to be married in the green coat you wore yesterday.

"P.S. No. 2. Do not, as you love me, dear Jean, mention this to a soul, and pray do not leave the school until a quarter to nine, in case papa should miss the clothes and jewellery I shall bring with me; neither, my dear Jean, must you speak one word, for I shall be so agitated, until we are under the school-house wall, on our way to the railway station; there, dear Jean, we shall be safe, and you may salute my lips with our first kiss of love.

"P.S. No. 3. Send me a few words very soon, love, to tell me that my bold act has not caused your heart to turn from me for ever, and I shall be happy."

M. Jean, with trembling fingers, wrote the following impassioned reply:—

"Cast you off, queen of my souls, delightful love? Oh, no! you are loved by a son of France, by one of the nobles of the old régime, who, but for the revolution, would have been able to have upon your forehead placed a coronet—but that being gone, has—but the heart is the same—and all he can write to the lady of his heart is that he dear loves her —stronger than anything else, and will be at the place when the clocks do strike nine, and then he will tell in words how he does love his belle Eleanor above everythings all else in this world, and with the kisses—the hundreds and hundreds of kisses—he says to the love of his heart, adieu, adieu, until nine of the clock.

"And for as long as the world do last he will be always the true lover,

"JEAN GAILLAND."

The grinning Mercury received the letter and asked,—

"Be I to take this letter where I got 'tother from?"

"Oui! oui!—yes, take it where you get the other."

Giles looked at the letter, then at M. Jean, then removed his gloves and wound up by agitating his hair and asking,—

"Be this all?"

"You must be one stupid," said M. Jean; "have I not told you to take this letter where you get the other?"

"'Ees, but hain't 'e goin' to gie I something?"

Thus enlightened, M. Gailland made a raid upon his pockets and finally produced a sixpence, a fourpenny piece, and a penny. Overflowing with joy at the contents of the letter he had received, he gave the whole amount to Giles, and that youth, without even a word of thanks, departed and left the door open.

M. Jean closed it, and, muttering something which sounded very much like *canaille*, he began to kiss the letter over and over again.

There were several round marks on the margin, which, had M. Jean been less excited, would have looked like dirty finger marks; but under the fever he suffered he thought they were impressions caused by the tears which fell from the gentle writer, and in kissing these spots he derived much gratification.

At the end of the long passage Giles shortly disappeared through an open door, and a moment after he was surrounded by the conspirators.

"Here's the letter," he said, giving M. Jean's production to Happy, "now gie I shilling and hankercher."

"All right, Chawbacon," said the chief, "here's your reward: now vanish, and if ever I catch you near the school unless I send for you, look out."

The rustic youth pocketed the reward and rushed down the stairs, and in crossing the playground he had to make good use of his legs to escape capture.

Being seen by about a dozen of the most mischievous lads in the school, one of the number raised a shout,—

"A lout! a lout! let's chevy him!"

Chevy him they did: if suddenly making a rush after Giles and shouting at the top of their voices was chevying, they were adepts at the art.

The conspirators had a war dance after M. Jean's letter was read, and in a high state of glee they looked forward to the *dénouement* of the well-laid plot.

Little did M. Jean imagine the loving epistle he pressed to his lips was the joint-stock effusion of Messrs. Dixon, Mallet, Stikkers, and Co. Possibly had he been less infatuated the composition of the billet would have struck him as being rather ridiculous, especially as it purported to have been written by an educated lady.

But he saw nothing of this; neither did he know that all the available talent among the conspirators had been used to concoct the epistle, to say nothing of all the letter-writers that had to be borrowed or surreptitiously abstracted.

It was a struggle to get it done in the time. Although they began (and several quires of paper were spoiled before the conclusion) at ten P.M., the sun began to struggle through the window frames before the last postscript was finished.

It was a hard night's work—not only the compilation of the letter, but the incessant watch they had to keep upon old Bill's movements. The old fellow, as ill luck would have it, was on the move until past one, and when he came near the room where the work was going forward the lights had to be extinguished, and those who were absent from their rooms had to make their escape and knock old Bill's light out to save themselves from being reported.

Six times was this act repeated, and antediluvian William, as he listened to the rustling of a dozen naked feet, growled savagely,—

"I'll catch 'em yet—then we'll see about putting my light out. Why, they've no respect for me at all!"

He tried by concealing himself in one of the recesses in the great passage to capture one of his tormentors, but, receiving a close discharge from several pea-shooters and the contents of a water jug, he gave up the attempt and beat a hasty retreat to his own particular den, to change his wet shirt—for the front was saturated—and get rid of the stinging sensation caused by the peas.

Poor old Bill! in spite of the tricks they played him, the boys loved the old man, and would have done much to have served him.

CHAPTER XI.
THE PREPARATIONS.

THE Mallet, young Stikkers, Jack Stanfield, and Happy-go-Lucky paid but little attention to their morning lessons, and much to their disgust they were doomed to stay behind until their uncompleted tasks were properly learnt.

The doctor left the delinquents seated side by side, and told them, in what the Mallet termed an aggravating voice,—

"When you are ready I will return to the school—the sooner you are ready the sooner you will be able to join your schoolfellows in the playground, and," the doctor added, "if I am not mistaken, there is a running match to take place; therefore, make haste with your lessons—I know you would not like to lose the sight."

With this the doctor left the unfortunates, and the faces, which had during his presence been earnestly bent over their books, were suddenly raised, and woful were the expressions thereon.

"I say," the Mallet said, "this is what I call luck, to be floored like this the very day we want the most time."

"Ugh!" growled Happy, looking savagely at his book; "I would not mind if we had everything ready for Frenchy—to be locked here for two hours is too much."

"Let's ask the head to let us off," suggested young Stikkers; "he'll do it."

"Will he?" said Jack Stanfield; "then again he won't."

"We can try," the Mallet remarked; "let's toss up who's to go to him."

"That's the idea," Happy said, fumbling in his pocket for a coin," "come on."

Among the four but two coins could be found; these, had they been good, would long since have been spent.

Happy had a French piece, Joe Stikkers a bad penny.

"I say," said the Mallet, "we can't go odd man with two coins; how is it to be done?"

"Easy enough," Happy said; "one coin between each two, the two winners to stand out, and the losers to go again."

So upon this they began, and Happy and his friend Jack stood out, thus leaving the palm between the Mallet and Stikkers.

The latter wanted to go the first five out of nine, but the Mallet overruled this, and they went "sudden death."

"It's the best way," said the Mallet; "the first time puts you out of your misery, and there's an end of it."

The Mallet came off victorious, and young Stikkers had to appear before the great man.

"What am I to say?" he asked; "I don't like the job."

"You'll have to go," Happy said; "so you'd better like it; no shuffling, or you'll get it hot."

"Let the young 'un alone," said Jack Stanfield; "he'll go right enough."

"He's an awful young beggar to sneak out of everything——"

"No I ain't. I'm not nearly so much afraid of going as some of you big chaps are."

"We'll see—now off with you and tell the

doctor that we shall be very much obliged to him if he will let us off."

"But," objected Joe, "I must make some excuse."

"Tell him," Happy said, "that in consequence of the match that is to come off, we cannot keep our attention fixed upon the books."

Stikkers departed upon this errand, and, as the door closed behind him, a face came to the open window, and a voice called out, gleefully,—

"Yah!—yah! kept in school! Look at the dunces!"

The trio turned just in time to behold Frank Summers grinning at them, and, as Happy made a charge across the hall, the boy darted off.

"I shall catch that young beggar before the day is over," remarked Happy, as he rejoined his companions; "and, when I do, I'll——"

"Look at 'em!—look at the dunces!"

The tormentor made his appearance at the door, but bolted before he could be captured.

This rendered the trio thoroughly savage; to be kept in school was quite bad enough, but to be taunted was worse.

"I say, you fellows," said Jack Stanfield, "that young whelp will be sure to come back again; so let's trap him."

"I wish we could," said Happy, "he'd remember it."

"It's quite easy," said Jack. "You hide inside the door, Happy—you, Mallet, crouch under that window, and I'll do the same under the other; so that, should he come again, we will grab him."

The suggestion was acted upon, and scarcely had they taken up their positions when Frank thrust his head in at the window under which lurked Jack Stanfield.

"Kept in school," he yelled, "and can't get ——o-o-o—ow!"

"Got you!" said Jack, grimly, as he seized his tormentor by the hair. "Come in, you young beggar—you shall have something!"

Happy and the Mallet came to their companion's assistance, and, despite Frank's yells and struggles, he was dragged inside.

"Table him," said Happy; "we'll learn him to be cheeky."

So Frank was tabled; and, while Happy and Jack held him down, the Mallet gave him a dozen smart cuts with a strap.

The punishment over, Frank was jerked upon his feet, then chased out of the hall.

His captors did not escape scot free; for Frank, to save himself from the blows they were raining upon him, suddenly threw a form across the hall, and the trio, before they could stop themselves, tumbled over.

Frank Summers gave a yell of delight when he saw them on the ground, and scurried off as quickly as possible.

Happy-go-lucky scraped his shin upon the sharp edge of the form, and as he stood ruefully regarding the wound he muttered a deep revenge against the author of his misfortune.

The return of Joe Stikkers caused them to forget their pain. Crowding round that hopeful youth, they impetuously began to question him upon the result of his mission.

"One at a time," said Joe; "but it was no good trying to get over the doctor."

"WHAT!" they exclaimed, simultaneously.

"He didn't see it," Joe said, savagely; "and, what's more, he's promised me a caning to-morrow for leaving the school-room without permission."

"That's it, is it?" Happy said. "Well, I'll make one to break the order he gave."

"I'll make another," said Jack. "We can't stop here; and it's half-holiday, too, and everything to be got ready for Frenchy."

Joe Stikkers and the Mallet were not so daring. Much as they would have liked to escape from durance vile, they had not the hardihood to follow their companion's suggestion.

"No." the Mallet said; "not for me. I shall stay. So I think the best plan will be to write a letter to Frenchy to put off the elopement."

"Yes," Stikkers said, "that will be the best. You big fellows don't get caned like us young 'uns, or you would not be so ready to disobey the doctor."

"Joe's thinking about the new cane the head brought down to the school this morning," said Happy, maliciously; "it is a thick one, and no mistake!"

"Poor Joe!" Jack said, taking the cue; "don't shout when he's laying it on. Keep up your pluck, young 'un!"

"I've had many a caning," Joe answered, "and never shouted yet. Still, you needn't chaff so much about it. I'd sooner have the cane than be served as you two will——"

"Shut up!" said Happy; "here's Mr. Randall coming."

The four noses went very close to the four books as the usher entered the school-room.

Walking straight to the delinquents, he looked over Happy's shoulder, and said,—

"Not much progress yet, young gentleman. The doctor has sent me here to hear your lessons."

"Look here, Mr. Randall," Jack said, looking up; "no fellow can do his task and a match coming off outside. You couldn't, I know, when you were a boy."

"I never kept my teachers a moment waiting to hear my lessons," said the usher; "neither during the whole of my school days did I receive one hour's punishment."

"You were lucky then, sir," said Jack.

"I'm afraid there are but few boys in Bircham who will be able to say the same when they leave."

"There are some, Stanfield," said the usher. "Young Godfrey, for example; look at that boy—how he rises from class to class. I'm afraid if some of you big lads do not pay more attention to your books and less to mischief he will out-distance you all."

"I hope he will, sir," said Happy, gravely. "Poor little Godfrey! he has no friends, and will have to work hard on his way through the world; not like us fellows, whose fathers have money enough to keep us without struggling on from day to day."

"I hope," said Philip, "that your opinion is not general."

"Why, sir?"

"Because," Philip said gravely, "it would bring but little credit to your instructors. You will all have to work, Stanfield, no matter what may be your position hereafter. The army—the navy—the law—or medicine, you must work, and work hard, before you can enter either of these professions. But come, we are wasting time; now begin with the matter before us, and show me the good stuff that is in you."

Thus he spoke to the boys, and little by little he brought their minds to bear upon the hitherto hateful task, and by assisting them over any difficult part, the lessons were finished by the time the dinner bell rang.

After dinner the friends met and began active preparations for the benefit of M. Jean Gailland.

A little difficulty was experienced respecting the feminine apparel. The young lady the conspirators had relied upon to furnish the disguise had refused the necessary aid at the eleventh hour; thus they were left in a fix.

"I'll tell you what it is, Happy," his friend Jack Stanfield said; "you must make up to the girl at the tuck-shop, or we are lost."

"I'll try," Happy said, as though the task was not very agreeable to him. "Fancy having to spoon with that red-headed girl! I'd almost as soon let Frenchy off."

"Be a victim for once, Happy," Jack said; "we don't get a prospect of such sport every day."

"No," Happy answered, "neither does a fellow get in for such a victimizing as I am in for."

"Never mind, Happy," said the Mallet, "it will not be worse than the dose that's in store for me to-morrow morning."

By long persuasion they at last got Happy from the playground to the small shop which kept a goodly supply of stale pastry, bad ginger beer, and damaged fruit for the refection of the Bircham boys.

The owner of this delectable store was blessed with a daughter, a lovely damsel of about sixteen summers—at least she would have been lovely but for two slight faults in her appearance.

These were, a pair of horribly squinting eyes and a fiery head of hair.

The boys, when the pocket-money was at a low ebb, and tick was necessary to procure the various delicacies dispensed by the fiery Venus, were wont to compare her locks to bright gold, and her eyes to stars.

This flattery seldom failed to procure the desired credit and a sweet smile from the young lady.

Nevertheless, she never forgot to chalk down an extra item against her flatterers, and when the score was being settled she would say, in reply to a customer's doubt respecting the correctness of the account,—

"Do you think I would cheat you, sir? I'm sure I am quite correct. Don't you remember you had the things about a week before the school broke up?"

She had them there. A boy's recollection could not under any circumstances carry him safely through all the sights and pleasures of the vacation; so the lady of the sunny locks had the coin, and the victims, out of revenge, used to term her a carrotty-headed, squint-eyed cheat.

This was said out of her hearing, for woe to those who openly waged war with the damsel. No matter how much their mouths watered for rosy apples, soft pears, or indigestible pastry; unless they could come down with the current coin, she would say,—

"Father told me I was not to give any more trust."

"But," the disappointed one would say, "you gave So-and-so tick yesterday."

"True, I did; but they are young gentlemen, and are never impudent to a lady."

It is, therefore, plainly understood that the damsel by degrees obtained an immense amount of homage from the youngsters, and whatever they had to say (and, as a rule, they had plenty), it took place far away from the damsel's presence.

"We'll go on a little way up the road," Jack Stanfield said, "while you negotiate with Carrots."

Happy sighed dolefully.

"I wish it was over," he said; "fancy that girl making eyes at a fellow! Don't go far away; I shall get through my misery as soon as possible."

They promised not to leave him, and Happy passed the dreaded portals of the tuck-shop.

Behind the counter he beheld the object of his hopes and fears; and the lady, who thought Happy the best-looking boy in the school, smiled when she saw him enter.

She knew her customers well, and as Tom Dickson was a little beyond the apple and tart age, she expected he had come to purchase a new line or a set of hooks, a selection of these articles being always kept in store.

"Good afternoon, Mr. Dickson."

"Good afternoon, Miss."

"Beautiful weather, Mr. Dickson."

"Yes; very nice, indeed."

"Yes—hem!—nice for fishing, Mr. Dickson?"

"Yes, for those fellows that like it; but I'm of Oliver Cromwell's, or Julius Cæsar's, or some fellow's opinion—I'm not certain which of these it was said it."

"What did they say, Mr. Dickson?"

"Not they, Miss; one said it—one only; and, now I come to think of it, I believe it was Dr. Johnson."

"Indeed, Mr. Dickson. What did he say about fishing?"

"Something about a fellow fishing has a worm at one end of the rod, and a fool at the other—that's what he said, or something like it."

"He!—he!—he! how funny!"

"Is it?" thought Happy. "I'm glad you find it so; and I wish you would not squint like that when you giggle. Hang the affair! How the deuce am I to begin about the clothes?"

The young lady, having suggestively giggled, asked,—

"I hope it's not your opinion of the matter?"

"Why do you hope so, Miss?"

"Well," she said, resting her elbows on the counter, and looking over her visitor's left shoulder (at least, so Happy imagined), "if it were so, I'm afraid we should not sell many rods or lines. Do you want a new line, Mr. Dickson?"

"No, not to-day."

The lady looked up, and the expression upon her face spoke as plainly as words,—

"What *do* you want?"

Happy felt this; and, nerving himself for the task, said,—

THE BOYS OF BIRCHAM SCHOOL.

M. JEAN ATTEMPTS TO SALUTE THE FAIR ONE.

"No; I don't think I shall have any more fishing-tackle this half. Now, I dare say you wonder, miss—that is ——" (Mentally—"Hang it! what am I to say to the carrotty-headed fright? She will think I have come here to do spoons with her.")

"I never wonder at anything you gentlemen do," she simpered, "you do change your minds so."

"Yes—oh—yes—that is, some of them do; but I don't think I should—at least, in some things—one thing especially."

The young lady's heart gave a throb as she thought of the possibility of her visitor having become smitten with her charms.

"And what," she asked, "is that one thing you would not change your mind in, Mr. Dickson?"

"Well," he said, "now, suppose I were very fond of a young lady—we'll say you, for example—I should never alter my mind."

"La! Mr. Dickson," she sniggered, as she

cast a languishing look towards the shop door. She intended this for Happy, but the glance shot off in an oblique direction.

Poor Happy! he had got thus far pretty well, but, as the crisis came, he began to feel hot and cold by turns.

"Don't you believe me?" he asked, desperately. "But of course you don't."

"Why shouldn't I? I'm sure, I always said to father, when he went on about the trust I gave, if there's one gentleman in the school, it is Mr. Dickson."

"Thank you," Happy said. "Now, if you have such a good opinion of me, I'm sure you would not mind doing me a favour."

"A favour, Mr. Dickson?"

"Yes, Miss, a favour, and one I would not ask any one else but yourself."

This was true; but he did not state the reason, so the lady felt flattered, and answered,—

"I'm sure anything that I can do I will."

"Thank you," said Tom. "You're a trump, that you are, and I shall never forget it."

This outburst was caused by the manner in which he had managed the difficulty, which at first seemed insurmountable.

"What is it you require?" she asked. "Is it trust, because I ——"

"No," Happy said, "I don't want any tick; but I want you to lend me one of your dresses and a cloak and a bonnet."

"You are joking, Mr. ——"

"No," Happy said, hurriedly, "I am not; quite the reverse."

"What a strange request!" she said. "Do you wish to use them yourself?"

"No," Happy said, volunteering an explanation; "one of my schoolfellows wishes to have some fun, that is all."

With an eye to the probable injury of her finery, the damsel said,—

"You won't tear the things, will you, Mr. Dickson?"

"No, Miss; everything will be returned as safely as I take them—that is, if you will let me have them."

"Yes," she answered—at heart sorry she had been so ready to oblige—"I will bring them down stairs for you now."

"Look here, Miss," Happy said; "I think you had better put the bonnet in a box, and the dress and cloak in another, then no one will know what I am carrying out."

"Will you take them now?"

"No," Happy said: "I had better wait until it's dark, hadn't I?"

"I think you had," she said.

Happy extended his hand, and the lady placed hers for him to take.

"Good bye," he said, "for the present. You don't know how much I shall think of your kindness."

He pressed her fingers, and, as though he had been escaping from a lion's den, made the best of his way to the door.

His companions were on the look out, and when they met, Happy said,—

"It's all right; Carrots is a stunner."

"Let's hear all about it, Happy," cried his friends.

So Happy told them, and they declared that he had managed first-rate.

"Should think I have," he said; "the boxes are the very thing. Won't Frenchy think he's got a prize?"

"He will," said the Mallet, "and no mistake. I say, suppose we stuff a small counterpane full of things, and put some brickbats in the centre. Frenchy is sure to carry them—he'll think it's the family plate."

This proposal was hailed with a shout of delight, and they went back to the school to prepare for the elopement.

CHAPTER XII.

M. JEAN GAILLAND FEELS A LITTLE ASTONISHMENT AT THE RESULT OF THE ELOPEMENT.

WORDS cannot express the state of ecstatic bliss which steeped the senses of our friend M. Jean.

The hours that intervened between the receipt of the letter and the time for the meeting with the disobedient young lady were the longest M. Gailland had ever known.

He could think of nothing but the happy moment, and, mercenary and selfish as he was by nature, the prospect was one of the brightest he had ever viewed.

Distance lends enchantment to the view, my Gallic friend, and the young lady's worldly effects are farther from your clutch than you imagine!

"I have but little quantity of money," mused M. Jean, "but she tell me in her note she will bring everything she have with her, and I hope there will be plenty of things."

Yes, M. Jean, brickbats especially—your young friend the Mallet will take care of that!

"She will have some money, too," he thought, "and I will borrow that; then, after it is all spent, I will sell the things she brings with her. Ha, ha, ha! The usher will go mad when he hears that she, the miss he love so much, has run away with Jean Gailland—ha, ha!—it will make him savage!"

Those in the secret had many a quiet grin that day as they saw the happy expression upon M. Jean's face, and it was as much as the Mallet could do to prevent himself from giving a yell of joy when he passed M. Jean in the playground.

He could not let the French master escape without a few words of annoyance, so, mingling with about a dozen youngsters, he called out,—

"Crickets! I have no more of them! My nose is broke with your crickets!"

M. Jean looked round for the offender; he suspected the Mallet, but that playful young gentleman was too busy examining a new bat which one of his schoolfellows had that day had from home.

"It's a stunner," he said; "a whalebone handle, too. You ask Frenchy, Ted; he's a judge of bats."

Ted was ignorant of the mishap that had befallen M. Jean in the cricket field, so, much to the Mallet's delight, Teddy walked straight to M. Jean, and, holding out the new bat for inspection, said,—

"Isn't this a good one, M. Gailland? You are a judge—what do you think of it?"

Poor Teddy! The words were scarcely uttered when M. Jean made a savage clutch at him, and, holding him by the collar of the jacket with one hand, boxed his ears with the other.

"You (slap) make (slap) funs of me (slap). I punish you, then—that what I do (slap, slap,

slap)."

Teddy tried to escape, but finding that impossible, he quietly endured the first edition of by no means gentle open-handed blows from his captor.

A little of this went a long way with Ted—so when tired of having his ears boxed, he gave M. Jean a sweep across the shins with his new bat.

The Frenchman yelled and clapped both hands to his legs, and the boy, released, rejoined his companions.

He looked for the Mallet, but that imp of mischief had disappeared.

"All right," Teddy remarked, "I shall not forget Mr. Daddy-long-legs for that—he'd better look out."

This was but one of the many dozen thrashings that were promised our facetious friend; and while these promises were fresh in the minds of his victims, the Mallet took especial good care to keep out of the way.

During the time M. Jean was gettin himself up for the meeting, five boys and the Mallet, garbed in female apparel, were making for the place of appointment.

Happy-go-lucky and Jack Stanfield staggered under a huge bundle; Joe Stikkers carried a bonnet box, and Charley Adlane another.

When they reached the spot, Happy and Jack threw their load to the ground, the latter remarking,—

"If Frenchy gets that load on his back he'll be broken in two."

"My arm is dislocated," said Happy; "I'm afraid we put too many bricks in it."

"Not enough," said the Mallet, from beneath his bundle, "I'd put a cartload in if I could have found them."

"You are too hard upon him, young 'un," said Happy, "and I'd——"

"No jawing," said Jack; "he'll be here directly, so pile up the plunder."

They made a heap of the bundle and the boxes, and the Mallet, assuming a sorrowful attitude, seated himself on the top.

"Don't forget to keep your handkerchief up to your eyes," said Jack Stanfield; "it will look the thing, and keep Frenchy from recognizing you."

"Where are you fellows going?" the Mallet asked, "you are not going to leave me in the lurch, are you?"

"No," Happy said, "you will be all right until you get beneath the school house; don't you remember, you have not to speak until you've reached there."

"I had forgotten that—off with you—I suppose you will be ready for us when we arrive?"

"Rather!" said Happy; "come on, boys, let's get the school out to see him come."

Keeping out of sight, they retraced their way back to the school, and began to collect all whom they could find.

They passed M. Jean near the school gate, and were much edified at the sight.

Whatever lingering doubts the Frenchman had felt respecting the young girl's love for him, they were dispelled when he beheld a female form seated upon the huge bundle, which had given Happy and his friend such a breathing to bring from the shed behind the playground.

"Ah!" he muttered, "she weeps! Yes; it is but natural she weep at leaving her father, although he has been too unkind to her."

The Mallet was indulging in a most delightful grin behind his white pocket-handkerchief.

"Here he comes," thought the hopeful youth; "now I must get up a good tremble."

He did so, and the white cambric was kept well over his face as the love-lorn Frenchman came close enough to obtain a better view of his bride.

"I come," he said, bowing and raising his hat as only a Frenchman can raise it—"ah! Mademoiselle, you weeps; but, oh, believe me, all your griefs turn to joy when you give yourself to me."

The Mallet nearly upset from his perch in giving an extra tremble.

"Let me," M. Jean said, "assist you—let me——"

The Mallet, well schooled in his part, pointed to the boxes, and slid down from the bundle.

"I take them, Mademoiselle," he said, "when you get off. Ah! I see you tremble very much. Let me——"

The Mallet bowed his head, and M. Jean, seeing the beloved one's hand so close to his lips, seized it and covered it with kisses.

"I can't stand this," thought the Mallet, as he drew his hand sharply away. "If he comes that again, I shall hit him on the nose."

M. Jean did not attempt it. He had begun to lift the heavy bundle, and, much to the fair one's glee, she beheld her lover with the goods fastened to his back by means of a cord across his shoulders.

"She has brought all the silver spoons and things," mentally reasoned M. Jean, as he staggered under the heavy weight. "Generous miss, she does know we shall want plenty of money soon."

The Mallet had to stuff the pocket handkerchief in his mouth to prevent an explosion of laughter as M. Jean, in stooping to pick up the boxes, nearly stumbled over upon his knees.

At last, after a long struggle to regain his equilibrium, the deluded Frenchman managed to possess himself of the boxes, and, nearly bent double, he walked slowly after the deceiver.

The Mallet chose the longest route to the school, and by the time they reached the sombre looking wall M. Jean was ready to drop.

"My back," he thought, "will not again get straight. She has brought too much with her. Ah! now I will have a rest——"

The spot was reached where he was empowered to salute the lips of the erring girl.

M. Jean, in the delight of the moment, forgot the weight of the bundle as, dropping the boxes, he stepped towards the fair one to claim the salute.

Mallet could hold out no longer. The Frenchman squeezing his hand and kissing his mouth was too much for the young rascal's nerves, so, much to the ardent lover's dismay, the boy threw up the veil, and, opening the cloak, roared out,—

"Not this time, Frenchy."

Before poor M. Jean knew well what had

taken place—before he could utter a word in reply—he was startled by a sudden shout, and, like magic, scores of heads became visible.

Over the school-house wall heads and grinning faces were thickly packed.

Behind the perfidious fair one he saw a group of his tormentors, and, unable to bear the sight, he cast the bundle from him, and fled, howling like a madman, from the spot.

CHAPTER XIII.

THE USHER TELLS HIS LOVE.

STANTON GLEDDELL and his friend Philip were walking arm-in-arm from the school gates when the French master fled from his tormentors, and, as ill luck would have it, Stanton, at the moment M. Jean came in sight, was laughing heartily at a remark made by his grave companion; and the Frenchman, scowling savagely at the pair, hurried past, vowing a deep vengeance against the happy handsome boy.

M. Jean felt convinced that Stanton Gleddell was the prime agent in the plot. The fact of the boy having laughed when the angry Frenchman passed forced the conviction deeper upon his mind, and had he dared he would have slain young Gleddell and his companion.

In happy ignorance of the dark cloud which the vindictive M. Jean would bring upon his life, Stanton and his friend went slowly towards Woodbine Cottage.

They passed close to the scene of M. Gailland's discomfiture, but all traces of the conspirators had disappeared.

The Mallet had seen the usher as he turned from the gates, and, giving the well-known signal, the boys scurried off in all directions, carrying the boxes and heavy bundles with them.

"Monsieur Gailland," Stanton remarked to his friend, "seemed greatly excited when he passed us."

"I did not observe him."

"You are a strange fellow, Philip," said the lad. "I verily believe at times that you are not aware of circumstances that pass within a dozen yards of you."

Philip smiled, a sad spirit-broken smile, as he answered,—

"I am at times lost to all save the remembrance of that fearful night——" he paused abruptly, then added,—"Not now, Gled. Another time you shall know why I seem so strange."

"I do not wish to penetrate the mystery which preys upon your mind, Philip," the boy said, "but I wish I could wean you from your melancholy."

The usher shook his head sadly.

"It is impossible," he said; "the malady is too deeply rooted to be eradicated."

"Not so, Philip. Mix more with your fellow-men; depend upon it solitude is about the worst physician you can have."

"I have often felt this," said Philip, "yet found it impossible to leave the quiet of my chamber."

Stanton Gleddell loved his friend, and he sought by every artifice in his power to lure him from his melancholy. The introduction to Eleanor Oakplank he had hoped would have brought about the desired effect, but as the time wore on he found, to his dismay, that Philip shunned rather than courted the lovely girl's society.

Stanton knew that Eleanor had more than a feeling of friendship for the usher, but of the state of his friend's heart he was in ignorance.

He had lured him from the companionship of a huge musty volume in the hope of drawing this secret from him.

"Have you," Gleddell asked, "ever thought how much the companionship of one of the opposite sex would alleviate your heavy sorrow?"

"I have, and the thought has given me pain."

"Why so?"

"Can I," Philip said, sadly, "seek the love of a pure-minded girl with the heavy blight that is upon my life?"

"Will it never pass away, Philip?"

"Never!" the usher groaned, his pale handsome face flushing, and his dark eyes glaring furtively around, as though afraid that the very trees were officers of justice, and he a hunted felon. "Never, Gled, never!"

His voice became hushed, and the last word came like a wail of agony, and was borne away upon the wings of the evening breeze.

Stanton was silent. Knowing how deeply Eleanor was attached to his friend, the utter hopelessness of her passion caused him the deepest sorrow.

They walked in silence until the quaint outlines of Captain Oakplank's cottage came in sight; then Philip paused abruptly, and, pointing to the cottage, said,—

"Not there, Gleddell! You are not going there?"

"Why," was the reply, and the speaker's face told the astonishment he felt, "why not there, Philip?"

"No, no; anywhere but that place. I cannot go there."

Gleddell bit his lip.

"How strange you seem, Philip. Is there anything so dreadful within these walls?"

"Nothing dreadful; but much for me to dread."

"Philip!"

"I repeat my words—much for me to dread."

"You speak in so strange a manner, Philip, that, did I not know you as I do, I should doubt your sanity."

Philip Bendall smiled—a strange mirthless smile; then, grasping his companion's shoulder, he said,—

"I do not wonder at your words, but you do not know all. You know me but as the usher of Bircham school. The dark life's cloud which hangs over me has not yet been lifted. When it has you will not wonder that I am afraid—yes afraid—to trust myself within the witching sound of that gentle girl's voice."

"Eleanor's?"

"Yes, Eleanor. It was a dark hour when I first beheld her."

Gleddell listened awe-struck at the wild expressions used by his friend; yet determined, if possible, to overcome this strange disinclination to visit Woodbine Cottage, he said,—

"I cannot understand you, Phillip, or I

should say I cannot understand the connection that exists between Eleanor Oakplank and this strange mystery which enshrouds your life."

"It is easy to understand," was the hurried reply. "My heart is filled with the lovely girl's image. Day by day have I struggled with the fatal passion, and the struggle has ended in making me, if possible, more wretched than before."

"You love her, then?"

Philip was silent.

"Speak," Gleddell said; "is it not so?"

"Unhappily, yes."

"Unhappily for me, Philip, for you have won her love, and——"

Philip pressed his hands to his brow, and almost shrieked,—

"Unsay those words! No! no! it is impossible!"

"It is true," Stanton said, angrily; "too true! Oh! Philip, why have you done this? Why did you not shun her companionship before she learnt to look upon you as she had never looked upon man before? Why have——"

"Cease, Gleddell. I cannot listen to your reproaches, although my heart tells me I deserve them. Why have I done so?—ha! ha! ha!"

"Philip, my friend, why this strange mocking laugh? It——here come the sisters. Calm yourself, Philip."

The usher raised his head, and every vestige of colour forsook his cheeks when he beheld Eleanor and her sister coming towards them.

"Heaven help me," he muttered, "and forgive me if I find my passion stronger than my will to do that which is right!"

Gleddell advanced to meet the young ladies, and Minnie, after the usual salutations were over, tripped towards Philip, and, playfully drawing him towards her sister, said,—

"Is this the way, O Knight of the Doleful Countenance, that you greet your lady love?"

"For shame, Minnie!" said her sister, her face crimsoning; "do not heed her words, Mr. Randall; she is—gracious heavens! how ill you look!"

"It is nothing," said the bewildered usher, "I—I have been reading too hard lately, that is all."

"Shall we stroll through the wood?" said young Gleddell, offering Minnie his arm, "or would you prefer returning home?"

"Through the wood," she said, archly; "unless you wish to assist papa in the extermination of the foe."

Gleddell laughed. He had upon more than one occasion suffered from the thorns on the captain's rose-trees when helping the old sailor to exterminate the green fly and other enemies to the captain's favourite trees.

Minnie passed her hand through the proffered arm, and the young pair went towards the green trees.

Philip, thus left with Eleanor, could do no other than follow the example of his friend, and, with swimming brain and throbbing heart, he felt the small gloved hand resting lightly upon his arm.

"You should not," Eleanor said, looking anxiously at his careworn face, "study so much, Mr. Randall, if it makes you so pale."

"I know not," he said, bending his head until his eyes met hers, "that I had a friend who cared so much for me until now."

She blushed, and, casting her eyes downward, answered,—

"It was very indiscreet of me to make such a remark, but the change in your appearance was so great that—that I could not help it."

He was yielding to the subtle fascination of her presence, and the memory of his great sorrow was passing away as the spell grew stronger upon him. "I am much changed of late," he said, "but I did not think my face would have so soon told the—the——"

He paused, and tried to crush back the words that came to his lips; but the sight of that beautiful face was too potent—the charm was too great to be broken, and he added,—

"The suffering I have endured of late——"

"Suffering!" she repeated, her heightened colour showing how much she felt his words.

"Yes, Miss Oakplank, such mental torture that I have at times prayed that death would come, and its cold grasp prove a Lethe for my sorrow."

She looked up at the twitching lips, and the depthless eyes became moist with tears.

"That prayer," she said, "was wicked, Mr. Randall. We have all to suffer, more or less, in this world, and should seek consolation rather than pray for death."

"We should," he said, sadly, "but I fear I am but as other mortals in my hour of affliction."

She looked at him interrogatively, and he answered her look by saying,—

"Rather than patiently endure the chastenings of spirit which make us better value the gifts of this world, we seek, or pray, to be rid of the earthly form of existence."

"You are but young," she said, "to wish to leave the world and its pleasures."

"The world has no pleasures for me, Miss Oakplank—the one object I would gain is beyond my reach, and life loses all its charms."

They were opposite a grass-covered mound, and around this grew a cluster of towering trees.

Towards this resting-place the usher led his companion, and by a silent gesture expressed his wish for her to be seated. She mechanically obeyed, and when he had taken his place by her side, she said,—

"Men seldom so easily relinquish an object so desirable for their welfare or happiness. You are too much shut off from the world, Mr. Randall, or you would not be so easily checked in the attempt to gain this one wished for——"

She paused, and a thrill passed over her as Philip gently took her hand between his.

"Your words," he said,—and his eyes lost their usual dreamy look, and became filled with a bright light,—"fall like balm upon my heart. I will not give up the hope of overcoming this seeming obstacle to happiness."

She did not attempt to withdraw her hand, and Philip, carried away by the torrent of blissful emotion which filled his heart, continued,—

"With you, Miss Oakplank, rests my future happiness or misery——"

"Sir—Mr. Randall!"

"Hear me, before you give utterance to words that may cast the idol I have raised to the ground—hear the cause of the anxious days and sleepless nights that I have passed since your witching voice and beauteous form awoke the hitherto dormant passion in my heart——"

She drew her hand away, but her face expressed more joy than anger at his strange incoherent words.

"I battled with the strong love which took possession of me," he said, "fought with it until I became the wreck you now behold—used all the sophistry I could call to my aid, but the result left me vanquished, ill, spirit-broken; and in the companionship of my books I sought to forget my presumptuous passion. I failed, and in all probability the grave would have soon been my resting-place, had not your words kindled anew the flame. Speak, Miss Oakplank—Eleanor—if I may dare address you by that sweet name—say the word that will elevate me to the highest pinnacle of happiness, or consign me to the abyss of despair."

Her head was turned from him, but his expectant ear caught her softly murmured reply.

"What am I to say?" she said. "I—I cannot—dare not answer you."

"Tell me," he cried, passionately, "dare I hope, or am I so distasteful to you that you cannot learn to love me?"

"Heaven help me!" she thought, "what can I do? I love him, yet I feel my father will never sanction our love."

"Still silent!" he cried, frantically. "Speak, Eleanor! do you love me?"

She turned towards him, and as her head fell upon his shoulder, she murmured,—

"I do!—yes, Philip, I love you!"

A wild cry came from his lips, and, clasping her to his beating heart, their lips met, and, as their hearts beat in unison, they partook of the first ineffable kiss of love.

The blissful embrace was broken by the return of Minnie and her companion. They had missed Eleanor, and when retracing their steps they beheld the lovers locked in that sweet embrace.

Minnie looked mischievously at her companion, and was surprised to behold his anxious troubled face.

"Come, Philip," Eleanor said; "here is my sister; we must return."

They arose and led the way to Woodbine Cottage, their hearts full of happiness, and their voices silent with excess of joy.

Stanton and Minnie followed close behind the happy pair, and when they had gone out of sight of the cluster of trees, a man emerged from the shade, and, watching the lovers, he slowly twisted the ends of his long moustache, and muttered,—

"A capital love scene. How fortunate that I concealed myself in time. So Philip Randall is here, and in my power. Come, that is not so bad. I came here to hunt up my French friend, and find another. Well, fortune favours the brave, and I think I know how much Philip will give me to prevent a pleasant little story from reaching that fair damsel's ears. Ho, ho, if I do not make this pay I deserve to be tucked up in a bed of red hot spikes, that's all!"

The stranger lit a cigar, and as he slowly went towards the school gates he continued,—

"So! my French friend is here, is he? Well I have no doubt he will be delighted to see me—as much so as my old schoolfellow. By Jove, I would not have missed that second edition of Romeo and Juliet for something."

The stranger laughed heartily, then, replacing the cigar between his lips, sauntered towards the school.

"H'm," he muttered, when he came in sight of the old house, "a comfortable looking place. I shall quite enjoy a few days down here. Delightful, and no sheriff's officers to hunt a fellow about. I wonder," he added, "what name my Gallic friend hangs out under. Oh! there's a boy; he'll tell me."

The stranger gave chase to one of the scholars, and from him learnt that a Frenchman named Jean Gailland was domiciled at Bircham school.

CHAPTER XIV.

THE CONSPIRATORS HOLD A GRAND COUNCIL.

PHILIP RANDALL and young Gleddell, when returning from Woodbine Cottage, met the tall handsome stranger near the school gates.

A sardonic smile wreathed the stranger's lips when he recognized the usher, and, coming towards him, he said, in a light bantering tone,—

"Well met, old friend! It is years since we saw each other."

Philip's eyes seemed as though they were about to start from their sockets, and, reeling backward, he clung to his companion, and gasped,—

"Edgar Greymore!"

"The same, Philip. Are you not delighted?"

The usher's eyes shot fiery glances at the speaker, and, clenching his hands, he strode forward and said firmly,—

"Out of my path, devil, or I will hurl you from me!"

The other laughed—it was such a laugh as the arch-enemy of mankind might have given when he was driven from Paradise.

"Come," he said—and his voice was as low and musical as a woman's—"this is but a scurvy way to welcome an old friend. Leave your companion, Philip. I have something, as they say in the play, for your private ear."

The fierce impulse passed away from the agitated man, and, clasping his hands with agony, he moaned, in a tone that was only audible to the astonished boy,—

"Fell fate! I knew the dream would soon be dispelled. Would that I had been sightless ere I again beheld that hateful face!"

"Come," Edgar Greymore said, "I am awaiting your pleasure, friend Philip. We have not met for so long, and I have much to say."

Philip Randall surveyed the speaker as though he were calculating the result of an encounter between them.

Greymore's slight but well-knit frame, his lithe movements, and the lurking devil in his eyes, showed how much he outmatched the usher in physical strength and deep ferocity.

Poor Philip, his frame enervated by the sedentary life he led, would have been powerless in the grasp of such an antagonist.

Greymore divined the other's thoughts, and, in his galling familiar mode of speech, he said,—

"Dismiss the idea, Philip. I did not come to quarrel; although," he added—and his white teeth gleamed unpleasantly—"I am prepared for even that. Come, step aside."

"What would you with me?" asked the usher, his voice low and broken. "Have you not worked me evil enough?"

"I——well, my friend, you must have mistaken. I worked you evil! A truce to this nonsense; let us retire for a few minutes, and I will tell you the object of my visit."

"What if I refuse?"

Greymore smiled.

"The consequence," he said, "would be unpleasant; very, I should say, were it known to the Juliet you so well played Romeo to, that her lover had——"

"Silence, fiend!" said Philip, as he left Gleddell's side, and walked towards the school house wall; "you shall have the interview you desire."

Greymore followed the usher, and for several minutes they stood conversing in low tones. Philip at first seemed as though resisting a proposal; the stranger, cool, defiant, seemed to threaten, until the usher yielded.

Then they separated; Philip rejoined his friend, and Greymore, gracefully raising his hat to Gleddell, sauntered carelessly away.

"Philip," Gleddell said, looking anxiously at his friend's pallid face and opening lips, "who is this dark handsome man?"

"A man!" the usher replied, "he is a fiend in human guise, a cold pitiless wretch, whose very presence pollutes the air, and he has threatened to disclose all to Eleanor." He caught Gleddell's hand as he added, fearfully, "I would sooner she were enfolded in the coils of the deadliest serpent than listening to the wily tongue of Edgar Greymore."

Stanton had been much struck by the appearance of Philip's terrible acquaintance—his graceful form, perfect chiselled face, the dark clustering hair, his hands, small and as white as a lady's, his soft musical voice, and the defiant expression of his dark piercing eyes formed a *tout ensemble* well befitting one of those graceful chivalrous bandit chiefs we at times behold upon the canvas.

The boy could not associate an evil mind with this hero-like exterior, and feeling that Philip had been somewhat too harsh in his opinion, he said,—

"It seems hard to believe that one so eminently gifted as this Edgar Greymore can be so black at heart."

"To you, Stanton," was the reply; "but to me, whose bitter memory is traceable to an early acquaintance with this man, his true nature is known; believe me, he is a devil incarnate, in spite of his outwardly fair guise."

Stanton bowed his head; he knew his friend's truthfulness, and, much perplexed in mind, he entered the school gates. In the long gloomy corridor he left Philip and went to his room, to ponder over the strange events of the evening they had passed together.

Philip needed quietude to calm his mind; he needed rest, to prepare for the struggle which awaited him.

He knew too well the pitiless nature of his boyhood's friend, and as he sat with bowed head, he covered his face and sobbed with agony.

"I could have borne his coming," he thought, "had not the fatal words been spoken which have linked my destiny with Eleanor's; he has seen her, and unless I accede to his slightest whim he will proclaim my crime, and she will be lost to me for ever. This," he added, rising, and leaving the room, "is the heaviest blow to bear."

Until the village church chimed the midnight hour the wretched man paced to and fro; then, worn out in mind and body, he threw himself upon his bed, and gradually sank into a state of blissful forgetfulness.

Within a few yards of the little chamber which contained the wretched usher, was situate the sleeping apartment of Happy-go-lucky, Jack Stanfield, and about a dozen of the lords of Bircham School.

This chamber was the envy of the lower form boys, and they looked forward to the time when they should reach the first form, and become magnates, whose words were law, and whose frowns were terrible.

Happy-go-lucky and his friend Jack had ordered their satellites, upon pain of being "smashed," to assemble in the first form room after hours.

The Mallet, Joe Stikkers, Charley Adlane, and their hopeful companions, after watching old Bill go his rounds, crept barefoot to the place of meeting.

Like a second Guy Faux, Tom Dickson had found a bull's-eye lanthorn, and as the conspirators arrived he drew back the slide, and, sitting up in bed, with his knees drawn up to his chin, thus addressed his auditory,—

"My noble companions! We have achieved a great victory, and from personal experience I can affirm that Frenchy's back must ache from the effects of that bundle which he carried. Now, first, we must return a vote of thanks to the Mallet for the able manner in which he made up the aforesaid bundle."

"I say," Joe Stikkers asked, "how are we to do the vote of thanks?"

"Ah!" Happy said, "yes. Why—don't you know?"

"No; do you?"

"Of course I do. It's easy enough. The Mallet sits upon the bed while we all stand up and say, 'For he's a jolly good fellow.' That's the way."

"Well," the Mallet said, "we'll put that off, in case old Bill might hear the row."

The leaders assented to this, and Happy's mode of doing his companion honour was postponed until a more fitting opportunity.

"Now," Tom Dickson resumed, "I have another plan to serve out our foe, and if we manage it carefully I think it will succeed."

"What is it?" asked the incorrigible Mallet, quite ready, as usual, to take his share any mischief.

This," Happy said. "Thanks to the way which young Stikkers scouted, we know all that passed between Frenchy and the young lady."

"Before you go any further, Tom," said Jack Stanfield, "remember that we can do nothing unless we have a rope ladder. Can any of you fellows get us one?"

Joe Stikkers resorted to his usual mode of

expressing exuberant delight; he stood upon his head and clapped the soles of his feet together.

From this position he was brought to the horizontal by Jack Stanfield hurling a boot at his back.

"Turn that up, Jack!" Stikkers said, rubbing his back, "that boot was heavy."

"I wish it had been heavier!" Jack said; "why don't you act like a Christian when you have anything to say?"

"I collects my thoughts when I'm in that position," said Joe, "so don't do it again."

"I won't, until next time—now out with the cause of your joy."

"You want a rope ladder?"

"Yes, that is the article."

"We can get one."

Happy was so delighted with the news, that he suddenly jerked out his legs and sent the Mallet flying from the foot of his bed.

"Where" he asked, "where is this pearl beyond price?"

"Eh!" Joe said, "drop that, Happy, or I shall have to bind up your paws with a strap."

"Now then, you beggars!" said Stanfield, "where is the rope ladder to be found?"

"In old Bill's room; he keeps it in case of fire."

Happy looked at Jack Stanfield, and Jack looked at his friend; they knew that none of the band would care to enter the old fellow's room.

The Mallet was quite ready for the emergency.

"We can manage it;" he said. "When the matter is talked over and argued, let's make a jolly row; old Bill is sure to come, and while he is searching the room, one of us must go and collar the rope ladder."

"Good," said Happy, "but would it not be an improvement if you were to be near old Bill's room when the row begins?"

"Well," the Mallet said, "I think as I have made the suggestion, some other fellow ought to carry it out."

"But you know the spot where to find the ladder, and it will be so easy for you to get it."

"Perhaps it will," the Mallet said, "well, I'll go."

"So far," said Happy, "so good—listen, all of you, to the plot, which if successful will beat the others into—into——"

"Fits!" suggested Joe Stikkers.

"Fits if you like, but the next time you interrupt, you'll find a bunch of fingers fitting your nose."

"I shouldn't if I were you, Happy," Charley Adlane remarked.

"Why?"

"You'd get your fingers cut with that spikey nose of his, that's all."

"Order!" Jack Stanfield said, "and let's return to business."

Young Stikkers growled out something about people being too fast, then became silent.

"This is the idea, boys," Happy said; "we must send another letter to Frenchy."

"He won't bite a second time," said the Mallet.

"He will," said Happy, "if we manage it properly: if you fellows will only be quiet for a few minutes I'll explain."

"The next mouth that opens," said Stanfield, "will be shut in less time than ever it closed before."

Jack armed himself with a water jug, and held the troublesome auditors in check.

"Go on, Happy," he said, "and make it as short as possible, for I'm getting sleepy."

Happy went on.

"He must have a letter," he said, "and in it some reference must be made to the scene in the summer-house; then the young lady must state that she came to the place of appointment at the proper time, and while waiting for Frenchy a number of boys came up, and she became so frightened that she ran home and left her luggage in the wood."

"Bravo!" yelled Stikkers.

"Order!" said Jack, "or you'll get this."

"She must tell him," Tom Dickson resumed, "that, to prevent a recurrence of a similar mishap, he had better come to the Cottage; and, to make sure that this elopement scheme has not been found out, he must bring a guitar and strike a few notes under her window."

Stikkers was about to stand on his head, but, detecting Happy's hand as it went in search of a boot, the hopeful youth became quiet.

"How about the rope ladder?" the Mallet asked.

"Oh! I had forgotten that. Frenchy must be told in the letter that a ladder will be hanging from her window for her to escape."

"Look here," Joe said; "how is the ladder to be fixed there, and what is it for?"

"I mean to let the old captain into the secret," said Happy; "he's sure to consent. Only, instead of the ladder being at Miss Oakplank's window, it will be at his; and when Frenchy is half way up we must cut away the bottom part, and leave him, like Mahomet's coffin, suspended in mid-air. Then, if the captain will do us a good turn, he will empty the water jug over Froggy's head."

The scheme delighted the youngsters, and they gave way to their joy by upsetting the beds and strewing the clothes about the room.

"Now," Happy said, "away with you, Daddy Longlegs, and hide near old Bill's room, and we'll kick up a row."

They gave the Mallet time to conceal himself, then lured the old fellow from his den by throwing the tin candlesticks about the passage.

Old Bill reluctantly tumbled out of bed, and, arming himself with a thick strap, ascended the stairs.

"It's no use reporting them," he muttered; "so I'll lay this about their backs."

A candlestick whizzing past his ears made him cautious in his mode of approach, and when he reached the room from whence the missile came every boy was melodiously snoring.

"Ah!" the old fellow said, "here's a nest empty. Where's the bird?"

A yell came from Jack Stanfield at this moment, and, with his hand to the small of his back, he rushed to his bed.

The porter made an entry against Jack, then toddled out of the room.

"What's the matter?" Happy asked, when

THE BOYS OF BIRCHAM SCHOOL.

M. JEAN FINDS THE ROPE TOO SHORT.

his friend took the flying leap out of bed. "if you had kept still he couldn't have seen you."

"Matter!" Jack ruefully answered. "When you hid that beastly lanthorn under the bedclothes you pressed the red hot bull's-eye against my back!"

CHAPTER XV.
THE SERENADE.

M. JEAN received the cleverly concocted epistle, and after several very careful perusals he began to mutter dark threats against certain of the Bircham boys.

He had no doubt of the genuineness of the missive, for the writer had taken especial care to mention little circumstances respecting the interview in the summer-house; and M. Jean fondly believed that none but himself and the young lady knew of that little scene.

The rope ladder which she promised to fasten to her window was another great stroke on the conspirators' part, and tended much to the success of the plan.

The guitar, too. M. Jean remembered having told the young ladies he possessed one of these lackadaisical instruments.

So, putting these things together, M. Jean felt assured that he should bear away the prize.

"So," he muttered, "the young pigs, they frighten the lovely miss away! I wish they were one snake, and I had that snake's neck in my fingers, that I could twist the neck of all of them at once—all of them!"

The hour named in the letter for the elopement to take place was ten o'clock; and M. Jean counted the minutes as the long hand outside the school-room time-piece slowly went its rounds.

He could think of nothing the whole day except the happiness that awaited him; and after the morning lessons were over the conspirators heard him strum-strumming upon the guitar, as he rehearsed the love song he intended to sing beneath the fair one's window.

Joe Stikkers stood on his head outside Frenchy's door during the performance, and derived much satisfaction from the repeated attempts M. Jean made to overcome a high note.

"Talk about cats' mol-rowing," thought Joe, "it's music to this row!"

Happy-go-lucky, with an assurance that was quite refreshing, waited upon the bluff old captain, and delighted the old fellow by reciting the mishap that had befallen M. Jean.

Captain Oakplank laughed until the tears came to his eyes at the vivid description our friend gave of the scene; and, finding the captain relished the joke, Happy said,—

"I've come, sir, to ask your consent to a fresh plan we have for curing Frenchy of his designs upon your daughter."

"Designs!" the old sea lion said; "the privateer! if he sails this way I'll fall foul of him and rake him from truck to keel."

"Then you will help us, sir?"

"Help you!—you Jack-a-napes, did I say I would?"

"No, sir; but I think when you hear the plot you will do so—it will be such fun."

Captain George Oakplank examined the point of his steel hook, and said,—

"Help you? Look here, my lad. I don't like sailing under false colours. You see this?"

He referred to the formidable appendage before mentioned.

"I do, sir."

"What I want is the rascally pirate to come here under my lee, and if I once grab him with this, he'll soon strike his colours."

"Yes, sir," Happy said, "you can do that, but I'm afraid you will not get him here unless you help us—perhaps, sir, you would like to hear about the trap we have laid for him."

"Eh?—will you cast loose your fishing-tackle?"

Tom Dickson told him the particulars of the rope ladder and guitar business, and much to his joy he saw the captain's face express the most intense delight as he proceeded.

"Hang your impertinence!" said the old fellow; "so you want me to hang the ladder from my window, eh?"

"Yes, sir, and allow Jack Stanfield and myself to be in the room underneath yours."

"Um!—dolphins and flying fish!—that's my store-room."

"Yes, sir; we won't touch anything."

"The jam, eh!—there's a cargo of that on the shelves."

Happy assured him that he had no liking for jam; as for Jack, he would faint at the sight of a jar of that sweet confection.

The captain entirely gave in, and Happy left the cottage, delighted with the success of his mission.

When he returned to the school the bell was ringing for the afternoon lessons, and Happy, hot and flushed from his long walk, only reached his seat in time to escape the doctor's searching eyes.

The remainder of the conspirators were in a fever of excitement to hear the result of their friend's mission, and sundry pieces of paper were passed under Happy's desk, inscribed with words that gave the young incorrigibles much joy.

When darkness set in Happy and his friend Jack carried the rope ladder to the cottage, and assisted the old captain to fix it inside the window.

They had to be very cautious in their movements, in consequence of the young ladies being at home.

"It will never do," said the captain, "to let the petticoats know our sailing orders, or they'll waylay the pirate."

Armed with a sharp table-knife, the lads were left in the store-room by the old sailor. He entered heart and soul into the fun, and, to prevent an invasion of the store-room during its occupation by Happy and his friend, the captain locked the door and placed the key in his pocket.

"Nothing like keeping the petticoats out," said the old fellow; "two of them would upset a fleet."

While the captain sat at the window, from which depended the ladder of ropes, the gentlemen in the chamber below found the darkness and confinement very irksome.

They could just distinguish the forms of their schoolfellows, as the latter concealed themselves in every available spot to have a good view of M. Jean's performance.

"I say, Happy," whispered Jack, "I'm getting tired of this; are you?"

"Rather," was the reply. "Talk about the prisoner of Chillon, no wonder his hair turned white! I believe mine would turn blue were I locked up for any length of time."

"Mine," Jack said, "would soon stand upright like frightful quills upon the oily turpentine."

"Don't mangle Shakspeare like that," said Happy, "but invent something to pass away the time until the pirate, as the captain calls him, arrives."

"I wish I could," said Happy, ruefully;

"there's nothing to be done, except breathe on the glass and sketch portraits."

"Tom," said his friend, "I smell some good things upon the shelves—oh, for a ray of light, that I could find the spot where lurketh the sweets."

"I say!" Happy said, "the darkness is taking effect upon you; let's have that speech over again."

"No," was the reply, "I go in search of the toothsome darlings, whose sweet scent brings the water to my longing mouth."

Happy heard his friend groping about among the jars, a goodly assortment of which stood upon a shelf within his reach.

Happy remembered his promise to the captain, respecting the sanctity of the jam, and called out to his companions—

"Come away from there, Jack; I promised not to touch anything."

"You needn't!" was the ready reply, "I'll forage for you, Happy!"

"But, look here, Jack, he'll find it out."

"Will he? Not much fear of that; I've robbed the old lady's corner cupboard too often to do it clumsily—Ha! here's a prize!"

"What have you found, Jack?"

Happy's resolution was gradually melting away; he, like his friend, longed to taste the good things within his reach.

"Found?" his friend repeated joyfully, "I think it's a jar of preserved damsons, by the feel."

A moment elapsed, during which brief space of time, Jack Stanfield had fetched out the largest of the "preserved damsons."

Another moment and Happy was edified by hearing his friend spluttering and gasping, as though he had partaken of something not good for his palate.

"What's the matter, Jack—are you taken bad?"

"Taken bad—oh, my mouth's on fire!"

"What is it?"

"Pickled onions!" spluttered Jack, "and I've chewed about a dozen red-hot Chilis."

Happy laughed heartily.

"Serves you right," he said, "that's a just punishment for—oh, here he comes!"

Jack Stanfield, his pocket handkerchief stuffed in his mouth, and his eyes streaming with water, ran to the window.

There was just sufficient light to distinguish M. Jean's well-known form, as, with a guitar under his arm, he slowly approached the cottage.

The pair beheld the duped Frenchman, as he placed his hand upon the rope ladder, as though to test its strength.

His next movement was the cause of Happy kicking his companion's shins to express his delight.

Slowly and cautiously M. Gailland ascended the ladder; at every step he paused and looked warily around. Stopping midway between the ground and the fair one's window, he placed the string of the guitar around his neck, and, much to the edification of the grinning pair, said,—

"I will show the lovely English miss how a son of France can serenade the lady of his loves."

After a little preparation they heard the guitar tink—a-tink—tink; then M. Jean's voice, as he began a little ditty of his own composition:—

"O lovely maid, O lovely maid,
   You have my heart in keeping;
Can you delight to hear me sing,
   Or to behold me weep-in-g?"

There was a dead silence for a few seconds after this effusion had left M. Jean's lips. In all probability the ropes would have been cut, had not the boys been so overcome with laughter that they found it impossible to do anything save roll about the floor.

"She opens not the window," muttered M. Jean. "Perhaps she is asleep, or waiting to hear my voice again. Yes, my leetle song that I have made has very much please her. So I will sing the grand verse."

He did, after the following style:—

"You, who by a father's cruelty,
   Have been from your lovier parted,
Oh, join with me in one big sigh,
   Or I shall be broken-hear-t-ed."

"I can't stand any more of this," whispered Happy. "Push up the window, Jack, and let's stop his howling."

Jack did so, and, to M. Jean's horror, the ladder was cut just below his right foot.

The guitar fell from his hands, and, with a yell that was heard far and near, he grasped the upper portion of the ladder.

Like a tribe of wild Indians, the boys emerged from their places of concealment, and danced and yelled beneath the luckless Frenchman. He saw that he had been duped, and began to invoke the direst curses on the heads of his tormentors.

In the midst of his savage speech, the window was thrown up above him, and M. Jean, with a hope that Eleanor would appear, looked up.

Horror!—out came a brawny arm, grasping a water jug, and, before Frenchy could lower his head, the captain roared out, in a quarter deck voice,—

"Pirates, ahoy! Look out for scaldings!'

Splash came the deluge in M. Jean's face, and, with a yell of rage and terror coming from his lips, he tumbled head foremost to the ground.

There was a general rush made by the youngsters to get out of his way, and M. Jean, drenched to the skin, and severely bruised by his fall, lay at full length beneath the window.

He had barely time to scramble to his feet, when the captain called out,—

"Ahoy!—ahoy! scaldings!"

Down came a second shower, but our Gallic friend was out of its reach.

A sadder, if not a wiser man, M. Jean slowly retraced his way to the school; and, throwing all the blame of this mishap upon Stanton Gleddell, he began to hatch a plot for the boy's ruin.

"So," he muttered, "he makes me what they call in English the butts of the school; he has done it for the last times, and should the chance of——"

A hand was placed upon the Frenchman's shoulder, and a pleasant voice said,—

"Pray who has incurred the blame of Jacques Cherdon?"

The Frenchman gave a stifled cry of terror, and turning beheld the handsome face of Edgar Greymore.

There seemed a subtle fascination about Greymore which riveted the Frenchman's gaze, and with lips shut and trembling limbs, he stood deprived of speech or power of moving.

The other—quiet, self-possessed, and evidently enjoying M. Jean's terror; coolly smoking a fragrant cigar, he seemed awaiting M. Jean's reply to the strange words he had used.

CHAPTER XVI.
MEPHISTOPHELES.

THE Frenchman's terror passed away, and assuming a boldness that his white face and trembling lips belied, he said,—

"You have made a mistake, sir, my name is——"

"Jacques Cherdon," said Edgar Greymore. "You play your part well, my friend, but not well enough to deceive me."

M. Jean checked his words, and looked as though he would have dashed the stranger to the earth; the other seemed to know these thoughts, and the mocking smile deepened upon his lips, and his small white hand carelessly caressed his long glossy moustachios.

"I tell you," M. Jean said, with savage force, "I am not the person you name. I am called Jean Gailland."

He would have passed on, but Greymore stood in his path.

"Possibly," he said, "such may be your appellation; but I think I can remember a certain Jacques Cherdon who helped an Englishman to commit a robbery at Chalons-sur-Marne. Do you remember that circumstance, my friend?"

"I do not," was the dogged reply. "I know neither you nor Jacques Cherdon."

"How strange," said Edgar Greymore, "that your memory should be so bad. Possibly you forget a certain Jacques who was chained to an oar at the galleys with his partner in the robbery——"

M. Jean bit his lip until the blood came, and again attempted to pass.

"Stay," said his tormentor, "we must not part until I have refreshed your memory."

M. Jean could not speak, but with strained eyeballs continued to gaze fearfully upon the speaker's face.

"Come, Jacques, or Jean, whichever you like, let us walk this way. I have not seen you for so long that a chat will be quite pleasant."

"Devil—I——"

"Let me see," continued Greymore, calmly, "since you and I escaped from the galleys fortune has played me some saucy tricks; you, my dear Jacques, seem pretty comfortable, except for the fact of being rather wet. Oh, by the way, Jacques, if you have any pretensions towards that black-eyed young lady, I should advise you to give them up, for *I mean to have her myself.*"

"*Diable!*" exclaimed M. Jean. "I will denounce you—I will——"

"Ha! ha! So you confess to knowing me—good. I thought you would listen to reason, and save me the trouble of going to that spectacled pedagogue and telling him a little of the private history of his French master."

M. Jean turned savagely upon his companion.

"Were you to do so," he said, "I would kill you——"

Greymore laughed derisively.

"Kill me?" he said, "a pretty threat to hold out to an old friend! Come, Jacques, give me your hand; we can be useful to each other."

He held out his hand as he spoke, but M. Jean turned contemptuously away.

"I want not your hand," he said. "I came here to live an honest life, but—but you have come like an evil——"

"Come—come," said Edgar, "I am not so much of the devil as all that. I will not mar your wish to live honestly, Jacques—I beg pardon, Jean—I came down here for certain reasons—I may as well be frank—I want money—a little to supply my present needs. Do me this favour, and we shall be good friends. I have a chance of doing a good thing for myself—I mean to have that girl—her father must be rich—and have her I will in spite of Philip Randall."

"Philip Randall, you know——"

"We are old friends, Jac—— Jean, and, like yourself, he would sooner read of my execution than see me here; for, again like yourself, he has a little secret which he would keep from the world."

M. Jean's eyes sparkled. Here at last was an opportunity to be revenged upon Philip.

He had no doubt about Greymore's willingness to assist him in any fell project he might form against the usher's peace.

With a view of sounding Edgar, the Frenchman craftily said,—

"This Philip Randall is a favourite of the young lady you ——"

"I know it, friend Jac—Jean, and I have spoken to him upon the subject."

"Well, what said he?"

Greymore smiled contemptuously, as he answered,—

"He refuses to waive his claim and defies me; but I shall settle that affair with him hereafter—for the present, my dear Jean, we will talk upon other matters. Can you assist me in a pecuniary manner?"

They were walking side by side now, and seemed as friendly as possible.

"I have but little money," said M. Jean; "my salary is but small. How much do you want?"

"A couple of hundred."

"Francs?"

"Devils!—no—pounds—yellow sovereigns or notes."

M. Jean halted abruptly. This demand fairly staggered him.

"Two hundred pounds!" he gasped; "I have not more than ten."

"Ten!" said Greymore, contemptuously; "you had better buy gloves with that, friend Jean."

They walked on silently for a few minutes, the wicked light in Greymore's eyes becoming deeper as he from time to time cast a sidelong glance at his companion.

M. Jean knew that a subtle plan was at work in his old companion's brain, and feeling how much he was in the smiling demon's power, the luckless Frenchman felt a cold uncomfortable sensation creeping over his frame.

"Friend Jean," said Edgar, breaking the long silence, "what caused your very damp appearance when we met?"

The Frenchman's face wore a savage look as he answered,—

"Those *canaille* play me a trick; they

make one fool of me twice—*mon Dieu*—but I have revenge for this—one great revenge."

"You know them, then?"

"I know one—I know that he made the others to do it. It is to him I have this revenge—the *cochon!*"

Greymore tapped his boot with a light cane he carried as he said,—

"Very proper, friend Jean—very proper; but as the affair is not interesting to me, suppose we return to the little favour I ask."

"I tell you before," said the Frenchman, "that I have only that little sum of money——"

"Which is useless, my friend; therefore the sooner you procure the amount I require, the better."

"*Mon Dieu!* how can I?"

"That is not my affair, my dear Jean; but have it I must, or a visit to the old pedagogue will be the result."

M. Jean hung his head, and looked imploringly at the speaker.

"I shall," Edgar Greymore continued, "give you until to-morrow night to make up your mind. So, until then, farewell, for I see my friend Philip coming this way. He is more reasonable, my dear Jean, than you are, for he brings me the little favour I have asked."

Greymore would have turned away, had not M. Jean caught him by the arm.

"Stay," he said, hoarsely; "I cannot get this money, no matter how long you may give me."

"Then, Jean, you will certainly soon see the last of the school, and find yourself in the hands of the police."

"You could not be——"

"Pardon; I could betray my own brother in a matter of this kind."

Nerved to desperation, the excited Frenchman said,—

"Do you want it——"

"Not so hasty, dear Jean. Come, listen to me. You have not the money?"

"No."

"Can you borrow it?"

"No."

"Then, Jean dear—you see I am getting quite familiar with your name—you must steal it."

"Steal it!"

"Yes. You look as much astonished as though you had never done such a thing before."

"You—you made me!"

"Yes; I made you do it, Jean. Well, we will admit that; and if you do it this time I shall have two of your sins to answer for."

"But," M. Jean said, despairingly, "I know not one who has so much of them."

"The schoolmaster, Jean, he must be rich; there, I give you the idea—now act upon it, and I will meet you here at ten to-morrow night."

Again the Frenchman detained Greymore.

"The doctor?" he said, aghast, "he will find it out, and I shall be transported."

"Bah! you are stupid, friend Jean; you wish to be revenged upon one of the boys, the ringleader of those who have twice befooled you; can you not fix the robbery upon him? It will be easy enough. Good-night. You won't shake hands? Well, I shall not be offended."

So whistling softly the refrain of a Parisian ditty, the graceful scoundrel sauntered towards a figure that came from the old schoolhouse gates.

M. Jean stood for some time, dazed by the tempter's words; then, as he beheld Philip Randall meet his old companion, he ran on, and did not feel safe until he had reached his room and bouble-locked the door.

With his wet clothes clinging to his body, he sat upon the side of his little bed, and covering his face with both hands, reflected over the devilish plan Edgar Greymore had proposed.

From this his thoughts went back to the time when he plied the oar beside the man who, like an evil spirit, had so unexpectedly appeared before him.

"I shall be ruined," he murmured, "if I do not satisfy his demands—ruined if I do, for there will be no peace for me. Every day will bring the fear of detection with it. Yet,"—and his eyes glistened savagely—"yet," he added, "if I can make that Gleddell guilty, it will be a great revenge, and a way to escape from the power of that devil, Greymore."

With this plan hatching in his brain, he undressed and went to bed.

Until the small hours, when the keen morning wind came playing among the trees, he lay tossing about, his mind torn by hopes and fears—the hope that he should be able to ruin the handsome boy, and save himself from Greymore; the fear that an attempt to rob the good old doctor would be detected, and followed by his banishment to the hulks.

In this state of mind he fell oft to sleep; when he awoke, the sun was streaming through the window.

He unclosed his eyes, and the undefinable sensation that some dreadful calamity was about to befall him came strong upon the unhappy Frenchman.

"At ten to-night," he muttered, "I must meet him; he will be there, and with a smiling face ask me for the money—money! curse the name of it! Would to heaven he had been dead before he came here!"

M. Jean held this self-communion in his native tongue, much to the edification of the boy who came to take away his soiled clothes and dirty boots.

All that day the figure of Edgar Greymore was before the French master's eyes, and once or twice, when he cast a furtive glance towards Philip Randall, he saw the usher's face wearing a gloomy look—such an expression as one might wear when he has lost all that is dear upon earth.

"He suffers," thought M. Jean. "I am glad! Much would I give to know the secret that gives Greymore power over this Philip."

The day passed, and night came; still the Frenchman was as far from following the scheme his tempter had held out as he had been on the previous night.

He had not the courage to attempt the robbery, neither could he calmly realize the inevitable effect of Greymore's disclosure to the doctor.

Vainly did he wring his hands, and pace to and fro his chamber for relief. There was but one way of saving himself—and he knew too well that Greymore would keep his word—he must rob the kindly old man, who had so oft befriended him. But how was he to attach the guilt to Stanton Gleddell?

A hundred schemes were formed, and almost as soon dismissed.

The time wore on, and he heard the clock chime the hour he had promised to meet Edgar Greymore.

It passed, and the Frenchman, the cold drops of agony standing thickly upon his forehead, pictured the dark handsome face of his evil genius as he stood among the elms awaiting M. Jean's arrival.

He saw in fancy the look of rage, and heard the hissing whispered words which came from Edgar's lips, when, tired of waiting, he left the place of appointment, muttering fierce threats for the morrow.

M. Jean threw himself upon the bed, and, burying his face in the clothes, tried to shut out the picture his disturbed mind created.

Suddenly, springing to his feet, he gazed out upon the darkness, and muttered,—

"To-morrow—to morrow he will tell the doctor everything, and I shall be ruined—turned from the school, and disgraced! Better," he added, "to do this—better to rob others, if I can. But, ah! that boy—that Gleddell—I would do it to get him sent to prison. But—but—I do not know the way to make it look like his work."

ANOTHER hour passed, and reflection added but to his agony; then, worn out in mind and body, he went to his couch, determined to risk all, rather than do the tempter's bidding.

With this resolution, he closed his eyes and slept.

From this state he was aroused by a noise outside the window.

"The bough of the tree," thought M. Jean, "blew against the glass."

He listened intently; and as the noise continued his limbs began to tremble, and his teeth to chatter with fear.

The window frame was being slowly opened.

The glorious queen of night was at her zenith, and the silvery rays, shining into the chamber, rendered every object as plain as though the noonday sun was shining.

M. Jean felt there could be but one that would visit him thus; and with every hair standing upright, he started up in bed and turned towards the intruder.

Horror! Edgar Greymore was entering the room; and within a foot of M. Jean's head was the deadly muzzle of a revolver.

CHAPTER XVII.

THE ROBBERY.

M. JEAN recoiled from the levelled tube, and in a voice husky with terror gasped,—

"Mercy! do not murder me!"

Greymore threw up the muzzle of his weapon, and laughed.

"Murder you?" he said. "What a bad opinion you have of me, friend Jac—Jean."

M. Gailland gazed strangely at the intruder, whose words were so much at variance with the peculiar mode of entry he had used.

Quietly lowering the hammer of the revolver, Edgar Greymore seated himself by the bedside, and continued,—

"The sight of a pistol, friend Jean, does not agree with your nerves. There, I have put it away; and when you have finished shivering I will tell you why I used it."

M. Jean was indeed shivering; he knew the merciless nature which was so well concealed beneath this outward guise.

"I—I—" M. Jean began, "did not——"

"Of course you did not," interrupted Greymore. "I can quite understand that. Now, 'list,' as the ghost said to Hamlet, and I will tell you why you received my welcome visit."

M. Jean devoutly wished the speaker had broken his neck when climbing the old tree which shaded the window.

"I came to the place appointed," Greymore said, "and not seeing you, I feared you were ill, friend Jean, and obeying the loving impulse which prompted me to discover the nature of your malady, I resolved to seek you out, and in the event of coming to the wrong room, I thought it best to place a pistol between myself and the individual—that is, had I entered the wrong chamber."

"You would not have used it——"

"Well, perhaps not the muzzle, but the stock is heavy, and would silence even a thick skulled nigger—here, look at it—it's a nice weapon, is it not?"

M. Jean drew back, and timidly gazing at the dark smiling face, wondered whether Greymore would use the butt of the weapon upon his skull if he refused to carry out the robbery.

"You don't like it, eh?" Greymore said, placing the pistol in his breast pocket. "Well, there's no accounting for taste;" then, speaking somewhat sternly, he asked in French, "Why did you not keep the appointment?"

Equivocation Jean knew would be useless, therefore he said in his native tongue,—

"Because I had not the money."

"Not obtained the money—what were you doing last night?"

M. Jean was silent.

"Ah, I see, friend Jean," said Greymore, "you were afraid to do it without my valuable aid, was it not so?"

"I was not afraid," was the answer, "but I could not think of any plan to bring the boy into the affair."

"Have you done so by this time?"

Jean replied in the negative.

"Well, it does not matter; we must trust to chance; but stay—at what hour does your foe leave his room?"

"The boys breakfast at eight."

"There is the opportunity, Jean—when he is at breakfast you must put a portion of the valuables in his box or hide them under his mattress; it will be a loss, but we must put up with it."

The Frenchman shrank from the scheme; it was not from any goodness of heart, but he feared detection, and fain would have given a portion of his life to have been rid of the tempter.

In vain he offered to send Greymore every penny of his salary as he received it, until the amount necessary to satisfy Edgar's greed was paid.

The other laughed at the offer, and, with a significance which was not lost upon the French master, he said,—

"Save your words, Jean; it must be done to-night, or I shall be compelled to relate a little story respecting an affair which took place at Chalons-sur-Marne, and, dear Jean, should the gentlemen doubt my statement, I have a copy of the trial report in my pocket. Moreover, dear Jean, there is the felon's brand upon your arm; so, under these circumstances, I think it will be best for us to work together."

"Devil!" muttered the Frenchman, angrily; "were you to do this I would ——"

"No, friend Jean, it would be no use for you to declare that I helped you to the galleys —not the least use—for I have been very careful in taking my measures to prevent any accident to myself should you denounce me."

Jean Gailland bit his lips until the blood came.

"Come," Greymore continued, "the day will soon be here; jump out of bed, and let us get this little matter over."

Much as he would have felt had he had to prepare for his execution, the Frenchman arose and dressed himself.

Greymore sat near the window, smoking a cigar, and quietly watched the wretched man until he had dressed.

"Do you think," he asked, "it would be safe to visit the doctor's bedroom, or shall we be compelled o take the heavier but not less valuable contents of the plate-chest?"

"The doctor's room!' said M. Jean, aghast. "No—not there '

"Very well, my friend, the plate-chest, then."

Greymore took from his pocket a leather case containing a miniature set of implements used by burglars.

There was a small steel saw, which, by its exquisite finish, looked as though it had been fashioned for a lady's use; yet the teeth were so finely tempered that it would have been an easy matter to have cut through an iron door in less than half an hour.

He had also a miniature crowbar, the top of which, fitting a flat piece of steel, was worked with a leverage which would force open the most securely fastened lock.

A tiny dark lanthorn and a diamond for cutting glass completed the contents of this box. From another pocket he took several gimlets, a screw-driver, a hammer, and a small bottle of oil.

M. Jean watched his companion as he fitted handles to the tools—watched him as he would have watched the hangman adjusting a noose for his neck.

When the preparations were complete, Greymore said,—

"Lead the way, Jacques."

The Frenchman's limbs trembled as he left the room, and when they reached a small chamber at the foot of the stairs he silently pointed to the lock.

Greymore applied a skeleton key and opened the door. There was another lock to be forced when they entered the chamber; then the good old doctor's little store was at the mercy of Edgar Greymore.

While M. Jean collected the plate his companion watched, and before they had finished their work a light became visible at the farther end of the long passage.

Like a tiger waiting for its prey, Greymore, pistol in hand, knelt behind the door and held it partly open. Nearer and nearer came the light, and as the long shadow fell across the doorway M. Jean's heart bounded with joy.

It was Stanton Gleddell who appeared.

CHAPTER XVIII.
THE FIRST SORROW.

WHEN the village postman brought the little heap of home loving epistles to the school, there was one letter edged with deep black, and addressed to Stanton Gleddell.

A mist came before the boy's eyes as his trembling hand closed upon the ominous looking envelope. The writing was unknown to him—but his heart foretold the contents. His mother was dead! He knew it—felt it; and stricken by the crushing blow, he reeled back, and would have fallen, had not Jack Stanfield been near.

"What is the matter, Gled?" the warm-hearted fellow asked.

Gleddell pointed to the letter, which had fallen from his hand, and said feebly,—

"Read that, Jack, read it for me."

Stanfield, silent and wondering, opened the letter, and in a subdued voice read:—

"*Sir,*

"*It is my painful duty to inform you that your mother departed from this life at 10 A.M. yesterday. Under the mournful circumstances, it may alleviate your sorrow to hear that she died blessing her boy.*

"*The interment will take place on the 14th (five days from this), that is, unless you otherwise wish it. We shall be glad to see you as soon as possible respecting the mournful arrangements; for owing to your late lamented parent having mortgaged her property to raise a sufficient sum for the completion of your education, we are without the necessary funds (unless the household effects are sold) to pay for the funeral.*

"*It pains us to write in this strain, but thinking it best you should know the worst,*

"*We are, sir,*
"*Yours very obediently,..* —
"JACKSON & SNIPE,
"*Solicitors.*"

"*Mr. Stanton Gleddell.*"

When Jack Stansfield, with a bursting heart and tearful eyes, had concluded, Gleddell gave a heart-wrung sob of agony, and his head falling upon his breast, he sat the very image of hopeless woe.

Jack took his companion's hand between his own honest palms, and, in spite of every effort to master his emotion, the tears came from his eyes, and dropped slowly upon their clasped hands.

The boy made no effort to soothe his friend. He knew that cheering words would be but an additional pang to the already surcharged heart.

He waited until Gleddell should speak, and as he thought over the contents of that letter, a burning spot came upon his cheeks.

He knew enough of his friend's affairs to cause this indignation; he knew that Messrs. Jackson and Snipe were the mortgagees, and, Shylock-like, would claim their pound of flesh, even had the poor widow to be buried in a parish shell.

"The vultures!" muttered the boy. "So they would break up poor Gled's home before disgorging even enough to bury his poor mother—the greedy rapacious hounds! I wish we had them here; they should know what the duck-pond meant."

Happy-go-lucky and his shadow, Joe Stikkers, came towards the mournful pair, both full of spirits, and ready for any mischief.

"Here's a go!" Tom Dickson said. "Why, here's Gled practising spoonying with Jack Stanfield!"

"Chic-or-um!" shouted Joe, throwing a summersault, "here's a lark! Hi—here, Mallet, come and see the exhibition! Gled and Jack doing spoons, practising so as to be ready when they get a sweetheart."

The Mallet made the best of his way towards his friends, but an exuberant youth, armed with a peashooter, gave the Mallet such a stinging volley in the right ear, that he yelled with pain, then turned and gave the assaulter vigorous chase.

Joe Stikkers fairly howled with delight when he beheld the Mallet's long legs disappear through the open door, and he would have stood upon his head had not Happy-go-lucky seized him by the hair.

Jack Stanfield, upon whose aching heart this mirth jarred unpleasantly, turned almost fiercely to the boy, and said,—

"Leave us, Tom; Gled's in trouble."

They saw, by the sad face of their usually boisterous friend, that something wrong had taken place, and in a moment their hearts were touched.

"What is the matter, Jack?" Happy asked, his voice scarcely raised above a whisper. "What is it that has cut you up like this?"

Poor little Joe Stikkers stood gazing wistfully at Gleddell's sorrowful attitude, and a most unpleasant choking sensation came to his throat.

"Gled's mother is dead," Jack Stanfield announced; and Happy's eyes expressed the deep sympathy he felt for one who had so suddenly been plunged in the lowest abyss of affliction.

Walking softly towards the sufferer, he placed his hand upon Gleddell's clustering curls, and whispered,—

"God's will be done, Gleddell, and may He give you strength to bear it."

A convulsive throb passed over the stricken boy's frame, and he replied to these beautiful words by pressing the speaker's hand.

Tom Dickson returned the pressure; then, taking little Joe by the sleeve, they passed out of the great hall to the playground, to spread the mournful intelligence among their noisy mischievous playmates.

A greater proof could not have been afforded of the kindly feelings which the good doctor had implanted in the hearts of his pupils than the reception of the loss Gleddell had sustained.

The news spread with wondrous rapidity, and the boys at once left their games and congregated in groups to talk over the sad tidings.

Stanton Gleddell had lost his only relative, and the boys of Bircham felt a gloom steal over them, a dark cloud of sorrow such as they had never felt before.

When the first violence of his grief was over, the boy raised his head, and in a voice that was scarcely heard by his friend, said,—

"Jack, the blow is heavy—very heavy for me to bear—motherless and penniless since yesterday."

"It is hard, old fellow," said his sympathising friend, "but, as Happy said, I hope the Power that took your mother hence will give you strength to bear it."

"I hope so, Jack; I will try; but those lawyers—it seems hard to believe there can be such men in the world."

"It does, Gled; but tell me, what are your intentions?"

"I scarcely know yet, Jack."

They were silent for a few minutes, then Stanfield spoke.

"Gled," he said, "you had better tell the doctor; he will let you go home, and——"

Stanton placed his shaking hand upon his friend's shoulder.

"Jack," he said, "I have no home, no friends, not a penny in the world."

Jack Stanfield thrust his hands into his empty pockets as he said,—

"I have no money, Gled; but, thank heaven, I have good parents, and they will send me some."

"What do you require it for, Jack?"

"For you, old fellow—you must go to London, and——"

Gleddell placed his hand lightly upon his companion's shoulder, and said,—

"Do not trouble about me, Jack. Although I have not a penny piece in my possession, *I shall have plenty by to-morrow morning.*"

Before Stanfield could ask his friend where he could obtain the money, little Godfrey Bransome came timidly to Gleddell's side.

The boy's blue eyes were glistening from recent tears, and his lips twitched nervously, as he said,—

"I am so sorry for you, Gled; I know how I felt when I lost my parents—poor Gled!"

Stanton patted the little fellow's head, as he answered,—

"Thanks, Godfrey. I believe if kind sympathy could ease my sorrow, I should soon forget my loss."

"I shall never forget mine," Godfrey said, sadly; "it's a long time ago, but I always cry when I think of it."

Gleddell turned his head away, and the boy left the friends.

The school bell rang soon after, and as the boys came trooping in from the playground, Stanton went slowly towards the doctor's study.

He met the kindly old gentleman, as in cap and gown he came towards the class room, and in a few broken sentences told the story of his sorrow,—

"Come in," the doctor said, opening the door, "I should like to hear a detailed account of the proceedings of these gentlemen."

He alluded to the mortgagees; and when the boy repeated the sad recital, the doctor's face became troubled in its expression.

"There's no hope," he said; "they have a legal claim upon your mother's property, but—" he added kindly—"do not let that trouble you, Gleddell: you are young, and thanks to the manner in which you have worked, a good scholar. You must win your way in the world, my lad, and with the talents you possess the task will be easy. What say you to becoming a master in the school? There

THE BOYS OF BIRCHAM SCHOOL.

M. JEAN COMES IN FOR A PELTING.

will be a vacancy soon."

"You are too kind, sir. When I have somewhat recovered from this affliction I shall be able to thank you for an offer which I gladly accept."

The doctor seemed pleased with this answer, and, rising, said,—

"When do you purpose going to town?"

"To-morrow morning, sir."

They had a little further conversation; then the doctor knelt beside the boy, and prayed that the chastened spirit would meekly accept the sudden bereavement. Then he besought the great Omnipotent to watch over and protect the orphan.

Gleddell listened, awed yet soothed by the earnest voice and the simple yet expressive words; and when the doctor had left the study, the boy mused.—

"Yes, the doctor is right; I ought to bear this without repining. Yet—yet, it seems hard—very hard—to do so."

With thoughtful kindness, the head master

No. 7.

had given Gleddell the use of the study until he was in a better mood to mix with his schoolfellows.

"You will be alone here," he said; "more so than you would be in your own room. Sympathy—although your schoolfellows will do it from kindness—will not alleviate your sorrow."

The day passed wretchedly with the poor boy, who, save from a visit from Philip Randall, was alone with his grief.

Towards evening, worn out in mind and body, he lay upon the quaint old couch, and slept until the night had far advanced.

When he awoke the moonbeams were playing upon the windows, and threw soft prismatic shadows upon the opposite wall.

Gleddell started from the couch, and, passing his hand over his brow, strove to repress the sudden return of the deep wretchedness which had weighed so heavily upon him.

"Two o'clock," he thought, "and Philip, I have no doubt, is sitting up for me."

He applied a match to one of the candles which stood on the table, then, divesting himself of his shoes, went softly down the wide stairs.

The usher's room was situated at the opposite end of the old building, and Gleddell, to avoid disturbing the domestics, whose rooms he had to pass, left his shoes in the library.

Little did the poor fellow know how this thoughtful act would be construed by even his best friends.

Like a spirit he glided slowly down the wide corridors, starting every now and then as his shadow, lengthened into gnome-like figures, seemed to dance before him.

Once he paused as the night wind swept round the gables and moaned weirdly.

"I am nervous," he thought; "first my shadow makes me start, then the wind—ha!——"

He was about to ascend the stairs which led to the wing where his friend's room was situate, when he saw, or fancied he saw, a faint gleam of light playing upon the wall.

This time it was not fancy. The small streak danced, will-o'-the-wisp like, first on the wall, then upon the floor.

For a moment it would disappear, as though an object had intervened between its disc and the wall.

CHAPTER XIX.

CIRCUMSTANTIAL EVIDENCE.

GLEDDELL shaded the light he carried with his hand as he slowly advanced—every step he took a suspicion that flashed to his brain resolved itself into a certainty.

He knew the light must proceed from a small chamber wherein the doctor kept his plate.

It was known as the strong-room, and more than once the boy had been sent there by the head master for his cash-box.

The thought that came to his mind for a moment caused him to forget his grief, and, regardless of the danger he incurred, he went boldly towards the door.

"Thieves!" the boy thought. "It can be no one else at this hour."

The idea was confirmed as he beheld the door of the strong-room slowly closed as he approached.

Stanton threw himself against the closing door, determined to clear up the mystery, and, as his weight forced it open, he heard a suppressed voice give utterance to a deep curse.

Then came a heavy downward blow full upon his head—the candle fell from his grasp as he sank to the floor, stunned.

When he opened his eyes again he heard the voices of many of his schoolfellows as they shouted,—

"Thieves!—thieves!—thieves!"

Gleddell sprang to his feet, and, to his horror, found himself alone in the strong-room, his candle burning upon the table, and the door locked on the outside.

To add yet further to his amazement, he could hear Tom Dickson saying,—

"Stay until the doctor comes before we pounce on the thief."

"Can I be dreaming?" Gleddell thought, pressing his hand to his head.

Alas, no! it was a fearful reality.

The Frenchman and his companion saw the opportunity of fixing the robbery upon Gleddell, when he threw himself against the door.

Like a tiger Greymore sprang to his feet, and with the heavy butt of his revolver felled the boy to the ground.

M. Jean uttered a cry of alarm, he knew not what had taken place, until he heard the dull thud as the weapon came in contact with Stanton's head.

Dropping the cash-box he sprang forward, and as his face and lips became of corpse-like hue he exclaimed,—

"You have killed him!"

Greymore laughed—his companion's terror amused him.

"Bah!" he said; "it would take more than that to kill—quick, friend Jean, open the window, and drop the plunder through the bars."

M. Jean stood petrified with fear; every limb shaking as though he had been suddenly stricken with the palsy.

A savage oath from Greymore caused him to start, and gaze wildly at the dark angry face before him.

"Open the window, fool!" Greymore said; "here has Fortune played into our hands, and you stand gaping like an idiot, in place of taking advantage of the fickle dame's favour."

"The window!" Jean repeated; "what good——"

"I will tell you the good it will do," Greymore said, interrupting M. Jean's interrogation; "I can carry away the spoil from beneath this window, and when you hear my signal you can raise an alarm; there will be a rush toward this room, and if the boy has not recovered, they will attribute his condition to a sudden fright—you understand me, fool —the terror he would feel at being discovered."

Jean gazed blankly at the speaker, who was busy dropping the contents of the plate basket out of the window.

"We will leave him the cash-box," Greymore said; "it is too light to be valuable."

M. Jean had by this time partially recovered from his terror, and fully understanding the diabolical plot which his companion had so quickly formed, said,

"If I make the alarm they will think I have something to do with it."

"Absurd; in the confusion that will ensue they will not enquire who first raised the alarm—do not be an ass, Jean—play your game properly, and all will be well."

Greymore had by this time collected his housebreaking implements, and when taking the skeleton key from the lock on the strong room door, he asked,—

"Do you know where the key of this room is kept? if we can but obtain this it will be a splendid affair."

"I have seen the keys," was the answer, "on the doctor's table."

"In his bedroom?"

"No, the library."

"Do you think the door will be locked?"

M. Jean replied in the negative.

"Bravo!" exclaimed the villain; "run down, Jean, and fetch the key—splendid! nothing could be better—any wooden-headed jury would swear that our quiet friend here, took the key from the library."

M. Jean would as soon have faced a loaded cannon as gone upon this errand, and in spite of the awe he felt for his companion, he refused to fetch the damning proof of Gleddell's seeming guilt.

"Coward!"—Greymore's lips curled contemptuously as he spoke. "Where is this room?"

M. Jean described the position of the library, and Greymore, with a swift noiseless tread, sped towards it.

The Frenchman's hair stood on end with terror when he was left alone with the senseless boy—he could think of nothing but the doctor suddenly appearing at the door; and so strong was this feeling upon him, that he crouched in the further corner of the room, when Greymore returned with a bunch of keys.

A small white tablet was affixed to one, and as Greymore placed it in the lock, M. Jean staggered from the room.

Everything transpired as the scoundrel had anticipated. None knew who first raised the cry that caused the lads to rush from their rooms and repeat the words which fell upon Gleddell's ears as he regained his senses.

The doctor, in dressing-gown and slippers, was soon among the half-frightened crowd, and had not Philip Randall held him he would have entered the chamber wherein the poor boy stood with his hand pressed to his throbbing brow.

"Do not go inside," the usher said; "we do not know how many ruffians may be there. I have locked the door, and sent for the police; they are the proper persons to apprehend the burglars."

The doctor yielded to this advice.

"How came my keys here?" he asked. "I left them in the library."

"I saw them in the lock when I came," Philip answered, "and at once prevented the escape of those inside."

"They may have gone before you came."

"No," Philip answered, "I heard a slight noise since I locked the door."

They would have heard Gleddell's voice calling upon them to release him, had not the door been cased with iron.

Joe Stikkers had been sent in quest of a constable, and met a mounted member of the force riding slowly up the green lane which led to the school gates.

The clatter of the patrol's sword scabbard upon the large stone hall caused the boys to rush towards the head of the staircase to behold the arrival of the important functionary.

Stikkers remained below, in charge of the constable's horse, and, boy-like, thought it must be an enviable life to ride about the country lanes, draped in a long cloak, and a sword dangling from his hip.

The youngsters much admired the bold manner in which the man unlocked the door and advanced into the room, and many were much disappointed that he did not draw his sword as he prepared to meet the fierce ruffians who had broken into the school.

Every eye was strained to behold the formidable robbers in the clutch of the stout constable, and when the latter appeared grasping Gleddell by the collar, a cry of mingled astonishment and horror came from the youngsters' lips.

Philip Randall was struck dumb at the sight, and the good doctor—the recollection of the conversation he had held with Stanton strong upon him—stepped forward, and drawing the boy from his sturdy captor, said, "There must be some mistake, policeman; this is not the thief."

"Not much mistake, sir," answered the man in blue; "he was the only one in the room, and there's all the things thrown about."

Gleddell was too bewildered to speak until Jack Stanfield came to his side.

"Speak, Gled," he said; "tell the doctor you are innocent—tell him how you came there. I'm sure you are not the thief."

The boy repeated the words wildly, and passed his hand over his throbbing brow.

"Good heavens! doctor, you do not think I could be guilty of this?"

"I do not, Gleddell," said the master. "Tell me how you came in that chamber; explain the mystery, that we may yet capture the midnight robbers."

The boy, with trembling lips, told how he saw the light gleaming from the half-opened door—told how upon entering he was felled to the floor, and did not regain his senses until he heard the voices of his schoolfellows outside the door.

The policeman's face expressed the disbelief he felt, and before the doctor could reply, he struck in with,—

"May be the young genelman is right, sir; but before we goes any further, hadn't I better make an examination of the place?"

"Do so," said Philip, speaking for the first time; "it will end your doubts respecting my friend's innocence."

There was a breathless silence as the doctor and the officer inspected the room.

"There has been two at work," was the policeman's remark when he saw the open window. "Is there much lost, sir?"

The doctor turned from the plate closet, and answered,—

"Everything portable has been carried away; also my cash-box."

"That ain't gone," said the executive, taking it from the floor and examining the lock; "but it's been operated upon, sir."

The doctor took the japanned box, and saw by the scratches on the front that a sharp-pointed instrument had been used in the attempt to force the lock.

No perceptible sign was visible outside the clasp-bound lock, and the policeman, after a careful survey, said,—

"This has been opened by its key, or else a first-class burglar has performed upon it."

"The key," said the doctor, "is attached to a bunch which I left upon the table in my study."

The policeman went towards the door as he said,—

"We'll see what's here, sir."

The doctor's face became very pale when the constable took the bunch of keys from the lock. In spite of his belief in Gleddell's innocence, this rather staggered him.

"Here's the keys, sir," said the officer; "you know best whether the young gentleman could get at 'em easily."

"Good God!" exclaimed the doctor, involuntarily, "he was in the library when I left those keys upon the table!"

The policeman pricked up his ears—the case to the official mind was as clear as the noonday sun.

"That's it, then, sir," he said, "he must have taken 'em and——"

The doctor waved his hand to imply silence, then going to the door, he beckoned for Gleddell to approach.

The boy obeyed mechanically, and Philip, seeing he could scarcely stand, walked by his side.

The doctor closed the door upon the wondering silent crowd, then turning to Gleddell said, in a subdued sorrowful voice,—

"I am willing to believe your statement, Gleddell, although the aspect of affairs is so much against you—willing yet to believe you innocent, if you can tell me how the keys I left upon the table in my study came here?"

"The keys!" the boy repeated, "a number of keys upon a ring?"

"Yes," the doctor said, "this bunch."

"Those keys," Gleddell said, in a firm voice, "were upon the table when I left the study."

The doctor looked pained as he glanced at Gleddell's feet, and said,—

"Did you leave your shoes there?"

"I did, sir."

Philip pressed his hand to his side, as though in pain. Poor fellow, he saw his friend's danger, and was powerless to save him.

"He cannot be guilty," he thought, "yet every circumstance that has transpired tends but to implicate him."

For the first time Gleddell became sensible of his peril, and raising his hands supplicatingly towards the doctor, was about to assert his innocence.

This movement caused a small steel instrument to fall from the outside pocket of his jacket; the sharp ring of the metal attracted the police officer's active gaze, and in a moment he had picked it from the ground, and by the flickering light compared it with the marks upon the cash-box.

"Fits to a hair, sir," he said, handing the box and the chisel to the doctor.

"I never beheld that implement before," Gleddell wildly exclaimed, "never saw it——"

He stopped abruptly, and turned to Philip Randall,—

"Philip, you do not believe this—you——"

The usher's eyes filled with tears, and grasping the boy's extended hand, he murmured in a broken voice,—

"Heaven forbid! Gled; heaven forbid!"

The good doctor's lips twitched convulsively as he nerved himself to give utterance to the words which would brand the boy he so well liked as a thief.

"Gleddell!" he said, as the friends stood hand locked in hand—"the discovery of that instrument has destroyed the last hope I had of your innocence."

The wretched boy sprang forward, and on his knees and with uplifted hands, said,—

"Unsay those words, sir—believe me, as I hope for mercy hereafter, that I speak the truth when I say I am innocent."

There was a sternness in the doctor's tone, as he said,—

"Can you in the face of this overwhelming testimony deny your guilt?"

Gleddell sprang to his feet—he saw that further supplication was in vain, and, folding his arms, he turned towards the constable, and said,—

"Take me to prison; perhaps the judge will have more mercy upon me than you, sir, who have known me so long."

"There is one chance yet, to save you from a felon's cell," the doctor said,—"I only ask that you will speak the truth—tell me why you made yourself the accomplice in a deed like this? answer me truthfully—tell me the name of your companion; for you must have had one to have carried away the——"

Gleddell could hear no more; every word stung him like the bite of a scorpion, and as his chest rose and fell with emotion, he exclaimed, wildly,—

"I have told you the truth, sir, told you how I became locked in this room; and were the rack or thumb-screw applied to my limbs I should answer the same."

"Stanton Gleddell!"—the head master's voice was husky as he spoke—"you still adhere to this statement—adhere to it in spite of the keys which I left in the room with you being found here, in spite of the marks made by that instrument which fell from your pocket. I am sorry you have acted thus, sorry for your sake—deeply grieved that such a disgrace should have fallen upon the school—and—and——"

The good old man's voice failed him; and motioning for the constable to take his prisoner, he turned away from the painful sight.

Philip Randall's heart felt as though it would burst, as he turned to the doctor, and begged for mercy for his friend.

"Philip!"—was the reply; "I gave him the chance of escaping the prison cell. You heard his answer."

The usher bowed his head; in spite of his brotherly love for Gleddell, he could not, in the face of such damning evidence, bring forward a plea to clear the boy from this heinous crime.

"What would you do," the doctor resumed, "were you placed as I am? Could you, after all that has transpired, believe Gleddell's words? God knows how deeply

I deplore the necessity which compels me to send him from here a prisoner, but I must do it; were he to stay there would be nothing but misery for him to endure—the envious and malicious would point and hurl the word thief at him; therefore, let him be judged by a proper tribunal—if he passes the ordeal scatheless, none will be more pleased than myself to give him a welcome."

Gleddell sprang forward, and taking the doctor's hand, said,—

"You are right, sir, quite right; this is no place for me, until my innocence shall be established. God bless you, sir, for all the kindness you have shown me!"

He could say no more; his long pent-up feelings choked his utterance, and compelled him to turn away.

There was a short but deeply affecting leave-taking between the usher and the hapless youth; then the officer led his charge from the room.

Silent and wondering, the group outside the door made room for them to pass; and many were the expressions of good-will and a firm belief in his innocence that came from his schoolfellows.

Jack Stanfield and Happy wrung their friend's hand—it was all they could do. Poor fellows! their hearts were too full to utter one word of farewell.

Many ran to the door to gaze at the sad sight, and Stanfield, when he beheld Gleddell's shoeless feet, ran to the bedroom and brought him a pair.

"Poor Gled!" he mused, "his cup of sorrow is indeed full."

The inmates of Bircham School went sadly back to their beds, and until the red sun began to appear they talked in subdued tones of the strange events of that night.

CHAPTER XX.

CAPTAIN OAKPLANK IN A RAGE.

In happy unconsciousness of the sorrow that was about to fall upon them, Captain Oakplank's daughters were busy with their needles, when the servant announced the arrival of a visitor.

"A strange gentleman, did you say, Mary?"

"Yes, miss. Here's his card."

Eleanor glanced at the small oblong piece of cardboard, and read,—

"Edgar Greymore,
R.N."

Minnie arose from her chair, and looked over her sister's shoulder.

"What a pretty name! Is he handsome, Mary?"

"Yes, miss," the girl answered, "very handsome, and not at all like the officers that come here to see master."

"Show Mr. Greymore in," Eleanor said. "You, Minnie, run upstairs to papa, and tell him he is wanted."

When Greymore entered the room, he saluted the dark-eyed handsome girl with a graceful ease which, in spite of his many grave faults, proclaimed him a polished gentleman.

"I fear," he said, seating himself near the young lady's work-table, "that my early visit is rather inopportune; but my anxiety to see a friend of my old commander's must plead for me."

"We are early people," Eleanor said, "and, living so far from town, dispense with its conventional habits."

"I am delighted to hear this," said Greymore; "for, like all sailors, I detest etiquette and all stiff-necked absurdities which custom sanctions, to the discomfort of those who worship certain stereotyped rules, under the name of fashion."

Eleanor smiled.

"I am afraid," she said, "that your opinions would find but little favour in fashionable society."

Greymore, in his assumption of the character of a careless naval officer, played his part to the very life.

"I do not," he said, "care sufficiently for the brainless set to value their opinion."

They conversed some time longer upon various subjects—Greymore for the purpose of drawing the young girl out; and Eleanor, pleased at the opportunity of conversing with one so eminently superior to her father's usual guests, answered his questions with a readiness that showed a well-cultivated mind.

"A sensible girl, and a pretty one," mentally remarked the affable villain; "far too good for my melancholy old schoolfellow, Philip—much too good; therefore he had better resign all pretensions to her, or prepare for an unpleasant result."

Eleanor felt that her father's visitor was, in spite of his pleasant manners, not quite natural in his assumption of the frank jovial sailor.

She knew not why this conviction came stronger upon her every moment. Perhaps it was the peculiar expression which came over Greymore's face as he from time to time fixed his eyes upon the young girl, that caused her first to suspect, then to dislike him.

Minnie having found the Captain sitting quietly by the side of the little stream which meandered past within a few minutes' walk of the cottage, they returned together.

Edgar rose at the old seaman's entrance, and with unblushing effrontery introduced himself by saying,—

"Lieutenant Oakplank, late of the *Semiramide* frigate?"

"The same," said the old fellow, as he surveyed Greymore; "but I don't believe I have ever seen your figure-head before."

"Possibly not," was the smiling answer. "I served as midshipman upon the *Jason*."

"The *Jason*! Ah, they've turned the old bark into a convict ship now, I believe?"

"They have, sir, and Captain Griffiths still commands her."

"Um!—the old fool—he clings to her like a barnacle."

"Yes. I believe the old *Jason*, sir, will be his coffin; she has been his cradle for many years."

"Yes," the old sailor said, warming at the sound of his old friend's name and vessel, "she was, long before you could have been old enough to clamber up her side."

"I was on board not many months since," was the answer—it was a truthful one—"and hearing the Captain speak so much of his old companion, I thought I would call, being in this part of the country."

"Quite right—quite right; I'm glad to see you. When do you join again?"

"Not yet," said Greymore; "the old vessel is docked for the present."

Had George Oakplank known the position occupied by his guest on board the *Jason*, he would, as he termed it, have fallen foul upon Edgar Greymore, R.N.

The ready-witted scoundrel, when he escaped from the galleys, was picked up by the *Jason*, and by keeping his ears open, had heard Captain Griffiths speak of an old friend named George Oakplank, who had lost his arm.

When he heard the name mentioned by Philip, the remembrance of Captain Griffiths' friend flashed to his mind, and with the aid of a few cards he determined to obtain an entry into the old fellow's house.

This done, he left everything to chance for the furtherance of his scheme respecting Eleanor.

With a degree of cunning that did him credit, Greymore answered all the old fellow's questions, and succeeded in thoroughly deceiving the bluff, open-hearted old sailor.

He was too politic to stay long upon his first visit, so, despite the old fellow's hearty invitation, he departed, well satisfied with the impression he had made; and as he sauntered from the house he muttered,—

"I would not give much for friend Philip's chance now; the girl was evidently impressed with my appearance."

Walking towards the school, he passed several of the boys, who, in place of running about the green lanes, and pelting any unfortunate bird down among the thick branches of the hedgerows, were somewhat subdued and quiet in their manners.

The sight recalled the events of the previous night, and with something like compassion in his voice he said,—

"I wonder how that poor devil feels by this time; it's a pity he had to be taken—but self-preservation is the first law, I believe."

With no more pity for the brave youth whom he had been instrumental in conveying to a felon's cell, he, with matchless effrontery, entered the school gates.

"Well," the Captain asked, when his visitor had gone, "what do you think of him, 'Lenor?"

"I scarcely know, papa," she answered, "I liked him a little at first, but before he left my opinion began to change."

The Captain used a seafaring oath, which, if wanting in elegance, was very forcible in its meaning.

"Shiver me from keel to truck, girl," he said, "if I did not feel the same; but he knows old Will Griffiths, and that's sufficient, I suppose; but"—he added—"his figure-head is most (something) like a pirate—I never saw a young blue jacket with such baby paws as he has got—eh, what?"

The servant answered.

"Oh! if you please, sir, there is one of the young gentlemen from the school."

"Mr. Gleddell?" Minnie asked, blushing.

"No, miss; a young gentleman that came here once with a letter from——"

The Captain wheeled round at this slip of the tongue, and frightened the girl by roaring out,—

"Came here with a letter, did he? And who was the letter for, you pirate in petticoats?"

Mary saw Eleanor's troubled face, and answered quickly,—

"For you, sir!"

"For me? eh, what, you——"

"Yes, sir—the time when the great cricket match took place, between the school eleven and the gentlemen who came from London."

"Ugh—I had forgotten all about the doctor asking us to see it—well, show the jackanapes in, and let's hear what he wants."

Jack Stanfield, looking pale and wretched, entered the room, and bowing to the young ladies and the Captain, said,—

"I should like to speak to you, sir, alone, for a few minutes."

"Speak to me, boy! why, what is the matter? come, out with it; no sealed orders here!"

Jack gave Minnie a pitying look, as he said,—

"I would rather not, sir; if you would be kind enough to grant me this favour, I shall be so deeply grateful to you."

"Make sail, you petticoats," said the Captain, "and keep out of sight until you hear my signal."

They left the room, and the Captain, turning to Stanfield, said,—

"Now, my lad, let's have the contents of your despatch-box."

The boy in a broken voice told him of Gleddell's imprisonment.

"I'm sure, sir," he said in conclusion, "that poor Gled is innocent; poor fellow, he had only received a letter telling him of his mother's death yesterday morning."

The Captain heard him patiently to the end, then his wrath burst forth in a volley of unintelligible expletives.

When his utterance became clearer, he gave vent to his feelings in this fashion,—

"Guilty! who the —— said he was guilty? who placed him in limbo? hencoops and furies! zounds! curse them all—why—why—he's the tautest lad among the whole of ye; and—and—I—yes, I, sir, had promised to get him aboard a fighting frigate when his term of learning a cargo of jaw-breaking words had passed—don't speak, sir—d'ye hear—tell me where he is—I'll scuttle the ship, and rescue him, or my name is not George Oakplank—and it is—d'ye hear that?"

During the time the Captain was giving vent to this incoherent string of angry expressions, he danced about the room like a madman, and finally sinking exhausted into a chair, he said,—

"Tell me all about it over again, I—I—but go on, hang you, go on!"

Jack Stanfield repeated the sad story, and his hearer, now calmer, listened intently to every word.

"It looks black against him, poor lad!" he said, "but I'd stake my old head that he is innocent, poor boy; and I loved him so well!"

The Captain's daughters, alarmed by the unusual angry words which came from the old fellow, entered the room at this moment.

"What is the matter, papa?" Minnie asked; "we came back, thinking you had been suddenly taken bad with the gout."

"Gout!" he yelled, "twenty gouts—fifty

bomb shells, crammed in my boots, would not be as bad as this—no, not if all the—— fuses were blazing up—tell 'em, you swab, tell 'em all about it, and be hanged to you!"

For the third time Jack Stanfield proceeded to tell the story of poor Gleddell's misfortune; but scarcely had he begun, when Minnie gave a cry of anguish, and fell to the floor in a swoon.

The Captain sprang from his seat, and flourishing his steel hook in dangerous proximity to Jack's face, roared out,—

"Hang ye, for a lubberly boy: why didn't you put your palaver in a milder way? don't ye know these petticoats have hearts as soft as a smashed pumpkin—hang ye! they're not like me—I ain't a bit put out with it."

The good-hearted old fellow finished his speech with a howl of rage, as he thought of his favourite boy being cooped up within the prison walls.

CHAPTER XXI.

THE USHER AT BAY.

ELEANOR raised her sister's head, and tried to restore her numbed faculties, and the Captain standing over them, muttered,—

"Aye!—I knew it—although they thought the old man blind, he could see how the wind lay; and he should have had her, too, when he came home with a gold swab on his shoulders and a commission in his pocket."

Minnie opened her eyes at this moment, and bursting into a flood of tears, cried hysterically.

"It cannot be true—unsay those dreadful words."

"It's too true, lass!" said her father, "he's bound up by the heels by these long shore lubbers; harkee, girl! had I but a boat's crew of the old craft at my back, I would rescue him from the foe. Now, cheer up, lass! we will go and see him."

Minnie looked wistfully at her father, and murmured,—

"You do not know, papa, how I——"

"Yes, I do—there, dry your eyes, and you shall see him; and hang me, if he does not grapple you with both fins, and give you a kiss that will be heard a cable's length off—I'll overhaul him, the jackanapes—that—that —I——"

The old fellow's voice broke down, and to prove that the news did not affect him, he went to the window, and gazed out upon the quiet wayside.

There must have been a mist upon the window panes, for the Captain had to use his silk pocket handkerchief to his eyes; then, as his grief-stricken daughter came towards him, he began assiduously polishing the glass.

"Well,"—he said, turning to Minnie, and making a brave attempt to clear his voice, "the pumps going still?"

She could not answer him; her lips moved, but the words she would have spoken died away, and with a stifled cry of hopeless grief she threw herself upon his breast and sobbed, "You will take me to see him, papa?"

The Captain blurted out a reply, but its meaning was lost by the energetic manner in which he used his silk handkerchief.

* * * *

After the interview with Captain Oakplank and his daughters, Greymore sought the usher.

He found him in his little chamber, surrounded by his books, one of which, a mighty old tome, was open before him.

The pale student's mind was far from the open page, and his eyes, sunken, yet burning with a fierce light, were fixed dreamily upon the open country, which, like a glorious picture, was spread before his sad earnest gaze.

His spirit, already crushed by the coming of that smiling handsome friend Greymore, was not equal to bear the terrible blow inflicted upon him by the calamity which had befallen his friend.

Had he been a brother, Philip could not have suffered more deeply, or felt his heart more scathed by the terrible uncertainty of the poor boy's fate.

He was thinking of him when Greymore entered the room. Picturing the lad broken down by the weight of his afflictions—no kind voice near to soothe his sorrow—no friendly hand to grasp—the picture was indeed black, and Philip groaned aloud at the too faithful reality his mind had conjured up. He had tried to form an hypothesis to account for the strange robbery, but none afforded him the least comfort. He felt that Gleddell was innocent—knew the boy too well to believe he could become a midnight thief—yet he must suffer—there was no means of escape. The more he thought over it and weighed each detail, the blacker the case seemed. There was not one ray of hope, not one streak of sunshine in the gloomy wretched hopeless prospect.

Greymore stood for some time regarding the wretched man, and when that groan of heart-wrung anguish burst from his lips, Greymore's face expressed the most diabolical glee.

Stepping softly to Philip's side, he placed his hand upon the wretched usher's shoulder.

The contact of that soft feminine palm seemed to burn the usher's very flesh—he knew the touch; instinct told him that none other than his most implacable foe could be there.

With a low cry, such as might have come from a startled panther, Philip sprang to his feet and faced the intruder.

Greymore, in spite of his wondrous nerve, shrank from the fierce blazing eyes of his hitherto meek victim.

He read therein sufficient to warn him of the danger which would accrue to him were he to further arouse the passion which, like a volcano, slumbered in Philip's breast.

They stood thus for some moments, their eyes fixed upon each other—Greymore calm; Philip trembling with suppressed fury.

In physical strength there seemed but little difference between them, although the usher was of the two the largest built; but this superiority was amply compensated for by Greymore's supple frame and well-developed muscles.

There was but a few months' difference in their ages, Greymore being about six months Philip's senior; but the latter from over-study looked considerably in advance of his years.

Philip was the first to speak. As the fierce light deepened in his eyes, he said, sternly,—

"You here?"

"Yes, Philip," was the reply. "The old

love for my boyhood's friend prompted me to call upon you."

"I am in no mood for your badinage," said the usher, calmly; "so state the object of your intrusion."

Greymore bit his lip. An angry retort came upon his tongue, but he smiled it down, and answered,—

"Since I must be candid, I came to learn the result of my advice to you."

"Your advice?"

"Yes. Did I not advise you to at once surrender all claim to Miss Oakplank's hand?"

"You did."

Philip uttered these words in a low fierce voice.

"I presume, then," said Greymore, "that you have done so?"

The usher was outwardly calm, but, from his clenched hands and panting breast, it was evident a fierce conflict was going on within.

"Listen, Edgar Greymore," he said. "I shall never surrender my claim; neither will I tamely see you wed that beauteous girl. So, beware!"

Greymore went ashy pale, and his lips twitched nervously, as he said,—

"You defy me, then? Well, be it so. Remember, I have always been your evil genius, and shall be so until I have worked out the one great aim of my life. Know you what that is?"

The usher was silent.

"Perchance," Greymore said, "you may remember a sweet girl, the daughter of our old preceptor, when we were at school. Philip, I loved that girl, young as I was. She was my star of happiness—my only joy upon earth. You came between us, and robbed me of that joy—you——"

"It is a base calumny," said the usher. "No word of love ever passed between us."

Greymore, unheeding the interruption, continued,—

"For the wrong you did me, I have caused you a lifetime's misery; but that is only part of the punishment I swore to inflict upon you."

Philip was calm, dangerously calm; and, basilisk-like, his eyes shot fiery glances at his visitor.

Greymore either did not or affected not to perceive this sign of the fierce passion which raged in the usher's heart.

"I had not until the present time," Greymore continued, "an opportunity of carrying out the second part of my revenge; but now"—his voice became like the hiss of a serpent—"the hour has come. You love this girl; she is dear to you,—dear as Nelly Galway was to me. As you robbed me of my heart's idol, so will I rob you. I have come, Philip Randall, to bid you resign all claim to Eleanor Oakplank. Do so, and I will leave you in peace; refuse, and, before the setting of another sun, I will proclaim you as a——"

"Hold," said Philip, "you have said enough. Again I repeat, no word of love ever passed between Nelly Galway and myself. She shunned your presence entirely through your misdeeds, not from any word of mine. This you know to be the truth."

"It matters not," Greymore said. "I lost her love when you, serpent like, whispered your foul calumny in her ears. Such is my belief—such I shall hold; and, as a first retribution, you shall behold Eleanor Oakplank my wife."

"Never!" Philip exclaimed, fiercely. "Never, while I have life! Do not goad me further, Greymore, or the consequences will be fatal to one of us."

Greymore surveyed the speaker contemptuously.

"I came not here," he said, "to listen to your melodramatic ravings. Answer me, will you resign you claim?"

"Never!" was the fierce answer; "so beware how you cross my path!"

"You defy me?"

"I do. Were you ten times the demon you are, I would do the same."

"Be it so. Before to-morrow has passed Eleanor shall know all."

Greymore was about to leave the room, his face reddened with an angry flush, and a triumphant light dancing in his eyes; he had not moved two paces towards the door, when Philip sprang before him, and placed himself against the closed door.

"Back!" he said, with fierce determination. "You shall not leave this room until you retract those words. Fiend! devil! have you not worked me misery enough without this? Abjure your purpose, or, by heavens, I will——"

"You will—what will you do?" said Greymore, interrupting him. "Stand aside, man; you are no match for me! I could hurl you through that window with as much ease as though you were an infant; so stand aside, if you value the safety of your limbs."

He advanced steadily towards Philip as he spoke, and, at the conclusion of his defiant words, placed his hand upon Philip's shoulder.

The usher gave a startled cry as he felt the contact of the other's hand, then, with a bound like a tiger, he sprang upon Greymore, and seized him by the throat.

Greymore uttered a fierce oath as he felt the usher's fingers close around his windpipe, and, drawing back his hand, struck Philip a heavy blow full in his face.

The usher reeled, but did not relax his grip but, throwing his whole weight forward, bore Greymore back.

The tables were turned; it was the pale student who now possessed the greater strength, and, despite the other's fierce efforts to wrench away the fingers that were entwined around his throat, he felt himself getting weaker every moment.

The foe he had despised, Greymore found, when they met hand to hand and foot to foot, was possessed of wondrous strength and a grim determination that he had little anticipated.

For the first time in his strange career Greymore had met his match—for the first time in his many encounters his heart began to sink within him, as he fixed his eyes upon the usher's face.

He read therein his doom—felt that his life hung but by the merest trifle.

Step by step he was being forced back to the open window, and as the horrible conviction that Philip would slay him came to his mind, Greymore gasped feebly for mercy.

"Mercy!" repeated the usher, "yes, you shall have mercy—such mercy as you showed to those shrinking wretches who sought to save themselves from the devouring flames.

THE BOYS OF BIRCHAM SCHOOL.

STANTON GLENDELL IN TROUBLE.

Devil!—fiend! such mercy shall you have!"

The window was reached, and Philip, with a display of strength which seemed superhuman, forced the supplicating wretch through.

One push and he would have gone whirling through the air—beneath was the paved pathway which led to the playground.

As a drowning man clutches at the smallest floating object, so Greymore clutched at the sides of the window-frame.

The love of life was strong within him, and Greymore, in spite of Philip's efforts to force him back, held on with a tenacity which despair alone could give.

He saw by Philip's face that a prayer for mercy would be useless; there was no hope for him unless he could wrest himself from the deadly fingers which were interlaced around his throat.

A numbing sensation was rapidly creeping over him; another moment and he must

No. 8.

succumb.

With a powerful strain upon his arms Greymore threw himself forward and forced the usher back. The victory was but momentary, for Philip, suddenly releasing his grasp, seized a heavy chair with both hands and struck his foe to the ground.

He hurled the chair from him when Greymore fell, then with a wild unearthly laugh coming from his lips, he raised the senseless man and was about to throw his burden through the window.

Before the deed could be consummated that would have brought Philip to the gallows, the door opened, and Jean Gailland, pale and frightened, entered the room.

The Frenchman's sudden entry recalled Philip to his senses, and lifting Greymore upon the couch, he turned and faced the intruder.

"You came but in time," he said, quietly; "another second and there would have been one villain less in the world."

M. Jean stooped over Greymore, and pointing to a thin streak of blood which slowly trickled down his cheek, said,—

"You have killed him!"

Philip's face, which had hitherto been crimson with passion, became colourless, and staggering towards the wounded man he gazed fearfully at the red stain.

He was calmer now the fierce whirlwind of passion had passed away, and he could now see the enormity of the crime he had so nearly perpetrated.

"Dead?" he said, in terrified accents, "no, no, it cannot be; he is not dead!"

M. Jean had taken a sponge from Philip's wash-stand, and as he cleansed the blood from Greymore's brow, the latter opened his eyes and uttered a deep groan.

Feebly raising himself upon his elbow, he fixed his dark eyes upon the usher, and in a voice of pitiless hate hissed,—

"You have signed your death warrant. Before the sun sets this day the authorities shall have the clue to the bur——"

He fell back upon the couch before he could finish the sentence, the dread meaning of which was only known to himself and Philip.

The latter stood motionless—statuesquely motionless—as Greymore spoke; and when he fell back upon the couch, Philip, with a wild cry, rushed from the room.

The afternoon lessons were over, and rich sunlight shed its gleesome beams upon the earth, as the wretched man strode through the school gates out upon the quiet country road.

He knew full well that Greymore would keep his word, and his soul shrank within him as the terrible knowledge of the law's dread penalty came in grim array before his eyes.

Until the sun had sunk in golden splendour below the distant horizon he wandered hopelessly about, and soothed by the quiet beauty of the hour, he returned slowly and sadly towards the old house.

There was an unnatural brilliancy in his eyes, and a red spot upon his cheeks, as he went towards his room, his lips too were firmly compressed, and showed that a fixed purpose had been the result of his wanderings.

"Better to die thus," he thought, "than to perish by the hangman's aid."

When he entered the little chamber, which had so long been his home, he looked around, as though expecting to find Greymore still there.

He had gone, and save for the few crimson spots upon the couch and the overturned chair, there was nothing to mark the late fearful scene that had been enacted.

Philip sank upon a chair and hid his face in his hands. Long he remained thus, and by the convulsive throes which from time to time passed over his body, the mental torture he suffered must have been terrible.

Suddenly springing to his feet, as the remembrance of Greymore's parting words came upon him, he looked at his watch and murmured,—

"They will be here soon to drag me to a felon's cell."

He seemed strangely calm as the terrible thought came to his mind, calmer still when he sat and penned a passionate and eternal farewell to the beauteous Eleanor.

This epistle he gave to one of the boys, and begged him to take it immediately to Woodbine Cottage.

From the biggest to the last new boy there was not one but would have been glad to have served their kind-hearted friend, Philip Randall.

Thus, the messenger he entrusted with the letter soon reached the old sailor's sweet little home.

Unconscious of the terrible blow awaiting her, Eleanor, when the boy arrived, was endeavouring to soothe her heart-broken sister.

Poor girl! she was soon to be plunged into as deep an abyss of despair as the gentle Minnie.

"From Mr. Randall, Miss," said the lad, when Eleanor came to the hall; "he did not say anything about an answer."

She thanked him with a sweet smile, and taking the letter, returned to her sister's bedside.

Philip's messenger, on his way back to the school, mentally wondered when he grew to be a man if he should have such a jolly girl for a sweetheart.

Happy boy! he had yet many years before he entered upon the uneven course which, according to the poet, never yet ran smooth.

Captain Oakplank, sitting over his untasted glass of grog, and his evening pipe not yet alight, was startled from a troubled reverie respecting his favourite, young Gleddell, by a sudden and piteous scream for help.

It was Minnie's voice, and the old fellow, jumping to his feet, ran upstairs, growling,—
"It will kill her—this boy being laid abeam by those cursed land sharks."

Great was the Captain's surprise when he entered the room at beholding Eleanor stretched upon the floor, an open letter tightly pressed to her bosom.

George Oakplank looked from the senseless form to Minnie, as though seeking an explanation.

"Something dreadful, papa," Minnie said, in answer to the look, "in that letter, for Eleanor cried out 'save him! save him!' then fainted away."

"What's in the wind now?" he said, as he bent over Eleanor, and tried to take Philip's letter from her convulsive grasp. "Eh, won't give it up?—suppose some pirate has been signalling to her, and now makes sail and leaves her as he would Portsmouth Bet. He'd better not. Come, girl, open your eyes."

A feeble moan came from Eleanor's lips, and the Captain, seizing the water-jug, was about to pour the contents over her, when Minnie interfered.

"Don't be cruel, papa," she said; "that is not the way to bring her to."

"Eh—bless my soul! not the way?" stammered the anxious old sailor, surrendering the water-jug to Minnie, "of course not; I ought to be keel-hauled for an old fool to think of it. Ah! she opens her eyes! Well, lass, what is it that has laid you like a——"

Eleanor struggled to her feet, and before her father could finish his speech she thrust the letter in her breast and cried wildly,—

"Save him! save him!"

"Save him!" reiterated the Captain, "who's to be saved, lass? Hang me if I don't think your mind has lost its sheet anchors, and you——"

Whatever nautical simile the Captain would have used was cut short by Eleanor suddenly saying,—

"It may not be too late—I will go to him. Take care of Minnie, father, until I return!"

Before the Captain could utter one word, either in reply or remonstrance, she fled from the room, and as he heard the front door close, the old sailor said,—

"May I never see pay-day again if the ship is not running stern foremost with the doings of these petticoats. Ugh! I wish they were boys, then I could rope's-end them; but these light craft, hang them!—they are not good for anything, except——"

"Papa, what can be the matter with poor Eleanor?"

"Poor de——I mean girl; how the brimstone do I know?"

The Captain was losing his temper, so Minnie forbore any further remark, until the little angry cloud should pass away.

Unmindful of the path she took, Eleanor ran wildly towards the school, and overtaking the boy who had brought the letter, she besought him to show her Philip's room.

He did so; and, entering, she found the usher—his head bowed upon the table, and one hand grasping a pistol.

"In time," she murmured, "in time to save him from a suicide's grave!"

Another minute, had not the brave faithful girl entered the room, that white brow, which was now bowed with mental agony, would have been shattered into a shapeless undistinguishable mass!

CHAPTER XXII.

A FIGHT.

THE second day of Stanton Gleddell's imprisonment was one of those gloomy, thorough English days, in which the rain falls in one continuous deluge, and the wind comes rolling and moaning round the eaves of the house, causing the most buoyant spirits to feel depressed, and the melancholy to stand at the closed windows and watch the rain-drops as they patter against the glass or, driven by the wind, sweep across the ground in fitful gusts.

Such days as these were not much liked by the boys of Bircham School—to be obliged to collect in groups about the large hall, and deprived of the recreation which the playground afforded, was not calculated to inspire them with the most amiable feelings.

Apart from the depression caused by the unpropitious weather, young Gleddell's loss had thrown a gloom over the school, and caused a state of party feeling which resulted in more fights in one day than usually occurred during a month previously.

Gleddell, though generally liked by his schoolfellows, had a few foes (who has not, whether saints or sinners?) These took the opportunity, now that he was in trouble, to openly rejoice at his misfortune, much to the anger of the poor boy's friends who manfully stood up for their favourite.

Among the staunchest of the latter were Jack Stanfield, Happy, Joe Stikkers, and the Mallet. Opposed to these was a loutish fellow, one of the biggest boys in the school, named Biggs.

Biggs was the son of a rich cheesemonger, and about as good a specimen of a purse-proud tradesman's son as could be found in any school.

He had a thorough contempt for such youths as Stanton Gleddell, Jack Stanfield, and Tom Dickson.

They were gentlemen—that was quite sufficient for Biggs, or "Cheesy," as he was called by those who did not care to toady into his favour for the sake of the large hampers he received from home.

"I've six times the pocket-money of any of those shabby-genteel fellows!"

This was "Cheesy's" continual boast, and the small fry who looked forward to a share in the riches were quite ready to tell him that he was ten times better than any of those fellows who pretended to be gentlemen, and had not a shilling in six months to spend at the "tuck" shop.

By a judicious use of his money he was able to keep a pretty numerous staff of adherents, who were always ready to do his bidding when a chance offered of annoying the opposite party.

So glorious an opportunity as the present was hailed with delight by the Biggs faction.

Only a week previous to Gleddell's apprehension, he had publicly thrashed Biggs for striking the poor orphan boy Godfrey Bransome, and thrashed him soundly, though Biggs was much the stronger of the two.

Up to this time Biggs had been the bully of the school, and every boy not sneak enough to toady to him was in hourly fear of having his ears pinched or his arm twisted by the great coward.

Until Gleddell, in school phraseology, "tackled him," the biggest among the Bircham boys stood in awe of Cheesy's large red hands and long limbs; but since that event Jack Stanfield and Happy-go-lucky had been on the watch for an opportunity to try their hands upon the bully.

Even little Joe Stikkers and the Mallet, both of whom had suffered more or less from Cheesy's viciousness had made up their minds, if ever they were again subjected to the ear-pinching or arm-twisting process, to "roll into" the cowardly brute, let the consequence be what it might.

The wet foggy day had its influence upon the amiable Cheesy, and as he sat upon a form opposite Jack Stanfield, he glanced viciously at Joe Stikkers and remarked,—

"Ugh! this place is as bad as being in prison."

Joe took the hint, and glancing at the Mallet, answered,—

"Don't know—never been there."

Biggs looked round at his parasites for approval as he said,—

"You had better go and see your friend; then you'll know."

The parasites grinned as a matter of course, but the grin was taken out of them when our lively friend the Mallet mischievously said to Joe Stikkers,—

"I hate this muggy weather, Joe; it makes everything smell disagreeable; but of all the smells that basket that came this morning for Biggs was the worst—I suppose he asks his father to send all the bad cheese to him to feed the hungry crew of sneaks who——"

Biggs jumped to his feet, his face red with passion, and, seizing the Mallet's wrist, began to give him a taste of the old mode of torture.

"Drop that!" said the Mallet, kicking at his persecutor's shins. "Come on, Joe, help me."

Stikkers, in obedience to the summons, clutched Cheesy by the hair, and in spite of his great strength, pulled him back.

The Mallet, as soon as he was released from the torture, threw off his jacket, and exclaimed,—

"A little of that goes a long way. I've had enough; let go, Joe, and come here; we'll give him something—he's always pitching his spite upon us."

Joe released his enemy's hair, and dodged cleverly out of the way of a blow that would have broken his jaw had it taken effect.

Biggs stood with clenched hands before the pair of small boys, and grinning savagely said,—

"What, do you mean it? I'll smash you."

There is no doubt, had he closed with the youngsters, it would have gone hard with them, but ere matters reached this pitch Jack Stanfield interfered.

"Stand back, you young 'uns," he said; "he's too much for you."

"No, he ain't," said the Mallet, resolutely; "let's have one round with him, Jack."

Stanfield pushed them aside, and said,—

"Look here, Biggs; don't you come that again."

"Why?"

"I'll tell you why, when you do it."

Biggs, in spite of his bullying, was at heart a rank coward, and as he stepped back from Jack Stanfield it struck him that the calm slight gentlemanly youth might give him a second edition of the pommelling he had received from Gleddell.

Though he felt this, he knew that unless he showed a bold front before his parasites, much of his prestige would be gone.

"Do you think," he sullenly asked, "that I am going to put up with this cheek?"

"You provoked it," Jack answered. "What right had you to hint about poor Gled's misfortune?"

"There's no hinting required," said Biggs, whose courage was reviving; "he's in prison, where every thief ought to be."

Jack Stanfield became red to the very roots of his hair.

"Gled's no thief," he said, "and look here, Biggs—if I hear you or any boy in the school make use of that word again, you had better look out."

Biggs was not warned by the angry expression upon Jack's face; unfortunately for him, one of the Cheesy faction said, loud enough for him to hear,—

"If taking all the silver things ain't thieving, I don't know what is. I know if I'd have taken 'em, people would have called me a thief, and wouldn't have got bullied for it."

The word bullied did the business.

Biggs, the reputed hardest hitter in the school—Biggs, who had more pocket-money than any three of the stuck-up shabby-genteel boys—Biggs, whose ears were always being filled by flatterers—Biggs, who had quite a train of sycophants, and whose word had been law—it was too much to calmly bear; too much—and the spirit which had prompted Biggs senior to risk the law's dread penalty when he gave short weight or adulterated his butter, arose in the breast of Biggs junior, when he contemplated the effect of standing calmly and being bullied.

His lips trembling with ill-suppressed passion, he answered Jack's threat by saying,—

"I shall make use of the word whenever I like."

"Bravo, Biggs! don't be bullied,"—this from a member of the faction.

"Whenever I like," repeated Cheesy, "and I shall do it now—he is a thief, and if any of his accomp——"

"Thud" came Jack's fist upon the speaker's mouth, and as Biggs reeled back and fell over a form, Gleddell's champion threw off his jacket and said,—

"If any more of you want it, you know where to get it."

There was a dead silence for a few seconds, then came a buzz of admiration from Jack's friends, a buzz that swelled into a shout as Biggs, bleeding from the mouth, scrambled to his feet.

Happy-go-lucky foresaw that a fight would be the consequence, and picking up his friend's jacket, he passed it to the delighted Mallet.

"Jack," he said, "you'll have to fight him."

"I know it, Tom, I——"

"Keep your eyes open; I'll be your second. Don't let him hug you; he's too strong—and keep to his face—you'll soon blind him."

Happy was the most scientific boxer in the school. He had taken lessons from an ex-pugilist, who kept the village ale-house.

Jack knew this, and bore the advice of his friend in his mind.

When Biggs scrambled to his feet, he also threw off his jacket, and baring his brawny arms, said,—

"I'll make you repent this;" then, as he saw Happy coming towards Jack, he added, "What, am I to fight the two?"

"No," Tom Dickson said, "but if he does not thrash you I will."

"You'll have the chance of trying," retorted Cheesy, "for I'll double him up in two minutes, and serve you the same afterwards."

"I shall be quite ready," said Happy, "by

the time you have doubled my friend up."

CHAPTER XXIII.
BIGGS VANQUISHED.

A FEW words, boys, before we begin the fight. Learn to box; it is a healthful recreation, and possibly may be of use to you some day. Learn to use the good old English weapons—but use them well. Should you see a disagreeable, quarrelsome, strong-built fellow bullying a boy who is too weak or too small to stand against the bully, then make use of your science. Should you, when manhood brings strength to your limbs, behold one man, armed with a knife, threaten one that is unarmed, smite him of the knife, and spare not; for the use of deadly weapons is un-English; and when you clench your hands remember you are an Englishman.

When the combatants stood face to face it looked anything but a fair match, Cheesy being at least two inches taller than his opponent, and his superior in length of limb and build. At first sight he seemed to have the advantage, but upon closer inspection Biggs's flesh looked puffy—a natural consequence attendant upon the demolition of the contents of the paternal hampers.

Jack Stanfield was slight, and his skin, placed in juxtaposition to Biggs's, seemed fair enough for a girl; but his friend Happy, about the best school authority upon the matter, had great hopes of his man, for when Joe Stikkers whispered, "Cheesy is too much for him," Happy replied,—

"No fear, young 'un, Jack is in good trim; for while Cheesy is gormandizing and loafing about, Jack's playing football, or climbing trees—look at his muscle, Joe."

Joe looked, but not understanding much about the matter, did not feel greatly edified.

Amid the shouts of the opposing factions, the fight began—Jack cool and watchful, Happ 's advice guiding every movement of his litheele gant form.

Biggs was hot, savage, and, relying upon his great strength, fancied he had nothing to do but win straight off.

There was but little damage done during the first round, it being little more than a display of sparring, during which each tried to find out the other's weak points.

"Don't let him close, Jack," Happy whispered; "he's too savage to fight quietly—wind him—how do you feel?"

"All right."

"Ain't in a funk?"

Jack smiled, and rose from his second's knee as time was being called.

The second round became a little more like business, Biggs rushing savagely at his adversary, and trying bear-like to hug him—Jack, as watchful as ever, and using his hands pretty freely upon Biggs's face.

At the conclusion of the second round both bore marks of punishment—one side of Jack's face began to swell, and his opponent's right eye looked most uncomfortably red.

"It's too slow," whispered Happy, as he held Jack on one knee: "you must draw him out, then go in and win—use your left a little more, old boy."

Time was again called, and Jack, after a short exchange of blows, began to retreat.

"Hurrah, Biggs!" shouted those of that party; "follow him up!"

"Stick to him, Jack," said the latter's friends; "don't funk.'

"He'll wind him," Happy thought; "bravo! that's it, bring him round!"

Inspired by the shouts of his party, Biggs followed Stanfield pretty close, and though giving and receiving some smart blows, he found he was as far from gaining the victory as ever.

For the first time since the fight began, he discovered how severely he had been punished—his right eye was rapidly closing.

Rendered savage by this, his blows became wilder, and pressing close upon Jack's retreating form, he received three ringing blows upon his left cheek.

This rendered him more furious than before, and, making a desperate effort to close with Jack, he became thoroughly winded; and feebly guarding his face, stood panting for breath.

Happy saw that the moment had come, so, running to his friend, he whispered,—

"Quick—go in, Jack, and finish him!"

As calm as when the battle first began, Jack went towards the panting breathless Biggs, and rained a shower of blows upon his face.

Cheesy struck out wildly—half blind and maddened with pain, he made no effort to guard himself; his only idea was to punish his opponent.

The effects of this was soon seen to be in Jack's favour, for Cheesy, finding he was too far gone to ward off any of the swift blows, began to retreat.

Then arose a shout from the opposite faction, and when Biggs's retreat became an undignified run, Tom Dickson called out,—

"Follow me, boys—let's charge 'em."

A responsive shout came from twenty throats as they bore down upon the foe.

There was a short struggle, a mass of hands and arms swayed to and fro—then Biggs and his party fled ignominiously from the hall.

Great were the rejoicings at this victory.

Gleddell's champion was carried shoulder high, and Joe Stikkers walked about the hall, his feet up in the air, and howled with delight.

CHAPTER XXIV.
IN PRISON.

THROUGH the gloom of that weary night which followed Gleddell's imprisonment, the boy suffered the most poignant anguish.

It was not the dread of being punished for the crime with which he was charged that gave him a moment's pain; his innocence of the robbery caused him no pangs upon that account; he felt that the magistrate would at the first examination give him his freedom. Poor boy! he little knew how oft the innocent have been punished, in spite of the laws which are held to be the best modelled in Europe.

How far this may be true, a careful perusal of our remarkable criminal trials will enlighten the reader.

Gleddell, so firm in his faith, gave but little thought to his position; but before his mind came the cold shrouded form of his only parent—it harrowed his loving heart to be thus placed, beyond the possibility of viewing the sweet face which had so oft been bent over him.

To once more kiss those lips which had taught his lisping tongue to call her mother! Was he never to behold her again, he frantically asked; and the cold stone walls of his prison seemed to take up the wild interrogation and echo it back in mockery.

The morning found him seated on the straw pallet, his head bowed and half supported by the palm of his left hand, and the governor of the prison, who, with his little daughter, was going his daily round, paused for a moment, and gazed with a pitying expression upon his face at the handsome intellectual looking boy.

No doubt the governor fancied he beheld another case of juvenile depravity—this time the offender one of a better class than the ignorant ragged hungry houseless street Arabs, who—God help them!—robbed because they knew not the difference between right and wrong; and their wise rulers built prisons and freighted convict ships to teach them better! Would not schools, I wonder, do the work cheaper and better? Perhaps not—the wisdom of our lawgivers is beyond our limited powers of understanding.

The governor's little daughter saw a sad pale face when the turnkey opened the cell door; she knew nothing of the juvenile depravity—which, by the way, is a disgrace to the present year of grace; so with child-like innocence she pointed towards the hapless prisoner and said,—

"Oh, papa, what a shame to put this young gentleman in here!"

Gleddell raised his head as the child's musical voice dispelled the horrible gloom of his prison, but ere he could catch a glimpse of her face, she was drawn away from the door; and his brain swam as he heard the governor chiding the child for speaking.

"If you do this again," he said, "I shall not bring you with me when I visit the cells."

"Why, papa—what have I done?"

"That boy, my dear, in spite of his good looks, is a thief—a common housebreaker, and will be transported for the——"

The door closed—then Gleddell, with a wild cry, sprang to his feet, and smiting his forehead, exclaimed, frantically,—

"Great heaven! am I mad?—can this be true?"

He gave a cry of such heartrending agony that it seemed the weight of his sudden sorrow had been too much for his brain, for with this piteous hopeless shriek he fell forward upon his face, and lay like one whose spirit had passed to the mystic regions of eternity.

When the jailor entered the cell, he found the boy still in this death-like trance, and with more mercy than could have been expected from one whose life was so blended with scenes of misery, he raised the boy from the cold stone floor, and placed him upon the wretched bed.

The man's hands were not skilled in gentle acts, for as he let the poor boy's head fall heavily upon the pillow, Gleddell recovered from his stupor, and, rising upon his hands, looked strangely at the face which was bent over him.

"What's the matter, young fellow?" asked the janitor. "I found you all of a heap when I came in."

"Matter!"—Gleddell repeated the word with bitter emphasis. "Ask the wild bird, when beating its frail body against the bars of a cage, and, could it answer, it would ask why it had been taken from the fresh sunlight?—seek the prisoner later, and you would find it bruised and senseless."

There was but little poetry in the man's nature, and Gleddell's simile was but little understood; but he caught the expressions bird and cage, which enlightened his faculties respecting the boy's meaning, and ere Gled could finish, the janitor said,—

"We puts birds in cages to keep 'em from flying away, and we keeps thieves in here for——"

Gleddell gave a cry such as might have come from a whelpless panther, as he sprang from the bed and faced the astonished gaoler.

"How dare you call me a thief?" he said; "repeat the word, and I'll brain you with this!"

He snatched the heavy earthen pitcher from the ground as he spoke, and the man, awed more by the lightning-like fire in the boy's eyes than the uplifted weapon, slowly retreated towards the door, and did not feel himself safe until he had shot the massive bolts in their sockets.

"What a devil of a temper that young fellow was in!" he muttered; "talk about eyes flashing fire—his did, and no mistake."

Gleddell paced the narrow limits of his cell until the angry flush left his cheeks paler than they were before this outburst of passion.

"I was foolish," he thought, "to give way thus. To this man I am but a criminal, and until my innocence is established, I must learn to bear tamely this terrible word. Thank heaven!" he added, as he threw himself upon the pallet, "my mother has not lived to behold her son the inmate of a felon's cell!"

He sat for some time brooding over the terrible misfortune which had so suddenly fallen upon him, and mingled with the thought of his dead parent came the form of George Oakplank's fair daughter.

"Minnie," he thought—and there was a world of unutterable anguish in the expression of his face—"she, too, will cast me off; in spite of her love, she will but think of me as a felon—an outcast, and one whose very presence would pollute the air she breathes. O God! what have I done, that I should suffer thus?"

Gleddell thought not of that sweet comfort to the bruised spirit, which is found in the beautiful expression that those whom God loves He chasteneth. When he gave utterance to his wild words, poor boy, he was chastened, and severely; and little wonder that in his dark time of trouble he should ask why he had been made to suffer thus.

Wearily passed the morn—and every footstep that came near his cell he would listen with bated breath, hoping that his keeper would come and take him before his judge.

He hoped in vain, for none stopped before his prison door; and as the hours rolled onward and the hope died away, he sank lower and lower in the depths of the dark abyss of hopeless despair.

Once he raised his sad woebegone face—it was to watch a sunbeam, that shone through the iron grating above his head.

It was but a passing gleam of the noonday flood of glorious light—this ray, which, shining for a few moments, disappeared, as though in penetrating that gloomy cell it had wandered from the bright green fields by mistake.

Sunshine with its gladness could bring the poor boy nothing but fresh misery—he watched the flickering beam, saw it leave the cold iron bars, and his thoughts flew to the old school house playground.

He saw in fancy the groups of laughing boys, as they trooped out of the great schoolroom, and filled the air with their gladsome shouts.

The ideal picture was hard to bear, and with it came the mental query—did one of those with whom he had dwelt so long feel a pang, when they thought of the wretched prisoner cooped up within those grey massive walls?

Could he have seen the majority of his schoolmates, he would have known by their sad looks, and the way in which they stood aloof from the merry games, that he was not absent from their minds.

From the bitterness which that gleam of sunlight had caused him, he was aroused by footsteps outside his door.

With head inclined forward, he waited breathlessly for the bolts to be withdrawn; and when the door was opened, he sprang to his feet and uttered a glad cry.

He saw in place of the sallow countenance of his janitor, the ruddy-faced old sea lion, George Oakplank.

The old fellow gripped the boy's hand, and his voice was husky as he said,—

"So they've laid you up like an old hulk, my boy, and run up a black flag over you—hang them!—a face like yours is the wrong cut to do such piratical work—how fare you, my boy?"

Gleddell could not answer the old fellow's question—he could think but of the kindly heart which prompted this visit, and with swimming eyes and faltering voice he said,—

"Oh, sir! you, then, do not believe me guilty?"

"Believe you guilty! No, lad, and all the big-wigs and those land-sharks, the lawyers, could not make me."

"Thank you, sir, for those words. This is the first gleam of hope which has shone upon my mind since I came within these hateful walls. And your daughter, sir — Minnie? Does she—she——"

The Captain turned towards the door, and said,—

"You had better ask her yourself."

A light form ran past the Captain, and the next moment Minnie, his first, his only love, was weeping with her face hidden upon his breast.

George Oakplank turned sharply upon his heel and walked towards the jailor, who stood just outside the door, and as he dropped a silver coin in the man's hand, he said,—

"You can close the door for the few minutes we have to be here."

The man looked at the coin, and then shut the massive door, the construction of which interested the old seaman so much that he did not look towards the young couple until that blissful meeting was over.

CHAPTER XXV.

AN INTRODUCTION.

WORDS were not required to express the joy of that meeting—they spoke in love's most eloquent language. When that passionate embrace was over, and they looked into each other's eyes, they saw how each had suffered; and sweet came the knowledge to the poor prisoner when he read that Minnie's faith was too firm to be shaken by the dark cloud which had fallen upon him.

Yet, lover like, he would have her lips confirm the joyful truth. As he sat with her small hand trembling in his grasp, he asked, in an undertone,—

"You do not believe me guilty, Minnie?"

She raised her eyes to his, and he saw the pain his words had caused.

"Forgive me!" he said. "Dearest, I meant not to pain you. The question was thoughtless—unnecessary, when your presence here tells me how much you love me in spite of all."

"I do love you, Gled," she murmured; "and happen what may, my heart will always be yours!"

"Bless you, dear one!" and he raised her hand to his lips and kissed it. "Now I can bear my sorrow better—braver, with this blessed knowledge to solace me. Have you seen Philip?" he added. "He does not, I hope, believe that I have fallen so low?"

The Captain heard Philip's name, and came forward just in time to prevent Minnie adding to Gleddell's misery by telling him that his friend was suddenly stricken with a deep sorrow, which had almost crushed his intellect, for he at that moment was confined to his bed, suffering from brain fever.

"Philip," George Oakplank said, "is your friend, Gled—what more can I say?"

"And the doctor? Have you heard——?"

"The doctor," answered the Captain, "will be the first to give you a welcome when you leave this cursed hole."

"When I leave," Gleddell said, sadly. "I have a foreboding that I shall suffer much before my——"

"Look on the bright side, lad," said the old fellow; "the log is pretty full against you, and the worst of it is that your best friends will be there to make the case blacker; but never mind that now—we must look to the present. You must go to London—you have a duty to perform there. To-morrow you will be examined—then I will do what I can to get you out on bail. Hang them! they can't refuse me that favour."

The janitor opened the door as the Captain ceased speaking—the few minutes allowed had expired, and they must go.

Gleddell felt less sorrowful after this visit. He had something to occupy his mind: the Captain's promise for the morrow—Minnie's looks and gently spoken words—were something to dwell upon; and the poor orphan boy felt less desolate—less alone in the world, now.

Even the cold grey walls which surrounded him wore a less cheerless aspect, and the small blue patch of sky visible through the narrow bars bid him hope for a safe issue from his tribulation.

The morrow came, and he met the stern magistrate with a face that bore the impress of truth. It was but a preliminary examination, and, after the boy was remanded, George Oakplank sought and obtained an interview with the law's high functionary.

The boon he craved was evidently not accorded with the readiness he had anticipated, for Captain George Oakplank left the presence, his face considerably flushed, and swinging his steel hook about in a manner that caused peaceable timid people, to give him a wide berth.

"The lanthorn-faced effigy!" he muttered, "what with his tacking and his double tacking, and his palaver, he would have left the poor boy laid abeam while his poor mother was being buried by the pirates who have taken all the spoil. It was lucky for him," added Captain George, savagely, "that he gave the boy liberty, or I'd have fallen foul of him, had he been the Admiral of the fleet, much less a tallow-faced big-wig."

The magistrate little knew the danger he incurred by his reluctance to accept the Captain's surety for Gleddell's reappearance when the trial was ordered to take place.

The old fellow did not regain his equanimity until he had Gleddell safely seated between his daughters in the quiet little parlour at Woodbine Cottage.

Gleddell saw that Eleanor looked much changed since they last met, and he would have inquired the cause, had not the Captain hinted that any allusion to the subject would be painful to the young lady.

The good-hearted old seaman did this for the best. He did not wish Gleddell to know that Philip was nigh unto death, and he had to use his strongest powers of persuasion to prevent the warm-hearted boy from rushing to the school and paying a visit to his old friends.

"No, Gled," he said, when the proposal was mooted, "to-morrow morning you must go to town. It's not many miles, certainly; but you will require all the rest you can get between this and the first train, which stops at our station."

Gleddell acquiesced; he wanted rest and quietude after what he had suffered. He had, as his old friend told him, much to go through, and he needed all the strength he could obtain before the dark time again came upon him.

It was early morn when Gleddell arose and prepared for his journey, and during the time the servant was preparing his breakfast the Captain entered the room.

To Gleddell's surprise, he saw that his friend was equipped for travelling; and in reply to his half-expressed query the Captain said,—

"I'm going to convoy you, lad. You are too light a craft to be left drifting about like a ship without her helm; besides," he added, "my old friend, the Admiral, is at the Nore, so, when you have done your duty to your parent's remains, we will run down and see him."

Gleddell's eyes sparkled; he had a strong love for the sea, and, boy like, thought not of the disagreeable duties and dangers of "those who go down to the sea in ships." The glad light soon passed when he thought of the uncertainty which awaited him when the trial took place.

"Should they bring me in guilty of the crime with which I am charged," he said, "your kindness will be——"

"Stuff!—they can't do it," said Captain George. "Guilty! I'll see to that, my lad. We'll bring a lawyer from London with us, and he'll palaver to the other land-sharks. Guilty! hang them, they can't make white turn black, so they can't make you do that which you have not done."

The boy drank greedily these hopeful words, and during their journey to London he gave way to a boyish day-dream of the glories of a sailor's life.

From this pleasing reverie he was aroused by the train stopping at the London Bridge terminus, and as he contrasted the great change which had taken place in his fortunes since last he stepped out upon that platform, the boy's heart became full of grief.

It was not yet three months since he parted from his only parent upon that spot; not three months since they stood waiting for the train, and talked hopefully to her who had passed away of the manner in which he intended to work during his last half-year's schooling.

"I shall be quite a man, mother," he said, "when I leave school. What a happy time it will be for us. I shall soon be able to earn money enough to keep myself and add to your little income. Good-bye, dear mother; here is the train—good-bye—God bless you! Remember, only six months—then I will always be with you."

He trod the very spot where this farewell had been taken, and every word, every look came with painful distinctness to his brain.

How much had transpired since that parting!—the last one between him and the gentle being he loved so well.

Then he was full of high hopes of the future, and looking forward to the time when he should be the means of making his widowed parent happy.

Now she had been taken from him, and all the bright hopes were changed into despair.

Little wonder that the poor fellow threw himself back in the cab and covered his face.

When he reached the small suburban cottage in which his childhood had been passed, a new trial awaited him.

They had borne the loved remains to the grave, and the boy, gazing for a moment at the cold empty dwelling, placed his hand to his forehead and moaned.

"Everything gone!—not one relic left—all, all taken away!"

Captain Oakplank's face expressed the indignation he felt at the avaricious greed of those who had taken the widow's little property, and as he drew his sleeve hastily across his face he muttered something about the pleasure it would afford him to have the rascally lawyers tied to a grating.

"Curse 'em! I'd flay 'em alive, the land-pirates! But come, boy, this is no place for you."

Gleddell craved one boon—that was, to visit his mother's grave; and the kind-hearted old sailor, while the boy knelt by the newly-raised mound, visited a stone-mason's shed which stood near the cemetery gates, and ordered a stone to be placed above the loved

THE BOYS OF BIRCHAM SCHOOL.

THE ESCAPE FROM THE SHIP.

and lost.

It was years after when Gleddell discovered the kindly hand which caused the erection of the monumental stone to mark his mother's grave.

When the Captain returned to his young friend the boy arose from the damp earth, and with drooped head and nervously twitching lips, he slowly and sorrowfully left the quiet grave-yard.

George Oakplank silently conducted him to the vehicle which awaited them, and when they reached the inn where the Captain had left his well-worn leathern trunk, he took the sad-hearted boy to the small chamber engaged for their accommodation and left him to his grief.

He knew that solitude would be the best antidote for Gleddell's melancholy, and his spirit would be better soothed than by words.

"He'll be better if left alone," the old fellow thought, as he went towards the residence of a clever lawyer whom he had determined should defend his favourite at the coming trial. "Poor lad! he has a cargo of grief to carry that would sink a heavier ship."

He was right. The poor boy was calmer when they went early the next morning to the railway-station.

"I do not know how it is," Gleddell said, "but since I visited my mother's grave I feel more resigned to God's will. Perhaps," he added, "it is for the best that she was taken away before this heavy trouble came upon me."

The Captain was silent. He was thinking at that moment of the terrible shock that his child would feel should the tribunal proclaim the boy a thief.

"I don't know," he mused, "but what it would be best for the lad to remain in the old *Glory*, and when she goes upon her cruise it would puzzle the big-wigs to find him. I'll stand the loss of the money, should they exact his recognizance. Yet, no! Let him face them. His log is clear, and it's hard if they can bring him in guilty."

So he thought; and the train whirled them onward to the seaport where the old *Glory* rode at anchor.

How eagerly Gleddell looked out upon the deep waters when they reached the beach, and his pale eager face had less of sorrow in its expression when they were seated in the boat which the Captain had hailed to take them aboard the mighty line-of-battle ship.

Gleddell saw—and his heart beat at the sight—noble frigates gliding over the waters, their swelling sails towering like a pyramid of snow. He heard the creaking of the masts and the sweep of the rope that came at intervals, as the vessels changed their course in obedience to helm and sail. Boats from the distant men-of-war gave life to the scene as they passed and repassed—some bringing the liberty men aboard. One containing several saucy midshipmen, one of whom, as they shot past Gleddell, pointed him out to his companion, then called out,—

"What ship?—going to join, sir? Hurrah! Pull, you lubbers!"

Their neat uniform and the golden crown in front of their caps attracted Gleddell's attention, and he mentally asked, "Shall I ever be one of these?"

A slight flush came to his pale cheeks at the thought, and he watched them until their boat shot past the bows of a liner.

"It's one of the *Glory's* boats!" exclaimed the old sailor, as he saw the lusty rowers toss up their oars. "What think you of being like these youngsters—eh, Gled?"

The old sea-dog's eyes sparkled with pleasure at the sight of the colossal ship, and many of the happiest scenes of his life passed before his mind.

"Shall I ever be like these?" Gleddell said, "Oh, sir, it would be the proudest moment of my life to board the side of a noble ship and feel that I was one of her glorious crew!"

"You shall do it yet, lad!" said George Oakplank, "you shall, in spite of all the land-sharks ashore—here we are!—huzza!—I feel ten years younger, Gled, at this sight."

The Captain had donned his uniform for the occasion, and when he stepped on the old *Glory's* deck he was received by the officer of the watch with a respectful salute, and in reply to his inquiry for the Admiral, the officer said,—

"He will be on deck immediately, sir."

"Tell him old George Oakplank is here, my lad—Oakplank, who sailed with him in the *Pallas!*"

The officer went towards the after hatch, and before Gleddell had time to indulge in more than a passing glance at the snow-white decks, the neatly-coiled ropes and the heavy guns, he found himself face to face with a grave elderly gentleman, in the uniform of an Admiral of the Queen's navy.

The greeting between the old companions was almost brotherly; and before they went below, Captain Oakplank placed his hand upon Gleddell's shoulder, and introduced him to the admiral.

"So you wish to become a sailor, my man?" the grave looking officer said, as he gazed at the boy's slight but elegant form and bold handsome face. "Well, I dare say we can find room for you on board; and with the introduction you have had it will be your own fault if you do not do well."

Gleddell's colour came and went as he listened to the Admiral's words, and a wild hope sprang within him that he was to remain on board.

He could not answer one word, his heart was too full; and the Admiral, understanding the boy's feelings, said to a youngster who was seated upon a gun and beating the devil's tattoo with his heels,—

"Take this young gentleman to the gun-room and amuse him till I send for you."

Gled followed his conductor, a boy of about his own age, and before they had gone half the length of the ship the middy quite confused his companion with the questions he asked—they came all in a breath—thus,—

"Going to stay aboard?—where's your kit?—got any money?—can you fight?—what's your name?—how old are you?—whose that old fellow with one arm—your governor, eh?—got any sisters?—are they pretty?—this way—ware shins—tumble down here—this is the easiest way."

So while poor Gled slowly descended the break-neck ladder, his inquisitive companion swung himself off by a rope which hung down the hatch, and before Gled had descended half-a-dozen steps, he heard the middy at the bottom call out to his companions,—

"Look out! here's a griffin coming, and we have'nt time to grease the steps!"

"A good-looking lad," remarked the Admiral, when seated opposite his old friend, "and, unless I'm much mistaken, he's got the stuff in him that will make a good officer."

"He's just the build," said George Oakplank, "for a mid. I wish to heaven I could leave him with you!"

"Is he not to stay?"

The old fellow told him how peculiarly Gleddell was situated—told of the crime with which he was charged—his recent loss—and wound up with a sweeping volley of denunciations upon the learned gentlemen of the law and a stout belief in the boy's innocence.

The Admiral knew his old companion was truth itself, and his interest being excited by the story of Gleddell's misfortunes, he offered to keep him on board and save the court of 'ustice the trouble of sitting in judgment upon him.

"No, old friend," was the answer, "he shall go, and have his name taken off the black list—then you shall have him."

They spent the day on board the line-of-battle ship, and when they left, Gleddell parted from the old *Glory's* gallant midshipmen with the hope of soon meeting again, and the boys, who had taken a fancy to the orphan, reciprocated the feeling.

CHAPTER XXVI.

THE TRIAL.

At length the hour came for Gleddell to appear before the tribunal whose fiat would condemn him to everlasting misery or restore him to freedom.

Pale, and calm in demeanour, the boy took his place in the felon's dock, and while awaiting the arrival of the judge, he gazed, in a startled, fearful manner, at the sea of upturned faces, every eye of which was turned upon the youthful prisoner.

He saw among the crowd many of his schoolmates, and his lip quivered when he beheld Jack Stansfield and Happy looking at him with a sad hopeless expression upon their faces.

For the first time since he had entered the court a cold chill passed over his frame.

This change was caused by the sorrowful manner in which his young friends gazed upon him. He could have felt more hopeful respecting the result of his trial had he seen the least sign of hope on their countenances.

Towards the gallery to the right of the felon's dock Gleddell dared not raise his eyes, and his cheeks burnt with shame and indignation as he felt the eyes of the gentle Minnie were fixed upon him.

He had caught a glimpse of the brave old Captain and his daughter as he stepped into the box, and the sight had done more to unnerve him than the thought of his perilous position.

He would have given ten years of his life had they not been there; yet, so strange is the human heart, he felt a gleam of joyful pride when he thought how deeply he was beloved by the beauteous creature.

"She obeyed the dictates of her loving heart," he thought, "when she came here, and when I am acquitted her sweet voice will be the first to welcome me."

He looked for Philip among the many he knew, but the usher was not in the court.

He felt disappointed at this, and sought to find a reason for his friend's absence. This reflection was interrupted by the entrance of the judge, and the boy collected all his energies to meet the accusation against him.

He listened to the charge with compressed lips and heaving breast, and when he was asked whether he was guilty, he raised his head, and looking the judge fearlessly in the face, answered,—

"Not guilty, my lord."

There was something in the manner in which he uttered these simple words that prepossessed the spectators in his favour, for a slight buzz of approval came from their lips. The noise, though slight, was at once silenced by a man who stood near the witness-box. Then the first witness for the prosecution was called.

It was the Doctor, and as he gave back the book upon which he had taken the oath, he raised his eyes and looked at Gleddell.

The boy read the pity that was in the old man's heart by this glance, and for a moment a mist seemed to swim before his eyes.

It was gone as quickly as it came, and he again stood calm and with that conscious expression of innocence upon his face which a guilty mind could not assume.

He heard the Doctor's evidence. It differed but little from that already known to the reader. The good old man was as taciturn as he could be. He merely stated how the alarm of thieves caused him to go towards the strong room and the finding of Gleddell by the policeman.

This functionary gave his evidence as policemen generally give evidence—he left nothing unsaid that could make the prisoner guilty.

The file that fell from Gleddell's pocket and the keys being found in the lock were made the most of, and the poor boy, when he heard the plausible story, felt his heart sink within him.

To Gleddell's surprise, when the policeman left the box, Jack Stanfield took his place.

He saw by Jack's face that he was no willing witness, and he wondered why he, above all the boys who saw him taken from the strong room—Jack Stanfield, his bosom friend, should have been chosen to give evidence against him.

Jack, upon being told to state all he knew about the robbery, somewhat electrified the court by saying,—

"My lord and gentlemen of the jury, it will save time if you will take the answer I gave to the constable when he ordered me to attend here—I know nothing whatever of the affair."

The judge looked surprised, and seemed as though about to ask why the lad had been called, but before he could speak, the counsel for the prosecution rose, and with a smirk towards his brother professionals, said,—

"Not so fast, young gentleman, you are a very important witness."

"Am I," Jack thought; "all you will get out of me won't take you long to write."

"Now remember," continued the counsel, "that you are on your oath."

Jack looked rather puzzled as he said,—

"I am quite aware of that."

"Now, where were you on the morning of the robbery?"

"Several places," answered Jack, saucily; "I was in bed, for one."

The barrister looked rather nettled, but smiling, as much as to say, "I'll have him directly," he said, after referring to a slip of paper he held in his hand,—

"Be kind enough to tell the court where you were at a quarter to nine on the morning of the 17th."

"In the schoolroom," said Jack.

"Do you remember any particular circumstances that took place that morning?"

"Yes!"

"Let the court hear them explained."

Jack's eyes twinkled rather mischievously as he began,—

"Well, there was a slight misunderstanding between myself and Harry Ogleby—he drew an ugly face in my grammar book and I punched his head for it."

There was much tittering among the spectators, and old George Oakplank could scarce refrain from giving a lusty cheer at the manner in which Jack answered the landshark.

"Come, come," said the barrister snappishly, "we require no nonsense here; now report the conversation you had in the schoolroom."

Jack looked as grave as an old owl, as he answered,—

"I had several conversations that morning, there was one with Happy-go-lucky, about serving out the fellow who collared our tommy at break——"

"If you persist in annoying me in this manner, sir, you will be committed for contempt of court, do you hear that, sir?"

The speaker's face looked uncomfortably red, and he flourished his hand most energetically; he could have saved himself the trouble, for all the effect it had upon Jack.

"Well," he said coolly, "that's a treat, I'm to be committed for contempt of court, and I'm doing all you ask me to do; you want me to repeat the conversation I heard in——"

"I mean the conversation with the prisoner," roared the barrister, redder than ever about the gills, "do you understand now, sir?"

"Oh, I see," Jack said, "had you told me that before, you would have saved your angry passions from rising——"

"My lord," and the lawyer fairly danced with rage as he spoke, "am I to be made an object of ridicule by this boy?"

The judge looked sternly at Jack, and cautioned him respecting his conduct.

"Look here, my lord," said the reckless fellow, "I've answered every question that he has asked——"

"I have heard your answers," said the great man, "and they were wanting in proper respect for the learned gentleman."

Jack mentally hoped the day would come when he should meet the learned gentleman in an out-of-the-way lane.

Jack always carried a cattapult in his pocket, and a round pebble, fired from behind a tree, would add an extra bump to those already possessed by the learned gentleman, if that rencontre ever came about.

"Now," the lawyer said, "perhaps you will repeat the subject of the conversation which took place between you and the prisoner upon the morning of the 17th?"

Gleddell wondered what this could have to do with the robbery; and feeling that whatever had passed between him and Jack Stanfield, could not in any way tend to prove his guilt, he felt perfectly at ease respecting his friend's statement.

"The tenor of our conversation," Jack said, "had nothing whatever to do with the crime with which the prisoner is charged."

"That," said the judge, "is far better left to the judgment of the jury."

Jack somewhat dejectedly related how his friend received the letter telling him of his mother's death, and the remarks respecting the loss of his little property, beyond this, they could not get a word from the boy.

"Now," the red-faced lawyer said, "I am in a position to prove that this witness has wilfully kept back part of their conversation —let Godfrey Bransome be called."

The little orphan boy came timidly to the witness-box, and after he had taken the oath the lawyer said,—

"Now my little man, tell his lordship the words you heard the prisoner use when he sat beside the last witness."

Godfrey looked piteously at Gleddell, and in a voice that was scarcely audible, said,—

"When I heard that Gleddell had lost his mother I went to speak to him, and as I came near enough to hear the answer he was making to his companion I heard him say, —'Do not trouble yourself about me, Jack; although I have not a penny-piece in my possession, *I shall have plenty by to-morrow morning.*'"

Gleddell started as though he had been stung by an adder. He remembered using those words when Jack said he wished he had plenty of money. The boy felt the danger this expression had placed him in, and clutching the rail in front of the dock, he bent forward and listened eagerly for the next link to be formed in this chain of seeming guilt.

Jack Stanfield had not left the witness-box, and when Godfrey made this statement Jack said,—

"Yes, I had forgotten that—he did say so; but surely you do not think it had any reference to this robbery?"

Poor Jack was ordered to stand down; and the case for the prosecution being ended, Gleddell listened anxiously to the counsel Captain Oakplank had employed for him.

He had no witnesses to prove his innocence, so when his speech had concluded the evidence was briefly summarised.

The fact of Gleddell having used the words repeated by Godfrey Bransome was looked upon as the first step to the robbery; then the Doctor's evidence of having left the keys on the library table, when the prisoner was in the room; then came a further proof of his guilt—he was found in the strong room without his boots—the keys in the lock, and the marks upon the cash-box corresponding with a steel instrument which fell from his pocket. Although Gleddell's counsel had urged the fact of none of the missing property being found upon him, the plea had no weight in the face of this damning chain of seeming guilt.

Gleddell felt there was no hope for him, and with blanched cheeks and staring eyes he watched the jury leave their box.

They were not long absent, and when they returned the foreman, in answer to the judge's question, said, in a loud clear voice,—

"Guilty, my lord; but, in consequence of his youth and the heavy affliction he was under at the time, we strongly recommend him to mercy."

The judge pondered for a few seconds over these words, then, addressing Gleddell, said,—

"Were it not for your youth and the jury's recommendation, I should pass the heaviest sentence the law allows for this offence—an offence which has been aggravated by your obstinacy in refusing to disclose the hiding-place of the stolen property, or the names of your accomplices. Under these circumstances, I feel it my duty to sentence you to be *transported for the term of seven years.*"

When these dread words left the stern man's lips, Captain Oakplank sprung to his feet, and would have spoken, had not Minnie given a scream of heart-wrung agony and fallen from her seat. He bit his lips to prevent the angry words that were upon them from being uttered, and seizing the senseless girl round the waist, he rushed from the court.

The effect of the sentence upon Gleddell seemed for a time to have deprived him of his faculties, for he stood as though turned to stone. Then, as Minnie's cry rang upon his ears, he clasped his forehead and cried out wildly,—

"Great God! am I to suffer thus Oh! mercy, mercy! I am innocent!"

With the last word ringing piteously upon the ears of that dense crowd, the boy fell to the ground in a state of coma, and when the gaoler bore him from the court he seemed like one who had passed the mystic precincts of the unknown world.

* * *

From the prison Gleddell was taken to the convict ship at Woolwich. Here, with upwards of a hundred of the lowest dregs of our great city, the helpless boy was cast.

Oh! the anguish that filled his innocent soul when he stood clothed in a suit of coarse grey cloth, and was compelled to hear the horrible language used by this loathsome gathering of young and old.

The sentence of banishment he had received was heaven compared to the sufferings he endured when he found himself levelled to an equality with the dreadful beings whose chief delight was to narrate their villanies — recitals which were received by the listeners with every manifestation of delight.

Gleddell had never thought he could have fallen into the slough of moral turpitude which his companions had, and he shrunk from their very presence as though they were the most loathsome of the crawling reptiles upon God's earth.

Death, he felt, would be preferable to the horrible vista which opened before him, for he would suffer more than tongue or pen could describe by herding with these creatures, whose brute instincts made them worse than the beasts of the field.

He was not without hope of ending his sufferings by this means, for the surgeon who had charge of the ship selected him and three others of the human freight to act as "captains of the deck"—such was the name given to the best behaved of the convicts, who were chosen by the medical officer to see his orders carried into effect, and to watch the various batches of criminals as they came on deck in their turn for air and exercise.

Gleddell's heart filled when he thought of the kind old Captain, whose intercession with the doctor had procured for him this little superiority over his degraded companions.

While performing this duty he would gaze with tearful eyes and bursting heart at the quiet water and the distant lights which twinkled from the windows of many happy homes.

"One plunge," he thought, "and all will be over. Better death—ten times better—than such companionship as this!"

So strong the resolve came upon him to find a Lethe for his sorrows in the dark waters of the Thames, that he waited and watched for an opportunity to carry his project into effect before the vessel should leave her moorings.

There was the haunting fear that he should be wounded—brought down by one of the guards who paced the quarter-deck—or he would have taken the leap when first the terrible prospect of spending so many years with his callous companions burst with its fearful reality upon his mind.

He had heard from the lips of one of the convicts what his fate would be if he attempted to cheat society of its vengeance, and the recital made his blood crawl and freeze the very marrow in his bones.

All the time he was upon deck he watched the vigilant guards, which consisted of twenty-four men, and did duty in three watches. Each man of the party, when on watch, paced to and fro with a loaded rifle in his hand.

"Could I but feel sure," Gleddell thought, "their bullets would kill me, I would not delay one moment in taking this step; but to be stayed by a shattered limb, and then taken below and ironed, and every chance of ridding myself of my miserable life gone—no, that would be worse, if possible, than I now have to endure."

The agony of mind he had suffered had left its marks upon his face, and the surgeon, who showed as much kindness as he dared to the poor boy, ordered that he should not be ironed when between watches.

Gleddell's eyes expressed his gratitude, and when the officer left a thrill of joy passed over the boy's frame.

"Perhaps," he thought, "when the prisoners are all down below and in irons the soldiers will be less watchful."

Filled with this hope he crept on deck and crawled towards the vessel's side. What joy! one spring and he would be upon the bulwarks—then their bullets, if he was struck,—would matter but little, for if wounded he would fall into the water - if shot in any vital part, so much the better—it would be a speedier death than drowning.

So praying to the great Omnipotent for forgiveness, he arose from his knees, and seizing a rope drew himself up.

Slight as was the noise he made, he was heard, and the nearest sentry sang out,—

"Who goes there?"

Gleddell made no answer—he was upon the bulwark, and clearing his feet from the coil of a loose rope, sprang into the sluggish water.

A piercing cry escaped his lips as his feet left the bulwark, and that cry was followed by the sharp report of the sentinel's rifle.

Though he had stood but for a moment before taking the leap, the soldier saw his intent, and, as quick as thought, brought his piece to his shoulder and fired.

Save for a few drops of blood which were visible upon the vessel's side, there was no trace left of the hapless boy.

In vain were the boats lowered—his body was not found, by those who so eagerly sought, and all on board the convict ship felt that he was dead ere the sullen plash told the waters had received another victim.

CHAPTER XXVII.

JEAN GAILLAND BECOMES THE POSSESSOR OF AN IMPORTANT SECRET.

It is difficult to conceive a worse position than Philip Randall was placed in after his encounter with Edgar Greymore.

He knew the pitiless nature of the man he had so nearly killed, and as he reflected over the threat Greymore had used, his heart sank within him at the fearful result of his mad attack upon the man who held so terrible a secret over him.

He tried by calm reflection to find a mode of escape from the danger that menaced him; but the more he pondered over his position, the worse he became.

There was one way which offered a means of escape. That was, to seek Greymore and offer to resign all pretensions to Eleanor's hand. Could he do this and live?

No; the gentle girl had become too dear to him to exist and behold her another's.

"This would kill me," he thought. "Yet if I do not do it I shall be dragged to the felon's dock and banished for ever from my native land—banished for a crime of which I am innocent! No; death before either alternative!"

He paced slowly to and fro the little chamber, strangely calm for one who was about to die by his own hand—to leave the world and its pleasures at the early age of six-and-twenty.

"I would not die," he mused, "and leave my foe to carry out his machinations against the poor girl. No; ere I seek a Lethe for my sorrow she shall know the serpent's nature which is hidden by so fair an exterior."

The thought was parent to the act. He sat at his writing-table and penned an impassioned farewell to his heart's idol—told her all—his connection with Greymore in a deed of guilt, committed when they were but boys, and drew such a faithful picture of the polished scoundrel's hidden nature that would have caused her, had she ever loved him, to have loathed his presence.

Philip concealed nothing from the gentle girl. He told her that life without her would be unbearable, and pointed out the eternal gulf which would be between them should he be taken by the authorities and sent to a convict settlement.

"It is better," he wrote, in concluding this extraordinary epistle, "to die by my own hand than to endure the fearful ordeal of hearing my name bandied from mouth to mouth as an atrocious criminal—better for us both. Eleanor, to you my disgrace would be a living torture, but by the means I am about to use you can mourn me as one who has passed into that mystic state where we can hope to be reunited until the end of time."

Such were the contents of that letter which caused Eleanor to swoon when she received it, and, when her senses returned, to seek the unhappy man, with the hope that she would be in time to save him from that fearful crime he contemplated.

She came softly to his side as he prayed, with bowed head, to his Maker to be forgiven for the heinous crime he was about to commit, and placing her hand upon his shoulder, she gave utterance to the single word,—

"Philip!"

He looked up and gazed at her pale lovely face like one who had been suddenly awakened from a dream; and, as his fingers relaxed their grasp upon the loaded weapon, he murmured,—

"Eleanor!—and here!"

"Yes, Philip," she said, "and, thank Heaven, in time to prevent you sending your soul into eternity laden with the crime of self-destruction."

She moved towards the table as she spoke, and taking up the pistol, continued,—

"Oh! Philip, you had but little reliance upon a woman's love and faith when you penned that letter. Think you that my heart would have changed towards you, though the whole world might have believed you guilty of the terrible crime the knowledge of which gives this man such a power over you. I have your word that you are innocent, and would believe that in spite of all."

She opened the window quietly, and *throwing the pistol over the playground wall*, went on,—

"There, it is gone now, Philip. Let us talk calmly over this terrible danger that menaces you. It will not be the first time that a weak woman has saved a man, even in greater difficulties than this."

He fell upon his knees before her, and clasping her hand, murmured—

"Angel!—surely heaven has sent you to save my erring soul from a great sin!"

She stooped over him and kissed his forehead, and that kiss came like balm to his perturbed spirit.

The wish to live now came upon him as strong as the wish he had felt to be rid of his troubled existence, and as he arose and drew her to his heart, he said,—

"Eleanor, I have been upon the brink of a great crime, tottering upon the verge of that mystic abyss—the strange world of the future. It was wrong, but—" He paused suddenly, and as one hand passed across his brow, he added, "perhaps, after all, it would have been best for us both had I carried out my resolve before you came, angel-like, between my soul and perdition."

"Philip!"

There was much of tenderness and reproach in this single word, and as he held her yet closer to him, he continued,—

"That one act, Eleanor, has linked my destiny with one who can at any moment bring me to the felon's cell; he has promised to do so, and ere the noonday sun shines upon the earth he will keep his word."

She made no comment, but the lovely head nestled closer to him, and one fair soft hand stole around his neck, its mute significance telling him how dear his existence was to her.

"Would you not," he asked, his voice low and tremulous, "sooner mourn me when dead, than live to behold the hour when I should stand before a tribunal, the mark for every finger, and my name loathed by all——"

She looked up, and their eyes met as she said,—

"You are innocent, Philip, of this crime?"

He pointed upward, and answered solemnly,—

"I am as guiltless as you are."

"Meet this charge," she said, "it will be more manly, more noble, than seeking death by your own hands."

A slight flush and a momentary lighting up of his eyes told that he had caught some of the hope which had dictated her answer—a hope that his innocence would carry him safely through the dark hour, should he stand before a tribunal charged with the perpetration of which Greymore alone was guilty.

The brightness of his eyes faded, and his face again became sombre in its expression, as he mournfully said,—

"No, Eleanor, there can be but one result, should I be dragged before a tribunal."

"That?" she asked.

"Banishment for life, or a term of years which would be the same in the end, for I should not long survive the disgrace."

She looked tenderly, pityingly, at the man whom she so well loved, and in fancy beheld him garbed in a suit of convict grey—his limbs bruised and the proud soul humiliated by the brutal treatment from a hard-hearted pitiless taskmaster.

The picture was one of horror, and as her heart filled with grief she murmured,—

"It would kill me, Philip, yet I would not that you took away the life which God has given you by your own hand. Can nothing be done to avert this? Can you not escape—there is yet time?"

"And you," he asked, "what will you feel when you hear my name bandied from mouth to mouth as one who has fled from the avenging awe of justice? Will not that add another link to my seeming guilt and be the cause of an eternal separation between us?"

She stood before him with clasped hands and moving lips, as though she were offering up a prayer to the Giver of all Good to guide and help him in this hour of dark trouble.

"Were I to leave England," Philip continued, his lips nervously twitching as he spoke, "I should seek an asylum in the New World—there, under an assumed name, I should try to win my bread until the sorrow upon my heart should do its work and take me from the world and its cares."

"Philip, this is dreadful!"

"A few words, dear one, and I have done. I dare not ask you to be the companion of my exile. I would not, though heaven knows how dear you are to me, have your name linked with mine under these circumstances; so, Eleanor—oh, God, that I should be compelled to utter those words—we must part for ever!"

She gave a wild cry and clung yet closer to him.

"No, no!" she sobbed, "you will return—time will clear your name of this injury—then we can be happy, so happy that our present grief will be but one small speck in the bright cloud of joy."

He made no reply. He could not mercilessly destroy the blissful vision she had created out of the dark dread and mystic future.

"Come, Eleanor!" he said, "the hour is late, I will accompany you home."

She drew her cloak around her and silently followed Philip from the room.

Across the lawn he led his fair charge, and passing out at a small wicket used only by Philip and the head master, they were soon traversing the quiet lane which led to the house.

They were in no mood for conversation—the quiet beauty of the house—the well-remembered walk they were traversing—the towering trees amid which so many happy hours had been passed, and the knowledge that they were to separate—perhaps for ever, had its influence upon them, rendering each silent, although they had much, very much, to say.

Passing out upon the road which led to the village, the twinkling lights at Woodbine Cottage became visible, and Philip, who saw in their gleam that the moment had come for him to part with all he held dear upon earth, came to a sudden halt.

"Eleanor," he said, "the time has come for us to say farewell. Now I ask that you will cherish my remembrance and still hope that we may meet again."

"I shall never cease to——but, Philip!"

"Dearest?"

"Is there no means of escaping this terrible banishment?"

"None, Eleanor—except *Greymore's death!*"

She looked up at his face and saw an expression thereon that caused her to recoil.

"Philip!" she said, "you would not kill——"

The lover gave a low cry of affright.

"Eleanor!" he said, "the fiend of darkness must have been near me when that thought crossed my mind—so much as he has wronged me, I could not raise my hand against him."

Her womanly instinct told her he was speaking the truth, and with sweet soothing words she bid him hope that their parting would be but for a brief time, and in the happiness of their reunion the past would be forgotten.

He listened—holding both her hands in his—and when the farewell words came from his lips his face bore such an expression of hopeless desolation that it wrung a cry of agony from the generous girl.

One close embrace—then Philip broke away, and plunged into the silent depths of the thick wood.

Eleanor stood as though turned to stone, and, clasping her hands, she cried wildly,—

"Gone! gone! Oh, Philip! Philip!"

The wind sighing among the trees bore away that hopeless cry, and ere it had died out, there arose a pitiless scream for help. It was a man's voice, and as the girl stood dazed and bewildered by the sound, it was repeated, and with startling vividness came the words,—

"Help! help! Murder! murder!"

An unaccountable impulse urged her forward, and as she reached a thick clump of trees a man dashed closely past her.

It was M. Jean Gailland. He had seen Eleanor enter the school-house, and with his ear applied to the keyhole had overheard every word of their conversation.

There was a snake-like glitter in his dark eyes when he heard Philip tell Eleanor that he would seek safety by instant flight, and, rising from his knees, he drew back as the sorrow-stricken pair emerged from the usher's small chamber.

Like a sleuth-hound he dogged their steps, and, crouching behind a tree, he beheld their sad parting.

"He will go;" so ran the Frenchman's thoughts, "that will be one out of the way—then Greymore—ha! devil as he is, I will put the police on his track when he leaves here. He must be got rid of by that—*or another way.*"

The sallow face became distorted as this thought crossed his mind, and had Greymore been near and knew his friend's thought, he would have felt that Jean was a foe not to be despised.

CHAPTER XXVIII.

PHILIP RANDALL ACCUSED OF MURDER.

THAT wild cry for help was followed by a death scream, which, sounding amid the hitherto sombre stillness of the wood, froze the blood in the veins of those who were hurrying in the direction of the evil sound.

Tired labourers, returning from the distant homesteads to their little dwellings, were startled by the strange sound, and rushed towards the place from whence it proceeded.

Many of the boys from the school, who were returning from their evening rambles, heard the shrill cry, and were quickly bending over a man's form, which lay huddled at the foot of a tall tree.

The white moonbeams, streaming through the thick foliage, fell upon a ghastly scene. There, with his face upturned, and the once handsome proud features bruised, disfigured, and bloodstained, lay Edgar Greymore.

A chill mysterious feeling came over the little crowd as they saw the proud man battling bravely with the grim destroyer; and one of the boys, going forward, raised the bruised and crimsoned head.

"Let me die in peace," gasped Greymore; "do not lift my head—it will but prolong my misery——"

He paused as Philip Randall came upon the scene, and with a mighty effort raised himself upon one arm.

The film that had begun to spread over his closing eyes was arrested when he beheld Philip, and gave place to a blaze of fierce and deadly hatred. The lips moved convulsively, as though he would have spoken, but the death faintness came upon him, and with a deep groan he fell back upon the ground.

Then came pitying murmurs from those who stood around, and one asked, in a tone sufficiently loud for the dying man to hear,—

"He has been murdered. Who has done it?"

With the last struggle of his departing life, Greymore raised himself, and pointing with outstretched finger towards Philip, he said,—

"There stands my murderer — there — Philip Randall—he——"

With this accusation falling from his lips, his head fell back, a convulsive shiver passed over his frame, then all became still.

He was dead, and the soft beams from the glorious queen of night fell upon all that was earthly of that strange being, whose dark proud wayward soul had made him the envy of his fellow men.

He lay so calm, his features seeming as though he had but closed his eyes in sleep; and Philip, whom the dead man's last words had for some moments deprived of speech or motion, now sprang forward.

He knelt beside the corpse, and placing one hand over Greymore's heart, felt that it had ceased to beat.

"Almighty Power!" he exclaimed, "can this be true? He is dead!"

That awful feeling which creeps over us when we stand in the presence of the dead held the little group of spectators silent until Philip spoke—then one of the men stepped forward and said,—

"Yes, dead, master—did you expect a man could live with his skull broken and shattered as his is?"

"His skull!"

"Aye," said the man quickly, "considering your hand did the business, I don't see that you need feel surprised!"

Philip reeled backward, and clasping his forehead, said,—

"You surely do not believe——?"

"Every word," said the man, "every word; he would not have gone before his Maker with a lie upon his lips."

Jean Gailland stood near the dead body, and as he looked at Philip he muttered,—

"Both gone—Greymore dead—and the usher taken by the police for murdering him—this is more good fortune than I expected—the lovely miss may yet be mine—ha! she is here."

Eleanor, with a wild and horrified look upon her face, came through the little group which surrounded Philip and the murdered man.

She stood for some time like a beautiful statue, her eyes fixed upon the pale rigid features, which looked so strangely horrible under the pale moonlight.

She was fascinated—and though the sight filled her with horror, she could not avert her gaze.

Philip arose from beside the corpse, his face blanched, and a strange wild light in his eyes.

He would have spoken, but his tongue clove to his mouth. It was a strange scene—strangely horrible in its details.

There stood the usher with outstretched supplicating hands; facing him, but divided by the rigid form of the dead, was Eleanor, one hand tightly pressed to her brow, the other extended towards Greymore's lifeless body.

The crowd were awed by the strange attitude of the wretched pair, and even the man who had stood by Philip, ready to detain him until a constable came, drew back and gazed wonderingly at the statuesque maiden and her lover.

Jean Gailland, his dark face expressing the joy he felt at heart, leant against a tree and furtively watched the poor girl's twitching lips, and the mute horror expressed in her eyes.

Philip read but too faithfully the thoughts that were passing through Eleanor's mind, and though he could not speak, he made a movement towards her marble-like form.

He came close enough to her to touch her extended hand—that touch, though light, recalled her dazed senses.

Had an adder stung her hand she could

THE BOYS OF BIRCHAM SCHOOL.

THE FRENCH MASTER PLAYS A GAME AT FOOTBALL.

not have recoiled with greater loathing than she did when Philip touched her.

The very contact of his fingers caused a cry of alarm to escape her lips, and holding forth her hands as though to prevent his approach, she cried out—

"Philip—Philip—has it come to this!"

He would have followed her had not the man who looked upon him as Greymore's murderer held his arm.

A tiger left whelpless in his lair could not have shown more fury than did Philip when he felt his forward movement checked by the labourer's strong grasp.

A cry of concentrated rage came from his lips, and before his would-be captor could step aside, Philip drew back his clenched hand and dealt the man such a powerful blow full in the face that he fell to the earth as though he had been shot.

He lay stunned and motionless, and the usher, with glaring eyes, looked around as though seeking a foe upon whom to vent his savage passion.

There were brave men in that crowd—men who would have faced any ordinary danger—but none who dared approach that slight elegant form; there was an expression in those dark eyes that warned them of the danger they would incur, and as he strode forward towards Eleanor, the crowd fell back and gave him a wide passage.

He came within a couple of paces of the wretched girl, but ere he could speak she gave a wild cry, and tearing from him fled from the terrible scene.

He would have followed had not the Venerable Doctor Bircham suddenly stood before him.

The good old fellow had been brought to the scene by one of the terrified boys, and hearing that Philip was in danger he hurried from his studies, hoping to be in time to save his friend from the clutches of the law.

"Philip," he said, placing his hand lightly upon the usher's shoulder, "what is the meaning of this?"

Philip answered this query with a vacant stare, and would have gone in pursuit of Eleanor had not the Doctor detained him.

The head master, failing to glean any information from Philip, turned towards the horrified crowd, and seeing M. Jean, he said,—

"You, M. Gailland, can possibly explain this mysterious affair?"

The Frenchman came forward, and, pointing towards Greymore, said,—

"There has been a murder, sir, and the dead man accused Monsieur Randall of the deed—the words were the last he uttered."

The Doctor's face whitened, and looking towards the usher, he said,—

"Philip, is this charge——"

He was interrupted in his interrogation by Philip throwing his hands up and giving a wild scream of more than mortal agony.

"Innocent! I am innocent!" he said, "yet she has fled from me as though I were an object to be loathed!"

His voice sank to a low murmur as he ceased speaking—then he electrified all who stood near by giving such a wild unearthly scream that caused the blood to curdle in their veins.

As the cry left his lips his hands clutched the air and he fell to the ground, bereft of sense or motion.

The events of that fearful night had been too much for the usher's overtaxed faculty, for when that cry left his lips his reason had fled.

The Doctor was well known to all who had gathered around the murdered man's body, and by his order the corpse was carried to the school-house and placed in a dismal chamber.

The usher, guarded by two men, was led to his chamber. He spoke but once during that fearful walk, and his words were those of a maniac.

The shock had been too much, both physically and mentally, for ere the morning came he had to be held in his bed by four strong men, and not until the medical man, whom Dr. Bircham had sent for, forced an opiate down Philip's throat, could he be with safety left alone.

When the effects of the potent drug wore off he was found to be upon the verge of the tomb—both his intellect and his bodily vigour had departed, and the watcher's lamp burnt beside a gibbering helpless maniac.

It was a merciful dispensation of Providence, this state into which the usher had fallen, for when the jury sat in inquest over Greymore's body they returned a verdict of wilful murder against Philip Randall, and the man who sat so unmoved in the stricken sufferer's room was an officer of justice.

He kept guard over his prisoner, waited and watched until he should become strong enough to be conveyed to a felon's cell.

All save one in Bircham School felt for the usher—the one who expressed any gratification at the terrible doom which threatened Philip was Jean Gailland.

Philip was his rival, and a dangerous one; so Jean felt that while he lived the passion he had conceived for Eleanor could not be requited.

Yet, much as he wished for the law's dread penalty to be inflicted upon Philip, he with matchless cunning daily visited the sick man's room in the guise of a friend.

CHAPTER XXIX.

THE CONTENTS OF THE POCKET BOOK.

HAD not the little world of Bircham been so much engrossed with the fate of their favourite, Stanton Gleddell, and the terrible charge against the usher, they must have noticed a great change which had taken place in M. Jean since the night of the murder.

The French master's features had become pinched and haggard, and his sunken eyes bore that strange fearful expression, as though he was in hourly dread of meeting a fearful apparition.

They would, but for the reason already stated, have wondered at the fear which M. Jean always evinced at the visit of a ruffianly-looking fellow, known in the village as Poacher Luke, or Luke the Poacher.

His first visit to M. Jean took place upon the morning succeeding the murder in the wood, and from that time he seemed to possess a wondrous power over the pale haggard French master.

Luke was the black sheep of the village, a grim sombre being, to whom report attributed all the evil that was done in the village.

Luke cared but little for the opinions of his neighbours—quite the reverse—his dark face would light up when he saw how much he was hated and feared.

His dwelling was in keeping with his nature—a small whitewashed cottage, situate amid a thickly wooded piece of waste ground known as the "old chase."

Here Luke and his wife dwelt, and none of the villagers cared to near the poacher's dwelling after nightfall; the light gleaming through the small window was to them as much shunned as the mariners shun the beacon light which tells of a sunken reef and the treacherous quicksand.

The reckless and high-spirited among the Bircham boys were great friends with Luke Jessop; to them the door of his small dwelling was always readily opened; and many who were closely intimate with the dreaded poacher were of opinion that a time had been when Luke had fulfilled a far different position.

The man's language and manners, despite the habitual sternness and ferocity of his features, told that his early days had not been passed among the ignorant class from which he received such scant courtesy.

The mystery that surrounded him caused the lads much speculation—and one and all who knew Luke were of opinion that he was labouring under some great sorrow, which had caused him to withdraw from the society of his fellow men, and seek in solitude a forgetfulness of the past.

Such was the opinion of the boys, and after events told how near the truth their perceptions had guided them.

Luke reciprocated the kindness he received from his young friends by teaching them to climb the most difficult trees, and pointing out where the choicest birds' eggs were to be found.

Nor was this all he did for the boys—Luke could manufacture the most cunning baits; and many of the finny tribe owed their sudden jerk out of their native element to the skilfully made fly or the tempting morsels Luke had provided for the angling portion of his young acquaintances.

He found equal favour with the upper form lads, who affected a partiality for the intellectual (!) pastime called ratting.

With these sportive youths he was upon the most familiar footing; and every terrier in the possession of these fast gentlemen had been under Luke's careful training; and, truth to tell, his instruction was highly prized by their happy owners.

In vain did the head master issue his edict forbidding the elder boys to visit the poacher's hut—the very spirit of opposition caused them to go the oftener.

The good old master, biassed by the stupid prejudice of the villagers against Luke, looked upon him as an object to be shunned.

The boys thought Luke a stunner, and no end of good at training terrier pups—aforesaid pups being surreptitiously kennelled in all sorts of queer places about the school.

Such was the man, of many enemies and but few friends, who had become such an object of terror to M. Jean Gailland.

It was upon the morning succeeding the murder that this acquaintance began.

M. Jean was sitting in his little room, rejoicing over the strange events of the preceding night, when the boy who held the enviable position of fag for the French master, entered the room and disturbed Jean's pleasant train of thought.

It was a crowning mercy, M. Gailland thought, to be rid of Greymore. There was no fear now of the dark secret respecting his past life ever coming to light. The knowledge that Jacques Cherdon, the escaped convict, and M. Jean Gailland, the French master at Bircham, were one (he rubbed his hands and chuckled gleefully at the thought), had perished with Edgar Greymore.

No wonder that M. Jean gave utterance to an angry exclamation when the boy's entrance disturbed his pleasant train of fancies and aerial structures respecting the Captain's beautiful daughter.

"Luke Jessop," the boy said, "wants to see you, sir."

"Luke Jessops?—I know not him. What does he want? Who is this Luke Jessops?"

"Don't you know, sir? Why, I thought everybody knew him."

Jean shrugged his shoulders, and turned the palms of his hands outwards, as he said, somewhat angrily,—

"I know not of him; tell me what he is, that I may know if it is me that he wants."

"Luke," answered the boy, readily, "lives in the old chase; we all know him, for he's the best hand out at telling us where to find the finest eggs; and can't he make stunning flies, that's all?——"

M. Jean gave utterance to something between a yell and a very short but wicked word in the French language.

It was evident the boy was no stranger to M. Jean's mode of expressing his displeasure, for he stopped abruptly in his enumeration of the virtues possessed by Luke the poacher.

"What is this to me?" said M. Jean, "I don't want to know about eggs or the flies."

"You asked me to tell you about him," said the youngster, "then you growl like a——"

"Bring him up," said M. Jean. "You have too much of the talk."

"Have I?" muttered the lad, as he left the room, "you ain't!"

M. Jean looked much astonished when his visitor entered the room, and the latter, without uttering a word of introduction, turned towards the door and locked it.

This action was not pleasant to M. Jean, and as he watched the familiar manner in which the poacher placed a chair close to the table near to which the astonished Frenchman was seated, he felt an uncomfortable sensation steal over him.

"We shall be free from interruption?" Luke Jessop began, interrogatively; "also from being overheard?"

M. Jean did not answer for a few seconds —he was too much astounded at the strange behaviour of his visitor.

"No one will come here," he said at last. "What do you ask this for? I do not know you."

The poacher smiled grimly.

"We shall be well acquainted soon," he said. "As a beginning to our friendship, I wish you to answer me a few questions."

M. Jean felt afraid of the speaker; there was a peculiar expression in the dark eyes that were bent so searchingly upon him which caused this fear to increase.

"Questions?" he repeated. "I will tell you when I know the object of your visit."

"You will know that soon enough!"

Again the grim strange mirthless smile wreathed the poacher's lips.

"In the first place," he said, "did you ever bear a different name to the one by which you are known here?"

M. Jean's face whitened, and he clutched the arms of the chair in which he sat, in a nervous spasmodic manner.

"My question," the poacher said, watching the Frenchman's countenance, "is answered by that start of surprise and your white face."

M. Jean set his teeth hard,—these words had dispelled the bright imagery in which he had but a few minutes before been so fondly indulging.

That he had never beheld Luke Jessop before he felt assured, and unless he were a police officer sent to hunt him down, M. Jean felt that he had no object in asking this question.

Whatever might be his visitor's motives, Jean determined to keep the required information to himself; and, at once acting on the defensive, he answered,—

"My name is Jean Gailland."

Luke Jessop's dark eyes were fixed with a keen searching look upon the French master's face, as he quietly said,—

"It is a lie; you had another name in France."

M. Jean sprang from his chair, and his bloodless lips moved, as though he were striving to give utterance to a denial of this unwelcome truth.

The poacher followed his movements as he took a brown leather pocket-book from his coat.

"Be seated," he said, calmly; "we shall understand each other soon, Jacques Cherdon."

The Frenchman repeated the name in a low whisper, and thick drops of cold perspiration oozed slowly from his forehead.

He reseated himself, and sat silent, awed and horror-stricken, opposite that dark grim-featured man.

Here, then, was an end to his roseate hopes. The secret he had thought only in the keeping of Greymore was known to another—that a perfect stranger.

Deceit he saw would be useless; and with a sinking heart, and a strange wild expression in his eyes, he watched his visitor take from the pocket-book several small sheets of closely-written paper.

Luke's next question caused him to feel as though a red-hot iron had been passed through his brain.

"What," the poacher asked, "did you do with your share of the spoil taken from the Doctor's strong-room?"

M. Jean fully believed he was in the presence of a fiend, whose wicked power enabled him to master the second secret, only known to him and the dead.

He could not answer. His tongue, hot and dry, refused to articulate a word.

"You heard my question?"

The poacher's words caused M. Jean to regain his power of speech, and from his quivering lips came this answer,—

"I had none of the spoil."

"Your friend," Luke said, referring to a piece of paper he held open in his hand, "has belied you, then."

"My friend!" gasped M. Jean.

"Aye, your friend—Edgar Greymore, *alias* the Chevalier Bois-de-Louy, Count Orfild, and a dozen other names. Knew you this gentleman?"

M. Jean saw the galleys from which he had escaped looming before him, and with a despairing cry he cast himself before his terrible visitor.

"Mercy!" he cried, "Mercy! Kill me, but do not take me back to that accursed place!"

"What do you take me for?" Luke asked.

M. Jean's pale face was upturned at this interrogation, and grovelling yet lower before the supposed officer, he gasped,—

"A police agent."

"Rise, man," said the poacher; "you are mistaken."

M. Jean staggered to his feet, and asked,—

"What are you, that know so well my secrets?"

"Your friend or your foe. It rests with yourself which of these I become."

M. Jean was bewildered by this answer; but as the horrible picture of the galleys faded away, his courage began to return.

"Come," Luke said, "seat yourself near me, and you shall know the purport of my visit."

M. Jean obeyed.

"Have you seen this book before?" Luke asked, holding the pocket-book towards M. Jean. "Look well at it before you answer."

The French master was about to take it, but as he extended his hand he caught sight of a dark stain upon the cover.

"It's—it's——"

"Blood," said Luke, with savage bitterness; "stained with the life stream of your companion at the galleys and your accomplice in the last robbery he committed."

M. Jean clasped his hands, and every limb trembled as though he had been suddenly stricken with the palsy.

"You know the book now," the poacher went on. "It was his—it is now mine. How it became so is known only to myself. You see these papers?"

M. Gailland silently assented.

"Some of them," Luke continued, "affect you, for the scoundrel has kept a diary of his evil deeds. Listen!"

The poacher read in a low tone, as follows:—

"September 14th.

"Fortune has sent me two friends—I must use them. So Philip has become a pedagogue's assistant! Well, I should have thought a sword would have been better in his hand than a pen. And under the same roof I find Jacques Cherdon, ex-galley slave, metamorphosed into Jean Gailland, French master at a large school!"

"Here is the next entry that affects you," Luke said, taking a second paper from the same pile. "Shall I read it?"

M. Jean made no reply.

"You can guess its purport," the poacher said. "It relates to the robbery which took place here, and for which an innocent boy has been transported."

The Frenchman covered his face with his hands, but no sound came from his tightly compressed lips.

"Here is an addition to this entry," resumed Luke. "Your late friend, had not death put an end to his villany, would have set the bloodhounds of the law upon you, had you not become his accomplice."

M. Jean looked up.

"I know it," he said: "he compelled me to assist in the robbery."

"And you reaped no benefit?"

"Not a sous."

"It's like him," muttered Luke, "from first to last. All who came in contact with him were made his dupes."

A discoloured slip of paper the poacher next selected, and holding it between his finger and thumb, he said,—

"Had you a foe, Monsieur Gailland, and that foe possessed these small pieces of paper, he could if he wished soon place you in the hands of the law. More than this, he could, with but little difficulty, *charge you* with being Greymore's assassin—there is sufficient in these papers to establish a motive for the deed."

M. Jean had risen to his feet, and while the poacher's sonorous tones uttered these dreadful words, he clasped the back of his chair with both hands to support his shaking limbs.

"Thus, you see," Luke went on, "how valuable these papers are to you; and if you will do me a service I will place them in your hands."

"I will do anything," gasped M. Jean, "anything you wish."

The poacher, with blazing eyes, glanced at the discoloured slip of paper he held.

"It is well," he said. "We can do each other a service. How many years is it since your acquaintance with Greymore began?"

M. Jean reflected for a few minutes, then answered,—

"Between six and seven."

The fierce light in Luke's eyes blazed fiercer as he said,—

"You knew him, then, at the time this entry was made in his diary?"

M. Jean looked inquiringly at the paper.

"The entry," Luke said—and his massive chest rose and fell as he spoke—"relates to a mock marriage with a young English girl whom he lured from a boarding-school at St. Omer."

"I have heard him speak of it," said M. Jean, "but never saw the young lady."

Luke spoke as though under the influence of some powerful emotion as he said,—

"It matters not. If you will supply the missing name in this paper, you shall have the documents which refer to your connection with Greymore."

He handed Jean the leaf taken from the pocket-book, and, after some trouble, he was able to decipher these strange words:—

"My little captive, still like a caged bird that wants its liberty, and, in spite of my sophistry, she adheres to her resolution. * * * * * Capitally managed! Pierre —— [the surname was blotted out] made a capital priest. We are married now she believes!"

M. Jean returned the paper, and to his surprise Luke Jessop's hand trembled as his fingers came in contact with the strange entry.

"That is the price of the evidence against you," Luke said. "Supply the missing name —you can do it. You must know some of the dead villain's old associates; set about the task at once—the sooner it is done, the sooner you will obtain the papers. I shall visit you every third day, and if within a reasonable time you cannot show me some proof of your having fulfilled your promise, this pocket-book and its contents shall be in the hands of the police."

He gathered the papers up from the table as he spoke, then, unlocking the door, strode from the room.

M. Jean pondered for some time over the poacher's parting words, and little by little the recollection of a story he had heard from Greymore came to his brain.

It was of a fair young girl whom he had deceived with a mock marriage, and when she discovered the manner in which she had been wronged, she ended her life in the dark waters of the Seine.

He remembered also Greymore telling him, when they were chained wrist to wrist at the galleys, that the girl's father had expended a fortune in trying to discover the murderer of his child.

He could see the dark handsome face of his fellow-prisoner as he laughed at the vengeful man returning to England, broken-spirited and beggared in purse, after the long and fruitless search for the subtle villain; and the longer M. Jean pondered over these things, the stronger became the wish to fathom the connection between Luke Jessop and Greymore's beautiful childlike victim.

CHAPTER XXX.

IN WHICH M. JEAN PLAYS AT FOOTBALL.

THAT inexorable old gentleman with the scythe and hour-glass went on his way, indifferent to the joys or sorrows of the world.

He had added a few months to the mystic record he kept, and the seasons, following his example, had shorn the trees of their foliage, and left them but cold dreary looking objects.

Bathing, angling, and cricket had become things of the past with our friends at Bircham. Sometimes, when a group were roasting their shins at the big fire, a few reminiscences of the cricket-field could be heard, such as,—"Billy Wharton was no end of good at 'stumping' a fellow," and Tom So-and-so "was the one;" he would be a stunner at bowling next year— he "bowls with his head."

Beyond this the national institution was but little noticed, for the time was close upon them for football.

Many learned discussions took place about the great game, and many regrets were uttered at the loss they had sustained when Gleddell left the school.

I don't know whether it is the same now, but in my schooldays we were wont to talk of those who had left as though they were heroes, and we should "never see their like again."

"Ah," was the general cry, " if we had poor Gleddell here now for our captain, we should not care much for the other side."

Then the (to the uninitiated) mystic words, "drop kicks," "touch down," "squashes," "run in," and "shinning," would be freely mingled in the conversation.

Beyond this there was but little change in the school or those connected with it. Philip Randall's madness had not passed away, but he had been taken from the school and placed in an asylum until he should be in a fit condition to appear before a tribunal of justice to answer the crime with which he was charged.

He was as quiet and as gentle as a child under this affliction, and the head of the madhouse, a gentleman well skilled in these matters, had every hope that his patient would regain his shattered senses; he would do his best, in order that the law should not be deprived of a victim.

M. Jean had much changed since the murder, and, strange to say, he was much better liked by the Bircham boys: there was a cause for this sudden change in their sentiments, and they were not slow in perceiving it.

The Frenchman's mind being filled with the task Luke Jessop had enjoined upon him, he had discontinued those petty annoyances towards the scholars which had produced the warfare against him—a strife in which he was invariably vanquished.

His foes—for British boys, whatever may be their faults, are, as a rule, good-hearted—seeing how haggard and careworn he had become, ceased hostilities, and allowed him to go his ways in peace; and M. Jean, grateful for this condescension, mixed a little more among them, and affected to take an interest in their (to him) incomprehensible games.

Truth to tell, it was not from the love he felt towards them that he did this; but in the fearful state of anxiety which he laboured under anything was preferable to the solitude of his room.

His existence now had but one aim—that to obtain possession of the papers in Luke Jessop's possession. To do that was no easy task. His relations with his native soil were not sufficiently friendly for him to feel the slightest wish for a closer intimacy than already existed.

Yet how was he to escape Luke Jessop's implied threat?

"THERE IS SUFFICIENT IN THESE PAPERS TO CONVICT YOU OF GREYMORE'S MURDER!"

These words, uttered by the poacher, were always before M. Jean's eyes.

"Supply the missing name of the man who officiated as priest at the mock ceremony, and the papers are yours—fail to do so, and you will rue the consequences."

Thus spoke Luke a few days before he left the hut in the old chase. He had gone none knew whither, and M. Jean's soul sickened when he thought of his return.

Little wonder he grew pale and haggard—little wonder his eyes became sunken and he dreaded the solitude of his room!

Unhappy man!—sleeping or waking, he was haunted by the fear of the poacher's return, should his task be unfulfilled.

Oft, as he lay in his bed, he would groan aloud with agony at the utter hopelessness of ever complying with the poacher's wish.

He could see no means of escaping the threatened doom. To whom could he apply for information? All he had known in France he felt assured would hold no communication with an escaped convict. If they did there could be but one result—it would reach the authorities, and he would be dragged back to the galleys.

Yet if he did not make the attempt to discover Pierre's surname and his whereabouts, the poacher would place the account of his participation in the robbery in the hands of the police, or worse, he would be charged with Greymore's assassination.

How bitterly he cursed the hour which had brought him into contact with the subtle tempter who now lay beneath a newly-raised mound in the quiet little churchyard.

Regret was now unavailing. He had but one alternative—either to risk a return to the galleys, or fall into the power of the English police.

He knew his fate should the latter come to pass, but with the former there was yet a chance that the friend he thought of applying to might not betray him.

So, after many sleepless nights and anxious days, he resolved to pursue the latter course.

He wrote to an old acquaintance in France, and when the letter dropped from his fingers into the post-office box he felt like a man who had placed his neck in a noose and did not know the moment it would tighten and choke out his life.

Returning from the post-office, M. Jean passed through the playground. It was the first day of the football's appearance in the enclosure, and the Frenchman's ears were almost stunned by the mighty shout the boys gave as the ball received the first kick off.

M. Jean watched it sail upward, followed by a shouting eager crowd, ready to meet it before it could touch the ground again.

It would be out of place here for the writer to give a detailed account of the manner in which this noble old English game should be played, for this reason—that no two clubs or schools play alike. Why there should not be an universal code of rules for football, the same as cricket, I cannot imagine: but while Eton sticks to her wall, Winchester her canvas, and Rugby runs with the ball, and persists in "hacking," I fear each school or club will adhere to their own rules, right or wrong.

The Birchamites troubled themselves but little about the doings of the great public schools in the matter of football.

They divided in two parties; Biggs was captain of one, Jack Stanfield of the other; a couple of goals were formed of upright poles, and standing about eighty yards apart.

The competitors being assembled, the first kick off was given by our lively friend Joe Stikkers; then Jack, leading on his side, tried to drive the ball through their adversaries' goal.

There was one rule among the Birchamites which was as unalterable as the laws of the Medes and Persians. This was, that any player touching the ball with his hands was declared "off-side," and, as a matter of course, not allowed to take part in the game for some time.

Shinning was not allowed—at least not wilfully, although in the excitement consequent upon a well-contested game there were sure to be a few shins barked—but on the whole they played as well as many of our large public schools play this fine old English manly game.

No general ever handled an army with better judgment than Jack Stanfield handled his fifty boys.

His eye was everywhere; and when their goal was once or twice menaced, he knew the best and pluckiest to call upon to repel the enemy's movements.

"Back, back, there, you young'uns! let the Mallet get at it."

Away rushed the youth named; but, alas! dazed by the honour which had fallen upon him in being the forlorn hope of his party, he kicks wild, misses the ball, and for a few seconds labours under the disagreeable idea that his leg has broken short off at the hip and gone skyward.

There is a rush and a shout by the Biggs faction—the goal is theirs!

"Charge it home!" roared Biggs; "hurrah!"

But the shout of triumph came too soon. Stikkers had seen the Mallet's right leg fixed as it were in mid-air, and with a determination to save the goal or get shinned in the attempt, he rushed forward just as Biggs had made ready for a kick.

Stikkers saw there was not a moment to lose—he aims a terrific kick—the opposing sides close round the combatants just as their feet come in contact, and the ball, struck a little on one side by Joe, is hoisted upward by Tom Dickson.

Then begins anew the rush and the struggle by Jack's party to get the ball in their adversaries' goal; meanwhile, Biggs and Joe Stikkers are limping towards their respective quarters, their right legs feeling very much as though the flesh was being perforated with red-hot needles.

"Follow it up!" shouts Jack; "bravo, Mallet!—down with Happy—that's it—up she goes!"

Without a thought for the defence of their goal, Biggs's party rush forward to stop the onward rush of the foes, and for a short time a fierce and determined struggle takes place midway between the goals.

M. Jean, in spite of the wretched state his mind was in, could not help being interested in the game.

Little by little he neared the players, and growing excited with the struggle, he began to long for an opportunity to join in the play.

His wish was soon gratified, but I am sorry to say it was dearly purchased, and, as in the memorable game at cricket, M. Jean came to grief.

He was standing a few yards in front of Biggs's goal when the short struggle took place in the centre, a struggle which ended in Jack Stanfield's party driving the ball close to the opposite side's goal, which goal, in consequence of the keepers running out to help their side, was undefended.

Straight as an arrow the ball rolled towards the centre of the goal, and owing to the rush which had just taken place, not one of the players could get near enough to kick it back.

On it came—another yard and the boundary would be passed, and Stanfield's side would be the victors. M. Jean mechanically moved out to meet the ball, and Biggs leaping up at the moment called out frantically,—

"Kick it back, Frenchy—kick it back."

At the same time the opposite party yelled, "No, no; let it alone—let it alone."

Before M. Jean could determine which of these cries to obey he was surrounded by the opposing players—one party trying to kick the ball away from the goal, the other to follow up the advantage they had gained and drive the ball home.

The rush and struggle were terrific—the best players on both sides fought hard; twenty kicks were delivered simultaneously, and the ball was hustled about the dense crowd, preventing it from rising.

Poor M. Jean! Two-thirds of those vigorous kicks took effect upon his shins. He was no player, consequently he got in the way of both parties, and more than once had the ball bounced about his ankles.

In vain he howled with agony—no one heard him—if they did the excitement of the game caused his cries to pass unnoticed.

It was not until Happy-go-lucky had charged the ball home, and his side had yelled their delight at the victory, that the bruised Frenchman was able to hobble away from the playground, mentally cursing the English and their games.

When he reached his room and sat ruefully bathing his battered shins, he thus expressed his opinion upon the pastimes of the English.

"They call it 'crickets,' these English, when they stand before some sticks and let another throw a hard ball at them; and footballs when it is nothing but knocking the skin all off the bones of their legs—it is brute games the English have—there!"

M. Jean is not the only foreigner who could not understand our manly but somewhat rough pastimes.

CHAPTER XXXI.
THE NEW USHER.

"I can't make him out, Jack," Happy said, "can you?"

"No," was the answer; "he's a queer-looking card for an usher—did you twig his coat?"

"I should say I did—it's got tails almost to his heels."

They were speaking about the usher who had taken poor Philip's place, and they were not far wrong when they called him a "queer card."

Mr. Jacob Snivel—not a very awe-inspiring name by the way—was a man whose age averaged anything between forty and sixty—his gaunt shrunken form, and the habit he had contracted of stooping as he walked, together with his thin grey locks which hung over his temples, gave him the appearance of having reached the latter age.

When close to Mr. Jacob Snivel it was apparent that he was in reality many years younger than he seemed.

His piercing grey eyes, cold and expressionless at times, but when aroused they shone with such an evil light that the small boys within their influence wished themselves far away. The hard lines of his somewhat receding mouth, and his deep voice, went far towards counterbalancing his grey locks and his habitual stoop.

As though not content with the strange appearance nature had given him, Mr. J. Snivel's garments were of the most ludicrous cut.

A rusty black dress coat—one of those abominable pieces of ugliness with tight sleeves, short waist, and long tails, a vest of the same material and colour, cut high in the neck; following a downward line, from this came black knee breeches, and silk stockings when at home. When Mr. Snivel trusted his precious self outside the school-house, his shrunken calves were covered with a pair of black cloth gaiters, a white necktie of somewhat clerical form, and a high pointed shirt collar completed the new usher's external appearance; and little wonder that the Birchamites felt but little awe of this strange figure.

Internally Mr. Jacob Snivel was gifted with some of the worst of human failings—he was vindictive, ill-tempered, and cruel, and, as the boys soon found out to their cost, he was a spy and a sneak.

Bircham did not benefit much by Philip's loss and the advent of this peculiar individual.

But when warfare was declared between the new usher and the boys, they were not slow in finding a mode of retaliating upon him all that he caused them to suffer at the Doctor's hands; to use Happy's expression, "They made it hot for him;" but of this anon.

Respecting Mr. Jacob Snivel's antecedents but little was known when he came to Bircham.

There was a rumour that he had been a master at one of the large public schools, but said rumour was not certain which of those places had been honoured by Mr. J. Snivel's services.

It was during this state of uncertainty respecting the new usher, and when speculation was rifest, Jack Stanfield and Happy gave utterance to the sage words with which we opened this chapter.

"It's my opinion, Jack," Tom Dickson said, "that we shall alter the shape of Mr. Snivel's coat before he's been long here."

"I think so; but what a name! Now is there any school in England that could pay respect to such a guy as that? And with such a name too—Snivel! Well, of all the——"

"H-s-h!" whispered Happy; "here he comes."

With a slow measured pace, and his eyes cast upon the ground, the subject of this conversation came towards them.

He raised his head when within a few paces of the fire, and, in a cold rasping voice, said,—

"It's past five, young gentlemen; you know it's against the rules of the school to be in the hall."

The boys looked up. This was the first time since they had dwelt in the old place that any notice had been taken of the upper form boys remaining in the hall to get ready for the morning's lessons.

In fact, although it formed one of the printed rules, it was generally supposed that the Doctor rather liked the biggest boys to be there, and, acting under this belief, they were wont to chase the younger and more unruly boys out.

Happy closed the book he had open before him, and said,—

"I have been here, sir, three years, and this is the first time that any of the upper forms have been found fault with for being here."

Mr. Jacob Snivel fixed his cold gaze upon the boys, and sternly answered,—

"Doctor Bircham has placed the upper forms under my charge—you belong to that portion of the school, and from you both, as being two of the eldest, I shall look for support; therefore, let us understand each other. I will not allow any rule—no matter whether custom has rendered it obsolete—to be broken; therefore let me request you to leave the hall at once."

"But," Jack began, "we will speak to the Doc——"

Mr. Jacob Snivel raised his hand deprecatingly as he said,—

"That will do. The Doctor is perfectly aware of the state of misrule which exists among the upper forms and by his orders I am to restore a state of discipline—in mercy to control thoughtless and rebellious youths."

Saying this, Mr. Jacob Snivel marched from the hall, softly rubbing his great red hands.

"Tyrant!" muttered Jack between his set teeth.

Happy watched the gaunt form until it passed from view, then, turning to his companion, said,—

"That's a beginning, Jack!"

Stanfield's proud passionate nature could ill brook the rebuke he had received from the new usher; so, hurling his book to the further end of the hall, he exclaimed, angrily,—

"Yes, a beginning, Tom, that will soon end, as far as I am concerned."

Happy looked interrogatively towards the flushed and excited speaker.

"You don't understand me, Tom?"

"Hardly."

"It's this, old fellow; I would sooner leave the school to-morrow than stay and endure that fellow's insolent tyranny."

"Look here," said Happy, less angered and of a cooler temperament than his friend. "I don't see the necessity for scamping the last three months of our stay here. Remember, Jack, we are about the oldest in the school, and possibly by remaining we can be of service to the poor little devils who have many a long year before them."

"Perhaps we can, Tom. But after the kindly-hearted fellow who has so long been our preceptor and friend, it will be a bitter dose to swallow this Snivel's coarse tyranny."

"Poor Philip!" Happy said, with a sigh; "he was indeed our preceptor and friend! Have you heard anything from the keeper we bribed to bring us news from the asylum?"

"Nothing since last week; then Philip's mind was in the same state. I hope he may never recover."

"So do I, unless there's a clue discovered that will throw a light upon Greymore's mysterious death."

"Do you know, Tom," Jack said, "it has often struck me as being somewhat singular that Gleddell and Philip should have been so suddenly plunged into such an abyss of seeming guilt."

"How, singular?"

"That I can scarcely explain," Jack said. "It seems as though a small inward voice continually tells me that both are innocent."

"What a strange feeling!"

"It is; and every day the conviction becomes stronger that we shall hear more of these strange things."

"I don't believe," Happy said, "that Gled knew anything of the robbery, in spite of the dark chain of circumstantial evidence which convicted him."

"About Philip, Tom? What think you of the case as it stands?"

"I should not like to give an opinion," the youth said, "before a stranger, but as you ask me, I will answer. Now, in this case there is a motive for the deed. Greymore and Philip quarrelled and fought some hours before the

THE BOYS OF BIRCHAM SCHOOL.

GEDDELL SAVED.

murder, and had it not been for the French master running in, there would have been murder done then."

"I suppose," said Jack, "your hypothesis is somewhat similar to that formed by the coroner at the inquest?"

"Precisely. He sought for a motive—here it is. They met, and, carried away by anger, fought again. Then, you see, the pistol which was found near the body was evidently the weapon which did the business, and every one who had been inside Philip's room knew it well."

"Yes," Stanfield assented, "the pistol, the quarrel, and the Frenchman's evidence will no doubt hang poor Philip, should he ever recover his reason. Still, I'm positive that he is perfectly innocent."

"We will not argue the point, Jack," said Happy; "but about poor Gled? I wonder if he has reached the colonies yet?"

"Yes, some time since; but why do you

ask?"

Tom Dickson placed his hand upon his friend's shoulder.

"You have often told me, Jack," he said, "that wherever I go after we leave school you would be my companion."

Jack Stanfield looked rather puzzled as he answered,—

"Yes, I have said so."

"Are you of the same mind still?"

"Yes; but what the deuce are you driving at?"

"This, old fellow: what do you say to going to Australia, eh?"

"Australia?"

"Yes; the backwoods or the diggings. It will be better, manlier, and nobler than being shut up all day in a dingy office, scribbling for a miserable pittance which will not more than suffice to keep us in seedy clothes. Think it over, old boy."

"I can give you the final answer now, Tom. Ranging over those primeval forests with a gun over my shoulder will be more to my taste than ekeing out a miserable existence as a clerk."

"Then you'll go?"

"Here's my hand, Tom."

They shook hands, and the compact was made; then, arm linked in arm, they left the hall.

"I've been told," Jack Stanfield said, as they went slowly down the long corridor, "that it is possible for the settlers in Australia to hire the best behaved convicts for servants."

Happy-go-lucky's eyes sparkled brightly as he said,—

"If so, Jack, we will hire poor Gleddell, and release him from his slavery."

"Yes, Tom; that's the chief reason for the voyage to the colonies, and——"

"Hi! Jack Stanfield and Tom Dickson, you are wanted."

The friends looked round and beheld Joe Stikkers sliding down the bannisters.

"This way," Joe continued, "here's Tom Radford from Oxford called to see you—here he comes."

CHAPTER XXXII.

THE BEGINNING OF THE STRIFE.

COULD that broad-shouldered be-whiskered fellow be the same Tom Radford that went away from Bircham little more than two years since?

Yes; none other but Tom Radford could laugh in that genial hearty manner; and the old corridor rang with his voice as he beheld his old schoolmates hastening towards him.

The hearty hand-shaking over, the Oxford man took a good look at his old friends.

"By George, you're both grown," he said at last; then, with a great laugh, added, "I shouldn't like to make you fag for me now. Do you remember the battles we used to have over the fagging?"

They all laughed, and Happy said,—

"Come up to my den, Tom; let's talk over old times. Well, you have improved—fancy, whiskers too!"

And Happy felt his cheeks, where the incipient down was struggling to make itself seen.

"Whiskers!" Tom Radford said, "Oxford's the place to make them grow. But, I say, I scarcely thought I should find you beggars here. It's nearly time you left, is it not?"

"The end of the half," said Happy; "then we leave."

"Coming to college?"

The friends gave a negative answer, much to Tom Radford's surprise.

"What's the matter with you fellows?" said Tom Radford. "You shake your heads and look as wise as a pair of owls."

"Well, it's this way, Tom," Happy said. "We have made up our minds to start on our own hook as soon as we leave here."

Tom Radford drew forth a short black meerschaum, and leisurely filling it from a rat-skin pouch, nodded for Happy to continue his explanatory answer.

"You remember Gleddell, don't you, Tom?"

He of the pipe emitted a cloud of smoke from between his lips ere he answered,—

"A fair-haired little chap—one of the lower fourth at the time I left?"

"The same."

"Yes; I remember him well."

"You have heard about his misfortune?"

"Eh?—no. We don't hear much of the old school at our place. Got any beer?"

Jack Stanfield had a bottle secreted in his cupboard, and when it was produced the university man, without any ceremony, appropriated it to his sole use, and during its consumption Happy related the particulars of Gleddell's apprehension, trial, and punishment.

"Poor little beggar!" Tom Radford said. "So you say he was innocent of the theft?"

"As you are, Tom."

Tom examined his pipe reflectively, and said,—

"It was a pity you had no proofs of his innocence. But what has Gleddell to do with your movements after you leave here?"

"Everything," answered Jack Stanfield. "He has not a friend on the earth except our two selves."

"But," Tom Radford began, "you cannot be of any service to him now."

Jack told him their plan respecting the colonies and their old schoolfellow. After a few moments' reflection, Tom said,—

"Well, independent of your desire to serve poor Gled, I do not know that you could do better than seek your fortune in that delightful land. Here the market is completely choked, and men of first-class abilities starve for the want of employment."

"Such is our idea," Jack said; "therefore going to college would be wasting precious time—months and years," he added, "that would do much towards fitting us for the somewhat wild life we shall have in the bush."

"True, lad," Tom Radford said, placing his short black pipe in its case; "you'll find a keen eye and a ready hand more useful than Greek or Latin."

They conversed for some time longer upon the same subject, Jack Stanfield and Happy painting ideal word pictures of a settler's life; Tom Radford quietly listening, and putting an occasional touch of colour upon the imaginative scene.

The topic was congenial to the boys'

thoughts, and it was near locking-up time before they changed the subject.

"By the way," Tom Radford asked, "you have not told me whether you like the man who has taken poor Philip's place. Is he a good sort?"

"We have seen but little of him yet," Jack answered, "and unless he improves upon further acquaintance, I'm afraid we shall have but a sorry time of it."

"Ah! is it like that? What's been the matter?"

Jack told him of the scene in the great hall.

"But that's nonsense," Tom Radford said, "Why, I've seen the Doctor pass through there, and he never said a word to any of the upper form boys being there; it was only those little beggars, who used to kick up such a jolly row that he forbad them there."

"So I told the new usher, but he soon put a stopper upon me."

"How, Jack?"

"He growled out something about the school being in a bad state of discipline, and having had orders from the head master to put us in order."

"H'm," said Tom Radford, "he'll have to be very careful how he goes about it, for there is nothing a fellow hates more than having a new master, especially if he tries to upset the old rules with his innovations."

"Exactly, and——"

A smart rap upon the door caused Happy to pause and ask,—

"Who's there?"

"Open the door, sir!" was the answer.

The boys looked at each other—it was the new usher's disagreeable voice; and being unused to these visits in Philip's time, they hesitated before complying with his request.

"Shade the light," suggested Tom Radford, "that's how we manage—or else say that we are reading."

"No!" Jack said, rising, "I'll let him in; this, I suppose, is the beginning of the strife."

Before he reached the door Mr. Jacob Snivel applied his knuckles vigorously to the panel.

Jack threw the door wide open, and the usher, as he strode into the room, darted a keen searching glance around, then came to an abrupt halt, and said sharply,—

"You have been smoking; pheugh! the place smells like a taproom—open the window, at once."

"It is snowing very heavily, sir," Happy said, "and if we open the window everything will soon be covered."

Mr. Jacob Snivel clenched his large red fingers as he turned savagely upon Tom Dickson.

"You have no right to have a candle burning at this hour," he said, "neither is smoking allowed in the school; it will be to your benefit to have only these offences to answer for to-morrow morning—do not add disobedience to them."

Jack Stanfield's face became crimson with anger, and, clenching his hands, he faced the usher.

"I do not understand you," he said—and the boy's lips twitched nervously as he spoke; "we have broken no rule of the house."

"A light burning after hours, and the room reeking with tobacco smoke—pray, what do you call this but rule-breaking?"

"In the first place," Jack said, "the upper form boys are allowed a light to read by; with respect to the smoking, an old friend thoughtlessly broke that rule."

Mr. Jacob Snivel lifted his eyes until his glance rested upon Tom Radford's face—the boys' friend—and he gave a start of surprise at beholding a stranger in the room.

"You will have to answer to the head master to-morrow morning," said Mr. Jacob Snivel, angrily; "now have the goodness to open the window, for I have many rooms to visit yet."

A silence followed this; neither of the youths made the least movement to carry out the usher's order.

Knitting his overhanging brows he looked Jack Stanfield in the face, and said,—

"Do you hear?—open that window."

In all probability, had not Mr. Snivel visited their room, the window would have been opened to carry off the smell of the tobacco; for neither Happy nor his friend had begun the use of the subtle weed; but as the case stood, the spirit of opposition came so strong upon them that they would have suffered any punishment rather than have given in.

"Do you hear my order?"

The words were repeated in a louder key, and the keen grey eyes began to blaze fiercely.

Still no response: the boys stood—hot, angry, and defiant.

Mr. Jacob Snivel looked from one to the other; then, in a slow menacing manner, said,—

"Be it so; you have begun by openly defying my authority—we shall see—we shall see!"

The last words were spoken as he passed through the open doorway, and Jack, whose hot blood was thoroughly aroused, struck the edge of the door forcibly and slammed it upon Mr. J. Snivel's retreating form.

The trio looked at each other for some time in silence, then Tom Radford said,—

"Jacob Snivel, by all that's good!"

"Do you know him?" they asked in a breath.

"Not personally," Tom answered, "but from the description I have heard——"

"Lock the door, Jack," said Happy. "We might as well be hung for a sheep as a lamb."

Jack complied with the request; then the three drew near the fire, and Happy asked,—

"What do you know of him, Tom?"

"No good," was the answer. "Fancy him being here! Well, I pity the poor little devils under his care!"

After giving utterance to this communicative remark, Tom again produced the short black pipe, and began to smoke in a reflective manner.

"I'll tell you what," he said, balancing the meerschaum between the thumb and forefinger of his right hand, "I will see the Doctor before I leave here in the morning, and make it all right about this affair."

"No, Tom," Jack Stanfield said, "we've begun the fight, and can carry it out without having any one to get us cried off."

"Jack's right," Happy said. "We're too big now for that sort of thing; besides the whole school looks up to us a little, and it will be better for us to know exactly what power the Doctor has placed in this tyrant's hands. We are sure to know that after first lesson to-morrow."

"But," objected Tom, "you may get expelled for to-night's work."

"No fear of that," Happy said; "we stand pretty well in the Doctor's favour."

"Well," the sage adviser said, "just as you like—perhaps, after all, you are right. I know I'd stand anything rather than have any one sneaking me out of a scrape."

"I thought you'd say so," said Happy. "Now let us know a little about this gentleman, old boy."

"Mind you," Tom said, "I cannot vouch for the truth of the statement, but from what I have seen to-night it tallies pretty well. I almost forget how it came up—I think a lot of us were talking about our old masters, when a fellow from a public school pitched us a queer story about one of the masters. He described this man's appearance to the very life, and set us in a roar of laughter when he said his sweet name was Jacob Snivel."

"Hush!" whispered Happy, "there's some one at the door!"

"Listening?"

"I think so."

Tom Radford slipped his boots off, and, taking the top joint of Happy's fishing-rod, crept softly towards the door.

The insertion of the thin bamboo cane in the keyhole was followed by a subdued oath; then the trio heard footsteps rapidly retreating from the door.

"Had his ear to the keyhole!" said Tom, with a grin. "That's the effulgent Jacob; he has a weakness for that sort of thing. However, he won't come here again to-night, for when I felt the point touch soft flesh I gave it a twist, and from the oath that followed he did not like it."

The boys laughed heartily at Tom's words, and rejoiced exceedingly at the successful use he had made of the top joint.

"We put gunpowder in the keyholes at times," Tom Radford said, as he seated himself, "so that we can tell who has been peeping."

"How," Jack asked, "can you tell?"

"Very easy—most of the sneaks are minus an eyebrow."

"Good idea," Happy said; "if Mr. Snivel is given to listening and peeping, he shall have a taste of it. But go on, Tom; let us hear about this amiable gentleman."

"Well, from what the fellow said," Tom answered, "Mr. Snivel's character may be summed up thus—he is a cold unfeeling tyrant, never happy except when peeping and prying about for the purpose of getting people into trouble—it is a passion with him; and the very reason he left the public school was caused by the number of boys who ran away. His tyranny and brutality were more than they could stand."

"A pleasant portrait—ditto prospect for us," Jack Stanfield said; "but from what I know of the fellows here they are not the sort to tamely put up with this sort of thing; they ain't used to it, Tom, and I'm afraid it will take a long time to get them to settle to the collar."

"I don't care a straw for my own part," Happy said, "but it's the poor little beggars that would come the worst off in a matter of this kind."

"Big and little," said Tom, "are all the same to him, for he's as cunning as a serpent, and seems to have a faculty for escaping all the snares set to punish him."

"We can but try," Jack answered; "he has begun the war, and it's hard if we can't hold our ground."

The trio soon after separated, Happy and his friend Jack not without some qualms respecting the upshot of this first skirmish with Mr. Jacob Snivel.

CHAPTER XXXIII.

THE POACHER'S HUT.

STERN and sombre as the poacher appeared to the outer world, he was gentleness itself to the pale but still handsome woman who shared his bitter poverty and the ignorant revilings of the unlettered villagers.

There was that in Miriam Jessop's speech and manners which betokened a time when she was other than a poacher's wife and mistress of the half-ruined hut in the old close.

The disposal of the few articles of furniture, the scrupulous cleanliness of the lowly dwelling, and here and there small bouquets of simple wild flowers placed in cracked earthen vessels, gave a neatness to the poacher's home, and showed that there was one who yet clung to him and lightened the stern man's heart of much of its dark saddening memories.

She was his wife in every sense of the word. Suffering, penury, and the world's frown had not changed the heart that had been given to his keeping when, in the long years gone by, they stood before the altar and became one.

And Luke, though their path had been rugged, and sorrow, like a black pall, had ever been their companion, still kept the one green spot in his heart. Thus his lover-like devotion to his wife.

They were seated at the little table, and between them was the pocket-book from which Luke had obtained such damning evidence against M. Jean Gailland.

Miriam's eyes were red with the tears that fell silently upon her pale cheeks; and Luke, the proud stern vengeful man, now sat with bowed head and fiercely burning eyes as he glanced from time to time at the small pile of papers which had opened afresh a depthless sorrow, which time had robbed of much of its bitterness.

They had sat thus for some time, and Miriam's fond furtive glances at her husband's face told that she wished to ask a question of him who had been so gentle to her; yet her speech failed, and the words died away under the strange spell that was upon her mind.

"I cannot," she thought, "endure this terrible anguish. I must, no matter what the result may be, ask him if there is——"

Her thoughts were broken in upon by her husband's voice, and so strangely had the horrible spell under which her mind laboured grown upon her, that she started, and her face went as white as though a spectre had risen before her.

The words he uttered were more in answer to his own thoughts than addressed to her who looked so strangely at his dark stern face.

"Yes," he said, in a tone barely audible; "I have waited and watched for his coming—hoped against hope—pictured him lying dead at my feet—my hand——"

Miriam gave a startled cry, and rising from her seat, stole softly to his side. He looked up as she placed one thin wasted hand upon his shoulder, and, looking steadily into his dark eyes, said,—

"Do not finish the picture, Luke. Oh, merciful Father! that it should have come to this!"

"Miriam—wife!" he said; "there is a strangeness in your manners that can but proceed from one cause. You suspect——"

"Your own words, Luke, have made that suspicion. Oh, husband! twenty-three years have our destinies been linked together, but never——"

Her voice failed her, and covering her face, she sobbed out the agony at her heart.

Luke's lips twitched nervously as he passed one arm around her waist; then, as she drew shudderingly away from him, he gave an angry cry, and sprung to his feet.

"Miriam!" he said, "is the contact of my hand so loathsome that you shrink from it? Is——"

"Luke! Luke!" she said, wailingly, "that hand is red—red with the life you have taken. Ask me nothing—do not touch me! I——"

He faced round abruptly, and, folding his arms across his massive chest, said, with a solemnity that carried the conviction of its truth with it,—

"Miriam, I am innocent of this crime—as innocent as that child who ended her blighted life in the dark waters of the Seine!"

She flew towards him, and throwing her arms around his neck, pillowed her head upon his chest and sobbed, joyfully,—

"Thank Heaven for this! Oh, Luke! since that night how I have suffered! Such suffering!—it seemed to sap my very life. It has been one horrible dream; and ever before my aching eyes I have beheld the scaffold, and your body hanging pendulous, stiff and cold! But it is passed now. Oh! Father of Heaven, I thank Thee!"

Her faith was strong in her husband's truth; mystical as Greymore's death was, she would not have asked him one question; he had told her he was innocent. It was enough; for lowly as he had fallen since their first troth had been plighted, Luke Jessop had never been known to lie.

"I suspected this, Miriam," he said, after pressing his lips to her forehead; "I deserved your suspicion, for I was guilty in thought, though not in deed"

"Luke!"

"Aye, wife; when I saw that devil's form coming from Captain Oakplank's house, I tracked him as a panther tracks its prey; there was murder in my very heart, and a knife in my hand. I thought of her wrongs, wife—thought that fate must have delivered him to my vengeance. And as I lurked behind a tree, ready to send his soul to perdition, he was joined by another man."

"The usher?"

"I know not—it was dark, and both face and form were hidden from my eyes; they met —angry words passed—there was a struggle— then came the dull thud of a heavy weapon as it fell upon his skull—then his fall—and his assailant with him——"

"Yet you did not interfere, Luke?"

"I could not; there was a strange fascination in the sight, which held me spell-bound, and before it passed away, Greymore's murderer broke from his victim's death-grasp and fled; but" he added, "not before I saw a mark upon him that will lurk in my memory as long as I live; a sign by which I shall know him again should we ever meet."

"That mark, Luke, may I know it?"

"Yes; as the figure left his dying victim, the moon's bright rays fell upon the ghastly scene, and I beheld the murderer examining his wrist—it was bleeding; and from an expression he used, as he wound a bandage around it, I 'learnt that Greymore's teeth had met, when in his dying agony he seized with his teeth his destroyer's hand. That mark, Miriam—*two semi-circular scars*—will never leave his flesh; and by that mark I shall know the man who saved my soul from a dark crime—a crime, none the less, although he merited death at my hands."

Miriam made no reply. Her brain was busy with thought as she resolved to gain access to the asylum in which Philip Rendall was confined.

Luke read her thoughts and said,—

"You had better let matters take their course, Miriam; they cannot punish him until his reason returns, and that I feel will never be."

"I will do as you wish, Luke; but for the sake of that gentle girl whose life has been blighted by her lover's misfortune. I should like to see him; she has been kind to me— to us, Luke; and could I but take to her the comforting assurance of his innocence, it would alleviate her sorrow."

"Poor Eleanor," said Luke, "perhaps you are right, wife; see him, and look for this mark, although its absence would not alter the chain of circumstantial evidence against him."

"You think not?"

"I am confident; for although I would gladly appear and state all I saw of the murder, I should not be believed."

He said this so bitterly that his wife's hitherto pale face crimsoned with shame and indignation—she felt the humiliation keenly.

"Besides," Luke continued, "I should place my own neck in the halter by stirring in this matter, though life has but little charms for me. I could not die until I have hunted down the dead villain's accomplice in the foul wrong that was done to our fair-haired child."

Miriam's eyes filled with tears when he spoke of that gentle girl—their daughter— Greymore's victim. She would, much as she had suffered, fain have dissuaded him from his determination of discovering the man who played the priest's part at Greymore's instigation; but in this she knew her pleading would but add to the vengeful feeling in Luke's heart.

"The pocket-book I took from the dying wretch," he resumed, "would be used against me. Thus you see, Miriam, how powerless I am to aid Mr. Rendall; that is, if I would aid him, I could not, the poacher, the outcast could."

"Stay, Luke," she said, "you speak as though it were known that you possess the murdered man's papers——"

"Even so, wife; have not the contents of the book been used by me as the means of compelling this Jacques Cherdon, or Jean Gailland as he is called at the school, to discover Greymore's ally."

"Yes, I am aware of this"

"Well, do you not perceive how gladly the Frenchman would seize the opportunity to escape the task I have given him."

"How, Luke?"

"Thus:—he would change places with me; the very fact of my appearance in a court of justice would give him the opportunity of demanding the papers which relate to himself, and if refused, he could threaten to denounce me."

"Why not give him those which concern his connection with Greymore?"

"Because!" Luke answered, "it would deprive me of the power, bearing the surname and whereabouts of this Pièrre——"

Luke stopped abruptly as a man's footsteps sounded outside the door.

"It is him," he said, "Jean Gailliand." The latch was raised, and M. Jean entered the hut; he bowed with a Frenchman's grace to Miriam, then, turning to Luke, said,—

"I have found out all you require."

"I guessed as much," said Luke; "your face, Monsieur Gailliand, told your success."

It did! the haunted expression had passed away, and in its place was the old, self-satisfied smile, or rather smirk; the latter being more suggestive of the habitual expression of M. Jean's face.

He seated himself in the rude chair Luke offered, then, as Miriam left the room, he took a letter from his pocket; it was written in French, and M. Jean, as he unfolded it, said,—

"I shall have to translate it for you, Mr. Jessop."

"There is no necessity for that," was the answer; "I am quite familiar with your language."

M. Jean opened his eyes, and handed Luke the letter.

CHAPTER XXXIV.

ISRAEL BEN LEVY, THE RECEIVER.

THE Frenchman watched Luke's face as the latter attentively read the letter; his scrutiny helped him but little, for beyond a nervous contraction of the brows, he seemed but little affected by the letter from St. Omar.

When he had finished its perusal, Luke folded the thin sheet of paper, then examining the post-marks, placed both letter and envelope in his pocket.

"You have done well, monsieur," he said, "here is your reward, and if I may give you advice, I would warn you respecting the connection you form in future."

M. Jean paid but little heed to the poacher's words, his eyes were greedily fixed upon the brown leather pocket-book from which Luke Jessop took the paper which placed our French friend in such a peculiar position.

He took the half sheets from Luke, and after glancing at their contents, tore them into fragments and cast the pieces upon the fire.

It seemed as though a heavy load was taken off his mind when the last piece of tinder arose from the surface of the ruddy fire, and, as M. Jean watched, it flew up the wide chimney, he arose and said,—

"Here our acquaintance ends, I presume, Monsieur Jessops?"

"Yes!" the poacher said, "and a more agreeable ending it has proved than I anticipated."

M. Jean smiled. "I wish you," he said, "a very good-night; remember me to madame; and should we ever meet again remember that Jaques Cherdon dissappeared with the burning of these papers."

"I shall not forget, Monsieur Gailliand. Good-night!"

To which the Frenchman responded, "Good-night!" and passed out of the hut.

This dialogue had taken place in French, and when the Frenchman had gone, Luke said in English,—

"Come, Miriam, I have news for you, and if all goes well, we shall soon be far away from this country."

Miriam came to her husband's side, and as a fierce light burned in his dark eyes, he said somewhat excitedly,—

"Fate has been kind to me, Miriam. I have learnt the name of Greymore's accomplice, and his whereabouts."

She came to his side, her face so sorrowful that Luke said,—

"You do not rejoice with me, Miriam, in this."

She looked sadly at him, and said,—

"Can I do so, Luke, much as my heart is embittered against this man, when I know that the knowledge will be danger to you."

Luke smiled grimly. "You are wrong," he said, "this man is now in a country where the law cannot interfere between man and man, there I will track him, then, hand to hand shall our quarrel be fought out."

Miriam made no answer to these strange words, so Luke, after a few minutes pause, resumed,—

"The letter this Frenchman has brought me will do much towards the identification of this Pierre Dublé; listen, wife, and much as you fear the result of my meeting with the wretch who helped to kill thy own child, you must feel that a higher power than man's has put me on his track."

He ceased, and opening the letter read to his wife its precious contents.

The writer in answer to M. Jean's enquiry for Greymore's companion said, that one Pièrre Dublé, a close friend of the handsome young Englishman, had left St. Omar a few weeks before the arrival of M. Jean's letter.

The writer also said that Pièrre Dublé, a man of mighty stature and immense strength, had gone to England to find his old companion, who had, during his time at the galleys, betrayed Pièrre to the authorities.

The colossus only escaped by killing those sent to arrest him; then hearing of Greymore's flight from the galleys, he left France resolved to crush out the life of his betrayer.

The writer, who was intimate with Pierre, had heard from him but a few days before the receipt of M. Jean's letter, and the giant had said in a hasty note that he was upon the point of embarking for Australia.

There was a postscript to the letter, which somewhat sarcastically said,—

"If you wish to see M. Pièrre Dublé you will find him in Australia. He is a man of immense strength, powerful build, and across his forehead there is the mark of a sabre-cut he received in the affray with the gendarmes."

"This description," Luke said, "will enable me to recognize Pièrre Dublé, and my hope is that we may meet in some unpeopled tract of that far-off country—then God defend the right."

Miriam heard him patiently, then asked how he could ever hope to reach the colonies.

"That," Luke said, "will be an easy matter. To-night, Miriam, we must go to London; there I shall procure more than sufficient to pay the passage out; then," he added, somewhat hopefully, "when my mission is accomplished, I may earn my bread honestly in that land of plenty."

The wan features beamed with gladness at these words, and in her heart she prayed that Pièrre Dublé and her husband would never meet, and hoped—ah, how fervently!—that Luke would carry out the concluding words of his speech.

* * * * *

Israel Ben Levy's shop to the uninitiated appeared nothing more than a receptacle for left-off clothes and old uniforms.

But old Israel could have enlightened and somewhat astonished those innocent gentlemen had he made known the fact that he cared not if he did not dispose of one garment in twelve months.

The ancient Hebrew had an addition to the "old clo'" business, which addition he carried on in the little dingy room behind the shop.

A pair of blue spectacles were balanced upon old Israel Ben Levy's nose, as he sat turning over the leaves of a ponderous ledger, and from the manner in which he occasionally chuckled to himself, it was evident the contents of the book pleased him vastly.

He came to one entry near the end, and placing his greasy forefinger upon it, gave utterance to his thoughts.

"Thish ish very strange," he muttered; "why it is more than a week and that good looking gentlemansh has not called—yet he tells me in his letter that he will come soon after I receive the parcel. I hopes he hash not been taken, he, he, he!—I do hopesh so, he, he, he!"

Rebecca, the old Jew's pretty dark-eyed daughter, put her head inside the room at this moment and said,—

"Father, a stranger wishes to see you."

The book was closed with affright, and old Israel, peeping over the top of his blue spectacles, said,—

"A stranger!—what stranger? Ish it—a —a—you know, girl?"

"I think not, father. No, he does not look at all like a policeman."

"That's good; perhaps he's a new customer. Show him in, Rebecca—show him in."

The girl withdrew, and ushered Luke Jessop into the room, and when she withdrew, the poacher, without giving Israel time to utter a word, said,—

"Is this your receipt?"

"Yesh, yesh; it was sent to a gentleman—one of my customers."

Luke's lips curled scornfully as he repeated,—

"Gentleman!—no doubt you have many such?"

"Yesh," said old Levy; "but what have you to do with that paper?"

Luke replied to his query by reading a list of silver articles which had been received by the Jew from the "gentlemansh," and when he had finished, he somewhat startled Israel by saying,—

"What have you done with these things?"

The receiver of stolen property made no reply, and Luke, who watched the wrinkled villain's face, was not far astray in the reason he assigned for Israel's silence.

"You can speak," he said, "I am not an officer—far from it. I am a friend of the gentleman from whom you received these things."

Israel Ben Levy gave a sigh of relief, and said,—

"Why did you not say this before? I did not know what you wanted. So you are a friend of that nice gentlemansh and very good customer of mine."

Luke inclined his head.

"And you wants to know about the goods?"

Another gesture of assent.

"You can tell your friend that the goods were very old—very old; so old that they make but little in the melting-pot."

Luke gave an impatient gesture.

"I do not wish for these details; I only require the price you intend to pay—let me have that and——"

"Yesh, yesh; but how am I to know that you haven't to receive it."

Luke held the list which Israel had signed towards the old rascal, and said,—

"By this."

Israel did not like the look which accompanied these words.

"Yesh; but, mine goot man, anybody might comes with——"

Luke uttered an angry exclamation, and striding fiercely towards Israel, said,—

"I have neither time nor inclination to listen to your shuffling excuses. Give me the value of these articles, or——"

"Mine goot friend, I swear to you—ah! I have just remembered it—the things are not gone to be melted yet."

"Are you speaking the truth?"

"I am, I swear by——"

"Sufficient. I believe you so far, but shall be better convinced if you will show me the articles."

Israel looked keenly at his visitor, and the small sunken eyes glistened for a moment, as a subtle thought crossed his mind.

"Yesh," he said, "I will show you."

Luke's face wore a pleased expression as he watched the old sinner unlock one of the iron bound chests which stood in the room.

"There," he said, "ish the goots. Now you believe me?"

"I do. Come, as you have been so far truthful, will you in the same spirit answer a question?"

"Yesh—what ish it?"

"This," Luke said: "what is the value of these articles in their present state?"

"Vell, to keep them as they are, they would be worth nearly von hundred pounds."

"Not more?"

"No; that is the full value."

"If they are melted, what difference will that make?"

"Mush—very mush. They von't be worth more than sixty pounds—pounds, mind, my goot friend."

"I understand," Luke said. "Lend me a pen—that will do—yes, a sheet of paper."

In a bold clear hand, Luke rapidly wrote out an agreement by which Israel Ben Levy advanced £50 upon certain articles, and in consideration of the loan the borrower agreed to pay £10 for the advance.

Luke also wrote out a duplicate of this agreement, and when this was finished he signed them, and requested the astonished Jew to place his name beneath.

Israel Ben Levy read the paper, then looked at his visitor as though doubtful of the latter's sanity; but the dark earnest face bore a determined expression which left but little to be imagined.

Luke saw that the Jew would not yield to this agreement without making an effort to alter it; so the poacher quietly closed the door, which had hitherto been partly open, then, pointing to the papers, said,—

"Sign them."

These words broke the spell which had fallen upon old Levy, and rising from his chair, his face distorted with passion, he cried,—

"What—what you take me for in this business? You robber—you——"

"Silence, old man, and listen to my words," said Luke, sternly. "The contents of that box are worth at least three hundred pounds. I require you to advance me the sum stated in that paper for one year. If at the expiration of that time I do not tender the paper which lies before you, the property will be yours. But understand me, Israel Ben Levy. Whoever brings you that paper with the money and the interest I have added is to receive the goods, as you term them. Now, having so far explained myself, I can only add, if you do not consent to these terms, I will bring the police here and denounce you as a receiver of stolen goods."

Vainly Israel tried to evade placing his signature to the paper. Luke was inexorable, and the Jew was compelled to yield and hand over the money.

"I shall keep the list of those articles," Luke said, "and this paper together. Meanwhile, Israel, you carefully retain the counterpart of our agreement, and unless the edges of the paper should match as these do—see, it is a sheet torn in two—do not surrender the property."

Luke left the old rascal writhing at the manner in which he had been overreached, and as he went to the place where Miriam awaited him, he mused,—

"Should all go well with me in this new land, I will send these papers and the money to redeem the articles to the good old Doctor."

An honest resolve, Luke Jessop. But will your dark destiny permit its accomplishment? Time alone can tell how far your hopes will be realized.

CHAPTER XXXV.

THE "FAIR ROSAMOND" ON HER PASSAGE OUT.

THE marine's shot cut away a piece of the shrouds above young Gleddell's head; it was a narrow escape—one inch lower, and the bullet must have shattered his skull.

He heard the shouts and hasty orders as the boats were lowered, but the tide, running strongly out, soon bore him out of earshot of the sound.

It was well for the panting fugitive that he had learnt in his early school-days to swim—learnt to regard the water almost as his native element; but for this, he must that night have sunk beneath the dark waters of the Thames.

When the lanterns were gleaming over the boat's sides, as the guard sought to recover his body, Gleddell quietly turned upon his back, and, without the least exertion, the tide carried him out beyond the mouth of the Thames.

It was a strange position for the boy, who had so narrowly escaped being shot down as he took that leap for life and liberty.

True he had escaped so far; but, as he floated slowly out to sea, the thought crossed his mind that he had but attained a short respite from the grim monarch's icy fingers; so as he looked despairingly at the leaden coloured sky, and the few pale stars which gleamed out at distant intervals, he mused,—

"Better had I died by that shot than have risen to the surface of the water! True I can sink, if I so will it; but while there's life there's hope, and feeling thus will cause me to struggle with the grisly tyrant."

He spread his arms out, and paddling the water with open palms, raised his head and looked around.

There was but little prospect of escaping a watery grave; behind was the closely packed mass of shipping, on either side the shores; and, turning to gaze in the direction in which the tide was taking him, the poor boy beheld the great ocean and its white-capped curling waves.

Poor Gleddell's thoughts went back to the happy time at Bircham School; he thought of his old companions, and in fancy heard their gladsome shouts as when they were wont to gather in the school-house playground.

From this his mind wandered to that fair girl who had in the gloomy prison walls told him that, no matter how the world frowned upon him, her heart would still be the same.

Gentle Minnie! So strong in her faith, she could not believe him guilty of the crime which had branded him with the felon's mark.

So as he felt his limbs being numbed and the hope of life slowly departing, the boy's mind was busy with scenes of the old and happy time.

He knew—and there was a world of hopeless anguish in the thought—that a few minutes would end his suspense and sufferings; and for the first time since he had left the absent ship, he began to despair of ever leaving the dark waste of waters into which he had plunged.

THE BOYS OF BIRCHAM SCHOOL.

OUR HERO'S INTRODUCTION TO BUSH LIFE.

When the first idea of escaping from the companionship of his fellow prisoners had entered his mind, the boy had dwelt upon the one point—that to escape from the ship.

Beyond this he had formed no definite idea; so as the conviction slowly came to his mind that he had but taken that leap to find a grave with the waters, he saw the folly of leaving the vessel until he had maturely planned his escape.

Yet he could not have escaped the dangers by which he was surrounded, unless he had had a boat awaiting the moment he should have risen to the surface.

He had no help now—no friendly hand to pluck him from death—nothing now but the black portals of the mystic future opened to his view: and as he felt the death faintness creeping upon him, numbing every sense, and mercifully depriving even death of much of its bitterness, he suffered his hands to fall, and prepared to sink to the unknown depths

No. 12.

of the dark waters.

So, as he felt himself going, he threw his arms upward, and cried out,—

"Lord, receive my soul!"

Could it be fancy? No! his hands in the descent came in contact with a hard substance, then, as his fingers felt a slimy substance recede from them, the tide brought his body against the lower part of the object his hands had vainly essayed to grasp.

The strange floating object the boy knew from its cone-like form, and as the renewed hope of life came strong upon him, he threw his arms around its narrowest part.

The buoy wheeled to and fro for a few seconds, but Gleddell drew himself safely above the water and coiled his legs round the floating sign-post which marked a dangerous shoal.

Gleddell's first thought was to return thanks to his Maker; then the full heart found a relief in the tears which welled up and trickled slowly down his pale cheeks.

He knew he was safe now while his strength lasted, and that he hoped would be until the morning light gladdened the waters.

Then a passing vessel surely would take him aboard—so during the long hours of the night he remained upon his strange resting-place: the only sounds that broke the monotony of his vigil were the rushing noise made by two vessels as they ghost-like swept past the lonely watcher.

He called out to them, but his voice was weak—so weak that those on the decks heard it not, although one phantom-like bark passed within a dozen yards of the buoy.

When the dark hour came which precedes the dawn, Gleddell, in spite of the strangeness of his situation, closed his eyes and slept, and so soundly that his past and present peril were forgotten, and in a sweet dream which came upon him he was once more at Bircham among his schoolfellows.

So strong was the vision that he passed through the duties of the school, and when evening came he found himself walking side by side with George Oakplank's lovely child. He thought they were crossing a rippling stream, and as he handed Minnie over the stepping-stones a dense blackness came over earth and sky, and the surrounding green fields became changed to one vast sheet of water.

He saw his sweet companion engulphed—heard her wild cry for help—and, with a start which nearly caused him to release his hold, he awoke, and found the hazy light of the new-born day stealing over the rippling waters.

Soon the sun lifted the mist, and Gleddell found he had been carried far beyond the confluence of the Thames and the salt ocean.

He was near the shore, and, faint from the exertions of the preceding night, he looked around for a means of deliverance from death.

His watching was rewarded ere an hour passed away; then to his joy he saw a large vessel coming towards him. She came across the waters like a thing of life, and the boy, in spite of his misery, could not help an exclamation of admiration as he watched the ship.

His cry was soon changed to one of terror, for as the large hull came down upon him he saw a glittering object in the bows.

It was the reflection of the sun upon a marine's bayonet, and as Gleddell saw the vessel closer he detected three similar discs of light among the cordage and lower spars.

He knew then that the vessel from which he had escaped was now close upon him, and his heart fell as he thought that the officers were perhaps at that moment looking through their powerful glasses at the buoy.

There was no time for reflection; so at once loosing his hold, he dropped into the water, determined to die rather than again fall into their power.

* * * *

The watermen at Sheerness had drawn their boats to the beach, and were either gone to their homes or spending the day's earnings at the low beershops which abound in that maritime town.

It was twilight, and they knew those who were wont to patronize their pleasure boats had left the beach.

The last of the rough-handed bronzed-faced men had scarcely left, when a boy's half-clad form was washed ashore, together with a plank, to which, even in his insensibility, he clung.

For an hour the inert form lay like one which had passed the portals of the ruthless leveller—the waves, as they broke upon the shingle, washing over the lower part of the bruised and drenched body.

Then suspended animation returned, and the waif thus thrown ashore arose and staggered towards the nearest hut.

It was Stanton Gleddell, who once more touched his native land, while the convict ship which was to have taken him to a living death passed on her way.

He was too weak, too ill, to crawl towards the waterside beerhouse, from which came the sounds of fiddles, the voices of the sailors, and the shrill laughter of women.

The inside of the boat was dry, and lying in the stern he saw a sail, left as it had been lowered by the careless owner of the boat, who had left it within a few feet of the water.

It was a haven of rest for the poor boy; and dragging his weary limbs over the side, he crept beneath the sail, with the hope that a few hours' rest would bring strength sufficient to enable him to go among his fellow creatures and beg a little food to keep him from suffering the hardest of deaths—that of starvation.

A groan escaped his lips as he drew the canvas over him; then, placing his head upon a coil of rope, his eyes closed, and soon a sweet oblivion came over his senses.

The waters rose as the night wore on. Lashed by the high wind, the surf rolled under the boat's keel, and little by little drew her to the very edge of the water.

Then a wave larger than the rest raised the bows, and when it receded the boat, with its senseless burden, was afloat.

How long he was buffeted about by the gale which followed Gleddell never knew, but he was awakened by the loud voices of men, and starting up in affright, he found himself within a few feet of the bows of a large vessel.

He saw the copper sheathing as the ship rose upon the billows; then came the crashing of wood, and, with that instinct of self-preservation which is inherent with us all, he clung to the object which had smashed his frail craft.

It was the gear of the vessel's striker, and as the bow dipped in the trough of the sea, Gleddell was struggling in the midst of the white shower of foam.

The next moment the vessel's forepart rose, and he found himself suspended over the turmoil of waters; and while he hung thus, his brain dizzy and his weakness so great that had the bow dipped again he must have loosened his grasp and been washed away, a voice above him—a gruff surly voice, but to Gleddell the words were softer than the sweetest music—said,—

"Hold on a minute, there—this comes of being out at sea in a cockle-shell like that." The speaker caught hold of Gleddell's collar, and as he hauled him on deck, asked, "Didn't you see our light, or was you trying to see old Davy Jones?"

When he reached the forecastle Gleddell had fainted, and a crowd of men soon gathered around, each doing his best to restore the boy's faculties.

"Take him down to the steerage," said a dark-featured man, who came towards the group; "the women will soon bring him round."

"Right, mate," said the sailor who had dragged Gleddell aboard, "they'll do the best for him ——"

The sailor paused and looked strangely at the man who had suggested the steerage as the best place for Gleddell to be taken.

The man's actions were singular enough to excite astonishment, for, after gazing for a few moments at Gleddell's face, he came forward, and, pushing back the seamen, took a knife from his pocket and cut the torn remnants of the convict suit from Gleddell's limbs, and threw them overboard.

His reply was as strange as his behaviour when the sailors began to interrogate him.

"I know the lad," he said, "and now know how he came here. Lend me a blanket, one of you, and I will place the lad under my wife's care."

The blanket was lent by one of the seamen, and the man lifted Gleddell as though he were an infant, and took him below.

Whatever comments were made by the crew respecting the passenger's strange conduct mattered little to the latter, who, being a man of powerful build and a determined will, was not likely to be pressed too closely for the motives which had actuated him in stripping the boy of the remnants of the accursed garb.

When Gleddell awoke he found a woman bending over him, and to his wondering gaze and eager questions, she placed her finger upon her lips to imply silence.

He could tell by the dull ripple of the water near his head that he was on board a vessel, and at last, in spite of the kindly admonition he had received, he asked,—

"Where am I?"

"On board the *Fair Rosamond*, outward bound to Australia," a deep voice answered; "let that suffice for the present—when you are better you shall know more."

Gleddell sank back upon the pile of blankets which had been hastily thrown together, and, closing his eyes, tried to remember where he had heard the voice which answered his question.

CHAPTER XXXVI.

JACK STANFIELD OBTAINS A VICTORY.

JACK STANFIELD'S words were prophetic when he said the strife had begun between the boys of Bircham and their new usher.

It did begin with a vengeance, and though the boys found out that Mr. Snivel was a good scholar and well qualified to teach them according to their different capacities, they also made the discovery that he was, in addition to the good qualities enumerated by Tom Radford in a former chapter, a very passionate and unfeeling man.

He was not many days in the school before he had levelled several boys to the ground with his great red fist, and more than one had lost a tooth by a heavy open-handed blow upon the side of the face.

Another and a favourite pastime was to hammer a poor boy's head with the hard edges of a book cover until the blood flowed.

The consequence of these acts was soon apparent; the big boys were seen in close conversations in the playground, and the small fry went about looking very gloomy, and rubbing the soft places upon their skulls, which yet felt tender from the effects of an application of the book.

Mr. Snivel was wont to observe, when delivering this mode of punishment,—

"If you cannot learn the contents of this book, and keep it in your head, you shall feel it outside."

He was as good as his word; they did feel it, and remembered it for weeks afterwards. Whether this mode of proceeding tended to sharpen the intellects of the dull lads I am not able to state, but this I know, from the biggest to the least, they most cordially hated Mr. Jacob Snivel.

There are limits to all human powers of endurance, and this limit was soon passed; and dark mutterings, followed by close and mysterious conferences, were the fashion of the Bircham boys under the new *regime*.

The mutterings were against Mr. Snivel; the conferences related to the various plans devised for the carrying out of the dark threats.

Happy-go-lucky and Jack, with their shadows the Mallet and Joe Stikkers, stood in the centre of one of these groups.

"Something must be done," Happy said; "here we are, and a week has gone by, and every day it gets worse instead of better."

"True," said Jack; "but what is the something we are to do?"

"I know what I should like," said Joe, "only I don't think we can do it."

"What's that, Joe?"

"Why," the hopeful answered, "I'd like to have a huge hogshead, and fix a lining of spikes inside, then put Snivel in it and roll him down Muswell Hill."

"A good project, Joe," Happy said, "but impracticable."

"Quite," said Jack. "Come, Mallet, have you nothing to bring forward?"

"Yes," said he of the long legs, "I have, but we must catch him asleep to do it."

"He's like a cat," Jack Stanfield said, "he sleeps with one eye open; but never mind that, let's have your idea, my cheerful Mallet."

To which the cheerful Mallet replied,—

"Well, I shall keep that to myself, until one of you brings me word he's asleep."

"What do you mean by that, you young wretch?"

"What?"

"Keeping it to yourself."

"Because it's the best plan, unless you want it known all over the school."

"I don't understand you," said Jack; "surely you don't think there's a sneak amongst us?"

"I do."

"Name—name!" a dozen voices called out.

"No," the Mallet answered, "I shan't give any name until I'm quite sure of catching the gentleman; until then, I advise you to be on your guard, for there's one who tells old Jacob all our plans; this you may know by the manner in which he's been able to escape the traps we've set for him."

"I believe you're right, Mallet," said Jack, his large eyes flashing brightly, "for every plan we have devised has failed at the very moment of fancied success—yes, there's a Judas in the camp."

"Well," Happy said, "all I can say is that if we catch the gentleman he won't sit down in a hurry."

The bell rang to summon them to the school-room, and during the lesson Jack Stanfield saw Biggs pass a slip of paper to Mr. Jacob Snivel.

"That's the traitor," the boy thought; "but how am I to prove it?"

He forgot all about the classics, trying to solve this problem; and the consequence was that when he went up to the desk the usher told him sternly to write out his task twenty times.

Jack winced at the punishment and was about to expostulate, when Mr. Snivel made a rush from his desk and seized an offender, from whose pocket a large rosy apple had rolled upon the floor.

Jack Stanfield blessed the culprit, for upon the desk and within reach of his fingers, he saw the slip of paper which Biggs, when he came to repeat his lesson, had given the usher.

So while Mr. Snivel was operating upon the offender's cranium, Jack seized the paper and walked quietly back to his seat.

That night there was a grand meeting in the sixth-form room, the result of a long deliberation being a sudden arming with slippers, straps, and, in some instances, joints of fishing-rods.

When all was ready Jack Stanfield gave the order to march, and twenty shoeless feet were pelting towards the room wherein reposed the traitor.

With the cunning of an Indian scout, Joe Stikkers went forward to reconnoitre, and opened the door for the main body.

His Effulgence the traitor Biggs was lying comfortably upon his back, snoring, in concert with about a dozen of his faction.

The invading army gave no signal of their approach until they came opposite the victim's bed.

Here they gave a loud shout. Before Biggs could spring from his bed and arm himself, he was turned over, face downwards, and . . . .

We draw a veil over the scene.

Many a day passed before the martyr could sit upon the hard forms without tears of agony.

Elate with the punishment they had inflicted upon their ancient foe, the executioners retired to the fastness of their dormitory—a stronghold which was soon after laid siege to by the Biggs faction.

But the defence was so stubborn, and the volleys from the pea-shooters so frequent and well-directed, that the foe retired, followed by a parting cannonade of the contents of the coal-box.

Bed was out of the question until the excitement of the late scenes had passed away; so the lively Joe Stikkers went forth upon an exploring expedition, and after five minutes' absence returned with the grateful news that Mr. Jacob Snivel was fast asleep, and, as good fortune willed it, his chamber door had been left open.

The Mallet shrieked with delight at the news, and much mystified his companions by fishing a slate pencil from the mystic depths of his pocket.

He added to their astonishment by fastening a penholder to the pencil, then, holding the latter between his forefinger and thumb, he held the slate over the flame of a couple of candles until it became white with heat.

His fellow conspirators danced round him with delight when he told them the pencil was intended for Mr. Jacob Snivel.

As noiselessly as the tiger steals upon its prey, the Mallet stole upon the common foe.

He had not been many minutes in the room when the old schoolhouse resounded with a succession of the most horrible yells.

The Mallet had placed the hot pencil along one side of the usher's nose, where it stuck until the skin rose in a white blister, and Jacob, like a wild Indian, rushed from his bed in pursuit of his active foe.

Mr. Jacob Snivel's gaunt form did not appear to advantage as he followed close upon the Mallet's heels.

Our long-legged friend was not to be caught easily, and although the usher had his long fingers close to his tormentor's hair, the Mallet, by jerking his head forward, escaped this terrible clutch.

From one end of the long passage to its outlet upon the boys' sleeping rooms the chase continued, and the Mallet, too wide awake to retreat into his own room, made a dash through the first door that stood open.

Ill luck willed that the Mallet's long legs carried him into the room wherein slept Happy-go-lucky and his inseparable friend, Jack Stanfield.

The first bed afforded the Mallet refuge, and as his body disappeared beneath the white hangings, Mr. Jacob Snivel sprang into the room.

Happy guessed the cause of the Mallet's flight, and making a dash at the wash-stand he seized the ewer, and as Jacob's long body stooped over the Mallet's hiding-place he emptied the contents of the jug down the nape of the usher's neck.

Jack Stanfield and the remainder of the fellows in the room were not slow in following the example of Happy; so as the usher grasped at the Mallet's ankles he was drenched with the cold stream.

Jack Stanfield, to appear as though he did not, in the dark, know that the usher was the unwelcome intruder, as he added a kick to the reception Mr. Snivel had met, said,—

"I know you, Biggs—take that."

Mr. Snivel, under this concentration of calamities, was compelled to release his hold of the Mallet's leg, and, white with passion, he jumped to his feet and with one blow of his hard fist levelled Happy to the floor.

The room was in darkness, therefore the blow was delivered at random; and as Happy fell, the usher, with a cry like a savage beast, dashed among the boys his flapper-like hands.

Up to this time Mr. Snivel had not spoken, so Happy, as he scrambled to his feet, shouted,—

"At him, boys!—it's Biggs—I know him by his great hands."

"Down with Biggs!" was the cry; and the youngsters, as usual in all cases of the midnight skirmishes, retreated to the furthest corner of the room.

Here they armed themselves with every portable missile, and commenced firing at the dim outlines of the gaunt shadowy form.

This was too much for Jacob, and as the shoes and pieces of coal came thickly around his head, he beat a retreat.

At the threshold of the door he turned and faced his assailants; then for the first time opened his mouth.

"You shall hear further of this," he said; "and you, John Stanfield and Thomas Dickson, as the leaders in this outrage, shall suffer for your mutinous conduct."

Hands that were uplifted to fire a parting salute remained stationary, and from more than one of those who had supposed Biggs was the assailant, came the words,—

"It's the usher!"

Jack waited until the heavy footfall died away; then, sitting upon the edge of his bed, he said,—

"Yes, the usher. Don't funk—Happy and I will bear the brunt of this. Light a candle, Tom."

When a light was procured, they found the casualties amounted to three very red faces, a lump on the back of Jack's head, and the skin taken off the Mallet's shins.

"Not so bad," Happy said, "considering the victory. Now, lads, to bed; here's the Doctor."

There was a rush and general scuffle; and before they had time to get up a respectable snore, the good old head master entered the room.

In one hand he bore a wax candle, and by its light surveyed the disordered state of the room.

There was more of pity than anger in the good old man's voice as he touched Jack Stanfield's and Happy's shoulders, and said,—

"I am sorry to see this, my boys, and you both so near the end of your time; but something must be done as an example, and as this is not the first time I have had complaints against you, I think it will be best for you both to quit the school at once."

The two boys sat up in bed, and resting their chins on their knees, Happy said,—

"Very well, sir, we will leave; but had Mr. Randall stayed with us, this would not have occurred."

"No," Jack chimed in, "never; but I'm afraid, Doctor, unless your new usher alters very much, there will be but little comfort in Bircham School."

"The new usher," the Doctor answered, "is a strict master, I'll admit; but in the end his control will be found beneficial to the minds of those who are entrusted to my charge."

"Perhaps so," said Jack Stanfield; "but you must make a little allowance, sir, for us, who have been so kindly treated by Mr. Randall, as the new usher's harshness is strange and hard to bear."

"I have done so," the head master said. "Twice have you been reported to me, and no notice has been taken of the reports—this offence is the third, and the worst."

"It is certainly bad," Happy said, "but not done without a cause; however, it's no use to attempt to cry off. We have to go, and perhaps it will be best for all parties when this takes place."

The Doctor bowed, and left the room.

CHAPTER XXXVII.
ILLJURRA THE BUSHRANGER.

WHEN the stately emigrant ship swept past Sydney Lighthouse, young Gleddell and the passenger who had so strangely befriended him were standing on the forecastle; both were eagerly watching the outlines of the beautiful city which bears such a striking resemblance to every thriving English town.

When the pilot came aboard, the *Fair Rosamond* glided slowly up the beautiful river, with its well-wooded banks, and here and there a villa or country house breaking upon the view amidst the many windings of the stream.

The water, too, was covered with boats, and kindly greetings were exchanged between those who had come out to meet the gallant ship and the expectant crowd which thronged her deck.

There were a thousand sights and sounds so different to everything the boy had seen before, and his handsome face flushed with excitement, and the bright eyes shone brighter still as he looked from point to point, everywhere meeting, kaleidoscope like, a fresh object to arrest his attention.

His companion, though of strong and somewhat sombre mien, was not an unmoved spectator of the scene, and his eyes shone with a gladsome expression as the land became more and more developed.

How different were the feelings in the hearts of Gleddell and his companion!

The former, with a boy's love for all that is beautiful in nature, feasted his eyes upon the fair scene, and his heart swelled with gratitude when he thought of the providential escape he had had from a watery grave.

The stern man by his side stood with folded

arms, his keen eyes searching eagerly among those who passed the *Fair Rosamond*.

He would watch the boats approach, and as the emigrant ship glided onward, and the face he sought was not among those who cheered the exiles, he would look shorewards and mutter,—

"Not yet!"

It was not for a friendly form that these quick searching looks were directed—far otherwise; he sought a foe, one he had left his native land to find : and although he had never beheld his enemy's face or form, Luke Jessop's instinct would have singled him out from the many hundreds who passed in their handsome pleasure boats.

It was Luke Jessop's ready hand that stripped the felon's garb from Gleddell's senseless body, and cast the torn pieces into the sea—into the depths of that mystic world —the grave of thousands, and the possessor of many secrets. The convict's brand had gone to the silent register, and none, not even the seamen who had dragged the boy from beneath the vessel's prow, suspected the cause of Luke Jessop's strange act.

When the boy became well enough to recognize his old school acquaintance, his astonishment was great—greater still when he heard the strange misfortune which had befallen poor Philip.

It was upon one brilliant night when the look-out on board sighted land, near Cape Otway, that Luke told the boy the story of the robbery, and Gleddell lost that weight of misery which hung like a cloud over his spirit.

"Should I," he said, "ever return to my native land, I can proclaim my innocence."

"You can," Luke said; "but at present they believe you were killed by the sentry. Let them retain that belief until the time comes."

Gleddell looked up and asked,—

"When will that be?"

"When," Luke said, gravely, "my mission is accomplished, and I have returned to the good old Doctor that which belongs to him ; then, my boy, you shall once more walk with head erect, and the consciousness that none can point at the escaped convict."

Much of the boy's sorrow had passed away so much that he listened quietly to Luke's words, and in the charm of the new life which had opened before him he felt that he could await the coming of that time to which the ex-poacher referred.

"I can wait," he said, "your wish, but—" and here the boy's face flushed, and he cast his glance upon the deck—"there is one I should wish to know of my safety."

"That one," Luke asked, "is Minnie Oakplank?"

"It is," Gleddell said, his face crimsoning. "Poor girl! she now mourns me as dead— worse than dead."

"Write to her," Luke said, "but tell her, as she values your liberty—nay, your life—not to mention to any, beyond her father or sister, the fact of your existence."

Gleddell's face was happy in its expression as he said,—

"I will do so; but even in doing this I see danger to myself."

* This Tale began in No. 8 of this Journal.

"Why?"

"My name. Will not her answer to me proclaim to the Government officers the fact of the existence of one they supposed dead?"

"True," Luke said, "I had not thought of that."

"It is easily remedied," the boy said; "can I not assume another?"

"You can, and if I may suggest one— may I?"

"I should only be too happy to be guided by you."

Gleddell looked at the dark face which was turned towards his, and that look caused Luke the most ineffable delight.

The close companionship which had existed between them since the night Gleddell had been picked up by the *Fair Rosamond*, had done much towards drawing the hearts of the two towards each other.

Gleddell had not one friend among the many hundreds which crowded the emigrant ship, save the man whose prompt action had saved him from being given back to the authorities as an escaped felon.

Gleddell found something of a kindred nature in his strange companion; he found, also, in spite of the somewhat rough garb and the doubtful repute in which Luke had been held when at the Old Chace, that the *ci-devant* poacher was a gentleman.

Under these circumstances it cannot be marvelled that the poor friendless boy should cling to the man to whom he owed so much.

Thus when Luke asked him to adopt the name by which he had been known to the boys at Bircham, Gleddell, with sparkling eyes, said,—

"I will try and be something more to you than I have hitherto been."

Luke gazed inquiringly at the boy's animated face and asked,—

"How, Gleddell?"

"You are childless," was the answer; "I have no kindred nor friends, save a few of my old schoolmates, and the father of the gentle girl I love. I will take your name, and try to fill that void in your heart."

Luke extended his hand—no words were spoken as they silently stood hand locked in hand.

"This compact," Luke said, "will be beneficial to us both. We are now approaching a land where a strong arm and a stout heart will do much to render our advancement quicker, and make us respected by those with whom we may come in contact."

"It will," Gleddell said, "for if you keep your vow there is many a weary unpeopled tract of land to be traversed ere you return to the old land."

"Many," Luke said : then placing his hand upon the boy's shoulder he added, "Look, is not that a beautiful sight?"

They had come abreast of the hill upon which Sydney is built, and its wide streets, massive buildings, and the innumerable spires of its churches formed a *tout ensemble* wondrously interesting to those who had been so long cooped up within the confined space of the emigrant ship.

Now came the bustle and excitement consequent upon the disembarkation of the *Fair Rosamond's* human freight, and before the evening came upon the waters the seven hundred human beings had dispersed and left no sign.

Luke, with his wife and young Gleddell, sought a humble looking inn, and the boy, when all beneath the lowly roof slept, wrote a long and touching letter to the gentle girl who held his heart in her keeping.

He saw but little of Luke the next day, but when he returned in the evening there was a glad sparkle in his eyes, and meeting Gleddell, who stood at the inn door, he said,—

"Fortune has been kind to me, lad. What think you has occurred?"

"Well," Gleddell said, "taking into consideration the fact that I have not been with you, my guess would be rather far from the truth."

"Come inside; I do not think the passing and repassing of those *currency* lasses will improve your powers of listening."

Gleddell followed him to the little room, where Miriam sat awaiting her husband's return, and when they were seated he asked,—

"What did you mean by applying the term *currency* to those girls?"

Luke laughed.

"I expected," he said, "you would be curious upon that point; so to save further trouble I will explain the names applied to the different residents in this country."

"Thanks," Gleddell said, "for I have been much confused to-day by the terms used by several men who stood at the bar."

"I can believe that," said Luke. "Well, the meaning of currency is, a local term used towards those who are born in the country."

"Thanks; and *sterling*, what does that apply to?"

"These are settlers from England—people who have emigrated—not convicts."

"Yes, I understand."

"Then, again," Luke went on, "to make a distinction among the liberated convicts, those who have by good conduct had their term of punishment shortened are called *emancipists*, and those who have served their time are termed *expirées*."

"Well," Gleddell said, "I should think it will be advisable during our stay in this peculiarly constituted community to be careful in distinguishing between *currency lasses, sterlings, emancipists,* and *expirées.*"

"Yes," Luke answered, "it is in truth an awkward assemblage, especially as some of the wealthiest men in the colony are emancipated felons."

Luke seemed in such good spirits that Gleddell caught the infection, and for the first time for many months the old joyous laugh came from his lips.

"What is the matter?" Luke asked; "you seemed amused."

"Merely a passing thought."

"A secret, I suppose?"

"No, I merely wondered how a fellow could with safety make love to the object of his affections, especially if he were a stranger to the antecedents of the loved one's parents."

"Why?"

"Thus, suppose the lady's father had left England at the wish of the Government, how could a fellow tell her he felt transported with bliss?"

"Not very well," said Luke, laughing; "she might think of the time when the word was used in a different sense—but a truce to this!—I must explain the words I used when I came in."

"Do, I had almost forgotten to ask about the good fortune."

Luke's brow became black, and the old fierce look lit up his eyes as he said,—

"Chance has put me upon the track of this Pierre Dublé."

"Already?" said the astonished boy.

"Yes—I have visited the shops of the many gunsmiths in the town for the purpose of purchasing arms, and at one place, while selecting a rifle for you, the gunsmith told me that a powerfully-built Frenchman, who came out in the last ship but one, had taken with him to a village up the river sufficient weapons to arm a dozen men."

"But," Gleddell said, "there are more men answering this description than Pierre Dublé."

"Perhaps so, but I am convinced this is my man."

"You must have more reason for the belief than you have told me."

"I have," Luke said, firmly; "curiosity prompted me to ask a few particulars respecting the Frenchman, and to my joy, the gunsmith mentioned that his customer had a mark across his forehead, apparently a sword cut."

Gleddell made no reply. Truth to tell, the boy was pained when he thought of the probability of Luke and Pierre Dublé meeting. He knew sufficient of his comrade's character to cause his mind much disquietude; and the more he thought over the matter, the firmer became the conviction that one, perhaps both, would die.

He had seen the letter written by M. Jean Gailland's friend in St. Omer, and this, coupled with Luke's announcement that Pierre had taken such a quantity of arms with him up the river, rendered it pretty plain that the French Hercules would be no mean or contemptible foe.

He said nothing of this to Luke, but the hope was strong within him that Pierre would escape the bloodhound-like tenacity with which Luke kept on his track.

"We must start at once," Luke said, after a pause. "He cannot be more than three or four days ahead of us. At any rate, we'll go up Sydney River and inquire at Paramatta."

"Paramatta?" Gleddell repeated; "is that very far?"

"About fifteen miles," Luke said. "We can walk that, but——"

He paused, and looked towards his wife, who, though she took no part in this conversation, was a most attentive listener. She saw his glance, and guessed the cause of the abrupt manner in which he paused.

"I can walk the distance," she said, in her sad gentle voice; "I am much stronger now."

"It will be too much for you, wife," he said; "therefore you had better stay here until I return."

Her eyes filled with tears as she pleadingly said,—

"I shall be no trouble to you, Luke. Do not leave me behind."

"I will not," he said; "but do not be deceived, Miriam. There is danger to yourself m accompanying us."

"There will be none if I am with you."

Luke would gladly have purchased a tilted cart to have conveyed his wife upon their romantic journey. He could not afford this luxury; so the poor woman was compelled to walk the whole of the weary distance, and though she suffered, not a sound escaped her lips.

With rifles thrown over their shoulders, and leather bags at their hips containing powder, shot, and a small quantity of food, the two began their journey.

It was a strange wild scene, after the peaceful English landscape, that met their eyes as they traced the wooded banks of the river.

Swarms of locusts caused the woods to resound with a shrill screech. Gaudy-plumaged birds of the parrot kind formed a pleasing contrast to the green foliage of the trees upon which they were perched.

The guana, or lizard, looking more like the excrescences of the bark upon which they clung, were also seen; and suddenly bounding across their path the light active kangaroo would appear and disappear before a gun could be cocked.

The stately emu and the golden regent-bird became their companions as they advanced farther inland, and gave them an idea of the pleasures to be derived in following the chase.

They found Paramatta to consist of a few scattered houses and one hostel. Here they rested for the night, and here Luke learned that a man resembling the description he gave had left the village some days before, in company with five ruffianly looking fellows, of whom the host gave anything but a pleasing character to his guests.

The innkeeper was an old settler, and his heart warmed towards those who had so recently left the old land. So when his buxom wife had taken charge of poor Miriam, he asked the party to step inside the snug little bar room and take a drink, just for the sake of the dearly loved land he had so long left.

The offer was gladly accepted.

"Well, stranger," said the burly host, "you don't know much of the road you're going, I guess?"

"Not an inch," said Luke.

"I thought not, or you wouldn't think about going after this Illjurra."

"Illjurra?"

"Aye—didn't I tell you his name before?"

"You did not," Luke said, "you merely told me that a man answering to the description I gave had stayed with you."

"Likely enough—I forget. Well, stranger, it's my belief I would not go a yard after him —at least not out of sight of the house, any how."

"I would follow him," said Luke, "no matter where."

"Well, every man, of course, can do as he likes. Come, liquor up, and pass the measure to the youngster, for may be it will be the last time you'll be under this place."

Luke smiled grimly, and cast his eyes upon his rifle, which stood in the corner of the room.

"Your words," he said, "are certainly not encouraging."

"They ain't, stranger, not anyhow encouraging. Shall I tell you why I can't speak better of Illjurra and his comrades?"

"Do."

"Well, it's just this. When a man comes to your house once in six months, and stays for a few days, drinking and spending a heap of money, and among their traps you find articles which you have seen in the possession of strangers, it don't look well, do it?"

"It does not," Luke said, "and were it to happen more than once, I should be much inclined to think that Illjurra's following was the reverse of honest."

"You'd think right, stranger; for it's my opinion that they are nothing more nor less than bush robbers. Now, after this, if you go it won't be my fault; for, to tell you the truth, them chaps is mighty fond of a good rifle, and yourn seems to be of that kidney."

"They are very good," was the quiet answer, "and those who want them will have to possess a sharp eye and ready hand to come upon me without getting a ball in their skull."

"That's the sort of thing out here," said the host, "but it ain't saved all on 'em that went that way—not by a mighty long chalk."

By "that way" the host meant the backwoods and the mighty Australian forests.

"How long has this Illjurra been in the country?" Luke asked.

"Can't say," was the reply. "I've only seen him twice—once about six months past, and the second time about a week ago."

The entrance of the landlord's wife put a stop to the conversation, and soon after Luke and the boy retired to rest.

They were afoot when the sun rose, and soon the little village was left far behind. During the long day that followed, Luke taught his young companion to use the rifle, and Gleddell's keen eye and steady hand did much towards perfecting the lesson, at the conclusion of which Luke gladdened the boy's heart by saying,—

"If you keep up at this pace, my lad, you will soon be a dead shot. Ha! what is that?"

They emerged upon a sweet little glade in the forest, and Luke beheld to his surprise a number of wild-looking men seated around a camp-fire.

They took no notice of the wayfarers' approach, save by raising their eyes towards Miriam.

Luke and Gleddell exchanged glances, and the former, as he passed towards the camp-fire, whispered,—

"Be on your guard; these fellows are bushrangers."

Gleddell replied by quietly drawing back the hammer of his rifle; then, dropping the butt to the earth, crossed his hands over the muzzle, and stood silent and watchfully awaiting the result of Luke's interview with these strange and terrible outlaws.

It was a strange scene. The mighty trees surrounding the opening, the rich grass as soft as the finest carpets from Persian looms, the flashing light of the wood fire playing upon the fierce sun-tanned faces of the group which were scattered around, the glitter of a shining knife-blade or pistol-barrel which hung from belts of raw hide—this, and the statuesque form of the handsome boy, as

THE BOYS OF BIRCHAM SCHOOL.

LIGHT-TOED TOMMY GETS TOSSED UP IN A BLANKET.

he stood between Miriam and the brawny outlaws, his eyes watching their every movement and his hand ready to assist his friend—thus they remained until Luke came close to the camp-fire.

CHAPTER XXXVIII.
JACK STANFIELD AND HAPPY DEPART FROM BIRCHAM, AND THE RESULTS THEREOF.

BEFORE the great bell summoned the boys to their morning lessons, a neat little chaise stood at the school gates.

Happy and Jack took their seats in this, and when the former took the reins and was about to drive off, the whole of the boys rushed out, and showed their love for their dismissed schoolfellows by such a ringing cheer that awoke the sleepy old house.

Mr. Jacob Snivel watched this ebullition of feeling as he stood by the roadside watching the departure.

No. 13.

"Two," he muttered, "and more will follow unless they alter."

With this charitable resolve, he turned from the boys and went inside, ready to pounce on any of the party who should be late after wishing their old comrades adieu.

"Good bye, old boys!" Jack called out.

"Take care of yourselves!" said Happy.

"Good bye!"

"Good bye, Happy!"

"Good bye, Jack!"

And there was much shaking of hands and waving of caps; then came a shout, and the chaise rolled away from Bircham with two of the best-hearted fellows that ever dwelt in the old schoolhouse.

There was another beside the new usher who beheld the departure with the keenest delight—it was Biggs and his party, who had been kept somewhat in check by Jack and Happy, now determined to wreak summary vengeance upon Joe Stikkers and the Mallet.

"We shall have them now, boys," remarked Biggs, "now those bullies have left, and we'll pay 'em for all the thrashings Happy has given you young 'uns."

To which the small fry were quite agreeable, only it was something like belling the cat, none cared for the honour of making war upon either Joe or the Mallet, for these young gentlemen were known to possess plenty of pluck, and could hit well from the shoulder.

The youngsters who had hitherto been protected from Biggs's bullying by Happy and his friend, soon began to feel the loss of their companions.

Cheesy was now the "cock of the school," and many were the tussles which took place between him and any chance young un' he found away from the main body.

Joe Stikkers and the Mallet were looked up to by their party as the successors of Happy and Jack, and at a general council, which was held behind the old shed at the end of the playground, Joe thus addressed his little band,—

"You see, you fellows," he said, "we shall be all right if we keep together; it's when they catch one by himself he gets it."

"I got it this morning," said young Fred Simmons, "and finely, too."

"What did you get, Fred?"

"You know when I went downstairs to get some warm water, Joe?"

"Yes."

"It was then—I'd just filled my jug and was running past Biggs's room when he spied me."

"Well?"

"Was it well—no sooner did the brute see me than he made a rush to take away my jug."

"Did he catch you, Fred?"

"No; but as I ran away I spilt half the water, and when I got half-way upstairs the big brute was close behind me, but he got more than he bargained for."

"Did he, though? What was it?"

"Well, you know, I saw it was no good running, for he'd sure to have collared me before I got to the top, so to prevent this I turned round, and sent all the water I had left smack in his face."

"Bravo!" Joe said; "that was the way."

"That's not all."

"Not all, Fred?"

"No, for the handle of the jug broke, and the other part hit him on the nose."

"Hurrah! that was fine. Did it draw the claret?"

"Should think it did," said Fred, who was proud of the exploit; "but the worst of it was he called out to some of the fellows in the room on the top landing, and they rushed out and gave me no end of a slippering."

"That was bad, Fred."

"Should say it was—for me at any rate."

"Well," Joe said, "that proves my words to be true; we must stick together, and if they touch us, we can give them as much as they give us."

A scout, who had been posted at the corner of the shed, came running towards the group.

"Biggs and two of 'em," he said, "are coming this way."

"Good," said Joe Stikkers. "Out you go, Mallet, and bring him here."

The Mallet emerged from behind the shed, and purposely crossed within a few yards of the bully and his companions.

"Ha!" growled Biggs, "here's one of 'em! Let's chevy him."

"No, you won't," said the Mallet, who overheard the kind proposition, "I won't be chased by you or any of your cheesy gang."

"Won't you?" said the tyrant, catching the Mallet by the wrist; "then I'll twist your arm round."

The Mallet's reply was the application of his boot toe to Biggs's shin.

The bully, in spite of the pain, stuck close to the boy, and would have put his threat into force had not the Mallet butted him with his head.

Biggs gasped for breath, and held both hands to that part of his anatomy known by the scientific as the wind.

He remained thus for a few seconds, then with a howl set off in pursuit of his active foe, who had by this time reached the corner of the shed.

He disappeared when Biggs came almost within arm's length, and the latter, blind with rage, dashed after him.

No sooner had he got out of sight of the boys who were in the playground, than he saw the imprudence of the step he had taken. He was surrounded by the foe—his cap knocked off and kicked over the school-house wall, then the youngsters, obeying a signal from Joe Stikkers, divided and formed a lane for Biggs to pass through. Each right hand grasped a knotted pocket handkerchief, and Biggs, much against his will, was compelled to run the gauntlet.

After this victory there was a few days' peace; but it was but the lull before the storm.

Biggs and his party had taken their time to mature a plan by which they could have ample revenge for the punishment their leader had suffered.

It may be asked, and justly, why the good old Doctor suffered this state of things to exist?

The answer is easy. He knew nothing of it, and the youngsters would have sooner been thrashed by their tormentors every day than have told him a word.

This course would have brought upon them the opprobrious term "Sneaks," a word hateful to the bold high-spirited boys; they determined to fight it out, although well aware that they were not strong enough to take the field against their foes; they could carry on a sort of guerilla warfare, more tiring and annoying than twenty pitched battles.

There was one who knew the state of party feeling in the school—that one Mr. Jacob Snivel; but he refrained from interfering, until it should suit his purpose to do so.

A sneaking, slimy, crafty gentleman was Doctor Bircham's new usher; but, unfortunately for the poor boys, the good old Doctor knew not the true nature of the serpent he had beneath his roof.

CHAPTER XXXIX.

BOB THE DODGER.

BOB HARLEY, or Bob the Dodger, was one of the strangest of boys—one of those peculiar-looking youths whose age might be anything between twelve and eighteen.

A strange description, the reader will think; but possibly he may be acquainted with many who would answer the description of Bob Harley.

Imagine a short stiff-built boy, with a face much too old for his apparent age, yet, withal —what shall I say?—well, a young-old face, yet an honest good-humoured "mug." Add to this, a pair of large red hands, and feet which had the appearance of having the stumpy legs planted in the centre.

Joe Stikkers, with more truth than politeness, was wont to declare that Bob's legs and feet were modelled upon the shape of a parish pickaxe.

Bob cared but little for his companions' chaff. He was never known to be out of temper—thus he became the butt, and at times the pet, of the school.

No one except the Doctor knew anything about Bob's birth or parentage, and the youth himself, not knowing or caring much about the matter, took things very coolly, though he was wont to say at times,—

"It must be awfully jolly to have a father and mother and lots of sisters, to send a big hamper, and all sorts of nice 'tuck' in it; but as I haven't got any, I don't much trouble about it, for the Doctor is very kind to me when you fellows go home for the holidays."

The Doctor was indeed kind to Bob; and evidently feeling for the lad's friendless state, he permitted him to do pretty much as he liked—a permission of which Bob availed himself to the fullest extent, by shirking and dodging out of every task imposed upon him.

A more artful dodger than Bob could not be found in any school. He would do anything rather than get off a dozen lines by heart; and as I before remarked, in evading this he became justly entitled to his *sobriquet* of Bob the Dodger.

The Doctor was too conscientious to permit the boy to pass the whole of his time without making an effort to master the subjects so distasteful to his sluggish nature; so, when he thought Master Bob had had sufficient skulking, he would send for him, and say,—

"Remember, Robert Harley, I expect *you* will learn this lesson before the clock strikes twelve."

The emphasis placed by the Doctor upon the word *you* left the hopeful Dodger with a face as long as it was possible for his round features to elongate, and he would walk away looking the picture of hopeless misery.

Bob belonged to the fourth form—that congregation of unruly youngsters, the terror of all schools, whether public or private.

Sidling to his place, the Dodger would, after a few minutes' vacant stare at the task, cast his eyes upon his classmates.

"I must dodge this," Bob would ruminate; "I wonder which of the fellows will do it for me?"

Bob's musing would lead to the selection of a smart boy in the class, and by dodging the master's vigilance, Bob would slip from his place and get beside his sheet anchor—there's a metaphor for you, boys! Having thus gained—or, as the boys said, dodged into the desired place—something like the following dialogue would take place:—

"I say, Ned."

Ned, who shrewdly guessed the purport of Bob's visit, would stick his nose close to his book, and pretend not to hear.

"Ned," Bob would whisper, accompanying the word with an expressive nudge; "Ned, I want you."

"What is it, Bob?—I'm busy now."

"Ain't you nearly done?"

"No—why?"

"Look here, Ned; I've got these two pages to do."

"Well, do 'em."

The Dodger devoutly wished he could.

"I can't, Ned," he would answer. "Don't you think you could find time?"

"Me? No, it ain't likely."

Bob's face would become expressive of the discomfort he felt within; and after ruefully regarding a thick cane, which Mr. Jacob Snivel could use with great effect, the discomfort would increase.

I daresay the schoolboy reader will easily understand this feeling. It is a disagreeable sensation felt just below the small of the back—the paroxysm increasing as the prospect of condign punishment became a certainty.

"I say, Ned."

By this time the voice would become quite pathetic, and one of the large hands would be busy agitating the straight light-coloured hair which graced poor Bob's skull.

The dolorous appeal would cause Ned' eyes and nose to appear above the top of his book, and in a provokingly indifferent manner he would demand, coolly,—

"Well?"

"Can't you do it for us?"

"No; haven't I told you once?"

"Yes; but you can get through your in no time."

"Look here, Dodger; it's no use—I do it this morning."

"Do try, Ned. I ain't got off a line and you know when the Doctor says, 'I expect *you* to do it'—I hate the way he says that word—it's a sure dose of cane if I don't."

"Very sorry, Dodger, but I'm so awfully slow this morning, myself. Go in to it, Bob; you'll soon get over it."

A doleful shake of the head, then a sigh which could have been heard at the end of the long desk.

"I can't, Ned; it's no use."

"Don't bother me."

"But, Ned!"

A long silence; then,—

"I say, Ned, I've been thinking that I don't want that new bat I bought out of my pocket-money last half."

"Eh, you don't?"

"No, Ned."

"Want to sell it, then?"

"No."

"What are you after, Dodger? Why don't you speak out?"

"Loud—and get a wunner on the head?"

"No, say what you mean."

The Dodger's voice became quite confidential as he answered,—

"Well, it's this, Ned—if you'll do my lines for me to-day, and six more days, I'll give you my new bat for your old one."

Ned did not grasp so readily at the offer as might have been expected. The reason of his diffidence was this,—

The Dodger, like most youths at school, was afflicted with impecuniosity to a painful degree, and it was not an uncommon occurrence for his worldly goods to be in the possession of a keen financial youth, who was known in the school by the name of "Uncle."

Uncle was equivalent to pawnbroker, and this youth, the son of an old bill discounter, inherited a large share of the paternal love of filthy lucre.

In fact he played the same part in the little world at Bircham as his sire played among the spendthrift gentlemen in the large city of two million people.

He was training to help his worthy sire, and he made the practice lucrative; for instance, a youth like the Dodger, inordinately fond of the sweet things called "tuck," and not having the necessary coin to purchase the delicacies, would visit "Uncle," and for the loan of a shilling deposit a cricket-bat, or mayhap a rod and lines, until the money was repaid, with an addition of threepence for the accommodation.

Ned, knowing full well that the Dodger was in the habit of dealing with the young financier, was cautious in his reply respecting the proposed exchange.

"Look here, Dodger," he said, "have you got the bat?"

"Well, I haven't exactly got it now, Ned; but I shall have enough pocket money on Saturday."

"Saturday?"

"Yes; you know you can keep your own bat till then."

This was generous, and as such appreciated by Ned, who said,—

"Well, you are a treat, Dodger. You don't think I'm going to give up my bat until I get yours, do you?"

"Of course not; but I thought you might, that's all."

"Did you? Well, now look here, Dodger, I've got some money——"

"Have you?—that's good; you can lend me a——"

"No, Dodger—not a copper."

"You might; I can pay you when the tip comes in."

"Can you? Considering all your traps are at Uncle's, I don't see how you can get them and pay your debts as well; so that won't do, Dodger."

The Dodger's eyes wandered with a longing look towards Ned's waistcoat pocket, upon the outside of which he saw—and his fingers itched at the sight, the impression of a coin.

"It is no use," Ned went on, "thinking about bleeding me, for I'm saving up to buy a knife with ever so many kinds of corkscrews in it."

"Are you?—how much would it cost?"

The Dodger would have liked a knife of this description, but he could never muster the funds for its purchase.

"Cost?" Ned answered, in an off-hand manner, as though this was but a minor part of the business. "Oh, about three half-crowns."

"Three half-crowns!" gasped the Dodger. "What, seven-and-sixpence for a knife?"

"Yes, and cheap too; why, some of 'em cost double as much."

"Do they though?"

The Dodger was mentally wishing he was the happy possessor of so much wealth—had he been in that blissful state, Betty, the tuck-shop woman, would have done a good business while it lasted.

Even now Bob's mouth watered as he thought of the cargo of apples, tarts, and nuts he would have laid in, and in fancy he beheld himself sitting up in bed, after the lights were put out, and having a surreptitious gorge.

Ned broke in upon his aldermanic dream by saying,—

"But about the cricket-bat, Dodger?"

"Yes, Ned—what about it? Can't we manage?—because it's getting late, and there's more than double the lines to do than I used to have."

Ned glanced at the Dodger's task, and saw that he could do it by the time appointed by the Doctor to hear his dodging pupil.

"How much," Ned asked, "has Uncle advanced you upon it?"

"A shilling."

"A bob! Well, look here, Dodger—I'll give him the coin, and hold both bats until you give me the money back."

The Dodger closed with the offer, but he added a mental resolution to borrow Ned's bat before the day was out, and, as a matter of course, stick to it.

He forgot that Ned would not finish the stipulated number of lessons unless the bargain was fully carried out by him, so somewhat too early chuckling to himself at the manner in which he intended to put the dodge upon Ned, he gave his lesson to the boy, and when the gaunt usher stalked past he was busy with Ned's already finished task.

When the inspection of tasks took place, the master, much to the Dodger's delight, said,—

"Very well, indeed; you see you can do your work when you like."

As the Dodger walked from the dreaded presence, he could not help feeling some qualms respecting the imposition of which he had been guilty.

"Ugh!" he thought, "if he'd have found me out, shouldn't I have got it hot?"

He would certainly have felt uncomfortable for a few hours had the discovery been made; but this reflection did not trouble the Dodger long. He was safe, he thought, for some days yet, and felt happy in consequence.

Since the departure of Happy and Jack Stanfield, Bully Biggs, as he was now termed, enlivened the long winter evenings, and gratified himself, by reviving a barbarous practice which Gleddell and the two dismissed boys had during their stay abolished; this was the infamous system of catching any of the youngsters who might incautiously have strayed from their rooms after nightfall, and taking them to the lower hall and tossing them in a blanket.

There was no lack of victims for the first two or three nights, but after that time the poor little fellows took especial care to hide from Biggs and his compeers.

The Dodger, who did not mind the tossings if they were careful not to let him down, improved the occasion by bringing his dodging faculties into play, and satisfying his cravings for the somewhat stale indigestible "tuck" sold by Betty.

CHAPTER XL.

A CAPTURE—A RESCUE—A TOSS IN A BLANKET—AND AN UNWISHED-FOR VISITOR.

ONE night, when the bullies had scoured the passages for a victim, but without any result, the Dodger waddled down to the great hall, and there delivered himself up to the disappointed crew who had just returned from their fruitless search.

"Look here," he said, "you fellows want some one to toss, and if you'll agree to my proposal you may chuck me up as long as you like."

"What's the dodge now?" Bully Biggs asked. "Are you so fond of it that you come here?"

"No, I ain't very fond of it," replied the Dodger, "but I'm hard up, so if you fellows will give me a halfpenny each you can fire away until you are black in the face."

"What do you say?" Biggs asked; "shall we give the little beggar the money or toss him up for his cheek in asking for it?"

"Toss him up," said a few; but the majority, in consequence of the Dodger's pluck in venturing into the lion's den, suggested that he should have the stipulated sum.

They carried the motion, and the Dodger, rich in the possession of twelve halfpence, was pitched into the blanket and propelled upward like a rocket.

Like a rocket at first, but, his weight being none of the lightest, those who held the blanket let him suddenly fall to the ground.

"What's that for?" the Dodger asked, as he stood rubbing his back; "you're worse than a lot of cannibals."

"What's it for, you little beggar—why, you've sprained all our wrists—why don't you get lighter?—we might as well have a lump of wood to toss up."

"Good job too. I wish I'd broken your arms."

With this Christian-like speech the Dodger decamped, jingling the halfpence in his pocket.

"Hear him!" shouted Biggs, "the cheeky little villain; let's catch him and shake the coin out of his pocket."

The Dodger heard the good thing in store for him, and, putting on the steam, got to cover before his pursuers could overtake him.

"Look here," said Biggs, savage at losing the artful one, "let's go and rout out a light 'un and toss him up; it will make up for the pain that young wretch has put in our arms."

The proposal was hailed with delight, and they at once began an active search in the room occupied by the smaller boys.

In the sleeping apartment of the lively Joe and his friend the Mallet they found poor little Godfrey Bransome, kneeling behind his bed.

The friendless boy was offering up a thanksgiving to his Maker for preserving him from evil during the day which had passed, and when the noisy tormentors came banging into the room he was about to rise from his knees.

"Halloa!" said Biggs, "here's young Methodist parson—let's have him."

"He's just the size," said one; "come here, young square toes, we want you."

The poor boy looked from one to the other, his pale face flushed, and his little heart beating rapidly with fear.

"Don't stand there," said Biggs, savagely; "put on your trousers, and come with us."

Godfrey clung to the bedclothes as though they would afford him protection, and with trembling lips said,—

"Don't toss me, please, I'm not well."

"Not well!" said the brute; "you be hanged for a canting young sneak—come on down, or we'll carry you as you are."

Neither the pale cheeks nor the boy's kind voice had had any effect upon the brutes, and the boy, seeing this, said,—

"I will not go with you—I am too unwell to stand such brutal treatment."

"You won't," roared Biggs; "say you won't again, and I'll drag you out by the hair of your head."

Godfrey's breath came thick and fast, as he drew himself up, and said, firmly,—

"I will not come. You can drag me with you if you are so brutal, but I warn you that I will ——"

"He'll blab to the Doctor," said one of Biggs's companions; "so let him alone, Bully."

Biggs made use of an oath not fit for ears polite, then said,—

"The whining little cur—I'll teach him to be cheeky to us and threaten to tell the Doctor."

"I did not say I would tell," said Godfrey, "neither am I saucy. I only ask you not to toss me, for I am too ill, indeed I am."

"Shut up, you howling brute," roared the bully, clutching the boy by his clustering curls, "come on."

They had dragged the boy to the door, where he clung, pale and shivering, until Biggs savagely knocked his arm away with such force that the little fellow uttered a scream of agony.

"Drag him along, Bully," said the captors

to Biggs, "or we shall have old Snivel down upon us."

"Halloa!" exclaimed the Mallet, who, in company with Joe, came along the passage at this moment, "halloa, what's up?"

"Never you mind," said Biggs, "or you may get something for yourselves."

Godfrey's appealing look and his pale face went to Joe's heart, and, walking straight up to Biggs, he said,—

"Look here, Cheesy, if you want any one to toss up why don't you take one as can stand it—he can't."

"He'll have to, then."

"No, he won't," Joe said, coming to his friend's side, "at least if the Doctor arrives in time to prevent it."

Biggs gave a howl.

"Listen to that," he said; "here's a young beggar going to blab if we don't let this little cur go."

"I don't want to blab," retorted Joe, "except you persist in taking that young 'un."

"Don't get into trouble for me, Joe," said little Godfrey, in his meek childlike voice, "for perhaps I may not be so much hurt——"

"You hold your tongue, young 'un," said Joe, "I say you shan't be tossed; so let them do as they like about holding you ——"

"Come on," said Godfrey's captor, "it's no use to stand here jawing, so come on."

Joe put himself in their way, while the Mallet made a run to the rooms to bring aid.

"Get out of the way, Joe," said Biggs, it's no use trying to get him until we've given him a good tossing."

"He's too weak for it," said Joe, the tears starting in his eyes at the sight of the half-nude shrinking form. "Let him go, and take me—I don't mind it."

"Take you! What? and let a light 'un like this go free? No, thankee, Joe, we've had quite enough of the Dodger for one night."

"You won't take me, then?"

"No."

"Well," Joe said, "then you don't have him."

"Out of the way, young 'un, or you'll get hurt."

"Don't care." Joe saw his ally, followed by about twenty boys, issuing from the end of the passage. "You can hurt me if you like, but you'll soon have something for it."

"Listen to the fool——"

Biggs got no further in his speech. The next moment he was sprawling upon the floor, having been levelled by a blow from the bottom part of the Mallet's fishing-rod; and before he could get to his feet little Godfrey had been rescued from his grasp.

The attack and rescue had been so sudden that the invading party had been taken by surprise—a condition from which they recovered in time to behold several pairs of legs disappear round the turn of the long passage.

"I should like to know the little beggar who gave me that clout," said Biggs; "he should remember it to his dying hour. Did you see who it was, Needle?"

Needle, or Needle-nosed Jim, so called upon account of the sharp pointed appearance of his nasal protuberance, answered,—

"I did not know anything about it until I saw you sprawling upon the ground."

The bullies held a few minutes' conversation, the result of which was a resolve to capture the first small boy they could find, and toss him up until they had satisfied their revenge for the loss of little Godfrey, whose light form they had looked upon as capable of touching the ceiling every time.

A luckless youngster was returning from a forbidden expedition to the lower regions, wherein cookee held sway—he was a favourite with the rosy damsel, and reappeared in this particular instance in the possession of a large slice of cold pudding, a luxury to the hearty schoolboy, and one that he would do much to obtain.

The gentlemen on the look out for a victim beheld the youth slipping along the lower passage, his shoes in one hand, in the other the half-demolished slice of cold "delight."

"Look at that hungry little wretch," said Biggs; "don't you think a good bumping against the roof will help that cold duff down?"

"Should say it would," assented Needle-nosed Jim, "but you'll have to be careful how you catch him, for he's a regular scudder."

Scudder was classical at Bircham for one who could use his legs.

"Who is it, then?" Biggs asked; "I can't see his mug from here."

"It's Light-toed Tom."

"Ugh! we had better slip our shoes off——"

"Hush!"

"What's the matter?"

"Don't shout, he's coming this way."

Such was the case. Light-toed Tom, after taking a careful survey of the dimly-lighted staircase, bolted the last morsel of his luxury and began to ascend the stairs.

Tom knew the hounds would be out in search of their game, and this knowledge caused him to walk without his shoes, and, like a red Indian, feel every yard of his way. With his foot upon the bottom step, he again paused, and mentally remarked,—

"They're very quiet, to-night; I wonder what's up?"

Had he been able to have pierced the gloom above he would have seen six heads over the bannisters watching his movements.

"I s'pose," Tommy went on, slowly ascending the stairs, "the beggars have got tired of hunting us up, for I don't hear any shouts from the hall."

Another step or two was taken, then a pause, and his head was turned first one side and then the other.

"All right, still; but they seem too quiet to be up to any good."

One of the masters' study doors opening at this moment caused the light-toed youth to go up the stairs three at once.

"Look out!" Biggs whispered, "and directly he gets to the top shove something in his mouth."

The fear of being seen by the master creeping about without his shoes, caused Tommy to run in the midst of the foe he so much dreaded.

His foot scarcely touched the landing when he was pounced upon; but Tommy was the wrong sort to surrender quietly.

He had, by good luck, a shoe in each hand, so when he felt the enemy was upon him he struck out right and left.

The heel of the right shoe landed upon the spikey end of that ornamental part of Jimmy's face—his needle nose.

The left hand missed the object Tommy had aimed at—this was the head of the bully, Biggs.

Tommy knew his fate should he be captured, so while Needle-nose held his hand to that ornament to stop the effusion of blood therefrom, Tommy was, for a moment, left with Biggs only to contend with.

Tommy espied the opportunity; he had missed the bully's head, so, lowering his skull, he made a butt at Biggs's stomach.

The blow took effect, and Biggs, looking for all the world as though he had accidentally swallowed a lump of cold ice, stood perfectly doubled up, making spasmodic gestures towards Tommy, who at once put his legs in motion.

The four who had been looking on at the scene between Tommy, Needle-nose, and Biggs, immediately gave chase.

Up the long passage they went, each doing his best—Tommy well ahead, until he came to the door of his room.

Here he paused, uncertain whether to go in or not; the latter seemed best, for he felt that, once inside, he would be dragged out by his pursuers.

Off he started, just as the four came within a couple of yards of the door; there was only one possibility of escape—this, to go down the stairs which led to the servants' offices.

Down these he went; but alas! within six stairs from the bottom there was a loose rod—Tommy's heel caught against this—his hands wildly clutched at the bannisters—the next moment he found himself upon the mat, a disagreeable sensation pervading his body—a feeling as though he had left all the skin off his backbone upon the edge of the stair.

The foe were soon upon him, and in triumph he was marched off to the hall, Biggs and Needle-nose bringing up the rear.

There was but little time lost in parley; four of the biggest held the blanket, and Tommy was pitched head first in by Biggs and Needle-nose.

"Once—twice—three times—and away!"

Away Tommy went with a vengeance.

The sensation of ascending was not unpleasant; it was the horrible feeling when the hands touched the ceiling, and the victim felt as though his inside had been left against the plaster.

Three times Tommy had gone up; the fourth time he was in the act of ascending when a footstep was heard outside the door.

Instantly the shouts and laughter ceased, and, to the horror of Biggs and his companions, in walked Mr. Jacob Snivel, his long cane tucked under his arm.

CHAPTER XLI.

LOST IN THE BUSH.

THERE was one man in that horrid-looking group whom Rembrant would have loved to paint; he was the embodiment of the fine reckless unscrupulous outlaw; one of those strange wild figures we meet upon the canvas of the old masters, but seldom or never in this go-ahead world.

This desperado's face had but little of that intelligence which makes men superior to the lower animals; rather the reverse: it was thoroughly brutish, both in form and expression; and the mass of uncombed red hair which encumbered the mouth and chin and swept his breast, added rather than detracted from the repulsive look.

In stature he was a very Hercules, and the facia of muscle visible below the sleeve of his raw-hide hunting-jacket stood out like knotted cord.

A conical-shaped hat with a wide brim covered his head, and partially concealed his features; a pair of red serge trousers, patched and discoloured, covered his legs as far as the knee, here a pair of long boots with wide tops met the red serge.

A dirty worsted scarf was wound round his waist, and visible above the folds were the butts of a pair of heavy pistols, and the buckhorn haft of a long knife; such was the appearance of Illjurra the bushranger.

There was one part of the equipment of these outlaws that struck Luke as being Spanish, that was a heavy stock-whip which each man had thrust through his worsted scarf.

This whip, peculiar to Australia, was composed of a rather short heavy myrtle carved handle, and a thong eleven feet in length.

The possession of this told Luke that the party before him combined cattle stealing with their lawless pursuits, and as his eye wandered over the group he could well understand that the seven police in the colony had

* This Tale began in No. 8 of this Journal.

but little chance in exterminating the many well-armed gangs that infested the bush on the track from Sydney to the Morrumbidger, a distance between two and three hundred miles of a parched and unpeopled country, we say unpeopled, for the few cattle-runs that dotted the distance with their keeper's wooden huts gave but little shelter to the travellers from the depredations of these wild men of the bush.

These or similar thoughts passed through Luke's mind as he slowly advanced towards the group, and the chee ring host's comment respecting the rifles which Gleddell and himself carried came with unpleasant force to his mind.

It was too late now to recede; and as his eyes became more accustomed to the gloom beyond the flashing fire, he saw the dark outlines of the bushrangers' horses, as, held fast by their hobbles, they cropped the scant herbage around their picket posts.

This sight told Luke that had he avoided the voluntary contest of the camping-fire, the rangers, had they been so disposed, could have jumped into their saddles and soon overtaken the foot-weary travellers.

When Luke had become close enough to the blazing logs for his powerful well-knit form to be plainly discernible to the grim party, the leader, taking a short dirty pipe from his mouth, looked up, and fixing his fierce snake-like eyes upon the emigrant, laconically demanded,—

"Well?"

This mode of address somewhat put Luke off his guard, but the next instant he was as calmly defiant as when he entered the glade, and dropping the butt of his rifle upon the ground, he crossed his hands over the muzzles and said,—

"A strange greeting for one who has been in the trade."

"Where are you travelling?"

"Sydney to Broken Falls."

"Broken Falls," repeated the ranger, his face scowling and fierce; "that's a good hundred miles on."

"I know it," said Luke.

"Are you afoot?"

"Yes."

The man with the red head exchanged a meaning glance with his companions, but the emigrant's eyes were upon him and noticed the look.

"A hundred miles, and afoot," said the Hercules; "its pretty plain you ain't long in the colony."

"But a few days."

"I know it, else you would'nt think of reaching Broken Falls without a dray, or cattle, this part of the year."

"Why?"

The ranger gave a rude laugh, and slapping his knee with the open palm of his left hand, answered,—

"For a good many reasons;—one, there's no road after you get to the Springs; another, the fogs are down pretty thick, and they'd puzzle the devil to find the track then."

"These are difficulties, certainly," said Luke; "but I did not come out here to find macadamized roads, with rows of gas lamps on either side."

"If you did," chuckled the ranger, "you would be taken in; but even that's no more than some of you gentry expects. But look here, stranger, I ain't told you quite all about the dangers of the road: there's another thing yet, and one that is quite as bad as the other two."

"What is it?" Luke asked, fully expecting the answer which followed. "I should have thought there could have been nothing more difficult than the obstacles you have mentioned."

"Ha! ha! ha! You did not think of the bushrangers, stranger!"

"The bushrangers!"

As Luke repeated the word, his quick eye ran over the group, and the gigantic fellow who had held this dialogue, guessing the thought which followed that keen gaze, gave another disagreeable laugh.

"Yes, stranger," he said, when the cachinnation had subsided, "the varmints, they're as thick hereabout as blackberries in the old country."

"So it would appear," Luke said, drily.

The ranger bit his lip, and an angry flash came over his face at these words, but subduing his rising passion, he said,—

"They would'nt let a kangaroo pass 'em without taking his skin, much less a traveller pass without having his."

"What," Luke asked, with a start, "his skin?"

"Have him?" shouted the ranger. "No, no, no; it's his movables I mean, and 'specially a gun like that one of yours."

"It's a double barrel," said Luke, with emphasis; "and those who take it will count at least two less in their gang."

The ranger and his associates exchanged looks.

"They don't do business like that down here," he said; "if they wanted that gun they'd shoot you down—stick you from behind the bush."

"My eyes and ears are sure," Luke said; "thanks for your warning; I shall fire at the first movement I hear, and with four barrels at my service it will be hard if I do not bring one or two down."

"Four barrels!" repeated the chief of the gang; "there's but two there."

"I have a companion," Luke said, "who, although young, is sure of eye."

"A companion!" the ranger said; "I did not know of that. He, too, is tired."

The assumption of surprise respecting the emigrant's fellow-traveller was so well put on, that it deceived even the ready-witted Luke Jessop.

"He is tired," the latter said, "for the young are less able to bear the hardships which leave no mark upon men of our age."

"True," said the ranger, with more friendliness in his voice than he had yet shown, "they are not; but come, stranger, bring your companion to our fire; we are but poor stock-drivers, but you are welcome to such fare as we have."

The invite, though coming from such a questionable source, was not to be despised, and although a slight smile flickered over Luke's face when he of the gigantic frame used the word stock-drivers, Luke threw his gun over his shoulder, and as he turned from the fire, said,—

"I gladly accept your invitation, for an hour's rest will do much to refresh my fellow-travellers."

"Travellers!" said the ranger; "you have more than one?"

He darted a quick glance at Luke as he spoke, and his hand went towards the stock of a long rifle which rested by the limb of a fallen tree. Luke construed this action to its proper source. The bushrangers had began to suspect that Luke, in place of being a peaceful emigrant, was one of the armed police in disguise.

Luke disabused their minds of this idea, by saying,—

"I had forgotten for the moment that I had not told you of my second companion's presence, though it is but of little consequence as far as the matter we have been debating—it is a woman, and my wife."

"She is welcome," said the chief; "doubly so, for we are not often honoured with the company of the opposite sex."

Luke briefly thanked the chief of the gang, and the next moment he had passed out of the circle where the fierce glare lit up the trunks of the trees and the interlining of the thick brushwood.

The distance was too great for Miriam or Gleddell to hear what passed during Luke's interview with the bushrangers, and the apprehension they had at first felt passed away when they saw that no hostile movement was made by the fierce-looking group.

Nevertheless, although any fears respecting his personal safety were thus set at rest, both were glad when he stepped out from the

THE BOYS OF BIRCHAM SCHOOL.

LUKE AND GLEDDELL SURPRISED BY ILJURRA, THE BUSHRANGER.

circle of trees.

"Is your conjecture confirmed?" Gleddell asked, loosening the hammer of his gun, "or are they, like ourselves, travellers in this wild tract of country?"

"Quite confirmed, Gled," was the low-voiced reply; "they are what I first suspected, but, upon the strength of the whips they carry, we must suppose, while we keep their company, that they are stock-drivers."

"While we keep their company?" reiterated Miriam, in evident alarm. "Surely, Luke, we are not to consort with those men?"

"But for an hour or so, wife," was the reply; "by that time we shall have rested, and can resume our journey."

Miriam never questioned her husband's acts, so, meekly inclining her head in token of assent, she waited until Gleddell and Luke had conferred together preparatory to entering the ranger's camp.

"It was a serious oversight, Gled," said the elder of the two, "setting forth on our journey without cloaks or food."

"Not so much our fault as the keeper of the tavern. He assured us that we could put up for the night at a shanty somewhere in this part."

"True," Luke said, smiling; "but we forgot to add the possibility of losing our way."

"Perhaps our lives," Gleddell added; "for, unless the human countenance is a lie to the nature within, those fellows around the fire would not stand nice at putting us out of the way."

"I must admit the truth of this," Luke said; "but if such is their intention, it will not mend matters by declining their hospitality."

Gleddell looked up inquiringly.

"It is simple enough." Luke said, in answer to the lad's look. "If we keep onwards, floundering through this trackless forest, nothing would be easier than those fellows following us, and thus bringing on the very calamity to which you refer."

"I did not look at the affair in this light," Gleddell said. "Yes; there will be more safety by appearing to trust them than by going forward."

"Quite so; therefore, if we take refuge from the black storm which is now threatening, and stay until daylight, do not allow your senses to be steeped too far in the embrace of the drowsy god."

"I shall not. But come, I see our amiable friends peering at us."

Luke gave his arm to his wife, and Gleddell following close behind, they entered the camping-ground.

There was a slight movement among the bearded outlaws, as the party came close to the fire, and the gigantic chief, rising, touched the edge of his broad-leaved hat by way of a salute to Miriam.

"Welcome, madam," he said, trying to soften the habitual rough manner in which he was wont to speak. "We have but little to offer, but such as it is, it is at your service."

There was, as I have before stated in this work, evident traces of more than ordinary beauty in Miriam's face, and to these rough men, who seldom saw anything more comely than the dark features of the native women, Miriam possessed sufficient attraction to call forth more admiration in the keen look of the speaker than Luke altogether relished.

"Thanks for your kindly welcome," she said in a low voice, "for we stand much in need of a friend in this wild place."

The red-bearded chief had by this time collected the cloaks and blankets from his companions' saddles, and with a rough attempt at politeness, spread them for Miriam to recline upon.

It may as well be stated that the stock-drivers and others in Australasia, when travelling, always carry a thick blanket or a cloak, made from the skins of opossums, strapped to their saddles.

This is their covering at night, and, with the saddle for a pillow, the tired bushmen sleep as soundly as those who "live at home at ease," and seek the drowsy god's embrace in soft yielding feather beds.

Besides the articles before mentioned, a mounted bushman's equipage are a pair of hobbles for his horse, a bag containing provisions, which in most cases consist of corned beef and a mixture of flour and water called "damper," a whip, and arms for defence, if the road is considered dangerous, completes his accoutrements, and with a good horse under him and thus primed, the bushman will travel between two and three hundred miles, and with the assistance of a dog drive a herd of cattle safely the whole of the distance.

To return. Miriam gladly accepted the red-bearded man's polite attention, and thoroughly worn out, she sank upon the hill and watched with interest the preparation of a meal for herself and companions.

A couple of tin pots, each containing about a quart, were placed upon the glaring logs, and one of the band stooping over them, watched for the bubble of the water to drop into it a good handful of tea, for a supply of this luxury is always to be found among the provisions carried by the bushmen.

The bubbles soon appeared, and the refreshing draught was made; then from beneath a small pile of brushwood another of the gang brought three slices of fresh bullock's meat and threw them upon the fire.

These in their turn were soon done, and a large cake of damper placed before the three completed the preparations.

Preparations which had been watched with more than common interest by the tyros in bush life, who, when all was ready, opened their knives and began a meal which seemed the sweetest they had ever partaken of.

CHAPTER XLII.
AN AUSTRALIAN THUG.

THE meal over, Luke filled his pipe and be to think that after all he might have somewhat too hastily formed his opinion respecting the group which sat round the fire.

"Perhaps, after all," Luke thought, "these fellows may be stock-drivers, for this hospitality does not seem like the act of a set of merciless wretches such as the bushmen are supposed to be."

His thoughts were broken in upon by the red-bearded chief suddenly raising his head and saying,—

"Did I understand that you were going to Broken Falls?"

"Such is my intention, if I can manage the distance."

"It's a long way," said the ranger-chief; "may I ask what are your intentions when you get there?"

"To seek employment."

The outlaw was silent for some moments. He seemed to be making up his mind upon a difficult point, then to dismiss the subject as hopeless.

This, at least, was the construction Luke put upon the changes which passed over the man's bronzed face.

"You're going a long way," he said at length, "to get a job."

"I know no one else in the colony," said Luke, "except the owner of Broken Falls, and being an old friend, he is the best I could apply to."

"Yes, under these circumstances: and if I remember correctly, there is a vacancy just now that would suit you."

Luke's eyes brightened as he asked,—

"What are the duties of the post you mention?"

"Everything," was the reply; "it's the overseer's berth which is vacant—he has lost the man he had."

There was something in the ranger's tone that caused Luke to ask,—

"Lost him?—How?"

"He was shot by the bushrangers."

Luke fancied a savage expression crossed the ranger's face as he uttered these words, but the next moment he felt that it was but the flickering light of the fire playing upon that harsh forbidding countenance.

"Shot by the bushrangers!" repeated Luke; "after such a mishap I suppose the berth is not much sought after?"

"Quite the contrary," was the answer; "there are a hundred who would take the vacant post."

"Yet it remains open?"

"Yes, and for very good reasons. The owner of Broken Falls labours under the idea that all who seek the situation are in league with the cattle-stealers."

"A strange belief—perhaps true?"

"There may be some," the bushranger said, "to whom this applies; but all are not tarred with the same brush."

"There was a cause for the late overseer's death, I suppose?"

The firelight again flickered upon the chief's face, as it underwent a similar change to that which Luke noticed before, as he answered,—

"Yes, there was a cause—*he was honest!*"

Luke Jessop gazed with silent astonishment at the speaker.

"You seem surprised," the bushman went on; "but it's easy of explanation. Do you know from whence the pests of this colony come?"

"The bushrangers you mean?"

"I do."

"No; I cannot say that I have more than a vague idea of the matter."

"What is that idea?"

"Well, I have imagined that the bush-robbers were composed of men who were too idle to toil."

"Well?"

"This is one class: the other I should imagine to be escaped convicts."

"How escaped?"

"Men who have fled from the gangs."

"In part you are right," said the ranger, speaking like a man who is complete master of the subject, "the greater part of them are escaped convicts, but not from the gangs—the slavery they broke from is ten times worse than that of Norfolk Island, and God knows that is so bad as to defy the power of words to pourtray the misery of those who are the victims of an unnatural persecution."

Luke saw that the speaker was moved by the remembrance of personal sufferings as he delivered himself of these words, and both he and Gleddell listened intently to what was to follow, feeling that any information they could gather would be of service in the new land.

"You know, I suppose," the bushranger resumed, "that convicts are hired out as bullock-drivers, farm-labourers, and, in some cases, cattle-drivers?"

"I have heard so."

"Perhaps you are not aware that the unfortunate wretches who are thus hired are the victims of the most cruel injustice man can ut upon his fellows?"

"My knowledge," Luke said, "is confined to the vague ideas which I have already related."

"You know but little of the subject of which I can enlighten you in a few words, that when a man is hired out he is always an object of suspicion; and no matter how contrite he may be for the crimes which he has committed, there is no chance of reforming out here."

"This seems strange."

"It does to those like yourself, but when you know the persecution to which the hired convict is subject, you will think as I do, that it is a wonder that more do not take to the bush. What do you think of a case which occurred down here not a month since: a poor wretch was sent to water a drove of cattle and because one of the beasts strayed from the run and fell into the hands of the bushrangers, he was tied up and flogged for neglecting his duty. This is but one of many cases I could name. Could you blame the fellow for taking to the bush after this?"

"Speaking honestly, I could not, if he were innocent of any connection between the cattle stealers."

"As innocent as you are."

"Has this," Luke asked, "any connection with the shooting of Mr. Russell's overseer?"

"It has not; he died, as I before said, because he was honest."

"I can scarcely follow your meaning."

The bushman smiled grimly as he said,—

"You must know that one-half the stock-keepers and foremen are in league with the cattle-stealers—this man was an exception, and when any beasts were missed from the farm, he was in the saddle, and in nine cases out of ten he recovered the stolen property. In this instance he met with a fierce resistance, and still persevering in his object, he was shot through the head."

"I fear," Luke said, "that I should have done the same, had I been in his place, for, admitting that men are driven to take to the bush, still, those who hold situations of trust should do their duty to those they serve."

"You will alter your mind before you have been long in the colony."

"I think not."

The ranger gave an incredulous smile, and stretching himself upon the ground, he was soon to all appearance asleep.

Luke looked at his companions and found that his wife slumbered soundly, and Gleddell, although his hands were clasped around the stock of his gun, also slept.

The scene was a strange one to the eyes of a man used to the peaceful waysides of England.

The fire had gone down to a mass of glowing embers, and threw a strange light over the outlaws' slumbering figures, glaring brightly upon their long knives and pistol-barrels, and giving the group an appearance which for one not used to such sights was sufficient to inspire with a feeling nigh akin to awe.

Luke's caution had returned with the story told by the gigantic bushranger, so before he stretched himself by the fire, he noiselessly drew back the hammer of his gun, and placing the forefinger of his right hand on the trigger-guard, he endeavoured to follow the example of his companions.

There is something touchingly melancholy in the aspect of nature in repose, and Luke, as he lay with closed eyes listening to the soft whistle of the lizards which clung to the surrounding trees, the hum of insect life, and the rustle of the leaves, felt a delicious sensation stealing over his senses.

It was not sleep—the responsibility which rested upon him strung his nerves to the highest tension, and as totally banished that which Will Shakspeare terms "nature's sweet restorer," as though such a state of repose was denied to mankind.

Luke felt that responsibility greater than ever when he listened to the gentle respiration of his sleeping wife, and in spite of the peaceful appearance of the bushrangers, he could not dismiss the idea that treachery lurked beneath this quietude.

Nearly an hour passed, and none of the party had changed the position they assumed when first they extended their rude forms within the influence of the smouldering logs.

Luke still lay with his eyes closed, and to all appearance asleep; but his brain was busy, thinking of the man who had helped to crush out the life of his child, and as he thought that the same land now held them both, a smile of anticipated revenge for a moment played upon his lips, and he muttered, like one mutters in sleep,—

"There will be no rest until I have hunted down Greymore's accomplice, Pierre Dublé."

At the lowly-spoken utterance of this name the gigantic bushranger raised himself upon one elbow, and gazing hard at the circle of recumbent forms, he repeated mentally,—

"Pierre Dublé! Was it fancy, or did I hear that name whispered?" He arose to a sitting posture and added, "It must have been fancy, none here can know that name!"

There was a wary expression upon the giant's features as he sat regarding the travellers' forms, and an evil glitter shone in his wild grey eyes as they rested upon Luke and his young companion.

"It's time," he thought,—"this man and the boy must be quieted; the police are upon our track, and they can, if questioned, 'jacket' against us. Yes, it's time; their guns and the woman are a greater prize than many we have put out of the way to obtain."

To make sure that the travellers slept, the ranger arose, and quietly stepping to the fire, he thrust a half-consumed stick into the reddest part of the embers.

The dry wood caught, and the man stooped over young Gleddell's form and passed the light across his eyes.

There was not the slightest motion of the lad's eyelids as the flame passed within an inch of his face; so the bushranger, as though satisfied that his intended victim slept soundly, repeated the experiment with Luke.

Here a like result followed, and the chief, placing his hand upon the arm of one of his companions, whispered,—

"It is time, Kidder."

The man awoke with a start, and his hand went to the haft of the knife at his waist, but, recognizing his chief, he quickly arose and asked in a whisper,—

"What is it?"

The answer was a finger extended towards Luke and Gleddell. Its significance was understood, and the man nodded and touched his knife-handle.

"Not that, Jack," was the fiercely whispered reproof; "a quieter way."

The Kidder made no reply, but unwinding a silk handkerchief from his neck, he proceeded to twist it into a rope-like form.

Luke Jessop's watchful faculties were roused by the bushranger poking the stick in the fire, and with a rapidly-rising pulse he followed every after-movement of the powerful miscreant.

The meaning of the twisted handkerchief was not lost upon the emigrant. He knew that it was the favourite mode practised by the Thugs of India in disposing of any travellers whom they had lulled into a false state of security.

It was a safe and silent mode of murder, for the sleeper's neck once in the silken folds, his life could be choked out before he could make the least cry or attempt at resistance.

He had not expected to have found this mode of destroying life in vogue among the rangers, and for a moment his wondrous nerves shook at the discovery.

There was but little time left for him to decide upon his course of action, for the ranger chief had followed his companion's example, and was now quietly preparing a similar weapon of destruction.

There are some moments when a man placed in imminent peril seems to gather strength in the exact proportion to the danger that manaces him.

This was the case with Luke. He saw by the very caution they used that the rangers did not wish to come to an open attack upon them.

This he justly argued was caused by the wholesome fear which the four loaded barrels inspired the miscreants with.

Knowing this, Luke felt there was but one chance for escape, and as the silent fiends were busy with their fierce preparations, Luke lay with beating heart waiting the moment to come to put his project into execution.

His first idea was to spring up and discharge both barrels of his piece at the murderous forms, but this he rejected after a second's thought as being too much based upon chance for a safe issue.

For perhaps both of the shots might miss. Should this occur, he knew his fate would be sealed and that of the boy, who still slept, unconscious of the danger which menaced him.

So, waiting with feelings that can be better imagined than described for the bushmen to begin their snake-like advance upon him, he slowly unclosed his eyes, and with a start, as though awoke by the sting of an insect, he sat suddenly upright, and, as though by accident, threw the muzzle of his fowling-piece toward the crouching pair, who had at his first movement stooped over the fire, as though warming themselves.

"Hillo, mate!" said Luke, addressing the chief, "have you, too, been disturbed?"

"No," was the surly response; "we are keeping watch while the others sleep."

"A proper precaution," Luke said, rising; "for there is need of a sentinel in these parts, unless I am much mistaken."

The two men over the fire exchanged glances, and Luke, stretching his limbs, continued,—

"I could have sworn when I awoke that I saw two or three forms creeping out of that bush—listen! I am not mistaken."

Luke faced round, and slapping the butt of his piece to shake the powder down the nipples, stood as though ready to fire.

The bushrangers gave a start and turned their faces in the direction of the spot indicated by Luke, and a second after, as much to the latter's surprise as the bushrangers', there came the sound of the snapping of dried twigs.

CHAPTER XLIII.

THE chief gave a peculiar low cry, and in an instant the remainder of the gang were upon their feet and standing by their arms; and the noise, though slight, awoke Miriam and Gleddell. The latter at once placed himself beside his friend, judging by his attitude that some danger menaced the party.

The snapping still continued, and from the breaking of the brushwood it was evident that those who caused the noise were passing from the vicinity of the camp.

The chief, by a silent gesture, caused his men to disperse, and, with weapons ready for instant use, they passed beyond the pale of the fire-glare and disappeared in the dark void beyond.

"From what I have heard of bush-fighting," Luke said to the gigantic chief, who was standing with his revolver ready to catch the faintest sound, "I do not think we could stand in a better place to make targets than we do now."

"True," said the ranger; "therefore you had better seek the shelter of those trees. I will also find a hiding-place."

The Hercules, as he spoke, glided towards the spot where the horses were picketed. Then Luke, followed by Miriam and Gleddell, sought a cover in the opposite direction.

He was no sooner out of earshot of his treacherous host than, in low hurried accents, he whispered,—

"Follow me, and quickly, for our lives depend upon the use we make of our legs for the next few minutes."

Unquestioned was the emigrant's act by his companions as they swiftly followed him towards an opening among the trees. Here Luke, taking a directly opposite direction to that pursued by the band, struck into the thick timber.

He held on his way for some time, and when the distant fire became a mere speck he halted, and told Gleddell the narrow escape they had had from being strangled.

"The ruthless miscreants!" said the boy, his cheeks reddening with indignation. "Think you we shall be followed?"

"To a certainty," said Luke, "when they strike upon our trail; but as they will require daylight for that, we must keep on, and trust to Providence for the rest."

They did keep on, neither knowing the path they pursued, until the day broke and revealed the surrounding scene.

The aspect of the country was much changed from that which they had stopped at with the bushmen.

There a large forest terminated in the bush, which extended far away to the left and right; while here the ground was broken, and destitute of trees, some torn, a few trunks. which appeared to have fallen by the destroying hand of time or the wrath of the elements.

"Not much shelter here, Gled," said Luke, "we must push on towards that forest flat in the distance, there, by dodging among the trees, we can hold our ground against twice the number of the scoundrels from whose clutches we have so providentially escaped."

The advice was good, and while going towards the forest Gleddell asked,—

"Have you any idea of the cause of those sounds which seemed to scatter the bushrangers?"

Luke smiled as he answered,—

"Yes, it was one of their horses who had broken loose. I saw the brute go towards the brushwood when I first spoke. Ha! what's that?"

The party came to a sudden halt as the lad said,—

"It's the hoof-strokes of horses."

"It is," Luke said; "but thank heaven! they come from the opposite direction to that were we left our foes."

As he spoke, four horsemen came in sight, and as they neared the wayfarers Luke said,—

"A police magistrate and three troopers, and I'll wager my existence they are in search of the gentry we have so unceremoniously left."

The fact of the men's uniform, and the pistol-holsters of a young determined-looking man who rode at the head of the small party, had guided Luke to the solution of this procession.

The officer, riding close up to them, raised his cap to Miriam, and said,—

"You are early about,—new arrivals, I presume?"

"Yes," Luke said, "and for one night I think we have learnt a pretty good lesson respecting travelling in Australia."

"Indeed!" the magistrate said; "have you been robbed?"

"No," Luke said, "for we have nothing to lose, except our lives—those we nearly lost."

"You were unfortunate," said the officer, patting the neck of his impatient steed; "may I inquire how you were placed in such jeopardy?"

Luke told him the story of his meeting with the rangers, their hospitality, and the contemplated Thugism.

"You have had a narrow escape," said the officer, "for that gang is about the worst we have in the colony; that you may judge when I tell you I have a proclamation in my pocket from the Colonial Secretary's office, offering a hundred pounds reward for the apprehension of their leader, the scoundrel Illjurra."

"Illjurra!" Luke repeated, "the very ruffian we were warned against in Sydney!"

"Do they know of the murder there?"

Luke looked up at the magistrate, and replied,—

"The murder, sir?"

"Yes, that miscreant shot the overseer at Broken Falls not long since."

"Would I had known it," said Luke, "I would have shot the fellow down in the midst of his band."

"You would have done the colony a service had you done so, and saved me much trouble, for I have been now for nearly a month on his track and not taken him yet. Can you remember the place you left this gang, that is, the direction you have taken since?"

Luke described the path he came since he left the bushrangers, and the officer's face brightened at the description.

"We shall house him yet—push on, men."

The horses were soon in motion, and the party, when they had watched the horsemen out of sight, turned and resumed their long march.

It was near noon when they halted, and Luke made a fire, to roast a couple of birds which Gleddell had shot during the early part of the day.

The meal was acceptable, and at its conclusion Miriam sought an hour's repose beside the trunk of a fallen gum tree, while her companions, seated upon the log, talked of the past and the uncertain future.

Whilst thus engaged, they were startled by the sound of horses' hoofs coming upon the track they had that day followed, and suspecting the sound denoted the return of the magistrate and his men, Luke leisurely turned his head.

What he saw caused him to spring to his feet and seize his gun, and the lad, following his example, turned and beheld the bushrangers jump from their horses, and with threatening looks and gestures came towards the resolute pair.

As a slight rampart, Luke and Gleddell placed themselves behind the fallen trunk, and, with their fingers upon the triggers, they awaited the coming of their foes.

The look, the attitude of the pair caused the rangers to pause in their advance, and both parties stood motionless for some moments, fiercely regarding each other.

CHAPTER XLIV.

IN WHICH BULLY BIGGS AND NEEDLE-NOSE ARE TRAPPED.

THERE is a vague remembrance in my storeroom of past events about which I have read or seen, and foremost in this heterogenous collection there is a something about somebody's head appearing and turning all who saw it into statues, stone statues, I think, but of this I am not certain—by the way, was this wonderful head called the Medusa's?—I think so, but as in the case of the statues, I will not be certain.

I am certain, however, of this fact, that the appearance of Mr. Jacob Snivel's head inside the door of the lower hall had quite a contrary effect to the head before mentioned.

For so far from changing those who beheld it into statues, no colony of rabbits could have made a swifter retreat to their burrows than did Bully Biggs and his compeers, to escape the thick cane which Mr. Snivel carried and knew well how to handle.

Needle-nosed Jim, with a frame of mind worthy of the assassin, blew out the lights, and when his companions scudded towards the door they heard the rasping voice of the gaunt usher, saying,—

"Tossing in the blanket, are they! the young villains?"

The door, I believe, is generally considered the place to escape from in a case of this sort, but Bully Biggs evidently thought the presence of the the thick cane at that place of exit necessitated a different mode of egress, and, acting upon this thought, he threw open one of the windows, and, followed by his sweet companions, tumbled most ungracefully though, and pelted across the lawn as fast as legs could carry them.

Poor Light-toed Tom, shaken by the unexpected collision his body had sustained with the floor, was for some moments unable to move, but when he did regain the power of moving, he saw Mr. Snivel in the act of relighting one of the candles.

Suspecting no chastisement, Tommy sat rubbing his back, and Mr. Snivel, after taking the cane from under his arm, advanced straight to him of the light toe, and, clutching his collar, put the cane in motion to such an extent, that Tommy began to yell most lustily for mercy.

The prayer was unheeded, and the martyrdom continued, until Mr. Snivel's arm ached, then, as he released the sufferer, the following remark fell upon Tommy's ears:—

"I hope this will be a warning to you!"

Tommy looked after the gaunt figure as it strode from the room, and ruefully muttered,—

"Well, after being tossed like that, to get it as hot as I've had it, is what I call a shame."

When I chronicle the fact of Tommy having been laid across the usher's knee during the punishment, the reader will readily imagine that the sufferer found the school-room forms anything but pleasant to sit upon next morning.

The youth of the light toe did not forget the gentleman who brought his misfortune upon him—far from it, for night and day it was his sole thought how to be avenged.

An opportunity occurred a few nights after, which came like balm to Tommy's heart—an opportunity, I need scarcely say, he did not allow to pass unnoticed.

Bully Biggs and Jem of the Needle-nose, finding that victims were scarce for the blanket-tossing, held a council as to the best mode of passing the long evenings, and light-toed Tommy, with his friend Bob the Dodger, happening to be prowling about the hall, saw the Bully and his companion sitting with their faces close together, and from the grin now and then perceptible upon their features, the two youngsters came to the conclusion that Needle-nose and Biggs were planning a new scheme against the peace of the small fry.

"Look here, Tom," whispered the Dodger, "they're up to mischief, don't you think so?"

Tom nodded affirmatively.

"What do you say," the Dodger went on, "to us slipping in at the other end of the hall, and listening to what they're up to?"

Light-toed Tommy shook his head, and sagely remarked,—

"Suppose we're caught?—shan't we have a thrashing, that's all!"

"We're sure of that," coolly answered the Dodger; "but if we're not nabbed, we shall be able to put Joe Stikkers and the Mallet up to their games."

Tommy reflected for a few moments; he was calculating whether the certain risk was worth the prospective gain.

"Don't funk," said Bob. "Suppose they do thrash us, it won't be the first we've had."

"You don't mind it, Dodger; but I had such a dose the other night that I can do for a little time without any."

"You certainly did get dropped on, Tom; but would'nt you risk all those two could give us to be revenged for that caning you got?"

The Dodger had touched his companion's weak point—revenge was uppermost in his thoughts, and the fear of being thrashed passed away before the bait held out to him of the light toe.

"Yes," he said, "I'd chance a dozen of their thrashings to get a chance of serving 'em out."

"Say no more," said the sturdy Dodger, "but let's be off."

They were soon at the bottom of the hall, then taking off their shoes, they one by one stepped through the baize-covered doors, and creeping upon their hands and knees, crept close enough to the conspirators at the fire to overhear all that was said.

Unfortunately, they were too late to hear the delectable scheme which Bully Biggs and Needle-nose had been concocting, for as they crouched behind the plotting pair, Biggs said,—

"Yes, that'll be the thing, we shall have lots of sport out of the young beggars."

"We shall," replied he of the pointed nasal; "and now as that's settled, what about the other affair?"

"Which other affair?"

"The beer!"

"Ah!" said Biggs, "I'm glad you reminded me of that, for our bottles are empty."

The Dodger nudged his companion and whispered,—

"That's where the Doctor's beer goes, is it?"

Tommy wagged his head in reply.

The mystery was explained—for a mystery it had been to the good Doctor, and his grey-haired servitor, how the cask, which was kept for the use of the head master and his family, so soon became emptied. Gleeful were the young ones' hearts at hearing these words quoted by Bully Biggs and the Needle-nose, and intense was the chuckle they gave when the two worthies again spoke.

"Did you know," Biggs asked, "that the old man has had a new lock put on the cellar door?"

"Yes, I found that out last night when I went down to get a jug full, and could'nt open the lock with my bent nail."

"Did'nt you get any?"

"Not a drop."

Biggs indulged in a laugh, then pithily remarked,—

"Well, you must have been a flat to have come away without the swipes."

"I don't see it; I could not get through the keyhole, could I?"

"No; but there was another place you could have got through."

"Eh?—where?"

"Don't you know," inquired Biggs, "that it's an old coal cellar where the Doctor's swipes are kept?"

"Of course I do."

"Well, did you ever notice a circular iron plate a few yards in front of the steps which lead to the paved yard?"

A light began to dawn upon the Needle-nose gentleman's faculties.

"Of course I have," he said, "is it——"

"Yes, that's the spot: for when they made the new cellar in front of the kitchen, the workmen left the iron plate in the paved yard."

But wasn't it fastened by a chain to a staple in the wall?"

"Such was the case, but I foresaw sooner or later the Doctor would smell a rat, and have a different lock put to the door, so I took the liberty of unfastening the chain, and very useful I have found that movable plate."

"Have you?" thought Tommy; "wait till I catch you inside, my gentleman!"

"Biggs," said Needle-nose, approvingly, "you're a stunner!—but what time is it?"

"Must be near locking-up time—but why do you ask?"

"I have a wish to taste the new barrel I saw rolled down yesterday."

"You shall,—oh, here comes old John with the keys."

A grey-headed old servant entered the hall, and, without taking any notice of the boys, began to rake out the fire.

"John, you old muff!" said Biggs, "you'll stifle us."

"No business here, young gentlemen," answered the old fellow, continuing his occupation, "it's past the hour now."

"Is it? I say, John, give us a jug of beer, old chap, you haven't been generous for a long time now."

The old fellow, after chasing a glowing cinder from side to side, suspended his labour and answered,—

"I don't mean to be generous any more."

"How's that, John?"

"Because there's a lot of young gentlemen here in the school that helped themselves so often that the beer ran short, very short."

Here the poker recommenced, and the last obdurate cinder was driven out from the grate.

"Helped themselves, you old muff!" said Needle-nose; "how do you know that?"

The old fellow chuckled, and, jingling his keys, answered,—

"How do I know—he—he—he!—I found a bent nail in the lock of the cellar door—he—he—he!—how do I know?—he—he—he!—that's how I know."

Biggs and Needle-nose exchanged glances, and old John, giving the keys another shake, chuckled out,—

"Got a new lock how—he—he—he !—bent nails no use—he—he—he !"

"It strikes me," Biggs said, when the old man had left the hall, "that some other fellows beside ourselves know the way to the Doctor's cellar."

"I'm of the same opinion," said Needle-nose, "for I was not fool enough to leave the nail in the lock."

"I know I did not," said Biggs; "but it's no use speculating upon the matter, we'll wait till the old muff has locked up, then we'll try the iron plate; so come on, Needle."

Linking arms, the precious pair sallied from the hall, and the concealed listeners, after assuring themselves that their foes had gone to their rooms, crept from their hiding-places and made their way to the paved yard.

They had not formed any particular plan of action, and while considering the best way to obtain their revenge for the many acts of tyranny they had suffered, they saw Biggs and Needle-nose, each carrying the water-jugs from their rooms, approach the iron plate.

The shadow of the stone steps concealed the youngsters, and when the two had removed the plate and slid down among the barrels, Bob the Dodger said,—

"Look here, Tom, you go to the Doctor and tell him we've heard some thieves in the beer cellar."

"That won't do," said Tom; "suppose they fill the jugs and get away before I come back ?"

"No fear of that," was the Dodger's reply, "for I'll clap the iron plate down and sit on it till you come back."

Tommy gave a helping hand, and the iron trap, much to the dismay of the beer-stealers, was suddenly dropt into its place, and the Dodger, sitting upon it, bade his companion make haste and fetch the Doctor—a piece of advice he of the light toe was not slow in following out.

"Got 'em this time!" chuckled the Dodger, as he felt the captured pair trying to lift the iron plate. "Won't they get it hot, that's all !"

The iron plate upon which the Dodger was so firmly seated was of the ornamental kind, there being half-circular pieces cut out all round the centre.

The Dodger had not noticed these orifices when he so gleefully squatted upon the trap. Better for him had he been more observant !

Bully Biggs and Needle-nose were not quite green enough to be trapped without making an effort to escape ; so, after the first few moments' dismay had passed, the former said,—

"We're nabbed, Needle."

"We are," was the reply, "and by some of the young'uns, if I'm not much mistaken."

"I thought the same myself, Needle ; but what's to be done ?"

"Get out, if possible."

"If possible !" repeated Biggs, savagely, "I don't see the possibility of it."

"Let's try."

They did so, but the Dodger's squat heavy form totally precluded all their efforts to raise the iron plate.

"The young beggar," said Biggs, "is sitting on it."

"A fact, Bully, beyond all dispute."

"Hang him !"

"Amen say I to that ; but if we curse until we are black in the face, it won't move him."

"Perhaps blessing him will."

"No, Bully, but I think this will do something towards it."

Biggs heard the click of a penknife as Needle-nosed Jim opened the blade, and, rubbing his hands with delight, said,—

"Shove it in, up to the handle, Needle !"

The Dodger, glued to the iron plate, was whistling melodiously, happy at heart at having such a chance of paying out his old foes ; but in the midst of his tune he suddenly gave a howl of pain and sprang from his seat.

Needle-nose Jim had pricked him with the knife. The part thus touched was tenderly felt by the Dodger, as he clapped his hand to it and rolled about the paved yard.

He stopped in the middle of a magnificent howl as he saw the iron plate begin to shift from its place, and, forgetting the pain he suffered, the Dodger scrambled to his feet, and, jumping on the iron, remarked,—

"No you don't !"

Neither did they, for his weight was sufficient to keep the means of egress closed, and despite the attempts of the captives to stick the knife-blade through his thick-soled boots, the Dodger stuck to his post with Spartanlike fortitude.

Bully Biggs and his companion, foiled at getting out of the cellar by force, tried the effects of bribery, and the former, putting his mouth as near as possible to one of the openings, said,—

"I say, young 'un, what's your name ?"

The Dodger, speaking in a high falsetto, which thoroughly disguised his voice, answered,—

"Wiggins."

Wiggins was a by-word in the school—a mysterious personage, who always found things before they were lost. Thus, a boy would lose a couple of choice fishing-hooks, and upon asking if any of his school-fellows had seen them, the answer would be,—

"I daresay Wiggins has got 'em, he found my finest bat yesterday and left it in the court."

Dire were the threats uttered against the invisible Wiggins ; but as he never appeared in the flock they were not fulfilled.

When Bully Biggs received this name as an answer to his query, he said coaxingly,—

"Come, young'un, don't lie, your name's Joe Stikkers."

"Is it !" screeched the Dodger, "you're wrong this time, Bully, I'm the invisible Wiggins, come to punish you for thrashing the little boys."

"I'd thrash you, if I could get out !" said Biggs ; "I know you, so let us go, and we won't do anything to you."

"You won't get the chance, Bully."

Biggs thumped the iron plate with his fist, and inwardly prayed that he should one day have his captor's head to serve in the same way.

"Look here, young'un," said Needle-nose, "you might as well let us go, we'd give you something for it."

"Don't you wish you may get it !" squeaked

THE BOYS OF BIRCHAM SCHOOL.

A PICTURE FROM LIFE.

the Dodger. "No, no, no; here's a lark! I say, Needle, did you ever see a piece called Wiggins's rogue, or the trapped beer stealers? —here comes the Doctor,—my eye! won't you get it!"

Biggs and his companion scudded off like two rats, and hid behind a huge barrel—in their flight taking all the bark off their shins against the corners of the beer-stands.

Cowed, and in pain from the shinning operations, they crouched yet lower as they heard the shuffling of feet on the pavement above.

Light-toed Tom had told the Doctor the names of the invaders of his cellar, and the old gentleman when he came to the top and saw the Dodger on sentry looked very grave.

He felt sorry for the misconduct of the two big lads, and stood for some time evidently perplexed how to act.

He felt that were the affair brought before

No. 15.

him during the time the school was assembled, he should be compelled either to severely chastise the culprits or dismiss them from the school.

Neither plan was compatible with his nature, he looked upon it as more of a boyish freak than an act springing from a badly-organized mind; so reasoning that undue severity would possibly be the means of doing more harm than good, he stood with his aged head bent in thought, until a soft cat-like tread behind caused him to turn.

It was Mr. Jacob Snivel, who, unfortunately for the thirsty pair, came across the paved yard at this moment, and the Doctor, believing that two heads are wiser than one, at once explained the cause of his perplexity.

The usher gave a grim smile, then drawing the head master out of the boy's hearing, suggested a punishment for the gentlemen below.

It was evident, from the manner in which the good old man doubted, that the usher's plan of punishment was too severe for the offenders; but the subtle reasoning of the gaunt usher at length prevailed, and Messrs. Biggs, the Bully, and Needle-nose Jim were fastened in the cellar until old John, who had received his orders from the Doctor, released them at seven next morning.

The long night's incarceration had the desired effect, for neither of the prisoners could look with composure at a jug of beer for months afterwards.

CHAPTER XLV.

IN WHICH M. JEAN GAILLAND'S COURTSHIP COMES TO AN ABRUPT TERMINATION.

WHEN M. Jean destroyed the proofs of his connection with the murdered Greymore, his mind became relieved from the ever-haunting fear to which it had been so long a prey.

He was free now to woo the beautiful girl whose image, in spite of the many rebuffs he had received in the prosecution of his suit, still remained indelibly fixed upon his heart.

He waited until he thought the bitterness of the heavy sorrow which fell upon her had passed away before he visited the cottage. When he did so, he was received by the heart-broken girls with a winning courtesy which caused the vain Frenchman to imagine that at last he had made an impression upon Eleanor.

Far different was the real cause of the welcome he received.

The Captain's daughters saw in him one who had been under the same roof with those they had both loved and lost, and to hear him speak of them was a balm to their stricken spirits.

No peacock ever strutted with greater pride than did our Gallic friend when he took leave of the young ladies, and that night, when surveying his sallow face in the small looking-glass in his room, he muttered,—

"To-morrow I go again, for that old animal their father will not have come back, and I will tell her how much I do love her, and she will have me for her husband. Yes, she must do that, or else she would not listen so pleased when I talked to her last night. M. Jean! when you return to la belle France you will take back one of the prettiest of the English misses!"

So much for the anticipated joy, M. Jean. We shall see how far the result will agree with your rosy visions.

M. Jean's sleep was that night rendered delicious by the repetition of his waking thoughts; time after time he imagined himself walking hand-in-hand with the Captain's beautiful daughter, and, strange to say, whenever he cast his eyes towards her, he beheld a plain gold ring shining upon the fourth finger of her left hand.

"Ah!" he soliloquized next morning, while scraping his chin, "they say here in England that if you do dream anything for three times it will sure to be true, and I have dreamt this four or five times, that she had the gold ring on her finger, so it is sure to be true. M. Jean, you are a lucky fellow to have such a pretty miss for your wife!"

Before that day had numbered many hours the love-sick Frenchman's nerves received a severe shock.

Among the small pile of letters which awaited the Doctor when he came down to breakfast was one bearing a colonial postmark.

The head master read the word Sydney two or three times over before he tore open the envelope, and after each reading he muttered,—

"Australia! bless me! I've no relatives in the colony, and I'm positive I know no one there. Perhaps, after all, it's not for me."

A second look at the superscription removed all doubts, and the Doctor opened the envelope, and, to his surprise, read the following letter:—

"*Sydney, New South Wales,*
"*September,* 1852.

"*Sir,—The enclosed list, signed by Israel Levy, relates to the property abstracted from your strong room, and for which an innocent youth has been banished from the land of his birth. The robber, as you will perceive by the enclosed name, has long since passed away from this life. The erasure in the leaf from Greymore's diary relates to one who was compelled by the last-named to assist in the burglary. You will observe that the sum mentioned in the Jew's bill will restore your property, so, if you should feel inclined to redeem them, I will, as soon as I have honestly raised the amount, which circumstances alone compelled me to use, send you a draft upon a London banker.*

"A FRIEND."

The Doctor sat for some minutes regarding this strange and hastily-written letter, then, opening the leaf Luke had kept from Greymore's diary, he uttered a heartfelt,—

"Thank heaven! the boy was innocent of that crime! Poor Gleddell!—poor lad!"

CHAPTER XLVI.

THE paper which had been drawn up by Luke Jessop for some time puzzled the old gentleman to properly understand.

At last a light dawned upon him, and carefully wiping his spectacles, he placed them on the desk.

"Fifty pounds," he thought; "it is not much, certainly, to lose in comparison to the amount of property taken from the strong room."

The Doctor, though not a rich man, would sooner have given twice this amount than one of his favourite scholars should have been taken from the school on so grave a charge as that upon which poor Gleddell was convicted.

"This soiled leaf," he resumed, placing his finger upon the portion of Greymore's diary, "will be better placed in the hands of the authorities, and no doubt, with the evidence the Jew will give respecting the person who deposited the plate in his keeping, will do much towards obtaining the poor boy's release from an ignominious captivity."

He had reached thus far with his musings, when M. Jean, who had occasion to speak with the headmaster, came to the desk.

Had a spectre suddenly arisen before him he could not have become more terror-stricken than he did upon beholding the leaf he so well remembered Luke Jessop retaining out of the murdered man's pocket-book.

Leaning against the black-board which stood against the desk, he remained white and speechless, his eye-balls starting from their sockets, and every limb trembling with deadly fear.

The Doctor was too much occupied with his own thoughts to notice the strange behaviour on M. Jean's part.

He would in all probability not have noticed the Frenchman had not the latter staggered forward, and, as though fascinated by the soiled piece of paper, clutched at the rails in front of the desk, and with chattering teeth and trembling hands tried to draw the terrible handwriting towards him.

The Doctor saw the shaking hand extended across the desk, and, lifting his head, exclaimed,—

"Monsieur Jean—sir—what do you require?"

M. Jean by this time had read the words upon the paper, and as he saw that his name had been erased, his fears vanished, and with a wondrous power of self-command he said,—

"Ten thousand pardons, sir; the writing upon that paper so much resembles that in a letter I found near the place where that poor man was shot, that it quite overcame me."

The worthy Doctor was far from suspecting that M. Jean's name had once figured upon that leaf, and, fully believing in the truth of the French master's words, he said,—

"I have every reason to believe this was written by the same hand. Pray step this way, and I will tell you how it came into my possession."

M. Jean gladly obeyed, and the headmaster told him of the strange letter he had received from New South Wales.

"I am filled with delight," said M. Jean, "to hear that you have got a clue to your silver."

"Thanks, 'Monsieur Gailland," said the Doctor, "I am sure you feel what you say; but I must confess, valuable as the stolen articles are, I feel more joy at the knowledge of that poor boy's innocence."

M. Jean, according to his words, was equally delighted; but in his heart he hoped that Gleddell would never return from the convict settlement.

It was some time before his nerves got over the shock they had sustained, for even the image of the beauteous Eleanor faded from his mind during the continuance of the shock.

By the evening he was a little like himself again, and when putting the last touch upon his somewhat elaborate toilet, he could not help thinking how different matters would have been had Luke Jessop forgotten to erase his name from the paper.

"I have had what they call in England a narrow escape," he thought; "never again, Jean, must you keep the company of men so wicked as that Greymore was."

There was no doubt, whatever faults Jean had committed while under Greymore's influence, he had amply atoned for them since by the mental torture he had suffered, and if the resolution which he made when Luke Jessop gave up the pocket-book was adhered to, a great change had taken place in the Frenchman, a change which promised to continue.

When he visited Woodbine Cottage that evening he found Minnie much happier than she had appeared on the previous day. The change, coupled with the intelligence he had heard from the Doctor's lips, led him to the conclusion that she had also received some gratifying news from the same quarter as that to which the Doctor was indebted for his letter.

"Diable!" muttered M. Jean, "surely that boy has not been pardoned and coming home! No, that is impossible, for the Doctor told me that he should have to tell the Home Secretary all about it first."

This reflection relieved his mind considerably, for M. Jean rightly conceived that the coming of Gleddell would put an end to all his hopes of an alliance with Eleanor Oakplank.

"I am much pleased," he said, the ready lie upon his lips, "to see Mademoiselle look so much better and happier; it seems more like the time before them dreadful things did happen."

"There must be a limit," Minnie said, casting her eyes upon the ground, "to our grief, Monsieur Gailland."

"Mademoiselle speaks truly"—he cast a quick glance at Eleanor's pale sad face as he spoke—"it would be but a very sad world were we always to mourn, and cherish hopes that are impossible to realize."

"There are some things which can never be forgotten, Monsieur."

"Yes, it is so," he assented; "but would it not be as well to try and forget things which only make life miserable by keeping them constantly before the mind?"

"That sweet feeling called hope," Minnie said, "often bids us do this, and I think in many cases those who are guided by this, sooner or later receive their reward."

The Frenchman looked steadily at the young girl's face as he said,—

"Perhaps Mademoiselle speaks from experience?"

The rich blush which mantled her face confirmed M. Jean's suspicions respecting the letter, and the faltering voice in which she answered made this confirmation doubly sure.

"What reason," she said, "has Monsieur Jean for saying this?"

"Several," he said, determined, if possible, to draw the truth from her lips. "Several—would Mademoiselle be angry were I to speak plainly—speak like an old friend?"

"I see no reason," she answered, "that I should be so."

"Then I have Mademoiselle's permission to speak all I think?"

Minnie inclined her head in the affirmative.

"Well," M. Jean began, "when I had the honour of seeing you young ladies last evening, you, Mademoiselle Minnie, looked so sad, so pale, that my heart felt for you very much. I come to night, and I see your face still pale, but in your eyes I read there has been something since I last saw you to make you much happiness."

Minnie tapped the carpet with her tiny foot as she asked,—

"What do you suppose can have occurred in this short time to make such a wonderful alteration in my appearance?"

This was a false move on the young lady's part, which M. Jean was not slow in following up.

"To-day," he said, "when the postman came with the letters to the school, I saw one among the bundle which had a foreign stamp, and was directed to——"

Minnie sprang from her chair, and facing M. Jean with flashing eyes and palpitating bosom said,—

"By what right, sir, do you pry into our affairs—what cause have you to do so?"

M. Jean also rose, and, shrugging his shoulders at the angry outburst from Minnie's lips, answered,—

"If Mademoiselle will only listen for one moment I will tell her that I did not pry into her business. Will Mademoiselle hear me?"

"Proceed, sir."

Assured now that she had received a letter from the same place as that which the Doctor's came from, he soon concocted a plausible story, which seemed so truthful that the young girl's indignation passed away as soon as it had arisen.

"You know, Mademoiselle," he said, "that I have many letters from my own country, and this morning, when I saw the postman come to the school I went towards him, for I was in a great trouble for a letter, and when he told me there was not one for me, I said, 'There is one with a foreign postmark there,' and he said, 'No, that is from Australia, and for Miss Oakplank.' This, Mademoiselle, is the truth."

"I believe your statement, Monsieur, and apologize for my haste, for I did not wish the receipt of that letter to be known to every one."

M. Jean placed his hand over his heart, and with a bow that would have broken an Englishman's back, said,—

"Mademoiselle can trust one whose family belonged to the old nobility of France—the knowledge shall never go beyond my lips."

"I am grateful for this assurance, Monsieur, for—for——"

"Do not let Mademoiselle distress herself, for the time will soon come when the young gentleman will be released from——"

Minnie gave a startled cry, as the thought of the request her youthful lover had made in his letter—a request that none should know of his existence, for he hoped that the guard's story of having shot him would be accepted, and in time he could return to England, under another name, and without that haunting fear of being recognized as an escaped convict.

Knowing his wish for secrecy, no wonder the astonished girl gave that exclamation of surprise when she heard M. Jean make use of an expression which revealed his knowledge of Gleddell's existence.

M. Jean paused as she gave utterance to this exclamation, but finding she remained without speaking, he resumed,—

"He will soon be released, for the good Doctor will see the Home Secretary, and then all will be right again."

Minnie smiled at the Frenchman's words, and before she could make any remark about the improbability of the great official M. Jean had named taking any interest in a request from the good-hearted schoolmaster, M. Jean suddenly asked,—

"Where is Mademoiselle Eleanor? Surely she will not go to the garden upon a night so cold as this?"

Minnie looked sadly at her sister, who was now slowly walking towards the little summer-house, wherein she had passed so many hours of happiness with poor Philip Randall.

She would have joined her sister, but M. Jean, with excessive solicitude, told her that the air was too damp and cold for her to leave the room until she had a warm wrapper over her shoulders.

"I will go, mademoiselle," he said, in conclusion, "and bring your sister back from her lonely walk."

Before Minnie could utter a word he passed out upon the lawn, and when the young girl saw him join her sister she went upstairs to fetch a shawl, in case poor Eleanor should re-refuse to return to the house.

When descending from her bedroom she was startled by the well-known hasty rap which announced her father's return from London, for the old fellow had been there for some time, trying to get sufficient interest to obtain a commutation of Gleddell's sentence.

Minnie opened the door to the bluff old fellow, and was much astonished when, instead of saluting her pouting lips, he rushed into the little sitting-room, and while divesting his neck of a thick woollen wrapper, he blurted out,—

"A whole week lost!—six days gone, and then they tell me the boy was shot by a d—— confounded marine—shot by a—a—ahem! red-coated, pipe-clayed marine!"

"Papa, what is the matter?"

"Matter—eh! Don't you know, eh?—don't you know they've sent our boy—your boy—my boy to Davy Jones, with an ounce of lead in his body, sent him—eh? what the dev—ahem—what are you laughing at? Don't I speak plain!"

"Quite plain, papa."

"Do you mean to say, you—you she-pirate, that you grin when I tell you a—ahem—rascally marine has put a leaden ball in our boy's back—in Gled's back, and sent him to Davy Jones? Do you understand that?"

"Yes, papa."

"Yes, papa! Hen-coops and jibbooms! six-water-grog and banyan days! Has the girl gone mad? Why don't you pipe your eye—go into squalls—capsize—do anything, but stand there grinning like a Gibraltar monkey with a pain in his side?"

The old sea-dog had worked himself into a state of passion at his child's supposed heartlessness, and by this time he was dancing round the room like a cat on a hot gridiron.

Minnie caught the old fellow as he was executing a war-dance in the corner, and putting her hands upon his shoulders, said,—

"He is not killed, papa."

"Eh? you pirate in petticoats!"

"Read this, papa; it came this morning."

Very hot and very red the old fellow perused the letter Gleddell had despatched from Sydney, and when he had finished, a broad grin broke over his face, and returning the precious missive to Minnie, he chuckled,—

"He has forereached upon them this time, girl! Ha, ha! the confounded big-wigs! Ho—ho—ho! But where's 'Lenor, you—— Ho! belay, there, you French privateer! you frog-eating son of a——"

The last word was inaudible, as he dashed into the garden, flourishing his stick. He had turned towards the glass door just in time to behold M. Jean drop on his knees before Eleanor, and in spite of her evident reluctance at his suit, the Frenchman was making frantic efforts to seize her hand, while he poured forth his protestations of eternal fidelity.

The Captain's hasty step and loud voice caused M. Gailland to gather himself up, and catching sight of the big stick the old sailor carried, he made the best use of his legs to escape.

With the agility of an elephant the startled Frenchman clambered over the gate, and just as he was in the act of descending over the other side, the thick oaken cudgel fell upon his head, and a voice called out,—

"Stop, you privateer!—stop, you—ha, ha, ha!—ho, ho, ho! he's caught like a fly in a spider's web!"

Poor M. Jean, in his hurry to clear the gate, the existence of a row of spikes escaped his notice, and by the time the Captain had closed with him he was fast to the top, the spikes having passed through a portion of his clothing, and held him—powerless to extricate himself—powerless to escape the swift and heavy blows of the old sailor's cudgel.

CHAPTER XLVII.

A FRIEND IN NEED.

No sound, save the lone cry of a wild-fowl in a neighbouring swamp, was heard for some minutes after the bushranger came to an abrupt halt before the muzzles of Luke and Gleddell's levelled pieces.

It was a strange scene: the wild picturesque forms of the bushmen—the two kneeling figures behind the fallen tree, and the pale-faced woman crouching in silent terror, her eyes alternately wandering from her husband to the savage-looking group who had halted at the sight of the determined man and his young companion.

Miriam looked wildly around in the hope of seeing the police magistrate and the armed troopers who escorted him; but nothing met her gaze save the undulating expanse of country, alternating in ridges and hollows like the waves of the sea.

At last the grim leader of the desperate gang spoke; and as he did so, his face had more of the brute than anything human in its expression.

"Tracked you to earth, you cursed varmints!" he said; "and now you shall pay for the way in which you set the traps (police) upon us."

"I am not a child," Luke said, "to be frightened by the words of a cowardly ruffian; so let me warn you that the first step you take, a bullet will find its way to your skull."

The coolness in which these words were uttered, the calm resolute expression of the speaker's face, were not without their effect upon the savage Hercules.

"We are six to your two," he said, "so you have but little chance of escape; but before I shoot you down like a durned skunk, as you are, tell me what you told the traps, that they came upon us before we had time to get our horses saddled? Do you hear that? we have lost our cattle, and——"

The fellow's rage got the better of him when the remembrance of this loss came upon him, and, pausing in his speech, he brought his rifle to his hip.

"Raise your gun another inch," said Luke, "and I pull the trigger! Remember, although I may fall the next moment, my first shot will be at you."

The bushranger mechanically lowered his piece; for, in spite of the brute courage he possessed, he had no wish to become a target, even though his followers should triumph in the end.

"Let us pursue our way in peace," said Luke, "although I should be but doing an act of justice were I to shoot you down where you stand, I will leave that to those who are upon your track."

"Why, you durned reptile!" shouted the ruffian, "you speak as though you were the stronger and we were the weaker party; so come out, and give up your arms, or the shooting will be on this side."

"You will not participate in it," Luke said coolly. "Remember my warning! the least attempt to use gun or pistol by you or your party, and I rid the colony of a murderer."

"Murderer!" repeated Illjurra. "Who the——"

He stopped abruptly as one of the men whispered a few words in his ear, and, when the fellow had finished, Illjurra, with a loud laugh, exclaimed,—

"Certainly; why didn't I think of it before? Away to the timber!"

His words were followed by the hasty retreat of his men, and before Luke had time to stay them they passed swiftly within the enclosure of a belt of trees wich faced the fallen log.

"The trick is not new," muttered Luke, "but, nevertheless, dangerous to us."

"They're gone," Gleddell said, joyfully; "thank heaven we have been spared the sin of taking away a fellow-creature's life!"

"Not so fast, Gled," said Luke, placing his hand upon the boy's shoulder, for in the excitement of the moment he had risen from his couchant position, and exposed his body above the prostrate trunk. "Keep down, lad, they have but taken to the trees as a better way of putting a bullet or two——"

"I see—I understand," the boy hastily answered; "they think to murder us without any danger to themselves."

"Right, lad; but if our ammunition holds out, we may be able to keep off those devils until the police officer and his troopers, attracted by our firing, returns this way. Ha! look out, lad!"

The warning came only in time, for the bullet fired by Illjurra cut a piece out of the bark of the fallen tree, then clipped a piece out of Gleddell's cap.

"An inch lower," the boy coolly remarked, "and it would have been my head instead."

Luke turned an admiring glance upon the lad, who could exhibit such perfect self-possession in a moment like this.

"Keep a sharp look-out," he said, "for any part of their body that may show when they take aim, but do not fire until you are sure of your ball taking effect."

Gleddell nodded an affirmative, and Luke, bidding his trembling wife to draw closer beneath the shelter of the log, quietly awaited the next move of their foe.

Between the belt of trees and the fallen log there grew a patch of brushwood; this again, being upon one of the ridges of the undulating ground, afforded Luke and his companion a partial screen from the bushrangers.

Thus, whenever they wished to fire a shot at the kneeling pair, it was necessary, in order to denote their position, for the bushmen to step a few paces forward from their place of shelter.

This advantage Luke was not slow to perceive.

"Gleddell," he said, "can you place your cap on the upper part of the log, as though it still remained upon your head?"

"Easily," replied the boy, suiting the action to the word.

"That," Luke said, "will bring a shot or two this way, so keep close while the lead is flying about, then as they make for the timber, keep that bush between you and fire. Be careful not to expose an inch of your body more than you can help."

"I understand," answered Gleddell, "and thanks to that bush, we have a slight advantage over those gentlemen."

Ping! came a bullet through the boy's cap, and Luke, who had waited with his finger upon the trigger, brought his gun to the shoulder and fired.

A yell of derision told his non-success, and six shots came in quick succession from among the trees.

Gleddell heard a smothered cry from Luke, and turning, beheld his friend place his hand to his shoulder.

"You are hit, Luke?" he anxiously asked.

"Merely a scratch—look out."

The warning was not lost upon Gled, who instantly dropped flat upon the ground.

Two of the bushrangers had ascended one of the tallest trees, and with their six-shooters began to pepper away at the resolute pair.

The elevation served Gleddell's purpose admirably, for during the time Miriam was binding Luke's arm, he shot down one of the pair.

"Bravo, Gled!" said Luke; "the second bird will not stay there long."

So it turned out, for the fellow, evidently dismayed by the fate of his comrade, began to drop from branch to branch, until he finally disappeared among the trees.

"I only hope," Luke said, "that my arm will not get stiff, for these fellows are trying a fresh move."

There was no trace of them visible for some time after the last shot of Gleddell's, and the pair began to entertain a sanguine hope that they could resume their journey in peace.

In another moment they would have left the shelter of the log, had not a warning cry from Miriam caused them to look towards a mass of underwood which grew in their rear.

Here the moving of the fragile tops denoted the passage of either men or animals through the closely-packed stems.

Luke Jessop's ignorance of the Australian country made him doubt for some moments that the movement was caused by anything larger than a hare or animal of similar size.

With Gleddell the case was different. He had gleaned much knowledge from books, so placing his finger reprovingly upon Luke's wrist, he whispered,—

"Be careful, the way in which those bushes are agitated proves the passage of something larger than a kangaroo."

Their suspense did not last much longer, for issuing from among the scrub came the heads of two of Illjurra's gang, and at the same instant from among the timber came Illjurra and two of his companions.

"Ho, ho, ho!" yelled the ruffian, "trapped ye durned varmints, trapped by ——"

He did not finish his impious word, for Luke, driven to desperation at seeing himself thus helplessly in their power, brought his piece to the present, and fired both barrels at the mocking desperado.

"You, at least," he said, "shall not live to triumph over our death."

Both bullets struck the Hercules in the chest, and with a wild scream of agony he threw his hands up and fell forward upon his face.

Luke clubbed his weapon, determined to sell his life dearly, for he fully expected the bushmen would at once close upon him, or at any rate come so near that he would be riddled by their revolvers.

Strange to say, the daring act seemed to appal them, for they stood looking at each other evidently expecting that Gleddell's piece would next deprive one of them of life.

Their irresolution was Luke's opportunity, so quickly recharging his piece, he placed the caps on the nipples, and, pointing to the two fellows who had crept through the brushwood, he whispered to Gleddell,—

"Let us drive these fellows back; it is better to have the foe on one side instead of two."

The boy was quickly beside the speaker, but before they had taken a dozen paces towards the ruffianly pair, the latter sprang to their feet and fairly turned tail and broke through the scrub, and were soon beside their companions.

"You see," Luke said, "how easy it is for men to become disorganized. The fall of their leader has rendered them almost powerless."

"A state," Gleddell said, "in which I hope they may continue until we are safe out of this scrape."

"Numbers will give them courage, and in a few minutes they will be as eager for our blood as a pack of wolves."

"The adders are not so bad as they were," Gleddell said, "so let us hope we are not doomed to leave our bones to bleach in this strange place."

"I hope not, lad. Ha! they are reviving! Come behind the friendly log—quick! for your life!"

The four ruffians had evidently made up their minds to end the strife, for, shoulder to shoulder, they advanced upon their stubborn foes, each armed with a pair of six-barrelled revolvers.

"Gled," Luke said, between his clenched teeth, "each of those fellows has twelve shots —forty-eight against our four. It is useless to hold out against them. I'll try what a scramble will do."

As the last word left his lips they began to open fire, then as suddenly faced about and made for the timber.

This act was so unexpected by Luke, that he could not refrain from sending the contents of his piece after them; and before he could reload, the patter of horses' feet was heard upon the soft grass.

"The mounted police!" said Luke; "thank God, we are saved!"

It was the magistrate and the constables, and as they galloped into the open between the bush and the timber, the officer said to his men,—

"Follow them, my lads! Remember the reward. Dead or alive, bring them back."

The troopers' spurs struck sharply into their horses' flanks, and in a moment they were out of sight.

BOOK THE SECOND.—CHAPTER 1.

A STRANGE DISCOVERY.

THE officer dismounted, and, turning Illjurra over upon his face, exclaimed,—

"Illjurra! and shot!—ha!"

His hand sought the butt of his revolver as Luke and Gleddell stepped out from their place of shelter, but, leaving the weapon as soon as he recognized the friends, he said,—

"This is your work I suppose?"

"It is," Luke answered. "We have been keeping these fellows at bay for the last two hours, and, if I mistake not, you will find another somewhere among those trees."

"You have done well," said the officer; "for not only have you rid the colony of a a nuisance, but earned FIVE HUNDRED POUNDS."

Luke repeated the officer's concluding words with a feeling akin to that of one who has been suddenly raised from poverty to riches.

In his present need this sum was to him a vast fortune, and dazzled by the unexpected manner it had fallen to his lot, he became lost to all that passed around him.

From this state he was aroused by his wife's voice, and her lowly-spoken words went to his heart as she said,—

"Touch it not, Luke. It is the price of a human life—one as precious as your own."

Miriam's words were not without an effect upon Luke, and the mind which a moment before had been dazed by the magnitude of the reward for capturing the bushranger, dead or alive, now recoiled from taking money for shedding a fellow-creature's blood.

"Wife," he said, as standing over the fallen man he looked strangely at the form which but a short time before had been ndued with life, "you are right; for although our present need would make a man take money from a source more questionable than this, I feel that a curse would attend the possession of the amount received for the wretched man's death."

Miriam thanked him with a look, and moved away from the vicinity of the fallen man; for the police-officer, with a coolness which the constant familiarity with such scenes had given him, turned the body over, and began to search his pockets.

He paused in his task, and suddenly springing to his feet, exclaimed,—

"He lives!"

Luke and Gleddell drew near at the officer's exclamation, and beheld the bushranger open his eyes and move, moan some indistinct words, the only one which could be understood was "Water!"

Gleddell waited not for the word to be repeated, but running to a small stream which flowed at the base of the belt of trees, he filled his boot with the sparkling liquid.

He drank greedily, and for a few moments seemed to be recovering his former strength; but as he attempted to rise, an expression of intense anguish came over his features, and he fell back with a groan of agony upon his lips.

"You do not bleed from your wounds," said the officer, "so do not allow yourself to believe you will ever leave this spot alive."

The glassy wild-looking eyes, and the face with death stamped so plainly on each lineament, vouched for the truth of the officer's words.

The bushranger knew it too, for after some vain gasping efforts to speak, he said, at intervals,—

"I know it—I feel it—do not move me—let me die in peace."

A ghastly serenity had come over the dying man's face as the bitterness of his physical agony passed away—once only his eyes lit up with a savage gleam, then it was when Luke, stricken with remorse at taking the life of a fellow-creature, knelt beside the dying man, and asked if he had any message to leave.

The fierce expression died away before Luke had finished speaking, and Illjurra in a feeble voice asked the police-officer to kneel beside him.

The magistrate obeyed, and, with an open book in his hand, prepared to take down in writing any directions the dying outlaw might wish to leave.

"Closer," he gasped, "everything is getting dark, and I see them coming to me — oh, God! they are here! — and you ——"

He raised himself upon one hand for a moment, as his mind became stronger than his physical power, and screamed,—

"You devil! you deserved it!—you, Greymore—fiend!—beast!—curse you!"

He fell back, and so still and rigid became the features after this outburst, that those who stood and knelt by him thought he had passed the mystic portals of eternity.

Luke Jessop, with every limb quivering with excitement, anxiously watched the lineaments of the bushranger's face, and feeling cold and hot by turns, as a dim suspicion that he had found the man he sought came across his mind.

"He's gone," the magistrate said, closing his book, "to a higher tribunal than he would have found had he lived; let us hope he will meet with more mercy there than he has shown to——"

"Gone! gone! impossible!" said Luke, excitedly; "he must live, if but to——. Hear," he added, placing his head close to the bushranger's ear, "Pierre! Pierre Dublé!"

The eyes here unclosed, and the death film must have been over them, for the bushranger, evidently filled with a powerful emotion by the utterance of that name, strove to see through the darkness which was closing around him, and gasped, faintly,—

"Who calls me by that name? I—I——"

Here the voice became inaudible, and the blue lips moved in the vain attempt to complete the sentence.

"See you Helen Walden's form, as dragged from the Seine's black waters your——"

A shiver passed over the dying prostrate form as Luke gave utterance to these words, and with an effort of the will which for a moment shook off death's cold fingers, he said,—

"Who speaks of Helen? She is avenged! Seek in that quiet English churchyard for that fiend's body, and they will tell you he was found dead—dead. My—my—hand sent him into—to——"

The death rattle choked his words, the white limbs quivered, then became still, and the magistrate rising, said,—

"He has gone!"

Luke moved not, but sat like one bereft of all power of volition. This condition endured for some moments; then wringing his hands in the bitterness of his despair, he said,—

"Merciful Father! give him but a moment's life that he may divulge that terrible secret and save the innocent!"

The magistrate's professional instinct was aroused by these words, and turning to look at Luke, he asked,—

"You have met this man before, then?"

This question recalled Luke to himself, and rising, he answered the magistrate,—

"Never! but by his agency I have been rendered childless. See you not the merciful unerring hand of an offended God in this? I came to this land to kill that man, and my vow has been kept."

"A strange coincidence," said the magistrate; "or shall I say a retribution guided by the unerring finger of the Deity? When you are calmer I should like to hear your story; it must be a strange one."

"It is," said Luke; and turning to Gleddell he continued, "Take my wife from this scene, lad, it is not fitted for a woman's sight."

Gleddell obeyed, and when he had led Miriam out of sight of that ghastly corpse, Luke told the officer how his child had been taken away by Greymore, and the mock ceremony of marriage which had taken place, the rigid form now before them having played the part of priest and deceived the child-like girl.

"I was wealthy then," Luke said; "and every shilling I possessed I spent in tracking the villain who stole my child. Three years passed in the wearying search. I returned to England a ruined broken-hearted childless man; but, Heaven be praised! I have been spared to avenge her loss upon one of her betrayers—would it had been the other!"

"That other?" said the magistrate, interrogatively: "is he alive?"

"Dead!" was the sombre reply; "killed by the hand of his——ha!"

Luke suddenly remembered the mark by which he should know Greymore's murderer, and stopping abruptly, he went towards the bushranger's cold form, and baring the right arm beheld the red scar where the dying Greymore's teeth had met.

The broad-brimmed hat had fallen from the outlaw's head, and there across the forehead was a diagonal scar.

"There can be no doubt of his identity now," Luke said; "here is the mark of the gendarme's sabre—here, again, is the impression of his victim's teeth."

The magistrate made a note of these marks, and Luke left the body and again stood by the officer's side.

"Had he lived but a few minutes longer," he said, "your evidence would have released an innocent man from the clutches of the law."

"This man's life," said the officer, "seems to have been a curse to all with whom he came in contact."

"Not so much his as the villain who died by his hand."

"This Greymore?"

"Yes," Luke said, "and for that crime an innocent man has been charged, and when I left England his intellect had been shattered by the unmerited disgrace which had fallen upon him, and he lay in a madhouse, awaiting but the return of reason to be brought before his judges."

"But," said the magistrate, "is the evidence so complete against him that you fear he will suffer for that murder?"

"Complete in every link. The murdered man had some weighty secret in his keeping respecting the accused, and they were known to have quarrelled and fought a short time before the deed took place. Again, Greymore, with his dying breath, accused the unhappy man of being the assassin, and to complete the chain of evidence, Philip Randall's pistol was found near the scene of the murder, the butt showing but too well how it had been employed. This, I believe, was the strongest

THE BOYS OF BIRCHAM SCHOOL.

JACK STANFIELD AND HIS FATHER.

point against him, for the fellow-weapon was found in his room."

"Philip Randall!" the magistrate repeated, musingly, "I once knew a boy of that name, an old schoolfellow——oh, here's my troopers returned, and empty handed."

As he spoke the men trotted through the trees, and pulled up when within a few paces of their chief.

"The rascals eluded us," said one of the men, "by taking to the bush."

"It can't be helped," said their chief, "one of you ride into the township for a dray, for we must get this body there for the coroner's inquest."

One of the troopers turned his horse's head away and was soon out of sight."

"Now," said the magistrate, "I think the best plan will be for you and your companion to mount a couple of the bushrangers' horses. Meanwhile my man goes in quest of them I will finish searching

No. 16.

Illjurra's pockets, for these rascals often have little things that come very useful to us in tracking others of the same profession."

The search was productive of but little in the shape of evidence against those who had escaped, and just as the officer was about to give the task up as hopeless, he felt a hard substance between the lining of the dead man's pocket.

"I thought so," he muttered, as he cut away the cloths and took out a flat tin box, the usual receptacle for the Australian's money and papers.

Unfastening the string which was bound several times round the tin case, he opened the lid, and found, beside a trifling sum in money, several pieces of paper, covered with writing in pencil.

After an examination the magistrate gave utterance to an exclamation of disappointment, then said,—

"Confound the fellow, he has kept his diary in French."

"I will translate it," said Luke, "my residence in the French capital has made me master of the language."

The officer handed the box to Luke, then lighting a cigar, awaited the arranging of the small pile of closely-written sheets, which Luke was carefully placing according to their various dates.

It was a task of no little difficulty, for paper had evidently become scarce after Pierre took to the work, and he had pencilled across the lines which were written before he came to the colony.

CHAPTER II.

A PICTURE FROM LIFE.

It occupied above an hour the reading of the strange jottings left by the dead bushranger, and when Luke had become sufficiently master of their contents, he found that Pierre's days had been but a succession of crimes, and had the death which that day overtook him happened ten years before, it would have been better for many who knew the renegade, who turned out to be an Englishman instead of a native of sunny France.

The out-station of the mounted police was not far from the place where the bushranger had met his death, so when the trooper returned with the led horse, Luke bestrode the charger which had so few hours before been ridden by Pierre Dublé; before him Miriam was placed, and when Gleddell had mounted his horse the magistrate said,—

"It may be some hours before the dray reaches here from the township, and as there seems every prospect of a storm. I think our best plan will be to stay at the huts until the weather clears."

Luke assented, and, led by the magistrate, the party were soon in motion, and going at a quick pace towards the station.

There is nothing so exhilarating as the pleasure one feels when seated upon a grand horse—to the youngest of the party, whose mind had been powerfully affected by the later sorrows, the sharp trot through the bush restored his somewhat languid mind, and he so far forgot the ghastly form which lay with upturned face towards that heaven which he had in life so often offended.

Luke was silent during the journey; his thoughts were evidently centered upon the strange workings, of what he could not but think was the hand of Him who notes our most trifling act.

Miriam, although her heart yearned to ask her husband some particulars of those papers which had been found on the bushranger, but knowing her husband's mood she refrained from breaking in upon his profound reverie.

The magistrate and his subordinate rode side by side, seemingly the only two that were at ease, for from time to time a burst of laughter coming from their lips would startle the remainder of the little cavalcade.

In this manner the station was reached, and Gleddell, with boy-like aptitude for adapting himself to his new life, assisted the trooper to hobble the horses and prepare the simple meal which the hut afforded.

A blazing log-fire soon boiled the water, for the Australian scarcely ever partakes of a meal without the cheering pot of tea, the pot, or billy as it is termed, by the way, serves both for kettle and teapot.

Gleddell also assisted in the manufacture of the damper; and by the time the meal was ready, Luke's brow was less moody, and he joined in the somewhat boisterous merriment of the frank genial young magistrate.

When the meal was over, the officer lit a cigar, Luke and the troopers their pipes, and the party, drawing closer around the ruddy logs, began to converse like men who had known each other for years.

The magistrate told several stories of daring adventures which had befallen him since he had been appointed chief officer of that district, and Luke and Gleddell listened with profound interest to the wild recitals.

"A strange community," said Luke, "this man who fell to-day is, I should say, a fair type of the outlaws who render the colony anything but safe for those who have farms or cattle runs in lonely districts."

"They would be safe enough," said the officer, "were it not for the collusion between the farm hands and the bushrangers."

"While this state of things exists," said Luke, "there will be no means of stopping the evil."

"I fear not," was the reply; "for the state of feeling against the employers is antagonistic, that no matter whether a man may be a good or bad master they suffer alike, and as a matter of course a good man will soon become as harsh as those who were the primary cause of the enmity between employers and employées."

"A sad state of things," said Luke, "and one I fear will not be altered until the colonists dispense with convict labour."

"Some time must elapse before that takes place," said the young magistrate; "for at present people emigrate with the idea of being rich in a few months, and prefer the danger of the gold-fields to accepting a remunerative situation upon a farm."

"There is some truth in this," assented Luke; "but time, I suppose, will bring all things right."

"I hope so," said the officer; "for I am heartily tired of the shooting down and hanging which goes on here from day to day and from week to week."

The patter of horses' hoofs outside the hut caused Luke to pause in his reply, and soon after a stalwart trooper entered the station, and told the officer that Illjurra's body was on its way to the township.

"Very well," said the magistrate; "lead your horse round to the stable, as we shall stay here to night."

The man saluted and withdrew; then the officer said to Luke,—

"I suppose you will stay here to-night? By the bye, are you going much farther?"

"To Broken Falls."

"Broken Falls, eh? I forgot. You wish to take the vacant overseership?"

"I do," Luke said; "and hope I shall not be forestalled."

"I think I can answer for that," said the young officer; "for Mr. Russell has determined to keep the post vacant until he can secure the services of a stranger."

Luke's eyes brightened.

"May he keep this resolution," he said, "until I reach the farm."

The magistrate glanced at Luke's determined face and muscular form as he said,—

"The place would suit you, and you the place; and should you accept it, I have a little advice to offer; that is, if you are open for advice.

"I shall esteem it a favour."

"Well," the officer said, "be guided by me, and do not place any confidence in any of the hands upon the farm, especially a clerical-looking Scotchman. I hate the fellow, and feel morally convinced that he is at the bottom of all the mischief that has been done lately; but hitherto he has been too cunning for the smartest of my fellows."

"What is his name and occupation?"

"His name is James M'Elvry—his occupation a shepherd."

"I will watch him," Luke said, "should I be fortunate enough to secure the overseer's berth."

"You will do that; for your promise I thank you much."

"It shall be kept."

It was, as will be seen hereafter, kept too well for Mr. James M'Elvry.

The conversation here turned upon subjects that would but weary the reader were it recapitulated, and the darkness soon after coming upon the earth, Miriam retired to the little chamber which the troopers had placed at Luke's disposal.

After she had left the room, pipes were again lit, some fresh logs placed upon the fire, and one of the men bringing a bottle of rum from his little store, the billy was filled with water, and the party prepared to pass the evening in more comfort than had hitherto fallen to the lot of the travellers.

The papers left by the dead bushranger were brought out by Luke, and amid an attentive silence he translated their contents into English.

The task was long and difficult, and the lovely moon had long been in her zenith when Luke read the last words of that too unhappily true picture of life.

It appeared from the disjointed fragments of that strange sinful career through which the bushranger had passed, that he once belonged to that wretched tribe of outcasts—that plague-spot upon the rich and mighty metropolis—the street Arabs. Thus, filling up certain gaps in the outlaw's autobiography, was the story told:—

"ILLJURRA'S HISTORY.

"My parents, at the time of my birth, lived in one of those pestilential alleys near Golden Lane, and among the ragged and degraded children of this locality was my infancy and childhood passed.

"My father was a labourer, and the little he earned by carrying the hod was spent a few hours after its receipt at the glaring gin-shop near the obscure nook in which we resided; a task, I may as well state, in which my mother was not slow to assist, and oft when they have been expelled from the gin-palace, penniless, drunk, and quarrelsome, has my thin carcase become a mark for their claws.

"They led a wretched life, those authors of my being—the man morose and brutal, the woman quarrelsome and a perfect mistress of the art of vituperative abuse. I often shudder when I think of my childhood, and wonder why people squander money in sending missions out to the blacks when there is so much need of their services in the very heart of London.

"It was not an unusual thing for my mother to have a pair of black eyes after a Saturday night. When my father was in work, as a rule, his head was swathed in a dirty pocket handkerchief, like my mother's organs of sight were they ornamented, for the gentle creature was in the habit of straightening the poker across my paternal parent's skull, and loud were her praises sung by the neighbours after one of these fearful scenes.

"Years have passed since they were placed in the quiet grave, but the memory of the scenes I then beheld is still strong upon me.

"Then came the cold winter, and when we needed fire and clothing my hapless parent was out of employ. Many a cold morn have I seen him leave our wretched room, a piece of bread tied in a dirty rag, and with this in his pocket has he walked miles in search of employ.

"With the darkness he would return, and if unsuccessful in his search, bitter was the greeting he received; if otherwise, I used to be bundled from the fire, and expressing her words with an oath, she used to tell me,—

"'Get out of the way, you unfeeling little wretch, and let your father sit down. Poor fellow! he has to get up and go to work to-morrow.'

"A warm basin of tea and sundry edibles would reward him for having obtained employment, but woe to the unhappy wretch if he had been unsuccessful.

"Then the shrill voice would be raised, and I become an object of interest.

"'Look at your poor child, you lazy hulking vagabond,' she would scream; 'see how his feet are frozen with the cold, while you, in place of working like a man, walk about like a gentleman.

"I have seen the piece of dry bread enveloped in its dirty wrapper when my father started in the morning, and listening to my mother's words, used to wonder whether gentlemen walked about with pieces of stale bread in their pockets.

"There was no warm tea upon an occasion of this sort, and the moody man, without deigning to reply to his helpmate's words, would sneak into his wretched bed and make up for the loss of food by an extra quantity of sleep.

"This life my parents led left me pretty much my own master, and with many as ragged and hungry as myself I used to wander about the dirty neighbourhood, fighting for the turnip-parings and cabbage-stalks which we found in the gutters.

"I had but little knowledge until I reached the age of fourteen, then I began to understand why some boys whom I alternately played and fought with, were suddenly taken away and put in prison for taking something. I was then ignorant that it was wrong to steal. I knew it was dangerous, so kept from it as long as I could.

CHAPTER III.

THE BUSHRANGER'S CONFESSION.

"ABOUT this time my parents died, and I was left to my own resources, and my first thought was how I could satisfy the cravings of hunger—for when the parish shells took away the bodies of my parents, the landlord seized the few miserable articles of furniture we possessed, and I was turned out to starve or steal.

"I chose the latter, and at first confined myself to purloining articles of food; but by degrees I became bolder, and panted to do something which would make me rich, for the possession of a few shillings was at that time a mine of wealth, and as I had never possessed a silver coin in my life, I ardently looked forward to the time when my longings should become an established fact.

"The opportunity came at last. A venerable gentleman, with some vague ideas of bettering the condition of the wretched neighbourhood, came amongst us; and to add more force to the lecture he intended to give about the squalor of the dirty courts, selected me as being the most ragged and deplorable of the filthy children to serve as an illustration of the truthfulness of our benighted condition.

"From some cause—possibly a dislike to having such a leper as myself amongst them—the philanthropic ladies and gentlemen would not attend the old party's lecture if I was brought in the room.

"He was not long in getting over the difficulty. He would have a picture from life! and I stood for the model.

"Never shall I forget the old fellow's delight when, seated before my picture, he shaded his eyes with his hands, and exclaimed to the artist,—

"'Capital! Capital! This must convince them!'

"It was pleasant to see the manner in which he rubbed his hands together, as he compared my pinched face and ragged clothes with the picture; and how my heart beat and my eyes glistened when I saw him count out quite a small heap of bright sovereigns to the artist.

"How my eyes greedily followed the painter, as he collected the price of his labour and placed them in a small drawer in the table against which I had been wont to stand, when the artist transposed my wretched figure to the canvas.

"For six days I had stood to the artist, and during the whole of that time I existed *honestly*. A doorway had been my bed-chamber, my bed the stones, my pillow an inch or two of the step which came beyond that door.

"The refuse vegetables and damaged fruit I picked up at Covent Garden Market had supplied me with food; the pump opposite the church had given me drink.

"I had heard, I don't know where, that artists were in the habit of giving large sums for people to sit as models, and putting down my reward as low as sixpence per hour, I calculated I should receive at least six shillings.

"What bright prospects I saw the possession of this sum would give me! I could buy a basket and sell apples, fish, shrimps, or any commodity which could be obtained for the prospective sum. And now the moment had arrived when I should be in possession of all this wealth.

"I could have cried with joy, but the pale stern face of the melancholy artist awed me, and I stood after the philanthropist had gone, trembling and frightened almost to breathe.

"The artist seemed to have forgotten me, for he continued to add little touches to the picture, until at last, wearied with his work, he put aside his pallette and brush, then, taking his hat and coat, was on the point of leaving the room, when his eye fell upon me.

"'Ah,' he said, 'I had forgotten. Here, boy.'

"His hand went to his pocket, I heard the jingle of silver, and involuntarily stretched forth my dirty hand; he placed a coin upon the ledge of his easel, and, pointing to it, said,—

"'Here, take this.'

"A wild hope sprang up within my breast; I thought a half-sovereign at least was placed there, and with a glad cry I sprang forward and clutched my treasure.

"One look told me the extent of the man's generosity, and crushed my hopes— *it was a sixpence*.

"I took the coin, and, without a word, left the room; but as I descended the stairs all the black passion of my nature was aroused, and as I wept bitterly at my disappointment, I determined to watch the artist from the house, and return and steal the gold I had seen in the drawer.

"I saw him leave, and, reascending the stairs, I found, as I expected, that the door was locked; this troubled me but little, for there was a small window over the door, and, to my joy, it was open.

"Ten minutes afterwards, my brain reeling with joy, I slunk from the house— twenty-eight sovereigns in my pocket.

"Once out of the street in which the artist lived, I ran until I reached the steps which lead from King William Street to London Bridge.

"I had no purpose in going there; I wished to get as far as possible from the scene of my first great crime, and as I sat on the steps panting for breath, one hand over my treasure, the reflection came that, although in possession of so much money, I dared not purchase a piece of bread.

"I had sense enough to know that my forlorn appearance would not tally with the possession of so much gold, and by attempting to change a sovereign I felt I should risk both my liberty and my wealth.

"I was both tired and hungry, and while sitting on the cold steps wondering how I should procure food and a change of clothes without exciting the tradesmen's suspicion, the recollection of the sixpence the artist had given me came to my mind.

"Unfortunately, the coin was in the same pocket with the gold, and so great was my fear that I should be detected, that I dared not take the money from my pocket to find the small silver piece.

"I had just come to the determination to wait until night before I looked over my treasure, when a gentleman passed me carrying a carpet-bag; he paused when about a dozen yards from where I crouched, then calling me to him, gave me the carpet-bag, and said,—

"'Carry this to the boat, my lad.'

"I followed the gentleman on board the steam-packet, which was on the point of sailing for France, and after he had rewarded me with a few coppers, I, boy like, was enchanted with the appearance of the ship, and felt how much I should like to be upon the blue water.

"The wish was parent to the act of secreting myself on board; for I well knew that were I once upon a foreign soil I should be safe from the police, a safety my native town denied, while the artist possessed so faithful a likeness of the robber of his gold.

"I don't think I should have left England had not my personal appearance been in the painter's possession, for I knew when he discovered the robbery the police would see the picture, and my apprehension would soon follow.

"I remained among the cargo until the vessel was out of sight of England, then, by a lucky chance, I made the acquaintance of a boy who assisted the steward, and from him obtained the best meal I had ever partaken of in my life.

"I found my new acquaintance quite willing to give me a suit of his clothes for a couple of the bright gold pieces; thus attired, I went boldly on deck, and, acting upon my new friend's instruction, I paid my fare, and told the man that I had not time to do so before the vessel started.

"I took up my abode in France, and soon acquired sufficient of the language to make myself understood, and before I had been there long I obtained a situation in the stables of an English gentleman, but after a few years spent honestly, I decamped one night with all the valuables I could reach, and left my master to return to England without me."

"I lived upon my wits for many years after this, and so perfect had I become in the French language, that I was never suspected of being other than a son of the soil.

"My name, too, had been changed from Jack Davidson to Pierre Dublé, and under this name I made the acquaintance of the handsomest and most polished scoundrel that ever lived.

"He must have had a strange fascination of subduing all with whom he came in contact, for I was his veriest slave.

"There is one deed I committed under his guidance which haunts me to this hour. Greymore had persuaded a beautiful girl to elope with him from a boarding-school. Poor child! she was as good as she was beautiful, and though she had taken the fatal step, in leaving those with whom her father had placed her, she would live with him upon no other terms than his wife.

"I performed the ceremony for them—accursed be my tongue for that act—and when Greymore tired of his victim, he brutally told her of the mock-ceremony which had taken place.

"She received the intelligence without a muscle of her face moving, but I could see in the wild glitter of her eyes that she meditated something dreadful. I thought it would be against her betrayer, that her head could be raised but a few hours afterwards. When going to the gaming-house I saw her lifeless body brought from the dark waters of the Seine. I understood the meaning of that fearful startled look."

Here Luke broke off abruptly, and covering his face with his hands, groaned with anguish.

There are times when an attempt at consolation but adds to the sufferer's agony, it was so in this instance; so the young magistrate and Gleddell, who were both aware of the singular connection between this part of the bushranger's confession and the man who now sat with lowered head and shivering frame, so they remained silent until he had sufficiently recovered to resume the narrative.

Luke was feebler than usual, and his fingers trembled as he held the papers close to the flickering candle, and it was some time before his voice lost that strangely tremulous sound which tells so plainly of the hidden suffering and the strong efforts made to conceal it from his companions.

"I was with Greymore," Luke resumed, "at the time, and when his eyes fell upon the fair face and the long wavy tresses of his victim, he drew me away from the scene, and as a sneering expression came upon his handsome face, he said,

"'All women are not alike, Pierre, some would have found a different mode of alleviating their sorrow in this gay capital.'

"I could not answer him, for bad as I was, I felt strangely horrified by the sight, and from that day I began to hate and loathe the sight of my companion, and I should have parted from him even had he not been taken by the gendarmes for stabbing a young noble whom he had cheated at the gaming-table."

* * * * *

Here followed a mass of close writing

which related to the various artifices by which Pierre obtained a livelihood.

"Suddenly I heard that," Luke resumed, after he had placed these sheets aside, "he had escaped from the galleys with Jacques Cherdon, a fellow-convict, and one whom Greymore had by his devilish arts won over to rob his employers.

"Soon after I heard of their escape I found that the gendarmes were upon my track. Greymore having divulged our connection during his imprisonment.

"Twice I was nearly in their hands, and the second time my forehead was laid open by a sabre-cut, yet I escaped them and fled from France—one object alone in my thoughts—that, revenge for the cowardly manner in which Greymore had rejected my servile attachment to him.

"No Indian ever tracked a foe with a firmer longing to shed his blood than I lingered to have that handsome devil's life.

"I was rewarded, when I reached a quiet little village, not many miles from London, becoming face to face with my betrayer.

"I must confess that the old spell came upon me, and I quailed beneath his bitter stinging words; but at last he goaded me to a pitch of frenzy, and I left him waiting but for the night to come on to put my plans into execution.

"When darkness set in, and while I loitered near a large school, a window was thrown open, and I caught a momentary glimpse of a white arm extended out into the murky light, and before I had time to take a second look something fell heavily a few feet before me.

"Whatever it was had been thrown by that white hand, the window closed immediately after, and, to my surprise, when I picked the object from the ground, I found it was *a pistol*.

"Without thinking of the weapon, which I held by the muzzle, I went to the confines of the wood, which stood between the schoolhouse and the village, and among the trees awaited the coming of Edgar Greymore.

"He made the appointment, and selected the woody spot to give me a small sum of money that I might leave England; this was the promise he held out, but when we met beneath the quiet moonlight I saw the fiend-like glitter of his eyes, and during our conversation detected the gleam of a keen stiletto in his hand.

"I knew the purpose for which he had made the appointment, and, before he could use his deadly weapon, I caught him by the throat and killed him with a few blows of the heavy pistol-butt.

"He fought to the last, and in his dying agony fixed his teeth in my wrist—it was the final effort, and the next moment he lay at my feet a corpse.

"I rifled his pockets, but, before I had quite finished, the sound of coming footsteps caused me to flee, and twelve hours afterwards I was on board a vessel bound for Australia.

"When I reached the colony, I found that unless I toiled for my bread I should not be better off than if I had stayed in England; and while seeking for employment at the various farms, I came up with a party of bushrangers near the Mittagong range.

"Their wild life was congenial to my tastes, and I became a member of their band, and soon, by using more ferocity than my companions, and shooting down a troublesome overseer or two, I was elected their chief, and ——"

Here the strange confession ended, and Luke, placing the papers together, said to the young magistrate,—

"I think you had better take charge of this packet, and by endorsing it with your name and position, it may yet save an innocent man from the scaffold."

"I shall place the matter in the hands of the Colonial Secretary," answered the officer; "he will, I know, do everything in his power to save the unfortunate man."

That night Gleddell obtained writing materials from one of the troopers, and before he sought the repose he so much needed, he wrote a detailed account of the revelations in Illjurra's history which so deeply affected the unhappy family at Woodbine Cottage.

CHAPTER IV.

WHICH FOLLOWS THE FORTUNES OF HAPPY-GO-LUCKY AND JACK STANFIELD.

THE two friends, after their expulsion from Bircham School, in spite of the advice of their relatives, adhered to the resolution they had formed of visiting New South Wales for the purpose of ameliorating the condition of their old schoolmate, Stanton Gleddell.

It was no easy task to convince their relatives that they were doing right by thus voluntarily seeking the dangers which beset the traveller in the sparsely-peopled district where the convicts were portioned out to the colonists.

The lads laughed at the dangers thus set before them, and Happy, in reply to a long tirade from his uncle, replied,—

"Well, admitting the truth of your argument, we shall have no more to undergo than the settlers have had."

"True, my boy; but remember, you are not compelled to risk your safety by a Quixotic expedition to all the farms and cattle-runs in the district of Sydney, for you will have to do so until you find the object of your search."

"Perhaps so; but we shall benefit by the opportunity it will give us to see the country; and as for the expense, it will be much less than a tour on the continent, and more to my taste than seeing a succession of ugly towns."

The old gentleman shook his head as he gravely remarked,—

"Things are different now to what they were in my young days, Tom. We never thought of travelling hundreds of miles. No, lad; we left school and went to business fresh, and stayed there until we—that is, I——"

"Yes, uncle, until you made a fortune; and very commendable on your part," said the young rogue; "but I'm sure you would sooner know that I am in good health and riding through that splendid country than to see me with the edge of a mahogany desk against my chest, and dying by inches?"

The old gentleman looked over his gold-rimmed spectacles at his nephew's robust frame as he repeated,—

"Dying by inches?"

"Yes, uncle," Tom Dickson gravely replied, "you don't know my peculiar constitution. I can assure you that sedentary occupation would soon send me me in a rapid decline, unless"—he added artfully—"I travel a little before I begin business."

The old gentleman was sincerely attached to his brother's only child, and, being a bachelor, he looked upon Tom as fondly as he would had the lad been his own child.

He was a man of immense wealth, and Happy, whose father had died penniless, was in consequence quite dependent upon his uncle.

It had been the old gentleman's long-cherished hope that his boy would, on the completion of his schooling, enter one of the universities for a short time, then enter a large mercantile firm to gain a knowledge of business; for the old merchant thought it essential that his heir should learn this in case of an unforeseen turn of fortune.

Having looked forward for so long to the boy at once fulfilling the programme he had sketched out, it was a source of much discomfort that this sudden fit for travelling had come upon him.

"Still," the old fellow thought, "if it is really necessary for his health, and he'll promise to be careful, and not expose his precious life—and not stay too long away—why perhaps, after all, I may as well let him go."

The boy read the thoughts that were passing in his uncle's mind, and his frank ingenuous face became expressive of delight.

"I will not stay long in the colony, uncle," he said, "for, careless as I may have been in my duty to you, I love you none the less—boyish thoughtlessness must be my excuse; believe me, want of affection is not, nor has been, the cause of——"

"There—there, lad," the old fellow said, interrupting Happy, "I have no fault to find with you upon that point, and whatever disappointment I feel at the resolve you have taken will be felt less keenly when I think that the promptings of a good heart have more to do with this expedition than the benefit your health may derive from the change."

Happy-go-lucky blushed.

"There, don't blush because I have penetrated the true motives of this unappeasable desire to leave England. I think none the less of you for it. Now when do you propose going?"

"As soon," Tom Dickson answered, "as I hear from Jack Stanfield."

"Where is the young gentleman?"

"At his father's country house, and from the time that has elapsed I fancy he has found the task rather difficult to obtain his father's consent."

"Very likely——"

The postman's rat-tat sounded through the house, and a servant brought a letter from Jack. Happy soon read his friend's big epistle, and to the old gentleman's look of interrogation said,—

"He will be in London within twenty-four hours after the receipt of this."

"When does the next vessel leave?"

"In four days, uncle."

"Very well. Mind you have every necessary for your comfort, and I will give you a letter of credit upon a banker's in Sydney."

Happy thanked the old gentleman for his kindness, and his head filled with a lad's longing for a sight of the deep blue waters of the fathomless ocean, and the new life which awaited him in that country beyond the sea.

Happy's conjecture respecting his friend was correct, for Jack, who was an only child, had some difficulty in obtaining his father's permission to visit New South Wales.

Sitting over their wine in the luxurious dining-room of the old-fashioned country house, Jack broached the subject to his father.

He waited until Mr. Stanfield had reached his sixth glass of wine; then he startled the old gentleman by saying,—

"Without for a moment questioning the wisdom of your ideas respecting my future, I should, were the matter left to myself, prefer travelling a little before entering the house of the tutor you have selected for me."

Mr. Stanfield paused in the act of carrying the glass to his lips, and said,—

"But, my dear boy, you will see plenty of the world when you obtain your commission in the army."

"To a certain extent I shall, sir, but it will be in a different way to that which I should like."

"Different—how different?"

"Thus, sir," Jack answered: "we will suppose I have gone through the cramming necessary to pass the required examination——"

"Yes, yes. By the way, you are not doing justice to the bottle near you."

"Thanks; I have had sufficient."

"H'm! good lad! Glad to see you do not abuse the privilege I give you."

This seemed favourable, so Jack, warming with the wish so strong at his heart, said,—

"Having passed—which I should judge an easy matter, by the number of dolts that wear the Queen's uniform—I join my corps, and stay a year or two in barracks, at some out-of-the-way town, or possibly one of the dreary camps, such as Aldershot, Shorncliffe, or the Curragh."

"Well, even so, you are no worse off than many of our young aristocracy."

"True, sir. But to return. After a year or two of this distinguished service, the regiment is ordered to Malta, or India; unless a war breaks out; then I might stand a chance of being frozen to death by red-tape, as many of our gallant fellows were in the Crimea, and——"

"Boy! boy!" said the old gentleman, aghast; "I never heard the service spoken against in this manner before. My lamented father gave quite a different idea of his career in the army."

"Possibly, sir; but I believe you will find that mine is about as truthful as any sensible——"

Mr. Stanfield threw himself back in his chair, and, after a quiet chuckle, said,—

"Go on, you young republican! go on!"

"No, sir, I am not a republican. No one believes in loyalty and that sort of thing (as far as it goes) more than I do; but for the sake of wearing a red coat, and receiving carpenter's wages for so doing, I am not blind to the reverse side of the glorious prospect held out by being an officer in the British army."

"You young dog!" said Mr. Stanfield, secretly pleased at the lad's words, "it is a good thing for you that duelling is out of fashion."

"Why so, sir?"

"Because you would have to cross swords with every officer who knew of the manner in which you spoke of the service."

Jack laughed as he replied,—

"I should not fear that, judging from the specimens I have seen of the officer and gentleman; for to tell the honest truth, there are few among them who know the use of the weapon which hangs as an ornament at their hip."

"You young rebel! Go on—go on."

"I have done, sir; but as we are upon the subject, I may as well state that it is only in deference to your wishes that I consent to waste my early years in the intellectual occupation consistent with the duties of a modern officer."

"Upon my word, young gentleman, you —— but go on, and pray tell me what those duties are?"

"Chiefly a desire to learn whether Private Brown has pipe-clayed his belts properly, Private Jones has cleaned his boots, Private Robinson has secreted a small article in the folds of his bedding; then at times there is a change, in the onerous duties of being a member of a force called a court-martial—a pleasant change, because you can amuse yourself drawing caricatures upon the paper placed before you while an old martinet badgers a poor devil who dares not reply. This and the vapid conversation at the mess-table forms about the chief occupation of a man who throws away his money in the purchase of a commission."

"Upon my word, young gentleman," said his father, "I believe there is some truth in your words, although it puzzles me where you have obtained your information."

"From an old half-pay officer, father; one who not having the money to purchase his promotion, although a good and brave soldier, wasted his life in the service, and saw day by day mere boys rising step by step above him—not from merit, but by the aid of a well-filled purse."

Mr. Stanfield was silent for some time; it had been his wish that Jack should become an officer, but after the expression of these sentiments, he knew it would be wrong to press the point with the lad.

He knew perfectly well, except in a few instances, that his boy had given a truthful picture of the most important and, unfortunately for our military system, daily lives of officers quartered in barracks or camps; so, with a readiness which both pleased and surprised Jack, he said, after a few minutes inward communion,—

"Well, my boy, you shall travel. But what part of the world do you wish to see?"

"The colonies," answered Jack. "New South Wales; the district of Sydney first."

"Absurd," said the old gentleman. "No, Jack, do the Continent—Rome, Italy —that's the sort of thing; you will derive some benefit by that; but the place you have chosen I shall never give my consent to your visiting."

"May I ask, sir, why you do this?"

"You may; but you will be no wiser for asking. I do not wish you to go—let that be sufficient."

The old gentleman, evidently judging from Jack's flushed face that a scene would follow this refusal, hastily finished his glass of wine, and left the room.

"Well," Jack muttered, as he looked after his father, "that's enough to dishearten a fellow; but poor Gled shall not be deserted for the want of another effort."

He did not revert to the subject for some days, but allowed the old gentleman sufficient time to reflect over the hasty decision he had given.

When Jack again spoke about his unalterable determination, he found that his policy was the best way to attain the desired end; for Mr. Stanfield, after a long argument, finally gave in, and accorded his full permission for the lad to leave England in quest of his friend.

* * * * *

When the young adventurers reached the rapidly rising town of Sydney, they bought a couple of strong horses, and in the holsters of the saddles each carried a pair of six-barrelled revolvers.

BOOK THE SECOND.—CHAPTER V.

THE FIFTH OF NOVEMBER AT BIRCHAM.

FROM the time when the old house became an establishment for the culture of the youthful mind, its inhabitants had been wont to commemorate the doings of that evil-disposed individual who

"Solemnly swore, with powder in store," &c.,

to give the King and his Ministers a rise in the world as sudden as it would have been disagreeable.

Perhaps the Bircham boys were rather demonstrative in their mode of perpetuating the memory of Messieurs Guy Fawkes and Co.; but this was not sufficient excuse for the arbitrary order which, written in bold letters, stared them in the face when they entered the large hall on the long-looked-for day dear to all lovers of explosive fireworks:—

BIRCHAM ACADEMY.

NOTICE.

No Fireworks, Gunpowder, or other Explosive Compound to be brought to the Playground. A severe punishment will follow the infringement of this Order!

(Signed) JACOB SNIVEL.

THE BOYS OF BIRCHAM SCHOOL.

JACK STANFIELD DEFINES HIS FRIEND.

Sturdy Bob, the Dodger, was the first whose eyes were gladdened by the sight of this notice.

"No fireworks!" muttered Bob; "and I've got two shillings' worth under my bed! Here's a go!"

"What's a go, Bob?" quoth Joe Stikkers, as he halted before the edict. "No fireworks, &c., and signed by old Snivel!"

"Yes, Joe; and he's a hard hitter, so we must do something to dodge him, or——"

"Hallo!" exclaimed the Mallet, as he came to a halt between his friends; "this is nice, so it is!—and I've got my pocket full of matches and crackers!"

The Mallet did not trouble himself about the possibility of the matches igniting and causing an uncomfortable commotion in his trousers pocket.

"Tell you what, Mallet," said Joe, "this won't do! so I, for one, will infringe the order."

No. 17.

"But the severe licking you'll get afterwards, my cheerful Stikkers!"

"I shan't get a licking if you'll all stick to me."

"I'll stick to you, Joe," said the Dodger; "so tell us what you are going to do."

The crowd had by this time thickened, and most of the Stikkers faction were listening to their leader's discussion.

"Look here," Joe said; "of course it's no use for us to openly go against old Jacob, because he could lick about twenty such miserable little beggars as we are."

A murmur of disapprobation came from the youngsters, but Joe was equal to the task of convincing them of the truth of his words.

"That's just the way with you little wretches," he said; "if a fellow speaks the truth, you begin to growl; but if he plums you up with all sorts of lies, you swallow it as long as your vanity is tickled by——"

"Shut up!" said the Mallet; "you're spinning yarn enough to make stockings for all the poor in the village. Go on, Joe; tell 'em what you mean in a few plain words."

Joe was a little staggered by this address from his friend, and from the manner in which he looked at the Mallet it was evident he was, as brother Jonathan remarks, considerably "riled" by it.

"I can do that," said Joe, "and punch your head afterwards, Mallet."

"Well, do the explanation first," said the Mallet coolly, "and the punching afterwards."

"I will. Now, you young beggars, I daresay, if I were to say to you, 'Come on, let's meet the usher as he comes down to the schoolroom, and pitch him over the stairs,' you'd all say——What would you say—eh?"

"Yes, yes; that's the best way."

"Is it?" Joe said: "I know better, you little wretches! you'd be off like frightened hares before he came down to you, and leave one or two of the biggest to fight it out."

"No, we wouldn't, Joe."

"Nonsense, you would. Didn't you all go brave enough last week to pitch into farmer Hempseed's cow-boys, and directly you saw one of the men come out with a horsewhip you took to your heels, and left me and the Dodger to have it out?"

"Which we did," said the Dodger, *sotto voce*, "and I can feel the sting of that whip quite plain now."

The youngsters were silent after Joe had finished this accusation against them; so the young orator stood upon a form and resumed,—

"You are not heroes, you young beggars, but a fair sample of English boys—capable of doing much mischief as long as you stick together. Beyond this your heroism does not go; and those who attempt to garnish a stupid novel by making a boy its hero, write that which is both false and stupid, and, unless I am much mistaken, receive but little thanks from any intelligent youngsters, who, judging by themselves, know that a boy, no matter how brave he may be, cannot be such a fire-eater as to lead grey-headed men to glory, or do battle single-handed with brawny-limbed fellows who could take him by the collar and shake their lives out."

"Steady a bit, Joe," said the Mallet. "I heard you say, when Happy and Jack Stanfield left the school, that should they enter the army they would turn out heroes."

"True," said Joe, "I did say so, and I publicly acknowledge it; but you do not surely place Happy, or Jack, or Gleddell upon a footing with us young beggars?"

"Why not?" queried the Mallet.

"Because," Joe said readily, "they are young men—that is, they are close upon their twentieth year, and the eldest among us is not yet sixteen."

"Quarter to nine, Joe," said the Dodger; "so be quick with your spouting, or we shall have the master down upon us."

"All right, Bob, as the story-book says, to return to the subject, which is this confounded order against letting off fireworks or having the usual bonfire."

"Yes," said the Mallet; "to think of a plan to have our old Fifth of November games, or we shall have but a dull day of it."

"I've a good mind," Joe said, "to ask the Doctor to rescind this order—"

"No," objected the Mallet, "no, let's fight it out with old Snivel without appealing to the Doctor."

"The Doctor's not here," volunteered one among the listeners, "he went away to London last night, and one of the servants up at the house told me he could not be back for a week or ten days."

"I'm rather glad of it," said Joe, "for it always goes against me to do anything to offend the head—for he is not to blame after all, and it's my opinion that if he were here we should not have been annoyed by the sight of this beastly notice."

"But," said the Mallet, "the Usher would not take upon himself to do this, he must have had the Doctor's orders before he left for London."

"I don't believe it," said Joe, like the rest of the elder boys, always ready to defend the Doctor, "it's all Jacob's doings."

"Can't see it," the Mallet said, "because the Doctor would be sure to call him over the coals if he acted without orders."

"Suppose he did," said Joe, "the old sneak would have one excuse—I know him so well—he'd say that he was afraid we should set the place on fire, therefore he forbid the usual demonstrations in the playground."

"I say, Joe," asked the Mallet mischeviously, "what profession are you going in for when you leave school?"

"Why, daddy long-legs?"

"I should like know, that's all."

"Well, I can't answer you, old broomstick-legs, for I don't know myself."

"What a pity, Joe, to see you waste so much of your talent for no purpose."

"Talent—waste—what does the spindle-shanks mean?"

"Only this, Joe: I thought you were in training for a lawyer."

There was a burst of laughter at this sally; before Joe could retaliate with the somewhat nasty saying used towards youths of spare habit, v.e., about training to go up gas-pipes, the school-bell rang and the assembly dispersed.

The Mallet, on his way to the schoolroom, acting upon a suggestion of a friend, removed the crackers and matches from his trousers pocket, and placed them in the outside receptacle for odds and ends which garnished his loose jacket.

Mr. Jacob Snivel looked unusually grim upon this eventful morning, and his restless grey eyes furtively scanned the fresh young faces, as though trying to discover the impression his edict had made upon the pupils.

With the exception of the lower fourth, he met no responsive glances; here, as usual, this turbulent class were in prime condition for a revolt. This is not not to be wondered at, as they acknowledged Master Mallet for their leader.

A transient smile was perceptible on Jacob's thin lips when he saw the defiant expression upon these youngsters' faces, and he was observed to examine his thick cane with more than ordinary care.

The Dodger winced at this as he peeped over the top of his book, for the artful one could not dodge Mr. Snivel as he had used to dodge the Doctor.

Bob tried it on twice, and the second time he had cause to remember it—and remember it he did for many days, as might have been seen by the careful manner in which he sat upon the hard forms; also the very careful manner in which he shuffled out from joining in a game at bait the bear.

Mr. Jacob Snivel, when matters in the schoolroom did not glide so smoothly as he could have wished, made it a rule to punish the biggest of the refractory pupils, and upon this memorable Fifth day of November, Anno Domini something, he kept his eyes upon the Mallet; for that sprightly youth, independent of being the biggest in the class, took every possible opportunity of showing the defiance which slumbered in his youthful breast.

The term silent insolence will better explain the Mallet's behaviour than aught else. For instance, he would suddenly raise his hand and stare at the usher until the latter, looking towards the lower fourth, their eyes would meet; then the hopeful youth would smile in a supercilious manner, and run the fingers of his left hand through his brown curly hair.

Mr. Snivel took no outward notice of this; he was thinking for our friend, and determined to pay him off with interest.

The poor Dodger was grinding away at his lesson most manfully during this by play between the Usher and the Mallet, but in spite of all he could do to fix his attention upon the book, the doggerel rhyme about the Fifth day of November would dance over the open pages before him.

He had to learn a half-page about tropical trees and plants: thus he mentally acquitted himself of the task:—

The Dodger, reading from book,—

"*The trunk of the Ceila tree is often thirty, sometimes forty, feet in circumference, and in height and expanse it is gigantic.*"

The Dodger, placing his forefinger between the leaves to keep the place, closes the book, and then repeats a portion of his lesson.

"The trunk of the Ceila tree is"—a pause, during which the Dodger closes his eyes and endeavours to remember the next word; he has it—"this Ceila tree—*please to remember* — is often—*the fifth of*—thirty feet — *November* sometimes—*gunpowder treason and plot*—forty feet. *We see no reason*—in circumference *why gunpowder*, and in height *treason* and expanse *should ever* and expanse *be*—it is equally *forgot* gigantic."

He had thus mastered the peculiarities of the silk-cotton tree, when Mr. Snivel's voice called upon all the victims pursuing the same book of learning with the Dodger to come beneath the shadow of that awful desk.

The luckless Bob, feeling so confident in his descriptive powers respecting the Ceila, did that which was very unusual with our dodging friend, he placed himself upon the right of his companions, and put his book in the Usher's wrinkled hand.

Mr. Jacob Snivel tucked the cane under his arm, and placing his hands behind his back, gave the customary,—

"Now, sir!"

This was the signal for the confident Dodger to begin. He did so, thus,—

"Please to remember—the Ceila tree is—the fifth of November—he is often forty feet long—the gunpowder treason and plot—and we see no reason why—the circumference of—gunpowder treason should ever be for——"

"Hold!—stop!—silence!" roared Mr. Jacob Snivel, appalled by the *pot pourri* the boy had made. "Silence, you rascal!"

The book fell from Jacob's left hand as his right drew the cane from under his arm. Then came an ominous "whiz" as the instrument of torture described a circle above the Usher's head.

Its descent upon the Dodger's cranium was the prelude for a yell which would not have disgraced the most warlike of J. F. Cooper's North American Indians.

The boy's cry of mingled pain and terror seemed to arouse the latent savageness in the Usher's nature, for he seized the lad by the collar of his jacket, and held him in a grip like a vice.

While thus helplessly at the Usher's mercy the poor lad was beaten until the agony he endured became too painful for him to utter a cry of either entreaty or pain.

Mr. Snivel continued the barbarous flagellation until his arm tired, and from more than one place upon the boy's face the blood began to ooze out; then he released his grip of poor Bob's collar, and the lad fell to the floor in a huddled senseless heap.

The Usher's eyes blazed with maniacal fury as he pointed to the boy with the cane, which near the end bore grievous evidence of its recent use.

"Take him to his room," he said, his lips quivering and his face white with passion; "and let this be a warning to all, that I will not be insulted by any boy in this school."

Not one of the lads came forward in compliance with the Usher's request; so turning his pale face and gleaming eyes towards the sixth form, he said,—

"Biggs and Lucas, take this boy from the schoolroom."

Cheesy and Lucas obeyed this mandate, and both being lads of a powerful build, they raised the poor Dodger from the floor and bore him away.

The eyes of his schoolfellows followed the boy's form, and by the contraction of their brows and the hasty whispers that were exchanged, it was evident some mischief was brewing neither creditable to the "Boys of Bircham" nor their really talented but bad-tempered Usher.

CHAPTER VI.

THE NIGHT OF THE FIFTH OF NOVEMBER.

SUCH a brutal scene had never before been enacted in the school, and the majority of the lads' faces burned with indignation at the brutal outrage.

The bad feeling which the edict against discharging fireworks aroused had become so firmly rooted in the lads' minds, that they awaited but a word from their elders to convert everything portable into a missile, to be flung at the Usher's head.

Mr. Snivel sent the remainder of poor Bob's class back to their seats, and clenching his great knuckles as he passed to and fro before the master's desk, he seemed on the look-out for a second victim.

In an evil moment his eyes fell upon the Mallet, who, in place of attending to his lesson, was whispering to the lad who sat next on the form.

A sardonic smile played upon the Usher's face when he detected this act, and pausing suddenly in his walk, he called upon the Mallet to leave his class.

The boy promptly obeyed, and by his clear flashing eyes and flushed face, it was evident that he was nerving himself to resent the punishment he felt was awaiting him.

"You called me, sir!" he said boldly, as he stood before the Usher; "but I am not quite ready to repeat my lesson!"

"So I imagined!" was the answer and the Mallet saw the red fingers close tightly upon the cane. "Had you paid more attention to your task, and talked less, you would have learnt more; give me your book, sir!"

The boy did so, and the light in his eyes danced fiercer.

"Now!" said Mr. Snivel, "let me hear you repeat them."

"I cannot, sir; I do not know the lesson; give me a few minutes and I will."

"You idle good-for-nothing scamp, what do you mean by telling me this? it is nearly eleven, and you have the assurance to tell me you have not learnt this task?"

"I have not, sir; I had done so, but the late horrible scene has quite driven it out of my head."

"I'll drive it back," said the Usher, "and in such a manner that you will not forget for some time yet."

The gaunt arm was raised quickly, but the Mallet jumped aside and thus escaped the blow, and the Usher losing his balance staggered forward and fell upon his hands and knees.

The sight was edifying to the youngsters, and they raised a pæan of triumph in consequence.

Mr. Snivel slowly regained the perpendicular, and turning to the French master said savagely,—

"From which quarter of the school came that derisive laughter?"

"From that class," said Monsieur Jean, pointing to the lower youths; "they all stand up and laugh when you did fall."

The Usher walked steadily towards the class, his keen grey eyes looking angrier than ever, and his pale face more ghastly with suppressed passion.

The Mallet, who had been the cause of Jacob's fall, quietly returned to his class when the Usher was in the position usually assumed by the four-footed beasts of the creation.

The Usher walked straight to where the Mallet sat, and compressing his thin lips said,—

"I have watched you the whole morning, and saw that you were eating in place of paying attention to your task; further, you have tried to make me an object of ridicule to the school."

He paused, and looking around the class, seemed trying to solve the thoughts of the anxious and angry faces.

He received only sullen defiance in their looks, and had not his black passion been stronger than his good sense, he would have paused ere he fanned the slumbering fire into a raging volcano.

"For this," he said, resuming his address to the Mallet, and his voice growing huskier every word he uttered, "I will publicly flog you; and would do so were you twice your age. Remember, I will have the same amount of respect as when the head of the school is present. Now, sir, stand out!"

The Mallet's face became very red; he was an old pupil of the Doctor's, and this was the first time he had ever been in danger of being publicly chastised.

"I shouldn't care," the boy thought, "did I deserve it; but I do not, and this is a wanton piece of cruelty and spite."

"Stand out, sir!" said Jacob, making a step forward. "Stand out, or I'll flog you where you stand!"

"You will do nothing of the kind," said the Mallet resolutely. "I do not deserve flogging, therefore I will not submit to it."

"Insolent young scoundrel!" said the Usher, nearly maddened by the boy's cool defiance. "Here, Biggs—Lucas—Harvey, drag him out!"

The Usher must have forgotten his position when he gave this order—an order, by the way, which the boys who belonged to Biggs's faction were only too glad to obey.

The Mallet saw them coming, and gave an appealing glance towards his classmates; then, clenching his hands, awaited the onset.

Joe Stikkers had been a quiet observer of the preceding scene, and now the moment for action had arrived, he left his seat and went to his friend's side.

"I'm here, Mallet," he said. "Let them come on! It strikes me there will be a little settling of old scores here to-day."

The Mallet's face bespoke his gratitude for this timely aid.

Biggs and his compeers were evidently disconcerted by the appearance of Joe, for the leader had yet a lively recollection of Stikkers's mode of hitting.

He was not very muscular, but what was wanting in strength was amply atoned for in the quickness of his movements when engaged in the fistic art.

"Return to your seat, sir!"

This was addressed by Mr. Snivel to Joe Stikkers, who made no reply.

"Do you hear, sir?"

Still the same silence; the boys had quite enough to do to watch the advancing trio without attending to Mr. Snivel's angry mandate.

"You had better," Joe said to Biggs, "let the Usher do his own work; he don't want the aid of such fellows as you in a matter of this sort, so go back to your seats, and let us settle the matter ourselves."

This was perhaps the most unfortunate speech Joe could have made, for it incited Biggs to carry out the Usher's orders in spite of the prospective resistance of the young pair.

Tom Harvey and Lucas were both of a better stamp than Biggs; they felt the Usher was about to perpetrate an act which the good old Doctor would not have sanctioned had he been at the school.

Feeling this, they were not so eager to aid in the outrage; thus, when Biggs made his rapid advance, he did so alone, and as his hand touched the Mallet's shoulder, Biggs received what is known by the appropriate name of "a stinger!"

Stung he was to all appearance, for he placed his right hand upon his nose, as though not quite certain whether that important member still distinguished his face.

By this time two-thirds of the boys were on their feet, some half-frightened—others thoroughly enjoying the scene.

Mr. Jacob Snivel's patience was by this time exhausted, and, regardless of the danger to the sundry heads in the way, he flourished his cane and made an onslaught upon the Mallet and Joe.

The first blow fell upon the Mallet's jacket pocket, and a succession of loud reports followed.

The Usher, in spite of his nerve, jumped back as though he had been shot; he was evidently under the impression that the Mallet had discharged a six-barrelled revolver at his head, for as he ran backward he called out,—

"Secure him! secure him! he is armed."

It was all very well to call upon the boys to secure the Mallet, but they gave him a wide berth as he ran about the school, the fireworks banging and fizzing, and a cloud of grey smoke enveloping the upper part of his body.

The Mallet, after the first feeling of surprise passed away, remembered the cause of this explosion, and began to rid himself of his jacket.

He did so but in time to save himself from a serious injury, for besides the crackers and squibs which his pocket contained, there were a number of catherine wheels; these soon became ignited, and their fizzing, combined with the explosion of the crackers and the hissing of several rockets, rendered the Mallet's garment anything but a desirable covering.

The sound of the fireworks and the clouds of grey smoke had a magical effect upon the boys, for soon, from all parts of the school, came numberless samples of the pyrotechnic art.

Where they had been concealed up to this time was a mystery, unless, like the Mallet, the lads had carried them in their pockets.

The various explosions gave the lads so much joy that they forgot the place they were in, and yielding to the excitement of the moment, they gave a lusty cheer, and more than one squib was hurled at the Usher's head.

"Monsieur Gailland!" called out the amazed Usher, "and you, Mr. Ford, help me to suppress this riot!"

M. Jean did not appear to care about the honour and glory attached to the business, and a cracker of gigantic proportions banging against his feet caused him to beat a hasty retreat.

The writing master, a pale, limp gentleman, like M. Jean, evidently did not see the utility of his becoming a target for the fiery missiles, so he retreated close upon the Frenchman's heels.

Mr. Jacob Snivel's lips bespoke the scorn he felt at being thus deserted by the pair, so, giving one savage glance at the rebellious youngsters, he rushed among the thickest of the crowd and began to use his cane most unmercifully.

Had the lads' heads been ears of corn and the Usher's weapon a flail, he could not have gone to work with greater disregard to the probable result of the affray.

Between fifty and sixty young Englishmen, some verging upon their eighteenth year, were not the sort to long endure the Usher's savage attack, especially as he was alone in the schoolroom.

Two or three had received severe cuts across the face, and one little fellow had his cheek laid open before there was any attempt at retaliation.

It came at last. Joe Stikkers, who had been hitherto a passive spectator of the tumult, now came forward and shouted,—

"Get together, lads, and drive him out of the room."

"Hooray for Joe! down with the Usher! hooray! who wanted to stop our letting off fireworks? Down with him, hooray!"

Such were the sounds distinguishable above the hubbub of voices which answered Joe's war-cry, and the lads, lost to all fear respecting their behaviour, rallied around Joe—many boldly discharging a blazing squib at Mr. Snivel's head.

The Usher's gaunt frame towered above his foes, as did Gulliver's above the Liliputians, and save for a firmer compression of the lips, he seemed not to have become conscious of the menacing attitude of high-spirited but disobedient boys.

"Back to your seats!" he said sternly, "back at once, or I will make such an example of the ringleaders that they will wish they had never been born."

A derisive shout answered this mandate, and from among the crowd came the words,—

"Who stopped our holiday? Down with old square toes!—turn him out!—pelt him!"

Up to this moment the insurgents had been at a loss to know the best mode of attacking the enemy, so the suggestion to pelt Mr. Snivel came at the right moment, and was acted upon accordingly.

Pelt him they did, the few remaining fireworks were first sent at the angry grim-looking master; then the contents of the coal-scuttle formed a capital ammunition store, and so well were the pieces of coal aimed, that Jacob was compelled to give way before the storm which raged about his ears.

Back—step by step he retreated, his hand ready, and his eyes watching warily for such of the enemy as came within reach of his long arm.

He caught two or three before he was driven through the doorway, and those who were martyred had good cause to remember the Fifth of November for some time after.

The Usher, once clear of the schoolroom, the boys made a rush to the playground, and such a scene was there witnessed which put to shame all previous commemorations of the escape of those whom Mr. Guy Fawkes—or Guido Faux, you can take your choice of the spelling—"bitterly swore with powder and straw," &c., to hoist higher then they would have wished.

The tuck shop did a grand business, for the old fellow had speculated largely in fireworks for the auspicious day, and his speculation turned out a grand success.

When night came on, the annual bonfire was blazing in the centre of the ground, and above it the rebels suspended the effigy of Mr. Jacob Snivel; and while the flames consumed the figure, the lads did their best to imitate a tribe of wild Indians, so far as the yelling and cheering was concerned.

BOOK THE SECOND.—CHAPTER VII.

JACK STANFIELD DEFENDS HIS FRIEND.

YOUNG, full of spirits, well armed, and bestriding their curveting steeds, they started upon their journey, and much to their disappointment met with no adventure until they were crossing that vast plain which still retained the native appellation of Manaroo.

Here the lads had their first and most terrible encounter with one of the lawless gangs which infested the region of the finest grazing ground in the colony.

"Well, Jack," said Happy, "what do you think of the country?"

"To speak candidly, Tom," was the reply, "I think a few houses would enliven the scene, especially as the chance of our reaching the station spoken of by that ill-looking fellow at Sydney will be very small should the darkness set in."

Truth to tell, the few days' ride they had had through the stony plains and interminable scrub, had somewhat taken a little of the romance out of our young adventurers.

In place of traversing verdant lanes, shady woods, and loitering by the banks of rippling streams, they had passed over large tracts of the country, the surface dotted with holes filled with glutinous mud: beneath the slush were numberless pieces of sharp pointed rock—alike dangerous to the horses' hoofs and the riders' seats when the animals stumbled upon these holes.

Then came a couple of scorching days, the thermometer standing at 115 in the shade; and in a few hours the thick mud in the holes became dried into dust; then the hot north-west wind would blow the gritty dust into their faces—penetrating eyes, nostrils, and ears in a manner anything but pleasant.

Leaving this sterile tract, they emerged upon a more level part of the country, and the view was a little enlivened with the white trunks of the gum tree and their drooping vertical foliage.

Here the adventurers halted, for the noonday heat was intolerable; and allowing their horses to graze upon the straw-coloured vegetation, but taking the precaution to hobble them in case they might stray too far away, the lads lit a fire, baked their damper, boiled the water for their tea; and this, with the corned beef Happy carried in a bag fastened to his saddle, made a tolerable and refreshing meal.

When the pipes were lit, and Jack was secretly congratulating himself upon their escape from the stony plain, a fresh cause of discomfort arose.

A swarm of sandflies made their appearance, and in such quantities that the ground was covered for miles with them; and so venomous were the little pests that Jack and Happy, when they went for their horses, found the poor animals kicking and plunging with pain and fear.

Upon searching for the cause of this strange behaviour, the adventurers saw the sandflies in myriads upon the horses' legs, chests, and flanks; and so severely were the poor brutes stung that the blood was perceptible upon their silken coats.

They had great difficulty in mounting the tortured creatures, and it was not until they rode through a creek where the water rose above the saddle girths that the little bloodsuckers were destroyed.

There was another pest, a species of ant, which caused the lads to shun any shady resting place which presented itself upon their route.

These little creatures, if they settled upon the hands or faces, stung the flesh until a blister arose upon the skin; then, unless they were driven off, the blister would soon become an inflamed sore; from this to a raw wound; and so far from medical advice as they were, the end might have been serious, had they suffered, as many have done, through not knowing the peculiarities of the insect world.

In England, the lads had been told that the climate of Australia was as soft as that of Italy; also that the insects were harmless.

How far their informant was correct, Happy and Jack knew by the time they had made acquaintance with sand-flies, gnats, ants, mosquitos, centipedes, scorpions, and the deadly tarantula spider. The bite of the latter, unless the flesh is cut out, proves fatal in nine cases out of ten.

After this digression, it is time to return to our travellers.

"I don't much care about reaching the station," Happy said, in reply to his friend; "for with our blankets, and the saddles for a pillow, we can manage well enough."

"That's true, Tom; but for my part I have had almost enough of that sort of thing for a while, and begin to find the freedom of this sort of travelling anything but superior to the swift railway in the old country."

Happy laughed at his less robust companion's words. True to his sobriquet, he was quite as content with the ground for his bed, a saddle for his pillow, and but a single blanket to keep off the night damp, as he would have been on the most luxurious couch.

"By the way," he said to Jack, who was caressingly patting the neck of his steed, "do you think we are upon the right track?"

"Yes, so far; the vessel to which Gled was taken left the Thames for Sydney."

"I know that!"

"Of course you do; but have a little patience, and let me recapitulate the result of our travels so far."

"All right, old boy, go ahead!"

"We heard at Sydney that the ship came safely to the end of her voyage."

"Have you a cigar light?"

Jack handed him one.

"Thanks, yes, she came safely to the end of her voyage. Well——"

"Then the convicts—at least, the greater part of them—were portioned out to the colonists, and if we are correctly informed, Gled was among those who were sent to the station beyond those hills."

"If we are correctly informed!" Happy repeated; "do you think we are?"

Jack turned suddenly in his saddle as he said,—

"Do you doubt the man's word?"

"I do," said Happy; "for since we left Sydney I have thought the matter well over, and each time my suspicion has become stronger."

"What cause have you for it?"

"Many," answered Happy; "the man's brutal looking face, the cunning glitter of his eyes, the longing manner in which he looked at our horses, and the leer upon his face when he asked if we intended to travel with our revolvers loaded."

"After all," said Jack, "there may be nothing in all this beyond a man having a disagreeable countenance, a natural admiration for a couple of good horses—and the question respecting the pistols may have proceeded from curiosity."

"I hope it may be so," said Happy, doubtfully, "but the fellow's readiness when we were inquiring about the convicts, and the peculiar looks which he exchanged with a man who stood at the bar, have caused me to think we have placed too much trust in the fellow's words."

"But," Jack said, "he described Gleddell's appearance so well that ——"

"Not so fast, old boy: this would not have been a very difficult matter after we had asked the mounted policeman if he had seen a young fellow disembark answering the description we gave. Now I come to remember, the trooper who was on duty when the convicts landed told us he had not seen any one answering to Gled's appearance, and by the time we had finished our glasses of punch this fellow came up with his ready information."

"You may be right, Happy," Jack said, "but I do not see how it could benefit the fellow to deceive us."

Tom Dickson's horse began to snort and prick up his ears, and would have stood still had not the spurs been pretty freely applied to his flanks.

"What's the matter with the brute?" Jack asked, as the beast he bestrode began to exhibit similar signs of fear.

The young wayfarers were passing a group of pines when the animals became restive, but when clear of the trees they became quieter, and save for an impatient tossing of their heads, seemed to have overcome this fear.

"Were it not broad daylight," said Happy, "I should be inclined to think that the horses were startled in consequence of some one being hidden among those trees."

"There's no one there," answered Jack, turning to look at the pines, "so for once the animal instinct, which the mouldy old naturalists aver never deceives either man or beast, has gone wrong."

"Don't be too confident, old boy," said Happy, "but push ahead, and let's get clear of these trees."

They pressed their steeds into a sharp trot, and were soon out upon the open country.

"By the way, Tom," said young Stanfield, "you did not answer my last query about ——"

"Yes, the cause, or rather, I should say, my suspicion of the cause which induced the fellow to give us false information."

"Exactly."

"Well, it's this, Jack. I fully believe that fellow belongs to one of the thievish gangs which infest the colony, and his reason for putting us upon this wild-goose chase in search of this imaginary station is to lure us into an out-of-the-way place, then shoot us down for the sake of our horses, arms, and money."

"If so," Jack answered quietly, "they will find our pistols are not carried for ornament."

"True, old boy; but these gentry prefer popping a fellow off from behind a tree—and, truth to tell, I firmly believe there was one of the fraternity among those pines, or our horses would not have shown such restiveness."

Jack laughed at his friend's words, and said,—

"Did I not know you well, Happy, I should be inclined to think you were nervous."

"Rather," said Happy, "you mean you would think I had but little pluck."

"It's more charitable to call it nervousness."

Tom Dickson made no reply: he was looking anxiously ahead for the wooden hut which his Sydney acquaintance had described as being situate near the plain they were now traversing.

There was no sign of the place yet, and the day was fast closing in, and as both the horses and their riders were fatigued, Happy pointed to a clump of white-trunked gum-trees, and said,—

"We'll halt there, Jack, for the night, if you've no objection."

"Not the least, old boy; quite the reverse. I shall be grateful for a rest."

Twenty minutes' sharp trot brought them to the spot, and, selecting the most sheltered place, they dismounted and unsaddled their tired steeds, and, after carefully grooming them, Happy undertook the task of collecting materials for a fire, while Jack led the horses to the best piece of grazing-ground near the camp.

Here Jack hobbled them, and left the animals to crop the luxuriant grass which had grown thickly under the shelter of the massive trunks of the surrounding trees.

This done, he returned to Happy, whom he found busy preparing the evening meal. Good teeth and ravenous appetites, and the blade of a strong clasp knife, made short work of the beef and dampers; then the pipes were lit, fresh fuel placed upon the fire, and the travellers, with their heads upon their saddle-bags, began to talk about the old country and those they had left.

They were laughing over poor M. Jean's various scrapes, brought about by the Mallet and his *confrères*, when one of the horses gave a neigh.

They were upon their feet in an instant, and a revolver was quickly snatched from the holster of each saddle.

Thus prepared, they listened intently for the cause of the animal's sudden cry.

"There's something moving between that large tree and those shrubs," whispered Happy; "cover it with your six-shooter, and if there's no answer to my hail, you fire. I'll keep watch this way, for there's something very like a light footstep coming behind us."

Beyond where the blazing logs threw their fitful gleams, Jack Stanfield saw the outlines of a man's form, and with compressed lips and beating heart he raised his weapon, just as Happy sang out,—

"Who's there?—speak, or I——"

The report of a pistol awoke the echoes of the place; a tiny red flash was seen near the dimly outlined figure, and Happy's word of menace was checked by a sharp pain, which began at the fleshy part of his right arm, and seemed to extend from there to the extremity of his leg.

A second report—a second flash—and Happy fell, struck by a bullet in the calf of his right leg.

He bit his lips to repress the cry of pain which arose to them, and said,—

"I'm hit in two places, Jack; run to your horse—save yourself, old boy; never mind——"

The reproachful look Jack gave his wounded friend told how deeply Happy's words had affected his generous heart.

"Leave you, old fellow?" he said; "never! Give me your pistol. I've twelve shots, and each shall take a life before I desert you."

"They'll shoot you down, Jack—ha! there's the fellow whose lying tongue lure us here!"

As he spoke several men issued boldly from the shelter of the trees, and advanced towards the two friends.

Like a lioness defending her young, Jack stood over his fallen companion, and with his pistols levelled at the ill-looking group, he said fiercely,—

"Cowards!—keep back, or there'll be red work if you advance another step!"

"Pistol him, Jerry," growled the fellow who had been instrumental in entrapping the lads, "or he'll use his barkers."

Jack saw the man addressed by the ill-looking scoundrel raise a revolver, but before he could bring it on a level with the lad's breast, the latter, carried away by the excitement of the moment, began to rapidly discharge the barrels of the revolver in his right hand.

The first shot broke the ruffian's arm who was about to bring down the boy, and as the pistol fell from his helpless grasp, others of the party began to return the lad's fire.

About a dozen shots altogether were exchanged between Jack and his adversaries —the result, two of the rangers wounded; on the other side, Happy was down and seriously hurt, and Jack was bleeding profusely from a wound in the neck.

The result of the contest would have been death to the gallant fellow, had not the firing attracted a number of horsemen, who came galloping towards the scene.

Their horses' hoof-strokes acted like magic upon the rangers, and all, save one who was shot in the thigh, turned and fled into the darkness.

CHAPTER VIII.

THE SOLITARY MOURNER AT GREYMORE'S GRAVE.

THE party who had so opportunely arrived were mounted upon strong stock horses, and, besides the heavy stock whip which each carried, the steel butt of a genuine Colt's revolver was visible above the outside pockets of their short jackets.

They were four in number—two men who were past their prime, the others just verging upon manhood; and as Jack raised his eyes towards his preservers he caught sight of a face he knew, though it was much browner than when he last beheld it, and he exclaimed joyfully,—

"Gled, as I'm alive!—then the rascal was right, after all!"

THE BOYS OF BIRCHAM SCHOOL.

THE SOLITARY MOURNER AT GREYMORE'S GRAVE.

One of the two young men threw himself from his horse, and, running to the speaker, grasped his hand warmly; then, stooping over Happy, said,—

"Jack Stanfield and Happy!—this is a surprise! Are you hurt, Tom? You look pale."

"Dear old Gled!" said Tom Dickson, forgetting the pain he suffered. "What a man you're grown! Your old pale face has gone, and——"

"Never mind my face, Tom; where are you hit?"

"Arm and leg," said the careless fellow. "I must apologize, Gled, to your companions for not rising to receive them. Help me up, old fellow; perhaps I can stand on one pin."

"You've been rightly named, Tom," said Gleddell; "you are indeed a Happy-go-lucky. Do sit still! Luckily, Martin Russell is with us—he's a surgeon, Tom;

No. 18.

so you will soon be all right."

The second young man of the party had by this time dismounted, and, kneeling by Gleddell's side, he felt Happy's arm lightly, and, much to that young gentleman's relief, said,—

"Nothing serious here, Gled; bind it up."

Gleddell took a loose scarf from his neck and began to wind it round Happy's arm, and young Martin arose, and was about to walk to the wounded bushranger, when he heard Tom Dickson say,—

"I say, Gled, ask your medical friend if he'll take a squint at my leg: for it strikes me I've got a red-hot shot there, it burns so confoundedly."

The young surgeon smiled at the sufferer's *nonchalance*, and, before Gleddell could speak, he was examining the wounded leg.

"You've had a narrow escape, young gentleman," said the surgeon; "the twentieth part of an inch to the right and that ball would have shattered the bone."

"What has it done now?" Happy asked. "It feels jolly hot."

"Not much harm," was the reply. "If we can get the bullet out, you will soon be all right again."

"Get it out by all means, then; there's a knife in my pocket."

The surgeon smiled.

"You must wait," he said, "until we get you to Broken Falls before that operation can be performed."

He left the youths talking, and went to the bushranger, whose leg just above the ancle had been shattered by one of Jack Stanfield's shots.

The elders of the party came to the three old schoolmates, and Gleddell said,—

"This is Mr. Russell, the owner of Broken Falls."

A stout gentleman acknowledged the introduction by bowing to the new comers, and, with a smile that showed his well-shaped teeth, said,—

"Welcome to New South Wales, gentlemen."

"I do not think I need introduce——" Gleddell began, and was interrupted by Jack Stanfield, saying,—

"Luke Jessop, by all that's good! Your hand, Luke. What is the next surprise in store for us?"

Luke shook hands with the young fellow, and said,—

"I'm afraid you must wait until we are on our journey again——"

Jack Stanfield interrupted Luke by whispering,—

"Poor Gled seems to have fallen into good hands, Luke; I did not think crim——"

"He is not a criminal," Luke said in the same low tone, and an angry spot came to his bronzed cheeks as he spoke. "Mr. Gleddell is assistant-overseer at one of the largest farms on the colony."

Jack looked the surprise he felt, and Luke, to stop further questioning, said,—

"We shall be at the Falls by daylight; by that time all will be explained. By the way," he added, "your old friend, Philip Randall, is innocent of Greymore's murder."

"I know it," Jack said; "but how have you made the discovery?"

"You shall hear at the place I have mentioned."

"Thanks; I shall be all anxiety to see the morrow dawn."

The horses belonging to Happy and Jack came as well as their hobbles would let them to the scene of the late fight—drawn thither by the presence of others of their species.

"Thank goodness!" said Jack, when the animals appeared, "the scoundrels did not take our steeds."

Happy was pleased to see his broad-chested, fine-limbed bay; but his face was a trifle sad when he glanced from his wounded leg to the horse's back.

"They might as well have taken my steed," he said, "for I shall not be able to put my leg across him for some time."

"True, old boy," said Jack, assisting his friend to rise upon the sound leg; "the next question is, how are we to get you away from here? I would give something, Tom, for the service of a dirty London four-wheeler."

"So would I, Jack; but as we cannot obtain any conveyance, I suppose I shall have to hop on one leg."

"We can manage better than that," Luke said, as he mounted his horse; "give your friend a leg up; he can sit before me. Steady! that's it."

Jack then helped the wounded bushranger upon Tom Dickson's horse, and Mr. Russell and his son having mounted by this time, the party resumed their journey.

Martin Russell and his father placed the outlaw between them, in case the slippery gentleman should make his escape upon the fleet animal; thus Jack Stanfield and Gleddell, riding on either side of Luke and Happy were able to converse freely, and Tom, in spite of the pains of his wounds, was far from being the least noisy of the party.

They had much to talk about; and great was the surprise felt by Jack and his friend, when Gleddell told them all that had happened since the time he had been sent to the convict ship.

Stranger still was the story told by Luke, the wondrous meeting when Gleddell's boat was cut in two by the *Fair Rosamond*.

The lads listened silent with wonder at the story—it seemed so marvellous that Luke should have the proofs of Gleddell's innocence; and their wonder increased when Luke came to the story of Illjurra's confession.

"The young magistrate," Luke said, in concluding his narrative, "placed the facts of the case in the hands of the Colonial Secretary, and I have no doubt the next mail will convey them to England—that is if they have not gone already."

"I hope it is so," said Jack, "for poor Philip will be sacrificed upon circumstantial evidence, should he become at all sane."

"He'll stick to the mad dodge, never fear," said Happy, "even should he wake up one morning and find himself all right."

"I hope he may," Gleddell said: "poor

Philip, he has indeed suffered for another's villany."

"Speaking about Greymore," said Jack, "reminds me of a scene I beheld in the little churchyard near our old school."

"The girl, you mean," said Happy: "yes, her connection with Greymore has often puzzled me; was there anything in the murderer's confession about a fair-haired blue-eyed girl?"

This question was addressed to Luke, and to Happy's surprise he felt the strong arm which held him upon the horse's back tremble violently.

The surprise he felt was not lessened, when he saw Gleddell making signs for him to change the subject.

"What's the matter?" asked Happy, unheeding Gleddell's evident discomposure and Luke's trembling form. "You fellows are full of mysteries—what is it, Luke?"

"Nothing, lad; nothing," answered the overseer; "you do not, of course, know the bitterness I have suffered through that handsome devil's villany."

"Greymore?"

Luke inclined his head affirmatively—then told how he had been rendered childless by the man who had fallen by his old companion's hands.

"She was fair and blue-eyed," said Luke in husky tones; "can you wonder that your words struck a chord which vibrated through every nerve?"

"I cannot," Happy answered; "but if the bushranger saw your child's body taken from the Seine there can be no——"

"No, no!" said Luke, his head bowed upon his chest, "she must have been another victim; but tell me, what was it you saw?"

Tom Dickson looked towards his friend, and Jack made a sign for him to tell the particulars of the scene in the quiet churchyard.

"It was this," Happy said. "Jack and I were crossing the graveyard—it was the nearest way, you know, to the school."

Luke inclined his head.

"It was the day upon which the murdered man was buried, and the coffin had been placed in the grave, but owing to another funeral taking place at the same time, the grave-diggers had left the filling in until the other grave had received its occupant."

"Exactly," Luke said, looking eagerly at the speaker, "pray—go on."

"Curiosity caused us to turn from the path and go towards Greymore's last home, but when we came in view of the spot, our footsteps were arrested by seeing a female form standing at the foot of the yawning pit.

"Her hands were clasped, and her eyes upturned in silent prayer, and her pale face had such an expression of hopeless woe stamped upon each feature, that we were more touched at the sight of that solitary mourner, than I for my part had ever felt before.

"I think Jack felt as bad, for he drew me away, and we walked silently towards the gates, and trod as lightly as we could, for fear we should disturb the broken-hearted girl."

"What age should you suppose the girl to have been?"

Luke asked this question in a steady unfaltering voice, but the trembling lips, heaving chest, and the variable colour which came and went upon his cheeks, told how the spirit was at work within.

"Two or three and twenty," was the answer; "but she looked older, in consequence of a settled expression of sadness upon her face."

"She was fifteen," thought Luke, "when that villain took her from St. Omer—that is six years since; she would have been verging into womanhood had she lived until now. The coincidence in their ages and personal appearance is strange; yet not out of the every-day occurrences of life. I must forget this folly: she is dead, murdered, and I——"

His reflections were broken in upon by Happy saying,—

"There is no difficulty in finding out the connection between the poor girl and Greymore, for just before we left Captain Oakplank's daughters took compassion upon the poor girl, and she's now living with them as a sort of companion and servant; so it will be easy for you to discover all about the affair."

"True," Luke said; "thanks; but, upon reflection, I do not believe there can be any affinity between the solitary mourner and my poor lost murdered child."

"Strange things have occurred," said Jack Stanfield; "in proof of this I need but instance the extraordinary events which you have recounted to us—the saving of Gleddell's life—the discovery of his innocence—the man who fell by your hand after he had escaped so many dangers—the fact of Greymore's mysterious murder coming to light—these things are more wonderful than this poor girl being your daughter, in spite of the bushranger's assertion that he saw her dead body taken from the Seine. She may have been senseless, but not dead."

Luke's eyes glistened tearfully as he caught at the hope thus held out, and, bowing his head, he murmured,—

"Pray heaven it may be so!"

The party rode on in silence for some time after this. Mr. Russell and his son, as the most experienced of the party, led the way, several horse's lengths in front of their companions: they were silent, and apparently listening for an expected sound.

Luke, wrapped in his sorrowful memories, took no heed of anything which passed around, and the three friends, respecting his silence, forbore to speak, although they had much to talk about and much yet to hear.

So they rode on, until the distant bay of a watch-dog came upon the breeze, and the cry was succeeded by a dozen hounds giving forth their knowledge that the travellers were heard, although the horses' feet fell softly upon the earth.

There was much wickedness abroad beneath the pale moonlight, and the owner of Broken Falls smiled when he listened to the baying of his faithful dogs.

It was that period of the year when the emerald tints of the foliage had begun to assume a rich brown, that the travellers emerged from the thickly-grown trees full upon one of the loveliest scenes that eye could behold or imagination conceive.

BOOK THE SECOND.—CHAPTER IX.

BROKEN FALLS.

THE silver autumnal moon was at its full, and the still radiance falling upon the earth rendered objects as distinctly discernable as though Diana's rival planet was at its meridian.

Below there lay Broken Falls and its twelve hundred acres of cultivated land, and Jack Stanfield, struck by the singular beauty of the place, turned to his companion and said,—

"This, then, is your home, Gled?"

"It is," was the answer, "and there is not a fairer spot within a hundred miles."

"It is indeed beautiful!"

As he uttered these words he gave his horse the reins, and again moved forward.

The homestead where dwelt the wealthy colonist was a large wooden structure, verandah all around, and conspicuous by the beauty of its form and the mass of bright flowered creepers which clung to the trelliswork beneath the verandahs.

In front was a large garden, tastefully laid out, and filled with flowering plants, whose many hues seemed like bright ribbons laid upon the dark moonlit earth.

Flanking the wooden mansion were the domestic buildings, the stores, and a handsome cottage, now occupied by Luke, as overseer; a little in rear of these buildings were the stables, the shearing shed, the huts for the farm hands, and the cart houses.

Then, stretching away to the base of a range of high mountains, was the cultivated land, divided by gleaming white wooden fences into between thirty and forty sections.

A running river had formerly washed over the spot where the flower-covered structure now stood, and its course had been stopped, and from the spot the travellers had emerged from, the water seemed to fall in mist-like spray over the homestead and the adjacent buildings.

When they reached the broad sweep which led to the house, Happy and Jack saw that the water had been diverted from its path by a mass of rockwork so constructed as to give it the appearance of being nature's handiwork, and after dancing over the rugged top, the clear stream fell into a pool-like basin, upon the surface of which floated several handsome pleasure boats.

To prevent this artificial lake from overflowing, a small canal had been cut to carry away the surplus water to the cattle ponds; here, again, to prevent an overflow, other and smaller canals carried the limpid stream to an opening at the base of one of the mighty hills which reared itself like a grim sentinel above the farm lands.

The travellers were received by a kindly lady, the owner's wife, and her daughter, a beautiful girl of sixteen summers.

It needed but few words to introduce the new arrivals, and Happy, when Martin had extracted the ball from his leg, had his wounds dressed, and as he lay at full length upon a soft couch, before the fire, he felt rather thankful to the bushrangers for making him such a tender object of solicitude to the lovely Ellen Russell.

During the early breakfast—for it was not yet daylight—the lads heard that Mr. Russell and his companions had been absent from the farm for three days in search of several herd of valuable cattle.

The search had been unsuccessful, and they were on their way homeward when the report of Jack's revolver attracted their attention.

After breakfast, the owner of Broken Falls and his family retired, and left Jack and Happy to that which they both needed, a few hours' sleep.

It was near mid-day when they awoke, and Tom Dickson was about to jump from his couch when a tinge of acute pain recalled the wound in his leg to his mind.

"Ugh!" he growled; and the noise awoke Jack, who was coiled up in a mass of blankets before the fire. "I shall have to stick to the horizontal for some time yet—hi!—Jack, wake up, you lazy villain, and go and hunt up Gleddell."

"All right," said Jack, rolling his eyes. "I was in the middle of a beautiful dream."

"What was it?"

"I thought the bushrangers were scalping us, after the fashion of those gentlemanly Indians who cut a fellow's hair so well that no barber is afterwards required."

"That's a beautiful dream, is it? Oh, here comes Gled."

The door opened and Gleddell entered the room and after a short conversation had taken place between the trio, Jack suddenly said,—

"I can't hold out any longer, Gled; I want you to tell us how Luke and yourself managed to get into such snug quarters."

"That's soon told," said the handsome youth, twining the twelve feet lash of his stock-whip around the handle; "so your curiosity will be at rest."

"I wish the confounded pain in my leg and arm would," said Happy. Then suddenly changing the subject, he asked,—"I say, Gled, what a beautiful creature that young girl is. You ain't—are you?"

"Am I—what?"

"Spoons? I hope not."

Gleddell laughed as he said,—

"No, Tom; but surely you have not begun to feel that way already?"

"Yes," said Happy, "I'm a gone coon. Just feel my heart, how it's pining away; it's all through that young lady. What's her name, Gled?"

"Ellen."

"Oh, Lord!" said Happy, "I'm done for in earnest. That's my favourite name!"

"It ought to be," Jack said drily, "for I can testify to the sixth young lady of that name you have been spoons on. You are too susceptible, Tom."

"I know," said the victim, "I was always so; but go on, Gled, tell us—oh, confound it, I'm sure there must be a lot of hot needles tied in that bandage."

"You'll do yourself no good." said Jack, "if you persist in turning and twisting about in that manner."

Happy became still, but the effort it cost him was something stupendous.

"I must make my explanation as short as possible," said Gleddell, "for we are off to the bush directly, and——"

"May I accompany you?" said Jack.

"We should be glad of your help; but how about Happy?"

"Don't mind me," said the invalid; "pray don't—I shall be all right. Pray go, Jack."

Gleddell and Jack exchanged looks and laughed; they had a pretty good idea of the cause which prompted Happy's readiness to be left at the farm without his friends.

"I must tell you, though," Gleddell said, "that we may have a brush with the cattle-stealers, for our informant told Luke the fellows had come to the determination of opposing our recapture of the cattle."

Happy gave a long howl when he heard this.

"What's the matter?" asked both friends in a breath.

"Nothing," said Happy, "only the pleasure I shall feel at being shut up here while you beggars are fighting in the bush."

"Miss Russell will keep your spirits up, Happy, until we——"

"*Koo-eh!*" sounded in a prolonged tone outside the house, and Gleddell, in response to his friend's inquiring looks, said,—

"It's only Luke calling the fellows to bring our horses. They are a long way off, and this peculiar cry is heard farther than calling out a man's name——listen, it is answered."

"*Koo-eh!*" came faintly from the huts in rear of the mansion; and Gleddell said,—

"The horses will be here in five minutes; so look to your pistols, Jack, while I tell you how Luke and I became located at Broken Falls."

So during the time Jack was employed cleaning his revolvers Gleddell related all that had befallen him since he arrived at the colony.

"It was a strange thing," he said, "that Luke should shoot the very man he had determined to slay; and, stranger still, that he attained the post rendered vacant by the murderous hand of this Illjurra."

"It was indeed," said Jack. "Before you proceed further just *koo-eh!* to that black fellow, and tell him to bring round my horses."

Gleddell did so; then resumed,—

"You may be sure that Mr. Russell soon closed with Luke's offer; and a first-rate overseer he makes: there's no skulking now among the farm hands—they are mostly convicts, you know."

"Yes; so I have been given to understand."

"And a peculiar lot they are," Gleddell went on; "but Luke stands no nonsense from them : at the least sign of insubordination down they go; and they begin now to understand the new overseer, and work accordingly."

"It seems rather a harsh way of managing," said Happy; "but I suppose it's necessary?"

"It is," answered Gleddell; "but there is no other course. By the way, before Luke came the cattle were in the habit of disappearing most mysteriously from the runs; but Luke and I soon found out the cause."

"Did you?" said Jack; "more bushrangers?"

"No; a shepherd, a fellow named McElvry, was collecting a nice little herd for his own use; and so skilfully had he managed the affair, that he had, in the space of two years, detached over four hundred head of horned cattle and two thousand sheep from the run, without exciting Mr. Russell's suspicions."

"This does not say much for that gentleman's perceptions."

"You'll be able to judge better," Gleddell answered, "when you have been a short time in the colony."

"Perhaps so; but I do not think any fellow could get over me to that extent."

Gleddell smiled, and said,—

"However, Luke and I tracks my gentleman, and finds out the hiding place of the cattle; and, much to the thief's surprise, drove them in the next day."

"What became of the Scotchman?"

"He has taken to the bush, I expect; and before he left the farm he managed to gratify his spite by relieving us of some of our best teams of oxen."

"It is to find them, I suppose, that you are going now?"

"Yes; and as they are known to be in the possession of the black gang, we shall have some fun before we come back."

"You won't find it fun," sighed Happy, "if you get a couple of revolver pills in your brains."

The two friends laughed at their companion's doleful face; and Gleddell said,—

"It's the fortune of war, Tom."

"Is it!" growled Happy; "then I'd have the misfortune of war next time."

"I say, Gled," said Jack, suddenly, "I wonder you were not afraid to tell this Mr. Russell your name."

"Why?"

"He is a magistrate, is he not?"

"Well?"

"Suppose he had heard of the escape of a certain Stanton Gleddell from the convict ship!"

"There was not much to fear upon that score; for the officers of the ship believe that I died from the effects of the sentry's shot."

"Then Mr. Russell does not know your strange story!"

"He does, every word."

Jack elevated his eyebrows, indicative of extreme surprise.

"Luke told him all," Gleddell said; "though we at first thought it would be best for me to take the name of Jessop; but mature deliberation assured me it would be the best to let things take their course, especially as Luke had such convincing proofs of my innocence."

"Which Mr. Russell believes?"

"Undoubtedly, or I should not hold the position I do."

"By the way, what is your position here!"

"Well?" Gleddell answered, "I am supposed to be bookkeeper and assistant-overseer; but, truth to tell, I am oftener in the saddle, using pistol or whip, than I am at the desk with a pen. I don't like such close work: there is something nobler in bestriding a good horse, and galloping about this beautiful country, than casting up the expenditure and profits of the farm."

"But how about the accounts, Gled?"

"Oh, Miss Ellen looks after them when I am otherwise engaged."

"What a blessing," said Happy. "I can help her. I say, Gled, where's the books kept?"

"In that cupboard over your head."

"Then she will come here to make them up?"

"Yes."

"I'll help her," said Happy; "so the sooner you take Jack away the better."

"Why?" Gleddell asked; "are you afraid his personal attractions will——"

"Oh, dear, no," replied Tom; "but you see he will be in the way; and when a fellow wants to say spoony things, another fellow within hearing is not agreeable."

The friends laughed; then, wishing Happy good-by, took up their weapons and left the room.

Tom saw them mount their horses, and a groan came from his lips.

The poor fellow would have given much to have accompanied his friends, and his eyes longingly followed the forms of Gleddell, Jack, Luke, and young Henry Russell.

"Just my luck," he growled, "to be laid up here like a—— oh, good morning, miss."

His growl subsided as Ellen and her mother entered the room; and by the time the ladies had asked about his wound, and the younger of the two offered to cheer his loneliness with a little music, he began to feel much better. And after he had watched the young lady's nimble fingers, as they ran over the keys of the piano, he thought it not a bad thing, after all, to be laid up in such comfortable quarters.

CHAPTER X.

A FAMILY COUNCIL, AT WHICH THE DOCTOR WAS PRESENT.

LEAVING one tail of his coat (Clankhammer coat the Bircham boys called it) upon the spikes, M. Jean escaped the unpleasant proximity of Captain Oakplank's stick; and the old sailor, detecting the trophy, came up the garden, shouting,

"Look here, girls! look here! the—ahem!—pirate has left his colours behind. Hallo, they've made sail!—hi! hi! Minnie —'Lenor, where the dev——"

He came to an anchor in the big arm chair, and resumed, in a less boisterous tone,—

"Well, I suppose it's no use to hoist a signal to such light-heel'd craft; so I'll stick to my moorings here until the wind brings 'em round again."

He sat for some time impatiently beating a certain dark gentleman's tattoo upon the table; but, finding no relief from the serenade, he growled,—

"There's nothing in this world like these petticoats for hoisting fog signals. Now, here's 'Lenor. When I went upon my cruise about the boy, she was going about the house like a sick monkey, because Philip had——"

Rat—tat—tat!

"Ugh! who's that? I suppose some crimp wants money. Hi! Mary! say I'm not at home, d'ye hear?"

"Yes, sir," answered the girl; "when will you return?"

"In six months' time: tell 'em I've gone for a cruise round the North Pole, and got icebound."

A few seconds after the old sailor heard Mary thus acquit herself,—

"No, sir; master ain't at home."

"Dear me," said the visitor, "how unfortunate! I wanted to see him most particularly. Have you any idea, my good girl, when your master will return?"

"Yes, sir; when he comes back from being frozen on top of North Pole."

"Iceland, you lubberly swab!" roared the old fellow. "How the dev——"

The visitor, hearing the Captain's voice, said,—

"I'm glad to hear your master has not gone upon such an unpleasant errand. Tell him Doctor Bircham will——"

"Come in, Doctor," said George Oakplank, going towards the door; "come in."

The venerable master entered the room, and while the pair were shaking hands, the Captain said to the girl,—

"Just try and steer right this time. If any one else comes, say I'm gone to the Red Sea. D'ye understand?"

"Yes, sir."

"Well, Doctor," said the old seaman, handing his visitor a seat, "how is the poor lad?"

"Much the same, Captain. The doctor tells me that a sudden reaction might restore his faculties; but he still refuses permission for your daughter to visit his patient."

"Skyscrapers and reef-points! What's the fellow afraid of? Is my 'Lenor a pirate, going to cut his prize out from the madhouse?"

"I believe," said the Doctor, "that the principal acts for the best."

"Best—best? How—how?"

"He has cause to fear that Eleanor's presence in poor Philip's cell would change the malady from its present passive state to that of a raving dangerous lunatic."

"I don't understand much of these matters," said George Oakplank; "but I know whenever I've seen the lad he has been so quiet, and conversed so rationally that, were it not for the wild expression in his eyes, I should not think his top screws wanted refitting."

"A worse sign in many cases than we are aware of."

"But," said the old seaman, "he always asks for 'Lenor, and speaks about young

Gled and the school so sensibly, that I wonder they do not bring him before the big wigs for the murder."

"Calm and retired as he appears, when his mind is under the influence of a brief return of reason, a most dangerous form of madness smoulders like a sleeping Vulcan in his breast. They have tried him; and the bare mention of Greymore's name turns him into such a paroxysm of grief, that it required six strong men to hold him."

"Poor lad!" said the Captain. "We must wait and hope that the true murderer will be found; then I believe we should have Philip with us again."

"No doubt the sudden knowledge that he was free to leave his cell would do all that is necessary. By the way, how fares the poor girl your kind daughters found at the murdered man's graveside?"

"She is much the same; quite, mournful, and evidently suffering from a grief too deep ever to be forgotten."

"Poor creature! she must have been very beautiful before them tell-tale marks of care came to her face."

"As lovely as a frigate under all canvas," said George Oakplank; "but now she's like a dismasted craft, drifting out to sea without an inch of canvas to save her from sinking."

The head master at Bircham did not follow the sailor's metaphor very closely; so he assented to the remark by an affirmative inclination of his head.

"I have been to London," he said, after a pause; "in fact I only returned this morning."

"I have been there to," said the Captain; "and only came back about half-an-hour since."

"Indeed: did you succeed in your object?"

"No," grunted George Oakplank; "they told me the boy had been shot by a confounded marine; and when I came home, Minnie had a despatch from the lad. By George, Doctor, he's foremasted the big wigs this time."

"He is innocent," said Doctor Bircham; "and to establish that and procure his pardon I went to London."

"Well, did they give it you?"

"No; I received the same account—he had been killed in attempting to escape when the ship lay in the river."

"Ho—ho—ho! And what did you tell them?"

"Nothing," the Doctor said; "for until this moment I was not aware that he lived."

"But how did you know of his innocence?"

"By a letter I received from New South Wales."

"Didn't that tell you he lived?"

"No; the writer merely said an innocent youth had been arrested for Greymore's crime."

"Greymore," repeated George Oakplank; "that man came like a blight upon the lives of —— ha! now I come to think of it there was something in Gled's letter about Greymore and Philip; but as I had to give chase to a pirate I did not read it all."

"Can I see this precious missive?"

"Yes, yes; Minnie has it: we'll have a council, Doctor, and see what's to be done."

"You shall have my assistance Captain."

The old seaman did not wait to hoist a signal to his daughters, but straightway marched up to their room and brought them down under convoy.

"More secret orders," he said, as the young ladies greeted the Doctor; "here's 'Lenor now left off crying; and when I ask them what's the cause of all the grieving and kissing going on between them, they tell me that I must have patience. Patience be—ahem!—I never had any."

"Papa speaks the truth, Doctor," said Minnie, laughing, "for a more impatient——"

"Silence, you privateer; would you mutinise before my face? Now bring out the secret despatch, and let the Doctor hear how the boy—our boy, you know, Doctor—has forereached upon old Davy, and taken his own orders for sailing."

Minnie felt like most young ladies of her age would have felt under the circumstances—not over well pleased at her father's order to show her first love-letter.

The good-natured Doctor guessed the reason for the pouting lips and the rosy-tinged cheek of the bashful young lady.

"Come, Captain," he said, "don't you think we are asking too much from the young lady?"

"Too much? Hencoops and capstan-bars! Am I not the commander of this ship? Out with your despatch, you minx."

"But, papa——"

"Well, what is it? I don't want you to read the soft parts; it's the part about Philip I want the Doctor to hear."

Minnie gave a sigh of relief, and took Gleddell's letter from her pocket. (I know it would be more romantic to say breast; but as pockets are more in vogue in these degenerate days, truth compels me to use the term.)

"Gleddell says in his letter," she said, "that one of those dreadful bushrangers left a confession in his pocket of the murder for which poor Philip has been made to suffer so much."

"How strange are the ways of Providence!" said the Doctor. "Pray continue, young lady. Has he told you whether any steps have been taken to forward that confession to England?"

"Yes," Minnie answered; "the magistrate who was with them at the reading of the papers told Gleddell that he would at once place the facts of the case in the hands of the Colonial Secretary."

"If so," the Doctor said joyfully, "we shall soon have Philip once more with us; for this news will, I feel confident, restore him to reason."

"I hope it may," said the Captain, "but it will be a long time before he will be able to feel at ease among those who are acquainted with his trouble."

"I am of the same opinion," said the Doctor; "his sensitive mind will recoil from his fellow men, and——"

"He need not stay here," said the Captain, suddenly. "That's a good thought, girls; he'll go out to the colonies. I've a little bag of shots in the locker, enough to buy a piece of ground big enough for us all. Eh, Doctor, what do you think of that?"

"Under the circumstances the very best for all parties. Would I were younger!—I would make one of the party; for there a man has breathing room; and—I beg pardon, but the ladies—what do they think of the arrangement?"

"We think with papa," said Eleanor. "I feel we shall be happier there, away from the former connections, the many busy people who even now look down upon us with contempt."

Captain Oakplank jumped to his feet, and, flourishing his steel hook, roared,—

"Have they? do they? Tell me this news? and !by George I'll shiver them from deck to truck. Look down upon my girls, will they?"

It was some time before the united efforts of the Doctor and the young ladies could pacify the old sailor. When they did so, he took his hat and coat, and said,—

"Come, Doctor; we will go and see the lad, and if they do not let him out of limbo I'll give 'em a broadside, as sure as my name's George Oakplank."

The old gentlemen left the house; and the happy sisters were so overcome by the breaking of the dark cloud which had so early saddened their young lives that they threw themselves into each other's arms and wept tears of blissful joy.

CHAPTER XI.
RE-UNITED.

ELEANOR sat alone in the little room which overlooked the garden. She seemed more like the stately beauty of yore as she bent her head over a faded flower, which from time to time was pressed fondly to her red lips.

Her father had not yet returned since he had gone with the Doctor to visit Philip.

Eleanor had asked her sister to leave her for a short time; and the laughing Minnie went to her room to read for the fiftieth time the precious epistle from across the seas.

From a drawer in one of the tables Eleanor took an album, and from among its leaves came the faded withered blossom which seemed such an object of solicitude to the beautiful maiden.

"He gave me this," she thought, "a few days before that man came like a blight upon our lives; and from the hour he was taken from me has this simple flower been——"

A hasty footstep nearing the door caused her to rise from her seat; and, as the colour went and came to her cheek, she sought to hide her agitation by fixing her eyes upon the withered petals of the flower Philip had given her in happier days.

Could she be mistaken in that footstep? No! The door is thrown open. She dares not raise her head. She fears to look upon the loved one's face after his long and wretched captivity; but when she feels a trembling hand upon her shoulder, and a voice husky with joy whispers "Eleanor," she drops the faded blossom, and, turning, hides her head upon his breast—that breast which was to be her shield and safeguard through life.

"Re-united, darling!" he whispered; "I had never in my moments of madness pictured such a scene as this."

She could not speak; but as he gathered her yet closer to him, she uplifted her eyes and stole a wistful glance at his face.

It was much altered: the brown curling whiskers had been shaven off; his cheeks were wasted and hollow; and beneath his eyes were the black marks which told the mental agony he had suffered—and suffered so unjustly.

It was some time before they became sufficiently calm to ask or explain the cause of that sudden and joyful liberation.

"I knew of the happy change yesterday," Philip said; "and the sudden knowledge that I was free to leave my prison broke the mental darkness which had fallen upon me."

"My father and Doctor Bircham left the house some time since, to tell you the good news."

"I have seen them, darling, and they are responsible for my appearance at the assizes."

Eleanor shuddered.

"Have they not given you your freedom?" she asked: "has not the strange confession of that man been sufficient to prove your innocence?"

"Amply sufficient, darling," he said; "but there are certain formalities which I must pass through before I am quite at liberty."

Eleanor became silent: she was apprehensive that the law would yet claim him for another's crime, which Greymore had, with his subtle management, fixed upon the poor usher.

"Philip," she said, "you promised me on that dreadful night that you would tell me the cause for the extraordinary power Greymore had over you."

"You fear," he said, "that it is for this I have to appear before the representatives of the law?"

"I do, Philip."

"Do not give the idea a second thought; for I am, thanks to the kind Doctor Bircham, able to prove my innocence."

"Was it anything very dreadful, Philip?"

"It was. Had it been true I should have been sent to the felon's dock to answer the only crime which is punishable with death."

"Murder?" she whispered.

"Yes, dear one. You shall hear a brief outline of the terrible mystery which hung so long over my life."

He told her that he had been a schoolfellow of Greymore's; and that the latter, although but a mere boy, began to show the reckless disposition which afterwards so fatally marred what might have been a bright career.

BOOK THE SECOND.—CHAPTER XII.
HAPPY-GO-LUCKY SAVES ELLEN RUSSELL.

IT appeared that Greymore was ever impatient of control; and upon one occasion he had, with two companions as daring as

THE BOYS OF BIRCHAM SCHOOL.

WE CAN'T ESCAPE HIM HE SAILS FOUR KNOTS TO OUR THREE.

himself, been confined to the school for some flagrant breach of rules.

The three, not relishing the punishment, broke out after bedtime by means of their sheets; and were discovered by one of the masters in the act of ascending the knotted sheets.

It was a large school, and the most stringent rules were necessary to keep order among the inmates; so for this offence the head master had the trio publicly flogged.

The indignity rankled deep in Greymore's mind; and the night after the flogging he set fire to the room beneath the master's bedchamber.

This room was Philip's study, and he at the time was absent supping with a friend who lived at the other end of the schoolhouse.

Greymore had his revenge, for the head master perished in the flames; and when the fire was subdued the men discovered the cause of the conflagration, and saw it was the work of an incendiary.

Philip, conscious of his innocence, would have given himself up, had not Greymore persuaded him to fly from the place before the police arrived. He offered as an inducement to accompany the frightened boy.

Philip consented, and his flight was considered a proof of guilt: nor was his innocence made manifest until the Doctor found another inmate of the school who assisted Greymore to set fire to the building. His confession saved Philip.

"It was this," Philip said in conclusion, "that weighed upon my spirits, Eleanor, for although years had passed since the night of the fire, I always felt my danger, and the dark prison cells were ever before my eyes."

"You have suffered!" she said, smoothing his pale forehead? "but it is all over now."

"For which mercy I humbly thank the great Giver of all Good," said the usher reverentially kneeling.

She also knelt, and together mingled their prayer and thanksgiving for the lifting of the black cloud which had obscured the brightness of their youth.

In spite of the motherly attention of Mrs. Russell, and the timid interest displayed by Ellen, Tom Dickson's wounds refused to heal, and the poor fellow used to lie on his couch, gazing with yearning eyes out upon the bold range of mountains visible from the window.

Much of his exuberant spirits had passed away, and a settled expression of sadness had come upon his handsome face; so different to the old joyous look, that his kindly nurses were more alarmed for his safety than they gave outward sign of feeling.

In a populous town, medical men are plentiful and skilful; but at Broken Falls, the ladies had good reason for their anxiety.

To make matters worse, the young fellow who had attended to Happy's wounds when he first came to Broken Falls, had gone with the party in search of the stolen cattle; thus there was no one to whom the ladies could appeal for advice.

The owner of Broken Falls and his party had been away nearly a fortnight when this change took place in Happy, and from intelligence brought to the station by one of the aborigines in Mr. Russell's employ, it would possibly be a week before the party returned.

This protracted stay was caused by the stolen cattle having dispersed and strayed beyond a range of thickly wooded hills.

There came a pang of sorrow to Ellen's heart, when she saw the pale sad face growing thinner and more wretched in its expression as the days wore on; for with a woman's keen perception, she guessed the reason of the youth's change—a change which came like a blight upon him, when he needed mental quietude to assist the healing of his bodily wounds.

She remembered the alteration had taken place from the afternoon of a bright sunny day, when she sat by the sufferer's couch reading a poem of Byron's.

They had been conversing upon a subject calculated to fill their minds with graver thoughts than usual for a youth of twenty and a maiden of eighteen—this subject, the mystic land which lay beyond the grave.

Ellen changed the somewhat gloomy thoughts engendered by this conversation, and opened the book of poems which stood upon a table near the sofa.

"Is that Byron?" Happy asked, gazing eagerly at the lovely face bending over the book.

"It is," she answered; "do you like his poems?"

"I'm afraid," Happy said, "I should confess a want of taste were I to answer in the negative; yet I am but a poor lover of poetry; and my preference, in this instance, is for the occasional pieces."

"Shall I read you some?" she asked smiling at the frank confession; "but I must warn you beforehand, that I shall not do justice to even the simplest of the great poet's productions."

"You do yourself an injustice," said Happy. "I must be the judge in this matter—pray begin."

She opened the book at random, and read that poem which ends with this verse:—

"Yet wilt thou weep when I am low—
Sweet lady, speak those words again:
Yet if they grieve thee, say not so—
I would not give that bosom pain."

Raising her eyes at the conclusion of the verse, she blushed and closed the book, and for the first time in her life felt a strange indefinable feeling steal over her heart.

Her eyes met Tom Dickson's, and they were fixed upon her face with such a steadfast expression that left but little to conjecture respecting the state of his feelings towards her.

She read this, and her mind being as honourable as it was pure, she summoned all the resolution she possessed to tell Happy how useless it would be for him to entertain any feeling but that of friendship for her.

She bent her head yet lower under his ardent gaze, and as her heart beat quicker, she sought for words to express herself without wounding the youth's too sensitive mind.

She was saved the painful task of breaking the subject by Happy, whose voice, in spite of his firmness, trembled as he asked,—

"Would you Miss Russell, weep for me were I laid low?"

She spoke so lowly in reply, that he had to lean forward to catch her words.

"Death," she said, "is such a sad thing, that even a friend's loss is at all times painful."

Happy saw she avoided a direct reply to his question, and being too well-bred to repeat the words, he said somewhat sadly,—

"Were I to die, I have but few that would regret my absence."

"There may be more than you imagine, Mr. Dickson."

"Friends, acquaintances," he said, "but

none save my father's brother that have any love for me."

"Friendship is love, Mr. Dickson."

"To a certain extent it is, but not the love for which my heart yearns."

Ellen felt they were drifting to the explanation she so much desired, and the knowledge gave her more pain than she thought herself capable of feeling.

"You will meet with one," she said, "to reciprocate your yearning, Mr. Dickson."

"I have met one"—and he epmhasized the words—"one who fulfills the ideal I have pictured."

The young girl's face became suffused with blushes, as she said,—

"Does she return—the—the feeling you have described?"

"I know not," he said; and the words came quickly from his lips, as though determined to know the worst at once, "and I am so great a coward that I feel it's no use for me to——Miss Russell, you are the *beau ideal*—you can but answer the question you asked."

"I—I—Mr. Dickson?"

The worst was past, and she nerved herself for the task before her.

"I am grieved," she continued, "to hear this, for we can never be more to each other than we are now."

"Never!" he said, turning pale; "that is a long time."

She looked up, and, gazing timidly into his eyes, said,—

"I must repeat the words, Mr. Dickson —we can never be more than friends."

"Am I, then, so distasteful to you?"

"You are not," she answered, frankly; "but there are circumstances which render it imperative that we should understand each other."

Happy lowered his head as he said,—

"Those circumstances preclude the consummation of my brightest fondest hopes?"

"They do. Look out from the window, and you will see the white fence which divides Broken Falls from the next farm."

"I see the fence," he said, wondering what reference the white rails had to the question at issue; "and, from what I can understand, they are the boundary of a vast tract of land under cultivation."

"You are correct; that land belongs to my future husband."

"There is, indeed, no hope."

He fell back as he uttered these words, and, covering his eyes to shut out the brilliant sunshine, seemed overpowered by the blow which had shattered his hopes.

There was a few minutes silence, then Tom Dickson groaned,—

"Would I had known this sooner! I——"

"Mr. Dickson," she said, rising from the chair, "I hope you hold me blameless. I have not given you, by word or sign, any encouragement for this unhappy passion."

"You have not," he said; "you are quite blameless. It has been my blind presumption which has led me on from day to day to picture joys upon which my fancy has fed until I believed the attainment within my grasp."

There could be but little doubt that the maiden deeply sympathized with the unhappy youth, and, when he became calmer, she told him more of her engagement to the owner of Table Lands—so the farm was called on account of the evenness of the immense tract of land.

It wanted but six months of her attaining the age of eighteen, and that day, according to present arrangements, had been fixed upon by her father for the nuptials to take place.

It appeared that Willoughby Addison, the owner of Table Lands, was a man about twenty years Ellen's senior; and although he had not won her love, he had so far gained her esteem, that in obedience to her parents' wish, she had given her consent to the marriage.

This step she had not regretted until she saw Happy, who had in a few days made an impression on her heart that would take years to efface.

She did not tell her listener this, nor did she dare, placed as she was, encourage the soft passion. Her parents and suitor had received her consent to the match, and Ellen Russell would have sacrificed every feeling to keep her plighted word.

The match was one of the best in the colony, for Willoughby had inherited the lands from his father, and was possessed of immense wealth: this, and the proximity of the two farms, had done much to render the marriage the height of Mr. Russell's ambition.

Happy listened to the details with a beating heart, and when Ellen left the room and he was alone with his misery, the wish uppermost in his mind was that Willoughby Addison would break his neck, or fall by a shot from a bushranger.

After this explanation he saw but little of Ellen, therefore knew not that the bloom of health left her cheeks, and she became pensive and sad—ay, as sad as he had become.

This, then, was the cause which retarded his recovery; and as the days went on he prayed for that rest which the grave alone can give to the troubled mind.

Within the week of the aborigine's return to the farm, Mr. Russell and his party came back, and Jack Stanfield and Gleddell, jumping from their horses, hastened to their friend's couch.

They had learned from one of the hut-keepers, as they rode towards Broken Falls, that the gentleman up at the house was very bad; and when they bent over the unhappy youth, both were shocked at the wreck of their once robust friend.

"What's the matter, Happy?" they asked, as soon as their astonishment passed away. "We expected to find you quite well."

"I had hoped to find myself so," said the poor fellow, with a faint smile. "I expect the air of Australia does not agree with me."

The friends exchanged glances.

"We must try what we can do to get you well again," said Jack; "possibly a little change may do you good."

"I think it would," Happy said; "the

sight of Table Lands has become rather monotonous and distasteful."

"I thought so," muttered Gleddell; "the moth has been singed. I ought to have warned him of her engagement."

The friends tried and succeeded in getting him from the couch he had thought never to leave alive, and when once he got beyond the dangerous vicinity of the lovely girl, he seemed in a fair way of being again the robust careless fellow who had landed in the colony a few weeks before.

The favourite amusement of the trio was to take a sailing-boat at the arm of the sea which washed the base of the mountain beyond Broken Falls.

In this light craft they would pass many hours of the day, and, if wind and weather permitted, venture out upon the broad ocean's surface.

One morning, when they were hoisting the sails, Ellen Russell, accompanied by a large dog, and a child belonging to one of the farm hands, passed along the base of the mountain.

She paused when she saw the three friends, and Gleddell, knowing her fondness for boating, asked her to accompany them upon a short trip.

At first she appeared irresolute; but an appealing glance from Happy caused her to accept the offer.

Passing through the inlet, they soon reached the open sea, and, deceived by the gentle breeze, went out some miles from the land.

Charmed by the exhilarating scene, they noted not a bank of struggling clouds rising in the westward, until Gleddell, in a voice which betokened alarm, said,—

"We shall have a stiff breeze soon, so we had better take to the oars, Jack."

Jack Stanfield seized an oar, and was in his seat by the time Gleddell was ready, and directing Happy to steer, they put the boat about.

They had not gone twenty fathoms when the wind came upon them, and before a hand could be raised the sail ropes were broken, and the canvas and the heavy boom swung round over the bows.

There was a faint scream from Ellen, as the boom swept her off the seat; the next moment the boat had left her and the child far behind.

The dog, a large retriever, sprang into the sea, and just as the poor girl, in her wild terror, loosened her grasp of the child, the animal seized the little creature's clothes and kept it above the surface.

So quickly had the sad accident occurred that the friends knew nothing of it until the dog jumped overboard, for they were using their united strength in righting the sail.

When Ellen's danger burst upon Happy's horrified gaze, the gallant fellow, without one thought for his weakened powers, jumped into the water and swam swiftly to her rescue.

There would have been two lives lost that day but for Gleddell and Jack, for Happy, although he reached Ellen as she was sinking, found his strength not equal to the task of supporting her to the boat.

He gave a piteous look towards his friends and said,—

"For heaven's sake help me—I am too weak to support her weight."

His appeal was answered, and in spite of the danger they incurred, the brave fellows left the displaced sail, and seizing the oars, were soon alongside the sinking pair.

They came but in time, for Ellen had swooned, and in another moment she would have gone to the ocean's strange depths.

When the boat came close enough Happy passed his arm around the rope which helped to support the single mast, and with the other hand held Ellen until his friends dragged them into the boat.

Happy thought the danger he had incurred well repaid, for as the light craft righted and sped towards the land, Ellen Russell's head was reclining upon his knee.

BOOK THE SECOND.—CHAPTER XIII.

THE TRIAL.

WHEN the time came for Philip to appear before the representatives of the law, so great an interest had been raised by the strange story of the discovery of Greymore's murderer, that the court-house was crowded before the judges took their seats.

The captain and his daughters were present, and the benevolent face of Dr. Bircham could be seen near the prisoner, and in the body of the building were several of Philip's former pupils.

So confident were Philip's friends that he would be acquitted, that the employment of counsel was thought unnecessary.

The proceedings began by the counsel for the prosecution recapitulating the circumstances which had caused the prisoner to be charged with Greymore's murder.

At the termination of this forensic display the judge asked Philip the usual question, to which he received an answer—

"Not guilty, my lord; and in confirmation of my words I beg to direct your lordship's attention to the confession which has been forwarded from the Colonial Secretary's office in Sydney.

Upon hearing this, Mr. Ferrett, the crown prosecutor, arose and electrified Philip's friends by saying—

"My lord and gentlemen of the jury, I am now in a position to state that some very grave doubts have arisen respecting the genuineness of those papers.

This statement seemed to occasion as much surprise among the members of the bar as among Philip's friends, for the judge said,—

"How is this, Mr. Ferrett? I should have supposed all legal doubts would have been at rest when the prisoner was released upon bail. The crime of murder is not a bailable offence in England."

"At the time, my lord, I was of opinion that all doubts were at rest; but from the evidence of an unimpeachable witness, I think I shall be able to show that there are many reasons for this change."

George Oakplank arose from his seat at this juncture, and would have spoken but for a warning gesture from Doctor Bircham.

Philip's face became pale, and he, for a moment, felt a cold sensation of dread creeping over his heart; it passed away as quickly as it came, and proudly conscious of his innocence, he looked assuringly towards the anxious party in the gallery of the court.

Eleanor's answering look was full of deep tenderness, yet mixed with dread for his safety.

"Pray, Mr. Ferrett," said the judge, "when did this unimpeachable witness tender his information?"

"Yesterday evening."

"Proceed," said the high functionary, "and explain the nature of these doubts."

Mr. Ferrett glanced at a slip of paper, then, in slow, measured accents, said—

"I believe, my lord, one of the signatures appended to the paper received from Australia is that of Luke Jessop."

"It is," said the judge, after a pause; "and the second is that of a magistrate who was present at the convict's death."

"This Luke Jessop," Mr. Ferrett resumed, "is not, I believe, unknown to many now present in this court, and from what I can glean, he bore but a doubtful character. I will call witnesses to prove this, if you think it necessary, my lord."

His lordship held a whispered conference with a colleague, then said

"It is not necessary."

"Very well, my lord. Taking this man's character into consideration, and the fact of his shooting down the supposed criminal from whom the confession emanated, it is not at all difficult to imagine that he wrote this confession, and imposed upon the magistrate, by stating that he had taken it from the dead man's pocket."

"Clue garnetts and devil's imps," roared the old sailor from the gallery. "What would ye ———"

"Silence in court!" said the usher, and old George reseated himself, his face red with passion.

"What motive could he have for doing this?" the judge asked.

"Probably no personal motive," said the lawyer; "but when we consider that the prisoner's most attached friend was the travelling companion of this Luke Jessop, it is not difficult to imagine that he would not have hesitated to oblige the prisoner's friend by making this effort to throw the guilt upon a dead man."

The judge looked very grave as he said to Philip, "Is this statement true respecting your friend?"

"It is," Philip said calmly; "he was at the time travelling with Luke Jessop, but how that knowledge came to this court astonishes me."

Mr. Ferrett regaled himself with a self-approving smile, and looked towards the jury as much as to say "You shall see my witnesses before long, gentlemen."

Philip had good reason to feel astonished at the lawyer's knowledge, for he believed that Minnie Oakplank was the only one besides her father and sister that knew of Gleddell's whereabouts.

"As the prisoner, my lord," Mr. Ferrett resumed, "admits the connection between his friend and the poacher, I will proceed to the next, and I may say more important portions of the evidence last night received."

An inclination of the head gave the judge's assent, and Mr. Ferrett resumed.

"You will be careful, gentlemen of the jury, to note this important fact, that the pistol which was found near the murdered man belonged to the prisoner. Also to note that the weapon was loaded and capped, and after the prisoner's arrest, the fellow pistol was found upon his table, also a portion of loose powder which had evidently fallen from the powder-flask when the pistol was loaded."

Philip grasped the rail in front of the dock, and looked towards his friends, and beheld, in place of the hopeful glances in return, bowed heads and evident signs of deep affliction.

Still the cold, measured tones went far, and the lawyer's words fell like drops of molten lead upon the face of the wretched Philip.

"In the supposed confession," the lawyer continued, "mention is made by the writer that he found the pistol outside the school house wall. Now, my lords and gentlemen, I leave it to your judgment whether a man, that I can prove had a strong motive for wishing this Logan Greymore out of the way, would load a pistol—mark this carefully—load a pistol, then throw it from the window."

The case began to wear a serious aspect, and among the closely-packed and interested listeners there was but little doubt respecting the truthfulness of the lawyer's statement.

That this feeling extended to the collection of intellectual (?) greengrocers, bakers, &c., which formed the jury was very plain, for the learned body were seen exchanging whispers and looking monstrously wise and important.

The judge was evidently the least biassed by the counsel's words; being a man of learning, and possessed of great mental perception, he saw certainly a wondrous combination of circumstantial evidence; but, as yet, no positive proof of guilt.

"I believe," he said, "you stated, Mr. Ferrett, that you could prove that the prisoner had a motive for the crime."

"I made that statement, my lord, and leave my witness to substantiate it."

"Let the witness be called."

CHAPTER XIV.

THE WITNESS.

THERE was a deep silence, and every face turned towards the witness-box as the crier called, "MONSIEUR JEAN GAILLAND."

Captain Oakplank, when the Frenchman's name rang out, disregarded Doctor Bircham's mute entreaty, jumped from his seat, and leaning over the front of the gallery, looked eagerly towards the door from which he expected Jean to emerge.

Accompanied by a policeman, M. Jean entered the court, and with a jaunty step came towards the place allotted for witnesses, and as he was about to take the oath George Oakplant, no longer able to control himself, burst out,—

"You ———!" these blanks must really stand for the captain's words; "you monkeyfied, crawling, loblolly son of a prig;

you set the limb of the law upon the poor lad; you apology for a man, by the figure-head of the old Bucephalus if I could get alongside you I'd—I'd——

The captain's greeting ended with a wild gesticulation, and the bright steel hook was seen cutting sixes and sevens above his head.

"Captain Oakplank," said the judge, "with all allowance for your feelings, I must beg that you will, as an officer and a gentleman, remember you are in a court of justice."

"Aye, my lord," said the old sailor, falling back into his seat, "I will be quiet, but man and boy I've been yard-arm to yard-arm with many a pirate; but one like that grinning——. I beg pardon; I've piped all my words down now; I'll say no more, but I wish I had that fellow tied to a grating, I'd take the lies out of him before all hands were piped to breakfast."

When M. Jean had taken the oath, he related all that is already known to the reader respecting the meeting between Philip and Greymore, and the struggle which took place in the usher's room, and he emphasized the words.

"When I went into the room, Mr. Randall was trying to push Greymore through the window."

"Did you," the judge asked, "see Greymore after this?"

"Yes, he stayed with me until he had recovered, then he left; and when next I saw him he was dying, and accusing Philip Randall of his murder."

This being the whole of M. Jean's evidence, he was ordered to stand down, but before he left the witness-box, the counsel for the prosecution said,

"One moment, monsieur; pray inform the court how you became acquainted with the fact of Luke Jessop's acquaintance with the prisoner's friend."

M. Jean hung his head; he was not prepared to answer this question.

"Come," the lawyer said, "remember this is a court of justice, and by virtue of the oaths you have taken, you are bound to speak the truth."

"I learnt this," M. Jean said, in a faltering voice, "from Miss Oakplank."

"She told you."

"Partly. I knew she had received a letter, and from another circumstance I guessed the writer."

"What was that circumstance?"

M. Jean glared furtively towards Doctor Bircham, and hung his head.

"Come, sir," said the inexorable lawyer, "the Court awaits your answer."

A peculiar smile was upon the doctor's lips when M. Jean looked towards the gallery; and when he whispered a few words to George Oakplank, the latter's angry face showed unmistakeable signs of satisfaction.

M. Jean saw it was impossible to escape the astute Mr. Ferrett, so lifting his head he said boldly,

"It was this—the Doctor received a letter from Australia, and I saw in the postman's hands one with the same postmark for Miss Oakplank."

"Well, sir, what has that to do with the question I have asked?"

"This," M. Jean said, "the letter Doctor Bircham received was from this Jessops, and it concerned, 'The young Mr. Gleddell's innocence of the robbery.'"

"Well."

"So when I heard this, I went to Woodbine Cottage; and found out that Miss Oakplank had a letter from Mr. Gleddell, so there could not be any mistake that Luke Jessops and Mr. Gleddell were together."

"That will do, you can stand down; but do not leave the court, we may want you again."

"Not at all improbable," whispered the doctor to his friend, "eh, Oakplank."

The captain rubbed his hands with manifest delight, but made no answer, for the judge was about to address the prisoner.

He spoke as became a man placed in his painful position, and Philip, who listened to every word, calm, pale, and more like a statue than a human being, awaited the conclusion of the lengthy address, then gathering his faculties, he commenced in a clear, distinct tone:—

"My Lord, I am grateful for the careful attention you have bestowed upon the statements which have been made against me. All I can say is that I am not guilty; yet every word the witness has spoken is perfectly true."

There was a slight buzz of astonishment at this; and many wondered at the prisoner proclaiming the truth of M. Jean's words.

"That struggle," he went on, "which took place between myself and the murdered man was the result of a quarrel between us respecting a matter too delicate to be spoken in this court; but after he left my chamber I became maddened by the danger which my hasty temper had brought upon me, and resolved rather than be placed at the felon's dock, to commit suicide: it was for that purpose I loaded the pistol which was found by the murderer beyond the schoolhouse hall. I can say no more, my lord."

Even to save his life Philip could not call upon the only being who could substantiate his words; but she, forgetting everything save her love for him, left her father's side and went to the witness-box, and in a faint voice said,

"I, my lord, can tell you how that pistol came beyond the schoolhouse wall."

"You, Miss Oakplank?"

"Yes, my lord; let me be sworn.

The oath was administered, and the brave girl told how she had sought Philip after the night of his letter bidding her farewell, and found him with the pistol in his grasp; how she had taken it from him and threw it from the window, and all who listened to her words felt the conviction of their truth.

The judge looked from the prisoner to the beautiful girl, then asked if she had the letter in her possession. She had not, but a messenger from the court was despatched for her writing-desk.

It came, and the letter was placed in the judge's hand.

"So far," said the grave representative of the law, "your evidence, Miss Oakplank, has shed a new light upon the mystery."

Then glancing at the papers he had received from the Secretary of State, he said,

"I find that the unhappy man who wrote this confession has made mention of a white arm appearing for a moment through an open window. You may stand down, Miss Oakplank."

In spite of these proofs of Philip's innocence, Mr Ferrett seemed determined to hold out as long as he could, and not until the letter Doctor Bircham had received from Luke was compared with Milman's confession, would he relinquish the idea that they were written by the same person.

The judge was about to address the jury when one of the Bircham boys elbowed his way forward, and as he came towards the witness box he added his testimony to the previous evidence by saying,

"If you please, my lord, I took that letter for Mr. Readall to Miss Oakplank."

"Topgallants and flying jibs," said the captain, "so he did, I remember the lad."

"We require no more witnesses," said the judge; "I leave the matter in the hands of the jury."

A moment after those learned gentlemen gave a unanimous verdict,

"Not Guilty."

So ended the strange trial, and as Philip stepped from the dock a free man, M. Jean who had sought to destroy the poor fellow out of revenge for the rejection of his suit by Eleanor, slunk from the place and hastily walked towards the school-house.

Here he put his effects together and before the doctor returned, to give him into custody for assisting Greymore to rob the strong room, the Frenchman had gone none knew whither.

But a few weeks after, those who read the French newspapers saw that a certain Jacques Cherdon, alias Jean Gailland had been arrested in Paris as an escaped galley slave.

He had trusted to the time he had been absent from France to escape recognition, but he was deceived, for within a month he was again chained to an oar.

How the Doctor came by the information respecting M. Jean's complicity in the robbery is soon told. Curiosity prompted him to decipher the name which Luke had partially erased from the leaf of Greymore's diary, and to his surprise he found it was that of the French master.

The kindly old man would have kept the knowledge a secret but for the malevolence the Frenchman had shown to Philip Randall; thus was the mode of turning the tables upon M. Jean that caused George Oakplank to exhibit so much satisfaction when the Doctor whispered to him in the court-house.

CHAPTER XV.

THE DISMISSAL OF JACOB SNIVEL AND BREAKING-UP OF BIRCHAM SCHOOL.

SEVERAL days elapsed after the Doctor's return before he discovered the events of the fifth of November.

There were two reasons for this:—First, the boys, content with the victory they had gained, and their dislike to tale bearing, refrained from making any communication to the headmaster respecting the usher's behaviour upon that particular day.

Secondly, Mr. Jacob Snivel held his peace, for upon mature reflection he came to the conclusion that his conduct in repressing, or trying to repress, the time-honoured although senseless custom of commemorating the doings of Messieurs Guy Fawkes and Co., was not supported by any authority from the Doctor, also bearing in mind the severe flogging he had administered to the luckless Dodger, he was quite content to allow the affair to pass over and sink into the oblivion of forgotten days.

Probably this would have been the case had not the Doctor one morning caught sight of the Dodger's contused and discoloured face.

The old gentleman knew sufficiently the use of the cane to at once determine the cause of the Dodger's marks, for, looking over his gold-rimmed spectacles, he enquired,

"What is the matter with you, my lad?"

Bob was silent. He did not wish the usher any harm, although the poor little fellow felt the effects of the severe castigation more than he acknowledged even to his companions.

"Come," the Doctor said, quietly and firmly, "I insist upon knowing who has marked you in this manner."

Bob hung his head and murmured, almost inaudibly,

"I'd rather not tell, sir."

"I desire you to do so. Now, let me hear the truth. Don't be afraid; I shall not have you flogged, even should you have deserved the caning you have already received. If you did not deserve it those who have beaten you will have to answer to me for the brutal act."

Bob stole a glance at his classmates, and, receiving an encouraging nod from Joe Stikkers, said,

"It was the usher, sir."

"Mr. Snivel?"

"Yes, sir."

"The cause?"

The Dodger told him in brief terms, and endeavoured, as much as possible, to throw the whole of the blame upon himself.

"I don't believe, sir," he said, in conclusion, "that Mr. Snivel intended to hit me in the face, but I tried to get away——"

"He held you by the collar, I presume?"

"Yes, sir; and——"

"That will do. You can return to your seat."

Those who were near enough to overhear the conversation between the Doctor and Bob were, at its conclusion, much surprised when they found the master went on with the ordinary business of the school, without taking the least notice of the matter.

They saw that the old gentleman was ill at ease, for at times he rose from his seat, and with his hands clasped behind his back, paced slowly to and fro the schoolroom.

Twelve o'clock came, and the boys were soon trooping to the playground, but before more than a third of them had passed through the doorway the Doctor called them back.

"There will not be any school this afternoon, my lads," he said, "and as it wants but two days to the Christmas vacation, you had better see about packing your clothes."

The announcement respecting the half-holiday was received with manifest tokens of satisfaction; and one boy remarked confidentially to another,

"Isn't the Doctor a stunner; he's no end of good at giving us half-holidays!"

The schoolroom was soon deserted save by the masters, and the Doctor, turning to Jacob Snivel, said:—

"I am sorry, Mr. Snivel, to find that my orders respecting corporal punishment have been so utterly disregarded by you."

The usher raised his eyes, and as a scowl passed over his forbidding face he answered,

"You refer to the boy whose face is a little marked."

"I refer to that boy," said the Doctor angrily, "whose appearance betokens having suffered from a most brutal flogging—such an one that I would not have permitted had I been present."

"It would not have been necessary had you been here," said the usher; "but your absence caused the pupils to assume such decided signs of insubordination that an example was necessary to keep order."

"Did the example," asked the Doctor, "produce the desired effect?"

Jacob saw that the victory the pupils obtained on the Fifth of November was known, so somewhat spitefully he answered,

"It did not."

"Such harshness never has any effect upon the bold spirited lads, sir," the Doctor said. "You must rule by love, not fear; and as I cannot have my establishment disgraced by a repetition of such a scene, you will oblige me by sending to my study for your cheque."

Jacob Snivel bowed.

"Am I," he said, "to understand that my services are no longer required?"

"Such is my wish, sir; for yourself and the school, it will be better that you resign at once."

"Would it not be as well to continue until the vacation takes——"

"Not another hour, sir!—not an hour! I am sorry for it, but there's no——"

"Quite sufficient, sir!" said the usher. "You can send the cheque to my room. I shall be ready to leave within an hour. Good morning, Doctor Bircham."

"Good morning, Mr. Snivel."

Thus they parted—the master looking after the usher's gaunt form as he started towards the door; and all were secretly pleased at the dismissal of their surly companion.

An hour later a fly stood at the gates, and the fact of the Usher having become "sacked" being pretty well known, he was met by the whole of the boys, and as the carriage began to move away, a parting salute came from the lads' lips.

One long and well-sustained groan, and as the respectable Mr. Snivel leant back in the vehicle, he could not help contrasting the present scene with that which took place when Happy and Jack Stansfield left Bircham School.

"He's gone, Joe," remarked the Mallett to his friend. "There's the second. Frenchy first, now old Snivel."

"You needn't have told me this," Joe said, as he turned towards the schoolhouse. "Have you heard the news?"

"What news, Joe?"

"About the Doctor—old Ann told me."

"Ain't heard a word, Joe, although I was in the housekeeper's room, just now—so out with it."

"Well, it's a secret, old fellow, so don't be blabbing it all over the place?"

"No fear, Joe; I'll keep it."

Joe Stikkers lowered his voice, and said in a very mysterious manner,

"The Doctor's going to give up the school, after he is gone."

"No!"

"It's a fact, but I don't hear much about it, though."

"Why, Joe?"

"Because I shouldn't come back any more; I'm going to be a middy."

"I wish you'd take me, Joe," said the Mallett; "I don't want to come back here, if anybody else keeps the school."

"We'll go on to town together, old chums," said Stikkers; "perhaps my governor can manage it for you."

"I hope he will, Joe; for after all the changes here, and you leaving, it won't seem like the old place."

"There have been some changes, Mallett," Joe said; "poor old Gled Happy, and Jack in Australia, Phillip and the Captain on their way out. Well, things do change."

"They do," said the Mallett.

Two days afterwards the large hall was ornamented with bags, boxes, and portmanteaus. And as the lads went away, the Doctor stood at the door, and shaking them by the hand as they passed out, wished them "Good-bye."

"I'm getting old, now," he said to a group of the biggest boys, "and feel I must give up the school. Good-bye, God bless you all."

"Good-bye, Doctor," said the spokesman of the party; "we all owe more than we can repay to you, and dear old Bircham School."

The Doctor waved his hand as a passing salute, then turned with a sigh towards the deserted school-room.

CHAPTER XVI.

FIVE YEARS AFTER.

THE curtain rises at Broken Falls; scene, the sitting room in the rich cattle-owner's tasteful residence.

Mr. Russell has grown stouter this last year or so, and his lady keeps pace with him, and looks plump and good natured as she playfully teases a blue-eyed little urchin who is seated upon grandpa's knees.

The child is about two years old, and by the love light which dances in the lady's eyes, it is pretty plain that Master Tommy stands a good chance of being spoilt by grandma, and truth compels me to add that grandpa' does his best to aid in this by no means difficult task.

No wonder they are so fond of the little fellow, it is Ellen's child, and as her

THE BOYS OF BIRCHAM SCHOOL.

BIG DRUM AND PIPES SEE AN OPPORTUNITY TO RETRIEVE THEIR FALLEN FORTUNES.

husband's farm adjoins Broken Falls, Master Tommy spends nearly all his time with the old couple.

Ellen is mistress of Table Lands, and the prettiest and happiest wife in the colony, but the master of these acres is not Willoughby Addison, for that gentleman did not stand the ghost of a chance with the young lady after the gallant manner in which a certain Tom Dickson alias Happy-Go-Lucky, saved her from death.

Willoughby was a sensible man, for when he saw the decided preference his affianced bride had for Tom Dickson, he at once released her from her engagement, and during the time Happy was in England, whither he had been suddenly recalled by a letter from his uncle, Willoughby Addison resolved to sell the farm and retire upon a well-earned fortune, partly his own accumulation, partly a comfortable balance in the Sydney Bank left by his father.

Happy came back before the farm was sold, and although tolerably enriched by his uncle's death, he abjured his resolve of retiring to England with Ellen and purchased Table Lands from his late rival.

Thus all things as far as the young pair was concerned, became all that Mr. Russell could wish, and he gave her to Happy with a better grace than he would had Happy wished to have taken her to the old country.

Tom would fain have shared his wealth with Gleddell, but the latter preferred an offer made to him by old George Oakplank, who with his two daughters and Philip emigrated soon after the late usher's trial.

The old captain, true to his love for the sea, rejected a snug little farm which was offered him for a sum of money considerably below its value.

"Drive bullocks and feed sheep," the old fellow said, facetiously driving his forefinger against Gleddell's ribs—for the lad, it is almost unnecessary to state, had taken up his abode with Philip and the Captain soon after they landed, "that may do for your long shore lubbers, but not for us, eh, Gled?"

"No, sir; we intend ploughing something different to the land."

"I was not aware of that, gentlemen," the agent said—he was a 'cute fellow, and had an eye to business—"if I can do you a service in any other way, I shall be happy."

"Well," the captain said, "perhaps you can. We want a good boat, a good sea-going sloop, one that can do the coasting trade in half the time it takes the flat-bottomed craft I see lying off Port Jackson."

"I know the article that will just suit you," said the agent; "one just fitted for the inlets and streams about here, and also able to stand a good sea."

"Very well," said old George, bluntly, "I don't want any go-betweens in this affair; you place me alongside the owner, and if I strike a bargain I won't forget your locker."

The captain did strike a bargain, and the sloop soon became known and famed for her bold runs under the old salt's guidance.

BOOK THE SECOND.—CHAPTER XVII.

FIVE YEARS AFTER.—(Continued.)

BRED to the sea from his childhood, he was able to handle his vessel when the other craft engaged in the coasting trade were compelled, through bad weather, to remain in port.

Gleddell was ever at the captain's side, and in less than two years he became capable of managing the sloop and keeping up the fame the old salt had attained.

When the young man had thus acquitted himself, George Oakplank gave him the ship, and the lovely girl who had been his first and only love.

They all dwelt together at Sydney, and the young wife often feels lonely when both husband and father are away, for the old fellow cannot resist the opportunity of accompanying Gleddell when the weather looks stormier than usual.

At these times she finds a little relief in visting her sister—Mrs. Randall—wife of Philip Randall, who has the largest school in the colony.

Mr. Randall is fond of his handsome wife and splendid house, for he established the large school from a very humble beginning. It is said, the foundation of his fortune had begun in two small rooms—one his sleeping chamber, the other a school-room, which he kept until the daily increasing number of pupils compelled a larger residence.

He is one of the many self-made men who are looked up to by the colonists for opinion and advice; and the time is believed not to be far distant when the rich schoolmaster will retire and take his place among the colonial legislators.

Luke Jessop, or, properly speaking, William Walden, resigned his post of overseer to Henry Russell, who fancied farming better than following the medical profession, for which he had been reared.

Luke's courage, quick perception, and indifference to danger gained for him a name both feared and hated by the Bushrangers, and this coming to the knowledge of the Colonial secretary, Luke was offered the command of the mounted police, an offer he accepted, much to the dismay of the skulking vagabonds from whom life and property were never safe.

Luke was soon rewarded for his services in repressing crime, and when he, after three years' service, was appointed magistrate and chief of a new district he bore more than one honourable mark of his conflicts and desperate encounters with the outlaws.

The old sad look has long passed from him, also from his wife, for the solitary mourner at Greymore's grave turned out to be his long lost child—Helen Walden. She was brought to Sydney by the kind old captain and his daughters, and the closest friendship exists between the stern magistrate and the chief owner of *The Minnie* trading sloop; and more than once has the magistrate frustrated a well-planned raid upon the captain's warehouse by the colonial banditti.

Helen Walden had a strange story to tell as she hid her face upon her sire's agitated heart.

She told him it was her senseless form which Pierre Dublé and Greymore saw dragged from the Seine.

She revived when taken to the *morgue*, and after staying in Paris until Greymore returned to England, then, barefoot and friendless, she tracked him from place to place, until the report of the murder caused her to drag her weary body and still more weary spirit to the little village, where his strange, wayward spirit found a long and quiet home.

The gloom which had so deeply overshadowed her young life began to clear away after she had found a haven of repose with her parents, and the wondrous beauty which had caused her so much sorrow, attracted many suitors in the new land.

She rejected them all. Her place, she feels is with her parents, who had so long mourned her as dead, and no offers of wealth have as yet shaken the resolution she has made to remain with them until the grim tyrant breaks in upon her newly found happiness.

Jack Stansfield came back to England with Happy, and being a dutiful son he gladdened his father's heart by at once entering heart and soul into the studies necessary to qualify him for the profession the old gentleman wished him to follow.

He was not long afflicted with the monotony of a barrack life after he obtained his commission, for the war with Russia caused his regiment to be sent upon active service.

Jack lost an arm at the memorable attempt to capture the Malakoff on the 18th of June, and for his distinguished bravery on that fearful day he obtained the legion of honour.

To use a school phrase, old Mr. Stansfield is "no end proud" of his handsome son, and whenever an occasion offers he looks at the empty sleeve and says:

"Jack was among the first to scale the battery, and had he been supported as he ought to have been he would have won the day. Tell them all about it, Jack; all about the trenches and men. You led a sortie right under the walls of Sebastopol.

Jack always humours the old gentleman, who seems never to tire of hearing of his boy's many and strange escapes from death. Jack is known now as Lieutenant-Colonel of the County Militia, and very proud they are of their officer who has been in a real battle.

END OF BOOK THE SECOND.

INTERRUPTING for the present the further narrations of the varied adventures of the

BOYS OF BIRCHAM SCHOOL,

We give our readers the opening of the life-like story,

"OUT ON THE WORLD,"

A story as full of deep pathos as of startling interest, and well calculated to enthral the sympathies of all who peruse its faithful incidents.

BOOK THE THIRD.

OUT ON THE WORLD.

CHAPTER I.

THE GIPSY.

A REMARKABLE trial closed the assizes which had been held in a quaint old city in the north of England—a trial in which the prisoner told so strange a story, that for once the dwellers in the quiet old place were awakened from the usual sluggishness with which they were wont to regard the judicial assemblages convened from time to time in the massive castle.

A proud old noble—Herbert, Earl of Falconmere—had been aroused from his sleep by the midnight intrusion of a member of a gang of gipsies which had for some time taken up their quarters on a piece of waste land adjoining Falconmere Chase.

The nobleman had grappled with his unwelcome visitor, and the struggle that ensued brought a number of stout servitors to his assistance, and the gipsy was soon safely under lock and key.

Early next morning he was conveyed to the county prison, and the damning evidence of his guilty purpose was placed in the governor's hands—a small crowbar, a set of skeleton keys, a dark lantern, and a file. As may be expected, the magistrate at the first examination fully committed the prisoner for trial, upon the charge of burglariously entering the patrician's room for the purpose of robbery; there was a second count, that of murderously assaulting the Earl of Falconmere with intent, &c., &c.

The prisoner—a tall, handsome fellow of about thirty-six, dark as a Spaniard, and with features which, had he not been a gipsy, would have been termed classical—pursued a dogged silence during the examination, and contenting himself with giving the earl a look of fierce disdain, was led away to await his trial.

It will be easily seen that under these circumstances the prisoner's singular story had but little chance of being credited, apart from the antipathy with which his unfortunate race had ever been regarded. The circumstances under which his apprehension was effected were quite sufficient to condemn him in the minds of the intelligent jury, long before the trial took place.

Whether the strange defence he made was true or not, the gipsy evidently knew that he had but little mercy to expect, for up to the last moment he refused every offer made by the tribe to provide him with counsel.

So the trial proceeded—the prisoner calm, defiant, and at times smiling at the pompous evidence of the six footmen who rushed to their employer's rescue; but during the time the Earl of Falconmere was speaking, his large eyes gleamed with a dusky fire, and he seemed to have great difficulty in preserving the silent, watchful manner which had marked his bearing since he first came into the dock.

Many among the few who had intently listened to the trial noted that the earl never once raised his eyes towards the prisoner, and, in spite of his seeming calmness, there was a nervous twitching of the muscles of the throat and face which bespoke an agitation within.

To the judge's question respecting his guilt, the prisoner folded his arms, and in a calm, yet bitter voice replied—

'NOT GUILTY.'

There was a slight stir when the clearly-spoken words rang out, and many looked towards the speaker, a half pitying, incredulous smile upon their lips.

'*Not guilty*,' he repeated, 'of the crime with which I am charged. That I was found in yon *murderer's* chamber I admit, but not for the purpose he has stated. You start at the word murderer; but look towards the rich titled scoundrel who has this day perjured his soul—behold that pallid face—does it look as though my words were true? See! he rises from his seat and stag——'

Here the gipsy broke into a wild laugh, and pointed with outstretched finger towards the Earl of Falconmere, who was at that moment leaving the court. Every face had mechanically turned towards the agitated old patrician, who seemed scarcely able to walk erect.

'Prisoner,' the judge said, sternly, 'do you understand the terrible charge which you endeavour to fix upon a man who has but done his duty in giving evidence against you?'

'Perfectly,' was the calm reply; 'yes, the Earl of Falconmere is a murderer, and his soul is heavy with the crime. My lords and gentlemen,'—the gipsy drew himself up and swept the sea of faces which were turned towards him as he added, solemnly—'*he has killed his only child!*'

A subdued whisper came from the excited listeners—a whisper that gradually swelled, as it was taken up from mouth to mouth, into a low cry of horror.

The gipsy saw the effect his words had produced, not only upon those who filled the hall, but upon the judge, the barristers, and the jury; he also saw an official hastily leave the court as though to detain the earl.

As the gipsy ceased speaking, the eyes of all present were turned towards the harsh, proud face of Falconmere's last earl.

He bore the scrutiny without a muscle of his features moving, and as the judge began to address the prisoner, he arose from his seat.

'Have you any witnesses,' asked the judge, 'in support of this most extraordinary story?'

'None, my lord.'

There was a slight buzz as the high justiciary arose to pass sentence, and as the first sound fell from his lips, the faint murmur subsided, and a dead silence reigned in the vast hall.

He spoke as a man who thoroughly believed the gipsy's statement to be a tissue of falsehoods from beginning to end, and wound up the homily by sentencing Ralph Morkar to be transported beyond the seas for the term of twenty years.

The prisoner heard his sentence without betraying the least emotion, and pointing to the earl, who yet remained standing, said in calm, measured tones—

'My lord, you have done but your duty in this instance. You are safe from the vengeance of my tribe, but let yonder perjurer beware, for from this time henceforth the zingaries will watch for an opportunity to avenge my loss.'

The Earl of Falconmere heard the gipsy's words with a scornful smile upon his lips, and making a gesture with his hand to imply that his words were intended for the astonished crowd in the body of the hall, he said—

'I cannot leave this court with the knowledge that this man's improbable story has passed unchallenged. You can judge how much reliance can be placed in his statement, from the fact that my only daughter was placed in the family vault two years previous to the woman's appearance at the Abbey gates.'

Then, as though he had said sufficient to clear his character from the inevitable effects of the zingary's defence, he bowed coldly to the judge, and left the court.

The prisoner was led from the dock by two warders, and as they were passing through a passage which led to the cells the gipsy made a rapid sign to a man, whose dark features proclaimed him one of the descendants of the ancient chivalry of Egypt.

The sign, though not perceptible to the gaolers, was seen and acknowledged by the loiterer.

He watched the condemned man until the grim-looking doors closed upon his form, and then turned sadly away.

Pasing the front of the prison, he beheld Earl Falconmere enter his carriage. For a moment the gipsy stood as though turned to stone, and as he watched the carriage roll away the veins stood out on his swarthy forehead, and from his compressed lips there came words of such dread import, that Herbert, Earl of Falconmere, would have quailed had he heard the zingary's oath of vengeance.

CHAPTER II.

THE CAMP.

A LIGHT blue wreath of smoke rising among the trees marked the spot where the gipsies' camp was situated.

The tribe, consisting of about twenty of both sexes, were grouped around a cauldron, from which came a powerful odour, sufficient to impregnate the air for some distance from the blazing wood fire.

Except a boy of about thirteen summers, the group were all characterized by the dark olive complexion and black elf-like locks which distinguish the wanderers to this day.

The men were, with one exception, young and lithe of limb, and the women were remarkable for their lustrous laughing eyes and white gleaming teeth.

The boy, though somewhat tanned by exposure to the sun, had that unmistakable fairness of skin which proclaimed him a stranger in blood to the dusky group by which he was surrounded. His hair, though long, and matted together from neglect, was of the richest brown, and falling in wild profusion over his handsome well-set head, added rather than detracted from his beauty.

The boy was reclining at the feet of a

venerable man, whose snow-white beard formed a strange contrast to his swarthy countenance and black fiery eyes.

The group were evidently expecting a visitor to the encampment, for, from time to time, several raised their heads and listened anxiously.

A tread suddenly broke the spell, and the aged chief, as he looked in the direction of the quick footfall, heaved a deep sigh.

'It is he,' he said; 'we shall now learn the worst.'

As the last word left the venerable gipsy's lips, the man who had exchanged signals with Ralph strode hurriedly to the centre of the silent, expectant group.

The eagerness with which they thirsted for his intelligence was perceptible upon every face; but, faithful to the laws which forbid curiosity to any of their race, none spoke.

The new comer fixed his dark eyes for a moment upon the fair-skinned boy, then turned abruptly towards the group of women, and as the wistful, anguished face of Ralph's wife became opposite him, his lips twitched nervously, and the words he was about to utter died away upon his tongue.

As though ashamed of this weakness, he set his teeth firmly, and in a low, but perfectly audible voice, said, in the strange, figurative language of their Eastern forefathers—

'Not until the swallows have crossed the seas, or the earth has worn a white pall twice ten years, will the wanderer return to his tribe; neither in the noon of day nor under the black pall of night will he come, until twenty long winters have passed and gone.'

Save the stifled shriek of agony that came from Ralph's wife, no sound came from the gipsies when this intelligence was made known; but the dusky fire that shone in their dark eyes told how deeply they felt the fate which had befallen their companion.

The old chief arose, and pointing upward to the vaulted canopy of heaven, said, in solemn impressive tones—

'In gloom, in sunlight, in sleeping or waking, and until Azrael, the angel of death, hovers over him with her dark wings—until then may the doer of this evil be accursed!'

From the angry group came in deep, savage accents—

'May he be accursed!'

The gipsy chief raised his head, and making a silent gesture towards the women, they arose and meekly left the spot, taking with them the beautiful fair-skinned boy.

'Now,' the old chief said, 'we will hear the black lies which have this day robbed me of a son, and you of a companion.'

The man who had brought the intelligence of Ralph's doom inclined his head in token of assent, then seating himself near the cheerful fire, he related all that had passed in the hall of justice.

They listened with grave attention, and at the conclusion of the recital the old chief, discontinuing the figurative mode of speech which had hitherto embellished his words, said—

'To-morrow messengers must be sent through the whole length and breadth of the land, that the district chiefs may search for the clue to substantiate the story Ralph this day told before those wise men of England. The knife would be a quicker mode of revenge, but it would not enrich the boy who has eaten of our bread. Once a proof of the boy's birth and relationship in our possession, then Herbert, lord of Falconmere, dies, and the outcast shall reign in his stead.'

'Until the clue is found,' asked Tinker Tom, 'is Falconmere to rest in peace while he we love so well drags out a dreary life in the convict settlement?'

'It must be so; but stay. What were his wishes? You spoke by signs before he was led away.'

'None. He bid me take care of the boy. No more passed between us.'

'Are you willing to do so?'

Tinker Tom mused for a moment, then raising his head, he answered—

'I am. More so, since he can become an instrument in my plan of vengeance.'

'Ah! How so? Remember the boy is to be kept sacred from harm.'

'No harm shall befall him,' said Tinker Tom. 'Have I your permission to unfold my plan?'

The chief bowed his kingly head.

'There is but one being in the world whom this stern noble loves,' said the stalwart gipsy; 'that one a blue-eyed child whom he has adopted. To lose her would bring a deep sorrow upon his heart, and, in part, avenge the loss we have this day suffered.'

He paused, that his words might have weight with the silent group whose permission would have to be obtained before he could begin his well-defined plot against the lordly owner of Falconmere.

'With the boy's aid,' he resumed, 'it will be an easy matter to lure her from the Abbey grounds. Once in my possession,' the gipsy added, vindictively, 'she shall be reared as a beggar. In the hands of an old thief-trainer she will become a fitting tool for my purpose.'

The gipsy chief pondered long over these words before he said—

'Under the supposition that the girl has become all you would make her, in what manner do you intend to use her *talents?* Is it against the earl, who has reared her from her infancy with a father's love?'

'It is,' said Tinker Tom, his eyes aglare at the thought of his plan of vengeance. 'Her degradation shall be the means of crushing the earl's pride. In the same spot that Ralph stood this day will I bring the earl's *protégée*, and he—her adopted father—shall give such evidence against her that will brand her with the convict's mark for ever; and when the final doom is passed, and not till then, will he know that the fair-haired child who has so oft nestled at his breast and the condemned convict are one.'

The vindictive spirit that prompted this subtle revenge cared not for the time that must elapse ere he could strike this crushing blow upon the lordly owner of Falconmere.

'We have heard you,' said the chief, looking towards the swarthy group; 'let the tribe say if your plan is good.'

The men were silent, and Tinker Tom, who knew the ominous sign, bit his lip until the blood came slowly from the punctured skin.

'Does my plan seem too long for the anger that is in your hearts?' he asked, turning to the tribe. 'Think you that the knife would be a fitter mode of revenge?'

'We do,' they answered. 'It is too long to wait. Years must elapse ere the first blow is struck.'

'Ay,' Tinker Tom said; 'years must elapse. Every year will be an age of sorrow for the man who has so deeply wronged us. Know you not that his love for this child is the only sign of human feeling he has shown since he drove his daughter to a suicide's grave? Picture the old man in his loneliness, waiting daily, hourly, for the return of the object of his love. Behold him when the child he has so long mourned has budded into womanhood — rich, possibly, in outward beauty, but her heart blackened by evil—a thief, a felon. Fill up the picture by the knowledge being suddenly imparted to him that the sweet child he nurtured has fallen so low, that she steals into her childhood's home and robs the sorrow-stricken being who has so long mourned her loss—think of this, and tell me, is the vengeance, though tardy, worth waiting for?'

The impassioned manner in which he spoke, the facial changes which accompanied every word, the fiendish delight with which he portrayed the earl's sorrow, had their weight, and a low buzz of admiration came from the assembly.

There was one whose thirst for immediate vengeance could not be appeased. He claimed a closer kindred with the condemned man than any who sat by the blazing camp fire.

Ralph Morkar had married this man's sister, and Black Moreau's fierce longing for the earl's life could ill brook the subtle schemes set forth by Tinker Tom.

He arose when the latter had ceased speaking, and pointed towards the huts where the women of the tribe could be seen grouped around the bereaved young wife, who looked upon the doom that had that day fallen upon her husband as an eternal separation.

'Look!' Moreau said, passionately, 'think you yon weeping woman can wait the long years your plan will take to develop? Think you that the knowledge of a coming vengeance will soothe her lacerated heart when her mind travels to that far-off land where her husband toils, with an accursed chain impeding every movement of those limbs that have been hitherto as free as the air we breathe? It is her we should consult in this great wrong—it is her voice that has said give the evil-doer's body to the knife, and level his proud walls to the ground. What say you, my friends? Shall it be so?'

To this excited harangue Tinker Tom replied with all the arguments he had previously used. To them he added the danger that would accrue from slaying the Earl of Falconmere—a danger he showed them that would, in all probability, end with the extermination of the tribe.

'In part, Moreau,' he said, in conclusion, 'your wishes may be met. We will fire the Abbey, and under cover of the flames I will obtain possession of those papers which have caused your kinsman to be taken from among us.'

Moreau heard him patiently—his dark eyes glaring with a savage light, and his white teeth gleaming between his parted lips, gave the stern passion-worked features a demon-like expression.

'And the earl?' he asked; 'is he to perish in the flames?'

'That,' Tinker Tom said, 'must be left to chance. The Abbey fired, the girl and the papers in my possession, we can be content for a while.'

The venerable chief would fain have altered the cruel work; but for once his words were without authority, and sighing deeply, he arose, and left the angry, fierce-looking group to mature their plans of vengeance.

CHAPTER III

LATOUR AND THE EARL.

EARL FALCONMERE'S body-servant was a Frenchman by birth, cunning and unscrupulous by nature, gaunt in form, and cadaverous in features.

His step was as soft and as stealthy as a cat's, and the small bead-like eyes seemed always peering and prying into the countenances of all he met, as though endeavouring to read the inmost thoughts and feelings of those who had the high honour of Monsieur Jules Latour's acquaintance.

There was none, save the earl, in the princely establishment who had a good word for the French valet. From the stable-boy to the pompous steward, one and all hated the soft, sneaking, cat-like gentleman who honoured the Abbey with his presence.

He seemed to possess an unlimited sway with the earl, and though his foes sought to shake the nobleman's confidence in his valet's fidelity, they signally failed.

That a secret of momentous import was in the valet's possession, the *ladies* and *gentlemen* in the servants' hall devoutly believed.

There seemed some truth in their belief, for when the earl returned from the trial he was followed into his study by the gaunt Frenchman.

There was a peculiar expression upon the valet's saturnine countenance as he glided behind his master—a mingled look of hate and triumph, so blended that it was impossible to tell which feeling predominated.

As noiseless as a shadow Latour passed inside the chamber; then carefully closing the door, he placed his back against it, and said—

'Is he put out of the way?'

The earl, whose haughty features now looked pale and careworn, sank into his chair, and briefly answered—

'Transported for twenty years.'

'Good!' said the valet; 'he will not trouble your lordship again.'

'Personally he will not,' said Earl Falconmere; 'but the tribe, or I am much mistaken, will seek a terrible revenge for the punishment their companion has this day received.'

'Does your lordship fear the vagrants?'

Latour's thin lips wore the faintest possible expression of scorn as he asked this question.

'Fear them?' the earl said, angrily; 'I fear no man, face to face, but I am powerless to cope with a score of cunning vagabonds who would use secret assassination as a retaliation for what has transpired.'

Latour rubbed his hands softly, and his

voice sounded more like the purring of a cat than aught else.

'My lord is sure,' he said, 'of the devotion I feel towards his person. If my lord fears a visit from a midnight assassin, we will, with your lordship's permission, exchange sleeping-rooms.'

Earl Falconmere looked at the gaunt figure before him, then glanced at his own massive and powerful limbs.

'By this proposition,' he said, with a slight laugh, 'it would appear you are better able to cope with an unwelcome visitor than I am.'

Latour saw the look, and divined its meaning, and still softly rubbing his hands, he answered in a low hissing voice—

'In strength, my lord, I am but a child, but in cunning I could outwit even the serpent. Will my lord suffer me to occupy his room to-night?'—he showed his discoloured teeth as he added—'it will be both prudent and wise. Your lordship rarely finds Latour's advice a matter of regret after.'

The earl paused for a moment, then raising his eyes, which had hitherto been fixed upon the carpet, he looked steadily at the Frenchman's immovable countenance.

'I thank you' he said, 'for this proof of your devotion, but as we shall leave the Abbey in a few days, I think the change will be unnecessary.'

Latour bowed, and was about to leave the room; his hand was upon the door-handle when the earl's voice arrested him.

'By the way, Latour,' he said, 'have you visited the vault since—since the Lady Alice was buried?'

'I have not, my lord.'

The earl again began to study the pattern of the carpet, and after playing with his watch-chain for a few seconds, he said—

'Do so. That fellow's story I have every reason to believe made an impression upon the jury; and should there be an inquiry, and, perhaps, an investigation into its truth, it will be necessary to have *everything prepared.*'

'Your lordship's wishes shall be attended to forthwith.'

So saying, the valet bowed and glided from the room. As he hurried down the broad staircase, an expression of baffled hate lit up his features, and from between his thin lips came the words—

'Foiled again. So he leaves the Abbey, fearful that the gipsies will wreak their vengeance upon him. So, so; this very fear may yet serve my purpose.'

The earl, when Latour had closed the door, placed his elbow upon the table, and leaning his forehead upon his palm, became lost in thought.

From the many changes his face underwent, it was evident his musings were of a most painful nature. The greater part of an hour passed and he moved not, nor would he then, had not the door suddenly opened, and a beautiful child of about ten summers bounded into the room.

She saw the deep grief visible upon the earl's face, and stopping short in the centre of the apartment, she looked wistfully at the stalwart form, awed into silence by the strange wild gleam of the earl's dark lustrous eyes.

The rich sunlight, falling through the stained glass windows, cast its prismatic hues upon the child's long golden hair, playing like a halo around the sweet infantile face; and as she stood with half-averted head, one little hand raised towards the earl, her attitude was filled with that grace which painter, sculptor, or poet would fain have imitated, but not excelled.

Finding, after a pause of several seconds' duration, that her entry had been unnoticed, she approached the earl, her foot falling as lightly as snow falls to the ground.

He felt the gentle touch of her soft delicate hand upon his arm, and looking up, beheld the child's blue eyes fixed upon him with a sad, inquiring glance.

There was no tie of blood between them, but he had been as a sire to the fatherless orphan, and she repaid this kindness by loving her benefactor with all the fervency of her affectionate nature.

'Little one,' he said, 'tell me what you have done since I went away this morning.'

The little arms were twined around his neck, and the soft damask cheek was placed fondly against his as she answered—

'I had my music lesson, papa, and read a little with governess. Then I went out with Flossy, and had such fun in the park—rare fun it was, for Flossy kept barking and jumping after the birds, and could not catch one; but I cried after that, papa.'

'Cried, my darling; what caused you to cry?'

'Jack Lennox, papa.'

The peer raised his eyebrows and repeated the name.

'Pray, Lily, who is Jack Lennox? one of the grooms?'

'No, papa; he is a poor little gipsy.'

The peer started, and instinctively drew the fair child close to his breast.

'A gipsy,' he said, gravely; 'surely my darling does not seek a playmate among the wandering vagrants who infest the wood.'

'No, papa; but poor Jack is not a gipsy, he says, and I don't think he is, because he is not so dark as that horrid man that came once, and had a fire hanging to the handle of —a—a machine, I think that sulky Latour called it.'

She paused, as though trying to recollect the explanation given by Latour of the various uses to which Tinker Tom put his knife-grinding machine, and the earl, who had been held spell-bound by her words, waited with bated breath for her to resume her childish explanation.

'There,' she said, 'I have forgotten all about it. But poor little Jack Lennox, papa —I'm sure you would give him a pair of shoes. I wish my old ones would fit him; but they—'

'Yes, darling, I will give him a pair; but what were you saying about the boy not being a gipsy?'

'Oh, I asked him one day.'

'One day?'

'Yes, papa; he often comes in the park when I am playing with Flossy. Poor little fellow, he did cry so, to-day; he made me feel so sad that I was obliged to cry as well.'

The earl frowned angrily, as he said—

'You have not told me the question you asked him yet, darling.'

'No, papa; I will. One day I asked him why he was not so dark as the men and women I had seen in the wood, and he told me that he was not a gipsy. He said he had no papa or mamma, and when he was very little the gipsies found him in a wood, and have been kind to him ever since; but I don't think they can be kind, because he has no shoes to wear; do you think so, papa?'

The earl did not answer; his face was now as white as a sheeted corpse, and his lips moved in that nervous, twitching manner which showed how deeply he struggled with the pent-up feeling in his breast.

'When I saw him to-day,' the child went on, 'he told me that the gipsy who had been so kind to him had been taken away; and he cried so—— What is the matter, papa?'

A deep groan had escaped the earl's lips in spite of every effort, and the alarmed child, kissing the ghastly face, said anxiously—

'You look ill, papa. Shall I call Latour?'

'No, no, my darling; I am better now. Run to your governess, and get ready for your afternoon drive; and mind, Lily, you never go in the wood again alone.'

'I will not, papa, if you do not wish it.'

'I do not, darling. Kiss me—here comes Latour. There, come to me after you have finished your afternoon lesson.'

As the child left the earl's side, Latour entered the chamber.

'*Everything is ready*, my lord,' he said, 'should your fears be realized.'

The earl inclined his head; then passing his hand across his brow to wipe away the big drops which had gathered thickly during Lily's prattle, he said—

'You wished me to exchange rooms with you, Latour. I accept your offer. How far is your chamber from Miss Lily's?'

'Directly opposite, my lord.'

'Good. Place my pistols upon the table before I retire, and see that the fastenings of the young lady's windows are secure.'

CHAPTER IV.

MONSIEUR JULES LATOUR'S PROSPECTIVE FORTUNE.

BY degrees the lights in the various chambers in Falconmere Abbey were extinguished, and all, save two, who dwelt within the sombre pile, were paying tribute to the drowsy god of night.

The earl and his valet had exchanged sleeping apartments, and though midnight had long since chimed, neither had sought repose.

In the valet's chamber the lamp had long been turned down, and in the silent gloom sat the peer, one hand supporting his throbbing brow, the other nervously clutching the butt of an exquisitely mounted pistol.

The wind, as it came sighing among the ivy, and sweeping around the quaint gables in fitful gusts, seemed to the lonely watcher like the footfall of a prowling marauder.

Time after time he arose, and hastily opened the chamber-door, and sought to pierce the deep gloom in the long corridor; then the wind would lull, and the silent, determined man, after listening to the little Lily's gentle respiration, walked moodily to his seat, and resumed his lonely vigil.

So passed the night with Falconmere's proud earl, and when the sunbeams stole through the window, they played upon a face older by ten years in appearance to what it looked when the rosy light gladdened the earth on the previous morn.

His eyes were wild and bloodshot, the features pinched and careworn, and his lips, though tightly compressed, wore the hue of one who had passed to another world.

There must have been a greater cause than his anxiety for the gentle child's safety to have worked this wondrous change.

In the darkness of that long night the memory of a great wrong perpetrated by the stern, pitiless man came strong upon him; the murky air seemed filled with strange shapes, and a low, wailing cry was ever ringing its mournful cadence in his ear.

He knew that the white shimmering forms, and the touching voice, were but the unreal creations of his brain; yet the strange spell that came over his faculties was none the less terrible, nor his sufferings the lighter, by the oft-repeated defiant words by which he tried to dispel the shadowy terrors that weighed so heavily upon his soul.

'The dead,' he would mutter, fiercely, 'never return; these gleaming forms, and that wailing cry, are but the result of this day's undue excitement.'

So he argued, mentally, yet his eyes, starting from their sockets, would follow the white, transparent shadow, as it floated through the darkness, and large beads of perspiration, cold and clammy, stood out upon his forehead, as the fancied cry of hopeless anguish smote, from time to time, upon his brain.

He would have struck a light, but the spell was too strong upon him. He dared not move from his seat, nor turn his head, for the wretched man felt a cold hand placed upon his shoulder. Though it seemed but small and fair, yet the weight kept him down, and rendered his limbs incapable of movement.

With the gladsome light these strange and terrible fancies departed, and as he buried his face in his hands, a deep groan of agony welled up from his heart, and the strong man's frame trembled like one stricken with the palsy. When he arose from this position, he walked to the casement, and, throwing back the long windows, found relief in the cool morning air, as it played around his burning brow.

'Not for the sea's worth,' he said, 'would I pass another night like this. Yes,' he added, musingly, 'conscience does indeed make cowards of us all.'

Long he stood gazing mechanically at the rich prospect which the sun's mellow tints were rapidly disclosing. To the east tracts of golden grain stood out in bold contrast with the rich emerald tints of the grass-covered fields, and the sombre hue of various patches of newly ploughed earth.

The darker shades of the hedgerows which divided the fields looked not unlike the boundary marks upon a large map.

The eye, wandering beyond this, beheld a pleasing extent of undulating country, and

THE BOYS OF BIRCHAM SCHOOL.

BIG DRUM AND PIPES BEGIN THEIR NEW ENTERTAINMENT.

the tiny white dwellings, nestling among clumps of tall trees, or half hidden in a sequestered valley, gave a peaceful charm to the scene.

Looking southward, the thick foliage of Falconmere Park shut out the distant view, and as the earl watched the tree-tops bend before the gentle breeze, a deep curse came from his lips, and the face—hitherto so pregnant with remorse, became distorted with passion.

A thin spiral column of smoke rising from behind the thick wood, showed where the gipsies' camp was situate. The sight aroused all that was evil in the earl's nature, and he stood glaring like a demon at the light blue cloud which gradually melted away.

As he stood thus a gentle tap at the door caused him to start, and look towards the weapons which lay upon the table.

The tap was repeated, and then Latour's well-known smooth accents were heard.

'Enter,' the earl said, smoothing his disordered hair, and striving to repress his agitation.

With his usual cat-like gait the valet stole inside the chamber, and, glancing furtively at the earl, he began rubbing his hands softly, and asked—

'Has my lord slept well?'

'No, Latour,' was the answer; 'over-anxiety has kept me awake the whole night.'

Latour was grieved—deeply grieved—that such had been the case, and offered to prepare the earl a cup of coffee. The servants not yet being awake, the slimy valet would, upon such an occasion as this, soil his spotless hands.

The offer was accepted, and the earl, taking the case of pistols under his arm, retired to his own chamber.

He saw by the appearance of the bed that Latour had not slept therein. A large wrapper, lying in a careless manner upon the antique sofa, showed where the valet had passed the night. Nothing else, to all appearance, had been disturbed, although the early part of the night had been passed in a strange manner by the crafty, treacherous Frenchman.

When Latour entered the earl's chamber he extinguished the lamp, which stood upon a table near the bed. This done, he took a small lantern from beneath a loose wrapper he carried, and withdrawing the shade by which it was darkened, began to search carefully among the miscellaneous articles upon the dressing-table.

Though absorbed in this occupation, he took especial care that the circular gleam of light should not rest upon the window.

'*Peste!*' he muttered. 'It is not here.'

And turning from the table, he searched the pockets of the clothes the earl had that day worn. Inside the breast of a light overcoat he found the object of his search, and his saturnine countenance glowed with triumph.

It was a small key of peculiar construction and elaborate workmanship, and as the valet held it before the light, he muttered, joyfully.

'At last—at last is my patience rewarded. Month after month, year after year have I tried to obtain this key. Ha, ha! he has slept with it beneath his pillow every night for nine long years. His first waking thought has been to place it safely about his body, but once, my lord of Falconmere, your caution has left you, and Latour has profited by the omission.'

To ensure against the earl's sudden entry into the chamber, he locked the door, then wheeled the sofa across, and in such a manner that the high back rose far above the key-hole.

'My lord might return,' he thought, 'and finding the door locked, would put his eye to the key-hole. This will make all safe so far. Now for the prize.'

The key opened a large oaken chest which stood in a recess near the head of Earl Falconmere's couch. To judge by the external appearance of this massive article, every precaution had been taken to render it impregnable. There was not a square inch of the wood visible. A double row of wrought-iron plates defended the edges, and the flat surface was covered by a thick sheet of the same metal.

The key was not above two inches long, but the openings in the upper part were of such minute and peculiar make that the most skilful whitesmith would have been baffled to have picked the lock.

When Latour placed the key in the small opening he paused before turning it, and as a cunning twinkle shone in his eyes, he muttered—

'There are such things as pistol-barrels fitted to these boxes. I must be careful.'

Placing the lantern upon the floor, he arose and went to the fireplace and brought the tongs. Then, keeping well away from the front of the chest, he gripped the key with the points, and, raising his hand upwards, the faint click of the lock sounded in his ears.

Latour paused for a moment as though in expectation of beholding the lid open, and hearing the sharp report of firearms.

Neither occurred; and the valet, releasing the key, applied the tongs to the rim of the lid. An expression of disappointment came over his face when he found the lid immovable.

But an instant's reflection told him that the iron plates and cover would be sufficient to cause this. Fearful that he should be unable to attain his wish, Latour, reckless of the consequences, seized the lid and threw it upwards.

Save a dull thud, which was caused by the iron rim striking the wall, there came no sound to alarm the excited Frenchman.

So with a glad cry he turned the light of his lamp upon the contents, and began his search.

There was nothing in the appearance of the discoloured rolls of paper, old letters, and a few sheets of closely-written parchment, to need this secure receptacle; and as the valet took out each article, and after a careful examination placed them on the floor, his face underwent many varying expressions.

At times, when his fingers clutched a roll of paper, his eyes would light up with exultant triumph; then, as he found they were not those he sought, the expression would change to one of blank disappointment.

So he continued until the box was nearly emptied; then in a corner, hidden by a number of old letters which had been thrown in loosely, he came upon the object of his eager search.

It was a small bundle of somewhat discoloured paper, the edges frayed, and the exterior bearing the appearance of having been long carried about in a pocket.

The small roll was tied with a piece of faded blue ribbon, and on the outside, written in the earl's bold hand, was the single word ALICIA!

Latour's fingers trembled with joy when he untied the ribbon, and, carefully opening the packet, he took therefrom a plain gold ring, two parchment certificates, and a long silken tress of sunny hair.

These he laid aside during the examination of the various letters. When this was concluded, he took the outer sheet away, and, with a roll of paper he had brought with him, made up a packet similar in size to that which he had opened.

The outer sheet he found was blank, save for the word written by the Earl of Falconmere. This he placed around the fictitious roll, then tying it with the ribbon, placed it on the carpet.

He then rolled the original, and, holding one in each hand, compared the appearance they presented.

In size they were as much alike as possible, but the edges wore quite a different aspect.

Latour opened the lantern, and pricked up the wick with the point of a penknife until it began to smoke.

Over this he held the ends of the packet he had brought to substitute for that in the earl's possession, and, as he proceeded in his cunning work, he held the soiled papers close to the light, until the new, smooth edges of the second packet became of the same hue as the old.

This done, he carefully frayed the ends with the point of his penknife; then again holding each end over the black smoke, finished his task.

He had succeeded in every way—the false roll of paper bore such a close resemblance to the original, that, unless they were opened, detection was impossible.

As he carefully replaced the contents of the oblong box, Latour's lips parted, and a low chuckle of triumph, mingled with expressions of peculiar import, broke from him.

When the task was finished he carefully closed the box, locked it, and replaced the key in the breast-pocket of the earl's overcoat.

This done, he gathered the abstracted letters, and putting the certificates and ring into a pocket-book, arose from the ground and went to the sofa.

Here, stretched at full length, he read the contents of the packet, and by the time he had concluded, the first streak of day began to struggle through the darkness.

The reading seemed satisfactory, for Latour placed the papers in an inside pocket and mused—

'So, by a codicil added to her uncle's will, Greyford, with its rent-roll of four thousand, was hers; in the event of her death, to pass to the boy, if they were lawfully married. They were. Well, in the event of the boy's death it passes to the earl. Ah! I begin to see a little clearer now. Yes, the earl is the happy possessor of this snug little windfall; but whether he will long possess it remains at the discretion of Monsieur Jules Latour, *valet de chambre* to the Earl of Falconmere.'

Latour closed his eyes and pondered over the knowledge he had achieved. He had no particular dislike towards his employer; but when he maturely deliberated over the affair, he came to the conclusion that it would be more chivalrous to befriend a homeless boy than to accept a heavy bribe from the earl to keep the secret.

'Besides,' he mentally argued, 'the boy will feel grateful to me for the interest I feel in his behalf, and he cannot do less than give me, his only friend and guardian, a thousand a year to sustain that important and very respectable position.'

He became so excited with this prospect, that he almost believed he had achieved the distinction and emolument he had marked out for himself.

When he had sufficiently indulged his fancies with this pleasant prospect, his mind again reverted to the mode of attainment.

'I wonder,' he soliloquized, 'how such a wary, careful man as this master of mine appears in all his transactions, should have kept the letter from the lawyer announcing the sudden change in the old curmudgeon's sentiments towards his fair niece. Let me see. The old fellow was the lady's mother's brother. Exactly; and with him the last of the name passed away. Let me see.'

He drew the packet from his pocket, and selecting a letter written in the unmistakable caligraphy of a lawyer's clerk, read the concluding paragraph.

Having done so, the paper was replaced, and put carefully away.

'Yes,' Monsieur Jules Latour resumed, 'should everything be correct respecting the boy's parentage, he takes the old family name and the money to support it. Now, I think the first step will be to secure the will, if it is in the box. I think my best plan will be to take it, and then take myself off.'

Monsieur Jules laughed at his little joke as he rose from the sofa and crossed the room. He was in such a genial mood with himself that he could have laughed at the merest trifle.

When he found the will he not only laughed, but capered about the room with a buoyancy that would have excited envy among the dancing dervishes of the beautiful but dirty city of the Sultan.

Monsieur Jules returned to the sofa after restoring the key to its place, and opening the lining of his coat, placed the will inside.

'The will, the certificate of marriage, also of the boy's baptism, in my possession,' he said, gleefully. 'I think the thousand a year much nearer than it was an hour since.'

He left off to rub his hands, and so energetically was this process carried out that the flesh became the colour of beet-root.

'Now to find the boy,' he resumed, when his fingers tingled with pain; 'then, if possible, to obtain the clothes he wore that night; but that will not be a very difficult affair if the gipsy spoke the truth yesterday. If the clothes are not obtainable, there is e mark upon the boy's body, at least, so the unfortunate lady states. Well, I shall see about this soon. Now I think the mode of operation pretty well laid out. Should—ah! why not?—If this is not the rightful heir, I must find one; that will be very easy. As for the earl, I think the little secret connected with the family vault will cause him to keep the peace towards my very excellent self. Monsieur Jules Latour, you can commence your thousand a year from to-day.'

He laughed so heartily at this that the tears came to his eyes, and a severe pain cramped his right side.

'Laughing does not agree with my tender frame,' commented Monsieur Jules, as he tenderly rubbed his side. 'I must be careful, and make a note of that. Now for the earl. I wonder how he has slept while I have been making a fortune?'

By the time Monsieur Jules reached the

earl's presence all traces of the late hilarity had passed away from his features, and he seemed the quiet, attentive servant of yore.

And when he brought the earl the promised coffee, he gently persuaded the nobleman to take a few hours' rest now that all danger was past.

The earl yielded to the advice, and while he slept Monsieur Jules was busy in his own chamber packing a leather valise ready for his contemplated flight.

Monsieur Jules, before placing the most useful articles of clothing in the valise, carefully unfastened one side of the internal canvas covering, then between that and the bottom he spread the precious papers.

A little glue refastened the canvas, and, as Monsieur Latour remarked, when rubbing his hands—

'No one would suspect that anything was hidden there.'

Long before the earl rang for his valet the preparations were complete, and Latour waited but for the opportunity to visit the gipsies before he bade an eternal farewell to Falconmere Abbey.

If there is any truth in the story told by the gipsy, and in Latour's musings, our ragged little hero is the grandson of an earl, and the heir to a fortune.

We must leave the solution to that grim old tyrant, Time, and the *disinterested* kindness of Monsieur Jules Latour.

CHAPTER V.
THE ABDUCTION.

No servant could have been more attentive in the discharge of his duties than Latour appeared when in attendance upon the earl that morning; he assisted the nobleman to dress for a hunt that was to take place that day, and while handing him his velvet hunting-cap he made a suggestion to the nobleman which met with the warmest approval.

'I have been thinking, my lord,' he said, 'that the men, as a rule, are not fitting companions for Miss Lily during her rambles in the park or the adjacent forest.'

The earl looked inquiringly at his valet, then turned to the glass to finish the arrangement of his neckcloth.

'I have had much to do with children,' Latour continued, 'before I had the honour of entering your lordship's service—(This was true; the rascal had a wife and family residing in a low suburb of Paris, deserted and destitute)—therefore I know the difficulty that exists at times in answering their questions.'

The earl gave an impatient stamp with his foot.

'Yes, yes; I understand,' he said. 'You think the grooms would, in consequence of their ignorance, be unable to answer a simple question Miss Lily's inquiring mind might suggest.'

'Precisely so, my lord; therefore, with your permission, I will accompany the young lady upon her morning walk.'

The permission was readily granted, and as the earl rode away from the Abbey, Latour watched him from the window, his face anything but expressive of the deferential mask he had so well worn during his attendance upon his master.

The reason Latour had made this offer was the result of a long debate with himself.

He wished to confer with one of the gipsies, also to make the acquaintance of the boy he felt so keen an interest in advancing.

By judiciously placing his ear to the keyhole he had overheard the conversation between the beautiful child and her benefactor. He had no particular reason at the time for doing this; it was merely the result of a confirmed habit—a passion if you like. Monsieur Jules could not pass a door when two persons inside were conversing.

He had a theory that, sooner or later, such a mode of proceeding must result in obtaining information that would be useful, though, to speak the truth, the little items of conversation he had overheard in the pantry and the housekeeper's room had not realized this theory; far from it, he had oft listened to the most scurrilous adjectives coupled with his own name from those chambers, and had been compelled to retire in consequence.

He heard the earl and the child speaking as he glided down the long corridor, and every word she had uttered flashed across his brain when he perused the packet of letters.

With Lily's guidance, he had no doubt of soon finding the boy she knew by the name of Jack Lennox.

Besides, as Monsieur Jules argued, it would not be prudent to be seen by any of the male domestics as he went in search of the gipsies. Under these circumstances his generous offer served two purposes—one to obtain speech with the boy, the other to approach the camp without been seen.

The latter he deemed necessary, not knowing how many days might elapse before he brought his negotiations to a satisfactory conclusion with the gipsy who had so long befriended the boy, who was to aid him in the possession of a thousand a year.

Monsieur Jules rubbed his hands when he thought how well his story had become verified; and keeping up the imperceptible cleansing, he went softly towards the young lady's room to offer his valuable services as companion during her ramble.

He met the beautiful child at the wide oaken staircase. She had a small basket in her hand to hold the wild flowers which she so fondly loved to gather.

The bright blue eyes dilated with amazement when Latour told her that the earl wished him to accompany her in her morning walk.

There was a little pouting and some slight show of resistance before she would accept her gaunt escort; but when Monsieur Jules told her that her ramble in the park would be forfeited unless he accompanied her, she gave in.

'I will tell papa,' she thought, as they left the Abbey, 'how much I should prefer being left to myself.'

She little knew that she had parted from the earl for many, many years, when she stepped forth from the grim old pile into the fresh brilliant sunshine.

Latour was too busy with his schemes to place much constraint upon his charge. At times, in eager pursuit of a bright-winged insect, she would become lost among the trees, and her guardian would have to rush in search of his precious charge.

Her happy face became clouded when he overtook her, and she would sit upon the grass revolving a childish plan to escape Latour's surveillance.

It was strange, this antipathy she felt towards the earl's valet. He had never offended the little lady in manner, yet she shrank from his touch as she would from a venomous reptile.

'I wish,' she thought, as she gazed upwards at the white fleecy clouds, 'it would rain. I don't like this man to be with me, and if I thought papa would not be cross with me for returning so soon, I would go back to the Abbey.

Monsieur Jules, leaning against the trunk of a tree, was mentally wondering when it would please the little lady to wend her steps towards the forest.

He was anxious to confer with the gipsies, still more anxious to obtain, if possible, the clothes worn by the future owner of Greyford when he fell among the zingarees.

Finding the child continued plucking the petals from a bunch of daisies she had gathered, he asked in his blandest tones—

'Would Miss Lily like to go in the forest?'

She looked pleased at this, and readily answered—

'Yes; but you must keep a long way behind, because—because——'

'I will, if mademoiselle wishes it; but why must I do so?'

He saw the child's face overspread with a rosy blush, and instantly the earl's injunction came across his mind.

'Ah!' Monsieur Jules mentally remarked, 'she wishes to meet this ragged playmate of hers, and fears that I shall prevent it.'

The little girl made no answer to Latour's query. She could not tell a lie, neither could she state the reason she wished Monsieur Jules to be as far as possible from her.

She had not forgotten the promise she had made the earl to hold no more meetings with the gipsy's *protégé*, but her heart told her it would be cruel not to see her little playmate once more, and tell him that her papa had forbidden her to meet him again.

She was thinking how this could be managed, when Latour's words solved the matter; so, without any attempt to form an excuse for the request she had made, she arose and walked slowly towards the confines of the park.

When nearly two hundred yards from the spot where she had been sitting, she paused, and looking into Latour's face, said—

'Oh! Monsieur Latour, I have left my basket behind—do fetch it for me.'

'Certainly, mademoiselle, certainly,' said the obliging schemer as he turned and began to retrace his steps. Don't walk fast; I shall soon overtake you.'

Lily watched the Frenchman until his lath-like form became lost among the trees; then, clapping her hands with joy, she turned towards the forest, and bounded away with the fleetness of a young fawn.

Her silvery laughter pealed out as she passed through a broken portion of the high fence that enclosed the park; then taking a path that led towards a clump of trees, she was soon lost to sight.

When Monsieur Jules Latour returned with the basket, his eyes opened wide with amazement. The little lady was gone, and though Monsieur Jules ran until he was out of breath, he failed to discover the path she had taken.

Consoling himself with the hope that he should come up with her in the forest, he passed through the fence, and began to look eagerly around.

Crouching behind a huge bushy tree, Tinker Tom and another of the tribe saw Monsieur Latour enter the forest, and as his gaunt form passed through the fence, the gipsies, quitting their place of concealment, ran swiftly in his track.

Tinker Tom's swarthy face beamed with triumph, and, drawing back the hammer of a gun he carried, he hissed between his set teeth—

'If that fellow interferes, I will put a bullet through his head.'

'Do so,' said his companion, 'and the report of your piece will bring a dozen keepers upon us. My plan is the best and safest.'

'Be it so,' said Tinker Tom, lowering the hammer of his fowling-piece; 'perhaps it will be the quietest way of doing the business. Have you the rope?'

The second gipsy held up a coil of strong cord in reply. Tinker Tom nodded, and renewed the pursuit.

Latour by this time had begun to feel alarmed at the sudden disappearance of his charge, and, running to and fro, he called her loudly by name.

Passing through a clump of trees, he came suddenly upon the gipsies' encampment. The tents were struck, and the beasts of burden laden ready for instant departure.

To his wild inquiries he received a surly answer, and was told to leave the camp.

Though in a state of wild excitement, Latour marked the aspect of the tribe, and comparing the sudden departure of the wanderers with the earl's fears, he felt assured that the young girl had fallen into their power.

This was not a matter of much moment to Monsieur Jules. He could have returned to the Abbey and escaped with his valise before the earl came home from the hunt.

So, with a forced laugh, he walked towards the venerable old chief, and was about to address him in furtherance of the design he had already formed.

Before he could utter a word, the old man waved him back, and said—

'You have been told to depart. Do so; we desire not your presence.'

'But a few words,' said Latour. 'I have a matter that may be of advantage to us both, if you will permit me to dis——'

Tinker Tom and his companion burst through the thicket at that moment, and, in obedience to a sign from their chief, seized Latour and hurried him away.

They paused when out of sight of the tribe, and before Latour knew well what had occurred, he was being tied to a tree.

'What means this?' he yelled. 'What have I done to you or yours?'

'Nothing,' Tinker Tom said, quietly; 'it is to prevent your doing harm that we do this.'

They had bound him hands and feet to the massive trunk, and were going away when his frantic cries rang out with redoubled force.

'Hear me!' he shrieked. 'Whatever may be the cause of this strange proceeding, believe me I shall not in any way interfere with you. I came as a friend, and would make a pro—— Curse them! they are gone, and I am left powerless.'

Monsieur Jules saw part of the pleasant fabric he had reared on the previous night tumble to pieces, and, struggling to free himself from his bonds, he invoked the direst curses upon the heads of his captors.'

Curses or struggles availed him nothing in this dilemma. This he soon discovered, and his bloodshot eyes were turned wildly from point to point in the hope of beholding a peasant or one of the keepers from the Abbey.

WHEN the child ran laughing at the success of her plan, she entered a small glade completely shut out by the surrounding trees. Here she was met by the fair, handsome boy, who was lying at the old chief's feet when Tinker Tom brought the intelligence of Ralph's banishment from the tribe.

He sprang gladly forward when the beautiful child entered the secluded spot, and, gazing inquiringly at her flushed face, he asked—

'Have you been frightened that you came so quickly through the forest?'

'No, Jack, not frightened; I was running to escape that surly Latour. Papa told him to come with me, and I don't like him, so while he went back to fetch my basket I ran away.' Here she became sad, and, dropping her voice, added—'But I must not stay; I only came to tell you that papa says I am never to speak to you again.'

The colour came to the boy's face, and, throwing back his handsome head proudly, he said—

'The earl need not have told you this, Lily, for we go away to-day.'

'Go away!' she repeated. 'But you need not go, Jack; you told me you were not a gipsy, so—so, you can stay.'

'I must go with them,' he answered, bitterly, 'though I do not like their mode of life; but I am not old enough yet to make my way through the world, or else I—— Hark! what is that?'

He caught the fair girl by the wrist, and as his face paled he bent down and listened intently.

'It seems like a man calling out for help,' the boy said; then casting a startled look around, he added—'It is the man that came with you. Tinker Tom and Aiken have caught him.'

Lily looked at the excited boy, and asked—

'What do they want with him, Jack?'

'I will tell you, Lily. They have been in the park all the morning watching for you; so run, Lily, run! Although they will beat me for not keeping you, I do not care.'

The child became confused; she felt alarmed at her companion's words, but did not comprehend the danger he had but hinted at. The full significance soon came, and for some moments held her spellbound.

'They intend to take you away,' he said, forcibly, in revenge for the earl having transported Ralph. Don't cry, Lily; I will take you back to the Abbey, although,' he added, 'the gipsies tell me the earl is my greatest foe.'

He grasped the fair small hand, and they ran silently from the little glade which had so oft rung with their happy laughter.

Jack Lennox knew that Tinker Tom would soon be upon their trail, and determined, if possible, to save the child, he made a detour to reach the front of the Abbey, thinking by this means to escape the watchful gipsy.

The spire of the old gateway was visible between the trees, and keeping this in view the fugitives ran swiftly onward. Another ten minutes and she would be safe; but ere half that brief space had passed, a quick footfall behind caused their hearts to sink.

'Stop!' a voice said—'stop! Do you hear, Jack Lennox? Stop! or I will put a charge of buck-shot in your back.'

The boy came to a sudden halt, and, as he turned fiercely and faced his pursuer, he clasped his hands tightly, and seemed as though about to spring at Tinker Tom's throat.

'He will do it,' said the boy. 'I would not stop, Lily, had he not that gun with him.'

Tinker Tom's face was purple with rage when he overtook the children, and, without a word, he seized the girl and threw her over his shoulder.

'Let her alone,' said the boy, trying to interpose his small frame before the child. 'I wish I had strength enough, you should not do this.'

Tinker Tom's reply was a sudden blow with the gun-barrel. It struck Jack Lennox across the face, and hurled him bleeding to the earth.

The gipsy would have left the senseless boy but for the fear he would have gone to the Abbey and brought the keepers out to rescue the fair child.

He lifted the boy with as much ease as he would an infant, then, with his double burden, he started swiftly after the tribe.

Fearing the earl's anger when he discovered the loss of his little favourite, they had wisely made preparations to remove from the vicinity of the Abbey, and by the time Tinker Tom had recognized the girl they were far beyond the confines of the forest.

CHAPTER VI.

OUR HERO'S FIRST STEP IN THE WORLD.

EARL FALCONMERE'S horse fell soon after the fox was hunted from his cover. The leap had often been exceeded by the powerful hunter, but upon this occasion he was brought up too quickly, and instead of clearing a ditch that lay beyond the quickset hedge, his hind feet slid down the slippery incline, and the earl, to save himself, inadvertently jerked the animal's mouth and brought him over.

The horse and rider struggled for some time in the slimy filth, and had it not been for two labourers who were at work in an adjacen field, the last Earl of Falconmere would have terminated his existence in the foul stagnant water.

Though terribly shaken the earl was able to remount, and rewarding the men, he turned the horse's head towards the Abbey and rode slowly away.

Covered with the mire from the ditch, the earl did not wish to pass the front of the Abbey. There was a near cut to the rear of the park by passing through the forest; this path the earl pursued, and to his amazement came upon his valet, bound hand and foot to the trunk of a tree.

To spring from his horse and loosen the bonds was the work of a moment, his heart throbbing violently, and his quivering lips refused to ask the cause of Latour's strange predicament.

He had guessed the truth before Latour could speak, and when the valet told him that Lily had disappeared, he sprang into the saddle and galloped towards the Abbey.

Latour saw the noble beast clear the high fence at a bound, and hurrying as fast as his cramped limbs would permit, he reached the park just as the earl, at the head of a body of keepers, grooms, and stablemen, issued forth in search of the little Lily.

The earl carried a double-barrelled gun in his hands; both hammers were drawn back, and by the wild gleam in his dark eyes, Latour knew that his master would slay the abductors of his adopted child with as little remorse as he would bring down a partridge.

'Come with us, Latour,' said the earl; 'you can identify the ruffians who fastened you to the tree.'

Thus commanded, Monsieur Jules had no alternative but to obey.

They reached the spot where the gipsies had encamped, and, save for the charred remains of a wood fire, there was no trace left to guide the pursuers.

The earl leant upon his gun, and looked around for a sign of the retiring gipsies. There was none; every footprint had been obliterated by several of the tribe drawing long green boughs after them.

This had effectually obliterated their footmarks upon the green sward, and though the men scanned every part within a hundred yards of the camping-ground, they were still at fault.

The earl bore the crushing blow without a murmur; his desire for revenge for the time was stronger than the effects of the sudden loss he had sustained.

There was still hope. The tribe could not have gone far, and the keepers, who had learnt a little woodcraft by so oft tracking poachers when they stole from the preserves, now took the lead in the pursuit.

Spreading themselves out, they keenly examined every tree and shrub, and after an hour's torturing suspense, the earl's heart was gladdened by the shout from one of his men, which told that the tribe had been discovered.

A small remnant of an old discarded red cloak had been held by the sharp thorns of a wild briar. This discovery kept alive the faint hope that had nearly left the earl's heart when he found how well the tribe had hidden the path they had taken.

He sprang forward at the cry, and as the faint light grew stronger in his eyes, he gave the men stern and peremptory orders to shoot down the first of the gang if any resistance was offered.

An hour's search brought them within sight of the gipsies; the tribe were leisurely pursuing the open road when the shouts from the keepers attracted their attention.

They paid no heed to the loud commands for them to stop; not one even of the women turned their heads to look from whence the cries came.

This indifference made the men yet more eager to overtake them, and dashing across a ploughed field the earl and his party intercepted the gipsies.

They would have continued their march, had not the injunctive earl, his frame quivering with passion, called out in a voice of thunder—

'Halt! or, by Heaven! I will send the contents of this weapon among you.'

They saw by the speaker's wild gestures, and the stern expression upon his pitiless face, that he would execute his threat unless they instantly complied.

At a signal from the grey-headed old chief, the gipsies became as though suddenly transformed to stone; then the venerable man, stepping to the front, asked in a calm voice the reason of this interference.

The earl made no reply, but pushing such of the gipsies that stood in his path aside, made his way to a small covered cart, and with savage violence tore the canvas away.

He had fully expected to have seen the sweet child beneath the rude covering, and when he found the cart contained little else save the cooking utensils and a few small articles of clothing, a terrible imprecation fell from his lips.

His ravings were those of a madman, and with a spring like an angry panther, he closed with the old chief and gripped him by the throat.

'Where is she?' he yelled. 'Speak, old man, or I will crush out your life! speak—tell me where you have hidden the child.'

The young men of the tribe would have helped their chief, but awed by the superior numbers of the earl's party, they were compelled to stand and quietly behold the aged man nearly strangled in the earl's strong grasp.

'Take your fingers from my throat,' the white-headed gipsy gasped. 'I cannot answer you—I am choking. Would you commit murder?'

'Ay,' was the fierce response as the earl relaxed his grip; 'I would dye this road with the blood of your accursed race for this foul crime. Tell me,' he added with passionate energy, 'where is the child you have stolen?'

The old man pointed upwards, and raising his eyes solemnly towards heaven, answered—

'By the great Omnipotent I swear I have not seen a child this day, save the little ones of my tribe.'

He looked like a patriarch of old as he stood thus, and even the fiery earl was for a moment struck with the simple grandeur of the humble gipsy.

Latour, who had scanned the faces of the men, bore out the chief's statement by coming to the earl's side and whispering—

'Neither of the fellows who tied me to the tree are here, my lord.'

The earl's face grew paler at these words, and turning to the aged man, he asked—

'Are any of the tribe absent? Speak truthfully—I am in no mood to be trifled with.'

'The gipsy,' said the chief, 'has no need to lie. Two of the tribe are away; they left us to join another party who are moving southward.'

The earl groaned with anguish. He realized the fearful truth, and, clasping his burning brow with both hands, moaned—

'Lost, lost, lost!'

The folly of the men who had taken the child joining this party became apparent to the earl's followers, and the head gamekeeper, whose long service placed him upon a more familiar footing with the earl than his fellows, now advanced.

'It may not be too late, my lord,' he said, respectfully. 'We can, by going cross country, reach the London road almost as soon as the men who have taken Miss Lily; that is,' he added, 'if they have gone in that direction.'

The earl caught eagerly at the suggestion.

'Is there no other road,' he said, 'except this and the high road to London?'

'None other, my lord.'

The keeper was left with half a dozen men to watch the gipsies, and rescue the child should her abductors join them.

This done, he turned from the road, and, forcing his way through the hedgerow, took the nearest path to the road that led to London.

When retracing the verge of the forest, the earl and his party were within twenty yards of the object of their search. They knew it not, and until night set in the pursuit was continued, then only abandoned when the men became worn out with fatigue.

The earl returned to the Abbey that night a crushed and broken-hearted man. He had lost all he loved upon earth, and cared not how soon the cold hand of death came upon him.

* * * * *

Tinker Tom carried the children through the forest, until the boy recovered his consciousness.

His first act was to struggle with the muscular gipsy, and with his puny fist to strike the fellow's dark, swarthy cheek.

Tinker Tom laughed at this show of spirit, and, placing him upon the ground, bade him follow and be silent.

The boy wiped the blood from his face, and, looking fiercely at the gipsy, said—

'I shall be a man some day, then I will make you sorry for taking her away.'

The burly gipsy was both pleased and amused at the lad's latent spirit, and, placing Lily on the ground, said—

'There, my young game-cock, take the little lady's hand, and follow me. No noise, mind, if we should meet any one in the forest, or I will give you another taste of this.' He touched the gun-barrel significantly as he spoke. 'And as for the girl, I will twist her neck.'

Tinker Tom had the repute of being what is termed a man of his word. Jack Lennox had upon more than one occasion seen him carry out a threat to the very letter, and fearing that he would strangle the fair girl, he promised not to call out for help, no matter whom they might meet.

Tinker Tom knew the boy would not break faith with him. Though so young he showed the better clay from which he was moulded, by a strict adherence to the truth, and an absence of the pilfering proclivities so common with the juvenile members of the vagabond tribe.

This matter settled, the gipsy threw his gun into the hollow of his left arm, and bidding the children go in advance, the walk through the forest was resumed.

The little girl felt less fear now the man had placed her upon the ground, and her hand was clasped in that of her young playfellow; she clung to him, and showed more calmness than could have been expected from one placed in such a strange position.

They had not gone far when the earl's stately figure was visible through the trees, and had not Jack reminded her of Tinker Tom's threat, she would have called out to him for help.

The gipsy made them creep behind a clump of bushes until the earl had passed, then he arose and urged them quickly forward.

They were near the road, which was at that moment being traversed by the tribe, when the earl and his party could be seen approaching. Again the children were forced into a place of concealment. Here they remained until the pursuers were seen returning from their unsuccessful visit to the tribe.

The trunk of an old tree hid their forms from the earl and his men, and as Lily stood clinging to her young champion, she whispered—

'Let us run when papa and his men come close.'

Tinker Tom stood some yards in front of them, both hands grasping his gun, and his dark face full of triumph as he watched the keepers breaking through the thick vegetation.

He heard Lily's whispering, and as he glanced at the advancing party, he said, savagely—

'Make the attempt, and I will kill you both.'

Lily shrank back, and clung yet closer to her companion; and he, as though to shield her from harm, passed one arm round her waist and clasped her hand.

Anger and despair were blended in the look he gave Tinker Tom; then turning his head towards Lily, he whispered—

'Never mind; I will try and take you to the Abbey to-night.'

She felt he would keep his word, and when the earl again passed within twenty yards of the place of their concealment she remained perfectly quiet.

Tinker Tom laughed mockingly when the men were out of hearing, and again driving the children before him he went after his companions.

They had just crept through a hedge when the gipsy, with a lowly muttered oath, dragged the young girl back, and forcing her down, crouched beside her in the shelter of a dry ditch.

Jack Lennox he had already disposed of by hurling him to the ground. The boy looked up in surprise at this sudden attack, and was about to ask the reason, when Tinker

THE BOYS OF BIRCHAM SCHOOL.

A STREET TRANSFORMATION SCENE.

Tom placed the forefinger of his right hand upon his lips, and with his left pointed towards a group of men who were partially hidden by the trees.

Jack knew the men at the first glance; some he recognized as gamekeepers, others by their livery were grooms in the service of Earl Falconmere.

These men were the party left by the head keeper to watch the road by which the gipsy tribe were travelling.

Until nightfall Tinker Tom and his young companions remained in their place of concealment. The watchers at times passing so close that their words were plainly distinguishable.

The boy's heart beat painfully when he heard the men. He knew that one cry would bring them to Lily's rescue, and several times the effort to repress the words that came to his lips was noticed by Tinker Tom.

He brought the muzzle of his gun in line

with the boy's head, and in a voice like the hiss of a snake said—

'Remember, the slightest cry, and I will pull the trigger.'

Jack Lennox cowed before the savage expression in the gipsy's eyes, and bowing his head, wept at the misfortune that had befallen the little girl—a misfortune, in spite of the strong wish within, he was powerless to avert.

He saw Lily's tearful blue eyes regarding him with an expression of mute entreaty, and construing that glance as it was intended, he remained silent; but his brain was busy with a plan by which he yet hoped to effect her deliverance.

There was not a selfish thought in this: he hoped only to take the trembling child to the gates of the old Abbey; then he would return and meet the punishment he felt assured would befall him. For this he cared not. Too oft had he been lashed by the gipsies for refusing to aid them in their petty thefts, to shrink when the liberty, perhaps the life, of the fair child was at stake.

'I'll do it,' he thought; 'and they may tie me to the cartwheel, if they like; even then I shall not care, if Lily is safe.'

The punishment he alluded to would have caused a stout heart to quail at the very thought. He had seen, and his flesh had quivered at the sight, strong men stripped to the waist and bound hand and foot to the cartwheel, then lashed with a whip, the thongs of which were composed of thin strips of cowhide. He had seen the flesh torn and lacerated by this inhuman punishment; yet he could bear it to save the little girl from the power of the vagrant tribe.

When the bright stars shone from heaven's vaulted canopy, Tinker Tom left his hiding-place. The men who had been left by the earl's order had gone towards the Abbey, tired of watching, and hopeful that the child they all loved would be recovered before their return.

The gipsy, holding the children on either side of him, started swiftly in the track of his tribe. The walk was long and arduous, for he kept inside the hedgerow, and before they reached the camp, Lily's feet were torn and blistered by the rugged ground.

They had travelled ploughed fields, the earth dried by the sun and wind until each piece was as hard to walk over as jagged stones. Oft, too, had the child become ankle-deep in mud, as her captor stumbled into a ditch. So, with aching limbs, aching heart, and the large tears falling silently upon her soft cheek, she was dragged to the presence of the vengeful gipsies.

The women of the tribe would have soothed her, but she shrank from them and clung to the boy, and with her head nestled to his breast, sobbed with agony.

He drew her away from the dark circle of these rude beings whose very presence filled the child with alarm, and as he bent over her, and smoothed the long sunny tresses which fell like a golden shower upon her neck, he whispered words of hope.

'Do not sleep to-night, Lily,' he said, 'and I will try and take you from these people. There is a withered tree near the road-side. Wait until everything is quiet in the camp, then go to that tree; I shall be there, and we will go back to the Abbey.'

She did not answer, her heart was too full. Then Jack, taking her by the hand, led her to the fire, and gave her a portion of the savoury stew from the huge iron pot.

'Eat,' he whispered; 'it will make you strong enough to undergo the long journey to-night.'

He saw the child's weary look, and his heart misgave him. He knew they would have to be fleet of foot to escape, and with the hope that her strength would return when she had partaken of the nourishing viands, he pressed her to eat that from which her delicate palate revolted.

The signal was given for the gipsies to retire, and Lily was led by one of the women to the shelter of the canvas tilt, which by day covered the cart, and at night served for a tent.

Jack Lennox lay near Tinker Tom, and as the night wore on, he heard the gipsy's heavy respiration increase as his senses became steeped in slumber.

The boy raised himself on his elbow and listened intently. Everything was quiet in the camp; even the restless watch-dogs—the gipsies' vigilant and trusty sentinels—were coiled up within reach of the warmth which came from the dusky fire-glow.

As noiseless as ever an Indian scout moved within the circle of an enemy's wigwams, the boy quitted his companion's side, and crept towards the cart.

It was but the work of a moment to draw Tinker Tom's gun from among the loose straw; then with a swift and noiseless tread he ran towards the withered tree.

Eager and anxious was the search he made around the gnarled old trunk, and when he satisfied himself that the fair girl had not yet left the camp, he leant upon the fowling-piece, and strained his eyes towards the dim outline of the gipsies' tents.

Half an hour passed—to him it was a lifetime—and then the brave little heart began to sink with apprehension.

'She will not come,' he said, in low, sad tones; 'what shall I do? Has she been detected in her attempt to escape, or has the exertion she has gone through this day caused her to sleep?'

He heard the sweet chime from a distant village proclaim the hour. To him the sound came like a knell; the child could not come to him, and all hope of seeing her would pass away.

So ran his thoughts. The morn was fast approaching, and daylight, he felt, would be his greatest foe.

He trembled with excitement as these thoughts passed through his mind, and in another instant he would have returned to the camp, and sought the fair child in spite of every risk.

His first step was arrested by the sound of a heavy footfall hastily approaching the place where he stood.

Well versed in the cunning mode by which the gipsies eluded the gamekeepers' search, the boy laid himself face downward, and with a noiseless, snake-like motion glided towards the dark hedgerow.

He had safely hidden himself beneath the overhanging bushes by the time the solitary wayfarer reached the tree.

There was sufficient light to discern the man's features, and Jack Lennox, as he recognized in the man one of the tribe, gave a start of surprise.

The gipsy had gone forth the preceding morn in company with Tinker Tom, and as the startled boy saw him pause and look back at short intervals, began to fear that the absence of this man boded ill to Falconmere's proud earl.

He had heard the threats of revenge when the gipsies met in council, and as he saw Tinker Tom's companion going swiftly towards the camp, a chill came over his young frame.

'If he awakes Tinker Tom,' thought the boy, 'I shall be discovered; then,'—he paused for a moment, then jumping to his feet added—'then I will use this gun before they shall do any harm to the poor little girl.'

The deep bay of a watch-dog came upon his ears, then the angry voice of the gipsy as he reproached the hound for not recognizing his footsteps.

With bated breath Jack Lennox listened to these sounds, and the ruddy hue of health faded from his cheeks, and left them as pallid as those of the sheeted dead.

Every sense was concentrated as he placed his ear to the ground, and his heart throbbed quickly, as he feared the savage tones of Tinker Tom's voice would follow the noises already detailed.

'I had better return,' soliloquized the boy, sorrowfully. 'Lily will not come now, and should I be missed, that brute will come in search. Ha! she is here.'

He ran eagerly forward as the fair-haired child advanced towards him. She had come, but in a different direction to that which he expected.

'I have been so frightened,' she said, as she placed her hand confidingly in his. 'I saw you take something from beneath the cart, and would have come from the tent but I was afraid.'

'Afraid, Lily?—of the woman?'

'Yes; she said such dreadful things to me that I have cried ever since, and the time seemed so long. Every time that the hour struck from the church I felt worse; but when two o'clock came I thought of you, and how sorry you would be, so I crept out and walked a long way round away from where the men are sleeping, to come here. I was afraid of the dogs.'

They were walking hand in hand upon the smooth footway as the child told her young champion how heavily the time had passed since she had been taken to the tent.

'I am glad you are here,' he said, 'but we must make haste, for fear they may discover your escape. Can you run, Lily?'

'I could, but my feet are sore; but,' she added, cheerfully, 'I will try.'

They began at a gentle pace, and the warmth stilling the pains of her blistered feet, their speed increased, and was continued until both were panting with exertion.

This run had placed a couple of hundred yards between them and the camp, and for the first time since he had stolen from Tinker Tom's side, Jack Lennox began to breathe freely.

He began to impart the joyful feeling of security to his companion, but she suddenly stopped his speech by abruptly asking—

'What have you brought that gun with you for?'

'I took it away,' Jack said, 'to prevent Tinker Tom from shooting us, should he come. Lily—Lily! here—hide quick—here he is.'

The words came from trembling lips, and as the young fugitives sought the shelter of the hedge, they heard a man's hasty steps coming towards them.

They needed no light to distinguish this form, for the dreaded voice of Tinker Tom could be heard calling upon Jack Lennox to stop.

The boy dropped upon one knee, and as a fierce light came to his eyes, and a terrible resolution nerved his arms, he raised the butt of the fowling-piece to his shoulder, and in reply to the fair child's exclamation of alarm, answered—

'If he attempts to take you back, Lily, I will shoot him.'

She cowered beside the handsome, resolute boy, her terror holding her speechless and spellbound.

Tinker Tom had been awakened by the man who had passed so closely where our hero crouched. He had missed the boy, and the truth at once came to his mind.

With a frightful oath he sprang to his feet and ran to the tent where Lily had been taken. She had gone; and the gipsy telling his companion to take the fields, he bounded to the road, and soon saw the dim outlines of the children's forms as they ran onward.

He saw them turn from the footway and disappear, and running hastily towards the hedge, beheld the boy's attitude of defence.

Tinker Tom was unarmed, and he knew sufficient of Jack Lennox's determination to cause him to pause ere he sought to recapture the little maiden.

'Put down that gun,' he said, hoarsely, 'and return to the camp, or I will have you flogged as the tribe flogs those who steal from each other.'

The boy's firmly spoken reply staggered the angry gipsy, and overawed him in spite of his brute courage and immense muscular power.

'I shall do neither,' he said, 'and as sure as the stars are above us will I shoot you if you attempt to take the little girl from my side.'

The muzzle of the fowling-piece was in line with the gipsy's head, and the finger that coiled around the trigger, though small, was but waiting for an hostile movement to send forth the heavy charge of buckshot with which the piece was loaded.

Tinker Tom stood silent with rage and astonishment, and grinding his teeth with passion he listened intently for the sound of his companion's footsteps.

'If he can get behind the young cub,' Tinker Tom thought, 'I can easily retake the girl.'

The man he so anxiously listened for must have wandered far away from the narrow path which ran parallel with the hedge, for some minutes passed and no sign or sound denoted his whereabouts.

Goaded to madness at the thought of the

child's escape, Tinker Tom made a sudden bound forward to snatch the gun from the brave little fellow.

He came within a foot of the dangerous muzzle, then a sharp report broke the stillness, and Tinker Tom fell to the ground, his leg shattered by the close discharge.

Jack Lennox waited but to see that his foe had fallen, then throwing the gun away he seized Lily's hand, and started forward at a pace that fear alone could have caused.

The ground was now familiar to the young fugitives; they were rapidly nearing the grand old park that stood in the rear of the Abbey. Joy, before another twenty minutes would expire, Lily would be safe.

They entered the earl's domain by passing through the broken fence. Here every tree was familiar to the young pair; here the boy had often entered to join the fair and beautiful girl in her childish sport.

He thought of this as she endeavoured to keep pace with him, an effort which gave her the most exquisite pain, for her limbs were weary, and but for the danger that yet menaced her she would gladly have sought a brief respite by lying upon the cold damp earth.

'We are safe,' he began—'safe, and I will now leave. See! What is that?'

Four streaks of livid light lit up the Abbey's sombre walls as this exclamation left his lips. Higher and higher rose the red light, and the points, like serpents' tongues, licked and crawled around the four high towers which formed the angles of Falconmere Abbey.

The children paused, awe-struck by the fearful sight, and as the windows reflected back the red fierce light, the fair girl clung to her companion's arm and moaned piteously—

'The Abbey is on fire! Poor papa, poor papa; he will be burnt!'

Lily's words roused Jack from the momentary stupefaction that had fallen upon him, and dragging her quickly forward, he exclaimed—

'It is their work! Quick, Lily; we shall yet be in time to give the alarm!'

The wind fanned the flame until it spread like a winding-sheet around the doomed walls. Showers of sparks began to start upward, and the roar of the terrible element could be plainly heard by the terrified children.

Their pathway was as light as if the noonday sun shone among the trees, and yielding to the excitement caused by the grand yet sad sight, they flew onward—pain, weariness, and danger alike forgotten.

The sudden pealing of the great bell was now heard even above the roaring flames, then came a confused and heart-rending succession of shrieks as the female domestics rushed wildly from the blazing pile.

The hurrying forms of men flitted like shadows before the children, and amid the wild scene of chaotic terror and confusion they reached the lawn in front of the Abbey.

The young girl's return was unsuspected in such a scene, and many who now rushed wildly to and fro, and passed the pale lovely child, were among those who sought so eagerly but a few hours before to snatch her from the power of the wandering vagrants.

Latour, carrying a leathern valise upon his shoulder, passed within a few paces of the boy who he hoped would finish the erection of the glowing fabric he had so well outlined.

He saw them not. The all-absorbing thought of saving himself and the precious contents of the valise from the fierce element, drove every other subject from his mind.

Every moment added to the remorseless power of the fell destroyer. One of the mighty walls had fallen in, and men who were risking life and limb to stay the advance of the insidious foe, shrank back terror-stricken at the terrible crash of the falling masonry.

There was yet another sight in the night's dread work—a sight that caused strong men to turn pale, and their hearts to stand still.

There came a cry from those who directed the stream of water upon the front of the building—a cry that was taken up until it swelled into a chorus of affrighted voices; and the fair girl who clung to her boyish companion hearing the dread sounds, gave a piercing scream, and fell to the earth.

Jack Lennox drew the senseless child away from the rushing feet of the excited men as they ran beneath the earl's chamber, and a hundred voices took up the dreadful words which had stricken the fair girl to the earth.

'Save the earl! Save the earl!'

Such were the words which betokened the nobleman's danger, and every eye turning towards the open casement, around which the hungry flames played, beheld the peer grasping the window-sill, and frantically calling upon those below to save him.

Men who had grown grey in the peer's service, and whose devotion to their master made them reckless of their own danger, reared a ladder amid the fire, and as they were beaten back, scorched and half suffocated, the flames caught the ladder, and consumed the lower part before the earl could even risk this fearful mode of escape.

A mighty cry came from the strong men's lips when they saw the charred fragments fall amid the hissing fire. That cry was echoed by one from the earl as the flames drove him back from the window; then came a fearful crash, a column of smoke and fiery sparks shot upward, and the front of the palatial mansion fell to the ground.

Jack Lennox had watched this fearful scene with distended eyes and bated breath, and when all hope of saving the earl had passed away, he turned sadly towards the recumbent form by his side, and the utter loneliness of their position broke upon him.

What could he do? He had not a friend in the world save the gipsies, and after what had passed between them he felt it would be madness to return.

He saw Lily's blue eyes unveiled, and heard her lowly-spoken words as she asked for her papa. The boy felt thankful that she had been spared the sight of the earl's destruction. A soothing reply was upon his lips, but ere it could find utterance, he caught Lily's hand convulsively and drew her further in the shade.

A gesture to imply silence answered her interrogative look; and, taking his finger from his lips, he pointed towards two figures which were crouching behind a tall tree.

The girl's face became pale, and her large eyes dilated with fear as she recognized the hateful forms of two of the tribe.

The children could hear their lowly-spoken converse, and mixed with the exultant expressions at the fate which had befallen the Abbey, were words of dread import to herself and her young protector.

'Lily,' whispered the boy, 'we must go away from here. You hear what they mean to do if we are caught.'

She clasped his hand, and, half stupified with grief at her sudden bereavement, suffered him to lead her from the scene of her great sorrow.

Once only they paused, and Lily looked sadly back at the smoking ruins of her childhood's happy home. She sobbed bitterly when she thought of the kingly man who had been her all upon earth. Then turning away, as she remembered her cruel persecutors were but a little distance from them, she looked in her young companion's face, and asked—

'Where are we going?'

'I know not,' the boy answered; 'anywhere to escape the tribe. London, I think, Lily, will be the best place. We are now *out on the world*, and without a home or a friend.'

The child had no knowledge of the meaning attached to these words. She knew not they meant hunger, thirst, and not a place to hide their heads from the cold damps of evening, or a shilling to purchase food. The poor little wayfarers were indeed OUT ON THE WORLD.

CHAPTER VII.

A ROAD-SIDE ACQUAINTANCE.

THE brave little fellow's heart was sorely tried by that long and wretched journey to the great metropolis. Eight days and nights were passed ere the ragged, wayworn pair beheld the dim outlines of the great city looming out, sombre and massive, in the twilight.

Eight days! What misery and despair had been compressed in that brief space! What strange scenes they had passed through, and how oft, in after years, they recalled the harsh rebuke they had met from those whom they had sought to relieve their dire distress!

Walking onward by day, and begging a morsel of bread at the open doors of the humble cotters; at night sleeping in a barn or beneath a haystack—save once, when a kindly woman gave them a shelter with her little ones.

She had little else to give the hungry children, for the scanty morning meal was not sufficient to satisfy the cravings of four flaxen-haired youngsters whom she had to support; but she could not see them go upon their pilgrimage without food, so a small portion was eked out, and they left the poor widow's humble cot with lighter hearts than had fallen to their lot during the five days that had elapsed since Falconmere's proud halls fell to the earth.

The sixth day was, perhaps, the worst time they had experienced. Twice Jack had sought charity. Each time he had been refused, and threatened, in the second instance, with a horsewhip if he did not leave the village.

The latent fire in the boy's nature blazed in his angry eyes at the brutal threat, and as he turned away to rejoin his companion, the small hands were clenched, and his eyes filled with tears at his inability to chastise the untaught peasant.

This fierceness left him when he looked upon Lily's pale pinched face, and as she ran forward with outstretched hands to receive the scanty morsel she expected, Jack burst into an angry flood of tears, and said, savagely—

'I have nothing, Lily; the—the——'

His passion would not permit him to finish the sentence for some moments, then he stamped his foot upon the ground, and re-resumed—

'I don't care for myself; it's you, Lily. I can go without until we get to London.'

He had a vague idea that in the 'million peopled city' every want would be supplied.

'Never mind, Jack,' the child said, placing her hand upon his shoulder; 'I am not hungry. See—I have found this while waiting for you, and eaten part.'

She held a raw turnip towards the boy. It had fallen from a pail of offal which a man was carrying to the piggery. He had kicked it into the road, and from thence it was taken by the hungry child—fit food for one who had been so delicately nurtured.

Jack Lennox was hungry. Fain would he have shared the prize; but even in this, as in all things else, he would not eat until the fair child had partaken of two-thirds of this wretched apology for a breakfast.

A refreshing draught from a small running stream finished their repast; then the journey was resumed.

With eager eyes they read the milestones as they passed, and each told that they were slowly decreasing the distance between them and the great city.

Ten miles the children journeyed that day, and when footsore and worn out, they were compelled to seat themselves upon a heap of stones by the roadside.

'XXI. MILES TO LONDON.'

They were opposite the stone which bore this inscription, and Jack, looking in the direction pointed out by a ghostly finger-post, repeated the inscription several times.

'Twenty-one miles, Lily,' he said at length. 'We have come nearly sixty. This won't seem much, will it?'

Lily raised her eyes; she had been watching a number of ants, and thinking how much better off the little creatures were than herself.

'They have a place to sleep in,' she thought, 'and plenty to eat; I have neither.'

She was wondering when the present wretchedness would terminate, when Jack's voice aroused her.

'I am glad we have not to go far,' she said, 'for I could not walk much more, Jack; but,' she added suddenly, 'what are we to do when we get to London?'

The abrupt question somewhat startled our hero, and as he had not the least idea of his course of action, he remained silent. He had heard wondrous stories of fortunate lads entering the smoky place with a fourpenny-piece in their pocket and becoming rich men, but how this was accomplished he had not the least idea. So while puzzling his brain how he should answer Lily's query, the words were repeated.

'I don't quite know yet, Lily,' he said, rising. 'Come, let us walk a little farther, to those houses in the hollow, and while we are walking I'll perhaps think of something.'

The cluster of small dwellings indicated by Jack was situated about half a mile from the place where they had been sitting.

They travelled about half this distance in silence, for the boy had not yet resolved upon any plan that seemed likely to better their condition.

Lily was silent, and her little lips were tightly compressed. She was suffering the most excruciating pain from the blisters which covered her feet; she felt weak and ill for the want of nourishment as well, and though every step sent a thrill through her frame, and she felt that it would be a priceless boon to lie quietly by the road-side, she uttered no word of complaint.

She knew how ardently the boy wished to reach the great city of the world, and as a reward for the trials and privations he underwent upon her account, she would have fallen upon the footway before a word or any indication of her sufferings came from her lips.

Both had their eyes cast down, when a light footfall caused them to look up, and within twenty yards of them they beheld a boy, apparently a few years older than our hero.

He was coming towards them, and by his glance as he passed he was evidently as much surprised to meet the young wayfarers as they were to meet him.

There was ample time for the children to examine the stranger before he passed, and they saw that as far as outward appearance went he was much on a par with themselves.

His clothes were stained, and very dusty, and from the fact of their not having been made for him, they looked infinitely worse than they really were.

The jacket would have buttoned comfortably round the chest of a youth twice the new comer's size, and the superfluous cloth in this article might have been added with advantage to the bottoms of his trousers.

He had a greater length of limb than our hero, but he wanted that lithe movement and well-knit frame which Jack Lennox possessed.

His feet were large, so were his hands, but his frame seemed small for his height; and that which struck Jack, as he took a sidelong glance at the stranger, was the 'old look' upon his features. He was not illlooking, but a shrewd, half-cunning expression, which seemed to have grown upon him, made the face appear older by many years than it really was.

When they had passed each other Jack involuntarily turned his head, and found the stranger was looking back also. A halfsmile lit up the latter's face, and evidently looking upon this as a wish for our hero to speak, he turned back, and was soon beside the young pair.

'You seem tired,' he said, in an easy, familiar manner. 'Have you tramped far to-day?'

Jack did not know whether to resist this overture, or to make a further acquaintance with the young gentleman who possessed such a plentitude of jacket.

A moment's reflection caused him to do the latter. The stranger had come from the village, and perhaps would take Lily to a cottage where she could receive both food and rest. This thought shaped his answer.

'Yes,' he said, 'we have come a long way.'

'So have I,' the communicative youth said, 'and no luck. Have you had any?'

The vision of the cottage faded from Jack's mind. The stranger, after all, did not belong to the village. Our hero felt sorry he had encouraged the stranger's advances, and was meditating whether he should give him to understand that his company was not required, when Lily struck her foot against a loose stone, and gave a scream of agony.

This caused Jack to lead the fair girl to a similar resting-place to that which they had before used, and ere she had sufficiently recovered to resume the journey, the two boys were as familiar as though they had known each other from infancy.

The stranger made Jack acquainted with the causes which led to this meeting without the least reserve, and our hero saw that, so far from discouraging the acquaintance, it would be well to court it by offering him a share in their Joint-Stock Company of Misery (Unlimited).

An offer which was received with evident pleasure. But, stay. I must first inform my readers of the causes which led to this arrangement.

The trio had not sat long upon the small pyramid of stones, when Jack asked his free and easy companion about the small village which lay in the tranquil-looking valley.

'Yes, I have been there,' the stranger answered. 'Not much to be made there, but——'

'We are not common beggars,' Jack said, proudly. He was not quite reconciled to the gentleman's peculiar manners then. 'It was not to learn how much or little was to be obtained——'

The stranger laughed, and placed his hand patronizingly upon Jack's shoulder, as he said—

'No offence—no offence, I hope. Common beggars? No, certainly not. But, come, now; speak the truth. You are—eh, you understand?'

Jack did not understand, nor did he like the facetious dig in the ribs which accompanied the words.

Jack made a fierce answer, and clenched his hands; but the stranger, so far from taking umbrage at this show of spirit, only laughed the louder, and made a quiet remark which totally put our hero's dignity and anger to flight.

He could not, for the life of him, forbear laughing, and Lily, in spite of her pain, joined in the merriment.

This opened the way to a better understanding, and Jack freely expressed the state of his affairs.

The stranger looked much concerned when he heard of the scanty meal they had shared before starting upon the day's weary travel.

A desultory conversation ensued after this. Then the topic changed to their meeting.

'I like you both,' the stranger said, frankly, when this subject was broached, 'and as you will require a guide when you get to London, I see no reason why I should not fulfil that important post. Suppose I tell you a little about myself as we walk to the village?'

The stranger skilfully out-flanked our hero, and placing himself between him and the young girl, began before Jack could alter this arrangement.

'A few words,' he said, 'will do, but as we have some distance to go, I will make it as long as possible. To begin, I never had the felicity of knowing my parents, if I ever had any. I was found, I believe, by a policeman, wrapped up in brown paper.'

Jack and Lily both laughed outright.

'What are you laughing at?' asked the strange youth.

'The policeman,' Jack answered. 'You said he was wrapped up in brown paper.'

'I meant myself,' said the stranger, 'not the policeman. Well, he took me to the workhouse until I was claimed, but as that event never came off, they kept me until I was fourteen; then I was apprenticed to a tailor, but as my master was fond of trying the strength of his sleeve-board upon my skull, we parted about a fortnight since, and I started to seek my fortune—a search by the way which has been very unproductive at present.

'My name? Oh, I had forgotten that. Robert Jawkins was the aristocratic one given me by the board. The sleeve-board? Bless you, no; by the workhouse board. Do I mean a board? Decidedly; but the workhouse board was composed of a number of wooden-headed men, and the other. Eh? Why did they give me that name? I believe it was in consequence of the initials R. J. being found upon my brown paper suit, but somehow this name was only used by the workhouse people. Everybody else came to the conclusion that my rightful name was Long Bob, for by this I have been known since my farewell adieu to the people who gave me over to the gin-drinking little tailor.

'Do I know much of London? Well, yes; a trifle. My master, when he was not engaged in the attempt to split his sleeve-board upon my cranium, was in the habit of standing in front of a gin-shop bar, and I, relieved for a time from the operation, found it more congenial to mix with the boys who were wont to congregate at the corner of the street. They were at first rather free with their remarks. At one time I was honoured by being called "work'us"; at others, "cabbage," "snip," and so on; but a few fights having set matters straight and several noses bleeding, they found out also that my proper name was Long Bob, and I found out from them much information about the great place called London; for though I had been left as a legacy to the old city, in consequence of the very strict rules of the boarding-school I was reared at, I knew as little about the place as you do. I will tell you about that another time. We are close to the village, and if your history is very long I shall not hear it to-night.'

After this direct hint Jack could not refuse imparting his history to Long Bob, and before they entered the single straggling street, the runaway apprentice was in possession of both Jack and Lily's history.

Long Bob seized our hero's hands when he had finished his simple narrative.

'Well done!' he said, admiringly; 'you have acted bravely in shooting down that rascally gipsy.'

He passed many flattering encomiums upon the little lady's courage in undertaking the long journey, and wound up by the assurance that he would stick to them until the party who wrapped his infantile form in brown paper offered a thousand pounds reward for any information that would lead to his recovery.

'As this will never occur,' he said, 'I do not think we shall part company very soon.'

Jack said he hoped not, and Lily echoed this sentiment. The young pair looked upon the alliance of Robert Jawkins as a most fortunate circumstance. They saw, in spite of his quaint manner and peculiar mode of speech, that he possessed a keen, perceptive power; this, added to his knowledge of the Great City, gave them brighter hopes of the hidden future.

When they reached the village, the hungry children stopped abruptly in front of a little shop devoted to the sale of such homely edibles as the inhabitants required.

There was a pyramid of fresh, crisp-looking loaves in one corner of the window; next to this tempting display was a dish of boiled bacon fresh from the saucepan. To the starving pair this sight had a strange fascination, and they stood wistfully regarding it with their pale pinched faces close to the glass.

Long Bob saw the true state of affairs at a glance, and, turning over a solitary two-shilling piece in his pocket, he muttered, 'Poor little things, they are indeed hungry; two shillings—now how can I lay it out to the best advantage? A loaf will be threepence ha'penny. What's that bacon a pound?—About tenpence I should think. Suppose I say half a pound of that. Three and a half and five makes eight and a half, then I shall have one, three and a half left. The shilling will get the poor little girl a bed; Jack and I will sleep in the fields——'

'I wish,' Lily said, plaintively, and the low painful words abruptly stopped R. J.'s meditations, 'we had a piece of that bread. Do you think the woman would give me a piece if I ask?'

There was a suspicious moisture in Long Bob's eyes as he blustered out—

'I'll go and see—you stand here.'

Two strides brought him to the counter, and face to face with a red-faced portly dame, the owner of the general store.

She had been watching the little hungry-looking faces since the sight of her viands brought the children to a standstill, and when Long Bob entered as she supposed to beg, her ruddy face became ruddier, and, extending her large red hand towards the door, she said—

'That is the way out, young man. We never encourages vagrants in the village, so be off!'

This reception somewhat staggered R. J., but he was soon himself again, and, looking contemptuously at the dame, he placed his solitary coin upon the counter, and said—

'Your speech, my rustic Venus, does your good nature credit; but as I have no time to tell you a little wholesome truth, no words need pass between us. I'll take a loaf and half a pound of bacon—here's the coin.'

The good lady whipped the money from under Long Bob's fingers, and, after biting it between her teeth, gave him the articles he desired.

There was not another shop in the village, or Long Bob would not have tamely put up with this. He thought of the little ones outside, and restrained his indignation until he had the possession of the food and the change of his two-shilling piece; then, looking solemnly at the woman, he said—

'Yes, it must be so; my mother never yet foretold a death but it always happened. Poor, miserable woman! last night, when the gipsies read the stars, one fell upon the roof of this very place; it foretold your death.'

He turned abruptly and left the shop, to prevent the woman seeing the difficulty he had to keep his risible muscles under control.

He had good cause for laughter, for the dame's ruddy face became as white as though she had already succumbed to the grim destroyer, and, when he peered through the window, he saw her clutching at a small coffee-mill which was fixed at the corner of a row of shelves.

'She won't get over that to-night,' thought Long Bob; 'the superstitious old fool!' Then aloud, as he rejoined the children, 'Here, Jack, divide this with your little sweetheart.'

How eagerly the poor boy clutched at and tore the loaf asunder; and, though his heart was full of gratitude for Long Bob's kindness, he could not utter a word of thanks until he had placed by far the largest portion in Lily's hands.

He forgot, also, to ask their companion to share the food with them; had he done so, R. J. would have refused, although he had not eaten since early that morn.

He saw the wolfish, ravenous manner in which the children tore the loaf piecemeal, and, turning his head away from the painful sight, tried to whistle the air of a popular song to keep down the choking, hysterical feeling that came in his throat.

Poor fellow! he had seen men and women suffering from hunger, but a sight like this was too much for him.

By the time they had finished the needful nourishment, Long Bob had managed to swallow the unpleasant sensation that came to his throat, he had also succeeded in getting up a very respectable attempt at finishing the tune, which attempt singularly failed at the commencement.

'Feel better now?' he asked. 'Come on, we will look out for a place for Lily to sleep.'

'Much better,' Jack said; 'how kind of you to buy us——'

'Fal de dal ral. I say, Jack, we shall be near London this time to-morrow. I wonder how old Snip gets on with his sleeve-board practice?'

The fair girl placed her small wasted hand upon Long Bob's wrist, and said—

'You were indeed kind, and we never even asked you to have——'

'Couldn't touch a morsel,' said Bob, interrupting her; 'I had dinner with Duke Humphrey to-day.'

The children looked in his face, and opened their eyes with astonishment.

'Had dinner with a duke?' Jack said, 'a real duke?'

Long Bob flourished his hand, and said—

'Duke Humphrey. Bless you, have you never heard of Duke Humphrey?'

'Never,' they both said in a breath.

'Well, to think of that!' said Long Bob. 'Why, hundreds of people have dined with him every day—breakfast and tea, as well, sometimes.'

'He must be very rich,' said Jack, simply.

'Well, yes; but, you see, the dinners do not cost him anything. Here we are. This is the only public-house here. You two sit down while I go inside.'

'It strikes me,' Bob thought, as he went to the bar, 'we shall have to dine with the duke to-morrow unless something turns up.'

By the time he had arrived at this conclusion he reached the bar. There was no one present, save the hostess, and Bob's perception of character having been considerably sharpened by his early training, he saw at a glance that the bustling landlady was of a more genial, kindly temperament than the proprietress of the grocery store.

With a frankness that won the good lady's heart, Bob stated the object of his visit.

'I have,' he said, 'a shilling and a few coppers; the shilling I will pay for the little girl's bed, and what is left for her breakfast; that is,' he added, 'if it can be done at the price.'

There was a half smile upon the good woman's face as she listened to Bob's offer, and before she gave him an answer, she asked where the two boys intended to pass the night.

'We don't much care,' he said; 'it isn't very cold yet, except just before daylight, so a roost in a barn or under a haystack will do for us.'

Lily and Jack were sent for, and the landlady heard from the little girl's lips the strange story in detail, and when Lily told how they had suffered since they started upon the weary journey, the good dame's cheeks were wet with tears.

'I am able,' she said, 'to befriend you to-night, but you must all leave early in the morning, as my husband does not like strange children in the house.'

She did not tell the child that for this charitable deed she would, if known to her husband, be beaten worse than a dog, by the man who had sworn, at the altar, to love and cherish her through life.

Happily for the children the brute had gone to a market town a considerable distance from the village, and would not return until the following morning.

THE BOYS OF BIRCHAM SCHOOL.

THE DISCOVERY.

That night the children were regaled to repletion, and the hostess who had taken a strange liking to Lily, gave the child a share of her bed.

Long Bob and Jack Lennox were shown to a small, comfortable chamber, and left to the undisturbed enjoyment of a cosy bed.

'Much better than the haystack,' remarked Bob, as he drew the clean bed covering over his chin. 'Good-hearted woman—eh, Jack?'

'Yes, she is. How kind to take poor little Lily to her bed-room.'

'She's a trump, Jack, and no mistake; and if ever I am claimed by a great man—it may happen, you know. Just fancy some fine morning a thousand hand-bills posted all over London, headed "Proclamation!" then the Duke of Yorkshire offering a large reward for the infant that was wrapped in a sheet of brown paper marked with the letters R. J. What are you grinning for? it might happen. If it does, I will make this good woman a rich present for her kindness. She deserves it—eh, Jack?'

Jack Lennox, in a sleepy tone—

'Yes.'

'Don't go to sleep old fellow. I want to talk to you.'

'I must sit up, then,' said the tired boy, 'for I cannot keep my eyes open.'

'Do; that is the best way.'

Although he would fain have closed his weary eyes the boy sat up, and kept awake until his companion's plans were discussed for the morrow.

'I'll tell you what it is,' Long Bob began, 'we must make some arrangement about getting our living when we get to London. We cannot eat the paving-stones, neither can we sleep in the streets. Have you any idea yet?'

Jack said he had not.

'Well, I think,' Long Bob said, 'my best plan will be to find my old companions, and get a few coppers from them; enough, you know, to get us a shelter for the night. They will be sure to give me a little. Next day we must try and get a situation—there are always bills up for errand boys. Should we succeed, we can take a room for the little girl, and keep her all right; if not, we must hold horses, or sweep crossings—anything, you know, will be better than starving.'

Poor Jack's heart sank. This was but a dismal picture, but he agreed with his companion that anything was better than starvation.

'I see you can scarcely keep your eyes open,' Long Bob put in, 'so suppose we go to sleep, and talk it over to-morrow.'

His bedfellow gladly heard these words, and no sooner had he placed his head upon the pillow than he became lost to the outer world.

The boys were aroused by the hostess soon after daybreak, and descending to the kitchen they were regaled with a hearty breakfast.

Lily was with them, and the child looked brighter and happier than she had looked for many days. When the meal was over, Long Bob's pockets were made the receptacle for sufficient food to last them that day, and the kind-hearted woman, giving the boys a shilling each, wished them good-bye.

She kissed Lily at parting, and put a half sovereign in her hand.

'God protect you,' she said, holding the fair girl in her arms. 'I hope you will soon be better off. Don't forget, my sweet child, if the worst comes to the worst, and you do not find a friend in the great London, that I will do all I can for you.'

Lily promised never to forget Mrs. Mason no matter what befell her, and returning the good woman's kiss bade her good-bye, and ran after her companion.

This was the happiest morn they had known since they started from Falconmere, and when Long Bob was made acquainted with the present Lily had received, he threw his cap in the air and shouted with joy.

'Thirteen and threepence halfpenny,' he said. 'We are all right, Jack, for some days, and if our luck sticks to us we may both be doing something for a livelihood.'

The journey that day seemed but a tenth part of the distance it was in reality, and when they entered the suburbs of London they were brought to a sudden standstill by Long Bob exclaiming—

'Oh! here's a treat. Two purfessinels eating bread and cheese.'

The children turned and beheld the cause of Long Bob's remark, and that individual stuck his hands in his pockets, and grinned impudently at the two 'purfessinels.'

CHAPTER VIII.

BIG DRUM DISCOURSETH ON THE INGRATITUDE OF MANKIND.

THE 'purfessinals,' as long Bob termed them, were not an uncommon sight to those whom business or pleasure caused to pass through the by-streets of the great and many-peopled metropolis, and by them would have been passed without a second look.

To the children—one had been brought up among the gipsies, the other in the seclusion of Falconmere Abbey—the 'purfessinals' were objects of more than ordinary interest.

Not so much on the men's part was this interest manifested as the instruments of their vocation. A large drum, emblazoned with an impossible lion and an equally impossible animal with a single horn growing out of the centre of its forehead, stood on one corner of the table. Beside it one of those tasting instruments *vulgo* a mouth-organ, but which looked not unlike a dozen pieces of cane fastened together with several layers of wax-ends.

The men seated near the instruments were a study in themselves. The gentleman to whom the drum appertained was short, stout, and fat. A battered white hat with a black band was placed somewhat rakishly upon his head, and from beneath the rim two shreds of iron-grey hair were tastefully twisted into a form closely resembling the figure six.

His attire consisted of a seedy-brown coat, seedier black, or, rather, once-had-been black trousers. Beyond this little else was seen, for the coat was closely buttoned over a blue spotted handkerchief; but whether to conceal the want of an under garment or to keep him warm was a matter that concerned only the individual himself.

But stay—his boots; they were, perhaps, the most peculiar part of his attire. The legs were Wellingtonians, and owing to a slight disarrangement with the bottoms of his trousers, the gap between the feet and calves was filled by the greasy brown legs of these feet coverings.

I pause and ask. can I describe the soles of these boots? No, I cannot, as I would wish. 'Why?' you ask, courteous reader. I will tell you. Because they were beyond my descriptive powers—far beyond.

In size they might have been fit coverings for the feet of Chang, in shape anything you please.

The owner of these boots had, owing to circumstances over which he had no control, been compelled from time to time to restore their wasted constitution; he had, in fact, done his own 'repairs neatly executed,' and done it with a solidity which must have brought tears into the eyes of any son of Crispin who by chance saw them.

Many thicknesses of guttapercha had been glued on, and to strengthen this some fifty of the most fomidable hobnails had been added; also a pair of heel tips, which would, upon an emergency, have shod a cob's forefeet.

Big Drum, for so he was called (and no one knew whether it was his baptismal name or not), was proud of those boots, proud of his skill in the repairing line, and when he sat to rest or refresh himself, the soles of his boots were always visible to the most casual observer; and he would indeed have been brave, in every sense of the word, could he have passed Big Drum's boot-soles unalarmed.

His companion, Pipes, was a direct contrast. He was tall, thin, and of the meekest temperament; he also had a habit —it was upon very cold days, when supplying the instructive music during the time the company made a 'pitch,' and they often did so—it was then he would pause and use the fringed ends of his dirty comforter as most men use a pocket-handkerchief.

Pipes also had boots which deserve a slight notice. They partook largely of the character of his carcase, being very long and narrow, and showing their meekness of disposition by turning up at the points, as though afraid to offend the stones by coming in contact with them.

Pipes' retiring mild, bashful temperament formed as great a contrast to his friend's as the difference in their appearance. The latter had a forcible manner of impressing his companion with the truth of his remarks, and Pipes, having suffered from sundry hard knocks either with the ever-ready drumstick or any weapon that chanced to be within Big Drum's reach, had grown wise, and, no matter how much he inwardly felt disposed to contradict his friend, he took especial care to outwardly assent.

When the young wanderers came to a standstill before the suburban public-house, the professionals were partaking of the humblest but hunger-satisfying fare, known as bread and cheese, 'inguns,' and porter.

Big Drum was in the act of finishing the last drop of the liquid, and sorrowfully regarding the maker's name on the bottom of the pewter measure—a scene caused by the absence of the necessary coin to refill the tankard.

He paused in the act, and Pipes did the same with respect to cutting off a piece of bread. The cheese and the fragments had long since disappeared, but Pipes, who believed that crust was good for the digestion, was determined to finish his share of the loaf.

'I told you,' said Big Drum, the pewter measure within an inch of his lips, 'that we should meet with luck.'

'Where,' Pipes asked, 'where's the luck?'

'It's come to us—it's here. Look there!'

Pipes looked, and beheld the trio, and mildly cutting off the corner of his piece of bread, remarked—

'Tramps.'

'Yes,' Big Drum said, 'tramps: perhaps they is. I hope so.'

'Do you? Why?'

'I'll tell you why, Pipes. If they is tramps, our fortin's made. Look at the figger of that gal!'

Pipes did so.

'A werry grand figger,' he said; 'but I don't see how it can make our fortins.'

Big Drum placed the measure upon the table without finishing the remains of the pot of porter, and said, just loud enough for Pipes to hear—

'Them two boys in tights, and the gal in muslin and beautiful plumes, how would they look, eh? Do you see now?'

Pipes nodded, placed his knife and piece of bread upon the table, took up the quart measure, lifted it, gave a sign, and answered—

'Yes, if they'd do it.'

'Do it?' Big Drum said. 'In course they will.'

Pipes gazed reflectively at the inside of the empty measure, and said—

'P'raps. I hopes they will.'

Big Drum set his hat straight, and looking towards the children, said—

'Well, my little dears, you seems to have come a long way. Ain't you tired?'

'Not very,' said Long Bob. 'Why do you ask?'

'Because,' Big Drum said, insinuatingly, 'I is fond of children, and—and—can't you come and set down for a minnit and take a rest? I'll stand a pot of——'

He paused, as a thought of the exchequer came to his mind, and shifting towards Pipes, nearly pushed that worthy from his seat, as he made room for the children beside him.

Jack Lennox went boldly forth, holding Lily by the hand; they were both tired, and glad of an opportunity to rest.

Long Bob sat himself upon the edge of the table, and took up Pipes' instrument, and began to discourse sweet music therefrom.

Pipes mildly took it from him, and asked—

'Would you like to be a musician, young man?'

'Should not mind,' was the answer; 'anything would be welcome just now.'

Big Drum brought his fist down upon the table, and exclaimed joyfully—

'Thought so! Will you join the purfession?'

There was the faintest smile upon Long Bob's lips as he answered—

'I shouldn't mind if you could take my companions as well.'

'Take 'em—take 'em?' Big Drum said, gleefully, 'in course I can; the very thing. Talk about the Buffler and the paper pole, they would be nothin' agin you three.'

'Should say not,' remarked Bob, although he had not the least remote idea of the meaning of Big Drum's words; 'that little girl would draw more coppers than all the bufflers in—— Hallo!'

Big Drum, carried away by the excitement of the moment, seized Long Bob by the hand, and began to shake it violently.

He did the same with Lily and Jack, and wound up by slapping Pipes upon the back, and saying—

'I told you so—a regular fortin.'

The heavy hand drove all the breath from Pipes' thin form, and he could only make furtive attempts at an answer—attempts that failed until he wiped the tears from his eyes with the end of his scarf, then he managed to gasp out—

'I knows you did.'

Big Drum went into the heart of the business at once. He made a proposal, and our little friends joyfully accepted what they believed would be a career of unalloyed happiness.

Long Bob was in ecstasies at the prospect Big Drum held out, and he longed for the hour to come when an admiring audience would behold him holding a ten-feet pole, or performing wondrous evolutions with the brass balls.

He fairly yelled with delight at the idea of the skin-tight suit Big Drum promised to procure.

'Now, my dears,' the manager of this company said, 'suppose we has a little drop o' summut to settle the bargain, then pack up our traps and—— What are you doing, you shadder?'

This question was addressed to Pipes, who brought the sharp edge of his square-toed boot in contact with Big Drum's shin.

Pipes brought his mouth close to his companion's ear and whispered—

'Wot's the use of talking about having summut by way of a clincher? Did not I share the last blessed coin in that 'ere pot o' beer?'

Big Drum rubbed his red nose until it assumed a polish painful to behold, then thrust his hands in his empty pockets.

'Right, Pipes,' he said. 'We ain't very flush just now, so we'll put the treat off till arter the first night of our performance. You ain't hungry, my dears, are you?'

They told him they were not.

'I'm glad of that, cos, under present cirkumstances, it would be inconvenient to be hungry; but what are we to do for a turn-in to-night? I wish we could give a performance at once, but we can't; and I'm blowed if I knows how we shall manage to live till you three gets well up in the purfession.'

Long Bob laughed.

'I s'pose,' said Big Drum, 'you don't thinks it a purfession. That shows how little you knows of the world, young man. Wot's the difference atween me and Pipes doing the music and you two performing, to a lot of fiddlers a scraping away and fellows doing the climbing business a top of each other's shoulders on the boards? We does it on the boards—at least you will, though your boards won't be inside a place all lighted up, and men and women a drinking and smoking. No, ours is the true purfession. Buffler said so, and he knowed a thing or two.'

Pipes, who had been sadly contemplating the empty measures, looked up when Big Drum came to this part of his speech, and in a sepulchral voice, said—

'The Buffler did know a thing or two, cuss him!'

He gave a deep-drawn sigh, then relapsed again to the study of the name stamped on the bottom of the pewter measure.

'That reminds me,' Big Drum said, 'I must tell you about the Buffler, and I hopes his conduct will be a warning to you all. You see Pipes there, and you see me, Big Drum?'

They answered in the affirmative.

'Well,' he resumed, 'you sees two victims of ingratitude—about the worst ingratitude as ever you or anybody ever heard.'

Big Drum shook his head, and came to a dead stop.

'When I thinks of it,' he said, after a moment's thought, 'I feels that the beasts of the forest is better than men is one to another—much better—and all I hope is you won't do as the Buffler did, that's all.'

'What did he do?' Long Bob asked.

'Do?' Big Drum said. 'Do? I'll tell you what he done. He bolted, sir—yes, bolted, after all the trouble and expense me and Pipes was at to teach him his purfession.'

'Bolted? I suppose you mean he pa'ted company with you.'

'Parted company?' Big Drum looked fiercely at Pipes, but as the latter was deep in the study of the lion's fore-legs—the impossible lion on the drum—he had no excuse to wreak his vengeance upon his mild and inoffensive partner. 'Parted company? Yes, he did, but that was not all. I wish it had been: but I'll tell you how it took place, then you'll be able to judge if the Buffler wasn't the most ungratefullest wagabone in the world.'

Pipes, in a melancholy voice—

'He was.'

'Nobody asked you to put your spoke in,' Big Drum said fiercely; 'hadn't it been for you he wouldn't have come over us as he did.'

Pipes subsided, and began this time to examine the unicorn.

'I say,' Long Bob said, 'we have come a long way, and if you don't look sharp with your story we shall not be able to get a lodging to-night.'

'That's true, young man, so I will begin.'

Lily and Jack drew closer to their new friend, both anxious to hear the nature of the offence of which the Buffler had been guilty.

'It was this,' Big Drum said, 'when Pipes and I began to perform together we met the Buffler. He was a smart-looking sort of chap, and a good figger. He wanted to join us, and we let him; but, blow yer, he was no more fit to do his part than that table is to throw a summersault.'

'Well, Pipes and I—not as Pipes did much you know—we taught the Buffler, and I can tell you he came out properly, and used to draw the coppers like one o'clock.'

'What did he do,' Long Bob asked, anxious to emulate, if possible, the clever but ungrateful Buffler.

'Do?' Big Drum said, 'why, hanythink; he could do a break-down or a hornpipe, balance a pole on his feet, and throw the balls to rights.'

Long Bob sighed; the prospective greatness was almost too much for him.

He heard with inward awe Big Drum's account of the Buffler's skill, and wondered if the time would come when his performance would merit such warm encomiums.

'Well, he stayed with us a long time, he did,' Big Drum continued, 'till at last we began to think about opening a hexibition, and showing off the Buffler as the Vaulting Lion of Bagdad.'

Pipes here rubbed his nose with the fringe of his necktie, and whispered the faintest possible whisper by the way—

'That wos my title.'

Big Drum faced round suddenly; so suddenly that Pipes edged away until he edged himself off his seat, and fell to the ground, clutching in his attempt to save himself the drum.

The light instrument came with a bang upon his head, and Big Drum, in agony, sprang to his feet, snatched one of the drumsticks from the ground, and before Pipes could escape began to belabour him.

'Who said it wasn't your title?' remarked the angry owner of the fallen drum; 'is that any reason you is to upset my instrument, and knock it out of tune, you horrible shadder? Now I tells you, once for all, that if ever you puts your spoke in when you're not wanted you'll get more than you like.'

The children were convulsed with laughter at the scene, and when Big Drum, making a furious blow at Pipes, caught his knuckles on the edge of the table, Long Bob rolled on the ground, well-nigh suffocated with merriment.

The blow caused the weapon to fly from Big Drum's fingers, and while he danced about in pain Pipes crawled away to a place of safety.

It was some time before order was restored, and Big Drum could be induced to resume his story. When he did so, he said—

'We should have got up the hexhibition, only we was waiting to get together a little coin to begin. Every day we used to put away a little, and yesterday we had altogether, in a leather bag, two pun two and fourpence ha'penny.'

Big Drum paused, cast his eyes up to the sky, then closed his fist, and glanced round as though in search of the ungrateful Buffler.

'We had all this,' he resumed, 'and last night as ever was Pipes there let the Buffler go round with the bag to collect.'

'I did,' groaned Pipes. 'I wish I hadn't.'

'It ain't any use a whinin' over it now,' said Big Drum savagely. 'You'd no business to let him go round at all. I always told you that.'

'I know you did. Oh, Lord! when I thinks of that two pun two and fourpence ha'penny, I feels dreadful.'

Big Drum turned away from his unfortunate partner, and, addressing his young listeners, said—

'He went round to collect—cuss him, the wagabone! To think, after all the trouble that I took with him to make him a "purfessionel," the dress I bought him, and—and—after all this, and a lot more, we done for him, he—he collected the coin, then bolted—yes, bolted, bag and all, and a whole box of properties—three beautiful brass balls, a dagger, ten hoops, and the beautiful pole he used to draw out of his mouth after eating paper—all these went along with the the Buffler and the bag.'

Big Drum ceased, his eyes closed, and pulling his battered hat over his forehead, he gave a groan.

Pipes groaned in sympathy, and cast a melancholy glance at the bright, but empty pewter measure. It was too much to remember without grieving, both in the spirit and most terribly loud.

'Buffler—two pun two and fourpence ha'penny!' this said Pipes to himself. 'Oh dear! oh dear! the ungrateful wretch.'

'Two pun two and the odd ha'pence,' groaned Big Drum, 'and the beautiful lot of properties. Oh! I shall die! Not a penny in my pocket to begin a new company.'

'I say,' Long Bob said, after quietly surveying the sorrowful pair, 'don't pile up the agony too much. We have a few shillings; leaving as much as will get the little girl a bed, you are welcome to the rest, if it will set us going in the new line.'

'How much is it?' Big Drum asked.

'Yes, how much?' queried Pipes, in a sepulchral whisper.

'Thirteen and threepence ha'penny,' said Long Bob.

Big Drum opened his mouth twice before he could speak. When able to articulate, he gasped out—

'Bless you, my boy, bless you! I can see you will not serve us as the Buffler did—generous, noble youth!'

'No fear,' Long Bob said; 'you act square by us, and we'll do the same by you.'

When Pipes heard the magnificent sum mentioned, he rubbed his nose with the dirty worsted fringe, and clutching the smaller of the pewter measures whispered—

'Borrow a shilling, Drum; borrow a shilling, to begin with.'

Big Drum acted upon the suggestion, and Long Bob supplied the money, one-third of which went to refill the pewter measure.

Talking over their future plans the party sat until night came on. As talking was apt to affect Big Drum's lungs, he managed to borrow two shillings more from the Little Lily's purse; and when this had been expended they arose, Big Drum promising to take them to a cheap but respectable lodging at the east end of London.

Pipes was so overcome by the recollection of the Buffler's perfidy that when he was called to accompany his companions they beheld him shedding tears over the pewter measure, and giving vent to his grief in audible but disconnected sentences.

'The Buffler—hic,' he sobbed, 'two pun—hic—brass balls—hic—bolted—good young man, lent us three shillings—hic—hic—bolted with the bag—hic—ungrateful rascal—all Big—ig—Drum's—hic—fault.'

They detached him from the object of his solicitude, and got him to his feet; but even then the recollection of the Buffler's villany was too strong for him to forget easily—so strong, in fact, that he rolled from side to side, and would have fallen had not Big Drum supported him.

So they entered the great city, and on the morrow they were to begin a new phase in their strange and eventful career.

CHAPTER IX.

A STRANGE STORY.

Soon after the condemned gipsy had been led to his cell, a warder of the prison waited upon the governor, and told him that a gentleman wished for a few moments' interview upon a matter of the greatest importance.

The governor gave the necessary permission for the stranger to pass the grim porter of the prison.

A tall distinguished-looking man entered the governor's private room soon after the warder had disappeared.

His face was bronzed by the sun of other climes, and his long beard and jetty hair was tinged with white.

In years, he was yet young; but there was an expression of such deep melancholy upon his frank face which told how deeply he had suffered.

He bowed with stately grace to the governor, and seating himself in the proffered chair, said—

'I have ventured to visit you, sir, with the hope that you will, although I know it is out of the usual course of prison matters, grant me an interview with the man who was yesterday sentenced to transportation for entering Earl Falconmere's bedchamber.'

The governor looked surprised, and mentally wondered what connexion could exist between the visitant and the felon gipsy.

The governor had, during his term of office, seen many strange things, and had become the depositary of many strange and awful secrets; thus his request did not cause him a second's thought.

'Of course you have weighty reasons for making this request?'

'I have,' was the answer, and the finely chiselled lips twitched nervously as he spoke; 'very weighty reasons.'

'I merely asked,' the governor said, 'because many have preferred the same request merely to gratify a morbid curiosity. Criminals,' he added, 'become objects of the most tender solicitude to many; therefore, in granting a similar request to yours, I have to be careful. You can understand. It is not pleasant to read an account in the next day's paper, published by one of those meddling, ill-judged people.'

The stranger smiled.

'My errand,' he said, 'is soon explained. That man alone can clear up a mystery, the very shadow of which casts such a blight upon my existence that, but for the hope of finding my boy, I should care but little how soon I lay beneath the earth.'

The governor became interested in his visitor, not so much from his words, but by his manner.

'If I remember,' he said, 'the convict told a most improbable story before the judge. Has your visit any reference to this?'

'It has; the helpless girl whose death he described was my wife, Earl Falconmere's daughter.'

'Great heavens! Yet the earl told the court that his daughter was buried two years before the woman spoken of by the gipsy appeared at the Abbey gates.'

'He lied,' said the stranger. 'She was alive at the time he mentioned, and with me in Italy.'

'Your evidence,' said the governor, 'to support the gipsy's story will be a serious matter for the earl.'

'He is dead.'

'Dead?' repeated the governor. 'Impossible!'

'He was destroyed last night by the fall of the Abbey walls — perished miserably amid the flames of his proud home—and Heaven has saved my hand from being red with the vengeance I swore to wreak upon the destroyer of my wife.'

There was a long pause, then the governor spoke.

'Was there not,' he asked, 'a boy belonging to the unfortunate lady?'

'There was. It is of him I wish to hear. Heaven send he may yet be left me!'

The governor, before they parted, heard a sad story from the bronzed stranger's lips, and when he left him at the door of the gipsy's cell, the kindly old man's heart was heavier than its wont.

The gipsy received his visitor with a scowling countenance; but when he gave utterance to a name he had heard from the suicide's lips, he sprang from his seat, and exclaimed—

'You are Walter Carlin! then I am saved from the horrors of a convict settlement.'

'I will do all in my power,' the stranger said; 'but we will talk of that anon. Tell me of my boy.'

'He is with the tribe, and will be given up to you when I am free and avenged.'

'You are avenged.'

'How? By your coming? That is not—'

'Earl Falconmere,' said the tall stranger, 'is dead.'

The gipsy uttered a shout of joy.

'Dead!' he exclaimed, 'dead! Slain by the hands of my people?'

'He perished amid the flames of his ancestral home.'

'They did the work well,' said the gipsy, calmly. 'Now, Captain Carlin, I will tell you all you wish to know.'

Our hero's father seated himself upon the side of the convict's pallet, and with an anguished expression upon his face, listened to the gipsy's story.

'It is now nearly nine years,' he said, 'since I found a bare-footed, broken-hearted woman, bent down with want and suffering, dragging her weary limbs through a lonely road that leads to Falconmere Abbey. She, though scarcely able to stand, had a child of some four years old in her arms.

'I saw the poor creature staggering beneath her burden, and offered to assist her—an offer she gladly accepted, and together we entered the gates of the proud domain. But little conversation passed between us, although I saw that the poor sufferer's attire, though at the time torn and ragged, was of far different material to that which usually clothed the houseless mendicant. I also noted that her hands were white, and of a shape that ill-accorded with her condition; yet, in spite of these things, I was dazed and stupified when she announced herself to be the only child of Falconmere's proud earl.

'I will not weary you with the details of that sad journey, sir,' the gipsy continued, his voice now tremulous and touchingly pathetic, 'nor will I repeat the story of suffering and misery I heard from the trembling lips, but pass on to the time when we stood cowering before one of her father's liveried menials. She, the daughter of a peer, had the door closed in her face; then she pleaded for an interview with her parent. The low plaintive voice yet sounds in my ear when she sent her message to that stern, unforgiving man, who now dares to lift his head in the bright sun, and takes his place among the lawgivers of his country.

'"Tell him," she said, "that I have come to ask his forgiveness before I die—to see him once more, if only for a moment."

'The man conveyed her supplicating wish to her relentless sire, and soon returned with orders to drive the mendicant from the door. The earl, said the man, had but one child, and she was dead, and her corpse could be seen in the family vault. He concluded by telling the poor shivering woman that unless she quitted the precincts of the Abbey he would have her placed in the stocks as a vagrant.'

'Though crushed for a moment by this brutal answer, the poor girl, as she clung to the doorway for support, reiterated her words, and taking a packet of papers from her breast, bade the lacquey convey them to the unnatural being with whom she claimed affinity.

'Never shall I forget the look of frenzy that gleamed from the suppliant eyes, when the man returned and told her that the earl had destroyed what he termed a packet of forged letters. She snatched the child from my arms, and, without a word, fled from the home of her childhood.

'I followed her as quickly as the darkness would permit, and I came up with her as she reached a deep pool of water. She paused upon the brink, and turned fiercely upon me. I saw her purpose, and sought to save her, but only succeeded in tearing the child from her maddened grasp; the next moment she was beneath the dark waters, held down by the weeds and rank grass that grew beneath.

'I took the boy to our camp, and tended him as though he had been my own child, and next morning we placed the poor drowned woman in her grave. Soon after we left this part of the country, and only returned a few weeks previous to my apprehension.

'Although so many years had passed, the boy's wrongs were not forgotten by our tribe, and I waited upon the earl to endeavour to soften his heart towards our *protégé*. His answer was an utter denial of the relationship, and I was driven like a dog from the Abbey.' The gipsy's eyes flashed at the remembrance of this indignity, and clenching his hands upon the rail before him, he added—'This, in place of causing me to desist from my purpose, had quite a contrary effect. I determined, from that moment, to obtain possession of the proofs necessary to carry out my plan.

'These proofs I knew were to be found in the packet of papers which the earl retained upon that night when his daughter found a resting-place beneath the dark waters of the pool. I felt assured that they were not destroyed, and twice previous to the night I was taken I entered the Abbey, and searched among the papers in the earl's library. Upon each occasion my search was fruitless, and I determined to return once more, and open a large escritoir I had seen in the bedchamber. You are aware of the result of that enterprise.'

He ceased speaking, and the brave officer who had faced death in the red field of strife, bowed his head in his hands and wept like a child.

CHAPTER X.
BIG DRUM HOLDS A GRAND REHEARSAL.

UPON the strength of the new company Big Drum rented a large room (upon credit), for the twofold purpose of sleeping and rehearsal. Lily, who was a favourite with the landlady of the house, had by this means a very small but clean room for her sole use.

It is true, when these arrangements were completed, there was a slight hitch respecting the commissariat department; but this difficulty Drum likewise overcame.

A chandler's shop, where he had been wont to purchase the staple articles of food, *i.e.*, bread and cheese, was visited, and owing to Big Drum's eloquence, the shopman agreed to supply the necessary provender until a performance should recruit the exchequer.

These matters settled, the rehearsals began in earnest.

A brother professional, now retired, and sole proprietor of a fish shop, sold his box of properties to Big Drum (he gave three weeks' credit), and to Drum's delight there was an old suit—partly clown, the remainder indescribable—in this valuable collection.

The suit fitted Long Bob, save a few alterations; these Pipes made, and, much to his self-gratulation, Mr. Robert Jawkins was permitted to appear in 'tights' upon the third rehearsal.

Pipes wept tears of joy when he beheld Long Bob's manner of throwing the gilt balls in the air. But when he beheld our long friend lying on his back, his feet elevated, and balancing a painted pole eight feet long, he gave a sepulchral laugh and faintly whispered—

'Beats the Buffler into nothing.'

'Should say it does,' Long Bob answered, as he spun the pole round with marvellous swiftness. 'Could the Buffler do this?'

Pipes was much affected, and shaking his head, murmured—

'Couldn't touch it. You is a regular fortin, that you is.'

Big Drum made no remark, he was too happy.

Seated upon an inverted apple-basket, he rubbed the tip of his fiery nose until it looked red hot.

When Long Bob had concluded, Jack Lennox took his place; the boy's lithe, muscular form seemed like india-rubber as he went through a number of postures suggested by Big Drum.

Balancing himself upon his right foot, he extended his left, keeping the leg straight; then grasping his ankle, he spun round like a teetotum, a feat which caused the quiet Pipes to gently clap his hands and whisper—

'Bravo!'

He would have uttered it aloud, but Big Drum sat so still, his hands upon his knees, and his head craned forward watching breathlessly the handsome boy's movements. Pipes was in too much dread of his impulsive companion to disturb him.

Jack wound up by throwing his hands backwards, and bending his body until his fingers touched his heels; then springing upward, he turned a summersault and came upon his feet.

'Brayvo!' shouted Big Drum. 'There ain't a Buffler in the world as could do that.'

'There ain't,' came in a whisper from the corner.

'Now, my little lady,' Big Drum lovingly said to Lily, 'it is your turn. Don't forget to spin round when you finishes the dance. Play up, Pipes.'

The melancholy one fumbled in his pocket, and brought forth his instrument of torture; then wiping his lips with the fringe of his scarf, he began assassinating the Great Eastern Polka.

The graceful child's figure looked to advantage as she went through her part, a feat she embellished with so much innate grace and elegance that Big Drum and Pipes both exclaimed when it was over—

'She'll draw, she will.'

Long Bob desisted for a moment in his frantic attempts to balance a long feather on the tip of his nose, and answered—

'Draw! Should say so, too. Why, the browns 'ill jump out of the people's pockets when she does the whirligig.'

This was Long Bob's term for the pirouette with which Lily concluded her performance.

'Hopes they will,' said Pipes—'hopes they will.'

'I expect,' Long Bob said, giving up the feather business as too much at present, 'that you will have to make that box of yours bigger to hold the coin.'

Pipes hoped so too, and wrapping his mouth-organ carefully in brown paper, he went to the cupboard and brought the viands to the table.

The young trio were hungry; and though the bread was stale and the cheese in form like a cannon-ball, in substance a close imitation of bees'-wax, they partook of it with as much gusto as an alderman would a civic dinner.

Jack Lennox went for the beer, and when he returned he somewhat startled the party by exclaiming—

'Tinker Tom is at the end of the court.'

A bomb-shell dropped upon the table could not have created more confusion than these words did.

Long Bob ran to the fire-place and seized the poker; Pipes drew forth his instrument, but whether to charm the savage breast by playing upon it, or to use it as a weapon of offence, must remain a mystery.

Big Drum, a drum-stick in each hand, placed his burly form before the door, and heroically said—

'Let him come.'

Lily ran and nestled close to Jack Lennox, and the boy, passing one arm around her waist, whispered—

'Fear not, Lily; he shall never take you from me.'

Thus they stood for several seconds, and Long Bob finding that Tinker Tom did not ascend the stairs, placed the poker in the grate and said—

'There's a tabloo! Bravo Drum! you looks like "Ajacks" a defying the moon, only he didn't wear his hat on the back of his chump.'

Big Drum certainly looked peculiar.

His broad back was placed against the door, his hands, clutching the drum-sticks, were above his head, and his face was turned towards the children expressive of the greatest dismay.

He fully imagined that Tinker Tom had come to rob him of his prospective fortune, and determined to resist to the last.

The children had told the story of their escape from Falconmere, and the danger likely to accrue should Tinker Tom discover them. Thus the mention of his name was sufficient to cause a panic among the embryo professionals.

Long Bob's remark brought them to their seats again, then Jack Lennox, placing his hand upon Bob's wrist, said correctively—

'Ajax defied the lightning, Bob, not the moon.'

'Did he? Well, it would have served him right if the light—— Hollo, there, Pipes! What are you up to?'

Pipes was quietly sewing a large parti-coloured rosette on the breast of Long Bob's dress, when this interrogation so startled him that he ran the point of the needle in his thumb.

'I ain't doin' anythink.'

'Except,' said Long Bob, 'making a horful ugly face. What's the matter?'

'Pricked my thumb.'

'Serve you right. Why didn't you let my dress alone?'

'I wish I had,' said Pipes, dolefully.

Lily and Jack were deprived of the pleasure they had hitherto experienced in accompanying Long Bob upon a ramble after rehearsal; the knowledge that Tinker Tom was upon their trail was sufficient to keep them within the house.

'Never mind,' said Long Bob; 'you will see plenty of London the day after to-morrow.'

He spoke of the time fixed upon for their first appearance before the public; and, child-like, Lily clapped her hands joyfully.

'Only one day more, then I shall wear that beautiful frock Mrs. Smith has been making. Have you seen it, Jack?'

'No,' he said; 'I believe I have been too much engrossed with the preparation of my own costume.'

'It's very beautiful,' she said; 'and poor Pipes, what patience he must have had to put all those pretty shining .... all over your dress.'

'Yes, Lil, he has been very kind; but do you know I don't think he is very happy.'

They were standing at the open window, out of hearing of their companions, who were employed in various ways preparing for the great *début*.

Big Drum was renovating his instrument by pipe-claying the cords; rubbing, or trying to rub several suspicious-looking dark circles from the parchment. People who were not particular in their remarks would have said these rings were tell-tale marks left by the

THE BOYS OF BIRCHAM SCHOOL.

various foaming pewter measures that had been placed thereon, when the Buffler and prosperity smiled upon Drum.

Pipes was busy with a flat-iron and a damp piece of cloth, taking the indentations out of his hat. A necessary repair, for, as Long Bob said, the battered tile bore a closer resemblance to a concertina bellows than ought else.

The last-named gentleman had his share the work. What little instruction he had received from the little tailor came in very useful upon the present occasion, and in a very creditable manner he repaired sundry rents in Big Drum and Pipes' garments.

Pipes was not idle; coiled round the forefinger of his right hand was a wet piece of flannel, and in a soft and melancholy manner he was washing the faces of the impossible lion and the equally impossible unicorn. Both animals seemed much refreshed by the operation.

No. 24.

Lily turned her head towards the wild beast cleaner, and said—

'Pipes not happy, Jack? Why do you think so?'

'He seems so quiet, Lil—so different to Big Drum, that I often wonder how they came together; but,' he said, suddenly changing the subject, 'I want to ask you a question, Lily.'

He had his arm round her waist, and her head with its golden shower was lying upon his shoulder.

'Is it,' she asked, 'a very serious question, Jack?'

'Serious! Why, do I look so?'

'You do.'

'Well,' he said, 'it is a little serious. I want to know whether you like this life we are about to enter upon?'

She paused a moment before answering him, then shaking her head somewhat sadly, said—

'I should have liked better to have stayed at Falconmere; but now poor papa is gone, and we have not a friend in the world, what can we do? We shall starve, unless we go out to perform. I would sooner do anything than be hungry again. You know how dreadful it was when I had to pick up a raw turnip and eat it.'

Jack's eyes filled with tears at the recollection of that miserable day, and, in a voice somewhat husky and low, he said—

'Yes, it was dreadful, Lil; and, at present we can do nothing except follow in the path chance has opened. Something better may be our lot some day, until then we must be content.'

The brave little fellow knew too well that the mode they were about to follow of obtaining a living would be one of toil; but, with the hope that fortune would yet be kinder to them, he nerved himself to face the battle of life with a degree of fortitude that would have well become one older and more experienced in the world's ways.

From the present and future their conversation turned to the unexpected appearance of Tinker Tom.

'I wonder,' Jack said, 'how he could have followed us so closely, Lil; we have not been in London a week, and he is close upon us.'

Lily shuddered.

She had an instinctive dread of that dark vengeful man—a dread that had wound itself around her heart until his very name caused her faculties to become deadened, and her spirit to sink, as though a heavy sorrow was upon her.

Poor child! Was it that her peculiar organization foretold that the gipsy would prove a crushing blight upon her early life—that his coming was like an evil shadow in her path? If so, the secret workings of her fears were not groundless, for the man was destined to become all her worst fears portrayed.

'It may have been chance that brought him here,' she said, in answer to Jack's words; 'yet something tells me that he will yet attempt to carry out the dreadful plan you overheard. He shall not,' she added, with a determination that was singular in one so young; 'I will never become what he would make me—never.'

Jack Lennox's face reddened, and closing his small hands he answered—

'Tinker Tom, shall not have you, Lily. His appearance here has warned us of our danger. Though I cannot protect you, Big Drum can. I wish,' he added, 'my strength would enable me to cope with him. But never mind, Lil, some day I shall have more; then let Tinker Tom or any one else look out that dares to look at you.'

Lily smiled at her companion's warmth.

'I know you would,' she said. 'You are a brave fellow, Jack, and I like you very much.'

His eyes sparkled brightly.

'Do you,' he asked, 'really like me, Lil? like the poor ragged gipsy boy who——'

She placed her hand over his mouth, and adroitly changed the conversation by saying—

'It was lucky we told Big Drum all about our escape from the gipsies. He will know best what to do, should Tinker Tom even meet us in the street.'

'Better than we should, Lil. I hope we shall not meet him.'

'I hope not.'

'Hullo, there, you two!'

The young pair turned and beheld Long Bob coming towards them, holding at arm's length the flesh-coloured continuations which he had been altering for Jack Lennox.

'Here, Jack,' he continued, 'here is your tights; take care of them—they'll fit now.'

Jack and Lily were loud in their praises of Bob's skill in thus producing such a glittering dress—praises which R. J. received with his usual modest manner.

'They ain't bad,' he said. 'I think if I had stopped long enough with my thirsty master I should have done pretty well, eh?'

'You would indeed, Bob. Why, no one could tell, surely, that so many places had to be darned——'

'Fine drawn, if you please, Jack.'

'Yes; I had forgotten—fine drawn. They look like new.'

'Better than new,' R. J. said. 'New ones might shrink—these won't.'

'How is that, Bob?'

'They have been washed too often—ha, ha, ha!'

'What are you laughing about?'

'Look at Pipes.'

They turned and saw the poor fellow in evident tribulation.

He had been busy with the repairs necessary to render his boots worthy of the great appearance they were about to make; for this purpose he had melted various pieces of gutta-percha to stop a leakage in the soles, but, owing to an absence of the necessary tools, he had run the hot solution on the back of his hand in place of the damaged boot soles.

Big Drum looked up when his companion's cry of pain sounded upon his ears, and asked—

'What's the matter, shadder?'

'Ugh!' gasped Pipes. 'Been and put the hot gutta-percha on my hand instead of the boots.'

'Ha, ha, ha!' laughed Big Drum. 'The gutta-percha know'd where it was most wanted. Keep it there, Pipes; people will think you've got fat. Ha, ha, ha!'

Long Bob came to the rescue, and detached the warm protuberances from Pipes' hand. Beyond an inflamed appearance upon the skin there was not much the matter.

'To-morrow, ladies and gentlemen,' Big Drum said, when Pipes had subsided into the darkest corner of the room, 'there will be a full dress rehearsal of the company arter brekfust, that is if the togs are all ready.'

'Properties all ready,' said Long Bob gravely, 'except the stage, that ain't visible.'

'Ah!' Big Drum rubbed his nose reflectively. 'That's an unfortunate circumstance, and I'm blowd if I knows what's to be done about it. Pipes!'

A whisper from the corner answered—

'Yes.'

'We ain't got no stage, Pipes; what's to be done?'

'Steal a shutter as we go along,' was the answer.

'You're a disgrace to the purfession,' said Big Drum, severely. 'How can we steal one when the people keeps 'em down the gratings in front of the shops.'

'I know,' Long Bob said. 'I know how to get one.'

'How, Bob?'

'Let's go out to-night; while you burke the boy that pulls the shutters up, I'll cut away with it.'

'Young man,' said Big Drum, 'did you ever go to school?'

'Should say I did.'

'Where?'

'That,' Long Bob said, 'is a question I cannot answer at present. Not as I think you'd split on me, but the people at the large academy where I was educated are so lost without my presence that they will give a suvrin reward for my apprehension.'

'I don't want to know anything about that,' said Drum. But if you went to school you used copy books.'

'Four,' Long Bob said. 'I dare say I should have had more only the tailors wanted a lad of genius to invent something new.'

'Did you ever, when you wrote, see a line on the top of one of the pages, which said, "Honesty is the way to be rich?"'

'Can't say I did.'

'Perhaps it wasn't in your books, but you have seen another line, which said, "Evil manners corrupt good communications."'

Long Bob laughed until the tears came to his eyes.

'You've put the cart afore the horse, Drum,' he said, 'Yes, I've seen that one. What about it?'

'This, young man. Your evil man——'

'Communications, Drum.'

'Communications, then!'

Big Drum was getting savage.

'Will corrupt the good manners of that well-bred little boy and the little girl; so if you can't think of anything better than burking a boy and running away with the shutter, all I have to say is——'

Bang!

The drum-head, which had been too much tightened while the parchment was wet, cracked, and the report startled the party, and stayed the manager's lecture.

Unhappy Pipes, as usual, met with the warmest thanks from the owner of the instrument.

'I know'd it,' said Drum—'I know'd it. I told you not to go washing them lions in the coat of arms. There, that's wot comes of your meddling, you shadder of ill-luck. I'm a good mind to smash you, I am. No stage was bad enough, no music wusser.'

'Its not my fault,' whispered Pipes, as he dodged under the table. 'I didn't touch the parchment.'

'It's your fault, I tell you again, and don't answer me, or it will be wuss for you. Oh lord, oh lord! No stage, nor no music, all through you.'

Pipes nose was just visible beyond the leg of the table, as he in a whisper louder and firmer than usual said—

'It ain't my fault, then, and I don't care what you say; as for music, ain't we got my instrument? Its a good job it was bust, people will be able to hear the notes when I play. They couldn't do it when that horrid thing was banging like a——'

This was adding insult to injury with a vengeance. So Big Drum thought, for he gave a yell, and seizing Pipes by the collar dragged him from beneath the table, and while shaking the offender with all his strength, he growled—

'Good job, was it—good job! That just explains the accident. So you, you mean wretch, you did it, because you wanted to do all the music yourself.'

'No, I didn't.'

'You did—your own words prove it. Your notes! What's that squeaking thing to do with the performance at all? Where would you be without the drum? Don't it bring a audience together? don't it make the performers go through their work better, eh? Answer me, you shadder, or—or I'll——'

'That'll do, Drum,' said Long Bob; 'don't shake him like that. It wasn't his fault; it was yours.'

Big Drum released his captive, and turned towards Bob, and rubbing his nose in a slow and calm manner, answered—

'This is too much, you to turn agin me. Ain't it enough that we are—there—there, young man, I am not surprised; after the Buffler's ungrateful conduct, anything wouldn't be too much.'

'Look here, Drum,' Bob said. 'Now, listen to reason. How could Pipes do that? just tell me how he could do it.'

Big Drum pointed to the break in the parchment, and dolefully said—

'Look! ain't it busted? Do you think I'd do it?'

'Certainly not; but never mind, I'll soon sew it up, and it will be as good as ever again.'

He did so; and Drum, after testing the sound, was affected almost to tears.

The music being all right again, a council was held about the shutter before mentioned, and to the delight of all, Long Bob got over the difficulty.

'I'll tell you what,' he said; 'there's the very thing down stairs.'

'Where?' said Big Drum, joyfully.

'Mrs. Smith uses it for a shutter in the kitchen. Wait a moment, I'll go and ask her to lend it us.'

He went; and Big Drum, now restored to good temper, turned to Pipes saying—

'That young man, Pipes, is a fortin in himself.'

'He is,' said Pipes, who bore no malice for the recent attack Big Drum had made upon him—'a regular fortin. Beats the Buffler into fits.'

'The Buffler,' said Big Drum, 'is nowhere. This young man, though his legs might be a bit straighter, is better than forty Bufflers.'

The subject of this remark entered the room staggering under the weight of a shutter, which Mrs. Smith had been prevailed upon to lend them

'Here it are,' said Bob; 'she wouldn't lend it at first; but I told her, unless we got it we couldn't go out, so she wouldn't get her rent. That touched the old gal—she let me have it in no time.'

The shutter was placed in the centre of the room, and Big Drum, after trying its firmness, went back to his seat, and rubbing his hands, said complacently—

'Here, this is all right, now, so to-morrow we will have a full-dress rehearsal; the day after we will start.'

'Yes,' whispered Pipes, 'and I shall be glad when we do; here's four days, and I haven't seen the colour of a coin. I say, Bob.'

'Well, old 'un.'

'Do you think Mrs. Smith would mind lending us a shilling.'

'What for?'

Pipes placed his mouth close to Long Bob's ear and whispered—

'To get some beer.'

'Pipes,' said Big Drum, 'I'm ashamed of you. Can't you wait till we has coin of our own to get what you want? you are a disgrace to our purfussion; you always was, Pipes.'

'I'm blest if his ears ain't as sharp as a rat's,' mentally remarked Pipes. 'Who'd a thought of his hearing that.'

A few alterations were made in the construction of the shutter so kindly lent by Mrs. Smith. This done, Big Drum said everything was as right as ninepence, and, like his company, prepared for the grand rehearsal on the morrow.'

The time came, and much to the edification of the lady and her two ragged children who lived beneath the manager's room, the rehearsal began.

The shutter was placed in the middle of the floor; Big Drum stood with his back against the wall, his instrument ready slung for use.

Opposite him stood Pipes, awaiting the signal to begin his dulcet notes.

Long Bob and Jack, both arrayed in tights, were in the corner doing the 'pyramid,' and laughing heartily at the mishaps that attended the mastery of this difficult feat.

Big Drum gave an impatient tap upon his namesake, and glancing towards the door, muttered—

'I wish she would come. What can the woman be up to with her?'

'Curling her teeth,' suggested Long Bob, as he turned a summersault, his heels flying past Pipes' nose.

They were waiting for Lily, and when she entered the room a spontaneous burst of pleasant astonishment came from the lips of the company.

The child was dressed in white muslin, the skirts cut short, and the body low; her tresses were loose, and swept her back. Her sweet face was flushed with the hurry of dressing, and perhaps a consciousness that her appearance had caused this outburst of admiration.

'Stunning!' Drum shouted.

Pipes gasped out something wildly, and wiped the top of his instrument with his dirty fingers.

Long Bob said—

'My eye! Talk about a fairy, eh, Jack?'

Jack was silent. The appearance of the lovely child caused his heart to throb quickly, and obeying an uncontrollable impulse he ran forward and clasped her in his arms.

'Lily,' he said, kissing her white forehead, 'you do look pretty.'

She blushed and gently disengaged herself from his embrace, as Big Drum flourished the drum-sticks about.

'Take your places all. Now, Pipes, tune up. Say when you are ready.'

Pipes ran up the scale, then finished with a wheezing bass note, and said—

'Ready, Drum.'

'Now, then,' said the manager, 'you must suppose these here walls is the street, and the windows the people. Now, Bob, you first. You come forward and go on the stage, and make a bow; after that, when me and Pipes plays, you begin to chuck the balls about.

'All right, Drum!'

'You, Jack, pick up that rope with the lumps on the ends, and swing 'em about just as though you were keeping the crowd back.'

Jack reluctantly left Lily's side, and did as he was directed.

'Stand back, Pipes; there ain't much of yer, but you is in the way.'

Pipes flattened himself against the wall, and Big Drum continued—

'All ready—go on, shadder!'

In a plaintive manner Pipes began, 'Why did my master sell me,' and Drum gave the necessary vigour to the air by a plentiful application of the drum-sticks.

Long Bob acquitted himself better than could have been expected, considering the short experience he had had of the profession.

The balls, the hoops, the dagger, and the rings were tried, and at a signal from Big Drum, Pipes left off swinging his head to and fro.

'Now,' Drum said, 'you must talk all the time you are taking the paper shreds out of the box, but you needn't eat the shreds to-day, 'cos we ain't got too many of 'em; only go through the motion.'

'All right! What am I to say?'

'Anything you likes; something to make 'em laugh, 'cos the more they laughs the more they'd dub up.'

'All right! something like this.' Bob went through the motion of taking a handful of shavings from the box, and cramming them down his throat, pausing every now and then, as he said—'There was only two men, ladies and gentlemen, that ever lived after doing this trick; they died, you see, from the effects of eating so much paper. All the thin ends gets round their hearts, and they couldn't breathe. Horful, warn't it?'

In taking a fresh mouthful he went on—
'Of course, you have all got eyes, and those eyes were given you to see with; you then see this is paper, and you must know that if I eat all this I shall die too. Ladies and gentlemen, I don't want to die, so I only chew the paper, but as I shouldn't like to show you the paper in that state, I will bring forth a pole out of my mouth, and the more coppers you drop into the cap the larger the pole will be. Go round with the cap, Jack. Give that gentleman change of a fourpenny-piece; he wants to give something, and I'm afraid he is too shy to ask for change. Will that do, Drum?'

'Fine, go on.'

'Drop 'em in ladies and gentlemen, drop 'em in, you haven't seen such a company before in the streets ever since you were born. There is no deception—everything is fair and square, and all we ask is a little encouragement. Go on, music!'

This was the signal for Big Drum and Pipes to commence, and while they filled the air with discord, Long Bob slowly drew out the paper pole.

He was seconded by Jack, whose elegant figure and well-shaped limbs added greatly to the effect of his performance.

He was accompanied by spirited music from the conductor, and when he concluded Lily came forward.

The child was a little timid when she began, but under the influence of Jack's encouraging voice, and the shrill notes from Pipes' 'torture,' she became more at ease; her tiny feet, encased in red shoes, moved with wondrous rapidity, and when she turned and curtsied gracefully to the admiring audience, Drum declared she would make their 'fortins.'

Pipes took his instrument from his mouth, and whispered to himself—

'I wish Bob would borrow a shilling, I'm awfully dry.'

So ended the rehearsal, and the company looked forward to the morrow with hopeful hearts.

CHAPTER XI.

BIG DRUM AND PIPES BEGIN THEIR NEW ENTERTAINMENT.

An eminent public orator was wont to recite his maiden speech in a field of cabbages; he compared them to a large audience, and, after a few discourses, mustered sufficient courage to appear before a crowded assembly.

He found a vast difference between the sea of faces that were upturned towards him and the cabbages, and he became so nervous that he was unable to proceed beyond the third sentence, and overwhelmed with shame and confusion, retired.

A friend asked the young orator why he had been compelled to make such an undignified retreat, and received for an answer—

'I have been in the habit of comparing an audience to a field of cabbages; but when brought before the many faces and restless eyes, I found them very different to my quiet listeners. I did not care for the faces, it was the eyes that did for me.'

Big Drum's company must have experienced some such sensation when they made their *début* after the rehearsal. When performing to the bare walls the matter was easy; but when the 'pitch' was made, and Long Bob stepped to the centre and began to throw the balls, his nerves became unsteady, and to make matters worse, one of the balls, in place of dropping on his hand, fell upon his upturned face, striking him between the eyes. and, as Bob afterwards expressed it—

'I saw all the lamps lighted up and dancing before me.'

The first 'pitch' was a failure in spite of the energetic music of Big Drum and Pipes, and when the crowd began to laugh and a number of boys to cast ridicule upon the performance, Drum threw his instrument on his back and started off in high dudgeon.

The second 'pitch' was no better. Long Bob had not yet recovered from the blow he had received, and when he had the balls well in play he sprang backwards to escape a second blow.

The consequence was a shout of laughter from the bystanders, and again they were compelled to pack up and depart.

R. J. was considerably chapfallen by this second failure, and as they moved briskly through the street he mentally debated a sudden dive down an unfrequented street, and a return to his late master.

He would have done so but for his affection for Jack and Lily.

'No!' So ran his thoughts. 'I'll try again, and if the balls all come in my face, and break my snout, I'll stick to 'em until I can do it to rights.'

Pipes stayed behind his brother musician until Long Bob came up to him. When they were walking abreast he bowed his head and whispered—

'Shut your eyes next time. It's the people that does it.'

'Right, Pipes,' was the reply. 'It's their eyes that makes me nervous; I can't stand 'em. But I will try your dodge next time.'

'Do, Bob, or else we shan't get a blessed penny, and there ain't a morsel of anything to eat when we gets home.'

'All right, old 'un,' Long Bob answered. 'I'll do it next "pitch" we make. You see if I don't.'

'Hopes you will, Bob—hopes you will.'

Pipes whispered this, then hurried after Big Drum, who, driven to desperation, was looking out for a favourable spot to make the third, and, if successful, the last 'pitch.'

Jack Lennox and Lily were walking side by side, both somewhat timid as to the result of their first essay before the public, yet anxious that Long Bob would finish his share of the performance with more credit than he had hitherto done.

'It is very unfortunate, Lil,' said Jack Lennox, 'that poor Bob should make such a mess of the business. I wonder how we shall manage when our turn comes.'

'I hope better than he has,' she said: 'yet I am afraid not.'

'Why so, Lil?'

'I feel so frightened,' she said, 'when I think of having to dance in the midst of a crowd, and the boys making all sorts of rude remarks.'

Jack's face reddened.

'They had better not,' he said, fiercely, 'say anything to you; if they do I will make them remember it.'

'You mustn't take any notice, Jack; for, as Pipes told me, public performers are obliged to put up with a great many insults without taking the least notice.'

'They may do so, I shall not.'

Long Bob joined them at this moment. His face expressed the misery he felt at his non-success, and as he sidled beside Jack, he said—

'Well, Jack, what do you think of this muff, eh? I ought to be kicked for being a fool.'

'You will get on all right next time, Bob.'

'I'm afraid not, Jack; I dare say I could manage it if the people wouldn't stare at me so.'

'Did the ball hurt you when it came on your face?' Lily asked; 'it sounded as if it did.'

Long Bob rubbed the tender spot, as he answered—

'Hurt me? I should say it did. I didn't know for a minute whether my eyes were knocked out or not, but,' he added, half savagely, 'the pain I felt when the ball fell was nothing to the back-ache this beastly thing gives me.'

He gave the dancing-board anything but a friendly look, as he spoke. Long Bob little knew, when he borrowed the heavy kitchen-shutter from Mrs. Smith, that it would fall to his lot to carry it about the street.

'Let me help you,' Jack said; 'I am not tired.'

'No,' said Long Bob; 'I'll stick to it. It's a punishment for being such a muff as I have been.'

They were passing down a wide street when this conversation took place, and, much to Bob's relief, Big Drum halted at the corner of a by-turning, and placed the strap of his instrument around the back of his neck.

'A pitch,' Bob said, advancing boldly to the centre of the road; 'keep your eye on me, Jack; I'm going in for a win this time.'

Jack nodded encouragingly, and Pipes, as Bob placed the half shutter on the road, whispered—

'Think of the coin, Bob. Not a farthing amongst us, and nothing to eat all day. Shut your eyes, and go in.'

'All right, old 'un; play up.'

Big Drum eyed Bob savagely as he began to unpack the conjuring implements, and his face became ruddier than ever when Pipes began the music without the signal from the drum.

'Can't you wait?' he said, fiercely. 'That squeaking noise will frighten the people away. They don't come to have the stummick-ache.'

Pipes became silent, and reflectively rubbed the end of his scarf across his nose.

'He allus pitches on me,' thought Pipes; 'if I hadn't have given that first bar of the polka the people wouldn't have stopped.'

Long Bob had by this time made his preparations, and with an amount of courage which startled Big Drum, and caused him to strike a false note, R. J. threw one of the gilt balls above his head, and called out—

'Now then, music! Don't you see the ladies and gentlemen a waiting to behold the Chinese juggler beat into nothing?'

The music began in earnest; so did Long Bob's performance, for, to the surprise of the company in general and the performer himself, Bob kept the three balls in motion.

He had gone in to win, and kept his word. After the first few seconds he forgot the crowd which had by this time gathered, and went through the part assigned him even better than at the rehearsal.

Big Drum was in ecstasies and the parchment suffered; so did the organs of hearing possessed by the bystanders.

The unexpected sight had a far different effect upon Pipes; it took his breath away, and though his head moved from side to side his instrument was silent.

This fact was unnoticed by all save Jack and Lily, and as she stood with her hands crossed upon the brave boy's shoulder, she whispered—

'Pipes is not playing a note.'

'Never mind,' Jack answered; 'Drum is making up for it. What are those boys laughing at opposite us?'

'At Bob, I think; his tongue is hanging out of his mouth, and makes him look so——'

She paused abruptly, and looked up as a hand was lightly placed upon her shoulder.

Jack's eyes followed her upturned face, and to his surprise he beheld Monsieur Jules Latour standing behind them. Earl Falconmer's ex-valet had not time to learn whether it was the young girl he had known under such different circumstances, for Long Bob finished the pole business just as Latour was about to speak.

'It is our turn, Lil,' said the boy, drawing her quickly away; then as they took their places upon the board he whispered, 'Did you see the Frenchman?'

'I did,' she answered; 'he seemed as though he wished to speak to me. What does he want with me, I wonder?'

'No good,' replied Jack; 'he has rogue written on his forehead. We had better not know him, Lil; if he speaks to us I will answer.'

During the time these words were exchanged the children were dancing opposite each other, and Monsieur Jules—a cunning smile upon his face—stood well forward, keenly watching them.

He was not certain yet of their identity, and to obtain a closer view he came within the circle, and received more than he wished.

Long Bob had taken the cord used to keep the crowd back from Jack, and, being elated with his success, began to twirl the ends over his head.

Whether by accident or design, one of the stuffed ends came plump in the face of Monsieur Jules, and filled his eyes with sharp gritty dust.

He stepped smartly back amid a shout of laughter from the crowd, the juvenile members of which began a series of remarks which added to Monsieur Jules's discomfort and anger.

Many wished to know the tradesman's name that manufactured the ex-valet's glossy hat; others made rude inquiries respecting the amount of stiffening used in the preparation of his collar.

Monsieur Latour likened the boys to pigs; but as he made the remark in his own language they knew not the meaning of his savage mutterings, and he was allowed to pass through them without a shower of nice thin, round stones, which the London street boy knows so well how to use.

The painful sensation increasing every moment in his eyes, Latour went inside a chemist's shop which stood near, and by the time the bathing business was over the street performers had disappeared.

The pitch had been as successful as could be expected, each of the performers affirming that Lily's graceful dancing had been the cause of the large receipts, which Pipes, as treasurer, carried in a small square box.

There was no doubt that Long Bob's misadventure with the Frenchman put the crowd in good humour, and caused them to part with the coin with more freedom than they would otherwise have done; at least, this holds good with a portion of the audience.

The remainder—and these were the most respectable—were charmed with the little girl and her partner's dancing. Perhaps their tender years and remarkable beauty had also a share in thus filling the exchequer.

It was a picture an artist would have been proud to have represented when Jack and Lily stood face to face on the board.

The girl's red shoes and flesh-coloured hose contrasted prettily with her snow-white spangle-bound skirt, and her long light tresses, floating like a golden mist, and her strikingly lovely face and white shoulders, brought to the imagination of the beholders the nymphs one sometimes meets in the works of the old masters.

In her dancing she kept time with the somewhat rough accompaniment which Big Drum dignified by the name of music, and often the orchestra, instead of playing for her to dance by their time, found themselves following the movements of her twinkling tiny feet.

There was a sunny look upon her face as she held the handsome boy's hand—a look that deepened into a rosy blush when he gave her a word of praise or encouragement. Then, at the whispered word—

'Now!'

She released her grasp of his hand, and placing the tips of her fingers together, raised them over her head; then, receding from her partner, she unconsciously assumed the most graceful and charming attitudes.

It was her heart that directed these movements, for whatever posture she assumed her eyes were fixed upon the boy's face, and though every action was in perfect harmony with her graceful form, and at times her head became averted, her depthless blue eyes never wandered from the flushed happy boyish face before her.

When they concluded, and the little performers bowed to those who stood around—and they were many, and among them, to judge by external appearances, were a few who were no strangers to the sight of the highly-paid dancers of Her Majesty's Theatre—a murmur of admiration came from their lips, and such exclamations as 'Bravo, little ones!—first-rate!—bravo!—bravo!' were heard; and, while Pipes went round with the box, Big Drum vented his joyful feelings on the parchment heads of his high-toned instrument. They gave three performances after this: then, night coming on, and the company being tired, Big Drum proposed a little refreshment before they returned to Mrs. Smith's.

Pipes, as usual, shed tears over a quart of half-and-half, and whispered to himself—

'They says, and I believe 'em, that everything happens for the best. Now, there was the Buffler. He sloped with the funds, and everything he could carry. That was for the best, 'cos we takes these youngsters into the purfession, and they brings in the coin like—like beer goes down Drum's throat,' he added, lost for a simile; 'yes, like it rolls down Drum's throat, and it does go down, too. Ah! the pot's empty again, and I ain't hardly tasted.'

Poor Pipes! He was troubled with a very bad memory, especially where beer drinking was concerned. To listen to his assertion. he never by any chance more than tasted. Perhaps this was the cause of his unsteady gait when they began their return homeward; or possibly it might have been the performances, which in the three last instances had gone off without the least hitch. Certain it was that he did roll from side to side, and mutter strange things in a thick undertone.

When crossing the well-known turning that leads from New Oxford Street to the Seven Dials, Long Bob came to a dead stop, and placed the heavy shutter on the pavement.

'What's the matter?' Drum asked. 'Is it getting heavy.'

'Like lead,' was the answer. 'I believe the old gal wouldn't have let me have it only she knew I should have enough of the beastly thing the first day.'

'You must take it home, Bob.'

'I know that, Drum; but I think I could carry it better if I knew it was the last time.'

Big Drum looked puzzled, and waved his hand majestically towards a crowd of little boys who closed round him when he came to a standstill.

'This is what I mean,' Bob said; 'down here there is a old chap as keeps a broker's shop.'

'What, Ben Isaacs, the Jew?'

'The very identical. You knows him then, Drum?'

'Yes,' the manager slowly answered; 'we once had a little business together—that is, he did the business, and I didn't want him.'

'Grabbed your sticks?'

Big Drum nodded.

'He's good at that,' said Long Bob. 'I've heard he once took three cracked plates and a kettle from a' old widow, because she couldn't pay her rent, but that ain't it. I've been thinking he might have an old dancing-board that would do better than this.'

'So he might,' said Drum. 'How much could you get it for?'

'Eighteenpence, I should think; anyhow, give us two bob. Pipes can take the shutter till I catch up to you. I shan't be long.'

Big Drum gave him the money, and Bob

ran off at full speed towards old Ben Isaac's.

When Pipes was told of the treat in store for him, he applied the fringe of his worsted scarf several times to his face, and eyeing the board, wofully remarked—

'I'm the solo reed instrument in the band, and don't carry the properties.'

Big Drum waxed very wrath, and seizing Pipes by the collar with one hand, pointed to the board with the other.

'Collar it,' he said, 'or you don't have a blessed farthing of to-day's coin.'

'I shan't touch it, so you needn't bully me.'

Jack Lennox overheard the squabble while he was busy threatening to punch a juvenile butcher's nose.

He parted Big Drum and Pipes, then trying to lift the shutter, said—

'Don't grumble about it, I will take it home.'

'You shan't,' Pipes said, leaning forward and taking it from the boy; 'I'll take it home for you, Jack, but to-morrow I cuts the concern; then,' as he raised the board to his shoulder, 'we'll see how you get on without proper music.'

'Better without you,' said Drum. 'I hope you will go; you've been long enough living on the fat of the land for nothing; for I calls whistling on that thing nothing.'

'Quite enough, Drum,' said the injured Pipes; 'remember to-morrow.'

'I'll make you remember to-night,' growled Drum, as he followed his companions, 'if you don't mind.'

They were soon overtaken by Long Bob. He had purchased the article required, and left it until the next day in old Ben's care.

He relieved Pipes of his burden, and much happier than when they started, they reached the dingy third floor back.

Mrs. Smith saw by their faces that fortune had been kind, and with a gushing generosity that made Long Bob wince, she offered them the loan of the shutter while they honoured her house with their presence.

'Thank'ee ma'am,' the long youth said, as he carried the Nemesis to the subterranean chamber to which it belonged, 'we are much obliged; but Drum and myself thinks it would be imposing on your good nature to take it again.'

'Oh dear, no, not at all; you are quite welcome to it—quite.'

'We know that, ma'am, that's the very reason we won't borrow; you see the stones may do it a lot of harm, and that would not be right.'

Mrs. Smith still protested her perfect willingness to lend the article, and Long Bob in like manner declined. When she was enabled to begin the ascent of the narrow stairs, Mrs. Smith, had she followed him, would have overheard him mutter.

'The old gal is too kind—her kindness is quite overpowering, at least it has been to me to-day. Carry that again! no, not if it was made of gold.'

When he entered the third floor back he found Big Drum and Pipes, and the two children, seated at the little table; the latter, he saw, were trying to abstain from laughing, and by Drum's serious face he guessed that something was wrong.

The box Pipes had carried was open, and the contents, quite a little heap, was piled before the manager, who commented thus—

'You see, that makes eleven shillings and fourpence ha'penny; the bad penny and ha'penny would have made eleven and a tanner. Now look here, the first thing is to divide it among us, and as Pipes is a going to leave us to-morrow, he shall have his share now.'

Pipes looked repentant, but made no remark.

'Now,' Drum continued, 'we must give five bob to the chandler's shop, five to Mrs. Smith; that's ten, isn't it, Jack?'

'Ten shillings down—balance, one shilling and fourpence ha'penny.'

Pipes rubbed his nose with his finger. The fifth share, he thought, was not much to retire with.

'One and fourpence ha'penny,' said Drum, 'to be divided. Let's see, how is it to be done fairly?'

'Let's go five out of nine for the lot,' suggested Long Bob.

'Young man,' Drum said, 'gambling ain't allowed in the company; remember you are a purfessional, and purfessionals are respectable.'

Bob screwed up his comical face behind the sage speaker, and caused Jack and Lily to burst into a fit of laughter.

Big Drum looked fiercely towards Pipes, but as that passive gentleman was studying a small hole in the ceiling, the look did not take the desired effect.

'One shilling and fourpence ha'penny,' said Drum, pushing his white hat aside, and burying the tops of his fingers in his unkempt air. 'I'm blest if I knows how to do it.'

'Give it to me,' said the incorrigible Bob; 'I'll spend it in ribbons for Lily.'

'Young man,' Drum said, severely, 'this ain't a time for buffoolery——'

'Buffoonery, Drum,' little Jack said, and Drum became red to the roots of his hair.

'Ah, so it is,' he said, looking round to ascertain whether there was a possibility of having a row with Pipes. The latter was too quick. When Drum turned his head, the melancholy one was silently studying a faded rose upon the paper on the wall. 'Yes, now I remember, you are right, Jack.'

He paused for a few seconds, and looked from the little pile of coppers set aside for distribution to Pipes's face, but failed to catch the solo instrumentalist's eye.

'The only way,' he said, 'at least, as I can see, to do it, will be to have threepence each all round; that will be one shilling and threepence, and——'

'I'll go you first time,' Bob jerked out, 'for the three ha'pence.'

Big Drum pretended not to hear this.

'The odd three ha'pence I propose we gives to Pipes, to help him on the road. Here you are, shadder; fourpence ha'penny. Count it.'

Pipes squinted down at the magnificent sum, and possibly dazzled by its magnitude, he closed his eyes, and whispered—

'Don't want it.'

Big Drum repeated the words.

'No,' Pipes said, 'I don't.'

'Take it, old 'un,' Bob said; 'it will help you on the road. Eh! What are you shaking

THE BOYS OF BIRCHAM SCHOOL.

THE UNWELCOME VISIT.

your head for?'

'I ain't going on the road,' came in a faint whisper, 'so I shan't want it.'

'Where are you going, then, old 'un?'

'To a place,' whispered Pipes,' 'where they don't want any money, and where I shan't be in anybody's way; that's where I'm going (sob), and the sooner I goes the better.'

Both ends of the dirty scarf were crowded in Pipes's eyes, as he gave vent to a flow of tears at the conclusion of these pathetic words

Big Drum was much affected.

He rubbed his nose with the back of his right hand, then mechanically rubbed the right palm with the back of his left; he was not aware that the right hand was already before his nose when he brought up the left.

He watched Pipes for a few seconds, then, unable to bear the sight any longer, jumped to his feet, and pulling the rusty scarf from his thin companion's eyes, blustered out—

'You ain't a going to drownd yourself, Pipes?'

'I (sob)—I is.'

'Don't,' said Drum; 'I didn't mean to offend you, Pipes; let's be friends again, and I'll stand two pots of cooper.'

Pipes unclosed one eye, and whispered—

'You can't, you've only got fourpence.'

Long Bob burst into a roar of laughter, then stood on his head in the centre of the room.

Lily and Jack joined in the laugh, the drollness of Pipes's remark was more than they could possibly endure.

'No more I ain't,' said Drum, 'but I can borrow some, so don't drownd yourself, Pipes.'

Pipes consented not to rob the musical world of his power after a proper amount of persuasion had been used, and by the time Long Bob—who volunteered to go for the beer—returned, the manager and the solo performer were good friends again.

'Now, you young 'uns,' Big Drum said, 'me and Pipes has been talking matters over, and we thinks the odd one and four and a half had better be spent in grub, so that we shan't go on tick any more at the chandler's shop; what do you say?'

'Motion carried,' cried Long Bob; 'and the chairman to be bonneted.'

Big Drum knew sufficient of his volatile young friend to cause him to take off his dirty white hat and place it beneath the table. He feared the bonneting would be carried out, and had too much affection for his valuable hat to risk it being damaged.

'Just as you like,' Jack said; 'I and Lily are agreeable.'

'Very well,' said Drum. 'Now, young man, go and lay this out to the best advantage, and remember you are a purfessional, and purfessionals never picks the corners off the loaf.'

'All right, old Gooseberry; hand over the filthy lucre.'

'Ochre!' Drum said. 'What is that?'

'The coin. Ha! ha! ha!'

'Never heard it called ochre afore,' said Drum. 'Ochre; what a name!'

'Do you know,' Bob said, 'what the immortal Shakespeare said about a name?'

'I don't; but Pipes ought to. He once performed in "Hamlet."'

'Did he?' said Bob, doubtfully. 'Well, he'll know this is what he says. Listen. *A name would smell just as sweet if it was a rose.* There, Drum; there's poetry for you.'

Saying this Bob disappeared through the door to return in ten minutes with the produce of the one four and a half.

'Block ornaments,' he began, 'sixpence; loaf fourpence, that's ten; quarter of cheese twopence, that's twelve; candle a penny that's thirteen; matches a ha'penny, thirteen and a half; tossed the tatur-man and lost, that's fourteen and a half.'

The 'block ornaments' as Bob terms them, were stale scraps of meat purchased at the butcher's; but uninviting as they looked, the company were so little accustomed to such food that they beheld in the 'ornaments' a foretaste of quite a luxurious repast.

They were without a fire, so our long friend went to Mrs. Smith, one hand carrying the paper which held the meat, the other holding the five shillings on account as a peace-offering to that most estimable lady of the very uncommon name.

With her sweetest smile she relieved him of the money, and grimly gave him permission to use the gridiron whenever he liked.

While Bob was thus engaged, Big Drum made known a project he had formed during their homeward walk, and strange to say, although both the children hailed it with delight, Pipes raised a loud dissentient whisper against it.

'I've been thinking, my dears,' Drum said, 'that as next Monday is the fust of May, it would not be a bad dodge to start a Jack-in-the-green; there's just enough to do the business comfortable. I'll do the music; you, Lily, shall be the lady, and go round with a brass ladle; you, Jack, shall be the gentleman, and wear a cocked hat; Bob will do very well for a clown, and if I do the music, which I shall, Pipes can be—'

'All hot, all hot!' cried Long Bob, rushing into the room with a plate of cooked block ornaments.

'What am I to be?' Pipes asked, wiping his mouth with the fringe. 'You didn't finish your speech, Drum. What am I to be?'

'You,' Drum said; 'why Jack-in-the-green, of course.'

Pipes gave a groan and turned his eyes upwards. He was quite overcome by this announcement.

CHAPTER XII.

JACK LENNOX BECOMES AN OBJECT OF INTEREST.

As the ivy clings to the fallen masonry of an old tower, so Simon Redley clung to the blackened remains of Falconmere Abbey.

He was the forest-keeper, and had grown grey in the service of the noble family which, by the earl's supposed death, had become extinct.

He had began by serving the earl's father, and like a retainer of old he felt proud of the family, and would have resented an insult levelled at the lord of the good old place with a fierceness that smacked strongly of the good old feudal days.

Like snow melting beneath the sunlight the crowd of domestics had left the charred and massive ruins, all had gone save Simon Redley, and he, with his grey hairs bowed low, sat at the open door of his cottage, looking sadly at the desolation which marked the progress of the fierce destroying element.

The morning was young—the orb of day just tingeing the dew-covered grass, and dank foliage of the trees—yet, at this early hour, the old forest-keeper was astir, and engaged in the work he had begun since Falconmere's earl perished amid the fallen walls of his palatial home.

He was looking for the remains of the proud, stern man amid the ruins, working alone, his only aid a small crowbar, by which he removed various heavy masses of the strange-looking heap.

The forest-keeper had stood by when the search was made for the earl's body, and though not a trace was found, he clung to a belief which had crept to his heart and caused him to work in the endeavour to learn its truth or falsity.

'He must be there,' he muttered, as he paused in his work; 'yes, there among those girders and heavy stones. Such is not a fit resting-place for the last of an old and noble family.'

He plied his crowbar again, and became so engaged that he did not notice a tall, bronzed, military-looking man, who crossed the keep and passed within a few feet of the forest-keeper.

He knew not of the stranger's presence until a deep and somewhat subdued voice said, in hushed accents—

'There has been foul work here, Simon.'

The old man looked up. The stranger's voice awoke a dim recollection in the keeper's mind, and passing his hand over his brow, he gazed at the calm, handsome, passionless face.

'Ay,' he said; 'may the hand wither that fired the old Abbey. May Heaven's curse blight those who did the fell deed.'

He continued to gaze searchingly at the stranger, and as though a flash of light suddenly passed through his brain, he dropped the crowbar and exclaimed—

'It is Lady Alicia's husband!'

'Yes, Simon,' was the answer, and the stranger grasped the old man's hand; 'years, I find, have not effaced my form from your remembrance.'

'I never forget,' Simon Redley said; 'you above all I should remember.'

'Sixteen years,' said the stranger, 'must have altered me much; it is a long time, Simon.'

'It is; but I should have known you had it had been sixty. It were impossible to forget the handsome boy who had so oft been my companion in happier times than this. So, Master Walter, you have returned, and she who should have been here to welcome you, has long since gone to the tomb.'

The stranger sighed deeply, and a gleam of passion was visible in his dark eye.

'Yes, Simon,' he said, 'I am alone in the world; my wife dead, and my children'—here his voice faltered—'God knows where they are.'

'Children!' repeated Simon—'children! Tere was a rumour—a strange one it was—that she came here to die; but I heard not the least mention of a child.'

'There were two,' said the stranger, sadly. 'Tidings of one I have gleaned, but the other—so like her fair, beautiful mother—has gone, none knows whither!'

The forest-keeper looked straight into the stricken man's face, and said—

'Your words are strange, Master Walter—you are Master Walter to me, though you have changed since we last met.'

'Much changed, Simon.'

'Ay,' the old man said, as though speaking to himself, 'he is; but children! It is the first I have heard that my lord's daughter was a mother, for they placed her in the vault, and her own name, not his, was upon the coffin.'

'That coffin, said Walter Carlin, did not contain the body of Lady Alicia.'

Simon Redley started.

'She did not die,' Walter continued, 'until ten years after that mock funeral took place.'

'Master Walter,' said the forest-keeper, 'are you speaking the truth?'

'As I hope for mercy,' he said, 'I am.'

The old man stepped close beside the speaker, and pointing to the cottage, said—

'Let us go inside; we can talk better there. Oh, God, that I should have lived to have raised my hand against his child!'

They went to the keeper's lodge, then the old man told the story of a report that a child belonging to the earl's daughter was among the gipsies. He told how the story had been discredited by the earl and his servants, and how the former had given the keepers orders to drive the gipsies from the place.

"I obeyed those orders," said Simon, regretfully, "and my hand was ever the first to strike the vagrants. One day, when I went my rounds of the park, I found a portion of the fence had been broken down, and soon after this discovery I saw a beggar urchin chasing a butterfly; the little fellow showed no signs of fear at my approach, and as I raised my whip to lash him from the grounds, he looked me full in the face and dared me to strike him."

The forest-keeper paused, and the stranger, who drank in every word with an eagerness that bespoke more than ordinary interest, compressed his lips, and as an angry spot reddened his cheeks, he bent forward and fixed his dark eyes upon the forest-keeper's face.

"I could not," Simon resumed, "carry out my intention—God be praised I did not—for as the sunlight streamed upon the lad's face I beheld the exact counterpart of your features."

Captain Carlin sprang from his seat and hastily asked,—

"When did this occur?"

"Not a month since," Simon answered; "and from that hour to this my mind has been tormented trying to satisfy itself as to the truth of those reports which were so rife some ten years since."

"Simon," said his visitor, his twitching lips belieing the outward calmness he assumed, "that boy was my son."

"I knew it, Master Walter, my heart told me so; yet—fool—dolt that I was not to act upon the dictates of my heart and take the boy under my care! I knew you would come, Master Walter, and it would have been a joyful hour for me to have given your beautiful boy to your arms."

A sigh came from the sorrowing father's lips, and he bowed his head in lonely submission to the great sorrow which had fallen so heavily upon him.

"He may be found," Simon said, in a voice so low that it scarcely broke the stillness; "there is hope, Master Walter. The newspapers and the police may do much for you, for there must be many who have seen the children since they left Falconmere."

"The child, is he not with the gipsies?"

"No, Master Walter. The tribe carried off a little girl that my lord loved as purely as though she had come from the old stock; they took her away in revenge for the earl appearing against one of their tribe who had broken into my lord's chamber."

"But the boy, what had he to do with the child's abduction?"

"They were playmates, Master Walter. The little girl, shut up in the great Abbey, and never suffered to go beyond the grounds, found a companion in the ragged boy, who, in defiance of my men, would climb the fences to meet the fair child. I have seen them together, Master Walter, and never before have my eyes rested upon two beings more gifted with outward beauty."

The stranger was now sitting with folded arms; his face turned towards Simon, and every faculty absorbed by the old man's words.

"When the tribe took him away," Simon continued, "the boy escaped with her from the camp. He showed the better blood that ran in his veins by the chivalrous manner in which he defended her from an attempt made by one of the tribe to recapture them. He fired upon the fellow, and shattered his leg."

The officer's face wore an expression of pride. He was a soldier, and the use Jack had made of the gun was sufficient to fill his heart with pride, and added to the yearning he felt to discover his noble boy.

He made a gesture for the old man to proceed.

"He left the gipsy prone by the roadside," resumed Simon, "and came to the Abbey—alas! it was to behold the grand old place in flames, and Lily's benefactor consumed by the raging fire. They must have been startled by the appearance of some of the tribe, for from that moment to this no trace has been found of them."

"Was there a search?"

"Ay, Master Walter; the tribe, baulked of their prey, were like bloodhounds upon the children's trail. They found out that the young pair had passed through Maybury, hand-in-hand, but after that they were at fault. The boy must have profited by the cunning the gipsies had taught him, to escape thus successfully."

"Thank heaven they have! for the passions of those lawless outcasts once aroused, they would destroy the boy to satiate their revenge."

"They're a bad lot, Master Walter, and I hope that one who has cause to hunt them down may never behold them again."

"Of whom do you speak, Simon?"

The captain's face was anxious—the danger to his boy which Simon's words foreshadowed for a moment caused a thrill to pass through his frame.

"I speak of the man whose leg was shattered by the boy—a powerful ill-looking ruffian who used to prowl about here while the smoke yet rose from the ruins—he will keep his word, Master Walter, should he once discover them."

"He had better never been born," said the soldier, firmly; "if he harm my boy, not the united power of his tribe would save him from my hand."

"It was but yesterday," Simon said, "that he was able to start upon their trail, for in the early morn he stood among those trees looking with such devilish triumph upon the fell event, that twice I had my gun raised to fire; but the thought of the boy's safety came to my mind, and I approached him as a friend, and learnt from his lips all I have told you."

"You acted wisely, Simon."

"So far, Master Walter, but I have thought since that there would have been less danger to the boy had I disabled the ruffian."

"It would have been useless—others of the band would have taken up the pursuit."

"Perhaps so, sir."

Captain Carlin took a small book from his breast pocket, and opening it said,—

"Give me as much information respecting this gipsy's appearance that I may know him when we meet."

Simon described Tinker Tom so accurately that his recognition would be easy.

"He limps," Simon said in conclusion, "for the wound is not yet healed, and nothing but the fierce passion for revenge could enable him to endure the pain he suffers."

"I shall recognize him," said the officer, closing his book, "if not by this description, which will point out my boy's foe."

"Master Walter," said the old keeper, rising, "I need not ask the question; you are going in search of your boy."

"I am, and until he is found shall know no rest, either of mind or body."

"If," Simon said, "an old man's assistance is of any service to you, I will go with you; for should the ruffian have come up with them it will require a strong arm to effect their release."

"No, Simon, I shall be better alone upon my errand. We shall meet again. Should I find my noble boy——"

"If you do not?"

"I shall find him, Simon, though the search may be long and full of peril. My heart tells me all will yet be well."

"Pray heaven your words may be prophetic!"

The soldier rose and moved towards the door, and Simon, as they walked slowly from the house, said,—

"You will be kind to the little girl, Master Walter, when you meet them. Think not of the wrong the man who loved her has done you, but let the fulfilment of the solemn duty you are about to go upon make you——"

Captain Carlin stayed Simon by a gentle gesture of his hand.

"I needed not this from you," the officer said. "I shall be kind to the girl, if, with heaven's help, I find them. But tell me, Simon, what child is this that so won the heart of that stern terrible man."

"She was taken to the Abbey by the late earl, sir, and, as far as I can learn, he first met her in the company of two tramps, a man and woman; the child was being beaten by the woman, and her screams for mercy and the manner in which she called for her mamma caused the earl to interfere. I believe the pair of wretches were only too glad to escape by giving up the child, for he—and you know, Master Walter, how terrible he was in his anger—accused them of having stolen the child —an accusation which was, upon questioning the child, found to be correct."

"Is this all you know about the child?"

"It is, sir."

They soon after parted; the sorrowing father upon his mission, and old Simon, the forest keeper, to return to the mound of fallen masonry, there to search for the cherished remains of his late lord.

Pursuing his way to the little village of Maybury, the soldier pondered over the strange story of the meeting between the earl and Lily.

"If," he thought, "Simon Redley's account of the meeting was true, there must have been a great change in Earl Herbert since my poor Alicia was thrust from the Abbey gates, and in her utter hopelessness sought a Lethe for her sorrows in the dark waters of the pool."

It was night before he reached the village, and entering the little hostel, he inquired for the landlord.

Boniface came; the advent of such a distinguished looking customer was not in the daily course of events.

Could he be accommodated for the night? The landlord said he could—he had a chamber which was fit for a nobleman. Mine host believed this himself, so little wonder that he endeavoured to imbue others with his belief.

"Refreshment, sir? yes—what would you like? We have eggs, sir, eggs poached and fried bacon; some of the finest you have ever eaten—my own curing, sir."

"Anything else?"

"Yes," said mine host, looking through the window at a venerable old fowl, who had gone to roost upon the lower branch of the tree on which was nailed the sign-board, "we have fowls, sir; but I am almost afraid we can't catch any to-night—they are such cunning beggars, sir, and always hide when they see a customer approach."

"Never mind, poach me a few eggs."

"Yes, sir."

The landlord left the room, delighted—he had again saved the life of the solitary old Spanish hen, without the character of his house suffering.

Boniface wished his visitors to understand that his poultry-yard was unlimited, and with the old fowl's assistance he managed to carry out the delusion.

"Wonder who he is!" said mine host to his wife; "he seems a gentleman."

The dame paused in the act of breaking the third egg, and answered,—

"You said the same when that there Frenchman came here, upsetting the place with his airs and graces."

"True, Margery, true; but you must confess that I am not often mistaken."

Margery would not confess to her husband's perceptive powers, but, with wife-like contradiction, refuted his words by bringing forward many instances wherein he had signally failed in his judgment.

To mine host's relief the bell rang, and he escaped the lecture he had so unwittingly brought upon his head.

"Yours is a very quiet little place," the stranger said, when Boniface entered the room.

"Yes, sir! We don't have much noise here when it's not hirings, and the like."

"Very few travellers pass through, I should imagine?"

"Not many, sir, since the Maybury station opened; though, after all, it isn't Maybury, for the place is a long way from here; and then, again, we don't have more than two trains a day stop. If it wasn't for the young gents as comes here to fish, I don't know what we should do, for, you see, sir, we are a poor lot in the village."

The stranger fell into the host's humour by telling him he thought so from the observations he had made when passing through.

"Ah!" the landlord said, "times are not as they were before the railroad came."

"I suppose not."

"Then, sir, we used to count upon two grand nights a week. That was when the commercial travellers came through on their way to Dover; but now the sight of a strange face is sufficient to talk about for a week after."

"If they have passed through here," thought the Captain, "I may yet be able to overtake them."

"Talking of strange faces," the landlord continued, "a queer thing happened this last week."

"Indeed!" remarked the traveller, startled, he knew not why, by the landlord's words.

"The fact of it was, two children came through the village, and after just staying here to get a drink of water and a mouthful of bread and cheese, which the missis gave them, they went on right out in the open country, and, from what I could see of it, they were in a most awful fright ——"

"John, John!"

"That's the missis," said the landlord, turning his head in the direction of the shrill voice, "and the supper is ready."

He hurried from the room, leaving his visitor's mind a prey to the most intense anguish. He would have called the man back, but fearful that his anxiety would be the cause of stopping any further conversation, he sat, silently watching and waiting for the landlord's return.

He repeated his host's words over many times. They were frightened—what was to follow? Had they been overtaken and brought back to the inn by the ruffianly gipsy; if so, what had become of them since?"

The feeling he experienced when mine host returned with the tray was as though a heavy cold hand had released its hold from his heart.

"Supper, sir, and done to a turn; what time would you like to retire?"

With a forced calmness the sad-hearted man pointed to a chair, and said,—

"Be seated, landlord; you have strangely excited my curiosity respecting the cause of the children's fear."

"Oh!" exclaimed mine host, as though astonished that his words had made any impression on the stranger's mind, "but the eggs are getting cold."

Walter Carlin pushed the tray from him as he said,—

"Finish your story, landlord; I cannot rest until my curiosity is satisfied."

Mine host's face was expressive of much surprise as he resumed,—

"They have not much to fear after all, sir!"

The listener breathed with more freedom.

"For no one came after them until the next day, then a tall thin foreigner came post-haste through the village, and made all sorts of inquiries about the boy—he didn't care much for the girl: he said it was the boy he wanted."

"Did he overtake them?"

"I don't think he did, sir; for you see, as they took to the open country, and our place being, as it were, right in the centre of the cross-roads, why, they ought to have come on the Gorton-road; then again, by crossing a field, they would have come on the London-road—so you see, sir, it just depends which way they turned."

"Exactly—I feared that the man's chance was but a small one."

"His was, sir—but the next day another came—on the same errand—a rough, savage-looking gipsy fellow—he wanted them both—and when he turned from the door, I told him he ought not to walk with such a leg as he had—why he could hardly crawl!"

"Well, well, what answer did he make?"

"Such a one, sir, as made my blood run cold: 'My leg will be all right when I find the young cub and the girl.' It wasn't his words so much, sir, as the way he showed his teeth."

Hurriedly bringing his recital to an end, he raised the cover from the dish of eggs, and, making a profound bow, left the room.

CHAPTER XIII.

A STREET TRANSFORMATION SCENE.

THE amazement depicted on Pipes's face when Big Drum announced the honour in store for him was exquisitely ludicrous, and caused the children to burst into a hearty fit of laughter.

"It ain't a bit o' use, Pipes," Drum said, "for you to turn up your eyes and make ugly faces, 'cos you'll have to do it."

"But," said Pipes, appealingly, "I don't know nothing about the business, and you do; why don't you do that part?"

He shifted out of Big Drum's reach, and held up the ragged end of his scarf as a protecting shield, at the end of this speech.

"Me do Jack-in-the-green!" said Big Drum; "me! you must be mad, Pipes; who's to see to the music?"

"That's easy enough," said Pipes; "I can take the drum for once."

Drum looked the disgust he felt. "You!" he said, "why, if a puff of wind was to come round the corner and catch the head of the drum, you'd be blown away."

Pipes swallowed this allusion to his spare figure, and whispered,—

"You can't do both instruments anyhow, and yours by itself won't do."

"It would do at a pinch," Big Drum said, "'cos it would draw; but as you is to be Jack-in-the-green, I'll take the two."

Pipes groaned dismally, and whispered to himself,—

"He'll spoil my instrument; that's what will happen."

"It's all cut and dried now," Big Drum said, "so we'll have the banquet, then go on again arterwards."

Pipes, overcome by the fall from solo instrumentalist to the part assigned him by Big Drum, had but little appetite for the repast, until Long Bob, who was plying his knife and fork with an energy quite refreshing to behold, said,—

"I say, Pipes, old 'un, you'd better eat 'em while they're hot; block ornaments ain't good if they once gets cold."

Pipes cast his eyes obliquely towards the plate, and, with a doleful shake of the head, replied,—

"I ain't a bit o' happytight, Bob, when my feelins is onced hurt."

The long youth stretched forth his long right arm, and made a clutch at Pipes' plate.

"Sorry to hear you're so bad, old 'un," he said, "and it's a pity that good things should be wasted: I'll finish 'em up for you."

Pipes drew the plate away before Long Bob's fingers could close upon the rim.

"I'll try and eat a little bit, Bob," he said; "not as I thinks I can."

Bob's eyes longingly followed the shreds of meat; then carefully wiping his plate with the last fragment of his share of the loaf, remarked,—

"It's bad, old'un, to eat against your will; it might give you the indigestion."

Pipes determined to risk the consequences, and in a twinkling his plate was as clean as though it had been unsullied by the contact of the "ornaments."

It was but a sorry meal for those two men and the hungry growing lads; yet Big Drum, though he possessed the five shillings he had set aside to give the chandler's shop keeper on account, would have gone without food rather than touch one penny piece of the debt.

To Long Bob's suggestion that he should invest a sixpence in beer, Drum answered,—

"Mr. Bob—when the man told us he never gave any 'tick,' I said to him, 'Out of the very first day's luck you shall have something towards paying what we owes'—and I know it's more than one pun five, so I can't give him less."

"Drum is right," said honest Jack Lennox. "Let us pay off our debts: then we can eat and drink, and feel all the happier because it will be paid for."

"But only a tanner!" said Bob. "I'll make that up again if we have any luck to-morrow."

Big Drum rose, and taking his hat from the floor, placed it on his head; then, buttoning his coat, marched out of the room, saying,—

"Not a coin, Bob. I'll go and pay the man; then you won't have it always before your eyes, which it will be as long as I keeps it here."

Pipes sighed as he beheld Drum walk out with such a mine of wealth in his pocket, and in a sepulchral whisper called out,—

"Bob!"

The long youth thrust his hands deep in his empty pockets, and went to his friend's side; and Lily, with her young companion, went to the open window to gaze upward at the small patch of blue sky just discernible amidst the interminable line of hot dry-looking tiles.

They spoke in low tones of the green lanes around Falconmere Abbey, and, with their arms around each other's necks, spoke hopefully of the mystic future.

"It cannot be always like this," the boy said. "We must bear with it, Lil, until a happier time comes."

"I am happy," she said—and her blue eyes were fixed upon her companion's face—"when

I am with you."

"I know you are, Lil; but how can I be so when I see you as you were to-day, limping homeward? I knew your feet were blistered—knew it by the tears that came to your eyes when we had to run across Oxford Street out of the way of an omnibus."

"It did not pain me much, Jack."

"I know better, Lil. You are a brave good little girl, but you are not fit for the life we have to lead. I wish," he added, "that I were a man, then—then——"

She noted the pause, and, placing her small soft hand upon his shoulder, asked,—

"What would you do, Jack?"

He was silent. He had a vague boyish idea that, as a man, he could win both fame and fortune, but how, or by what means, he was at fault.

"I don't know," he said, bluntly; "but I should then be strong and independent, and could work; then, dear Lil, you should live better than you do now."

"I have support," she said, "and Mrs. Smith gives me a very nice bed. What more do I require, Jack?"

"Much," he said; "much more. You have been brought up as a lady; you have had servants to wait upon you; and your slightest wish has been law. After all this, Lil, to have fallen so far beneath your former mode of life must make you wretched. I know it does me."

"Naughty boy!" she said, playfully, "have I not told you I am happy? So why need you make yourself so miserable?"

"You have told me so," he said, moodily, "and I believe you, Lil; but I cannot, when I hear the coarse speaking of these rude men, believe that I am doing right by allowing you to stay with them any longer."

She opened her eyes very wide at this, and was about to speak, but the boy interrupted her by saying,—

"I know what you would say, Lil. You feel that these men have been kind to us. They have, I'll admit. Also that, in spite of their manner and appearance, they are honest. But, Lily dear, the life of a street performer, the penury, hardship, and toil, will soon make an inroad upon your delicate health. Then, should you be ill, what will become of us? They will send you to an hospital, and I shall not be able to see you, and——"

His pride gave way under the picture thus conjured up, and leaning his hand upon the window-sill, he burst into tears.

"Jack, dear Jack!"—and she threw her arms round his neck—"do not go on in this manner. We shall be better off soon; I know we shall."

He sobbed out a reply, the words of which were undistinguishable for a time.

"Bob Jawkins," he sobbed, "told me that all this would happen if you were taken to the hospital, and you would have to go, Lily dear, because we have no money to pay a doctor."

Her soothing words soon won him from his grief, and as he wiped the tears from his eyes, and strove to be cheerful under the bright hopeful words she uttered, a gleam of sunshine lit up the murky chimney-pots.

It was Sol's last ray, as the glorious orb sank with dusky majesty in the far west.

"Look, Jack!" the hopeful child said, "see the sun, how different it makes everything look. Be happy, Jack, under the circumstances in which we are placed, and like the blessed sunshine, happiness of heart will make our path lighter.

"Lily," he said, drawing her to him, "you are a brave girl, and your courageous little heart shames me, who should be of the two the bravest."

"You are brave, dear Jack," she said, caressingly smoothing his forehead, "but your bravery is different to mine."

"How, dear Lil? I don't quite understand you."

"It's this," she said. "When the gipsy came to take us back to the encampment, you fired that dreadful gun at him; that was brave of you—but when you think of the hard life we have you grow miserable, and all your courage leaves you. Not so with me. I could not have shot at that dreadful man, no matter where he had taken me; but though I am often in pain when I dance or walk over these hard hot stones, I wipe away the tears that come to my eyes, and think that some day it will be different, and that thought makes me forget all I have to suffer."

The germ of patient endurance—so strong in the softer sex—was being early developed in this gentle child.

Lily's words gave our hero much thought, and he came to the conclusion that if she could suffer so much uncomplainingly, he could, were he to try, do the same.

He was about to tell her so, when Long Bob's voice startled him.

"Have some!" R. J. shouted, holding a cracked yellow jug above his head. "Come on, young'un—do you good."

The dilapidated jug contained nearly a quart of Pipes' favourite mixture—half and-half.

Jack Lennox took the venerable vessel from R. J., and with careful forethought he poured a little into a handleless teacup for Lily.

"Fancy it's tea," he said to the child, who gently refused it, "it will do you good—do, only a little—there, that's a good girl."

Much to his joy the child moistened her lips with the plebeian beverage, then taking a small portion himself, he gave the jug back to Long Bob.

When Pipes called our long friend to his side, he whispered—

"Like some beer, Bob?"

"Don't aggravate me," answered the youth, "after that beast Drum walking off with five bob in his pocket!"

"That's just it," said Pipes. "Of course he'll go and pay the man the coin, and then they'll have at least a pint over it."

"Hope it'll choke 'em," said Long Bob, charitably; "don't you, Pipes?"

"No, I don't hope that, but I wish I was there to have a share. I say, Bob!"

"Well, old un', say on."

"How does you and the old gal down stairs stand?"

"Pretty well. She wanted me to take her shutter out again."

"Did she?" Pipes said reflectively; "that's a good sign—and lent you the gridiron?"

"Yes."

"Ah! that's another good sign."

"Sign of what? What are you driving at, old un'?"

Pipes brought his mouth close to R. J.'s ear and whispered, "Don't you think she'd lend you a bob?"

"Ah!" exclaimed R. J., "good thought! I'll try."

"Do," Pipes said, rubbing his hands; "if she does, bring a pot of the best."

"Like a bird!" said R. J., as he disappeared through the open door.

Whatever arguments he used, they were to the purpose, for, to Pipes's ineffable joy, he came back five minutes afterwards with the beverage.

When Jack Lennox had resigned the precious vessel, Big Drum's footsteps were heard as he ascended the stairs; and Pipes, in his hurry to finish the contents of the jug, nearly suffocated himself.

When Drum entered the room he saw the thin one wiping his eyes with his dirty fingers, and, turning sharply, said, "What, snivelling again, you crocodile, eh?"

"Yes," said Long Bob, readily; "it's tears of joy, Drum. He's thinking of the figure he'll make as Jack-in-the-green."

"Ugh!" growled Drum, "some people can be merry!"

"What's the matter?" asked Bob.

"Not much," Drum replied, heroically; "only the man at the chandler's shop sent for a pint on the strength of the coin I gave him."

"I said so," Pipes whispered.

"And," Drum continued, "I'm blest if the gal didn't fall down and break the jug."

"Of course he sent for another," R. J. said, with a side glance at Pipes; "he couldn't do less."

"Couldn't he," Drum said savagely, crushing his hat under his arm, "but he did though, and after me almost fancying I had the taste in my mouth, I didn't get a toothful."

Long Bob and Pipes grinned behind the disappointed one's back.

"Now then, all of you," Drum said, "let's go into the business, 'cos we ain't got much time."

"All of them" came and gathered round the great man, who thus arranged for the new entertainment.

"Joe Mullins, the sweep," he said, "is coming round to make the green, so it will be all right and up to the mark."

"I say," interrupted Long Bob, "ain't he going to measure Pipes for it?"

"Measure?" Drum said, interrogatively.

"Yes," continued the incorrigible, "I know he'd like it to fit him. My eye, Pipes, won't it be a treat when he beholds your queer looking mug a grinning through the leaves! Talk about a owl in a ivy bush—ha! ha! ha!"

And R. J. danced a break-down, much to Pipes's annoyance.

"Look here, young fellow," Drum said, "don't you interrupt. I've got all the business in my head, and if you begins your buffoonery it won't be there long, so sit down and be quiet."

Long Bob tried to do so; but long before Drum had finished the programme, R. J. had slily fastened a pin to the end of a stick, and, much to Pipes's dismay, he received several sharp pricks, and looked beneath the table for the cause.

At last Bob sent the pin with some force into Pipes's leg, and the solo instrumentalist sprang from his chair and gave a yell.

"What's the matter?" Long Bob calmly asked, as he dropped the stick behind his chair.

"Matter!" said Pipes, "something stuck in my leg!"

"Order!" shouted Drum. "Now listen, all of you. When we get a good crowd—audience, I mean—you must all keep dancing as long as I plays."

Pipes's face became a woeful length as he said,—

"But the Jack-in-the-green don't dance with all that lot over him!"

"Don't he?" said Drum; "that's where you are wrong. The Green dances longer and quicker than anybody else. So look out, if you don't keep time with me."

"Oh Lor!" gasped Pipes, as he sank into his chair. "I shall never be able to do it!"

Joe Mullins came on the next evening, and, tired as the company were, they set to work with a will to help their sooty ally.

The night previous to this new experiment the funds were all exhausted in providing new dresses for the company. Long Bob's get-up was superb, and, as a finish, he drew Pipes's likeness, life-size (the head and face), on the breast of his close-fitting dress.

Drum was in ecstasies with Lily's costume, and declared she looked "stunning;" as also did Jack in his swallow-tailed coat and lace-bedizened cocked hat.

The only sombre face visible in that little room was Pipes's. He sat, as usual, in the darkest corner, casting from time to time savagely spiteful glances towards the green pyramid that seemed to his eyes about as pleasant an object as the rack to a hapless captive in the dungeons of the old Inquisition.

"Beastly thing!" muttered Pipes. "I hope it will all tumble to bits direckly I begins to dance."

His hope was not fulfilled—as, to his sorrow, he discovered before the day was half over.

Never in the course of his existence had his legs moved so nimbly as they did beneath the leafy covering.

Big Drum, having to manage both instruments, had given Long Bob strict orders to keep Pipes a-moving—orders which R. J., in his capacity of clown, found but little difficulty in carrying out.

Poor Pipes, puffing beneath the accumulation of misery which oppressed him, would pause to regain his breath during one of Drum's most spirited passages with the pair of instruments.

In vain, by moving his body to and fro, he sought to keep up a semblance of joining in the dance—the leaves, the artificial flowers moved, but Bob's keen eyes were watching Pipes's square-toed boots, and in an instant he would detect the dodge, and, much to the edification of the bystanders, he would shout, loud enough to be heard above Drum's performance on the instruments,—

"Now then, old un', keep it up. Go on—chuck your hoofs about."

The audience would laugh as the green pyramid began to bob about, and then Robert,

THE BOYS OF BIRCHAM SCHOOL.

BEFORE THE COUNTRY JUSTICE.

seizing the opportune moment, would call out,—

"Don't forget the coppers, ladies and gentlemen; drop 'em in the ladle. Go round, Lily; there's a gent has sixpence for you. Keep it up, old 'un—remember we have got to perform before the Emperor of Rooshia when it comes the first of May in that country."

After thus making the circle into a good humour, he would join hands with Jack and Lily, and the trio, forming a ring, would dance round Pipes until that suffering individual was, as he afterwards declared, ready to drop.

Big Drum's coat pocket began to feel heavy towards night; never in the whole of his "purfessional" career had he experienced such a day of good luck.

At every pitch they made Lily came to him at its conclusion, with the brass ladle filled with halfpence, and more than once he detected the gleam of a small silver coin among them.

Long Bob, who had danced all day with a vigour that threatened to dislocate his limbs, began to feel weary, and, to Pipes's joy, proposed that they should "cut it."

"One more," Drum said, "opposite that public, then we'll close."

They made a pitch opposite the gin-palace, and when Long Bob gave the signal for the children to join hands, a cry of terror came from Lily's lips, and Jack, raising his eyes, beheld Tinker Tom, his arms crossed upon a post, and his dark sinister eyes glaring vengefully upon the young pair.

The boy gave an angry cry, as he placed himself between Lily and their foe; then Long Bob, who at once recognized the gipsy by the description Jack had given, clenched his hands, and went towards the burly ruffian.

Tinker Tom would have liked to have seized the boy and girl, but, seeing he was recognized, he turned from them and passed into the public-house.

CHAPTER XIV.

THE DETECTIVE.

WALTER CARLIN traced the fugitives step by step, until he became lost in the mazy windings of the great city.

Then his fondly cherished hopes fell, and, sadder at heart than of yore, he gave up the search.

In one of those quiet streets leading from the Strand to the banks of the polluted Thames, he took apartments.

From his solitary rooms he could wander forth in the hope of yet finding the boy; but day after day passed—each night the weight became heavier upon his heart, and the proud head, before so erect, became drooped, his step less elastic, and among his dark raven locks streaks of glistening grey deepened as the time wore on.

He supped in silence—not a friend had the broken-hearted man to share his misery; and day by day the iron went deeper and deeper to his soul.

During one of his fruitless rambles his eyes caught the inscription upon a brass plate of a door—

"PRIVATE INQUIRY OFFICE."

He repeated the words over and over again, and finally, placing one foot upon the doorstep, seemed irresolute whether to enter the dingy office, or pass on to his lonely home.

While thus irresolute, the office door opened, and a grave elderly man was about to pass through.

He came to a sudden standstill when he saw the officer's pale wan face, and holding the door open, said, blandly,—

"Will you step inside?"

Mechanically obeying, Captain Carlin found himself face to face with the clever private detective.

The soldier at once entered upon the matter nearest his heart, and the detective, with a grave smile, drew a chair close to his visitor, and prepared, note-book in hand, to jot down such items as would prove the most useful in the matter.

"I scarcely know" said the officer, "how to begin; in fact, not having contemplated a visit to your office, I am unprepared to state the difficult task I should like you to undertake."

The detective played with his watchguard as he said,—

"It requires but little explanation to set my men upon the track of those who have often baffled the most subtle officers from Scotland Yard."

"Indeed!" exclaimed the visitor, startled for a moment by this frank acknowledgment.

"You seem surprised, sir," said the gentlemanly chief of the private detectives, "at my words."

"I am," was the answer.

The chief of the private inquiry office tapped the table with his white fingers.

"You would be more so" he said, "were I to enumerate the series of hidden crimes and the deep mysteries my men have unravelled during the last five years."

"Crimes and mysteries which the regular detectives failed to discover?"

"Even so," was the answer; "now, sir, in what, pray, can I serve you?"

The officer, in as brief terms as possible, related all that is known to the reader, and the grave listener smiled once or twice during the recital.

"I tracked them," said the officer, "from the village near Falconmere until they reached a roadside public-house in the southern suburbs of London."

The detective asked the name of the house.

"The Red Lion," answered Captain Carlin; "there I was informed that the children, in company with a youth older than my son, made the acquaintance of two men, who, from the description I have been able to glean, must have been connected with a company of street performers."

Another note was made in the small book, and the detective nodded for his visitor to proceed.

"From that hour," Captain Carlin said, "up to the present time I have failed to discover the least clue."

"I think," the detective said, "I may safely promise that before a week has passed your son will be found and placed in your care."

The officer shook his head sadly, and the detective, noticing the action, said,—

"You think I overrate my powers?"

"No," he answered; "but I fear that those upon the boy's track have before this discovered him, and I tremble to think of the consequence."

"Those upon his track—is there more than the vengeful gipsy?"

"There is a Frenchman, who, until the wall of Falconmere fell a prey to the flames, served the earl. Since then he has devoted every energy to the task of finding my boy."

"Have you no idea of his purpose?"

"None."

The detective pondered for a few moments over this statement—then, raising his head, said hopefully,—

"Even with this difficulty to cope with, I think I may safely repeat my words."

The soldier's face flushed with joy, and, taking the detective's hand, he exclaimed,—

"Do this, and I will reward you beyond your most sanguine expectations."

The detective returned the fervid grasp of

his visitor's hand, and said,—

"I will do my best."

He rose to open the door for his visitor, and Captain Carlin, turning upon the threshold, asked,—

"Can I call daily, and hear how you progress?"

"I think not—no; it will be better not to do so. Should anything occur that leads me to the belief that we may conclude our task before the week has expired, I will send to you."

"Be it so; I will hopefully await the passing of the next six days."

He turned from the door-step; his pa careworn face looking brighter than it had for many weeks.

The detective watched his visitor until he passed from view; then, re-entering the office, he looked carefully over the notes he had made.

'There will be no difficulty," he thought, "if we can get possession of the gipsy—the Frenchman, too; he must have some motive in thus closely following the children. What can it be?"

A few moments' thought suggested a trap to catch Monsieur Jules Latour.

Rapidly the pen glided over the paper as he wrote—

"If the French gentleman who followed two children from Bridgenorth to London will call at the Private Inquiry Office, No. 1,—, he will hear something to his advantage."

Pressing the white knob of a call-bell, a lad appeared from an inner room.

"Take this," the chief said; "write it out, and leave a copy with each of the daily papers."

The lad took the paper, bowed, and disappeared behind the noiseless baize-covered door.

"So much for the Frenchman," he thought; "now for the gipsy."

He pondered long over many plans to lure Tinker Tom to the private inquiry office, but knowing the ways of these wanderers, he dismissed plan after plan as hopeless.

"The same bait," he thought, "that may hook the Frenchman will not get a nibble from the gipsy."

Striking the call-bell twice brought a stout, well-dressed man to his presence.

"I'm glad you are not out, Harvey," the chief said, "for I have a case that is peculiarly in your line."

He explained a portion of the captain's statement to his subordinate, and when describing the strolling players, a smile passed over the man's features.

"I do not think," the chief said, "that it will be necessary to go out of London to find these men."

"I think not."

"Should you find them, bring the boy away at once—that is," he added, "if they are together. If not, go at once upon his track, and do not return here without him."

The man bowed, and left the office. As he passed through the busy street he muttered,—

"Big Drum and Pipes, for a thousand pounds! I wonder what they will think of their old friend in his new line. Poor old boys! I'll warrant Pipes has shed many tears since we parted."

The well-dressed agent was the ungrateful Buffler.

Passing the Mansion House, a boy of the Shoeblack Brigade touched his hat to the private detective.

"Clean your boots, sir?" then, in an under tone, "have 'm cleaned; I've seen him."

The Buffler nodded, and the boy, taking his box a few paces down a quiet turning, spread the brushes out, and, turning up the bottoms of his customer's trousers—a very long job, by the way, in this instance,—

"I watched for him," the boy said, while the Buffler, with an affected carelessness, watched the vehicles as they whirled past, "but he didn't come till this morning."

"Ha! what hour?"

"About ten, sir."

"Proceed."

The right boot was being elaborately blacked by this time.

"He came up the steps from Thames Street," said the boy, "and at the side of the bridge which is just over where the steamer goes from, he met a man."

"Describe him."

"A stout-built fellow. I could not see much of his face, because he had a seal-skin cap pulled over his forehead."

"Well?"

"I tried, though, and as I asked them to nave their boots cleaned, I saw that the man with the cap had a mark across his cheek."

"A red streak?"

"Yes, sir."

"Timothy Adkins," muttered the Buffler. "I thought there was more than one in the job. Well, boy, what became of them?"

"The man with the mark on his cheek and the fair nice-looking young gentleman walked to the railway station."

The private detective bit his lip.

"I followed them, and luckily a gent had his boots cleaned close under the place where they give out the tickets."

"Yes, yes."

"I heard the man with the cap say 'Boulogne,' and the young gentleman gave him a brown pocket-book. That's all, sir."

"What became of the youngest?"

"He called a hansom, and went away, just as the train started."

The boots were by this time finished, and the boy's eyes sparkled as two half-crown pieces were placed in his hand.

"You have done well," said the agent, "I have another job for you."

"Yes, sir;" and as he slipped the coins in his pocket the begrimed but intelligent face became very pleased in its expression.

"Have you seen any street performers lately?" the agent asked.

The boy reflected for a few moments before he answered,—

"Yes, sir; several."

"Describe them."

"Yesterday there was a man with a monkey and a——"

"No use. The party I want, I have every reason to believe, will consist of four—two men, a boy, and a girl."

"Tumblers, sir?"

"The boy most likely will do that; the girl, I expect, will dance; and the two men

—one short and stout, and the other tall and thin. The stout one will have a drum, the other a mouth-organ, and, in all likelihood, a small box suspended round his neck by a strap."

The boy shook his head, and said,—

"I ain't seen 'em, sir. The last lot I saw was up Shoreditch way; but that was Jack-in-the-green day."

"It was not those I seek."

"No, sir; but there was a fat man with a drum, two boys, and such a pretty little girl, besides a man doing Jack-in-the-green."

The private detective reflected for some minutes.

"In numbers," he thought, "they seem to tally with the chief's description. But I should scarcely expect Drum would leave his legitimate line for this."

"The little girl," the shoeblack said, breaking in upon the detective's thoughts, "had the most beautifullest hair in the world —all like gold, and hung down her back a long way."

"Her description!" exclaimed the detective, struck by the boy's words. "Well, the boys—what were they like?"

"One was bigger than the other, and an awful cheeky one, too. He kept chaffing the people and the man inside the green, but the other boy did not say a word; I don't think he looked as though he liked the job."

"Perhaps not. Well—about the man with the drum."

"He was short and fat, and wore a white dirty hat with a black band round it."

"How did he wear it?"

The boy looked up, rather puzzled at this interrogation.

"I mean," the detective said, "did he wear it drawn over his eyes, on the back of his head, or how?"

"Neither," the boy answered; "now I remember, it was all on one side."

"Big Drum!" muttered the agent; "this boy is invaluable."

"Is it them, sir?" asked the shoeblack, the prospect of two similar coins to those he already possessed looming pleasantly in the distance.

"I hope so," was the reply. "Now, Sam, you must leave off cleaning boots to-day, and try what you can find out about the Jack-in-the-green party."

"Yes, sir; what am I do?"

"You saw them, you say, near Shoreditch?"

"Yes, sir."

"Well, you go among the keepers of the stalls which line the road, and inquire—some one is sure to have seen them—follow every clue you may get, and if possible discover where they live."

"Yes, sir—where shall I see you?"

"I will be opposite the railway-station in Bishopsgate at nine o'clock."

"Very well, sir; I will be there. If I meet them to-day, what shall I do?"

"Do not lose sight of them until they are safely housed."

"All right, sir!"

Then, throwing his box on his back, the boy dived among the crowd of vehicles and disappeared.

The private detective walked quickly to the telegraph office at the railway station and much surprised the clerk by sending the following message to a brother officer at Dover.

"Adkins—en route for Boulogne—brown leather pocket-book—scar over cheek—sealskin cap—packet leaves 10 this evening—the other safe yet—parted this morning."

He paid for the transmission of the message, and left the clerk wondering what sort of people they were who could make anything out of the above message.

The detective paused outside the telegraph office, undecided which way to turn.

He had great confidence in his young ally, and believed that the boy would do as much good as far as the search was concerned as he could.

"He can work the west-end to-day," thought the agent; "I'll take a turn southward."

Passing over the bridge, his mind reverted to the different cases which had so completely baffled the regular and the private detectives.

A merchant's office safe had been broken open, and the contents stolen; but, strange to say, the office door and the outer doors bore no marks of having been forced; yet the robber or robbers must have passed through them before reaching the safe.

The peculiar construction of the locks put an end to the blue-coated official's hypothesis that the thieves had entered by using skeleton keys.

When the case was given over to the head of the private detectives, the Buffler joined Big Drum and Pipes, in order that he could watch the movements of the merchant's son.

For upon this youth the detective's suspicion fell.

He alone had charge of the keys, and they were morally certain that the young fellow had a share in the robbery.

But how to prove it?

The merchant's son was under his father's roof from the time the office was closed until the next morning, and the keys were in his possession—so he stated—the whole time.

It was a case that required the most delicate handling, and the Buffler, as he called himself when he joined Drum's company, took charge of the affair.

He spent a month with the street performers, but without gleaning the least clue to the mystery.

Other matters compelled him to suddenly leave his friends, and the chief, looking upon the affair as undiscoverable, gave the Buffler another case.

The latter's pride was a little touched by his failure, and though he entered upon the new affair, he had not lost sight of the old one.

The detectives, to glean information, are compelled to use peculiar means.

Costermongers, crossing-sweepers, and shoeblacks are very useful to them.

The Buffler took one of the latter, and pointed out the merchant's son to him, and told the boy to watch him closely.

The result has been detailed.

Adkins, a returned convict, had been seen lurking near the office by the detective, when performing at the corner of the street.

To find out the suspicious-looking fellow's name was easily accomplished by the Buffler.

To link this man's appearance with the

robbery was easy, and the detective's mind at once grasped the whole facts of the case.

But ere he could act upon his conviction it was necessary to obtain a proof of the collusion between the merchant's son and Timothy Adkins.

The shoeblack had obtained this, and as the agent walked slowly towards the Borough, his eyes searching for his old companions, his thoughts were occupied with the bullion robbery.

"It's as clear as the noonday's sun," he mentally argued; "the lad is rather fast—fond of billiard-rooms and betting; the old fellow has a due regard for the value of £ s. d.,—the boy wants money—he lends Adkins the keys of the outer doors—the safe is broken open, and none's the wiser for his share in the affair—so he imagines; but the clumsiness of the key business betrayed him. Now, how am I to act—will the father hush up the affair for his son's sake, or——"

"Rub-a-dub-dub, toot-te-to-toot."

From the depths of a narrow turning came the sounds of a drum and a mouth-organ, and the detective, postponing the solution of the question he had begun to argue, started in the direction of the sound.

CHAPTER XV.

THE BOUNDING BROTHERS OF BARCELONA.

THE appearance of Tinker Tom put our "purfessional" friends on their guard, and as they dragged their tired limbs through the by-streets en route to Mrs. Smith's hospitable mansion, Lily was closely guarded by her companions.

One small hand was drawn through Jack's arm, and tightly clasped by the bold handsome boy.

Long Bob walked in front, the heavy brass handle gripped ready for instant use should the foe make his appearance. R. J., though somewhat loosely put together, was possessed of wondrous muscular power, and armed as he was, Tinker Tom would have found his master had he attempted to take the girl from their keeping.

Big Drum and his tired friend brought up the rear—Drum elated at the weight of his pockets—Pipes depressed in consequence of having to carry home the leafy covering he had suffered under for so many hours.

Except having to endure the cutting remarks of various boys, our friends reached home without any event worthy of recording.

A rest and some refreshment did them much good; then Drum, in the capacity of orchestra, manager, secretary, general director, and treasurer, began to count over the day's receipts.

The number of threepenny, fourpenny, and sixpenny pieces he found among the copper coins, for some time took away his breath and stayed the counting.

"I'm blest," he remarked, looking fondly at the little heaps, "if this ain't a good day's work!"

"How much is there?" Long Bob asked.

"In silver?" questioned Drum.

"No, altogether," said R. J. mildly.

"There ain't any bad 'uns—the silver 'mounts to nineteen and tenpence."

Pipes pricked up his ears and began to entertain visions of numberless pots of the "favourite."

"The coppers," Drum continued, "'mounts to eleven and sevenpence ha'penny—that's how much altogether, Jack?"

"One pound eleven shillings and fivepence halfpenny," the boy answered, readily.

Pipes wiped his mouth with the dirty fringe, and Long Bob stood upon his head in the centre of the room, and the children, who looked upon this amount as a fortune, clapped their hands joyfully.

"One pun' eleven and fippence ha'penny," said Drum; "the one pun' must go to the shop round the corner—the rest we divides."

Pipes pulled a long face at this, and R. J. came to his feet much quicker than he had tended.

"I think," Drum continued, "it will be the best way for us to have two bob a-piece, and put the extra one five and a-half away."

"Look here, Drum," said Long Bob, "can't you give the cove ten bob less and pay the rest afterwards?"

Big Drum shook his head.

"No, Bob," he replied; "it won't allers be the fust of May—I wish it was."

"Does you?" said Pipes; "I don't, then."

"Hold your noise, shadder; we's talking about business."

The shadder subsided, and Drum resumed,—

"It's this way, you see, Bob; arter that black-looking gipsy chap being so close upon us to-day, I don't think it will be safe to stay in the streets—not as we need care much, but it's our little gal we must look arter."

"Right, Drum," Long Bob said; "we must look after her, but what are we to do?"

"This is what I've been thinking," Drum continued; "there'll be a fair going on at a little town I know not far out of London—s'pose we works our way down there—and if we is lucky we can get enough to start a booth, eh—what do you think of that?"

"Capital," said R. J. "But we must get up some sort of performance to draw the yokels."

"That's just it, Bob; now what can we do?"

Long Bob's inventive genius soon solved the matter.

"Look here, Drum," he said, "of course we shall have to make a show outside."

"Exactly."

"And to do the thing to rights we must have a big canvass poster along the top of our booth."

"Yes, Bob, that must be done—but what can we put on it?"

"There's plenty of things we might have; for example—Pipes might be the Living Skeleton, and we could get a penny extra by admitting the public to see him drink beer."

Pipes shuffled about on his seat; he did not particularly relish being shown as a living skeleton, but the beer-drinking part of the programme made him hope the arrangement would be carried into effect.

"No," Drum said, "the public don't care much for these sort of things,—they have had plenty of skeletons and fat women lately. Can't you think of something else?"

"Yes," R. J. said, giving Pipes a mischievous glance, "we can black lead the old 'un all over, and stick up, 'To be seen alive, the great and mighty chief of Jumbo Island;" and when the people come in and begin to wonder how it is he is so thin, you can tell 'em that it is in consequence of the chief not having any of his wives to roast and eat for breakfast that makes him so."

The idea was not a bad one, Drum thought, yet it was not the thing.

"Look here, Bob," he said, "what's you and the young un's to do?"

"Oh, we'll do the outside. I'll be clown, Jack can be harlequin, and Lily columbine."

"Yes," Drum said; "but ain't there anything else?"

"I hopes there is," whispered Pipes, "cos I ain't going to be black-leaded when there ain't no beer in the part I has to perform."

Long Bob drew his considering cap well over his head, and after a few minutes' pause he slapped Drum on the back and called out,—

"Yes; I've got it!"

"Where, Bob, where?"

"Here, down in my nut, and I think it will do to-rights."

Drum hoped it would, and prepared himsel to receive the long youth's brilliant thought.

"This is it," said Bob: "we'll have stuck up in large letters, 'This way for the Bounding Brothers of Barcelona and the young Princess of the Thingamybob Mountains.'"

"That'll look fine," said the delighted manager; and "if we gets a trumpet, Pipes can shout it out every minute while I goes on with the music."

"Yes," said Bob enthusiastically; "we must have three dresses, you know, Drum: one to do the outside business, and the others to do the Bounding Brothers of Barcelona."

Drum saw the necessity for this, and at once began to plan how the material for the dresses was to be obtained.

Long Bob's skill was of great use to the company in making up the material, and, to do him justice, he did the work wonderfully well, considering how little he had learnt from the gin-drinking little tailor.

He tried hard to have poor Pipes black-leaded and transformed into the terrible chief of the Jumbo Island, but Drum overruled this, much to the slender one's relief.

"We can't very well do it, Bob," said Drum, "in conserkance of wanting the shadder outside to holler through the trumpet."

"I don't see why we couldn't. He could just as well wash his face, and come out, as not."

"No, Bob; it ain't to be thought on. Why, he'd have to wash hisself every time, and the washin' would be too much for him."

"Why?"

"Because," said Big Drum, with a grin, "by the time he had got hisself washed like that, he would only be the size of this here drumstick handle."

"I say," whispered Pipes, "when you is both done making game of me, prap's you'll leave off."

"All right, old un'," said R. J.; "you don't know what good things we shall have for you."

"Had quite enough of good things for one day," said Pipes, spitefully. "So if you thinks to black-lead me all over, you won't."

"Shut up!" said Drum; "we don't want your spoke in the business. I think the best thing you can do is to go out and sell the green."

"What! that——"

"Yes. Somebody will buy it, if it's only for the timber that's in it."

"Whether anybody 'ud buy it, or not,' Pipes said, "I won't take it out."

BIG DRUM'S fury was ungovernable. To be thus set at defiance by his hitherto meek companion caused his very nose to turn blue; so, before Pipes could finish his defiant answer, Drum's white hat struck him across the mouth.

Long Bob wanted to back the old un' to go in for a little of the fistic business, but Pipes would not come up to the scratch.

* * * * *

The appearance of Big Drum's company at the fair excited the envy of less fortunate proprietors than our stout red-nosed friend.

From morn to closing time the front of the booth was crowded by a closely-packed collection of grinning rustics.

Long Bob became brilliant as clown, and sorely chaffed the "chawbacons" who did not comply with his request to "walk up."

Jack Lennox made a splendid Harlequin, and little Lily, as columbine, caused many exclamations of admiration from the crowd.

Big Drum was in the seventh heaven, as, seated behind his drum, he belaboured the parchment.

Pipes had wrapped his mouth-organ carefully in brown paper, and appeared behind a huge speaking-trumpet; and when Drum gave him an opportunity, he refreshed the crowd by making the most unearthly noise.

It might have been an imitation of a man with a sore throat, or a dying bull's roar; yet it was not either; and though many a puzzled agricultural gentleman asked another agricultural ditto, 'What this chap be doing with the horn?' they could not obtain a decided answer.

A piece of canvass, stretched, as Long Bob observed, from "pole to pole," bore this telling announcement in large black letters—

"The Great Bung, and the Bounding Brothers of Barcelona! The Young Princess, from the Thingamy Mountains! Walk up! One Penny each to see the whole of the performance!"

Nearly opposite Big Drum's show, a powerful rival had taken his stand, and the following announcement drew many eyes from the feats of the "Bounding Brothers of Barcelona."—

"The Laughing Pig! also the Calculating Pug! Alive! Alive!"

The first hour or so after the company had thrown open their show, Long Bob saw with dismay that the laughing pig and his friend the calculating pug drew tremendously, and in spite of Drum's performance, Pipes's trumpets, and his own splendid wit, the crowd, after gaping with open mouths at the exterior of the show would ungratefully walk to the rival exhibition.

"This 'll never do, Drum," said Bob; "that feller takes all the custom."

Drum looked wistfully at a small crowd who were cheerfully paying their pennies to behold the pig and the pug.

"It won't, Bob," he said; "is there any paint left?"

"The black paint Pipes used for the

canvass?"

"Yes, Bob."

"There is a little, Drum. How much do you want?"

"Not much; only enough to stick up a fresh attraction that'll smash that feller."

"Him with the Pug?"

"Yes. Fetch the paint, Bob, and we'll get Pipes to write up—The Talking Herring—the Dancing Helephant—and the Whistling Crab."

"That won't do," suggested Pipes, "unless we have something to show like 'em."

"You'll do for the Herring," said Drum, savagely.

"And you," Pipes retorted, "will make a fine Helephant."

Long Bob, Jack, and Lily were highly amused at this; and Jack suggested,—

"Bob, as Drum and Pipes will manage their part, suppose I personate the crab?"

"Can't see how it is to be done, young un'. You might do the Crab by going outside and whistling through the canvass, but the Elephant and the Herring is too much."

"No, it ain't," growled Drum. "We can, after you three have gone through your performance, set up a cry, and say the Helephant has broke loose."

"Good," said Bob, "that will do. Now, old un', fetch the paint, and go at it; we'll spiflicate the pug in no time!"

Beneath the first announcement Pipes added,—

"*Also the Laughing Herring—the Dancing Elephant—and the Whistling Crab. One Penny admittance to the whole entertainment.*"

"Talking herring," said Drum, pointing to the alteration; "you've put laughing."

"That will do much better," Long Bob said. "Now, then, here come some Chawbacons; go it, music; now, Jack and Lil, let's have a round."

They joined hands and spun round, to the sepulchral groanings of Pipes's trumpet and the deafening noise of the drum.

The fresh announcement and this display soon drew a crowd: then Long Bob came forward, and pointing to a rustic youth whose sturdy frame was arrayed in a dirty yellow smock frock, said,—

"Come back again, have you?"

The rustic opened his mouth very wide—he had not been near the show until now.

"What a mouth!" Long Bob said. "I shouldn't like to be a potato——"

"I say," one of the bystanders called out, "where do you keep the elephant?"

Long Bob was quite ready for this query.

"Well," he asked, "where do you think?"

"Dunno—don't believe you've got one."

"Come," R. J. answered, "I'll bet you a sovereign we have—here, will any gentleman hold the money?"

No gentleman came forward, and Bob, to convince the sceptics respecting their possession of the huge animal, whispered as he passed Pipes,—

"Put your trumpet inside, old 'un; I must go and make the elephant roar."

During the time the crowd were laughing at Long Bob's sallies, Pipes slipped inside and took his instrument out of brown paper and left the speaking trumpet inside the doorway.

"All right," he whispered behind Long Bob, "just in the doorway."

The announcement Bob turned to advantage by answering Pipes and talking at the crowd.

"Broken loose, did you say, and dancing all over the place?—I'll soon settle him."

R. J. made a frantic rush inside the show, and, placing the trumpet to his mouth with one hand, with the other he seized a hammer and began beating the seats as an accompaniment to the bellowings of the trumpet.

The crowd were convinced of the elephant's existence, and many began to speculate upon the outlay to view the whole of the entertainment.

Long Bog wound up the business in a most effectual manner by swinging the elephant's trunk two or three times across the open doorway.

"There he be! there he be!" exclaimed one, as Bob gave a louder roar through the trumpet, and again his long trunk was seen.

"He be fightin' wi 'im," remarked another. Our long friend, ever ready witted, had stuffed one of the sleeves of his jacket with shavings, and, trusting to the deep shadow, he swayed it about inside.

Truth to tell, Big Drum and the remainder of the company were much more astonished by this sight than were the crowd.

Big Drum so much so, that he rapped his fingers on the edges of the drum : Pipes stood watching the dusky looking affair, evidently wondering what it was, how it came there, and feeling thankful that Long Bob had joined their company.

"I've quieted him," said R. J. as he came to the front. "Now, gentlemen, walk up, walk up—it's getting near dinner time—if you don't come now you will be sorry—this way, sir, pass inside, sir—he'll collect the money inside—go it music—now Jack, another round—hold tight, Lil—the elephant's trunk did the business. Eh! what was it? The sleeve of my old jacket!"

"Bravo!" Jack said softly, "there they go; we must have at least twenty inside."

"The crib will hold sixty—loose hands and do a jig."

Pipes wheezed and squeaked upon the mouth organ—Drum belaboured the parchment—and the trio danced until they were breathless.

A loud bang on the drum brought the outside performance to a close, and during the time occupied by Pipes in collecting the money, Long Bob and our hero were beneath the stage, changing their dress preparatory to appearing as the Bounding Brothers of Barcelona.

The audience were too thick skulled to applaud or condemn the performance; so, with mouths agape, they sat until the Bounding brothers had concluded, and little Lily, her graceful form draped with rose-coloured gauze, was led forward by Jack Lennox.

The hobnailed gentry were not proof against the child's winning grace and faultless face and form.

They did not clap their hands, shuffle their feet, whistle, or yell "Encore!" when the girl retired, but in lieu of those demonstrations so peculiarly the fashion of the town gods, Messrs. Baconrind, Fatpork, and Co. looked after the child, and remarked,—

"She be a pretty 'un—don't 'ee think so, Giles?"

"Ees, lad, she look purty loike, but these darned play actor people do look loike that when they be dressed up."

"Hold thee tongue, lad; there be t'elephunt coming."

"Whur?"

"Don't 'ee hear 'un roaring loike mad?"

"Ees, I do. Here comes young chap to tell us summat."

Jack Lennox came to the front of the rough stage, and making a profound bow, said boldly,—

"Gentlemen, I am requested by the manager to tell you that the elephant is, from some unknown cause, very savage just now; and when in that state it is dangerous to bring him out of his cage."

Long Bob, who was behind the canvas back of the stage, gave a succession of unearthly moans through the trumpet.

"That noise, gentlemen," little Jack resumed, "is the elephant's cry when he is angry."

"Bring 'un out," shouted a red-headed farmer's lad; "we paid our money to see 'un, and it don't matter to us if he be savage."

"We should have much pleasure in doing so," said Jack, coolly, "but we dare not endanger the lives of the public by——"

Here Long Bob gave a most terrible roar.

"You hear that," Jack continued, scarcely able to refrain from laughing outright. "He's getting worse every minute."

"Where's t' herring, then?" asked the rustic Rufus; "*that* beant savage too?"

"No," Jack said, ".but unfortunately the elephant is now standing over the glass dish which contains the herring, and we dare not take it away."

"Where's t' crab, then?"

"The crab?" Jack said—"Hush!"

The rustics held their breath and listened, as Long Bob began to whistle through a hole in the canvas.

"Bring 'un out—bring 'un out!" shouted the discontented portion of the audience."

Now was the moment for Long Bob to interpose and save the credit of the company.

Rushing upon the stage, armed with a hammer, he began striking wildly at about an inch of the stuffed sleeve which Pipes kept lolling through a rent in the canvas.

"There be trunk, lookee!" exclaimed one; "he'll be coming out directly."

"Run about, Jack," whispered Bob, "then make a bolt towards the chawbacons."

Jack got up a good counterfeit of sudden terror, and after running to and fro the narrow limits of the stage, asked, loud enough for the audience to hear,—

"Is he loose?"

Big Drum, who had the trumpet, made a terrific noise through it; Pipes moved the stuffed sleeve quickly about behind the canvas; Lily gave a scream, and Long Bob, as he plied his hammer, shouted,—

"Yes, he's broken his chain—run, Jack, and fasten the doors; if he gets out he will kill every stranger he ——"

This, coupled with Jack's sudden flight towards the door, had the desired effect. In an instant every rustic sprang to his feet, and, amid cries and shouts of fear, they rushed madly towards the door.

Big Drum kept them to it by sending forth such fearful growls through the speaking trumpet as caused the panic to increase, and the show was emptied in a wonderfully short space of time.

The last of the gulled yokels had disappeared before the sensation was brought to a conclusion.

Then the company, no longer able to contain their long-suppressed feelings, gave way to shout after shout of laughter.

"That may do for once," Long Bob remarked; "but we must not come it again."

"What's to be done?" asked Drum. "You see it didn't draw without having something else besides the Bounding Brothers and the Fairy Princess."

"That's true," said Bob; "it shows their bad taste. I don't see anything that we can do, unless we get up another dodge."

Drum rubbed the tip of his nose reflectively.

"Look here!" Long Bob exclaimed, "I have it!"

"Eh! have you?"

"Yes, Drum. We'll get up a terrific combat between the Wild Elephant of Nova Scotia and the Daring Hunter of the Chum-chum Forest!"

"That sounds well," remarked Pipes. "Now, how is it to be done?"

"Very easy, old un'. I'll go over to the man that let us have this booth, and borrow an old cowhide I saw there."

"Good," Drum assented. "You'll dress yourself up, eh?"

"Yes, and Pipes can work away with the stuffed sleeve; and if I can get an old hatchet we shall do."

"We shall, Bob."

The fame of the whistling crab and the enraged elephant having spread after the first performance, the company found it impossible, in consequence of a sudden rush of visitors, to put the Daring Hunter of the Chum-chum Forest upon the stage.

Agricultural gentlemen began to pour in— some in cow-gowns; others in waistcoats and ties of all colours that were known and unknown—some (and these were accompanied by ruddy-cheeked Venuses) came in white hats, the nap a good inch in length, and standing out defiantly.

The second audience demanded the production of the laughing herring and the whistling crab—they were satisfied respecting the elephant; they ought tohave been, for the animal's roar was tremendous, and the manner in which he beat his trunk against the canvas caused many a scream from the female patrons.

Bob took advantage of these sounds of fear, and Jack was deputed to go forward and make a speech.

"Ladies and gentlemen," he said, "we are sorry that we cannot bring forward the laughing fish and his companion the whistling crab, in consequence of the elephant, whose roar you can hear, and whose trunk you may observe beating against the canvas, as he madly tries to get hold of his keeper and crunch him up. This savage beast, ladies and gentlemen, will not allow us to touch his companions, but if you will be silent, you shall hear them go through their performance."

There was a little outburst of dissatisfaction, but it was soon quelled by the rustic Venuses taking Jack's part.

When everything was quiet, they heard the

THE BOYS OF BIRCHAM SCHOOL.

SAVED FROM A WATERY GRAVE.

herring laugh (Pipes), and the crab whistle a tune (Long Bob); and much to the satisfaction of the company the audience retired, fully satisfied with the entertainment set before them.

CHAPTER XVI.
LILY IN TINKER TOM'S POWER.

A REPETITION of these dodges brought the first day's performance to a satisfactory close, and with bright hopes of the morrow the company partook of a sumptuous supper before retiring.

Drum and his thin friend slept upon a pile of straw in one corner of the stage: Long Bob and Jack, upon a similar shake-down, stretched their weary limbs in the opposite corner.

The little girl had quite a tasteful retreat at the back of the stage. Jack Lennox and Bob had devoted many hours to the construction and fittings of the fairy princess's chamber.

True it was but a tiny space, and the sides were but canvas; but the boys had cunningly concealed the dingy reality by sundry strips of pink glazed calico.

They had also erected a bedstead with a few pieces of wood, and this, with a little flock bed and a blanket, made, under the circumstances, a very comfortable apartment.

Poor child!—had it been the hard cold ground, she would have slept quite as soundly. The dancing outside had completely exhausted her tender frame, and scarcely had her wearied head touched the pillow when her eyes closed, and she fell into a deep sleep.

Everything remained quiet until near daybreak; then the tired company were suddenly aroused by the fearful alarm of fire.

They were upon their feet in a second, and simultaneously a cry of horror came from their lips, as they beheld the canvas at the back of the stage burst into a sudden blaze.

"Lily!" exclaimed Jack, as he dashed towards the place, "Lily, wake up, or you will be burnt."

No answer—no response to his wild appeal; and the boy, trembling with a dread apprehension that his little companion had fallen a victim to the suffocating smoke which hid her resting place from his view, rushed madly forward and tore down the canvas.

The bed was empty, and part of her clothes, neatly folded, lay upon a small box beside it.

The lad was dazed, bewildered, and held spell-bound at this mystic disappearance; and had not Long Bob suddenly pulled him away, he would have been scorched by the rapidly rising flames.

"Lily," exclaimed Long Bob, "is she——"

He could not utter the dreadful word—it seemed too horrible—to ask if that fair young creature had died!

Jack Lennox's manner suggested the worst; his head had drooped upon his breast, and his hands were compressed tightly across his eyes, as though to shut out some dreadful sight.

In a voice choked and husky he said,—

"She is gone—gone, taken away!"

Long Bob breathed freely.

"It might have been worse," he said. "Cheer up, Jack, we shall soon find her again. Come, Drum, give me a hand, and let's pull down this part of the booth before the fire catches it."

A few minutes sufficed to stay the progress of the flames, and, save for the back of the stage being destroyed, there was little damage done.

An event like this soon caused the proprietors and others connected with the various booths and shows to assemble, and, with that kindness which the poor at all times show to the poor, a proposal was at once set forward and acted upon.

It was for all to set to work and repair the damage, each booth proprietor to contribute a certain amount of wood and canvas.

Many hands make light work; and so before the day had fully dawned the still smouldering canvas was replaced, and, but for the sudden loss they had sustained, the company would have returned to that state from which they were so rudely aroused.

Unconscious of all that passed, Jack Lennox sat upon one of the seats, his heart heavy and his eyes wet with tears.

A bluff red-faced man, the proprietor of a caravan wherein was to be seen a giant eight feet two inches high (the caravan was not six from floor to ceiling), placed his hand upon Jack's shoulder and roughly but kindly asked the cause of his grief.

The boy looked up, but could not speak; so Long Bob, who stood near our hero, answered for him,—

"A little girl," he said, "that we had with us, has disappeared very strangely—it preys on his mind, sir."

"The child that danced outside?"

"Yes, sir."

The red-faced man brought his open hand smartly down upon his leg, and made use of a very strong expletive.

"I thought," he said, "I know the child again; I saw her, when the crib was on fire, in the company of a man."

"A man!" Long Bob repeated; "a man—was she going willingly?"

"I did not notice, but I saw them coming from the fire as I ran out."

"Tinker Tom has got her," said Pipes huskily; "poor little girl!"

"Did you," Long Bob asked, "notice the man at all, sir?"

"No; he passed me so quickly, and had the little girl by the hand. But, now I come to think of it, he had gaiters on, and seemed to limp as he walked."

Long Bob looked from Big Drum to Pipes as he muttered,—

"He's got her at last!"

There could be no doubt now poor Lily was in the hands of her most inveterate foe, and the trio—for poor Jack took no part in the conversation—talked in a low tone about the poor child's danger.

Big Drum would have set forth at once in pursuit of the abductor, but Pipes and Bob dissuaded him from it.

"It won't do any good," Bob said. "We shall do better by being quiet for a day or so."

"I don't see that," said Drum.

"It's this way," Bob said: "if we follow him at once he will take good care to keep out of the way, but if we remain quiet he may come here again and try to get Jack. If he does we shall be able to get her back."

"Very well," Drum said; "I gives in, but, I don't think we shall ever see her again."

"Never!" sobbed Jack. "Poor Lily!"

The council ended with a resolution to give that day to the fair, and to start early next morning in quest of the loved and lost Lily.

Poor Jack suffered the most acute anguish when performing, and the day seemed as though it never would end.

Long Bob, although his heart was sad, seemed ten times more witty than ever as he stood upon the platform bandying words with the crowd.

Roars of laughter followed his description of the bellowing of the elephant, together with his companions, the whistling crab and the laughing fish.

This part of the entertainment they were compelled to give up; none had the heart to carry on the humorous deception of the previous day.

The show drew wonderfully. The report of the fire had made the place popular, and crowds came to view the interior—to behold the ravages the fire had made, as much as to see the performance.

There was a choking feeling in Long Bob's throat as he facetiously told the next crammer—that the elephant had with a wondrous sagacity taken the laughing herring and the whistling crab upon his back, and escaped with them during the fire.

Towards evening they found the audiences becoming smaller and beautifully less each representation.

Little wonder, for the Bounding Brothers of to-day and the light elastic forms of the previous day were totally different.

"Look here, Drum," Long Bob said at last, and the tears came to his eyes as he spoke; "we can't stand any more of this, so let's pack up and go in search of poor Lil."

Jack Lennox pressed his hand in silent thankfulness, for though the chance was but small of recovering the sweet child, yet the fact of being in search of her would be better than remaining there another day.

So the booth was taken down and returned to the owner; then, with heavy hearts and bowed heads, they left the noisy scene to go in quest of the sunny child whose gentle manners had won the strong love of these rough men—and made her loss so deeply felt, that they would have faced any danger to free her from her captivity.

Long Bob said but little; but there was an expression in his eyes that boded ill for Tinker Tom should they meet.

So they commenced their search; every child's form they saw in the distance causing a throb of pain and disappointment when they found it was not the loved and lost Lily.

CHAPTER XVII.

THE CAPTIVE.

TINKER TOM, like a sleuth-hound, had dogged the steps of the company since the day he had beheld Lily and Jack performing in the street transformation scene.

The vow the gipsy had so solemnly registered was not forgotten, and sleeping or waking he looked forward with savage joy to the moment which should place the helpless girl in his power.

Gloatingly he crouched behind the canvas booth, and when night came upon the earth he cut an opening through the frail covering and crept inside.

With the panther's wary gait, and a fierce dusky gleam in his eyes, he stole to the little slumberer's bedside, and gazed with fiendish triumph upon his victim.

"Safe," he muttered, as he opened a clasp knife. "When I have settled the young serpent who stung me, I will come for you."

Prowling noiselessly about the stage, he came to Jack Lennox's wretched couch, and so great was the joy that filled his heart, he could scarce repress a cry of exultation.

The pale moonlight shining through an opening in the roof fell upon the boy's handsome face, and that of his companion, the quaint but good-hearted Bob Jawkins.

There was murder in the gipsy's heart as he stooped over the prostrate form, and but for Bob being suddenly disturbed in his sleep, the gleaming knife would have done its fell work.

Long Bob started as the gipsy placed his hand upon the bed covering, and, half rising, muttered,—

"Stir up the elephant, Jack—stir him up!"

The words were scarcely distinguishable, and the intended assassin, his evil thoughts rendering him a coward, thought he was awake and speaking to his companion, and glided away as noiselessly as he came.

Standing motionless for some time, he waited, ready to spring upon the first that came towards him, until Bob's mutterings ceased. Then, afraid to return and complete the deed his diabolical passion had prompted him to contemplate, he crept to the back of the stage, and struck a silent congreve.

Applying this to a small coil of well-tarred hemp, he set fire to the canvas, and, as the flames began to spread, he again went to Lily's bedside.

He made a small bundle of the child's clothing, then, pressing one hand upon her mouth, with the other he snatched her from the bed, and, before she became conscious of the harm that had befallen her, she was being borne swiftly through the cold night air.

A caravan, standing upon the outskirts of the fair, was reached at the moment the canvas began to blaze.

It was then Lily began to shake off the deadly fear which was so strong upon her, and as her eyes met the dark features of her abductor, she tried to remove the heavy hand from her mouth.

"Quiet!" growled the ruffian, "or I'll choke you!"

The cry that came to her lips died ere it found utterance, and, every limb trembling with fear, she gazed helplessly at the dark stern face and savagely gleaming eyes.

Men, alarmed by the cry of fire which rang out, rushed past the shivering girl and her captor.

Tinker Tom saw his danger, and, running behind the caravan, placed the child upon the ground, and threw her clothing at her feet.

"Dress yourself," he said, "and attempt to move one step, and I'll cut your throat."

She saw the moonbeams glimmer upon an open knife, and, though help was within reach of her voice, she was too much cowed to speak.

When the child had donned her clothes, Tinker Tom took her hand, and, dragging her tired limbs over the rough ground, the fair was soon left far behind.

Along the quiet country road he sped, until the delicate feet refused to do their office.

Tinker Tom threw her across his shoulders, and as the sun began to dispel the morning mists he knocked loudly at the door of a quiet roadside public-house.

Here they remained until night again came upon the earth. Then the journey was resumed: the gipsy savage, silent, and sullen; the child pale as a spectre, and praying that death would relieve her from the grasp of her abductor.

So the journey continued until they reached London: hiding while the blessed sunshine gladdened the earth, and travelling when the night-loving bat and owl were on the wing.

In the upper room of a low water-side public-house Tinker Tom determined to stay until all possibility of being overtaken should have passed away.

Here the ruffian, gloating over his captive, indulged freely in the use of ardent spirits.

Here the poor child would cower in a remote corner of the dingy room, and with distended eyes watch the man as, overcome by drink, his head fell forward and his eyes seemed closed with sleep.

It was then the sudden thought of liberty came to the child's mind, and stealing quietly across the room she tried to open the door.

It was locked!

Lily clasped her hands in mute anguish, and, losing her heart, wept bitter tears.

Hark! what is that sound which causes her to raise her head and run eagerly to the window?

It is a long way off, but the well-known music which had so oft occupied the movements of her tiny feet was near, and with them she knew came help and her release from the power of her savage guardian.

Tinker Tom heard the sound, and unclosing his heavy eyes he glared towards the pale frightened captive.

"Come away from the window," he said, his voice thick and scarcely distinguishable from the effect of his deep potations; "come away—do you hear?"

He followed the command with an oath which sent Lily cowering and shivering back to her murky corner.

By the time she had seated herself upon the little three-legged stool the beating of the well-known parchment had ceased, and she was again left to wonder what her fate would be should her friends not come.

* * * * *

"I'm nearly tired of this, Jack," said Long Bob, as they were putting their coats on after a very unsuccessful pitch; "here we have been up and down these streets and not taken a penny."

"I am tired," said Jack, "but if the woman spoke the truth we may yet come upon the place where Tinker Tom has taken Lily."

"Don't believe a word," growled Long Bob; "what did she know about it? It's my opinion he's made for the country, not come this way at all. What do you think, old 'un?"

"I don't know," answered Pipes, "what to think; we must have been pretty close on him all the way, but as to finding 'em here down any of these streets, why——"

"You knows nothing about it, you shadder," said Drum; "the old woman said she'd seen a man and a little girl go past the corner of this 'ere street."

"Well, that's nothing, there's plenty——"

"Lots of your jaw, so shut up until I've finished. Rats afore mice any day."

Pipes wiped his mouth with the old article, and muttered,—

"Yes, and a good fat rat you is."

"Then," Drum continued, "when I asked all along each side of the way, nobody hadn't seen 'em pass out at t'other end."

"Then," said Long Bob, "the case is just this—if they have not gone away in the night, they are in one of these houses."

"That's just it," assented Drum, "but how is we to find out which is the house?"

"This is my idea," said Long Bob; "we can make several pitches here, and as the houses ain't very high, we can do a pyramid, and Jack will be able to look through the first floor windows."

"You won't be high enough," whispered Pipes, "you wants another."

Long Bob measured the distance with his eye, and found Pipes was quite correct.

"There's only one way to do it, Drum."

"Which way is that, Bob?"

"You must give your instrument to Pipes, and let him do the two."

"Well?"

"Then off with your coat and tile, and do the bottom in the pyramid."

"Do—do the what?" said Big Drum, aghast. "Me do the pyr-a-mid?"

"Now, look here, old 'un, it's no use being obstinate, so you'll have to do it."

"Shall I?"

"Well," Bob said, "if you don't, why I shall know that you don't care much for poor little Lily."

"Don't I? Quite as much as any of you."

"Yet you won't do this little thing for us."

"Why don't you ask Pipes?"

"Well," Long Bob said, "do you want us to be taken up for manslaughter?"

"We ain't as heavy as all that."

"No, Drum; but you must remember that Pipes is so thin that he will be sure to break in two, and there would be an end to the company."

Drum rubbed his nose reflectively.

He would have done anything to have rescued the child from the gipsy—that is, anything reasonable.

But this Drum thought was too much, and for a time his insulted dignity would not allow him to listen calmly to Long Bob's proposition.

Jack Lennox came beside his stout friend, and placing his small hand upon Drum's wrist, looked up and said,—

"Won't you do it, Drum, just for once; it's our only chance to find poor Lily?"

Drum looked at the pleading face, wavered, and finally gave way with the words,—

"Well, I will, Jack, but it's only for this once—mind that!"

So Drum took off his coat and hat, and Pipes, with a ghostly grin, suspended the instrument around his neck, and waited to begin.

"Go on," growled Drum, "if you has the two instruments, use 'em."

Pipes did so, and, resigned by the dulcet strains, Long Bob scrambled upon Drum's shoulders, then, lowering his hands, assisted Jack to ascend.

Several false notes were made by Pipes as he joyfully watched the tribulation that had fallen upon his friend.

The memory of his own sufferings when he had appeared as Jack-in-the-green should have made him more merciful; but, strange to say, the contrary effect was produced.

He beheld with glee Big Drum waddle across the street, and blew a louder note upon the mouth-organ when he saw the roadway had been recently repaired with fresh granite.

Nice three-cornered pieces, each piece of needle-like sharpness, suggestive of more than wonted suffering for those of tender feet.

Poor Drum! he belonged to this class—though the soles of his boots were thick, he felt the angles of the loose roadway as plainly as though his flesh were undefended.

Long Bob felt like a mountain upon the unhappy Drum's shoulders, and every movement made by Jack as he swayed to and fro on Bob's shoulders.

Human nature could not endure more than a certain amount of this; and, as Drum was but human, he began to find that, unless the upper portion of the pyramid descended at once, he should be compelled to succumb to his agony.

"Bob," he whispered, "do come down—I can't stand it much longer."

The entreaty was lost upon R. J. in consequence of Jack at that moment uttering an exclamation of horror.

Long Bob upturned his face, and asked,—

"What's the matter, Jack?"

To Bob's dismay, the boy sprang from his shoulder, and, before our long friend could recover from the backward jerk, he came to the ground, bringing the hapless Drum with him.

Pipes stopped the orchestral performance when this calamity took place, and stood, with mouth agape, looking at his fallen companions.

Long Bob was the first to recover from his fall, and, assisting Drum to rise, he exclaimed,—

"Jack's gone!"

"What?"

"Jack's gone—jumped off my shoulders, and bolted through that window."

"Then," said Drum, "she are there, and I —what! the Buffler!"

Pipes here paused, and stood by his friend's side, and face to face they stood with the Buffler, who came upon the scene at the same moment that Long Bob had beheld his companion disappear through the window.

The Buffler cut their surprise very short by saying,—

"I'll explain everything by-and-by. Where's the children?"

"The child—children!" said Drum, aghast. "What do you know of the children?"

"Everything," was the answer. "Were they with your troupe?"

"One," said Drum; "but he's gone."

"Gone! speak, man, I am——"

"He's sloped through that window there."

"Then," said the Buffler, "we will follow him."

CHAPTER XVIII.
AT THE MERCY OF TINKER TOM.

WHEN all hope had passed away from the child's aching heart, the joyful sound which indicated the proximity of her friends caused her to spring to her feet, and in spite of the ruffian's menacing look, she ran to the open window.

Grinding his teeth with rage, Tinker Tom seized a bottle that stood upon the table, and leaning towards the child, said,—

"Make the slightest noise, and I will smash your skull with this!"

Lily retreated from the savage, and burst into tears

"Cry," he growled; "it will do you good; keep it up—it will make an addition to the noise your friends are making—Ah, I've caught the cub as well!"

He sprang to his feet as Jack, with a gladsome shout, jumped from Long Bob's shoulders to the window sill.

A moment he stood to recover his balance and stepping lightly upon the table, said,—

"Lily, dear Lily, you are saved!"

The boy had scarcely uttered these words, when Tinker Tom sprang upon him—there was a dull thud, as the ruffian's huge fist came crashing upon Jack's forehead, and vainly trying to grasp at the hand which smote him, the boy fell to the ground bereft of sense or motion.

The house in which this scene took place was one of the lowest of its class, a dirty beer house, frequented by the rough waterside labourers, and kept by a man who would have sold his own children, had such an opportunity offered.

With this vagabond Tinker Tom, anticipating a close pursuit and probable discovery, had made a bargain for the use of one of the murky cellars beneath the house.

So when the boy lay a huddled heap upon the floor, he raised him with one hand, and throwing Jack's light form across his shoulder, seized Lily by the hand, and hurried as quickly as his wounded leg would permit him down the rickety stairs.

The quick passage through the air somewhat revived Jack Lennox, and he began to struggle with his captor just as Tinker Tom kicked open the cellar door.

Once inside, the gipsy threw the boy from him, and, closing the door, folded his arms and gazed with savage triumph upon the young captives.

Though they were at the mercy of the pitiless wretch, Jack Lennox threw his arms around the girl, as though to shield her from him, and turning desperately upon their gaoler, said,—

"Coward! your triumph will be but short. My companions will never leave this house till we are found."

"You think so," was the answer. "Do you see that spade?—before they shall reach this place I would kill you both and bury you. Look—the place is soft, and will not require much time to make a hole that will hide your bodies."

The girl clung closer to her companion, and a shiver passed over her frame as she looked from the rusty spade to the dark vengeful face of their captor.

Jack Lennox's brave little heart quailed not at this fearful threat; he did not believe the merciless gipsy would dare for his own sake proceed to such extremities.

He knew not the character of the man, or he would have been less hopeful; for the gipsy, in the dark mood that was upon him, would have slain them as remorselessly as he would have crushed out the life of a snared rabbit, or twisted the neck of a noisy fowl that resisted the hen-roost being pillaged by the midnight robber.

"You dare not kill us," he answered; "it would bring your neck to the halter, did you but attempt such a deed."

"I have done more than this in my time," was the sullen answer. "So beware should your friends pass this door. The first cry you give will be the signal for your deaths."

"What have we done," Jack asked, "that you should seek to harm us? Let us go, and I'll promise that no one shall be the wiser."

"Let you go!" he answered; "let you go, when I have dogged you day after day, week after week? Let you go?—No! no! no! You should know enough of the rules of our tribe to know how the Zingaris keep an oath made beneath the stars."

"What has this poor child done? She did not cause your companion to be transported. Was not the destruction of the earl's mansion and his death revenge enough? Let her go with those who are now seeking us, and I will return with you to the tribe."

"You shall both return to the tribe," he answered, "and, stretched upon the wheel, you will be repaid for shattering my leg."

"I did it but to save her," said Jack; "and I would do it again were the same need to present itself."

The gipsy's eyes blazed fiercely at the boy's bold words.

"You dare tell me this!—he hissed—"tell me that you would raise your hand against me, and here alone in my power!"

"I would tell you so"—the boy's eyes sparkled as he spoke—"were your fingers entwined round my throat, and the words the last I uttered. Here, alone as we are, I tell you to beware what you are about, or you will suffer for this outrage——"

"Viper!" hissed Tinker Tom, between his clenched teeth; "another word, and I'll choke you!"

"Do your worst," said the boy, angrily; and, springing lightly across the cellar, he seized the spade, and, swinging it backwards, added—"stand from the door, or I'll cut you down, ruffian as you are!"

The heavy weapon described a swift circle, and, had not Tinker Tom sprung nimbly aside, he would have been seriously hurt; for the boy, driven to desperation at the thought of his friends leaving the house without discovering their hiding-place, seemed, for the moment, to possess the strength of a man.

The sharp corner of the iron blade sank deeply into the panel of the door, and Tinker Tom, with a howl like an enraged panther, sprang upon Lily's brave defender.

His superior weight bore the lad to the earth, and, as he pressed one knee upon the panting chest, and entwined his fingers round the small throat, he hissed,—

"Curse you, that blow shall be your last!"

Lily screamed aloud in her agony, for the boy's pale face was becoming of a dark red hue as the ruffian's fingers grew tighter, and checked back the life current in Jack's veins.

But for that cry there would have been a fell murder in that murky chamber, for the lad's struggles to rise were becoming still, and his face, as the terrible sense of suffocation became stronger upon him, lost its identity, and carried an expression that was horribly grotesque.

While the echoes of her shrieks even yet seemed to cling to the dank walls, there came the sound of a well-known voice, then the door was burst in, and Tinker Tom, with a cry such as a tiger would have given had the brute been disturbed from its prey, turned and faced the deliverers.

* * * * * *

Long Bob was the first to enter the Waterman's Arms, the Buffler next, then Big Drum and his genteel friend—the two last much astonished at their old companion's appearance, and the manner in which he stopped any questioning respecting their past connection.

Drum's wonder increased every step he followed the cool and somewhat commanding Buffler; and glancing downward at his own clothes, he felt morally certain the contents of the lost cash-box had been expended in adorning the ungrateful Buffler's person.

"That's him," whispered Pipes to himself; "he slopes with two pun two and fourpence ha'penny, and before we asks him a word about it he tells us to shut up. I wonder," he added, " how he knew about us having the two kids with us? I allers said he was a knowing cove, and so he is—but the two pun two four and a half, vere's that gone to? I shall ask him if Drum don't."

Long Bob was too much concerned about his companion's disappearance to give a thought about the Buffler's sudden appearance; but with that instinctive perception which had been early developed in the rough school wherein he had been reared, R. J. saw that the Buffler was a man who could help them through the task they were upon.

"He's no street performer," was Bob's mental remark; "looks more like a peeler in disguise. If he is, so much the better for us."

They met the landlord of the Waterman's Arms emerging from a dusky den, called by courtesy the bar-parlour.

He gave a keen look at the private detective, and, throwing open the tap-room door, said,—

"This way, gentlemen, this way."

"Stay," said John Harvey, placing his hand upon the landlord's shoulder.

The contact of the private detective's hand with the greasy coat-collar sent a thrill through the landlord's veins. He knew from experience the peculiar touch that signified the unpleasant companionship with the dreaded officers of the law.

There were countless acts upon the landlord's mind which merited a visit to one of her Majesty's prisons, and not knowing which of these had been discovered, a shivering seized his limbs.

The private detective saw the mistake the landlord had made, and, knowing the advantage he possessed, he said,—

"Where is the boy that came into your house a few minutes since?"

"Boy!" reiterated the landlord; "I have not seen a boy."

This was the truth; and the Buffler, although he felt certain that Tinker Tom and the child were in the room when Jack entered, yet had no positive proof.

"I cannot," he thought, "frighten the fellow into an admission of the gipsy's presence here, so must manage to search the place for the boy."

"I'll tell you what, landlord," said Long Bob, slowly turning up his sleeves, "it's my opinion there was a gipsy fellow in that room with a little girl he stole from us; so you had better tell us where they are."

The landlord knew his guest was by this

time safely hidden in the cellar, so, with an assumption of boldness he did not feel, he said,—

"You are quite at liberty to search my house, gentlemen. I know nothing of gipsies or children being here."

"That's a lie," thought the Buffler, who watched the man's face as he spoke. Then aloud he added, "We intend to search for them, and if they are found you will suffer for aiding in the abduction of the child, as well as other matters."

This was a random shot, caused by the fellow's ill disguised terror when they first entered.

The landlord evidently thought it the wisest course to conciliate the supposed policeman, so, calling him aside, he said,—

"You are a detective, are you not?"

"Why?"

"Look here. It's no use denying it—you are."

"Well?"

"Have you come here for anything else besides the child that has been stolen?"

"That will depend how much you may assist me to rescue her."

"Suppose I give you the direction where to find them, will you leave here without—without——"

"Taking you," Harvey said, supplying the words. "Tell me where they are, and for the present you will be safe."

The landlord breathed freely. He had a few days before purchased a quantity of valuable goods stolen from a vessel by the men employed in unloading her, and his guilty mind pointed out this as the cause of the detective's visit.

Finding that a betrayal of Tinker Tom would save him, he said,—

"Go down those stairs, and directly opposite you will see a door; inside you will find those you seek."

John Harvey lowered his voice, then, joining the company, told them the intelligence he had gained.

"I cannot," he said, "interfere in the matter myself; therefore, to keep the landlord out of mischief, I will stay here until you return."

Long Bob went down the stairs three at once, closely followed by his companions.

When they had reached the bottom the landlord asked the detective to step inside the bar parlour.

"I would rather," he said, "you did so, for I do not wish my customers to see too much."

Harvey complied, and, taking a seat, waited impatiently for the return of his companions.

Scarcely had the trio reached the bottom of the steps when Lily's scream of fear was heard, and Big Drum, throwing himself against the door, burst it in.

He was the first inside the cellar, and, placing the drum upon the ground, turned towards Tinker Tom, a stick in each hand—his warlike spirit aroused by the sight of Jack's peril.

Luckless Drum! He had not moved more than three paces from his instrument when Tinker Tom sprang to his feet, and rushed upon our stout friend. The first blow Drum received knocked his hat over his eyes—the next caught him in the chest and sent him clean through the head of his beloved instrument.

Long Bob, in spite of his anger at the brutal outrage which they had arrived in time to prevent coming to a fearful result, could not forbear smiling at the ridiculous sight which poor Drum presented as, poised in the shell of his damaged instrument, his hat over his eyes, and his arms hanging over each side, he gasped for breath.

Pipes, with a wise discretion, kept behind R. J.; and the latter, seeing he had a formidable antagonist, but not a whit afraid of the encounter, put himself in a posture of defence, and, well stopping the gipsy's first blow, cried out,—

"Come on, you skulking cowardly hound; see if you can get me down as you did that poor little fellow—take that!"

He delivered such a facer that Tinker Tom, strong as he was, reeled back, his eyes flashing as though a thousand lights had been before him.

As far as strength went, Tinker Tom was much superior to his opponent.

But he wanted that activity and skill which Bob possessed—could he have once closed with R. J. the fight would soon have been over; but our long wiry friend, knowing this, kept his foe well at bay.

Slowly and cautiously he worked round the gipsy, and for every blow he received Tinker Tom received three in return.

"I shall blind him soon," Bob thought, "if my eye does not close up."

There was every probability of this occurring, as Bob, in the outset of the fight, received a blow over the left eye, and already a black circular mark began to appear and increase in colour every moment.

R. J. did not despair. He had already severely marked Tinker Tom's face, and every mad rush the gipsy made to close, Long Bob skilfully shot under his guard, and like lightning his fists played upon his opponent's face.

Tinker Tom's savage haste to grapple with his wiry foe soon rendered him breathless, and Long Bob, preserving his strength for a final effort, watched his opportunity to end the combat.

It came sooner than he expected. The gipsy, maddened by the severe punishment he had received, determined, in spite of R. J.'s science, to grapple and throw his antagonist.

Bob saw the intention, and as Tinker Tom came rushing upon him, he stepped aside and delivered a right-hander straight from the shoulder.

The blow struck the spot R. J. had long been trying to reach—behind the gipsy's ear—and as though he had been felled by a pole-axe Tinker Tom dropped to the ground.

"Had enough?" R. J. asked, as he floored the baffled ruffian; "there's plenty left."

"Hooray!" shouted Pipes, rushing from his corner, armed with the spade, "shall I smash him, Bob?"

The Buffler came to the door as Pipes planted one foot upon the gipsy's breast; and, fearing Pipes would use the edge of the spade (he little knew our thin friend's valour had not appeared until Bob floored his opponent), he called out,—

"Don't strike him; I have sent for a policeman."

Tinker Tom tried to rise, and Pipes beat a hasty retreat.

"Lie still," said Bob, clenching his hands, "or I will knock you down as fast as you can rise."

The Buffler soon relieved Drum from his uncomfortable position, and the constable appearing upon the scene, took charge of the gipsy and marched him from the Waterman's Arms.

The excitement beginning to die away, Long Bob looked round for the children. John Harvey answered his inquiring glance by saying,—

"When they came upstairs I sent the boy for a constable; the girl, I expect, went with him."

"But," Bob said, "they ought to be back before this."

"I expect they are up stairs waiting for us."

"Of course they are," said Bob, tenderly feeling his damaged eye; "suppose we leave this cheerful spot."

Poor Drum was the last to ascend. The damages he had received were to him infinitely worse than any bodily punishment.

His renowned hat was like the bellows of a concertina in appearance, and one head of his drum was ruined for ever.

When they reached the bar, the landlord, in answer to R. J.'s inquiries, told him that the children had not returned since they went for the police officer.

The Buffler uttered a cry of alarm—a cry that was repeated by those who had come so bravely to the rescue; and like madmen they rushed outside.

The street was deserted, and like a thunderbolt the truth came upon them that the children had fallen into a fresh danger.

No one had seen them leave the house, and not knowing which way to begin their search, the party slowly and sorrowfully left the Waterman public-house, their hearts heavy with apprehension for their little friends' safety.

CHAPTER XIX.

A CHANGE OF FORTUNE.

WHEN Jack Lennox was released from the brutal grasp of Tinker Tom, he seized Lily's hand and fled from the cellar.

At the top of the steps he was met by John Harvey, and desired by him to fetch a constable.

Scarcely understanding the words addressed to him, the boy passed through the door, as the private detective descended the steps.

A few paces from the Waterman's Arms he met a police officer, and Lily, running eagerly forward, said,—

"Pray go and save poor Bob: they will kill him."

The officer looked puzzled at the child's strange words, and was about to ask their meaning, when Jack said—

"Go to that public house. He is there."

These words were scarcely more intelligible than Lily had used, but the officer, gleaning sufficient information that told him he was wanted at the disreputable beer-shop, left the children and ran towards the house.

Poor Jack, his brain in a whirl, and his senses confused by the late brutal treatment he had received, knew not what he did.

Still retaining his grasp of Lily's hand, he staggered more than walked from the Waterman's Arms.

The street was but a little distance from the main road, and when in the busy thoroughfare, the noise of the heavy vehicles suddenly recalled his scattered senses.

He put his hand to his thrilling forehead, and, turning to retrace his steps, said,—

"We must go back, Lil—I did not mean to —to—"

Lily uttered a cry of alarm as her companion suddenly released her hand, then reeled backward and fell prone upon the pavement.

The excitement he had felt for a time subdued his physical agony, but as that left him, he felt the effects of the ruffianly ill-usage, and the blood rushing in a volume to his head deprived him of sense or motion.

A few seconds sufficed to collect a crowd, and they looked pityingly at the pale beautiful child, as she raised the boy's head and wept bitter tears of anguish at this fresh misfortune.

"Is he in a fit?" asked a puny gentleman, pushing rudely through the crowd, "look up, girl, and answer."

The child raised her tearful face at these words and looked blankly, hopelessly, at her questioner. Her little heart was too full to speak.

"It's a dodge!" the puny gentleman said, looking round at the crowd for approval; "they ought to be given to the police!"

"Shame!" a sturdy mechanic said, as he placed his basket of tools upon the ground; "don't you see the boy's head is cut and bleeding!"

He went to Lily's assistance, and with his faded cotton handkerchief wiped the thin crimson streak from Jack's temple.

The crowd, as usual, easily led either for good or evil, began to give the puny gentleman a little of their mind; and a rosy-cheeked butcher's lad suggesting a bonneting for the old gentleman, the latter made the best of his way from the impending dangers.

A tall gentleman, attracted to the spot by the children's strange attire, uttered an exclamation of joy, and, moving forward, placed his hand upon Lily's shoulder.

"Miss Lily," he said, "what is the matter?"

"Oh, Monsieur Latour," said the girl, for once glad to behold a face she had so thoroughly disliked, "I am so glad you have come. Pray take us back to Big Drum and Bob; poor Jack is so ill."

"Do you know these children, sir?" asked the mechanic, as he chafed the boy's hands.

"I do," said M. Jules; "if you will get me a cab I will take them away from this."

The man looked from the stylishly dressed Frenchman to the children, then went in search of a vehicle.

One was soon obtained, and with the mechanic's assistance the senseless boy was placed in the cab, and Lily, glad to escape from the crowd, followed.

M. Jules gave the man half-a-crown, and told the cabman to drive to the Strand.

The cab was scarcely out of sight when Big

THE BOYS OF BIRCHAM SCHOOL.

TINKER TOM'S SURPRISE

Drum, Pipes, Long Bob, and the private detective made their appearance.

John Harvey eagerly questioned all who came in his way respecting the children, and to his mortification discovered the cause of their disappearance.

"A gentleman," he asked, "put them in a cab, you say?"

"Yes, sir."

"Can you describe him at all?"

"I didn't take particular notice of him, sir," was the reply, "but I think he must be a foreigner."

"The Frenchman!" muttered the agent; "this is indeed unfortunate—they have slipped through my fingers—which way did the cab go?"

"There, then turned to the left."

"Hansom!" Harvey called to a passing vehicle, and, jumping in, he added, "drive quickly; a four-wheeler has just turned the corner—a sovereign if you overtake it."

No. 28.

"Right, sir."

The small trap closed, and the hansom rolled away, much to the edification of Big Drum and his companions.

"Gone!" Pipes said, "gone, afore I could ask him about the box!"

"We're ruined," said Drum, "my instrument broke, and the young uns gone—wot unfortunit wretches we is."

Long Bob thrust his hands into his pockets, and muttered,—

"What next, I wonder? I wish we——hallo!"

The policeman who had taken Tinker Tom to the station placed his hand upon Bob's shoulder.

"Why didn't you come?" he said, "the inspector's waiting to take the charge."

"We've lost the young 'uns," Bob said, "that's why—but lead on, we are ready to prove everything."

So they went to the station-house, and after having the satisfaction of seeing the gipsy led away, the company went slowly towards Mrs. Smith's hospitable mansion with slow and dejected steps.

When Jack Lennox returned to consciousness, he found himself lying upon a sofa, his head bandaged and very painful. Opening his eyes wide with astonishment, he saw Lily sitting at a table examining a book of prints.

"Lil!"

The girl was by his side in an instant.

"Lil," he repeated, "where are we?"

"Hush!" she whispered, softly. "The doctor has been here; he said you were to be kept very quiet. So you must not talk—at least," she added, "not yet."

Jack raised himself upon his elbows, and looked strangely around the well-furnished room.

"Not speak?" he said. "Why am I not to speak?"

"It was the doctor's orders, dear Jack; he ought to know better than you or——"

"But," said the boy, impetuously, "I am not ill. Never mind the doctor; tell me how we came here."

"Mind," she said, not able to keep her promise with the medical man, "you must not tell the doctor, or he will not let us be together."

"I will not tell him a word, Lil."

"Very well; I will tell you all about it; but," she said, musingly, "it seems so strange that I can scarcely believe it myself."

"Believe what, Lil?"

"The sudden way in which we came here, and——"

He uttered an exclamation of impatience, and checked the child's speech.

"Tell me, Lily, dear," Jack said; "this affair seems so strange, that I am lost in wonderment."

"Do you remember," she asked, "when you were about to return to Big Drum and Bob?"

Jack passed his hand over his brow, as he answered,—

"Yes—yes; but something must have happened since then, for I remember nothing until I awoke here."

"Yes," she said, "something did happen, Jack. You were very ill, and fell down, and you looked so white that I thought you were dead."

"Poor Lil, you must have been frightened."

"I was, Jack, very. Well, a crowd gathered round; and had not Monsieur Latour come up at the moment, I'm sure I don't know what would have happened."

"Latour—the Frenchman that used to be at the Abbey?"

"Yes."

"Well, Lil, what did he do?"

"He was so kind!" she said, enthusiastically; "kinder than I ever thought he could be. You know, Jack, I used to dislike him so when we were at the Abbey."

"Yes—yes; pray go on, Lil."

"Well, when he came to us, he sent for a cab, and brought us here."

"Strange," Jack thought, "this man should take such an interest in us."

It seemed as though the girl understood her companion's thoughts, for she added, quickly,—

"When we came to this house, good Monsieur Latour sent the servant for a doctor, and I heard him say that he knew me under——under—let me see—yes, under better circumstances. The doctor said it was kind of Monsieur Latour to take us from the street; then, after he had looked at your head, he told me I must not disturb you."

"Did you hear him say what caused me to fall in the street?"

"I did, Jack—it was something about the blood being forced up in your head and flowing on your brain."

"That wretch nearly killed me, Lil—he did —but he cannot do any more harm now."

"The policeman, I hope, took him away, —poor Drum, I saw him"—Jack, in spite of the pain he felt, could not help smiling— "doubled up in his instrument; poor old Pipes, too—I wonder when we shall see them again."

Lily shook her head.

"I don't think we shall be with them any more: are you glad, Jack?"

BEFORE the boy could reply, the door softly opened, and Jules Latour, with the cat-like gait of yore, glided into the room.

He held out his hand to the boy, and in his blandest tone said,—

"Ah! I see you are awake, my little friend. Do you feel better?"

"I do," Jack said, shaking hands with the Frenchman, "and very grateful to you, sir, for your kindness."

"Do not speak of that—" Monsieur Jules said this as though his heart was brimful of disinterested philanthrophy, and the fact of bringing two children to his handsomely-furnished apartments was a matter of daily occurrence. "I am glad I met you when you were so bad—so glad."

Lily came forward, and, placing her hand upon the Frenchman's wrist, said,—

"We ought to be glad, Monsieur: what could we have done without you?"

"Ah! well, my little lady, we will say we are both glad." Poor little girl—the hypocrite caressed her sunny hair. "My heart did ache when I saw you in that dress, for you know, Miss Lily, I felt that I ought to do something for you, and if you will let me I will, and for your brave young companion as well—for I do——"

A rap came to the door, and stayed M. Latour's speech.

"Come in!" he said.

A smart servant girl entered, and, gazing curiously at the children, said,—

"The dressmaker, sir!"

"Ah! thank you—will you go with the servant, Miss Lily? You must leave off these clothes; they are not fit for you to wear."

"Oh, Monsieur Latour," she began, and her blue eyes sparkled with delight. "Am I to——"

"You must not say one word, Miss Lily, but go and get all things that are required—tell her to go," he said in an undertone to Jack, "for I want to talk to you, my young friend."

"Go with the servant, Lil," said the boy.

The child silently obeyed, and he was alone with the disinterested Monsieur Latour.

The Frenchman looked after the girl, and shaking his head, remarked—

"She will be glad to leave off those tawdry clothes, I should think; poor little Miss Lily my heart did ache when I saw her."

He was skilfully working upon the boy's most vulnerable point: yet Jack did not feel quite at ease respecting his friend's goodness of heart.

"He must have a motive in this," the boy thought, "yet I do not see that he can. Perhaps, after all, it is because he knew Lil when she was at the Abbey."

Satisfied with this reason for M. Jules' queer behaviour, the boy said,—

"Yes, sir, she will indeed be glad to change that dress, for although she has gone through the hardship and misery incidental to a poor company of street performers, her heart was never in the business."

"I can understand that," said M. Jules Latour—"she was reared in too much luxury; but you, my young friend, how did you like it?"

"But little," Jack said, quickly, "but as it was all that stood between me and starvation, I was compelled to follow it, and shall, I suppose, until a change of fortune has taken place."

"The change has taken place," said the ex valet, "if you like to accept it."

Jack's face wore a strangely puzzled look as he said,—

"The change has taken place, if I will accept it?"

"Yes," M. Jules said; "and for the poor little girl's sake I should think you would not refuse Fortune's smile."

"I do not exactly understand," said Jack; "pray explain."

"It is very soon explained, my young friend. I can place you in a position that will make you rich to most people."

"If you mean," Jack said, "that I am to live with you and do nothing for a return, I do not think I can consent, for sooner than live upon the charity of others, I will remain a street performer all my life."

"Very well spoken," said M. Jules, with affected enthusiasm. "I admire you for those words; but I think, for poor Lily's sake, you should be glad of anything that will keep her from the life she has been compelled to follow lately."

"I could do much for Lily," said Jack, "and I should be happy were it in my power to save her from the wretched mode of gaining a livelihood we have been compelled to adopt."

"You can do so," said M. Jules; "you can do more."

Jack looked at the speaker interrogatively.

"I mean it," M. Jules said; "you can place your little companion in a position nearly as good as that which she formerly occupied."

"How—tell me how?"

"At present," was the reply, "I cannot say more."

"I cannot bear to be kept in suspense; if there is anything to tell me, why not do it now?"

Monsieur Jules rubbed his hands softly, as he sat on the edge of the sofa, and as a cunning gleam shone in his eyes, he asked,—

"Suppose any one could put you in possession of an estate worth four thousand pounds a year, what would you give the person out of it?"

"Well," said Jack, smiling, "when such a thing comes to pass I shall be very generous."

"You do not think it possible, then?"

"No," was the blunt answer.

"Well, we'll suppose such a thing possible; now what do you think would be a fitting reward?"

"Well," said Jack, laughing outright at what he thought an absurdity; "I think I would give away half. But who could do this for me?"

M. Jules gave a silent chuckle as he placed a clearly-written sheet of paper before the boy.

"There," he said, "put your name to that, and if I do not, in less than a month, put you in possession of an estate worth the sum I have mentioned, I will forfeit my life."

Jack Lennox read a few lines of the document, then, taking the proffered pen from M. Latour, he wrote his name at the bottom.

"The man must be mad," he thought. "They say you should always humour a madman; so I have signed a paper binding me to pay him one thousand pounds a year."

M. Jules carefully blotted the signature, then, rising, said,—

"This is good; we have soon come to an understanding. Now, my young friend, get well as soon as possible, then we will begin the business."

"Mad as a March hare," Jack thought, "but quite harmless;" then aloud—"I am quite well enough to do anything you may require."

He jumped from the sofa as he spoke, and Monsieur Jules, pointing to his flesh-coloured tights, said,—

"Ah, I had forgotten. We must have a tailor for you; then we will leave here, and go to another part of London."

Jack had no objection to the tailor, but, before he consented to leave their present abode, he said,—

"What am I to do about my late companions? They have been kind to me, and I should like to see them again."

"You will be rich soon," said M. Latour; "then you can repay their kindness."

"And have them to see me?"

"If you like'."

"Very well," said Jack, fearing he could detect the gleam of insanity in M. Jules's eyes; "be it so. Send for the tailor; then we will leave here."

The next day M. Jules left his apartments, and took the children with him; and when the cab which conveyed them stopped at their new residence, M. Jules looked up at the roof, and uttered a cry of horror.

"What's the matter?" the children asked, in a breath.

"Ruined!—ruined!" said the ex-valet, wringing his hands. "The valise and all the papers are gone!"

Leaving the astonished boy and his fair companion standing upon the doorstep, Latour jumped on the box, and urged the cabman to drive quickly back over the course he had traversed.

"Well," Jack said, "I expect, Lil, we shall soon have to return to Big Drum, for the Frenchman's malady is getting worse."

"He's not mad, Jack," she said. "Depend upon it, there is something more in this than you or I can understand."

The boy shook his head, and, opening the door of the house, they went inside.

CHAPTER XX.

BIG DRUM'S INTERVIEW WITH THE BENCH.

THE loss of Lily and Jack was a blow from which Big Drum and his companions could not easily recover.

Apart from the use they were in filling the at all times scanty exchequer, the trio were much attached to the children; and with a dogged faithfulness they wandered about the great city in the hope of gleaning tidings of their little friends.

But as the days passed forward, this hope became fainter and fainter, until at last, after a long wretched day, they returned to Mrs. Smith's—tired, hungry, and penniless.

They had tried several times to collect a few coppers by giving a performance, but the public did not seem to appreciate a representation where the orchestra exceeded the company.

"We can't live with Duke Humphrey much longer, Drum," remarked Long Bob, as he stood gazing hopelessly upon the tops of smoke-begrimed chimney pots; "and the public don't care about us now Jack and Lily are gone. Poor little things! I wonder what has become of them!"

"That's just it, Bob," said Drum. "I ain't thought about hunger, nor thirst, nor anything else when we had hopes of finding them; but now I feels as though a something was a gnawing away at my inside—its horful!"

"Not had nothing since last night," said Pipes; "then we only had a thin rasher of bacon, biled with the kollyflower I got with our last penny."

"I wish," said Bob, "we had the same dose again to-night, for I feel reg'lar knocked up."

"It's no use giving in," Drum said, unloosing his necktie; "let's go to roost, and see what to-morrow will bring us."

"Not much," said Bob, "I'm afraid; however, we may as well turn in, for, after what Mrs. Smith said this morning, I don't think we shall have a place to put our heads to-morrow night."

"What did she say, Bob?" asked Pipes.

"I was thinking about asking her to lend us a shilling in the morning."

"No good, old 'un. I've tried. I went to her after I tried the chandler's shop, and she told me we had better find a fresh lodging, for she expected, now the little girl had gone, we shouldn't have money enough to pay rent."

"The old cat!" said Drum, savagely; "after the way I paid her up, to turn round upon us like that!"

"She's no worse than the chandler's shop man," whispered Pipes; "not so bad, because we've dealt there reg'lar ever since——"

"I say!" Long Bob called out from beneath a mysterious-looking heap which he dignified by the term bed, "it won't do any good you two sitting there croaking about our luck. Why don't you turn in? They ain't a bit worse than the rest of the world. They all do it when a fellow's down on his luck."

Drum and his companion turned in, and the tired trio were soon asleep—Drum to dream of showers of gold being heaped upon his head; Pipes to dream of roving at large in an immense cellar filled with barrels of the frothiest beer.

Long Bob's dream was yet more tantalizing. He thought himself seated at a sumptuous banquet, and every time he conveyed a luscious morsel to his lips, a demon, with a face not unlike Mrs. Smith's, whisked the delicacy from his fork and conveyed it to a capacious bag which hung by his side.

The three awoke early, and a consultation was held respecting the matutinal meal.

"We might raise something on the drum," said the owner of that unfortunate instrument, "if that gipsy fellow had not smashed the head in."

"Ah!" Long Bob exclaimed. "Lucky thought! This is the day we have to attend before the magistrate."

"So it is," said Drum. "Prap's he'll allow something for the damage the instrument received."

"Hope so," said Pipes. "Hope it 'ull be a suvrin, at least."

"What time shall we go?" Drum asked. "'Cos if we gets anything, I'd like to have it soon."

"Eleven o'clock's the time, Drum. So let's have another snooze; it will save us wearing out our toothpicks. Ugh! how hungry I feel!"

"So am I," groaned Drum. "I wonder whether we shall have anything more to eat!"

Pipes covered his head with the bed-clothes, and groaned audibly.

The darkest hour comes before dawn; so it was with our poor friends.

At eleven the trio appeared before the magistrate, who had remanded Tinker Tom until the police had made a few inquiries respecting the gipsy's antecedents, and the active officer having found sufficient to help Tinker Tom in the attainment of a free passage to a convict settlement, the prisoner was placed in the dock.

The first witness examined was our stout friend, and his peculiar answers caused even the magistrate to turn aside his head to hide the laughter he could not control.

Before Drum stood the broken instrument; beside this the spade which had been found in the cellar.

"What do you know of this charge?" the magistrate asked, when Drum, after being duly sworn, stood fumbling the brim of his battered hat.

"I knows all about it, your wertchop."

"Let me hear your statement."

"Yes, your wertchop. Am I to begin at the fair, your wertchop, or only when we found out where he had taken the little girl?"

"The fair," whispered the magistrate to a grave looking man, who sat beneath the judicial seat, writing.

The grave party whispered a reply, and the magistrate, smiling at Drum's attitude, said,—

"You had better do so."

"Wery well, your wertchop. This is how it was. This here feller, as is looking at me as though he'd like to eat me with a grain of salt, come one night and set fire to our show."

The clerk's pen went very fast over the paper; he was making a note for his superior's guidance.

"We knowed," Drum continued, "that he was arter the little girl, so we kept a sharp look out arter her, but not sharp enough, your wertchop."

"So it appears."

"Well, when the fire broke out, the little boy as we had with us went straight to where Lily slept, and when he got there she was gone."

"Where is the boy?" asked the magistrate. "You should have brought him with you."

"I wish we could, your wertchop, for, worse luck, he's gone, and the little girl too."

The magistrate leant over and whispered to his adviser,—

"We cannot go on with the case if the prosecutrix does not appear."

The old gentleman at the lower table handed his superior a slip of paper bearing the words,—

"He has committed an assault upon these witnesses, and there are other charges against him."

The magistrate glanced at the paper, then hed it in the palm of his hand.

"We cannot proceed further," he said, "with the charge of abduction, as the principal witness is not present."

Big Drum's face was a study, as he looked blankly at the magistrate and said,—

"What! is he going to get off arter blacking Bob's eye and spiling my instrument?"

"You can proceed with the second charge."

"Yes, your wertchop." Then, aside to Bob, "What does he mean?"

"The assault," was the answer. "Go on, Drum; tell him about the nose-ender you got in the cellar."

"Well, your wertchop, when we found the place where he had put the little girl, we goes down to the cellar and I sets my instrument down."

"Is that the instrument?"

"Yes, your wertchop, that's it; and no sooner did I put it down, than the prisoner turned round and let fly with both hands."

"Let fly?"

"Yes, your wertchop, hit me, your wertchop, one of his fists come on my nose, and the other hit me in the chest, and before I knowed where I was, I found myself sticking in my drum."

He held it up, and showed the damage.

"That will do: you can stand down."

"Yes, your wertchop; but ain't I to have nothing for the hole he has made in it?"

"His worship," said one of the officers, "is waiting to hear the next witness."

Drum very reluctantly left the witness-box, and Long Bob took his place.

R. J. gave his evidence with great brevity, and wound up by calling the magistrate's attention to his yet discoloured eye.

Pipes was next examined, but his evidence was nipped in the bud, by the magistrate telling him to stand down.

Tinker Tom viewed the witnesses with a contemptuous smile upon his lips. He cared but little for the trifling punishment the bench could inflict for an assault, but when the magistrate asked if anything was known of the prisoner, his face became ghastly, and as his hands tightened upon the rail in front of him, he writhed with passion.

In answer to the magistrate's query, a constable said,—

"The prisoner is connected with a gang of vagrants, who some time since set fire to Falconmere Abbey; and, if the information I have received is correct, he is the man we have long wanted. I will not detain your worship with details of his supposed crimes, but merely ask for a remand until we can supply the link that is missing in the chain of evidence."

Long Bob, with much inward satisfaction, beheld the gipsy conveyed to the cells by two gaolers.

Drum watched the proceedings with a puzzled expression upon his face. He had a vague idea that Tinker Tom could make reparation for the damage he had caused. When he saw him taken from the dock, he began to feel there was but little chance of raising a breakfast out of the broken drum.

Much to the astonishment of all present, he turned towards the magistrate, and said,—

"If you please, your vurtchup, make him give me something for damaging my instrument. It won't sound now, your vurtchup, and when I carries it down the street, the boys shies stones in where the parchment is broken."

"I am very sorry, my man," was the magistrate's answer, "that it is out of my power to assist you."

"It's werry hard, your wertchop," said Drum; "all through that feller we ain't been able to give a performance—we can't do it without music, and one head won't do without the other, so we is got regularly hard up, and ain't took a copper this two days."

The magistrate hoped they would be more fortunate, and tried to get rid of his troublesome witness.

It was no use. Drum had a fixed idea that either the magistrate or Tinker Tom should make the damage good; and when his worship told him that Long Bob was infinitely worse off than Drum, the stout one answered,—

"He may be, your wertchop, but I can't see it."

"But his face is bruised by that ruffian."

"Yes, your wertchop, but the drum is broke. Bob's face 'ull get well, and no one ever heard of a drum healing up after one of the heads had been smashed in."

His worship had the greatest difficulty in restraining his laughter, and having several petty cases to hear, he ordered Drum to have two shillings from the poor-box.

Before the money was paid a tall distinguished-looking man entered the court, and earnestly begged the magistrate to help him to gain possession of his children.

The trio opened their ears as the gentleman stated the case, and Drum became so interested that he quite forgot the money he was to receive.

The gentleman stated that he had not seen his children for many years, but through the agency of a private detective he had discovered their whereabouts, but ere they could be brought to him they fell into the hands of a Frenchman, and he, from some inexplicable cause, refused to give them up.

The magistrate pondered over this extraordinary statement, then asked,—

"Do you know where the children are?"

"I do not," was the answer. "In escaping from a ruffian, who would have injured them, they fell into the power of this Jules Latour."

"I can only issue a warrant for the man's apprehension," said the magistrate. "Possibly I may then be able to compel him to deliver them up to you."

"Drum," whispered Long Bob, "did you hear what that swell said?"

"I did. We'll follow him when he goes out."

"Like wax we'll stick to him. Fancy, Drum, if he should turn out to be Jack's father!"

"Well, what if he does?"

"What if he does? You antediluvian duffer, it will be the making of us—that's what if he does!"

"Can't you two be quiet!" Pipes whispered. "He's going!"

The sorrow-stricken man, with bowed head, left the court, and Drum, throwing his instrument over his shoulder, closely followed.

They had gone some distance from the court-house before Drum remembered the money the magistrate had promised him. When this recollection flashed across his mind, he wheeled suddenly round, with the intention of speaking to Long Bob.

But a yell from Pipes caused him to stand petrified with astonishment—a state of mind which was not improved when the unfortunate genteel member of the company said,—

"You ugly porpoise, I know you did that on purpose."

"Did what?" Drum asked, wistfully gazing at his companion. "What did I do?"

Pipes was standing with both hands pressed to the side of his head, and tears of pain stood in his eyes. He had good reason for this, for Drum, when he turned so sharply, struck the unfortunate Pipes with the damaged instrument with such force as to knock him backwards.

Poor old Pipes! he was trotting closely by the stout one's side, and, not anticipating such an astonishing hit, made sure, when the sharp edge of the instrument came against his face, that his skull was broken at the very least.

"Do! can't yer see?" and Pipes looked at the palm of his hand, as though expecting to see it crimson with blood. "Been and nearly knocked my brains out!"

"Brains," said Drum, contemptuously; "you'd better find 'em first."

Pipes muttered something which sounded like "hard-hearted beast," and, giving the Drum plenty of room, toddled after his companions.

Long Bob, after indulging in a hearty laugh at Pipes's misfortunes, went forward, and overtook Captain Carlin.

Our elongated friend had a tolerable share of self-assurance, so, without any preface, he went into the thick of the business at once. Touching his cap respectfully, he said,—

"I beg pardon, sir."

The Captain turned and gazed curiously at the figure by his side. R. J.'s appearance at the time was anything but prepossessing. One side of his face was yet discoloured, a ragged cap adorned his brows, his thin legs were covered by a pair of dirty cotton drawers (tights); to complete his somewhat peculiar attire, an old coat, quite large enough to fit Drum, depended in loose folds from his shoulders.

The Captain's look of surprise Long Bob interpreted correctly, and before our hero's father could ask the meaning of this strange interruption, R. J. said,—

"I know I'm not very fashionable, sir; but if you like to try me, I think you will find I can do more to find little Jack than the beak and all his warrants."

"Who are you, my good fellow?" the officer asked.

"I'm called Long Bob, sir; proper name. Robert Jenkins."

This intelligence was not sufficiently explanatory to the Captain.

"Well," he asked, "what may be the nature of this offer you have made? Be kind enough to explain."

Long Bob, with great brevity, told the Captain how he first became acquainted with the children, their connexion with Drum's company, and Lily's abduction.

"This black eye, sir," he said, "I received from the gipsy when we found out where the young 'un's were stowed. When I heard you speak about the Frenchman, I knew you must mean that Jack and Lil were the children. Now, sir, don't you think I can be of some use to you?"

The Captain reflected, before he answered.

"This youth," he thought, "loves my boy. I noted the husky voice and twitching lips as he spoke. Yes, I will trust him."

Long Bob awaited the Captain's reply with feverish impatience. Poor fellow, he thought his appearance would deter the bronzed officer from accepting his offer, but when the answer came his heart leapt for joy, and he could fain have wept.

"I will accept your proffered assistance," said Captain Carlin, "you know my boy; and if my heart speaks truly his companion is my daughter——"

"Your daughter, sir!—little Lily your daughter—Jack's sister!—well, I always thought there was a likeness between them, that I did."

"I am not certain that such good fortune is in store for me," was the sadly spoken reply;" "suspicion and hope bid me think so—at any rate you will do your best—you know this Frenchman, I presume?"

"I do, sir; I have seen him once, and I should know him among a thousand."

"I am glad of that. We cannot arrange matters here; let us step inside this tavern;" looking towards Drum and his companion, "these men are your friends?"

"They are, sir."

"Bring them with you."

Pipes's mouth watered as he followed R. J. inside the public-house, and when they were seated in the parlour his heart filled with joy at the sight of the foaming tankard, flanked by a new loaf and a goodly dish of cold meat.

CHAPTER XXI.
LONG BOB UPON THE TRAIL.

THE arrangements were soon completed, and when the Captain left the house, R. J. had a crisp bank-note in his pocket. Big Drum and his astonished friend were possessed of similar pieces of paper; for the bereaved father, though his sorrow was so great, forgot not those who had been kind to his homeless boy.

They sat long after their generous benefactor had gone. The task set before them was of more than ordinary difficulty, for the officer, in obedience to that instinct which prompted him to believe that Lily was his child, had told Drum and Pipes if they could discover the tramps from whom she was taken by Earl Falconmere, their reward would exceed all that he had yet done for them.

He waited upon the chief of the private detectives, after leaving the trio, and found to his sorrow that the children had so unfortunately disappeared when tracked to their hiding-place by Nicholas Harvey.

"It is not often," said the chief, "that my men fail at the very moment of success; but in this instance the peculiar circumstances of the case were such as to extenuate him from all blame."

"I am aware of that—have you been more successul with the inquiry respecting the girl?"

The chief's face brightened.

"We have," he said; "and I am happy to say that my suspicion has turned out correct."

"The child is my lost daughter?"

"Yes, this is the substance of my agent's report."

Opening a drawer in the writing-table, the chief took therefrom a book, and as the Captain, with suppressed breathing, listened to his words, he read,—

"As per instructions I visited the various casual wards, and when I began to give up all hope of discovering the tramp from whom the child was taken, I learnt the following information:

"By describing the part of the country in which the Abbey is situate, and speaking of its owner, I attracted the notice of an ill-looking vagabond, who soon found an opportunity of joining in the conversation. He had visited the place I described, and amid the coarse jests of the assembled vagrants, told how he had robbed a lady on the road, not only of her purse, but of her child——"

The listener sprang to his feet, and exclaimed,—

"My poor Alicia! my poor wife!"

"I will not," said the detective, closing the book, "pain you with the details written here. I can supply the information in less time, and more compatibly with your feelings."

The listener silently acquiesced to this arrangement, and the chief resumed:

"My agent learnt that the child was not long in these wretches'—for there were two, a woman being with the fellow at the time—power, for when passing a large mansion the child saw a horseman coming towards them, and was rescued by him."

"That horseman was Earl Falconmere, my most pitiless foe."

"Strange," said the chief, " that Providence should have made him the guardian of your child."

"More than strange," was the answer; "but pray continue; I am anxious to hear the end."

"A meeting, apparently a chance one, took place the next day between my agent and the tramp; the natural result was an adjournment to a public-house; once there, the tramp's tongue became loosened, and he told his companion that among the valuables taken from the mother of the child was a gold chain and a cross, studded with precious stones."

"My gift to my ill-fated wife upon the anniversary of our marriage," said the officer, in a broken voice. "Little did I imagine, when I placed it around her neck, that it would be torn away by the hand of a common footpad. Did your agent glean any tidings of this?"

"He did. It appears the fellow was afraid to offer it for sale, and up to the time he entered the public-house with his supposed boon companion, had it around his neck."

"Ha!"

"I see you anticipate the sequel. The man I sent drugged the rascal, and here are the chain and cross; and from what I can judge it is worth an immense sum."

The soldier took it without a word, and pressed it to his lips then, as the muscles of his face twitched convulsively, he placed it in his pocket-book, and said,—

"There can be no doubt of the child's identity, now."

"I am glad we have been successful so far, and hope ere long to repair the mistake made by the man when he suffered the children to fall into the Frenchman's hands."

"Tell me," said the Captain, scarcely heeding the chief's words, "does not your agent incur the risk of being prosecuted for robbery?"

"With regard to the chain?"

"Yes."

The chief smilingly answered,—

"Not the least risk. The fellow for his own sake will be quiet."

"I am glad to hear it. Give this to the man for the intelligence he has gleaned."

The chief glanced at the figures upon the bank-note, and said,—

"You are too generous, sir."

Captain Carlin made an impatient gesture with his hand, then said,—

"I t.... to be made happy by the sight

of my children. With your aid, and that of others, I have hit upon the Frenchman's track. I do not think he will escape us long."

"I hope not. The man Harvey is like a sleuth hound, and when once on the scent, he will run his game down."

They soon after parted, the lonely man to seek his cheerless abode, the detective chief to attend upon a veiled lady, who passed our hero's father upon the door-step.

* * * * * *

"Madam," said the gentlemanly agent, when he had listened to his visitor's statement, "your case is not hopeless. I think I may safely assert that your husband and children still live."

"My husband!" she exclaimed, wildly. "Impossible! He died upon the battle-field."

"Permit me, madam, to correct you—he was wounded, carried off by the foe, and returned as slain by his friends."

"Can this be true?" She clasped her hands imploringly. "Oh heaven! how much I have to thank thee for!"

"Quite true, lady. If you will leave your address, I will communicate with you when I discover the whereabouts of those you love."

She gave him a card, a coronet above the name engraved thereon, below this an address in pencil. Then, as the tears began to course down her cheeks, she rose, and left the office.

"A strange and complicated affair this," muttered the principal; "the strangest I ever had in my hands."

He watched the lady enter a brougham, and drive away; then closed the door, and soon became immersed in the perusal of a pile of letters.

It was, indeed, a strange case, though not stranger than many that are daily occurring in our midst.

* * * * *

"Now, Drum," said R. J., "I think the best thing we can do is to spend some of this money in togs—what do you say?"

"I think so, too. Eh, Pipes?"

"Yes," whispered the thin one; "but hadn't we better have a little drain more afore we goes?"

"Not a drop, you guzzling shadder," said Drum; "so get up, and let's toddle!"

They did so; and when they reached the street, Long Bob suggested a cab—a suggestion which was carried, and, much to the edification of Mrs. Smith, her lodgers made their appearance in a four-wheeler.

If the good lady's surprise was great when she beheld this unexpected sight, it was greater when our long friend emerged from the house shortly after in well-ventilated apparel, and returned arrayed in a fashionable suit of clothes.

Wonders were never to cease, for, soon after this, a man wearing livery, and what Mrs. Smith termed a smoke-jack attached to his hat, brought a letter for Mr. Robert Jenkins.

The letter was from the Captain, desiring R. J. to lose no time in setting forth upon his mission, and telling him that he had discovered the necessary information respecting the tramp who had possession of the little girl.

"You two won't be wanted," R. J. said, when he had finished reading the letter. "So the best thing for you to do is to get yourselves some togs while I'm out. After that, drink the Captain's health."

"Yes," said Pipes, "that's the best. We'll drink the Captain's health."

R. J. soon after left them to their by no means unpleasant task, and, as he swaggered up the street, under the influence of his ready-made suit and the jingling cash in his pocket, he excited many envious remarks from the boys, who had been wont to chaff the professionals when returning from their daily toil.

"Vulgar young ruffians," soliloquized Bob. "I don't suppose they ever saw a gentleman down this street before."

It seemed not; for, ere our friend could emerge from the narrow turning, a ragged urchin yelled out,—

"Yah!—yah! Ain't he grand since he went down Petticoat Lane. Yah! twig his tile!"

OUTWARDLY our long friend gave no sign that his equanimity was disturbed, but in his heart he cherished a hope that the time would come when he should have that precious youth's right ear between his thumb and forefinger.

"That comes of living in such a low street," soliloquized Bob; "never mind, if I find the young 'uns,' good bye to Mrs. Smith's sky parlour!"

Our friend, with great forethought, made his way to the spot from whence Jack Lennox had been taken by Monsieur Jules Latour.

"Now!" Long Bob thought, "the next thing will be to find the cab—a difficult thing I know—still it is to be got over—ah, of course, the Cabman's Club, that will be the place, and as I am pretty well off for coin, and cabby as a rule never refuses to drink, I shall not have much difficulty in making their acquaintance."

So to the Cabman's Club room Long Bob wended his way, and when he reached the beery, smoky den, he made the best use of his time, and by standing any number of "go's" of hot he soon became on a friendly footing with the man he sought.

While the astute Buffler was losing time going from cab rank to cab rank, to discover the vehicle which conveyed Jack and Lily to the Frenchman's apartments, our long friend was in close conversation with the man who had taken the children and Monsieur Jules Latour away.

R. J. left the smoky den much elevated; and tossing his hat in the air, he exclaimed—"Hurrah!—Long Bob is on the trail!"

CHAPTER XXII.

THE FACE AT THE WINDOW.

WHILE Latour was gone in search of the missing cab, the children talked about the paper our hero had signed.

"I do not," Jack said, "feel that I have been doing right by signing that paper."

The girl, in her childish innocence, knew but little of the world's evil ways.

"Wrong!" she repeated, "why wrong?"

"I do not know," he said; "but still, I feel that it is so."

"Then I would try and get the paper," she said, "and burn it."

"I will," said the boy.

That night the paper was abstracted from Latour's valise: he found it a few yards from the door, it having fallen from the roof of the

THE BOYS OF BIRCHAM SCHOOL.

THE RETURN.

cab.

Jack watched it burn, and when the tinder fell from his hand he crept into bed trembling, as though he had been guilty of a dreadful crime.

The Frenchman raged like a demon when he found the paper had been abstracted, and seizing the boy by the shoulder, he fiercely demanded,—

"What have you done with that paper?"

"I have destroyed it!" Jack replied, boldly; "I don't feel that I was doing right by putting my name there."

Latour spoke calmly, but it was the calmness which excessive rage can only give.

"If you do not," he said, "sign another, I will turn you out on the street—so make up your mind by to-morrow morning."

Jack Lennox pondered over the Frenchman's offer, and the result of this deliberation was a determination not to sign the paper.

The children talked over the matter—Lily,

her heart filled with gratitude for Latour's kindness in rescuing them from the streets—Jack, thankful, yet his suspicions aroused respecting the disinterestedness of Latour's motives.

"I may be wrong," the boy said, "to refuse such a chance of becoming rich, but I shall do so, Lil, until he explains how he has it in his power to place me in such a position."

Lily wondered how her late patron's valet could have the disposal of so great a sum in his power.

"I don't," she said, "quite understand it, Jack; but he must be very rich to offer you such a lot of money every year—perhaps, after all, it is because he likes you, Jack."

The boy smiled bitterly, as he said—

"People nowadays, Lil, are not in the habit of giving strangers three thousand pounds a year because they like them—no, Lil, there is something wrong, or he would not want me to sign that paper."

"You know best, Jack," she said; "sooner than you should do anything wrong I would take off these fine clothes and go back to Big Drum and ——"

The door opened and Latour entered, with his soft cat-like tread. He darted a quick inquiring glance at the young pair, then, seating himself near our hero, he said,—

"Well, my little friend, what do you think of the grand prospect I have offered to you?"

Jack made a gesture to Lily, who immediately left the room.

"I must," the boy said, "still decline it, Monsieur. Thankful as I am for your kindness. I feel that I should be doing something wrong were I to do as you wish."

Latour's brow darkened, and he had much difficulty to restrain the angry reply that came to his lips. He did so; and, with his face wearing a smile, and his voice persuasive enough to shake a stronger resolution than Jack Lennox had made, he said,—

"Something wrong! I wonder what you mean by that—how can you do something wrong?"

"I do not know," the boy answered, "yet I feel that it is so."

"Why—why—what makes you feel this?"

"The large amount of money and the necessity for me to sign a paper before you tell me how it is that you have the power to —— "

Latour jumped from his seat and gave vent to an angry expletive.

"You want to know all this?" he said; "you want me to tell you everything? I will when you sign this paper."

"That," Jack said, "will never be unless I am assured that I am not wronging any one. Poor as I am, I would ten thousand times sooner go back to my hard life on the streets than be rich at the ——"

"You shall!" Latour exclaimed, savagely; "you shall, both of you, go—go as you came here, in rags, and—and ——"

He paused. Rage choked his utterance, and for some moments he paced to and fro the room like a madman.

Jack Lennox had made a small bundle of his tumbler's dress, and during the time Latour was pacing backwards and forwards, the boy began to divest himself of his new garments.

The Frenchman turned suddenly, and, snatching the small bundle from Jack's hand, threw it out of window.

"You shall not go back," he said, "to those people you like—*diable*, I will find some other place for you."

An angry spot came upon Jack's cheek as he tried to save the worn garments from being thrown through the window.

"By what right," he asked, "do you do this? I am now convinced that you have been trying to make me commit —— "

"Silence!" roared M. Jules; "you are a fool, and stand in your own light,—but I will find another, and he shall have your money—more, I will send you away to a monastery in France, where you will not interfere with me."

Jack Lennox looked strangely at the excited plotter.

"You dare not," he said; "I will claim the protection of the law."

"Dare not?" hissed Latour, "you shall know when you are shut up in the walls of a monastery, and the girl you do like so well shall go to a convent. We will see then what I dare do."

Latour left the room as the last word came from his lips, and to Jack's dismay he heard the key turned.

He was a prisoner; and although the window was but a few feet from the ground, he could not escape, for Latour had taken with him the clothes the boy had taken off preparatory to donning his old suit.

He stood in the centre of the room, lost in wonderment at this sudden change of fortune; and before he could form any plan to guide him, a tapping upon the window caused him to turn.

Was he dreaming? There was the well-known face of his companion in misery, Long Bob—not the ragged Long Bob of yore, but now somewhat showily dressed.

"Bob," he cried, running to the window, and raising the lower sash, "I am so glad you have come; how did you find me?"

They shook hands, and Bob said,—

"Pretty easy, young 'un. I found out the cabby who brought you here, and as I was walking past, taking stock of the place, I got this bundle slap against my head——"

"My clothes," Jack said, joyfully; "Latour threw them through the window."

"Did he? I wish he had observed that I wore a new tile before he aimed at my head. Now, young 'un, as I've found you, where's Lily?"

"She's here."

"That's all right," said Bob. "Get on your things; I shan't be long before I'm back."

"But, Bob, stay; I'll come with you. We can easily get Lil——"

"You'll stay where you are, young 'un—that was my orders, and when I return I will bring somebody that you will be glad to see; shan't be long—good bye. You are a lucky fellow, Jack; so you will say soon."

Before the boy could reply, R. J. descended, by clutching at the thick ivy which covered the front of the house.

Long Bob hailed a hansom, and telling the man to drive like somebody unmentionable, he soon reached the Captain's temporary residence.

To the pompous hall porter R. J. said,—

"Captain Carlin—he is here I suppose?"

The pampered menial surveyed Bob in a supercilious manner as he answered,—

"Y-a-s, we have such a party staying at our hotel."

"I know that, Buttons," Bob said. "I asked you whether he was here."

The lacquey's dignity was hurt, and again surveying Bob, he was about to speak, when the Captain hurriedly descended the stairs.

He had seen the cab stop at the door, and R. J. alight, and, impatient to learn the cause of our friend's arrival, came down in time to prevent an angry reply from the gentleman in plush and buttons.

A few words told the glad tidings, and when the cab reached Latour's lodgings the Captain sent Long Bob to the Private Inquiry Office, to inform the chief that the missing children were found.

To R. J.'s surprise the grave looking gentleman put on his hat, and, entering the cab, told the driver to take them to a fashionable west end street.

"He is not there," Bob said. He was anxious to return to his employer.

"I know that," was the reply, "but there is another person who is much interested in your little friends, who will be happy to join the party."

Long Bob wondered whom this could be, and his wonder increased when the cab stopped.

The joy of that meeting between the father and his long-lost children must be left to the imagination; it was a scene that pen could not faithfully describe.

Poor little Jack, when he found his gentle companion was his sister, wept with joy.

They had all suffered, but the reward was great—greater than their wildest dream could have portrayed.

CHAPTER XXIII.

LAST.

WITH an arm around each of his children, the happy father stood before the baffled plotter, and Latour, seeing the castle he had raised fall to the dust, sought to turn aside the Captain's wrath, by telling him of the discovery he had made in the earl's chamber.

"I tried to find the young gentleman," he said, "after the fire, but did not do so until a few days since, and even had you not have found him, I should have given him the papers which I found."

Our hero had told his father all that had passed between him and Latour, and the Captain, too happy in his new-found joy, forgave the Frenchman for the deceit he had used, and when Latour left the room to fetch the papers relating to the Greyford property, the Captain, in a low voice, said to his children—

"There is but one cloud upon our happiness—that, my dears, is the melancholy fate which befell your poor mother."

He had scarcely spoken, when a carriage stopped at the door, and soon after, the lady who had entered the Private Enquiry Office as the Captain left, came into the room.

She gave an hysterical cry when she beheld her husband and children, and the Captain rushing towards her, cried out—

"Alicia!"

"Walter, my husband!"

They were locked in each other's arms, and the children, with wistful young eyes, gazed at their parents.

The embrace over—the embrace of those who had mourned for each other as dead—the lady came to her children, and, holding them in a close embrace, wept tears of joy.

* * * *

Where the blackened remains of Falconmere's proud towers stood, a splendid edifice was raised by the earl's daughter, and the workmen in clearing away the *debris* of the terrible conflagration, came upon the dead body of the proud Earl Herbert. He had lived for some days after the Abbey fell, for the spot where he was found had been to him a living tomb.

Across, a low wall a mass of masonry had fallen, and in such a manner that it formed a perfect chamber.

Inside this the earl was imprisoned, and in the darkness of that fearful tomb he had written sufficient on a blank leaf of his pocket book to restore his only child and her children to their heritage. He also implored her husband's forgiveness for persecuting them, and, when too late, saw the folly of giving way to the pride which had caused all their misery.

* * * *

The mysterious reappearance of the Lady Alicia was soon explained.

She had sought her father, when she believed her husband had fallen on the field of battle.

The proud man, enraged at her marriage, had sworn to punish her. For this purpose he had her conveyed to a private madhouse, and filling a coffin with stones had a mock funeral performed. He was ignorant of the children's existence—for the young mother, dreading his vengeance, had left them with her maid.

It was this girl who was robbed by the tramps, when on her way to the Abbey with the little girl.

She had started with the intention of trying to soften the earl's heart towards her mistress, whom she had not seen since the day she was conveyed to the asylum.

The loss of the child preyed upon her mind until her reason became unsettled, and, blaming the earl for the misfortune that had befallen her, she suddenly took it in her head to personate her lost mistress, and for this purpose she took the boy by the hand and sought an interview with the earl. The result of that attempt drove her to desperation, and she plunged into the pool of water near the Abbey and died, as the condemned gipsy told the Captain after his trial.

She had thought to carry out the deception by using the Lady Alicia's papers and jewels, which had been left in her charge.

* * * *

In the lower part of the new mansion three servants were seated—three privileged servants, to judge by the cosy room they had for their use.

One was a stout pompous individual, holding the position of butler in that vast establishment. The second was a gentleman of somewhat spare form. He held the office of steward, and, if all accounts are true, he looked well after the interests of his employers.

The third personage was a smartly-dressed young man—the young master's valet.

The butler helped his thin friend the steward to a glass of wine, and with much self-complacency remarked,—

"Yes, Pipes, I always do say that it was a lucky day that young Master Walter met us."

The steward sipped his wine like one who understood the taste of a good rich old port, and answered,—

"Yes, Drum, it was, and if he was here he'd say the same himself."

"Perhaps you'll explain," said the young master's valet, playing with his watch-chain; "really, I think the luck is all on the other side."

"Do you?" said the butler, who was rather severe; "that is where you are mistaken, Bob. Come, I'll put it to you this way. Do you think he would ever have got three such servants as we are, eh, unless he had been lucky enough to meet us when, along with Miss Alicia, he was OUT ON THE WORLD?"

END OF OUT ON THE WORLD.

CHAPTER XVIII.
AND LAST OF BIRCHAM SCHOOL.

FIVE years!—though but a few grains in the glass of time, many of those with whom you and I, reader, have been interested have other matters to think about than school games, half-holidays, and schoolboy mischief.

They are now men, or verging into manhood, and a new set inhabits the old schoolhouse—carves names and faces upon the forms, torments the masters—in fact, acts precisely as their predecessors acted, and as each successive generation will act; for boys were much the same a century ago, and will be a century hence.

The old house has changed a little since the Doctor stood at the door upon that cold December morning. The front has been scraped and painted, the window-frames painted, and upon the large door there glistens a brass plate, bearing the words—

Luton Vale Grammar School.

And a neat circular, printed on superfine note paper, is to be seen at the adjacent railway station, bearing the following announcement:—

Luton Vale Grammar School.

Principal—The Rev. J. Bently.

Assisted by Twelve efficient Masters.

Pupils prepared for the Oxford and Cambridge examinations, and for the Naval, Military, and Civil Services.

Prospectuses on application.

The quiet wood where the boys in Doctor Bircham's time loved to wander, is also much changed, two-thirds being already in the hands of the builders and a legion of noisy bricklayers, whose coarse language takes the place of the sweet songsters which dwelt among the old trees.

Within a few minutes' walk of the school resides a white-haired old gentleman, whose chief delight is to come to the playground and watch the youngsters as they play the old games, and fill the air with their many voices.

The principal treats the white-haired old gentleman with great respect; and when a new boy arrives at Luton Vale, an oldster confidently says:

"That's Doctor Bircham; he had the school before Mr. Bentley bought it; it was a school then, and our head paid no end of money for it."

Bully Biggs, two years after he left Bircham's, succeeded his father in the "business," and may be seen daily not a hundred miles from St. Paul's, manipulating prices of butter, and bullying the luckless shopmen.

Little Godfrey Bransome, when the school broke up, was taken by the Doctor, and in time went to Cambridge; and the old gentleman's heart is gladdened by the news that Godfrey will take the highest honours attainable in that famous old place.

Joe Stikkers had his boyish longing gratified. He became a midshipman, and two years afterwards was wrecked on the coast of Algiers.

Joe was picked up by a merchant ship, and the vessel was soon afterwards pursued by an Algerine corsair. Joe, instead of sharing the general panic, calmly buckled a cutlass to his belt, and urged the captain to fight the pirate.

The captain was more inclined for peace than war; and, much to Joe's disgust, stood hour after hour at the side watching the stranger through a glass.

The chief mate and the seamen would fain have dissuaded Joe from his warlike project; but the lad, pointing to the distant sail, said:—

"We can't escape him; he sails four knots to our three. So there is nothing for it but to make the best defence we can, or this good ship will fall into their hands. Then," he added, "I would not take a lease of our lives."

"But, sir," the captain said, closing his glass, "we have but two small guns and only powder for signals."

"Any small arms?" Joe asked.

"Not more than a dozen muskets, and as many cutlasses."

Joe's pluck was contagious, and the men who were but a few minutes before doing all in their power to escape the pursuers, became quite eager for the work.

Joe loaded the two guns with nails, and when the Algerines came within range, they received the double discharge with every sign of disapprobation.

"Now, lads," Joe said, taking advantage of their confusion, "empty your muskets, then follow me."

For this gallant act Joe received from the wners of the vessel a magnificent silvero cup and a costly sword.

Reader, my task is ended; and if you regret (as much as I do) that we have come to the last scene, I shall feel that my labour has not been in vain.

THE END OF BIRCHAM SCHOOL.

Milton Keynes UK
Ingram Content Group UK Ltd.
UKHW032229021224
452012UK00011B/136